"Another crowd-pleaser . . . This case begins with the brazen kidnapping of an infant. Before it's over, readers will be treated to some chilling insights from one of the earliest practitioners in psychology; plunge into a courtroom battle pitted against none other than Clarence Darrow; and follow Teddy Roosevelt with a handpicked batch of sailors through the gang-infested streets of lower Manhattan."

—Minneapolis Star Tribune

"Suspenseful . . . Through the observations, discoveries, and confusions of his idiosyncratic detective squad, Carr deftly scrutinizes 'the secret sins of American society' and the perpetual proposition that the greatest mystery is the human mind."

—Los Angeles Times Book Review

"Here's New York circa 1897, city of unparalleled corruption and splendor, city of fine dining and seedy taverns. . . . Few writers are as adept [as Carr] at fashioning careful revelations that detonate, chapter by chapter, like carefully positioned explosions."

—Chicago Tribune

"[A] labyrinth of crime and psychology . . . What worked so well in the first book—late-nineteenth-century New York City with all its splendor and warts—is just as engaging in the second. . . . Is *The Angel of Darkness* as good as its predecessor? No. It's better."

—San Diego Union-Tribune

"Fascinating . . . good courtroom drama . . . In a brilliant bit of historical casting, Clarence Darrow, a rising courtroom wizard from Chicago, turns up to . . . defend the villain at a tense upstate New York murder trial."

—Time

BY CALEB CARR

Surrender, New York

The Legend of Broken

The Italian Secretary

The Lessons of Terror

Killing Time

The Angel of Darkness

The Alienist

The Devil Soldier

America Invulnerable (with James Chace)

Casing the Promised Land

THE ANGEL OF DARKNESS

THE
Angel
OF
Darkness

—

A NOVEL

—

CALEB
CARR

RANDOM HOUSE
NEW YORK

2018 Random House Trade Paperback Edition

Copyright © 1997 by Caleb Carr
Map copyright © 1997 by Anita Karl and Jim Kemp

Published in the United States by Random House,
an imprint and division of Penguin Random House LLC, New York.

RANDOM HOUSE and the HOUSE colophon are
registered trademarks of Penguin Random House LLC.

Originally published in hardcover in the United States
by Random House, an imprint and division of
Penguin Random House LLC, in 1997.

ISBN 978-0-345-42531-7
Ebook ISBN 978-0-307-43272-8

Printed in the United States of America on acid-free paper

randomhousebooks.com

468975

Book design by J. K. Lambert

To my mother and father

"It is not having been in the dark house,
but having left it, that counts."

—THEODORE ROOSEVELT

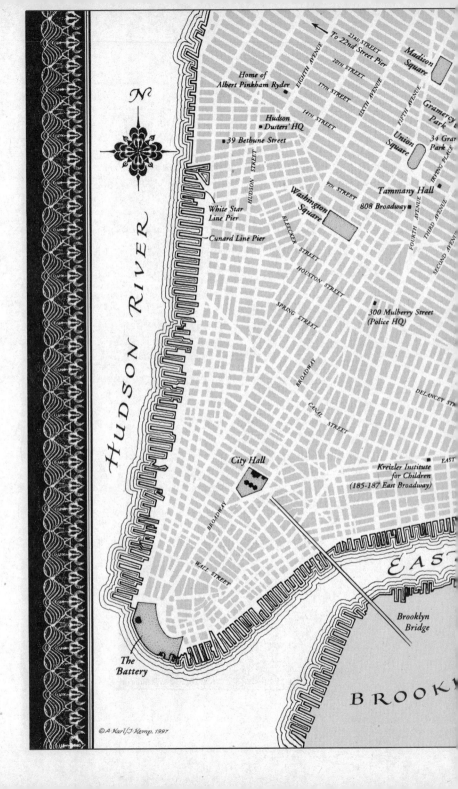

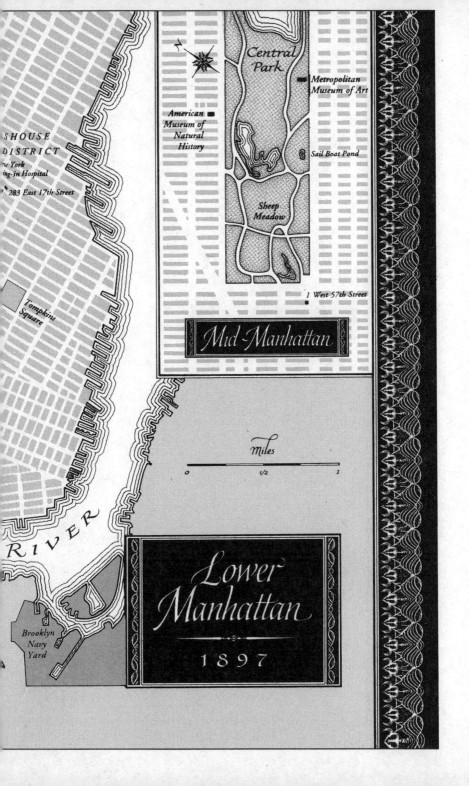

Central
Park

Metropolitan
Museum of Art

American
Museum of
Natural
History

Sail Boat Pond

Sheep
Meadow

1 West 57th Street

Mid-Manhattan

SHOUSE
DISTRICT

w York
ing-in Hospital

283 East 17th Street

Tompkins
Square

Miles

0   1/2   1

RIVER

Brooklyn
Navy
Yard

Lower
Manhattan

1897

THE ANGEL OF DARKNESS

CHAPTER 1

June 19th, 1919

There's likely some polished way of starting a story like this, a clever bit of gaming that'd sucker people in surer than the best banco feeler in town. But the truth is that I haven't got the quick tongue or the slick wit for that kind of game. Words haven't figured much in my life, and though over the years I've met many of what the world counts to be the big thinkers and talkers of our times, I've stayed what most would call a plain man. And so a plain way of starting will suit me well.

The first thing to do, along these plain lines, is to say why I've closed the shop up and come into the back office on a night when there's still plenty of business that might be done. It's a fine evening, the kind what I used to live for: a night when you can take in all the affairs of the avenue with nothing more than your shirtsleeves for cover, blowing the smoke of a dozen good cigarettes up to the stars above the city and feeling, on balance, like maybe there's some point to living in this madhouse after all. The traffic—gasoline-powered automobiles and trucks these days, not just clattering old nags dragging carriages and carts—has slowed quite a bit with the passing of midnight, and soon the after-supper ladies and gents will be over from the Albemarle Hotel and the Hoffman House to pick up their fine-blended smokes. They'll wonder why I've closed early, but they won't wonder long before heading for some other shop; and after they've gone, quiet will settle in around this grand Flatiron Building with a purpose. She still lords it over Madison Square, the Flatiron does, with her solitary, peculiar silhouette and her fussy stone face, all of which, at the time she was built, had architects and critics going at each other tooth and nail. The Metropolitan Life Tower across the park may be taller, but it doesn't have near the style or presence; and next to the Flatiron, buildings like Madison Square Garden, topped by its once-shocking statue of naked Diana, just seem like hangovers from another age, an age that, looking back, feels like it passed in the space of a night. It was a gay night, many folks'd say; but for some of us, it was a strange and dangerous time, when we learned things about human behavior that most sensible people would never want to know. Even the few that might've been curious got all the grimness they could stand from the Great War. What people want now's a good time, and they want it with a vengeance.

Certainly that drive is what'll be powering the type of folks who'll be on their way over to my shop to try and buy the smokes they'll need for long hours at the city's gaming tables and dance halls. The weather alone would rule out any darker motivations. The breezy, light arms of the night air will wrap themselves around all those keen, hopeful souls, and they'll tear into the town like a meat district dog who's smelled out a bit of bone at the bottom of an ash heap. Most of their activities won't amount to nothing, of course, but that doesn't matter; part of the strange fun of getting rooked into thinking that anything's possible on the beaten, dirty streets of this Big Onion is knowing that if you don't find what you're looking for tonight, it's all that much more important that you try again tomorrow.

I remember that feeling; I had it many times myself before I reached my present lamentable state. Being forever on the verge of coughing up a lung has taken away much of my joy in this existence, for it's hard to relish the world's pleasures when you're leaving pools of blood and pus wherever you go like some wretched, wounded animal. Still, though, my memory's as good as ever, and to be sure, I can recall the raw joy that nights like this used to bring, the feeling of being outside and on your own, with the whole world stretched out and waiting. Yes, even with the hack I know that you don't come in from a night like this without a damned good reason. But that's exactly what Mr. John Schuyler Moore has given me.

He came in about an hour ago, drunk as a lord (which will surprise exactly nobody what knows the man) and spewing a lot of vitriol about the cowardice of editors and publishers and the American people in general. To hear him talk (or maybe I should say, to hear the wine and whiskey talk), it's a miracle this country's made it as far as we have, what with all the secret horror, tragedy, and mayhem that infest our society. Mind you,

I don't argue the man's point; I spent too many years in the house and employ of Doctor Laszlo Kreizler, eminent alienist and friend to both me and Mr. Moore, to write my guest's gloomy estimations off as a drunkard's ravings. But as oftentimes happens with your inebriates, my visitor wasn't going to let his bitterness stay generalized for too long: he was looking for somebody specific to go after, and in the absence of anybody else it was pretty obvious that I'd do.

His particular complaint had to do with the book he's been writing these last several months, ever since President Roosevelt died. I read the thing, we all did; gave Mr. Moore our thoughts on it, and wished him well; but there wasn't one of us, including the Doctor, what seriously believed he had a prayer of finding a publisher for it. The manuscript told the tale of the Beecham murders, the first case that the Doctor, Mr. Moore, Miss Sara Howard, the two detectives Isaacson, Cyrus Montrose, and I had occasion to undertake together: not the sort of tale that any publisher in his right mind is going to place before the public. True, there's them what likes to get a little scare out of their evening read; but there's also a limit to how far that particular taste goes, and the Beecham tale was as far over that limit as you could likely get, in this day and age. Maybe it *is* a story that needs telling, like Mr. Moore claims; but there's plenty of stories that need telling what never get told, just because people can't bear the listening.

My first mistake this evening was to make that little observation to Mr. Moore.

He gave me what's a rare look, for him: hard and truly angry. I've known John Schuyler Moore since I was eleven years old, which would be some twenty-four years, and I would be hard-pressed to name a fairer, more decent, or generally kinder man. But he does run deep, and like most that do, there's a pool of hurt and bitterness inside him that sometimes can't help but stream on out. I've seen different things bring it on, but it's never been stronger than tonight: he *wanted* the Beecham story heard, and he was in a genuine rage with all them what were going to prevent him from telling it, not to mention anybody that might even try to understand such skittishness. Which in this case—unfortunately—was me.

He isn't young any longer, Mr. Moore isn't, and the ruddy ripples of skin around his starched collar tell of how he's lived his life; but in the angry eyes was the same fire that's always driven him when faced with injustice and what he sees as stupidity. And the man doesn't back down at sixty-odd years any more than he did when he was my age. Knowing all this, I figured a fine airing of opinions was on its way, and I climbed up one of the wooden ladders in the store to fetch a large jar that contains a particularly pricey mix of Turkish and Georgian leaves. Then I set a second wicker chair out under the little striped canopy that covers my two front windows—S. TAGGERT, TOBACCONIST, FINE FOREIGN AND DOMESTIC BLENDS in the best gold leaf—and set to work rolling the goods in my tastiest English papers. In that setting the two of us had at it, the May breeze continuing to carry the nastier smells of the city off to points east.

"So, Stevie," declares the great journalist himself, in the same tone of voice what's gotten him fired off newspapers up and down the East Coast, "I take it that in the end you, too, are going to prove a willing partner to the conspiracy of silence that surrounds the private horrors of American society."

"Have a smoke, Mr. Moore," answers yours truly, the unaware conspirator, "and think about what you just said. This is *me,* Stevie, the same what has gone on ungodly pursuits like the Beecham case with you since he was a boy."

"That's who I *thought* I was talking to," comments my companion unsteadily, "but your tone led me to wonder if I might not be mistaken."

"Light?" says I, whipping a match against my pants as Mr. Moore fumbles in his pockets. "It ain't that you're mistaken," I go on, "but you've got to know how to approach people."

"Ah!" says he. "And so now I, who have worked for the finest journals in this country, who currently comment on the greatest affairs of the day in the pages of *The New York Times,* now *I* do not know how to approach my public!"

"Don't take on airs," I answers. "The *Times*'s given you the sack twice that I know of, exactly because you *didn't* know how to approach your public. The Beecham case was strong stuff, maybe too strong for your readers to take first horse out of the gate. Could be you should've eased them into it, started with something that didn't involve talk about slaughtered boy-whores, cannibalism, and eyeballs in a jar."

A smoky hiss comes from the great scribe, and the smallest nod indicates that he thinks maybe I'm right: maybe the story of a tormented killer who took out his rage on some of the most unfortunate young men in this city wasn't the best way to acquaint people with either the psychological theories of Dr. Kreizler or the secret sins of American society. This realization (if I'm right and he's having it) obviously doesn't set Mr. Moore up much. A deep, whining groan that comes out of him seems to say: I'm taking professional advice from a petty criminal-turned-tobacconist. I laugh at this; I have to, for there's more of a pouting child in Mr. Moore's manner, now, than there is of an enraged old man.

"Let's look back on it for a moment," I say, feeling better now that his anger's giving way to a bit of resignation. "Let's think about all those cases, and see if we can't find one that might be less of an out-and-out shocker but still suit the purpose."

"It can't be done, Stevie," Mr. Moore mumbles, depressed. "You know as well as I do that the Beecham case was the first and best illustration of the things Kreizler's been trying to say all these years."

"Maybe," I reply. "Then again, maybe there's others as good. You always acknowledged that I had the best memory of all of us—it may be that I can help you think of one." I'm being a little coy, here: I already know the case I'd put forward as the most puzzling and fascinating of all we ever worked on. But if I advocate it too fast and with too much vigor, well, it'll just be the rag in front of the bull to a man in Mr. Moore's condition. He produces a flask, is about to take a pull, then jumps a foot or so in the air when a flatbed Ford motor truck backfires like a cannon out in the avenue. Your old folks'll react that way to such things; haven't ever quite got used to the sounds of modern times. Anyway, after he settles back into his chair with a grunt, Mr. Moore allows himself a minute to think my suggestion over. But a slow shake of the head indicates that he's come full circle to the same hopeless conclusion: in all our experiences together, there's nothing as good, nothing as clear, as the Beecham case. I take a deep breath, followed by a drag off my stick, and then I say it quietly:

"What about Libby Hatch?"

My friend goes a little pale and looks at me like maybe the old girl herself's going to appear from inside the shop and let him have it if he says the wrong thing. Her name'll produce that effect on anyone who ever crossed paths or purposes with her.

"Libby Hatch?" Mr. Moore echoes quietly. "No. No, you couldn't. It's not—well, it—well, you just couldn't . . ." He keeps on in that vein until I get enough room in edgewise to ask exactly *why* you couldn't. "Well," he answers, still sounding like a half-terrified kid, "how could you—how could anyone—" And then some part of his brain that hasn't been clouded by drink remembers that the woman's been dead for better than twenty years: he puffs up his chest and gets a little bolder.

"In the first place," he says (and up goes a finger, with more at the ready to indicate that there's a whole arsenal of points coming), "I thought you were talking about a story that wouldn't be as gruesome as Beecham's. In the Hatch case you've not only got kidnappings, but murdered infants, grave robbing—and *we* did the grave robbing, for God's sake—"

"True," I say, "but—" But there's no buts—Mr. Moore is not letting reason get into this. Up bangs another finger, and he bulls on:

"Second, the moral implications"—he does love that little phrase—"of the Hatch case are, if anything, even more disturbing than those of the Beecham affair."

"That's right," I chime in, "and that's just why—"

"And finally," he booms, "even if the story weren't so damned horrifying and disturbing, *you,* Stevie Taggert, would not be the man to tell it."

This point I find a little confusing. It hasn't actually occurred to me that I *am* the man to tell the story, but I don't much like the statement that I couldn't be. Seems to imply something.

Hoping I've taken his meaning wrong, I ask straight out just what's to prevent me from relating the terrible saga of Libby Hatch, if I so desire. Much to my disappointment, Mr. Moore answers that I haven't got the education and I haven't got the training. "What do you think?" he says, his stock of injured pride still not tapped out, "that writing a book's like doing up a sales receipt? That there's nothing more to the author's craft than there is to peddling tobacco?"

At this point, I become a little less amused by the inebriate next to me; but I'm going to give him one last chance.

"Are you forgetting," I ask quietly, "that Doctor Kreizler himself saw to my education after I went to live with him?"

"A few years of informal training," huffs Mr. Editorial Page. "Nothing to compare to a Harvard education."

"Well, you just catch me where I go wrong," I shoot back, "but a Harvard education hasn't done much to get *your* little manuscript out to the world." His eyes go narrow at that. "Of course," I continue, rubbing the salt in, "I've never taken to liquor, which seems to be the main requirement for gentlemen in your trade. But other than that, I figure I measure up okay against you scribblers."

That last word gets some emphasis, being an insult my companion is particularly sensitive to. But I don't overplay it. It's a remark designed not so much to pierce as to sting, and it succeeds: Mr. Moore doesn't say anything for a few seconds, and when he does open his mouth again, I know it's going to be something to equal or outdo my slap. Like two dogs in a pit down in my old neighborhood, we've barked and nipped and sized each other up enough—it's time to go for an ear.

"The cowardice and stupidity of New York publishers and the American reading public have nothing to do with any lack of ability on *my* part in telling the tale," Mr. Moore seethes firmly. "And when the day comes that I can learn something about writing, about Kreizler's work, or, for that matter, about *anything* other than tobacco leaves from *you*, Taggert, I'll be happy to put on an apron and work your counter for one solid week!"

Now, you need to know something here: Mr. Moore and me, we are both betting men. I ran my first faro racket when I was eight, for other kids in my neighborhood, and Mr. Moore's always been one to take a flutter on just about any interesting game of chance. Why, it was gambling that formed the first basis of our friendship: the man taught me everything I know about the ponies, and I'll acknowledge as much, even *with* all his patronizing. So when he makes that last challenge, I don't laugh; I don't shrug it off; I don't do anything but stare him in the eye and say: "Done."

And we spit on the wager, which I taught him, and we shake on the wager, which he taught me. And we both know that's that. He stands, takes a last drag off his butt, and says, "Good night, Stevie," pretty near pleasantly, like none of our earlier conversation ever happened. The whole thing's moved to another level: it's not what he'd call an intellectual exercise anymore, it's a wager, and further talk would only desecrate it. From this point on there'll just be the playing out of the game, the run to the wire, with one of us ending up a winner and the other a loser; and likely I won't see him much or at all 'til we know which of us is going to be what.

Which leaves me alone for tonight (and, I'm guessing, for many nights to come) with my memories of the Hatch case: of the people what gave us a hand and what got in our way, of the friends (and more than friends) what were lost to us during the pursuit, of the peculiar places we were led to—and of Libby Hatch herself. And I don't mind saying, now that Mr. Moore's gone and I've had a chance to think it over some, that most of his statements were square on the mark: in many ways, the tale of Libby Hatch was more frightening and disturbing than anything we ran across in our hunt for the butcher John Beecham. Under ordinary circumstances, in fact, the bumps on my skin and the shivers in my soul that are right now multiplying with my memories might even tempt me to concede the wager.

But then the hack starts in: out of nowhere, rough, racking, shooting bits of blood and God-knows-what-all onto the page before me. And funnily enough, I realize it's the hack that'll keep me writing, no matter what mental jitters I get. Dr. Kreizler's told me what this cough probably means; I'm not sure how many more years or even months I've got left on this earth. So let Libby Hatch come after me for trying to tell her story. Let her strange, sorry ghost take the breath out of me for daring to reveal this tale. Most likely she'd be doing me a favor—for along with the hack, the memories would end, too. . . .

But Fate would never be so merciful, and neither would Libby. The only place her memory will haunt are the sheets of paper before me, which will serve not the purposes of a publisher but to settle a bet. After that, I'll leave them behind for whoever happens across them after I'm gone and cares to take a look. It may horrify you, Reader, and it may strike you as too unnatural a story to have ever really happened. That was a word that came up an awful lot during the days the case went on: *unnatural.* But my memory hasn't faded with my lungs, and you can take this from me: if the story of Libby Hatch teaches us anything at all, it's that Nature's domain includes every form of what society calls "unnatural" behavior; that in fact, just as Dr. Kreizler has always said, there's nothing truly natural *or* unnatural under the sun.

CHAPTER 2

I t was a scratching sound that started it all: the light scrape of a boot
against the stone-and-brick face of Dr. Kreizler's house at 283 East Seventeenth Street. The noise—familiar to any boy who'd had a childhood
like mine—drifted through the window of my room late on the night of
Sunday, June 20, 1897: twenty-two years ago, almost to the day. I was
lying on my small bed trying to study, but without much luck. That
evening, too, was far too charged with the breezes and smells of spring
and too bathed in moonlight to let serious thinking (or even sleeping) be
an option. As was and is too often the case in New York, early spring had
been wet and cold, making it fairly certain that we'd get only a week or
two of tolerable weather before the serious heat set in. That particular
Sunday had been a rainy one earlier on, but the night was beginning to
clear and seemed to promise the onset of those few precious balmy days.
So if you say that I caught the sound outside my window partly because I
was just waiting for some excuse to get outside, I won't deny it; but the
larger truth is that, ever since I can remember, I've kept careful track of
night noises in whatever place I happen to find myself.

My room in the Doctor's house was up top on the fourth floor, two stories and a half a world away from his splendid parlor and dining room
below and another twelve vertical feet from his stately but somehow spare
bedroom and overstuffed study on the third floor. Up on the dormered
plainness of the top story (what most folks would write off as "the servants' quarters"), Cyrus Montrose—who split the Doctor's driving and
other household duties with me—had the big room at the back, and off of

that was a smaller room what we used for storage. My room was at the front, and not near as big as the rear one; but then, I wasn't near as big as Cyrus, who stood well over six feet tall. And the front space was still plenty plush by the standards of a thirteen-year-old boy who'd been used to, in order since birth, sharing a one-room rear tenement flat near Five Points with his mother and her string of men, sleeping on whatever patches of sidewalk or alleyway offered a few hours' peace (having first left said mother and men at age three, and for good at age eight), and then fighting his way out of a cell in what the bulls laughingly liked to call the "barracks" of the Boys' House of Refuge on Randalls Island.

Speaking of that miserable place, I might as well get one thing straight right now, being as it may make a few other things clearer as we go along. Some of you might've read in the papers that I near killed a guard what tried to bugger me while I was confined on the island; and don't think me coldhearted when I say that in some respects I still wish I had killed him, for he'd done the same to other boys and, I'm certain, went on doing it after my case was swept under the rug and he was reinstated. Maybe that makes me sound bitter, I don't know; I wouldn't like to think of myself as a bitter man. But I do find that the things what angered me as a boy still rankle all these years later. So if it seems that some of what I'll have to say in the pages to come doesn't reflect the mellowing of age, that's only because I've never found that life and memories respond to time the way that tobacco does.

There was only one other room on the top floor of Dr. Kreizler's residence, though for all the practical purposes of the household the chamber had long since ceased to exist. Removed from Cyrus's and my rooms by its own short hallway, it was usually occupied by the maid of the house; but for a full year it had been uninhabited by any living soul. I say "by any living soul" because it was, in fact, still occupied by the few sad possessions and the even sadder memory of Mary Palmer, whose death during the Beecham case had broken the Doctor's heart. Since that time we in the house had been served by a number of cooks and maids who came before breakfast and left after dinner, some of them capable, some of them downright disastrous; but neither Cyrus nor I ever complained about the turnover, for we had no more interest than the Doctor did in taking on somebody permanent. You see, the both of us—though in very different ways from the Doctor, of course—had loved Mary, too. . . .

Anyway, at about eleven P.M. on that June 20th I was in my room attempting to read some of the lessons Dr. Kreizler had assigned to me for that week—exercises in numbers and readings in history—when I heard the front door downstairs close. I felt my body tense the way it always did and still does when I hear the sound of a door at night; and then, listening, I made out one heavy, strong set of footsteps on the blue-and-green Persian carpet of the stairway. I relaxed: Cyrus's gait was as recognizable as the deep breathing and gentle humming that always accompanied it. I fell back onto my bed and held my book at arm's length above me, knowing that my friend would soon poke his broad black head in to check on me and waiting for him to do so.

"Everything quiet, Stevie?" he asked when he reached my room, in that low rumble that was at once powerful and gentle.

I nodded, then looked over at him. "He's staying at the Institute, I guess."

Cyrus returned my nod. "His last night for a while. Wants to make use of what time he's got . . ." There was a quiet, worried pause, and then Cyrus yawned. "Don't be up too late, now—he wants you to fetch him in the morning. I brought the barouche back—you'll want to take the calash and give one of the horses a rest."

"Right."

Then I heard those heavy feet and legs lumber off toward the back of the house and the sound of Cyrus's door closing. I set my book down and took to staring blankly, first at the simple blue-and-white-striped wallpaper around me, then at the small dormered window at the foot of my bed, out of which I could see the rustling, leafy tops of the trees in Stuyvesant Park across the street.

It didn't make any more sense to me then than it does now, how life can pile troubles up on a man what don't deserve them, while letting some of the biggest jackasses and scoundrels alive waltz their way through long, untroubled existences. I could see the Doctor at that moment clear as if I was standing next to him down at the Institute (that being the Kreizler Institute for Children on East Broadway): he'd long since have made sure the kids were all bedded down safe, as well as given late-night instructions to the staff about any new arrivals or troublesome cases, and by now he'd be at the big secretary in his consulting room working on a mountain of papers, partly out of necessity and partly to avoid the thought that it all might be coming to an end. He'd stay there under the glow of his green-and-gold Tiffany lamp, pulling at his mustache and the small patch of beard under his mouth and occasionally rubbing his bad left arm, which seemed to bother him at night worse than other times. But it'd likely be many hours before weariness began to show in those sharp black eyes, and if he did manage to get some sleep it would only be when he laid his long black hair on the papers before him and dozed off fitfully.

You see, it had been a year of tragedy and controversy for the Doctor, beginning, as I've said, with the death of the only woman he'd ever truly loved and coming to a head with the recent unexplained suicide of one of his young charges at the Institute. A court hearing to discuss the general state of affairs at the Institute had followed this last incident, resulting in an injunction. For sixty days the Doctor was to keep clear of the place while the police investigated the matter, and those sixty days were set to start the next morning—however, I'll have much more to say about all that later.

It was while I was lying there counting the Doctor's troubles that I heard the small, sudden scraping noise I've mentioned coming from outside my window. Like I say, I made the sound right away—my own feet had produced it too many times for me not to. As my heart began to race with a little nervousness but even more excitement, I thought for a second of fetching Cyrus; but then a quick succession of amateur slips in the climbing steps outside made me realize I wasn't about to get a visit from anybody I couldn't handle. So I just set my book aside, slid over to the window, and poked the top of my head out.

It makes me smile, sometimes, to think back on those days—and even more on those nights—and realize just how much time we all spent crawling around rooftops and into and out of other peoples' windows while most of the city was sound asleep. It wasn't a surprising or new activity for me, of course: my mother'd put me to work breaking into houses and lifting fenceable goods as soon as I could walk. But the image of the Doctor's respectable young society friends jimmying windows and cramming themselves through them like a batch of garden-variety second-story men—well, I did and do find it amusing. And nothing ever gave me a bigger smile than what I saw that night:

It was Miss Sara Howard, busting just about every rule in the housebreaker's bible, if there ever was such a thing, and cursing heaven like a sailor all the while. She had on her usual daytime rig—a simple dark dress without a lot of fussy, fashionable undergarments—but uncomplicated as her clothes were, she was having a hell of a time keeping a grip on the rain gutter and the protruding cornerstones of the house, and was a rat's ass away from falling into the Doctor's front yard and breaking what would most likely have been every bone in her body. Her hair'd obviously started out in a tight bun, but it was coming undone along with the rest of her; and her pretty if somewhat plain face was a picture of heated frustration.

"You're lucky I'm not the cops, Miss Howard," I said, crawling out onto the windowsill. That brought a quick turn of her head and a burning light into her green eyes that any emerald would've envied. "They'd have you out at the Octagon Tower before breakfast." The Octagon Tower was an evil-looking, domed structure on Blackwells Island in the East River, one what, along with two wings that branched off of it, made up the city's notorious women's prison and madhouse.

Miss Howard only frowned and nodded at her feet. "It's these blasted boots," she said, and, looking down at them with her, I could see what the problem was: instead of wearing a sensible, light pair of shoes or slippers that would have let her get her toes into the gaps in the masonry, she— being a novice—had put on a pair of heavy, nail-studded climber's boots. They weren't unlike the ones the murderer John Beecham had used to climb walls, and I figured that that was where she'd got the idea.

"You need rope and gear for those," I said, grabbing hold of the window frame with my right hand and extending my left arm to her. "Remember, Beecham was climbing sheer brick walls. And," I added with a smile, as I pulled her onto the windowsill with me, "he knew what he was doing."

She settled in, caught her breath, and just barely glanced at me sideways. "That's a low blow, Stevie," she said. But then the irritated face turned amused, in the way that her looks and moods always changed: suddenly, with the speed of a doused cat. She smiled back at me. "Got a cigarette?"

"Like a dog has fleas," I said, reaching inside the room for a packet and handing her one. I took one for myself, struck a match on the windowsill, and we both lit up. "Life must be getting boring over on Broadway."

"Just the opposite," she said, blowing smoke out toward the park and producing a pair of more conventional shoes from a satchel that was hanging around her neck. "I think I've finally got a case that doesn't involve an unfaithful husband or a rich brat gone bad."

A word of explanation, here: after the Beecham case, all the members of our little band of investigators besides Miss Howard had gone back to their usual pursuits. Mr. Moore'd gotten his old job back, doing criminal re-porting for the *Times,* though he continued to butt heads with his editors as often as ever. Lucius and Marcus Isaacson, meanwhile, had gone back to the Police Department, where, having been promoted by Commissioner Roosevelt, they were promptly demoted back to detective sergeants when Mr. Roosevelt left for Washington to become assistant secretary of the Navy and the New York Police Department fell back into its old ways. Dr. Kreizler had returned to the Institute and his consultation work on crimi-nal cases, and Cyrus and me had gone back to running the Doctor's house.

But Miss Howard couldn't face returning to the life of a secretary, even if it was at Police Headquarters. So she'd taken over the lease at our former headquarters at Number 808 Broadway and opened her own private investigation service. She limited her clients to women, who generally had a hard time securing such services in those days (not that it's any easy trick for them now). The problem was that, as she'd just said, about the only ladies who could afford to hire her tended to be biddies from uptown who wanted to know if their husbands were cheating on them (the answer generally being yes) or what the wayward heirs to their family fortunes were doing with their private time. In a year of business Miss Howard hadn't been involved in a single juicy murder case or even a nice, sordid bit of blackmailing, and I think she'd begun to get disenchanted with the whole detecting business. Tonight, though, her face reflected her statement that something genuinely racy might've come her way.

"Well," I said, "if it's so important you could've tried the front door. Would've saved you some time. Lot less chance of breaking your neck, too."

Now, if any grown man had made a crack like that to Sara Howard, she'd have whipped out the derringer that was always hidden somewhere on her person and situated it uncomfortably close to his nose; but, probably because I was so much younger, she'd always been different with me, and we could talk straight. "I know," she answered, laughing a bit at herself as she took off the nail-studded boots, shoved them into her satchel, and put on the more sensible footwear. "I just thought I could use the practice. If you're going to catch criminals, you've got to be a bit of one yourself, I've found."

"Ain't *that* so."

Miss Howard finished tying her laces, rubbed out her cigarette, and scattered the tobacco in the butt on the wind. Then rolled the remaining paper into a tight little ball and flicked it away. "Now, then—Dr. Kreizler's not here, is he, Stevie?"

"Not a chance," I answered. "Down at the Institute. Gotta be out by tomorrow morning."

"Yes, I know." Miss Howard bent her head in heartfelt sympathy and sorrow. "He must be crushed," she added quietly.

"That and more. Almost as bad as—well, you know."

"Yes . . ." The green eyes turned toward the park with a faraway look in them, and then she shook herself hard. "Well, with the Doctor away, you and Cyrus will be free to give me a hand. If you're willing."

"Where we going?"

"Mr. Moore's apartments," she said, doing her hair back into its usual bun. "He's not answering his doorbell. Or his telephone."

"Probably not home, then. You know Mr. Moore—you should get over to the Tenderloin, check the gaming houses. His grandmother's only been dead six months, he can't have lost *all* his inheritance yet."

Miss Howard shook her head. "The man at the door to his building says that John came in over an hour ago. With a young lady. They haven't left again." A small, mischievous smile came into her face. "He's home, all right, he just doesn't want any interruptions. *You,* however, are going to get us in."

For the briefest moment I thought of the Doctor, of how he'd been trying hard to discourage me from my lifelong tendency to get into the kind of goings-on what Miss Howard was currently suggesting; but, like I say, my moment of consideration was brief. "Cyrus just came in," I said, returning her smile. "He'll be game—this house's been like a morgue, these days. We could use a little fun."

Her smile grew into a grin. "Good! I knew I had the right man for the job, Stevie."

I nodded. "Yeah," I said, crawling back inside the room. "You just had the wrong shoes."

Miss Howard laughed once more and took a swipe at me as we headed in to rouse Cyrus.

I hadn't been wrong in thinking that, after a year of things going badly in the Seventeenth Street house, Cyrus would be ready for something that might break the routine. In a matter of seconds he was back in his light tweed suit, starched shirt, and tie, and as we headed down to the front door he pulled his favorite old bowler onto his head. The pair of us listened as Miss Howard explained that it was urgent we get Mr. Moore to Number 808 Broadway, where a lady in great distress was waiting for her return. The matter, Miss Howard declared, had "not only criminal but quite possibly international implications." More than that she didn't want to tell us just yet, and more than that neither me nor Cyrus needed to know—what we wanted was a bit of action, and we both knew from personal experience that, given our guide, we were likely to get it. Lengthy explanations could wait. We fairly shot through the foyer and out into the iron-fenced front yard, Cyrus—ever the careful one—pausing just long enough to make sure the house was securely locked up before we made our way down the small path to the gate, started west on the sidewalk of Seventeenth Street, then turned north on Third Avenue.

There was no point in either getting the horses and barouche back out of the small carriage house next door or wasting time trying to hail a cab, as it wasn't but four and a half blocks' walk to Number 34 Gramercy Park, where Mr. Moore had taken apartments at the beginning of the year after his grandmother's death. As we moved from one circle of arc light to another under the streetlamps that ran up Third, passing by simple three- and four-story buildings and under the occasional sidewalk-wide awning of a grocery or vegetable stand, Miss Howard locked her arms into Cyrus's right and my left and began to comment on the little bits of night activity that we saw along the way, plainly trying to control her excitement by talking of nothing in particular. Cyrus and I said little in reply, and before we knew it we'd turned onto Twentieth Street and reached the brownstone mass of Number 34 Gramercy Park, the square bay and turret windows of a few of its apartments still aglow with gas and electric light. It was one of the oldest apartment houses in the city, and also one of the first of the kind they called "cooperative," meaning that all the tenants shared ownership. After his grandmother's sudden death, Mr. Moore'd given some thought to moving into one of the fashionable apartment houses uptown, the Dakota or such, but in the end I don't think he could face moving so far away from the neighborhoods of his youth. Having lost the second of the only two members of his family he'd ever been close to (the other, his brother, had fallen off a boat after jabbing himself full of morphine and drinking himself senseless many years earlier), Mr. Moore had tried hard to keep ownership of his grandmother's house on Washington Square, but her will had stated that the place had to be sold and the proceeds divided up among her squabbling blue-blood heirs. Being suddenly and completely on his own in such a deep way was confusing enough for Mr. Moore without venturing into unknown neighborhoods: in the end, he came back to Gramercy Park, to the area where he'd grown up and where he'd learned his first lessons about the seamier side of life while slumming as a teenager over in the Gashouse District to the east.

As we started up the steps to the brown marble columns that surrounded the stained glass of the building's entrance, I kept a sharp eye on the shadowy stretch of trees, hedges, and pathways—two blocks wide, one block long—that was Gramercy Park behind us. Oh, it was surrounded by wealthy houses and private clubs like the Players, sure enough, and was enclosed by a wrought-iron fence some six or seven feet high, to boot; but any Gashouse tough worth his salt could've made short work of that fence and used the park as a hiding place from which to jump unsuspecting passers-by. It wasn't until I saw a cop walking his beat that I felt all right about turning away from that dark mass and joining Cyrus and Miss Howard at the door.

It was locked up tight at that hour, but there was a small electrical button set in the frame. Miss Howard put a finger to it, and then we heard a bell ring somewhere inside. Soon I could make out a small form moving slowly our way behind the stained glass, and in another few seconds we were faced by an old gent in a striped vest and black pants who looked like somebody should've buried him about ten years back. His wrinkled face turned sour at the sight of us.

"Really, Miss Howard, this is most irregular," he grumbled in a hoarse, wheezing voice. "Most irregular. If Mr. Moore does not answer his bell, then I'm certain—"

"It's all right, Stevenson," Miss Howard answered, cool as ice. "I've reached Mr. Moore by telephone, and he's told my friends and me to come up. Apparently there's some problem with the bell. He's told me where he's hidden his spare key, in the event it happens again."

The old corpse took a long, snooty look at Cyrus and me. "Has he, indeed?" he mumbled. "Well, I'm sure *I* won't be held responsible if there's anything untoward about this. Most irregular, but . . ." He turned toward the elevator door behind him. "You'd better come on, then."

We followed the man as he pulled open first the outer wooden door and then the inner metal grate of the plush elevator. Taking a seat on the little cubicle's velvet-pillowed bench just to tick the old doorman off (successfully), I studied the polished mahogany and brass around me, wondering what poor soul had to spend half his life keeping it in that shape. If it was the old man in front of us, I allowed as he had good reason for his cantankerousness. Closing the grate and then the door again, the man put on a pair of worn, stained leather gloves and then gave a hard tug on the elevator's greased cable—which came up through the floor and ran on through the ceiling in one corner—to set the thing into motion. We began a gentle glide up to the fifth floor, where Mr. Moore occupied the apartments that faced the park on the building's north side.

When the grate and door clattered open again, Cyrus and I followed Miss Howard down a beige-painted hall that was interrupted at various points by still more polished wood doors. Arriving at Mr. Moore's, Miss Howard knocked and then made like she was waiting for Mr. Moore to open up. Turning to the doorman, who was continuing to watch us carefully, she said, "It's late, Stevenson. We mustn't keep you up."

The doorman nodded reluctantly, closed the elevator up again, and headed back down.

As soon as he was gone, Miss Howard put an ear to the door, then looked at me with those green eyes dancing. "All right, Stevie," she whispered. "You're on."

Reformed as I may have become since moving in with Dr. Kreizler two years earlier, I still carried some of the tools of my old trade with me, as they could, on occasion, come in handy. Among these was my little set of picks, with which I proceeded to make short work of the fairly simple tumblers inside the lock in Mr. Moore's door. With a gentle little click the door popped ajar, and Miss Howard beamed with delight.

"You really have got to teach me that," she murmured, patting my back silently and pushing the door farther open. "Now, then—here we go."

Mr. Moore had decorated his apartments with as much of his grandmother's furniture as his family would let him get away with, as well as with some fine English country pieces what Dr. Kreizler had helped him select. So the place had a kind of split character about it, feeling in some spots like an old lady's house and in others like a rugged bachelor flat. There were some seven rooms in all, arranged in a kind of crazy order that wouldn't have made much sense in a regular house. In a stealthy little file we made our way down the darkened main hall, being careful to stay on the runner carpet all the while, and as we did we began to come across various articles of men's and women's clothing. Miss Howard frowned when she saw all this, and her frown only got deeper when, as we got close to the bedroom door, we began to hear giggling and laughter coming from inside. Drawing up in front of the door, Miss Howard balled one hand into a fist and made ready to give it a good rap—but then the door suddenly opened, and out popped a woman.

And this was, I can say now with even more appreciation than I could then, a *woman*. With long golden hair that hung down to her waist and robed in only a coverlet that she clasped with one hand at her side, she had a set of stems on her what started in a pair of slender ankles and didn't seem to end till somewhere up around the ceiling—and the ceilings in that building were high, mind you. She was still giggling as she came out, and we could hear Mr. Moore inside the room, pleading with her to come back.

"I will, John, I will," the woman said melodiously through rich red lips. "But you must give me a moment." She closed the door again, turned toward the bathroom what was situated down at the end of the hall—and then caught sight of us.

She didn't say anything, just gave us a sort of puzzled little smile. Miss Howard smiled back, though I could see it was a struggle for her, and then held one finger to her lips, urging the woman to be quiet. The woman aped the same gesture, giggled once more—she was obviously drunk—and then continued, without any further word of explanation from or to us, on her way to the bathroom. At that Miss Howard smiled much more genuinely—not to mention a little wickedly—and opened the bedroom door.

The dim light from the hall didn't let us see much more than a jumbled mass of sheets on a very large bed, though it was clear there was a person under the mass. Cyrus and I stayed by the door, but Miss Howard just strode right on up to the bedside, standing there like she was waiting for something. Pretty soon the mass under the sheets started to move, and then the top half of Mr. Moore's naked body appeared, his short hair tousled, his handsome face a picture of happiness. His eyes were closed, and in a kind of childlike way he reached out and put his arms around Miss Howard's waist. She didn't look too happy about it, but she didn't move, either; and then, feeling her dress, Mr. Moore mumbled:

"No, no, Lily, you *can't* get dressed, you *can't* leave, this night can't *ever* end . . ."

That brought out the derringer. To this day I can't tell you where it was that Miss Howard managed to keep it so that it was always out of sight yet always so available; but in a flash it was in front of Mr. Moore's closed eyes and smiling face. The smile disappeared and the eyes popped open, however, when Miss Howard pulled back the hammer.

"I think, John," she said evenly, "that even through the sheets I could clip off both your testicles with one shot—so I advise you to unhand me."

Mr. Moore darted away from her with a shriek, then covered himself completely with the sheet like a kid who'd just been caught abusing himself.

"Sara!" he shouted, half in fear and half in anger. "What the hell do you think you're doing? And how the hell did you get in here?"

"The front door," Miss Howard answered simply, as the derringer disappeared into the folds of her dress again.

"The front door?" Mr. Moore bellowed. "But the front door's locked, I'm sure I—" Looking to the doorway, Mr. Moore caught sight first of Cyrus and then of me—and that was all he needed to see. "Stevie! So!" Patting his hair down onto his head and trying to compose himself, Mr. Moore stood, still covered in his sheet, and drew up to the fullest height he could manage. "I would have thought, Taggert, that the bonds of male honor would have prevented you from playing a part in a scheme like this. And what have you done with Lily?"

"She's in the bathroom," Miss Howard answered. "Didn't seem at all disappointed to see us. You must be losing your touch, John."

Mr. Moore only frowned and looked to the doorway again. "I shall direct my comments to you, Cyrus. Knowing you to be a person of integrity, I can assume that there is some good reason for your being here."

Cyrus nodded, with the ever-so-slightly-patronizing smile that often came onto his face when he spoke to Mr. Moore. "Miss Howard says there is, sir," he answered. "That's good enough for me. You'd better ask her about it."

"And supposing I don't wish to speak to her?" Mr. Moore grunted.

"Then, sir, you'll be a long time getting an explanation . . ."

Faced with no other option, Mr. Moore paused, shrugged his shoulders, then plopped down onto the bed again. "All right, Sara. Tell me what's so all-fired important that it's got you breaking and entering. And for God's sake, Stevie, give me a cigarette."

As I lit up a stick and handed it to Mr. Moore, Miss Howard moved around in front of him. "I have a case, John."

Mr. Moore let out a big, smoky sigh. "Splendid. Do you demand the front page, or will the inside of the paper do?"

"No, John," Miss Howard said earnestly. "I think this is real. I think it's big."

Her tone took a good bit of the sarcasm out of Mr. Moore's voice. "Well—what is it?"

"A woman came to Number 808 this evening. Señora Isabella Linares. Ring a bell?"

Mr. Moore rubbed his forehead hard. "No. Which gives her something in common with you. Come on, Sara, no games, who is she?"

"Her husband," Miss Howard answered, "is Señor Narciso Linares. Now, does *that* ring a bell?"

Mr. Moore looked up slowly, intrigued in a way that clearly pleased Miss Howard. "Isn't he . . . he holds some position in the Spanish consulate, doesn't he?"

"He is, in fact, private secretary to the Spanish consul."

"All right. So what's his wife doing at Number 808?"

Miss Howard began to pace around the room purposefully. "She has a fourteen-month-old daughter. Or had. The child was kidnapped. Three days ago."

Mr. Moore's face turned skeptical. "Sara. We are talking about the daughter of the private secretary of the consul of the Empire of Spain in the City of New York. The same Empire of Spain that Mr. William Randolph Hearst, our friend in the Navy Department"—by which he meant Mr. Roosevelt—"certain of my bosses, some of the business leaders, and much of the populace of this country have been openly insulting and trying to goad into war for years now. Do you honestly think that if such a child were to be kidnapped in New York, said Empire of Spain would not make the most of the chance to cry foul and declare the barbarity of its American critics? Wars have been fought and avoided over less, you know."

"That's just the point, John." As Miss Howard went on, both Cyrus and I drew closer, now very interested in what she was saying and not wanting to miss a trick. "You *would* think that the Spanish officials would react that way, wouldn't you? But not at all. Señora Linares claims that the kidnapping occurred when she was walking alone with the baby in Central Park one evening. She couldn't see the abductor—he came from behind and hit her on the head with something. But when she went home to tell her husband what had happened, he reacted strangely—bizarrely. He showed little concern for his wife, and less for his daughter. He told her that she must tell no one what had happened—they would wait for a ransom note, and if none came, it would mean that the child had been taken by a lunatic and killed."

Mr. Moore shrugged. "Such things *do* happen, Sara."

"But he didn't even *try* going to the police! A full day passed, no ransom note came, and finally Señora Linares declared that if her husband wouldn't go to the authorities, she would." Miss Howard paused, wringing her hands a bit. "He beat her, John. Savagely. You should see her—in fact, you're *going* to see her. She didn't know what to do—her husband said he'd do worse if she ever talked of going to the police again. Finally, she confided in a friend of hers at the French consulate, a woman I helped out with some minor marital rubbish a few months ago. The Frenchwoman told her about me. The señora's waiting for us. You've got to come and talk to her—"

"Wait, wait, wait, now," Mr. Moore answered, holding up his cigarette and trying to salvage his night of pleasure. "You're forgetting a few things here. In the first place, these people are diplomatic officials. The laws are different. I don't know exactly what they *are* in a case like this, but they're different. Second, if this Linares character doesn't want to pursue it, then who are we to—"

Mr. Moore was interrupted by the sudden appearance, behind Cyrus and me, of the woman he'd just minutes ago been in bed with. She'd apparently retrieved her clothes from the hall and was fully dressed and ready to depart.

"Excuse me, John," she said quietly. "I wasn't sure what these people wanted, but it does sound important—so I thought I ought to go. I'll see myself out."

She turned to leave, and Mr. Moore suddenly looked like he'd done a few seconds in the electrical chair: He cried "No!" desperately, secured his sheet around himself again, and bolted toward the bedroom door. "No, Lily, wait!"

"Call me at the theater tomorrow!" the woman answered from the front door. "I'd love to take this up again sometime!" And with that she was gone.

Mr. Moore stalked over to Miss Howard and glared at her what you might call hotly. "*You*, Sara Howard, have just destroyed what was well on its way to becoming one of the three best nights of my life!"

Miss Howard only smiled a bit. "I won't ask what the other two were. No, really, I am sorry, John. But this situation is desperate."

"It had *better* be."

"It is, trust me. You haven't heard the best part yet."

"Oh. *Haven't* I . . . ?"

"Señora Linares came to me in the greatest secrecy, after normal business hours. In order to make sure that she wasn't followed by anyone from the consulate, she took the Third Avenue El downtown. When she got off the train at Ninth Street, she walked along the platform toward the stairs down to the street—and happened to glance into the last car of the train."

Miss Howard stopped for a moment, causing Mr. Moore to get a bit agitated. "Sara, you can dispense with all these dramatic pauses. They're not going to improve my mood. *What* did she see?"

"She saw her child, John."

Mr. Moore's face screwed up. "You mean she *thought* she saw her child—wishful thinking, that kind of thing."

"No, John. *Her child*. In the arms of a woman." Miss Howard allowed herself one more smiling pause. "A white *American* woman."

Mr. Moore digested that little tidbit with a kind of tormented but interested moan: the newshound was winning out over the libertine. He turned to me, still not looking much happier, but clearly resigned to his fate. "Stevie—as a means of atoning for this invasion, will you help me find my clothes? Then we'll get down to Number 808 and, God willing, find out what this is all about. But so help me, Sara, derringer or no derringer, if this case is a bust you will regret the day we ever met!"

"Oh, I regretted that ages ago," Miss Howard answered with a laugh, one that Cyrus and I picked up on. "Come on, Stevie. Let's see if we can't get our distraught friend here cleaned up. We need to move quickly."

CHAPTER 3

It was a walk I hadn't made in a year, that down to Number 808 Broadway, but you wouldn't have known it from the way my body moved along the route. I remember reading in *The Principles of Psychology*—that doorstop of a book what Dr. Kreizler's old teacher at Harvard, Professor William James, had written some years back, and which I'd fought my way through along with the rest of our team during the Beecham case—that the brain isn't the only organ that stores memories. Some of the more primitive parts of the body—muscles, for instance—have their own ways of filing away experience and recalling it at a moment's notice. If so, my legs were proving it that night, for I could've made the trip even if somebody's cut my spinal cord below the cerebral cortex and left me running on nothing but my brain stem, like one of those poor laboratory frogs what Professor James and his students seemed to be always chopping into little pieces.

As we made our way along Gramercy Park and then down Irving Place, I once again kept a sharp eye out for any Gashouse boys what might be out to pick off drunken swells who were on their way home from the gaming houses of the Tenderloin. But there wasn't any trouble hanging in the air, just the same moist, clean scent that'd followed the day's rain, and as we moved south I began to loosen up. Miss Howard still didn't want to divulge any more information concerning her case until we got to Number 808 and actually met the lady in question, so our efforts were applied with singleness of purpose to getting Mr. Moore to that location. This job was a little trickier than it might sound. We'd chosen to go downtown on

Irving Place because we knew that if we headed over to Fourth Avenue and then south to Union Square we'd pass by Brübacher's Wine Garden, where many of Mr. Moore's drinking pals would doubtless still be engaged in the customary activity of that establishment: laying bets on whether or not passing pedestrians, carriages, and carts would be able to successfully avoid grievous collisions with the streetcars what came screaming down Broadway and tearing around the square at top speed. Faced with such a temptation, Mr. Moore would likely have proved unable to resist. But Irving Place had its own distraction in the form of Pete's Tavern at Eighteenth Street, a cozy old watering hole what had once been a favorite retreat of Boss Tweed and his Tammany boys, and where in recent days Mr. Moore could often be found passing the evening with several of his journalistic and literary friends. Once the glowing orange lights in the smoky windows of Pete's were behind us, however, I could tell that Mr. Moore knew his last chance for salvation had also passed: his grumbling took a decided turn toward whining.

"I mean to say, tomorrow *is* Monday, Sara," he protested as we reached Fourteenth Street. The deceptively chipper front of Tammany Hall rose into view on our left, looking the way it always did to me, like some crazy giant brick wardrobe. "And keeping up with what Croker and those swine are doing"—Mr. Moore pointed toward the hall—"requires constant and irritating effort. Not to mention the Spanish business."

"Nonsense, John," Miss Howard replied snappily. "Politics in this city are dead in the water right now, and you know it. Strong's as lame a duck as ever sat in City Hall, and neither Croker nor Platt"—by which she meant the Democratic and Republican bosses of New York, respectively—"is about to let another reform mayor win in November. Come this winter it's going to be back to business as filthy usual in this city, and nobody needs you to tell them so."

As if to punctuate Miss Howard's point, a sudden roar of laughter cut through the night as we waded through the rain-thinned horse manure and urine that coated Fourteenth Street. Once across, we all turned around to see a small crowd of well-dressed, drunk, and very happy men emerging from Tammany Hall, a fat cigar sticking out of each of their mouths.

"Hmm," Mr. Moore noised in some discouragement, watching the men as he followed the rest of us west. "I'm not sure it's quite *that* simple, Sara. And even if it is, that doesn't clear up the larger issue of the Cuban crisis. We're at a critical point in our dealings with Madrid."

"Hogwash." Miss Howard paused just long enough to grab Mr. Moore's sleeve and pull him along faster. "Even if your area *were* foreign rather than metropolitan affairs, you'd be stymied for the moment. General Woodford"—referring to the new American minister to Spain—"hasn't even *left* for Madrid yet, and McKinley doesn't intend to send him until he's gotten a full report from the special envoy to Cuba—what's his name, that man Calhoun."

"How the hell," Mr. Moore mumbled despondently, "am I supposed to argue with a girl who reads more of my damned paper than *I* do . . . ?"

"All of which," Miss Howard finished up, "means that you'll have nothing more to occupy your attention at the office tomorrow than the usual run of summer violence—oh, and there's Queen Victoria's jubilee, no doubt the *Times* will milk that dry."

Mr. Moore couldn't help but laugh. "Right lead column, all the way through the festivities—there'll be special photos on Sunday, too. My God, Sara, doesn't it ever get *boring* knowing all the angles?"

"I don't know them on this case, John," Miss Howard answered, as we started down Broadway. The sounds of the carriages in the street became a bit smoother as they hit the Russ pavement of the avenue, but the slight softening of the clatter didn't ease Miss Howard's edginess. "I don't mind telling you, it frightens me. There's something terrible about this business . . ."

A few more silent seconds of apprehensive walking, and they hove into view: first the Gothic spire of Grace Church, reaching up and above the surrounding buildings with a kind of easy majesty, then the yellow bricks and cloisterlike windows of Number 808. Our old headquarters was actually closer to us than Grace, bordering the churchyard on the uptown side as it did, but in that part of town you always saw the spire before anything else. Not even the ever-bright windows of McCreery's department store across Broadway or the huge cast-iron monument to huckersterism that was the old Stewart store on Tenth Street could hold a wet match to the church. The only building that came close was Number 808, and that was because it had been designed by the same architect, James Renwick, who apparently had it in mind that this little crossroads of Broadway should be a memorial to our medieval ancestors instead of a pure and simple marketplace.

We approached the swirling, pretty ironwork of Number 808's front door—*art nouveau,* they called it, a name what always struck me as pretty pointless, since I figured that the next artsy fellow who came along was always bound to lay claim to the *nouveau* part—and then Cyrus, Mr. Moore, and I all paused before entering. It wasn't fear, so much; but you have to remember that just a year ago this place had been our second (and sometimes first) home during an investigation that'd seen unimaginable horrors brought to light and friends of ours mercilessly killed. Everything on Broadway looked pretty much the same as it had during those dark days: the department stores, the shadowy, ghostly yard and parish house of the church, the fine but not too fussy St. Denis Hotel across the street (also designed by Mr. Renwick)—all was as it had been, and that only brought the memories more vividly to life. And so we just waited a minute before we went inside.

Miss Howard seemed to sense our uncertainty and, knowing it to be well grounded, didn't push too hard.

"I know I'm asking a lot," she said, glancing around the street and speaking with rare uncertainty. "But I tell you—all of you—if you see this woman, talk to her for just a few minutes, hear her describe it—"

"It's all right, Sara," Mr. Moore interrupted, abandoning complaint and softening his voice to suit the scene. He turned first to me and then to Cyrus, as if to make sure that he was speaking for us all. We didn't need to tell him he was. "It takes a moment, that's all," he went on, looking up at the façade of Number 808. "But we're with you. Lead the way."

We passed through the marble lobby and into the great cage that was the elevator, then started the slow, laborious drift up to the sixth floor. Looking at Cyrus and Mr. Moore, I could tell they knew as well as I did that, all nervousness aside, we weren't going to come back down again without having gotten into something we might regret. Part of that was our mutual friendship for Miss Howard; part of it was, well, something that born New Yorkers just carry in their blood. A nose for *the thing*, call that thing whatever name you want: the story, the case, the ride—any way you cut it, we were getting on board. Oh, sure, we could pray that it wouldn't involve the kind of devastation what the Beecham case had; but pray was all we could do, for we didn't have the power to back out now.

The elevator came to the kind of heavy, sudden stop typical of commercial jobs, for Number 808 was a commercial building, full of furniture builders and sweatshops. That was part of the reason Dr. Kreizler had picked it in the first place: we'd been able to carry out our investigative affairs under the harmless cover of small businesses. But secrecy was no longer an issue for Miss Howard, and through the elevator grate I could see that she'd had a very tactful sign painted on the sixth-floor door:

THE HOWARD AGENCY
RESEARCH SERVICES FOR WOMEN

Drawing the elevator grate aside, she unlocked the door and then held it open as we all filed in.

The big expanse of the near-floor-through room was dark, with only the light from the arc streetlamps on Broadway and McCreery's upper windows across the street throwing any illumination inside. But that was enough to see that Miss Howard had made only a few changes in the decor of the place. The furniture what Dr. Kreizler had bought at an antique auction the previous year—and what'd once been the property of the Marchese Luigi Carcano—still filled the room. The divan, large mahogany table, and big easy chairs rested on the green oriental carpets in their usual spots, giving the place the sudden, unexpected feel of a home. The billiard table was now in the back by the kitchen, covered with planking and a silk drape. It wasn't the kind of thing, I figured, that would have given Miss Howard's lady clients much reassurance. But the five big office desks were still there, though Miss Howard had arranged them in a row rather than a circle, and the baby grand piano still sat in a corner by one of the Gothic windows. Seeing it, Cyrus went over and lifted its lid with a little smile, touching two keys gently and then looking to Miss Howard.

"Still in tune," he said softly.

She nodded and smiled back. "Still in tune."

Cyrus put his bowler on the bench, sat down, and gently started to play. At first I figured he'd go for one of the operatic tunes what the Doctor always had him give out with at our house, but I quickly realized that it was a slow, sad rendition of some folk melody what I couldn't immediately place.

Mr. Moore, who was staring out another window at the barely visible glimmer of the Hudson River in the distance, turned to Cyrus and beamed with a little smile of his own. " 'Shenandoah,' " he murmured quietly, as if to rightly say that Cyrus had found the perfect tune to summarize the strange and melancholy feelings what had only grown stronger in each of us at the sight of the room.

In another shadowy corner, I could see that Miss Howard had made an addition to the furnishings: an enormous Japanese screen, its five panels fully open. Peering out from behind one end of the screen was a section of a large black standing chalkboard, bordered in oak: *the* board, as we'd always known it. How long had it been hidden away? I wondered.

Miss Howard, having given us a few minutes to adjust to our return, now rubbed her hands in anticipation and again spoke with a kind of hesitation what was unusual for her.

"Señora Linares is in the kitchen, having tea. I'll just get her."

She glided back toward the rear of the building, where a dimly lit doorway indicated some sign of life. Again automatically, I walked over and jumped onto one of the windowsills that overlooked the church garden— my accustomed roost in this place—and took a small knife out of my pocket, using its blade to trim my fingernails as Cyrus continued to play and we heard the seemingly faraway sound of the two women's voices in the kitchen.

Soon a pair of silhouettes appeared against the faint light in the kitchen doorway, and even in the near darkness I could see that Miss Howard was helping the other lady walk—not so much because the woman was physically unable to stand on her own (though she did seem in some pain) but more to help her overcome what I sensed was a kind of terrible dread. As they came into the center of the room, I could see that the woman had a fine figure and was richly dressed in black: layer upon layer of satin and silk, all of it crowned by a broad hat from which drooped a heavy black veil. She held an ivory-handled umbrella in one hand, and as Sara let go of her arm she steadied herself on it.

The rest of us got to our feet, but Señora Linares's attention was fixed on Cyrus. "Please," she said, in a pleasantly toned voice what had obviously suffered through hours of weeping. "Do not stop. The song is lovely."

Cyrus obliged but kept his playing soft. Mr. Moore stepped forward at that point, offering a hand. "Señora Linares—my name is John Schuyler Moore. I suspect that Miss Howard has informed you that I'm a reporter—"

"For *The New York Times*," the woman answered from behind the veil as she shook Mr. Moore's hand lightly. "I must tell you frankly, señor, that were you in the employ of any other newspaper in this city, such as those belonging to Pulitzer and Hearst, I should not have consented to this meeting. They have printed abominable lies about the conduct of my countrymen toward the rebels in Cuba."

Mr. Moore eyed her carefully for a moment. "I fear that's so, señora. But I also fear that at least some of what they've printed is true." Señora Linares's head bent forward just a little, and you could feel her sadness and shame even through the veil. "Fortunately, though," Mr. Moore went on, "we're not here to discuss politics, but the disappearance of your daughter. Assuming, that is, that we may be certain the two subjects are not connected?"

Miss Howard gave Mr. Moore a quick look of surprise and disapproval, and Señora Linares's head snapped back up into a proud position. "I have given my word to Miss Howard—the facts are as I have represented them."

Miss Howard shook her head. "Honestly, John, how can you—"

"My apologies," he answered. "To you both. But you must admit that the coincidence is rather remarkable. War between our two countries is spoken of as commonly as the weather these days—and yet of all the children of all the diplomats in New York to mysteriously disappear, it's the daughter of a high Spanish official."

"John," Miss Howard said angrily, "perhaps you and I had better—"

But the Linares woman held up a hand. "No, Miss Howard. Señor Moore's skepticism is, we must grant, understandable. But tell me this, sir: If I were a mere pawn in some diplomatic game, would I go to these lengths?" At that the woman pulled her veil up and over the black hat and moved further into the light that drifted through the window.

Now, in the part of the Lower East Side where I was born and spent my first eight years, you tended to get pretty used to the sight of women who'd been worked over by their men; and given my mother's taste in male companions, I'd gotten some especially close looks at just how that work was done. But nothing I'd seen in all those years exceeded the outrages that somebody had committed against this very comely lady. There was an enormous bruise that started above her left eye, then moved down to swell the eye shut and end in a gash in the cheek. A rainbow patch of purple, black, yellow, and green spread out on either side of her nose and reached under her right eye, the one she could still see out of, showing pretty clearly that the nose itself had been busted. The flesh of the chin was all scraped away, while the right side of the mouth was dragged down into a continuous frown by another bad gash. From the painful way she moved, it was pretty apparent that the same kind of injuries had been inflicted to the rest of her body.

At the sound of the simultaneous hisses that came out of Mr. Moore, Cyrus, and me, the señora attempted to smile, and the faintest spark flashed in her lovely, deep brown right eye. "If you were to ask me," she murmured, "I should say that I fell down the marble staircase of the consulate—after fainting from grief following the death of our child. You see, my husband and Consul Baldasano have already decided that, at those times when an explanation to outsiders is unavoidable, I am to say that my daughter was taken by illness. But she is not dead, Señor Moore." The señora staggered forward a step or two, leaning on the umbrella. "I have seen her! I have—seen—" At that she seemed about to faint, and Miss Howard moved to her quickly, guiding her into one of Marchese Carcano's plush easy chairs. I turned to Mr. Moore, and saw his face light up with a whole batch of reactions: anger, horror, sympathy, but above all consternation. He waved a hand in my direction vaguely. "Stevie . . ."

I already had the packet out and was lighting a stick for each of us. I handed him his, watched him pace back and forth a few times, and then got out of the way when he bolted for the telephone what was sitting on a desk behind me. "We're way out of our depth here," he mumbled, picking up the receiver. Then, in a stronger voice: "Operator? Police Headquarters on Mulberry Street. Central Office, Bureau of Detectives."

"*What?*" Miss Howard said urgently, as a look of terror filled Señora Linares's face. "John, no, I told you—"

Mr. Moore held up a hand. "Don't worry. I just want to find out where they are. You know the boys better than that, Sara. They'll keep it unofficial if we ask them to."

"Who will?" the Linares woman whispered; but Mr. Moore turned his attention back to the 'phone.

"Hello? Central? Listen, I have an urgent personal message for the Detective Sergeants Isaacson—can you tell me where they are? . . . Ah. Good, thanks." He hung up the phone and turned to me. "Stevie—apparently a body's been discovered over at the Cunard pier. Lucius and Marcus are looking into it. How fast do you think you can get over there and get back with them?"

"If Cyrus'll help me commandeer a hansom," I answered, "half an hour. Three quarters at the outside."

Mr. Moore turned to Cyrus. "Go."

The pair of us sprang toward the elevator. Before reentering it, however, I paused just long enough to turn back to Mr. Moore. "You don't think we should—"

Mr. Moore shook his head quickly. "We don't know what this is yet. I won't ask him to come back to this place until we're sure."

Cyrus put a hand to my shoulder. "He's right, Stevie. Let's go."

I stepped into the elevator, Cyrus slammed the grate, and we moved back down the shaftway.

Because the Hotel St. Denis was right across the street, Number 808 had always been an easy spot to catch a cab at almost any hour of the day or night: there were two lined up outside the hotel when Cyrus and I crossed to it. The first was a four-wheeler, captained by an ancient geezer in a faded red liveryman's jacket and a beat-to-hell top hat. He was nodding off in his seat and stank of booze from six feet away. His horse, however, was a good-looking grey mare who seemed game.

I turned to Cyrus. "Get him in the back," I said, jumping into the driver's seat and starting to haul the old man out of it. "Hey—hey, pop! Up and at 'em, you've got a fare!"

The old man made some drunken, confused sounds as I shoved him toward the little iron step on the carriage's left side and down to Cyrus: "What—what do you think—what're you doing?"

"Driving," I answered, seating myself and taking the horse's reins.

"You can't drive!" the man protested as Cyrus forced him into the passenger compartment and sat alongside him, closing the little doors.

"We'll double your rate," Cyrus answered, keeping a good grip on the man. "And don't worry, the boy's an excellent driver."

"But you'll queer me with the cops!" the old fool bellowed on, removing his top hat and showing us the license what was fastened to it. "I can't have any trouble with the law—I'm a licensed hack, see?"

"Yeah?" I looked back at him, grabbed the hat, and shoved it onto my own head. "Well, now *I* am—so sit back and pipe down!"

He did the one but not the other, and was still wailing like a stuck pig as I cracked the reins against the mare's backside and we bolted out onto the pavement of Broadway at a speed that more than justified the quick measure I'd taken of the animal.

CHAPTER 4

By the time we rounded the corner of Ninth Street, we were moving at such a crazy pace—even, I'll confess, for me—that the cab near went up on two wheels. The Cunard Line pier, in those days before the launch of the company's really big liners (the *Mauretania* and the sad old *Lusitania*), was still located down at the foot of Clarkson Street, a short block above West Houston; but I was going to avoid that latter thoroughfare for as long as I could. Even late on a Sunday night it'd be a thick mass of whores, cons, and their drunken marks, one what had only gotten thicker in the months since Commissioner Roosevelt had left for Washington. The volume of their business would slow our movement badly. As it was, after we raced through the quiet residential blocks of Ninth Street, passed over Sixth Avenue, and headed west on Christopher, we began to see noticeable signs of what Miss Howard had mentioned earlier on our walk to Number 808: the criminal elements were conducting their affairs outside their dives, dens, and brothels in considerable numbers and with a total lack of the concern what Mr. Roosevelt had, if only briefly, drummed into them. Completing all this activity was the occasional sight of cops doing all those things that the commissioner had, by himself roving the streets at night on inspection tours, worked so hard to prevent: collecting graft payments, drinking outside dance halls and saloons, cavorting with whores, and sleeping anywhere they could. Yes, the old town was truly waking up to the fact that Roosevelt was gone and his reform-minded boss, Mayor Strong, would soon follow suit: the gloves were coming off of the underworld.

As we reached Bleecker Street, something snagged my eye (and, I'll confess, my guts), and I reined up hard, somewhat to Cyrus' surprise. "What's happened, Stevie?" he called to me; but I could only stare across the street in momentary confusion at a patch of faded blue silk and an enormous head of blond hair. From Cyrus's tone, I could tell he'd caught sight of the same thing, and I knew he was frowning: "Oh. *Kat* . . ."

I cracked the reins again and charged over to the blue silk and blond hair, both of which belonged to Kat Devlin, a—well, let's just call her a friend of mine, for the moment, who worked at one of the kid dives and disorderly houses down on Worth Street. She was with a decked-out man who was old enough to be her grandfather, for Kat was but fourteen; and as they tried to cross Bleecker, I steered the grey mare into their path.

"We don't have time for this, Stevie," I heard Cyrus say, gently but with intent.

"One minute, that's all," I answered quickly.

Kat started at the sudden appearance of the mare and looked up, her small, pretty face and blue eyes going furious. "Hey! What the hell do you think you're—" Then she caught sight of me. Her look softened, but she still appeared perplexed. A smile managed to work its way into her thin lips. "Why, Stevie! What're you doing over here? And what're you doing with that cab, besides trying to frighten off my trade?" At that she turned the smile up to the old man she was with and locked her arm in his tighter, making my heart burn hotter. The man patted her arm with an expensively gloved hand and grinned sickeningly.

"I was gonna ask you the same thing," I said. "Bit west for you, ain't it, Kat?"

"Oh, I'm moving up in the world," she answered. "Next week I move my things out of Frankie's for good and go to work on Hudson Street. At the Dusters' place." At that she suddenly sniffled hard and painfully, laughed a little to cover it, and wiped her nose quick. Her moth-eaten glove came away with a trace of blood on it—and all, as they say, became clear to me.

"The Dusters," I said, the burn in my chest turning into fear. "Kat, you can't—"

She could see what was coming and started to move across the street again. "Just a friend of mine," she said to the man she was with. Then she called over her shoulder to me, "Stop by Frankie's and see me this week, Stevie!" It was as much a warning to back off as it was an invitation. "And don't go stealing any more cabs!"

I wanted to say something, anything, to get her to leave her mark and come with us, but Cyrus reached up and gripped my shoulder hard. "It's no good, Stevie," he said, in the same soft but certain tone. "There's no time."

I knew he was right, but there was no resignation in the knowledge, and I could feel my body tighten up to the point where, for an instant, my vision went all cockeyed. Then, with a sudden, short yell, I grabbed the cabbie's long horsewhip out of its holder, lifted it above my head, and lashed it toward the man who was crossing the street with Kat. The whip caught his high hat at the crest, cutting a nice hole in it and sending it flying six feet into a puddle of rainwater and horse piss.

Kat spun on me. "Stevie! Damn you! You can't—"

But I wasn't going to hear any more: I cracked the reins and sent the grey mare flying back along Christopher Street, Kat's curses and protests loud but indistinct behind me.

I suppose you've figured out by now that Kat was something more than just a friend of mine. But she wasn't my girl, by any stretch; wasn't anybody's girl, really. I couldn't and can't tell you just what place she held in my particular world. Maybe I could say that she was the first person what I ever had intimate relations with, except that such a statement might conjure up happy images of young love, which was far from the reality of it. Truth is, she was a question and a puzzle—one what would get even more perplexing in the days to come, as her life took an unexpected turn what was destined to intertwine it with the case we were only beginning to unravel.

By the time we reached Hudson Street I was still in a hell of a state, and I made no effort to slow the mare as I pulled the reins hard with my left arm and gave the animal the word to turn downtown. Once again we near went up on two wheels, and though the cabbie screamed in fear I heard no sound of protest from Cyrus, who was used to my driving and knew I'd never overturned a rig yet. Passing by the faded red bricks of old St. Luke's Chapel on our right and then the saloons and stores of lower Hudson Street, we reached Clarkson in just a few more seconds and made another wild turn, this time west. The river and the waterfront suddenly sprang into being in front of us, the water blacker than the night and the pier at the end of the street unusually busy for the hour.

As we cleared the warehouses and sailors' boarding hovels what lined the last couple of blocks of Clarkson Street, we could begin to make out the shape of a big steamer docked at the long, deep green superstructure of the Cunard pier: she was the *Campania,* not yet five years old and lying at proud rest, with strings of small lights on her boat deck that illuminated her two deep red, black-crowned funnels, her handsome white bridge and lifeboats, and the stately line of her hull, all of which impressively hinted at what wonders the company that'd pioneered transatlantic travel was going to achieve in the none-too-distant future.

On the waterfront near the pier was a fairly large group of people, and as we got closer I could see that a lot of them were cops, some detectives and some in uniform. There were a few sailors and longshoremen, too, and, strangely, a few young boys dressed in nothing but soaking wet pants what had been cut off at the knees. They had large sheets of canvas wrapped around their shoulders and were shivering and jumping up and down, half from the chill of the river water they'd apparently been swimming in and half from excitement. A few torches and one longshoreman's electrical lamp lit the scene, but there was no sign as yet of the Detective Sergeants Isaacson. Which meant nothing, of course—they could easily have been at the bottom of the Hudson in diving helmets, searching for clues that the average New York detective would've considered useless.

Once we reached the waterfront, Cyrus pulled some money out of his billfold, stuffed it into the cabbie's shaking hand, and said only, "Stay here," a command that the man was in no condition to disobey. Just to make sure he didn't bolt, though, I kept his hat and license on my head as we started to make our way through the crowd.

I let Cyrus do the talking to the cops, given that whatever little respect most New York City cops had for blacks, they had even less for me. I'd already spotted one or two officers that I'd crossed paths with during the years I'd been known as "the Stevepipe" and had been, I'll admit, justifiably infamous around Mulberry Street. When Cyrus inquired after the Isaacsons, he was what you might call reluctantly directed toward whatever business was taking place at the center of the crowd, to a cry of "Nigger to see the Jew boys!" We shoved our way forward.

I hadn't seen the detective sergeants in a few months, but it would've been impossible to imagine them in a more typical setting. On the concrete embankment of the waterfront, they were hunched over a wide piece of bright red oilcloth. The tall, handsome Marcus, with his full head of curly dark hair and big, noble nose, had a tape measure and some steel gauging instruments out, and he was busily recording the dimensions of some still unrecognizable object underneath him. His younger brother Lucius, shorter and stouter, with thinning hair what in spots revealed an always-sweating scalp, was poking around with what looked like the kind of medical instruments Dr. Kreizler kept in his examination room. They were being watched over by a captain I recognized—Hogan was his name, and he was shaking his head the way all the old guard did when faced with the work of the Isaacsons.

"There ain't *enough* of it to make any sense of," Captain Hogan said with a laugh. "We'll be better off dragging the river to see if we can't find something that might tell us a little more—like, for instance, maybe a *head*." The cops around him joined in the laughter. "*That* thing ought to go straight to the morgue—though I don't know what even the morgue boys'd do with it."

"There are a lot of important clues in what we have here," Marcus answered without turning, his voice deep and confident. "We can at least get an idea of how it was done."

"And transferring it from the scene will only result in the usual damage to additional evidence," Lucius tacked on, his voice quick and agitated. "So if you'll just be good enough to keep these people back and let us finish, Captain Hogan, there'll be time enough for you to make your delivery to the charnel house."

Hogan laughed again and turned away. "You Jew boys. Always thinkin'. Okay, folks, step back, now, let's let the *experts* do their job."

As Hogan glanced our way, I pulled the top hat down over my eyes in the continuing hope of not being recognized, while Cyrus approached him. "Sir," he said, with far more respect than I knew he felt, "I have a very important personal message for the detective sergeants."

"Do you, now?" Hogan answered. "Well, they won't want any Zulu boy taking them away from their scientific studies—"

But the Isaacsons had already turned at the sound of Cyrus's voice. Seeing him, they both smiled. "Cyrus!" Marcus called. "What are you doing here?" The detective sergeant glanced around, and I knew he was looking for me. I already had a finger in front of my mouth, so that when he saw me he'd know not to say anything. He got the message and nodded, still smiling, and then Lucius did the same. They both got up off their haunches, and for the first time we could see what was lying on the oilcloth.

It was the upper part of a man's torso, which had been cut off just below the ribs. The neck had likewise been severed, in a way what even I could see was not the work of any expert. The arms had also been hacked off of the hunk of flesh, which looked fairly fresh. That and the fact that there wasn't much of a stench seemed to indicate the thing hadn't been in the water all that long.

At a nod from Cyrus, Lucius and Marcus drew aside with us, and friendlier greetings were exchanged in whispered voices.

"Have you changed professions, Stevie?" Lucius asked, indicating my hat as he mopped at his head with a handkerchief.

"No, sir," I answered. "But we needed to get here in a hurry. Miss Howard—"

"Sara?" Marcus cut in. "Is she all right? Has anything happened?"

"She's at Number 808, sir," Cyrus answered. "With a client and Mr. Moore. It's a case that they seem to think you may be able to help them with. It's urgent—but it's got to be unofficial."

Lucius sighed. "Like anything else that might actually advance forensic science these days. It's all we can do to keep this bunch from taking these remains and feeding them to the lions in the Central Park menagerie."

"What happened?" I asked, again looking at the grim quarter of a corpse on the oilcloth.

"Some kids saw it floating out in the river," Marcus answered. "Pretty crude job. Dead less than a few hours, certainly. But there're some interesting details, and we need to record them all. Can you give us five minutes?"

Cyrus nodded, and then the detective sergeants went back to their work. I could hear Lucius as he began to list various details of the thing to the other cops, his tone showing plainly that he knew it was useless and growing maybe just a little haughty as a result: "Now, then, Captain, you will note, I'm *certain*, that both the flesh and the spine have been cut with some kind of crude saw. We can rule out the possibility of any medical student or anatomist stealing body parts—they wouldn't want to damage the organs in that way. And these rectangular patches of missing skin are extremely interesting—they've been deliberately cut away, in all likelihood to remove some kind of identifying marks. Tattoos, maybe, since we're on the waterfront, or perhaps simple birthmarks. So the murderer almost certainly knew his victim well. . . ."

Having seen enough of both the butcher's work on the ground and the way that the cops alternately laughed at and ignored what Lucius was saying about it, I turned to look at the boys who'd found the body. They were all still full of the shock and excitement of the thing and were continuing to jump around and laugh nervously. I took note that I knew the skinniest of their number and drifted over to talk to him.

"Hey, Nosy," I said quietly, at which the skinny kid turned and grinned. I didn't have to tell him not to call out my name in front of the cops: he belonged to the gang of boys what ran with Crazy Butch, one of Monk Eastman's lieutenants, a group that I'd served with for a time before my incarceration on Randalls Island, and he knew I wouldn't want any contact with the bulls, being as, once you were a kid that they'd marked as a troublemaker, they took a kind of sick pleasure in riding you wherever they found you, whether you'd done anything wrong or not.

"Stevepipe!" Nosy whispered, pulling his sheet of canvas tighter around himself and rubbing at the large, oddly shaped protrusion on his face that'd given him his name. "You *cabbyin'*? I thought you was workin' for that crazy doctor."

"I am," I said. "Long story. What happened here?"

"Well," he said, his feet starting to dance in excitement again. "Me and Slap and Sick Louie, here"—I nodded to the other boys as Nosy indicated them, and they returned the greeting—"we was just walking the waterfront, you know, seein' if maybe there was any unclaimed baggage lyin' around the pier—"

I chuckled once. " 'Unclaimed baggage?' Jeez, Nosy, that's rich."

"Well, you gotta call it somethin' if the bulls grab you, right? So, anyway, we's workin' our way down to the pier, and we seen this red package just floatin' out there. Figured it might be somethin' tasty, so we dove on in, as we's in shorts, anyway. Got it up here okay—but I guess you can figure what it was like when we opened it." He whistled and laughed. "Brother. Sick Louie musta puked eight times—only got half a stomach, anyway—"

"Hey, hey," Sick Louie protested, "I told ya a million times, Nosy, it's my *intestines*, I was born widdout a buncha my intestines, dat's what does it!"

"Yeah, yeah, whatever," Nosy said. "So we went for a cop, figurin' maybe there's a reward involved. Shoulda known better. Now they won't let us go—figure maybe we had something to do with it! I ask you, what would we be doin' sawin' people up? And *how*, for Chrissakes? I got one kid's an idiot"—he flicked a thumb at the boy called Slap, who, when I took a closer look, didn't seem to be catching much of what was going on around him—"and another kid with half a stomach—"

"I told you, Nosy!" Sick Louie protested again. "It's my—"

"Yeah, yeah, your intestines!" Nosy shot back. "Now shut up, willya, please?" He turned back to me with a grin. "Fuckin' morons. So—whattaya got goin', Stevepipe, what brings ya here?"

"Ah," I said, looking back at the crowd around the piece of a body and seeing that they were starting to break up. "Came to fetch a couple of pals." Cyrus and the detective sergeants had started to move my way. "And

I gotta go. But I'm coming down to Frankie's this week. You gonna be around?"

"If these cops ever let us go," Nosy answered with another cheerful grin. "Imagine tryin' to hold us for a thing like this," he went on as I moved away. "It ain't logical! But nobody ever said cops was logical, eh, Stevepipe?"

I grinned back at him, touched the brim of the top hat, and then rejoined Cyrus and the Isaacsons, hurrying with them back to the hansom.

The cabbie had passed out again, though when Cyrus climbed back in he woke up with a start and whimpered a little, like maybe he was hoping the whole ride down had been a bad dream. "Oh, no . . . no, not again! Look, you two, I'm going to the cops if—"

Marcus, who had perched his feet on the little iron step on one side of the cab as his brother did the same on the other, flashed a badge. "We *are* the cops, sir," he said in a firm tone as he slung a satchelful of instruments over his shoulder and then laid a solid grip on the side of the passenger compartment. "Just sit back and be quiet, this won't take long."

"No, it won't," moaned the old man, resigned to his predicament. "Not if the ride down was any measure . . ."

I got into the driver's seat and cracked the reins, and we crashed back onto the cobblestones of Clarkson Street, leaving behind the strange scene on the waterfront and figuring—wrongly, it turned out—that we'd seen and heard the last of it.

My mind was still full of thoughts of both that bloody sight and my disheartening encounter with Kat and her mark as we dashed back east. But when we reached Hudson Street again and turned north, my attention was finally distracted by a familiar and—given the situation and my brooding—welcome sound: the Isaacson brothers, taking off after each other as soon as there were no other cops around to hear.

"Just couldn't resist, could you?" I heard Marcus say over the din of the mare's horseshoes on the stones.

"Resist what?" Lucius answered in a kind of squeak, already on the defensive as he clung for life to the side of the cab.

"You just had to take the opportunity to lecture them all, as if we were in some elementary school classroom," Marcus answered in irritation.

"I was recording important evidence!" Lucius answered. Glancing back once, I could see that they were leaning in toward each other over Cyrus and the bewildered cabbie, like a pair of bickering kids. Cyrus just smiled at me—we'd seen a hundred scenes like this before. The cabbie, however, seemed to be thinking that the strange spat was further evidence that he'd been abducted by lunatics.

" 'Recording important evidence,' " Marcus echoed. "You were grand-standing! As if we don't have enough problems in the department right now, without you acting like an old schoolmarm!"

"That's ridiculous—" Lucius tried. But Marcus wasn't having any of it.

"Ridiculous? You've been that way since you were eight years old!"

"Marcus!" Lucius was trying to get a grip on himself. "This is no place to bring up—"

"Every day, when we'd get home from school—'Mama! Papa! I can re-cite my whole day's lessons, listen, listen!' "

"—no place to bring up personal—"

"Never occurred to you that Mama and Papa were too goddamned tired to listen to your entire day's lessons. No, you just went right ahead—"

"They were proud of me!" Lucius hollered, abandoning all attempts at dignity.

"What were you thinking?" Marcus bellowed as I drove the grey mare past Christopher Street and then east on Tenth, in order to avoid any chance of seeing Kat again. "That Hogan's going to go back to Mulberry Street and say, 'Jesus, Mary, and Joseph, those Isaacson boys certainly know their business—showed us a thing or two!'? One step closer to get-ting forced out, that's all we are now!"

The "discussion" went on in that vein right up until I turned the cab north on Broadway and spun it around in front of the Hotel St. Denis. There weren't two better detectives in all the world than the Isaacsons, they'd proved that much during the Beecham case: trained in medicine and law in addition to criminal science, they kept up with advances in tracking theories and techniques from every corner of the world. It was their knowledge of the still unaccepted science of fingerprinting, for in-stance, that'd put the first crack in the Beecham case. They had an arsenal of cameras, chemicals, and microscopes that they brought to bear on any problem what might seem totally incomprehensible to your average de-tective; but they did love to bicker, and most of the time they went at it like a couple of old hens.

Cyrus gave the cabbie a little extra cash and I gave him his hat back as we left him to recover his wits in front of the hotel. Then we walked quickly over to Number 808 and got back into the elevator. Once inside, the detective sergeants brought the volume of their argument down, but not the passion.

"Marcus, for God's sake," Lucius seethed, "we can talk about this at home!"

"Oh, sure," Marcus mumbled, straightening his jacket and smoothing back his thick hair. "When you can bring Mama into it."

"Meaning?" Lucius asked in some shock.

"She'll take your side. She always does, because she can't stand to hurt your feelings. Sure, she'll *tell* you she always loved to listen to you recite. But she was actually bored stiff. Trust me—she used to say so when you weren't around."

"Why, you—!" Lucius started; but then the elevator reached the sixth floor and bumped to its usual weighty stop. The sign that Sara'd had painted on the door seemed to jolt the brothers back to adult reality, and they both fell silent, dropping the whole thing as suddenly as they'd picked it up. As for Cyrus and me, it'd been all we could do to keep from laughing out loud during the elevator ride. But as we stepped back into the old headquarters, seriousness of purpose returned to us, too.

CHAPTER 5

W e found Mr. Moore, Miss Howard, and the señora more or less
where we'd left them, though it was clear from the way that Mr.
Moore had drawn a chair up close to the Linares woman and was listening to her intently that she'd made quite an impression on him. A large
part of that, of course, was Mr. Moore's always being an easy mark for a
charming lady—and Señora Linares definitely had charm, even through
the scars, the bruises, and the veil, which she'd pulled back down over her
face. Miss Howard, meanwhile, paced and smoked, horrified, I think, not
only at the violence that had been done to this woman but at how often
such violence was done to so many other women, rich and poor, without
their being able to do a damned thing about it.

Señora Linares watched the Isaacsons enter the office with the same uneasiness she'd displayed on first meeting the rest of us, but Mr. Moore
stepped in quickly to put her at her ease.

"Señora, these are the men I was telling you about. The finest pair of
detectives in the entire New York City Police Department. Despite their
official capacities, however, their discretion may be completely relied on."
He then looked up with a grin to shake hands with Lucius and Marcus.
"Hello, boys. Bad doings on the waterfront, I hear."

"John," Marcus answered, returning the smile with a nod.

"Just another murder that looks unsolvable to Hogan's crew," Lucius
added. "Though if you ask me, it's a simple case of—"

"Yes, but they didn't ask you, did they?" Marcus said, at which Lucius
shot him a final look promising true rage if he went on. Marcus let it go

and turned to give Miss Howard a polite but very sincere hug. "Hello, Sara. You look wonderful."

"You're an excellent liar, Marcus," she answered. Then she went over to give Lucius a peck on the cheek, knowing that he'd never dare get physical with her on his own. "Hello, Lucius."

The peck brought a flush to the younger Isaacson's whole head, and he quickly pulled out his handkerchief to mop at his brow. "Oh! Why, hello, Sara. It's—it's wonderful to see you."

"I wish the circumstances could be happier," Miss Howard answered, turning to her guest. "Gentlemen, this is Señora Isabella Linares."

Both the Isaacsons' eyebrows went up. "The wife of Consul Baldasano's private secretary?" Marcus asked quietly.

The señora only nodded slightly; Mr. Moore, for his part, turned away, shook his head and mumbled, "I *am* a reporter, I really *ought* to know these things . . ." Then, aloud to the Isaacsons, he went on, "Listen—why don't I take you fellows into the back for a cup of coffee. Fill you in."

The detective sergeants, confused but intrigued, readily agreed and went along. The rest of us were left with a slightly awkward moment, which Miss Howard, ever skillful at such things, stepped in to smooth. "Cyrus? The señora said that she very much admired your playing. Perhaps you know something from her homeland?"

"No," the señora said, gratefully but with purpose. "No, señor, I am— in no mood for such melodies. And memories . . . the tune you played, it was of your people?"

"It's an American folk melody," Cyrus explained, moving back to the piano and sitting. "Like most of its kind, it doesn't belong to any one people."

"It was so moving, truly," the señora answered. "Might I hear another?"

Cyrus inclined his head, considered the matter for a moment, and then softly began to play the old tune "Lorena." The Linares woman sat back in her chair and sighed heavily, just listening for a few minutes. Then she put a hand on Miss Howard's arm. "I pray we are doing the right thing, Miss Howard. And I pray that I am not, in fact, mad."

"You're not," Miss Howard answered firmly. "I've had some—*experience* with lunatics."

"Your Señor Moore, he seems less certain."

"It's his way. He's a journalist. They come in two varieties, cynics and liars. He's of the first group."

Señora Linares managed a small, painful chuckle at that, and then Mr. Moore and the Isaacsons returned to the room. Marcus paused at the drapery-covered pool table and set the instrument satchel down on it. As he then moved further toward us with Mr. Moore, Lucius opened the satchel and began to carefully lay out the gleaming tools that were inside it.

Marcus stood by Miss Howard, while Mr. Moore crouched by the Linares woman. "Señora, in order for us to help you, we must be sure of several things: first, the extent of the injuries to your face and skull, and second, the details of what happened in Central Park and at the El station. With your permission, these men will examine those injuries and ask you some questions. You may find it tedious—but I assure you, it *is* necessary."

Another heavy sigh came from Señora Linares, and then she sat forward, lifted her veil, and removed her hat altogether, saying only, "Very well."

Marcus immediately fetched a standing electrical desk lamp from nearby, placed its shade above the señora's head and face, and then spoke softly: "You may want to close your eyes, ma'am." She complied, shutting the one lid that she could move, and then he switched on the bright light.

Seeing her injuries, Marcus's face tightened into a wince—and mind you, this was a man who'd just been studying a body that'd been decapitated, dismembered, and sawed in half. The woman really was a wicked mess.

Lucius joined his brother, holding several medical and measuring instruments, some of which he handed to Marcus. Though Cyrus's attention was riveted on the scene taking place under the little half shell of bright light in the center of the room, he kept on playing, sensing that it was calming Señora Linares. As for me, I jumped back up into my windowsill and lit up a cigarette, not wanting to miss a minute of the proceedings.

"Sara," Lucius said, as he moved toward the señora's head with what looked like two steel probes, "I wonder if you wouldn't mind taking notes?"

"No, no, of course not," Miss Howard answered, grabbing a pad and pencil.

"All right, then, we'll begin with the injury to the back of the head. That occurred when you were attacked in the park, señora?"

"Yes," she answered, a little pain revealing itself in her face. But she didn't move.

"And that was exactly where and when?" Marcus asked, also studying the wound.

"Thursday evening. We had just left the Metropolitan Museum of Art. I often take Ana—my daughter—I often take her there. She is very fond of the sculpture hall, I don't know just why. The figures make her so excited, full of smiles and wonder. . . . At any rate, we usually sit afterwards by the Egyptian obelisk outside, and she sleeps. The obelisk, too, has always fascinated her, though in a different way."

"And you were hit right there—right out in the open?"

"Yes."

"Yet no one witnessed it?"

"It seems not. It had rained earlier in the day and was threatening to do so again—perhaps people wished to avoid it. Although there were several very kind persons about when I awoke."

Lucius glanced up at Marcus. "You see the angle? And there's no laceration."

"Exactly," Marcus answered, his tone also businesslike. "Probably no concussion." Then, to the señora: "Any unusual physical side effects after it happened? A ringing in your ears, perhaps, or bright spots in your vision?"

"No."

"Dizziness, a feeling of pressure inside your skull?"

"No. I was examined by a doctor," Señora Linares continued, becoming a little more sure of herself. "He told me—"

"If you don't mind, señora," Lucius said, "we'll try to disregard other reports. We've had a lot of experience with New York City doctors—and their opinions—in cases like this."

The señora grew quiet at that, looking kind of like a little girl who'd spoken out of turn at school.

"No concussion, then," Marcus mumbled. "Pretty neat job."

"Perfect angle," Lucius said. "Somebody good—*unless* . . . señora, you say you never saw the person who struck you?"

"Not at all. I was unconscious immediately, though I don't think for very long. But by the time I awoke, he had fled. With Ana."

"You say 'he,' " Marcus remarked. "Any reason?"

The señora looked suddenly confused. "It—I don't know. It never occurred to me that—"

"That's all right," Marcus said. "Just asking." But then he glanced up and looked at Miss Howard—and from the apprehensive expressions that came into both of their faces, I could tell that there was no way in hell he'd been "just asking."

Marcus returned to his questioning: "How tall are you?"

"Mmm—a little over five feet and five inches."

Marcus nodded, murmuring, "Straight blow across. Not a sap."

"Point of impact's too distinct, too hard," Lucius agreed. "Piece of pipe, I'd guess. They've started work on the new Fifth Avenue wing of the museum. Plumbing's going in . . ."

"Lot of pipe handy." Marcus looked my way. "Stevie. Get over here."

A little surprised, I followed the order and moved between Marcus and Lucius to take a gander at the nasty bump on the back of the señora's head. "Look familiar?" Marcus asked me with a small smile.

"You been through my file at Mulberry Street?" I asked.

"Just answer the question," Marcus went on with the same small grin.

I took another look, then nodded. "Yep. Definitely coulda been. Nice little piece of lead pipe."

"Good," Marcus said, sending me with a nod back to my windowsill.

(All right, so now the world knows how I got my nickname—and for those who want an even more detailed explanation, don't worry, that's part of this story, too.)

The Isaacsons then moved around to the front of the Linares woman's head, at which she quickly closed her right eye again. Lucius took in the bruises and the broken nose very quickly, nodding all the while. "This'll be the husband's work."

"Very characteristic," Marcus said. "And completely different from the other."

"Exactly," Lucius added. "Which further suggests—"

"Exactly," Marcus echoed. "You say neither you nor anyone else at the consulate ever received a ransom note, señora?"

"No, never."

The Isaacsons exchanged somewhat confident looks and nods, through which the barest beginnings of excitment showed clear. "All right," Marcus went on, crouching down on one knee. The señora started a little as he took her hand: it seemed like he was just trying to reassure her, but then I noticed that one of his fingers went up to the inside of her wrist. "Please keep your eyes closed," he said, drawing out his pocket watch. "And tell us everything you can remember about the woman you saw with your child on the train."

Mr. Moore turned to Miss Howard, mumbling something under his breath and looking like his skepticism was returning.

"Try to keep quiet, John," Lucius called over to him. "We'll bring you up to speed in a few minutes. But it's getting very late, and the señora will be missed at home—"

"There is no difficulty about that," Señora Linares said. "I shall go from here to a good friend who works at the French consulate—the same woman who sent me to see Miss Howard. She has engaged rooms at the Astoria Hotel, and we have told my husband that we are spending the night in the country."

"The Astoria?" Marcus said with a grin. "Beats any night in the country *I* ever had." The señora smiled along with him, at least as much as her battered mouth would allow her to. "Now, then," Marcus continued. "About the woman . . ."

At the words Señora Linares's face filled to brimming with the same dread what had flitted around her all evening, and she couldn't help but open her good eye. "Never have I been so afraid, señor," she murmured. "So—struck by evil." Marcus indicated with his finger that she should shut her eye again, and she followed the instruction, after which he looked at his pocket watch again. "Not at first, though. No, at first she was simply sitting down, holding Ana. She was dressed in the clothing, it seemed to me, of a children's nurse or a governess. Her face, when she looked at Ana, seemed affectionate enough—even loving, in a way. But when she looked up and out the window"—the señora gripped the arm of the chair hard with the hand that Marcus wasn't holding—"they were the eyes of an animal. Like a great cat, entrancing, and yet—so . . . *hungry*. I thought I had been afraid for my Ana before I saw that face, but it was only then that I knew real fear."

"Do you remember the color of her clothes?" Lucius asked. It seemed to me that the question involved more than just a minor detail to him. But the señora said that she could not recall the color. "Or if she was wearing a hat?" Again the señora drew a blank.

"I am sorry," she said. "It was the face—I was so concentrated on the face, I noticed little else."

Miss Howard was busily transcribing all these statements, and I saw Mr. Moore glance over at her and then roll his eyes a bit, as if he thought all this dramatic detail was just the rantings of a hysterical woman who'd been through what even he'd conceded was a terrible tragedy. But the Isaacsons turned to each other with very different expressions: knowledge, confidence, anticipation, they were all there. And I could see that Mr. Moore was a bit deflated about missing whatever they were getting.

"And you're certain the woman didn't see you?" Lucius asked.

"Yes, Detective. I was well under the roof of the platform as I ran alongside the train, and it was already dark. I did scream and leap at the window as it left the station, but it was already moving too fast. She may have seen *someone,* but she could not have known it was me."

"Could you estimate the woman's height and weight?" Lucius asked, returning to look at the wound on the back of the señora's head once more.

The Linares woman paused to consider this. "She was seated," she finally answered slowly. "But I would not say that she was very much taller than I. Perhaps heavier, but only slightly."

"I'm sorry this is taking so long," Marcus said. "But just one more thing—do you happen to have a picture of the child? You can open your eyes to get it, if you need to."

"Oh—yes." Señora Linares turned in her seat. "I brought one for Miss Howard, she asked—Miss Howard, do you have the photograph still?"

"Yes, señora," Miss Howard answered, taking a mounted image about three inches by five off the mahogany table. "It's right here."

As Miss Howard handed the picture to the Linares woman, Marcus didn't move a muscle, keeping a grip on the señora's right hand, which forced her to take the picture with her left. Marcus watched her as she glanced at the image, all the time checking his watch, and then she handed the picture to Lucius, who held it in front of Marcus's face.

"It was taken only a few weeks ago," Señora Linares said. "Quite remarkable—Ana is so full of life and energy, and it is rare to find a photographer who can capture the true spirit of a child. But this man succeeded quite well, wouldn't you say?"

Both the Isaacsons gave the picture what you might call the quickest of glances, and then Lucius, not knowing quite where to put it, looked my way. "Stevie—would you—?"

I jumped down again to retrieve the photograph and return it to Miss Howard, who was once more busily taking notes. Pausing just a second or two to look at the thing, I was kind of—well, struck, in a way. I've never had much experience with babies, and as a rule I'm no sucker for them. But this little girl, with her swatch of soft dark hair, her huge, nearly round black eyes, and her big cheeks swelling around a smile that said she was game for just about any amusement life could throw at her—well, there was something about it that kind of tugged at you. Maybe it was because she seemed to have more of a personality than the usual infant; then again, maybe it was because I knew she'd been kidnapped.

As I returned to my windowsill, Marcus—his eyes still on his watch—murmured, "Good," very slowly. Then he finally let go of the señora's hand and stood up. "That's very good. Now, señora, I think you should rest. Cyrus?" Cyrus finally let up on the piano and stood to cross to Marcus. "Mr. Montrose will, I'm sure, be happy to see that you get safely to the Astoria. You have nothing to fear under his protection."

The señora looked at Cyrus with gentle confidence. "Yes. I sensed that." Confusion came back into her features. "But what of my daughter?"

"I will not lie to you, señora," Marcus said. "This is a very difficult case. Your husband's forbidden you to go to the police?" Señora Linares nodded miserably. "Easy, now," Marcus went on, guiding her to the door as Miss Howard fell in with them. "That may, in the long run, turn out to be an advantage."

"But you are policemen yourselves, yes?" the señora asked in confusion, as Cyrus opened the elevator grate for her. She put on her big black hat, fixing it to her hair with an eight-inch, stone-headed pin.

"Yes—and no," Marcus answered. "The important thing is that you mustn't give up hope. The next twenty-four hours will, I think, be enough time for us to give you an idea of what we can do."

The señora turned to Miss Howard, who only added, "Please trust me when I say that you couldn't be in better hands than those of these gentlemen."

Señora Linares nodded again, then stepped into the elevator and pulled her veil down. "Well, then—I shall wait." She studied the office once more and then quietly added, "Or rather, I think, we shall *all* wait . . ."

Mr. Moore looked at her in some surprise. " 'All'? What shall we all wait for, señora?"

The Linares woman indicated the room with her umbrella. "There are *five* desks, no? And you all seem as though . . . yes. I think we shall all wait. For the man who sits at the fifth desk. Or once did . . ."

I don't think there was one of us who didn't shiver a bit at the sound of her quiet words.

Without even trying to argue the point, Marcus nodded to the señora and then spoke to Cyrus: "Straight to the Astoria, then meet us at the Lafayette. We'll be on the outdoor terrace. There are questions that only you and Stevie can answer."

Cyrus nodded and pulled on his bowler as Miss Howard gave Señora Linares a final encouraging look before closing the office door. "Try to have hope, señora." The señora only nodded, and then she and Cyrus were gone.

Marcus began to pace as Lucius packed up the medical instruments. Miss Howard turned to the front windows and walked toward them, staring kind of sadly down at Broadway. Only Mr. Moore seemed particularly anxious.

"Well?" he said finally. "What did you find?"

"A great deal," Lucius answered quietly. "Though not enough."

There was another pause, and Mr. Moore's arms went up high. "And are you going to share your information, gentlemen, or is it a secret between you and the señora?"

Marcus chuckled once thoughtfully. "She's one smart lady . . ."

"Yes," Miss Howard added from the window, with a little smile of her own.

"Smart?" Mr. Moore asked. "Or just crazy?"

"No, no," Lucius answered quickly. "A long way from crazy."

Mr. Moore seemed just about ready to bust. "All right. Look, are you people going to tell me what's on your minds or not?"

"We will, John," Marcus answered. "But let's get to the Lafayette first. I'm starving."

"That makes two of us," Lucius said, picking up the instrument satchel. "Stevie?"

"I could eat," was all I said. The truth was that I, too, was anxious to know what the detective sergeants were thinking; but I'd also felt the full hit of Señora Linares's parting words, and wasn't in what you might call an optimistic mood.

Miss Howard turned to take a small jacket off of a wooden rack near the door. "Let's go, then. We'll have to take the stairs—nobody left in the building to bring the elevator back up."

As we filed toward the back door, Mr. Moore fell in behind us, still frustrated. "What's gotten into all of you?" he demanded. "I mean, it's a simple enough question—*is* there a case here or not?"

"Oh, there's a case," Marcus said. He turned to Miss Howard. "You got your wish there, Sara."

She smiled again, still looking melancholy. "One really *must* be careful about wishes . . ."

Mr. Moore put his hands to his hips. "Oh, and what's *that* supposed to mean? Look, I'm not going *anywhere* 'til *somebody* gives me some idea of what's happening! If there's a case, why are you all so damned dejected?"

Lucius groaned as he pulled the satchel over his shoulder. "The short version is this, John: there's a case, all right, a very perplexing one. And I hardly need to tell you that, given the players involved, it could turn into something very big. Very big—and very ugly. But the señora was right. Without *him*"—Lucius turned to look at the desk that sat to the right of the other four—"we don't have a prayer."

"And given what he's been through," Miss Howard added, as we all filed on toward the fire stairs near the kitchen, "I don't think any of us can really say that he'll do it. Hell, I'm not even sure it would be right of us to *ask*." She paused and turned to me. "Questions, as Marcus says, that only you and Cyrus can answer, Stevie."

I felt all attention in the room settle on me—not the kind of position I've ever been comfortable with. But it seemed like I had to say something. "Well—I should wait for Cyrus, I guess, but—"

"*But?*" Marcus asked.

"But," I answered, "for my money, it all hinges on tomorrow morning. How he takes leaving the Institute. And you're right, Miss Howard—I don't even know that it's right to ask . . ."

She nodded and turned away, disappearing through the black stairway door; and in that somewhat uncertain state of mind, we all started the long, dark descent to Broadway.

———

CHAPTER 6

As we ate supper in amongst the iron trellises and overhanging greenery of the Café Lafayette's outdoor terrace on Ninth Street and University Place, the Isaacsons told us what they believed they'd learned from their interview with Señora Linares. The theory put their talent for drawing unexpected conclusions from what seemed like a confused jumble of facts on ample display—and, as usual, kept the rest of us shaking our heads in amazement.

The blow that the señora'd taken across the back of the head, the detective sergeants said, presented us with two choices as to her attacker: either a good sap man, a specialist who'd had a lot of experience rendering people unconscious, or someone of much more limited strength who'd landed a lucky shot that didn't do any really severe damage. There were real problems with the first idea: if the attack had been the work of an expert, he'd have to've been about the same height as the señora, given the angle and location of the hit, and he'd have to've put his sap away in favor of a much harder and more risky weapon, such as a piece of pipe. Even more important, though, was the fact that he'd risked being spotted in what was a very public and popular location—right outside the Metropolitan Museum—at an extremely risky time of day.

Given these considerations, the detective sergeants were prepared to dismiss the idea that the Linares baby had been taken by a professional kidnapper, whether someone working for hire or in business for himself. Such characters just wouldn't take the risk of whacking somebody on the head with an unpadded piece of pipe, and they certainly liked to make their moves in more isolated spots than the Egyptian obelisk in Central Park. That left us with the notion of an amateur, one probably working without a plan—and it was very possible, maybe even likely, that said amateur was a woman. The fact that the señora herself had referred to her attacker as "him" didn't count for anything: she'd admitted that she'd never gotten a look at the person, and, coming from an upper-class diplomatic family, she'd just assumed that no woman would be capable of such an act. But the blow itself was consistent with a woman of average strength who was about the señora's size—and the description that she herself had given of the woman on the train matched these specifications.

What about that description, anyway? Mr. Moore wanted to know. What made the detective sergeants so ready to accept what she said? Wasn't it an awfully detailed story for someone with one good eye who'd just caught a quick glimpse of her missing child—and was in a sudden state of shock as a result—to come up with? Not at all, Lucius answered; in fact, the señora's description had lacked certain details that what he called "pathological liars" (which, I knew from the Doctor's work, meant people who were so far gone that they actually believed the lies they told) would've included. For instance, she could say generally what kind of clothes the woman was wearing but not what color; she could give a vague idea of the woman's size but nothing more; and she couldn't even remember if the woman'd had a hat on. And there were other, more subtle reasons to think that she'd been telling the truth at just that point— "physiological reasons," Lucius termed them.

Apparently, some bright bulbs in the detecting world had recently been floating the idea that people undergo physical changes when they lie. Some of the possible symptoms, these types said, were a quickening of the pulse rate and respiration, increased perspiration and muscle tension, and a few other, less obvious alterations. Now, there was no actual medical or what Lucius called "clinical" support for any of this; but all the same, Marcus had, as I'd noticed, kept one finger on the señora's wrist while they were discussing the mysterious woman on the train. At the same time, he'd kept a steady eye on his watch. They'd been talking about some very upsetting subjects, but there'd been no change in Señora Linares's pulse rate at any time, not even when she looked at the photograph of her daughter. Like so many of the Isaacsons' techniques and conclusions, that one wouldn't have meant anything in a court of law, but it gave them further reason to buy what she was saying.

All this was enough to quiet Mr. Moore's doubts about the señora—but the more important issue continued to be whether or not Dr. Kreizler would be willing to get involved in the case. I took a lot more grilling on this score, along with Cyrus, after he got back from the Astoria, and I'll confess that the both of us grew a little defensive after a while. Whatever our own fascination with the case, our first loyalty was to the Doctor, and the Linares business was quickly growing into something much deeper and more challenging than a night's diversion. Neither Cyrus nor I was sure that the Doctor was in any shape to go getting involved with a venture what was so demanding. It was true, as Mr. Moore pointed out, that given the court order, our friend and employer would have some time on his hands; but it was also true that the man was in sore need of rest and healing. Miss Howard respectfully observed that the Doctor always seemed to find the most peace and solace in some kind of work; but Cyrus answered that he was at a lower point than any of us had ever witnessed before and that sooner or later every person has to stop and take a breather. There was just no way to call it in advance, and by meal's end we'd come back to the same conclusion I'd voiced to the others as we'd left Number 808: the Doctor's reaction to the idea was going to be determined by how hard he took his departure from the Institute. Cyrus and I promised that one or the other of us would phone Mr. Moore at the *Times* as soon as the Doctor was back home. Then we all went our respective ways, each bearing the queer feeling that the actions we took in the next day or two could have ripples what would reach far beyond the confines of Manhattan, an island that suddenly seemed, somehow, smaller.

I managed to squeeze in a few hours' sleep when we got home, though it wasn't of a quality what could really be called restful. I was up at eight sharp—realizing, as I launched out of bed, that it was the first official day of summer—and found that the last of the rain clouds had disappeared and a fresh breeze was blowing in from the northwest. I got into some clothes and managed to comb my long hair into something that resembled order, then headed down to the Doctor's narrow little carriage house next door to give Frederick, our always reliable black gelding, a few oats and a morning brushdown in preparation for his day's labors. Heading back into the house, I concluded from the clanging of pots and pans in the kitchen that our latest housekeeper, Mrs. Leshko—a woman who couldn't boil water quietly—had arrived. I contented myself with a quick cup of her bitter coffee, then got onto the calash and under way.

I took my usual route—Second Avenue downtown to Forsyth Street, then left onto East Broadway—but I didn't push Frederick, knowing he'd worked hard the night before. It was a route that took me past many of the dance halls, dives, gambling hells, and saloons of the Lower East Side, the sight of which only made it harder to understand how in the world things had so fallen out as to make this trip necessary in the first place. Oh, the specific reason was apparent enough: a twelve-year-old boy at Dr. Kreizler's Institute, Paulie McPherson, had woken up in the middle of the night a couple of weeks back, wandered out of his dormitory and into a washroom, and there hung himself from an old gas fixture with a length of drapery cord. The boy was a small-time thief with a record so short none of my old pals in Crazy Butch's gang would have owned up to it; he'd been nailed, if you can believe it, trying to pick a fly (that is, plain-clothed) cop's pocket. Because of his inexperience, the judge had given him the option of spending a few years in the Kreizler Institute, after the Doctor'd examined the kid and made the offer. Now, Paulie was small time, but he was no chump—he knew what the alternatives were, and he'd accepted right away.

There wasn't anything unusual in all this: several of the Doctor's students had come to the Institute by similar routes. And there hadn't been any outward signs of trouble with Paulie since his arrival on East Broadway, either. He was a little moody and uncommunicative, sure, but nothing more than that, certainly nothing that hinted he was getting ready to string himself up. Anyway, word of the suicide had made its way through the city government and the parlors of New York society like, if you'll pardon my being plain, shit through a sewer. The incident was offered by many armchair experts as proof positive that Dr. Kreizler was incompetent and his theories were dangerous. As for the Doctor himself, he'd never lost a kid before; that, combined with the unexpected and unexplained nature of the suicide, tore the hole in his spirit that'd been ripped open by Mary Palmer's death even wider.

And out that hole had drained much of what had always seemed a bottomless well of energy with which the Doctor'd been able, for so many years, to meet the almost daily attacks of the hostile colleagues, social thinkers, judges, lawyers, and average run-of-the-mill skeptics that he ran into during the operation of his Institute and his work as an expert witness in criminal trials. Not that he ever quit; quitting wasn't in him. But he lost some of his fire and confidence, a portion of the mental belligerency that'd always kept his enemies at bay. To understand the change, I suppose you'd have had to've seen him in action before it took place—as I had, firsthand, some two years earlier. Brother, had I seen it. . . .

The encounter had taken place in Jefferson Market, that imitation of a Bohemian prince's castle what always struck me as entirely too beautiful to be a police court. Like I've said, I'd been mostly on my own since I was three, and fully so since I was eight, having at that time gotten fed up with breaking and entering to support my mother and her various men friends. The final straw'd come when my old lady's taste ran beyond booze to opium and she started frequenting a den in Chinatown run by a dealer everybody called You Fat (his real Chinese name was unpronounceable, and he never seemed to get the insult contained in the very appropriate nickname). I told her I wasn't running into a lot of other eight-year-olds what stole to support their mothers' alcohol and drug cravings—the kind of statement that's pretty well guaranteed to get a kid a good beating around the head. As she flailed away at me, she screamed that if I was going to be such an ungrateful little wretch I could just fend for myself; I pointed out that I already was, mostly, then left for the last time to take up with a bunch of street arabs in the neighborhood. My mother, meantime, moved in with You Fat, using her body instead of my larceny to secure an endless supply of her drug.

Anyway, my gang and me, we looked out pretty good for each other, huddling together over steam vents on winter nights and making sure we didn't drown when we cooled down in the city's rivers during the summer. By the time I was ten I'd made a pretty good name for myself as a banco feeler, pickpocket, and general criminal handyman; and though I wasn't big, I'd gotten to be fairly expert at defending myself with a short section of lead pipe, which was where I got my nickname, "the Stevepipe." A lot of kids carried guns or knives, but I found that the cops went easier on you if they didn't find you armed to the teeth; and God knows I was getting into enough trouble with the law by then for that to be a real consideration.

In fact, my record and my reputation eventually reached the point where I was approached by Crazy Butch, who, like I've also mentioned, was in charge of the kids who worked for Monk Eastman's gang. I'd always liked Monk, with his flashy derbies and his rooms full of cats and birds (or, as he said it, "kits 'n' boids"); and though Crazy Butch was a little too deserving of his title for my taste, I jumped at the chance to move up in the underworld. Instead of picking pockets on my own, I was soon stripping whole crowds of citizens with my gangmates, along with waylaying delivery vans and lifting whatever we could from stores and warehouses. Sure, I'd get caught sometimes, but generally I'd get released, too; because we were such a big team, it was generally pretty hard for a prosecutor to make a charge stick to just one of us. On top of that, I was only eleven, and I could usually play the innocent orphan when I needed to.

But the judge I got that one day at Jefferson Market, he wasn't buying any acts or any excuses. The cops'd nailed me for breaking a store dick's leg over at B. Altman's joint on Nineteenth Street while me and the gang were picking shoppers' pockets. I could usually control my trademark weapon better than that—I generally tried to leave a nasty bruise instead of a break—but the store detective had me by the throat and I was that close to choking. So, quick as spit, there I found myself: in the main courtroom at Jefferson Market, getting one hell of a lecture as I sat under the tall turret of the courthouse's fine clock tower.

The old windbag on the bench called me everything from a nicotine fiend (I'd been smoking since I was five) to a drunkard (which showed how much he knew—I never touched the stuff) to a "congenitally destructive menace," a phrase which, at the time, meant a whole lot of nothing to me—but which was, it turned out, destined to be the key to my salvation. You see, it happened that a certain crusading mental specialist with a particular interest in children was just outside the courtroom that day, waiting to testify in another case; and when the judge let out with that "congenital" phrase and then went on to sentence me to two years on Randalls Island, I suddenly heard a voice rise from somewhere behind me. I'd never heard anything quite like it—certainly not in a courtroom, anyway. Tinged with a combination of German and Hungarian accents, it rolled with all the thunder and righteousness of an old-time preacher.

"And precisely *what*," the voice demanded, "are your honor's qualifications for coming to so precise a psychological conclusion concerning this boy?"

At that point all eyes, including mine, turned to the back of the courtroom to get a glimpse of what was, for most of them, a familiar sight: the renowned alienist Dr. Laszlo Kreizler, one of the most hated yet respected men in the city, charging in, his long hair and cloak floating behind him and his eyes burning with coal-black fire. I had no way of knowing that one day I'd become accustomed to that sight, too; all I knew then was that he was the damndest person, with the damndest nerve, that I ever saw.

The judge, for his part, put his forehead into his hand wearily for a moment, like the good Lord had just sent a rain of toads down on his little patch of earth in particular. "Dr. Kreizler—" he started.

But the Doctor already had an accusing finger up. "Has an assessment been done? Has one of my esteemed colleagues given you any reason for using such language? Or have you, like most other magistrates in this city, simply decided that you are qualified to speak expertly on such matters?"

"Dr. Kreizler—" the judge tried again.

But with no better luck: "Do you have even the slightest idea of what the symptoms of what you call 'congenital destructiveness' are? Do you even know if such a pathology *exists*? This insufferable, unqualified, inflammatory rhetoric—"

"*Dr. Kreizler!*" the judge bellowed, slamming a fist down. "This is *my* courtroom! You have nothing to do with this case, and I demand—"

"No, sir!" the Doctor shot back. "*I* demand! You have *made* me a part of this case—myself and any other self-respecting psychologist who is within earshot of your irresponsible declarations! This boy—" At that he pointed in my direction and, for the first time, actually looked at me—and I'm not sure I'm up to describing all that was in the look:

His eyes sparkled with a message of hope, and the smallest, quickest smile told me to have courage. All in a rush and for the first time in my life, I felt like someone over the age of fifteen truly gave a good goddamn about my existence. You don't really know that you've been living without that commodity until someone makes you aware of the possibility of it; and when they do, it's a very peculiar sensation.

The Doctor's face went straight and stern again as he snapped back around to the judge: "You have said that this boy is a 'congenitally destructive menace.' I demand that you prove that assertion! I demand that he be given a new hearing, conditional upon the findings of at least *one* qualified alienist or psychologist!"

"You can demand anything you like, sir!" the judge responded. "But this is *my* court, and my ruling stands! Now kindly await the call of the case for which you have been retained, or I'll hold you in contempt!"

A bang of the gavel, and I was on my way to Randalls Island. But as I left the courtroom, I looked again to the mysterious man who had appeared—out of thin air, it seemed to me at the time—to take up my cause. He returned the look with an expression what said the matter was far from settled.

And so it was. Three months later, inside my leaky brick cell in the main block of the Boys' House of Refuge, I had that "encounter" with a guard what I've mentioned. Now, the simple truth is that you can find a bit of lead pipe almost anywhere if you look hard enough, and I'd found one pretty quick after my arrival on the Island. I kept it hidden inside my mattress, figuring the day would eventually come when one of either the boys or the guards might force me to use it—and the particular bull that finally did will be forever sorry for it. While he was busy trying to hold me down and undo his pants I laid hold of my pipe, and inside of two minutes he had three fractures in one arm, two in the other, a busted ankle, and a mass of bone chips where his nose used to be. I was still going at him, to the encouraging shrieks of the other boys, when a couple more guards finally pulled me off. The superintendent of the place asked for a hearing to decide whether or not I should be transferred to an insane asylum, and word of the incident got out to the press. Dr. Kreizler caught wind of it and showed up at the hearing, once again demanding that no sentence be pronounced without a proper psychological assessment being done first. The judge this time around was a lot more reasonable, and the Doctor got his way.

For two days, he and I sat in an office on the Island, doing little more than talking—and for most of the first day we didn't even talk about the specific facts of my case. He asked me questions about my childhood and, even more important, told me a lot about his, which went a long way toward easing my discomfort at being in the presence of a man what I was grateful to but who nonetheless filled me with a kind of nervous awe. During those first hours, in fact, I learned many grim facts about the Doctor's life that almost nobody knew or knows—and I can see now that he was using his own past as a way to coax mine out of me.

It was peculiar: as we talked, I began to comprehend—to the extent that an uneducated young boy could—that I might not just be doing things at random, that maybe I'd decided on a life of crime and mayhem as much out of anger as out of necessity. This wasn't an idea that the Doctor planted in me; he let me come to it myself by showing sympathy for all I'd been through and even a kind of admiration for my attitude. In fact, he seemed to find the fact that I'd survived what I had and was doing what I was doing not only remarkable but in a way amusing; and I quickly got the feeling that I was providing him with something more than statistics—the man was enjoying himself.

That was the real secret of his success with kids: it wasn't charity work to him, it wasn't the kind of wooden-nickel generosity you'd get from mission types. What made troubled children, rich and poor, trust the Doctor so much was the fact that *he* was getting something out of helping *them*. He loved it all, really loved spending time and effort on his young charges, in a way that was at least partly selfish. It was like they made the miserable parts of the adult world what he inhabited so much of the time—the prisons, madhouses, hospitals, and courtrooms—easier to take: gave him hope for the future, on the one hand, and pure and simple amusement, on the other. And when you're a kid, you look for that, for the kind of adult who isn't giving you a hand just to get in good with Jesus

Christ but is doing it because he enjoys it. Everybody's got an angle, is all I'm saying, and the fact that the Doctor's was so obvious and uncomplicated made it all the easier to trust him.

At my sanity hearing the Doctor used all the things that we'd talked about to make short work of the idea that I was crazy, backing his claims up with a little theory he'd worked out over the years, one he called "context." It was the core idea behind all the rest of his work, and the basic gist of the thing was that a person's actions and motives can never be truly understood until the full circumstances of his or her early years and growing up are brought to bear on the discussion. Straightforward and harmless enough, you might think; but in fact it was no small job to defend this notion against the charge that it ran counter to traditional American beliefs by providing excuses for criminal behavior. But the Doctor always maintained that there was a big difference between an explanation and an excuse, and that what he was trying to do was understand people's behavior, not make life easier for criminals.

Luckily for me, on that particular day his statements found a receptive audience: the members of the hearing board bought the Doctor's analysis of my life and behavior. But when he went on to propose that I be enrolled at his Institute, they balked, apparently still feeling that so notorious a young hellion as "the Stevepipe" needed to go someplace where he'd be kept on a shorter leash. They asked Dr. Kreizler if he had any other ideas; he thought about the matter for some two minutes, never looking at me, and then announced that he'd be willing to take me into his employ and his home and assume personal responsibility for my actions. The members of the board grew a little wide-eyed at that, and one of them asked the Doctor if he was serious. He told them that he was, and after some more consultation the deal was set.

For the first time, I felt a little unsure; not because I'd seen anything in the Doctor to distrust but because the two days I'd spent with him had set me to thinking about myself and wondering if I'd ever really be able to change my ways. These doubts nagged at me as I cleared my few belongings out of my cell and headed off through the grim old courtyard of the House of Refuge to meet the Doctor at his carriage (he had his burgundy barouche out that day). My confusion wasn't eased by the sight of an enormous black man sitting in the barouche's driver's seat; but the man had a kindly face, and as the Doctor stepped out of the carriage, he smiled and held a hand up toward his companion.

"Stevie," he said. "This is Cyrus Montrose. It may interest you to know that he was on his way to the penitentiary—and a fate far worse than yours might've been—before we crossed paths and he came to work for me." (I later learned that Cyrus had, as a younger man, killed a crooked Irish cop who'd been beating the life out of a young colored whore in a brothel where Cyrus played piano. Cyrus's parents had been killed by an Irish mob during the Draft Riots of '63, and at his trial the Doctor'd successfully argued that, such being the context of his life, Cyrus had been mentally incapable of any other reaction to the situation in the brothel.)

I nodded at the big man, who tipped his bowler and gave me a warm look in return. "So," I said uncertainly, "am—*I* gonna work for you, too, is that the deal?"

"Oh, yes, you'll work," the Doctor answered. "But you'll study, as well. You will read, you'll learn mathematics, you'll investigate history. Among many other things."

"I will?" I said, swallowing hard; after all, I'd never spent a day in school in my life.

"You will," the Doctor answered, taking a silver cigarette case out, removing a stick, and lighting it. He looked up to see me staring hungrily at the cigarettes. "Ah. But I'm afraid *that* stops. No smoking for you, young man. And this," he went on, stepping over and examining the little pile of things I was carrying, "will no longer be necessary." He pulled my piece of lead pipe out of some clothes and threw it away onto a patch of thin, ratty-looking grass.

It was looking like I was going to be left with nothing but studies, and that fact was not causing me to be any less edgy. "Well—what about the work?" I finally said. "What'll I do?"

"You mentioned," the Doctor said, climbing back into the barouche, "that when your activities with Crazy Butch involved waylaying delivery trucks, you were generally assigned to drive them. Was there any particular reason for this?"

I shrugged. "I like horses. And I took to the driving pretty good."

"Then say hello to Frederick and Gwendolyn," the Doctor replied, indicating with his cigarette the gelding and mare what stood in front of the barouche. "And take the reins."

My spirits picked up considerably at that. I went over, patted the handsome black gelding's long snout, ran a hand along the brown mare's neck, and grinned. "Seriously?" I asked.

"You seem to find the idea of work more comforting than that of study," the Doctor replied. "So let us see how you manage. Cyrus, you may as well come down and help me with this appointment schedule. I'm a bit lost. It seems, from my notes, that I was scheduled to be at the Essex

Street court house two hours ago." As the big black man got down from the driver's seat, the Doctor glanced up at me once more. "Well? You have a job to do, don't you?"

I gave him another grin and a quick nod, then jumped up into the driver's seat and cracked the reins against the horses' haunches.

And I never, as they say, looked back.

Yes, they were fine days, those, when we'd never heard the name John Beecham and Mary Palmer was still alive. Fine days whose return, I realized, we now had good cause to doubt. Those people what had always fought the Doctor and his theory of context (and were driven, it seemed to me, by fear of the way his investigations into violent and illegal behavior led him to poke around in the area of how Americans raised their kids) had generally countered his arguments by saying that the United States had been built on the idea that every man is free to choose—and is responsible for—his individual ideas and actions, no matter what the circumstances of his early life may've been. The Doctor didn't really disagree with them on a legal level; he was just looking for deeper scientific answers. And so, for many years, there'd been a kind of stalemate in the battle between the controversial alienist and them what he unnerved so badly. When little Paulie McPherson had hung himself, though, it'd given the Doctor's enemies a chance to break that stalemate—and they'd grabbed at it.

But the judge who'd presided over the first hearing on the matter had been a fair-minded man, and he didn't just flat-out shut the Doctor down. Instead, he ordered the sixty-day investigation period I've already mentioned, making the kids at the Institute wards of the court for that time and putting the place in the temporary charge of one Reverend Charles Bancroft, a retired orphanage superintendent. The Doctor himself was forbidden to set foot inside the Institute during that time: for a man of his antsy temperament, sixty days—with no sure knowledge of what would come after—could be a genuine eternity. And the question of how hard he'd take leaving the Institute didn't involve just him, either. The kids themselves would play a crucial part, for if even one of them snapped while he was gone—and some of those kids were wound pretty tight—the Doctor would, I knew, take all the blame onto himself. He'd always taught his charges to draw strength from the fact that at least one person believed in them and to be ready to use that strength in future times of trouble. But would they be able to do it when the stakes were so high and the outcome was so uncertain . . . ?

The sudden thunder of a gunshot bellowed out of an alleyway just after I'd turned onto Forsyth Street, causing Frederick to rear in fright and me to stop daydreaming and jerk my head around to locate the source of the trouble. It'd come from back by an old rear tenement building, the closest thing to Hell that any living person ever called home. I jumped off the calash to calm Frederick down by stroking his powerful neck and feeding him a couple of cubes of sugar what I always kept in my pocket when I was driving. Keeping my eyes locked on the alleyway, I soon saw the agent of the mayhem: a crazed-looking man, small and wiry, with a big, drooping mustache and a slouch hat. He came wandering out of the alley carrying an old side-by-side shotgun, brazen as can be, with no apparent thought to who might be watching. A scream followed him out, but his only answer was to declare, without turning around, "*Now* I'll take care of your fuckin' little boyfriend!" He then disappeared at the same quick pace around the corner of Eldridge Street. There wasn't a cop to be seen, of course; there rarely was in that part of town, and if one had been around, the sound of the gunshot would in all likelihood have sent him scurrying in the opposite direction.

I got back onto the driver's seat of the calash and made for the Institute at a quick pace. Reaching Numbers 185–187 East Broadway—the two red brick buildings with black trim what the Doctor'd bought and converted into one space many years back—I found that there was a young patrolman stationed at the foot of the steps to the main entrance. Jumping to the ground, I gave Frederick a few more pats on the neck and another lump of sugar, then approached the cop, who was too green to know me by sight.

"I don't suppose you'd be interested to know that there's a mug wandering up Eldridge Street with a shotgun," I said.

"You don't say," the cop answered, looking me over. "And what business might that be of yours?"

"None of mine," I said with a shrug. "Just thought it might be some of yours."

"My business is right here," the cop announced, straightening his light summer cap and puffing himself up so that his blue tunic looked near to busting. "*Court* business."

"Unh-hunh," I said. "Well, maybe you could tell Dr. Kreizler that his driver's here. Seeing as getting him off the premises seems to be the main point of the court's business."

The cop turned toward the steps, giving me a glare. "You know," he said, as he went up to the door, "an attitude like that could get you in some tight spots, sonny."

I let him get inside before shaking my head and spitting into the gutter. "Go chase yourself," I mumbled. "*Sonny.*" (Maybe I ought to note here that one of the things all my years with Dr. Kreizler never did affect—besides my taste for smokes—was my attitude toward cops.)

In a few minutes the patrolman reappeared, followed by Dr. Kreizler, a small group of his students, and a pious-looking old bag of bones what I took to be the Reverend Bancroft. The kids, some of the Doctor's younger charges, were pretty typical of the range of types he generally had at the place: one was a little girl who came from a rich family uptown and who'd refused throughout her life to speak a word to anybody but her nanny—until she met Dr. Kreizler, that is; another was a boy whose folks owned a grocery business in Greenwich Village, a kid who'd taken more than his fair share of beatings for no greater reason than that his conception'd been an accident and neither of his parents could stand having him around; then there was another girl, who'd been found by a friend of the Doctor's working in an adult disorderly house, even though she wasn't but ten years old (just how the man happened to find her in said disorderly house, the Doctor never inquired too closely about); another was a boy who hailed from a big manor house in Rhode Island and who'd passed most of his eight years breaking everything he could lay his hands on in a string of unending tantrums.

They were all dressed in the Institute's gray-and-blue uniforms, which the Doctor had designed himself and required the kids to wear so that the richer ones couldn't lord it over the poorer. The first little girl, the one what had never spoken to her family, had a firm grip on one of the Doctor's legs, making it tough for him to move as he walked alongside the reverend and gave him some last bits of instruction and advice. The other girl was holding both her hands behind her back and looking around like she wasn't quite sure what the hell was going on. The two boys, meantime, were laughing and taking playful jabs at each other from opposite sides of the Doctor, using him as a shield. All in all, a pretty typical scene for the place; but if you looked close, there were clues that something unusual was up.

Chief among these was the Doctor himself. His black linen suit was rumpled and wrinkled in spots, making it pretty clear that he'd been up working all night. Even if the clothes hadn't given him away, his face would've: it was drawn and exhausted, and the look of contentment what could be found in his features only at the Institute was nowhere to be seen. As he spoke to Reverend Bancroft, he leaned forward with a kind of uncertainty that was unusual for him, and the reverend seemed to sense it: he put his hand on the Doctor's back and told him to just relax and try to make the best use of the weeks to come, that he was sure everything would work out for the best. At that point the Doctor stopped talking and just shook his head in resignation, rubbing his black eyes and suddenly becoming conscious of the kids what were all around and over him.

He smiled and tried to perk up as he first pried the one little girl off his leg and then got the two boys to calm down, speaking to them like he did to all us kids, with affection but directly, as if there was no wall of age between them. When he looked up and caught sight of me at the curb, I could see that he was trying to hold himself together long enough to make it to the calash—but the second little girl proceeded to make that job a lot tougher. Out from behind her back she brought a bunch of roses, wrapped in the plain paper of a local flower shop but still showing the full glory of the new summer in their white and pink petals. The Doctor smiled and kneeled down to take them from her, though when she threw her arms around his neck, that former fallen angel what the Doctor'd given a second lease on childhood, his smile disappeared and it was all he could do to keep his composure. He stood up quickly, told the boys one more time to behave themselves, then shook hands with Reverend Bancroft and near ran down the steps. I had the carriage door open, and he shot in.

"Get me home, Stevie," was all he managed to say, and like spit I was back up top, whip in hand. The kids continued to wave as I turned the calash around and headed back the way I'd come; but Dr. Kreizler made no reply, just sank further into the maroon leather seat of the carriage.

He remained silent during the trip uptown, even when I mentioned my near run-in with the shotgun-toting maniac. I glanced back just a few times, the first to see if he was even awake. He was; but though the morning was only growing more beautiful, with the breeze continuing to blow the smells of fresh, full greenery and leaves around the street so that they near overcame the stench of garbage piles and horse manure and urine, he didn't seem to take note of it. He had his right hand balled into a fist that he tapped against his mouth as he stared intensely at nothing, and with his left hand he clutched at the bunch of roses so tight that one of the thorns stabbed him. I heard him hiss a little in pain, but I didn't say anything—I didn't know what I *could* say. The man was a spent bullet, that much was clear, and the best thing for me to do was get him home in a hurry. With that in mind, I gave Frederick a little ripple of the reins and told him to pick up his pace, and soon we were moving back around Stuyvesant Park.

Once inside the house at Seventeenth Street, the Doctor, his face by now ashen with exhaustion, turned to Cyrus and me. "I've got to try to get some rest," he mumbled, starting up the stairs. He stopped and flinched a bit at the sound of a bucket overturning in the kitchen hallway with what was, even for Mrs. Leshko, an amazing crash. The racket was followed by a long stream of what I figured were Russian curses.

The Doctor sighed. "Assuming it's possible to communicate with that woman, would you please ask her to keep the house quiet for a few hours? If she's incapable, give her the afternoon off."

"Yes, sir, Doctor," Cyrus said. "If you need anything—"

The Doctor only held up a hand and nodded in acknowledgment, then disappeared up the stairs. Cyrus and I looked at each other.

"Well?" Cyrus whispered to me.

"It isn't good," I answered. "But I've got an idea—" Another crash and more curses came from the kitchen. "You handle Mrs. Leshko," I said. "I'm going to telephone to Mr. Moore."

Cyrus nodded, and then I bolted down through the kitchen hallway and past the muttering, mopping mass of blue linen and stout flesh that was Mrs. Leshko. I kept on going through the white ceramic tiling and hanging pots and pans of the kitchen itself and finally got into the pantry, where there was a telephone on the wall. Closing the pantry door, I grabbed the 'phone's small receiver, yanked the stem of the mouthpiece down to my height, and got hold of an operator, telling her to connect me to *The New York Times*. In a few seconds, I had Mr. Moore on the other end.

"Stevie?" he said. "We've had some developments. Interesting ones."

"Yeah? Any word on the baby?"

"Only confirmation that she is, in fact, missing—none of the help at the consulate have seen her in days. I didn't want to question anybody higher up, though, not with what the señora's been through. But tell me—what's the word on your end?"

"Well, he's in pretty bad shape right now," I answered. "But he's gone up to rest. And I think—"

Mr. Moore paused, waiting for me to go on, and I could hear the clack of typewriters in the background. "You think—?"

"I don't know—this case. If you were to put it to him just the right way, he might . . . I mean, the whole connection to the Spanish business—and the señora, if we could get him to meet her . . . and that picture of the little girl . . ."

"What are you saying, Stevie?"

"Only that . . . he's in a mood, all right. And if this case leads in the direction it might—"

"Ahhhh," Mr. Moore noised in a happier tone. "I *see*. . . . Well. Your education's starting to pay off, kid."

"It is?"

"If I get you right, you're saying that this case may end up revealing some pretty unattractive things about the same kind of society types that're trying to shut the Doctor down. And the fact that it involves an innocent baby is just so much gravy. Right?"

"Well, yeah. Something like that."

Mr. Moore whistled. "I'll tell you what, Stevie—I've known Laszlo since we were younger than you are. I don't care how fed up and exhausted he is, if that doesn't get him going, we can start planning his funeral *now*—because he's already dead."

"Yeah. But we gotta slip the idea to him right."

"Don't you worry about that. I've already figured it out. Tell the Doctor the rest of us are coming by for cocktails." I heard a voice call to Mr. Moore in the background. "Yeah?" he answered, away from the mouthpiece. "What? *Bensonhurst?* No, no, no, Harry, I cover *New York!* I don't care what Boss Platt says, Bensonhurst is *not* New York! But it wasn't my story to start with! Oh, all right, all right!" His voice grew more distinct in my ear. "Got to go, Stevie—some fool doctor tried to shoot his family in Bensonhurst last night. Apparently the authorities don't like the way we reported the story. Listen, don't forget—we'll be by for cocktails."

"But you haven't told me about the other developments—"

"Later," he answered.

The line clicked dead, leaving me with no choice but to wait until that evening to find out what in the world Mr. Moore could've been talking about.

CHAPTER 7

Dr. Kreizler managed to sleep until midafternoon, after which he called Cyrus into his study. I popped my head in, too, to let the Doctor know that Mr. Moore, Miss Howard, and the Isaacsons intended on coming by for cocktails, a prospect what seemed to give him some consolation. Then he and Cyrus started to sort through all the mail the Doctor hadn't attended to in recent days. While they were closeted away with this work, I tried to get a few hours of study in, though my effort wasn't exactly wholehearted. Excusing myself with the thought that most kids weren't required to do schoolwork in the summertime, I headed down to the carriage house to have a secret smoke and give Frederick some more oats and another brush-down. Then it was Gwendolyn's turn, which she waited for with her usual patience. She was a good horse, as strong as Frederick but without his spunk, and spending time with her helped to ease some of my anxiousness.

Our guests showed up at near 6:30. The sun was still bright behind the two square, squat towers of St. George's Church on the west side of Stuyvesant Park, what with it being the longest day of the year, and all reports said that the weather would hold through most of the week. Mr. Moore and the others trotted up the stairs to the parlor, where the Doctor was reading a letter and listening to Cyrus play and sing a sad, lonely operatic number that most likely had something to do with people falling in love and then dying (such being the general concern of operas, from what little I've ever been able to make out about that particular musical form). I watched the scene that followed, as was my habit, from a shadowy corner at the top of the next flight of stairs.

The Doctor rose and shook each person's hand warmly, while Mr. Moore smacked a palm against the Doctor's back.

"Laszlo—you look like hell," he announced, immediately making for a silver box of cigarettes that contained a nice blend of Virginia and Russian black tobaccoes.

"It's good of you to notice, Moore," the Doctor answered with a sigh, indicating the easy chair across from his to Miss Howard. "Sara, please."

"As ever, John is the soul of tact," Miss Howard said as she sat down. "All things considered, Doctor, *I* think you look remarkably well."

"Hmm, yes," the Doctor noised doubtfully. "All things considered . . ." Miss Howard smiled again as she realized how backhanded her compliment had been, but the Doctor smiled back, letting her off the hook and telling her he appreciated the thought. "And the detective sergeants are here as well," he went on. "This is indeed a welcome surprise. I've had a letter from Roosevelt today—I've just been reading it."

"Really?" Lucius said, moving closer to the Doctor's chair with his brother. "What's he say?"

"I bet he's not terrorizing the sailors the way he did our beat cops," Marcus added.

"I hate to interrupt," Mr. Moore said from across the room, "but we *did* come for cocktails. Are we free to fix them ourselves, Kreizler?" He indicated a nearby glass-and-mahogany cart what was loaded down with bottles. "I trust that battle-axe downstairs isn't going to do it. What is she, anyway, some kind of refugee or something?"

"Mrs. Leshko?" As he spoke, the Doctor nodded toward the liquor cart, and Mr. Moore ran for it like a dying man in the desert. "No, I fear she actually is our current housekeeper. And, to my everlasting regret, our cook. I have Cyrus trying to find her another position—I'd rather not let her go before she has something else."

"You don't mean to say you actually eat her food?" Mr. Moore said, setting out six glasses and filling each of them with gin, a little vermouth, and a dash of bitters: *martinis,* he called them, though I've heard bartenders label the drink a *martinez,* too. "Laszlo, you know what Russian cuisine is like," he went on, handing the drinks around. "I mean, they only eat it over there because they *have* to."

"I'm painfully aware of that, Moore, believe me."

"What about the letter, Doctor?" Miss Howard asked as she sipped her drink. "What does our esteemed assistant secretary have to say?"

"Nothing good, I'm afraid," the Doctor answered. "When I last heard from Roosevelt, he told me that he and Cabot Lodge had been spending rather a lot of time at Henry Adams' house. Henry himself is in Europe at the moment, but that absurd brother of his seems to be holding court in his dining room while he's away."

"Brooks?" Miss Howard said. "You find that troubling, Doctor?"

"Surely you don't think anyone actually *listens* to him," Marcus added.

"I'm not entirely certain," the Doctor replied. "I wrote to Roosevelt to tell him that I consider Brooks Adams to be delusional, perhaps pathologically. In this letter he says that he's inclined to agree with me but that he still finds merit in many of the man's ideas."

Lucius's eyes went round. "That's a frightening thought. All that talk about 'martial spirit' and 'warlike blood'—"

"Contemptible nonsense, that's what it is," the Doctor pronounced. "When men like Brooks Adams call for a war to reinvigorate our countrymen, they only reveal their own degeneracy. Why, if that fellow ever found himself near a battlefield—"

"Laszlo," Mr. Moore said, "relax. Brooks is the fashion of the moment, that's all. Nobody takes him seriously."

"No, but men like Roosevelt and Lodge are taking his *ideas* seriously." The Doctor stood and walked over to stand next to a large potted palm by one of the open French windows, shaking his head all the while. "They're down there in Washington now, scheming like schoolboys to get us into a war with Spain—and I tell you all, such a war will change this country. Profoundly. And not for the better."

Mr. Moore smiled as he drank. "You sound like Professor James. He's been saying the same things. You haven't been in touch with him, have you?"

"Don't be ridiculous," the Doctor said, slightly embarrassed at the mention of his old teacher, who in fact he hadn't spoken to for many years.

"Well," Lucius said, trying to be evenhanded, "the Spaniards *do* have some reason to be resentful—we've called them everything from swine to butchers for their treatment of the Cuban rebels."

Miss Howard displayed a puzzled smile. "How is it that a person can be a swine *and* a butcher?"

"I don't know, but they've managed it," Mr. Moore answered. "They've acted like sadistic savages, trying to suppress the rebellion—concentration camps, mass executions—"

"Yes, but the rebels have been vicious in return, John," Marcus countered. "Captured soldiers massacred—civilians, too, if they won't support 'the cause.' "

"Marcus is right, Moore," the Doctor threw in impatiently. "This rebellion is not about freedom or democracy. It's about power. One side has it, the other side wants it. That's all."

"True," Mr. Moore conceded with a shrug.

"And *we* appear to want some sort of an American empire," Lucius added.

"Yes. God help us." The Doctor wandered back over to his chair, then picked up the letter from Mr. Roosevelt and scanned it one more time. Folding it up as he sat back down, he put the thing aside with another noise of disgust. "But—enough of that." He rubbed a hand over his face. "All right, then, suppose you all tell me what brings you here."

"What *brings* us?" Mr. Moore made a show of innocence and shock that would've done any Bowery variety star proud. "Why, what *should* bring us? Concern. Moral support. All of that."

"*Only* that?" the Doctor asked suspiciously.

"No. Not only that." Mr. Moore turned to the piano for a moment. "Cyrus, do you think we could have something a little less funereal? I'm sure we're all sorry that old Otello mistakenly strangled his lovely wife, but given the display Nature's putting on outside I think we might forgo such sentiments. You wouldn't happen to know anything less—well—stuffy, would you? After all, friends and colleagues, it's summer!"

Cyrus answered by gently breaking into "White," a popular song from the forties, what seemed to set Mr. Moore right up. He beamed a big grin at the Doctor, who only looked at him with some concern.

"There really are moments," the Doctor said, "when I doubt your sanity, Moore."

"Oh, come on, Kreizler!" Mr. Moore answered. "I'm telling you, everything's going to be fine. In fact, we've brought you living proof that things are starting to go your way." Mr. Moore indicated Marcus and Lucius with a little nod of his head.

"The detective sergeants?" the Doctor said quietly, looking to them. "But what can *you* have to do with any of this?"

Marcus glanced at Mr. Moore with some annoyance, then handed him his empty glass. "That was truly graceful, John," he said. "Suppose you stick to bartending."

"My pleasure!" said Mr. Moore, dancing back over to the cocktail cart.

The Doctor gave up on expecting sense from his journalistic friend and turned to the Isaacsons again. "Gentlemen? Have Moore's nerves given way altogether, causing him to bring you here for some imaginary reason?"

"Oh, it wasn't John," Marcus answered quickly.

"You can thank Captain O'Brien," Lucius added. "If 'thank' is the right word."

"The head of the Detective Bureau?" Dr. Kreizler said. "And what can I thank him for?"

"The fact that you'll be seeing quite a bit of us in the next sixty days, I'm afraid," Marcus replied. "You're aware, Doctor, that the court ordered a police investigation of affairs at your clinic?"

What was coming next clicked in my head right then, as I'm sure it did in the Doctor's; nevertheless, he said only, "Yes?"

"Well," Lucius continued for his brother, "we're it, I'm afraid."

"What?" There were both shock and relief in the Doctor's voice. "You two? But doesn't O'Brien know—"

"That we're friends of yours?" Marcus said. "Indeed he does. That was part of the amusement for him. You see—hmm. Now, how do we begin this?"

As the detective sergeants' explanation of what had gone on earlier that day at Police Headquarters was peppered with their usual squabbling over who'd been responsible for what, I may as well boil the tale down myself.

It'd started with the piece of a body that Cyrus and I'd seen on the waterfront by the Cunard pier the night before. (Well, really it'd started when the Isaacsons joined the force in the first place, for their advanced methods and peculiar attitudes, linked with the fact that they were Jewish, had made them instantly and almost universally disliked. But so far as this incident in particular was concerned, it was the body that'd set it off.) It'd been obvious to everyone, from the patrolmen on the scene to Captain Hogan and then up to Captain O'Brien of the Detective Bureau, that the section of torso was likely to develop into quite a sensational case. Summer in New York is just not complete without a big, splashy murder mystery, and this one had all the earmarks, starting with the probability that more pieces of the body would soon start to wash up in other parts of town (which they did). There'd already been and would likely continue to be a lot of press coverage of the thing and great attention paid to whoever worked on and solved it. But the deal had to be played just right: the cops had to represent it to the public as something what'd be tougher than shoe leather to work out, so that they could cover themselves with laurels when the time came.

The Isaacsons had been dispatched to the scene in the middle of the night, when Captain O'Brien was asleep and nobody knew what was waiting down at the pier; otherwise, they never would've gotten so close in the first place. O'Brien would choke before he gave what looked to be the summer's biggest catch to a pair of detectives who spent near all their time telling him that his methods were so out of date as to be laughable. But the Isaacsons had really finished any chance what they might've had of working on the thing by writing up an initial report along the lines of what we'd heard Lucius saying that night by the river: all indications were that it was a crime of passion committed by someone close to the victim, someone who knew his identifying marks and had carefully cut them away—someone, in other words, whose main concern was hiding the victim's identity and throwing suspicion off of themselves. But for the brass at the Detective Bureau, such wasn't good enough. They preferred the idea of a crazed anatomist or medical student dealing in body parts, the kind of spooky tale what always sparks the public's imagination. And that's just what they started to give out to the papers that very night. The fact that everything about the body spoke directly against such an idea, well, that kind of thing never bothered the Detective Bureau much. A real solution to a crime never rated against an invented story that could be used to their advantage.

Anyway, when Monday morning rolled around, Captain O'Brien saw the Isaacsons' initial report and decided that if he was going to milk "the mystery of the headless body" for all it was worth, he'd have to keep the brothers as far away from it as possible. It so happened that he also needed to make an assignment that morning of two detectives to investigate conditions at the Kreizler Institute for Children and the apparent suicide of young Paulie McPherson; and he took no wee bit of fiendish Irish pleasure in informing the Isaacsons that not only were they off the torso case, they were on the McPherson business. He knew that they were acquaintances of Dr. Kreizler's—but, like most cops, O'Brien had no liking for the Doctor and would only be tickled by making the situation even more difficult for him than it already was. If the thing turned out bad and the Isaacsons had to come down on their friend, well, that would just be a bigger laugh; and if nothing came of it, O'Brien would at least have succeeded in keeping the brothers out of the more important "headless body" business.

"And so," Marcus finished up, "here we are. I'm sorry, Doctor. We'll try to make it as convenient and—well—dignified for you as we can."

"Indeed we will," Lucius tacked on anxiously.

The Doctor moved in quickly to put them at their ease. "Don't let yourselves feel odd about it, either of you. There was nothing you could have done. Such a move was to be expected, really. We must try to make the most of it." His voice became touched by sadness for a moment. "I've racked my own mind, and those of my staff, for any clue as to what drove the McPherson boy to take his own life—without success, I'm afraid. I'm as certain as I can be that there was no incident at the Institute to spark it, though you must of course decide all that for yourselves. I do hope you know, however, that there are no two people in the world I would sooner trust with the matter than yourselves."

"Thank you, sir," Lucius mumbled.

"Yes," Marcus said. "Though I'm afraid we'll be a damned nuisance to you."

"Nonsense," Doctor Kreizler added—and I could hear in his voice that the relief he felt over things working out this way was growing into a kind of happiness. I glanced at Mr. Moore and Miss Howard and found them smiling in a fashion what said they were positively delighted things had worked out this way, and it was no big job to figure out why: while the Isaacsons' new assignment would only increase the chances of the Doctor taking on the Linares case, it would also cinch it that we'd have the talents of the detective sergeants on tap twenty-four hours a day. Such was cause for smiles, indeed.

"It's all a lot of noise over nothing, anyway," Mr. Moore said as he handed a second round of drinks to everyone. "The word at the *Times* is that this whole affair is going to blow over."

"Is it?" the Doctor mumbled, not too reassured.

"Absolutely."

As Mr. Moore reached the Doctor's chair, I noticed that he bent over somewhat suddenly to hand the Doctor his cocktail: and as he did, a packet of papers and letters came flying out of the inside pocket of his jacket.

"Oh, dammit," Mr. Moore said, in a voice that might've sounded completely genuine if I hadn't known that the larger purpose of the evening was to get the Doctor to sign on for the Linares case. "Laszlo," he went on, indicating the papers and handing a drink to Lucius, "would you mind . . . ?"

The Doctor reached to the floor and picked up the scattered documents, giving them a quick once-over as he arranged them back into a pile. He suddenly stopped when he reached something:

It was the photograph of little Ana Linares.

As I'm sure the cagey Mr. Moore knew he would, the Doctor paused to study the thing. And as he did, he began to smile.

"What a charming child," he said quietly. "The daughter of a friend, John?"

"Hmm?" Mr. Moore noised, all innocence.

"Well, she's entirely too beautiful to be a *relation,*" the Doctor went on, to which the others laughed a little: their first mistake, for the Doctor had not shown the picture to any of them. If they knew the smiling, pretty face it displayed, then something was up. The Doctor glanced at them all carefully. "Such being the case," he said quietly, continuing to address Mr. Moore, "who is she?"

"Oh," Mr. Moore answered, retrieving the packet of letters and folded documents, "it's nothing, Laszlo. Forget it."

As this little dance continued, I saw Detective Sergeant Lucius pick up the evening edition of the *Times* and plaster it over his face nervously, though it was obvious he wasn't reading a word.

The Doctor leaned toward Mr. Moore. "What do you mean, 'it's nothing'? Have you taken to carrying pictures of anonymous children?"

"No. But it's—well, it's nothing you should worry about."

"I'm not worried," the Doctor protested. "Why should I be worried?"

"That's right," Mr. Moore said. "No reason."

The Doctor eyed him. "Is it something *you're* worried about?"

Mr. Moore sipped his drink and held up a hand. "Laszlo, please— you've got enough on your mind. Let's just skip it."

"John," the Doctor answered, standing and speaking with genuine concern now, "if you're in some kind of trouble—"

He stopped as Miss Howard reached up to touch his arm. "You needn't press John, Doctor," Miss Howard said. "The fact is, it's a little matter *I'm* looking into. He's been giving me some help, that's all. I lent him the photograph."

Leaning back and turning to Miss Howard, the Doctor grew less concerned and more intrigued. "Ah! A case, Sara?"

"Yes," was her simple answer.

I could see that the Doctor was continuing to make much of his friends' holding back, and his next remark was a bit more pointed: "Detective Sergeant," he said to the ever-nervous Lucius, "I believe you'll have more success reading that paper if you turn it right side up."

"Oh!" Lucius answered, fixing the problem with a rustle of newsprint as Marcus let out a little sigh. "Yes, I—suppose you're right, Doctor."

There was another moment of silence, after which the Doctor spoke again: "I take it you two are also giving Miss Howard some help with her case."

"Oh, not really," Marcus answered uneasily. "Not much, that is. Still, the thing is—interesting, in a way."

"Actually, Doctor," Miss Howard said, "we could use your thoughts on it. Informally, I mean. If it wouldn't be an imposition, that is."

"Of course," the Doctor replied; and the way he said it, it seemed to me that he was beginning to form an idea of what was going on and might be agreeing to take the first few steps down the road toward getting involved.

Sensing that they'd gotten the hook in, Mr. Moore brightened and looked at his watch. "Well! We'd better discuss all this at dinner. I've got a table at Mouquin's, Kreizler, and you're coming along."

"Well, I . . ." Ordinarily, in recent days, the Doctor would have found a way to bow out of this social engagement; but that night he was too intrigued to even try. "I would be happy to."

"Right," Mr. Moore said. "And Cyrus'll be happy to drive—won't you, Cyrus?"

"Yes, sir," Cyrus replied cheerfully.

Mr. Moore turned to the staircase. "Stevie!"

"On my way!" I answered, bounding down.

"The barouche, if you please," Mr. Moore told me. "Cyrus, get the Doctor ready for a night on the town, will you?"

Cyrus nodded as I ran downstairs and out the front door to get Gwendolyn and Frederick harnessed and hitched up to the barouche.

By the time I drew the carriage up to the front gate, the others were coming out of the house. I turned the reins over to Cyrus, and as the rest of them climbed in the Doctor reminded me to make good use of the evening and get to bed early.

As they drove off, I could only laugh at that idea.

CHAPTER 8

Anticipation of the kind that'd eaten me up all afternoon set back to work on my insides that evening. I went down to the kitchen and told Mrs. Leshko that she could go home early, as I'd see to the glasses and such in the parlor. She gave me a big grin and near wrenched my cheeks off in gratitude, then got her things together and departed. I went up to the parlor and straightened up the cocktail wagon, taking the glasses downstairs to wash them. Then it was upstairs for several hours of the history of ancient Rome and half a packet of cigarettes, all of which was interrupted by the occasional trip to our new icebox for something to nibble on, periodic bouts of nervous pacing, and long minutes of wondering whether or not the Doctor would agree to help find little Ana Linares.

After dropping the others off at their respective homes, the Doctor returned to Seventeenth Street at about midnight. Such was early by the group's usual standards, but in recent weeks the Doctor hadn't allowed himself anything like so much leisure, so I took the time of his return as a good sign. He entered the house alone—Cyrus was next door tending to the horses—and as I heard him come in I started down for the parlor, where I knew he'd be pouring himself a nightcap. I'd taken the precaution of getting into some nightclothes and a robe, and as I walked slowly down the stairs I ran my hands through my hair once or twice to muss it up. Then I did my best to look sleepy, giving out with a quiet yawn as I entered the parlor and found the Doctor sitting in his chair with a small glass of cognac, once again going over his letter from Mr. Roosevelt.

He looked up when I came in. "Stevie? What are you doing up? It's late."

"Only midnight," I answered, walking over to the window. "Must've dozed off, though."

The Doctor let out a small laugh. "An excellent attempt, Stevie. But a trifle transparent." I didn't say anything, just kind of chuckled and shrugged. Setting his glass aside, the Doctor walked over to stand at the other window. After a moment, he quietly said:

"You realize, Stevie, what they want me to do?"

The question might seem to've come out of nowhere, but I guess I was expecting something like it, being as I answered without much hesitation, "Unh-hunh. Pretty much."

"And how long have you known?"

"Miss Howard told us about it last night."

The Doctor nodded, smiling for just a second, then kept staring out the window. "I'm not sure that I can."

I shrugged again. "It's your decision, I guess. I mean, I do understand—with what happened—"

"Yes." He didn't turn as he added, "We almost lost you, last time around."

That was a surprise: I'd been so convinced that Mary Palmer would be foremost in his thoughts when it came to considering the Linares case that I'd clear forgotten that *I'd* had a pretty close brush with the Reaper during the same attack that'd left her dead—and so had Cyrus, a fact what I quickly reminded the Doctor of.

"Cyrus is a grown man," he answered. "If he tells me he is willing to take the risks involved with this case, then that is his decision. God knows the Beecham affair should have given him a—point of reference . . ." He paused, then took in a very deep, tired breath and let it out in a slow hiss. "But you are a different case."

I pondered the thing. "I never thought—I mean, I figured you'd be thinking of—"

"I know," the Doctor answered. "It wouldn't have been like you to think anything else. You haven't had many years of believing that you're important, Stevie. But you are. Mary was, too, I don't have to tell you that. But she's—gone now." It was as much as he could bear to say about her, and more than he ever had, to me.

"Still doesn't seem natural," I said, letting the words out before I'd had time to think. "Not having her around."

"No. And it never will." The Doctor pulled out his watch and began to fiddle with it in a way that was strange for him: like he wasn't sure just how to say what was on his mind. "I—do not expect to ever have children,

Stevie. Of my own, I mean. But if I *were* to have a son—I could only wish that he would have your courage. In all ways." He tucked the watch away. "I can't let my actions put you in danger again."

"Yeah," I said. "I get that. But—" Words were becoming a problem for me, too. "But I was in danger my whole life. I mean, before I came to live with you. It ain't that big of a thing—so long as there's some kind of sensible reason for it. And this case—well, you seen that picture of the little girl. And it's pretty obvious what could be hanging on the thing." I stamped my foot once, lightly, trying to be clear. "I wouldn't want to think that I kept you out of it, that's all. The rest of them, they all know they need you. If I'm in the way, you can—I don't know, ship me off someplace. But you oughtta help them. Because like Detective Sergeant Lucius said, this thing could get real big and real ugly."

The Doctor smiled at that and gave me what you might call a scrutinizing look. "And when did he say that?"

I laughed a bit, knocking a fist lightly to my forehead. "Oh. Right. That would've been last night, I guess."

"Ah."

For what seemed quite a while but couldn't actually have been more than a few minutes—not even enough time for Cyrus to finish up in the carriage house—we both just stood there, looking out at Stuyvesant Park. Then the Doctor said:

"The detective sergeants found the weapon this morning—did they tell you?"

I spun toward him in excitement. "No. Mr. Moore said there'd been developments, though. What was it, a piece of pipe?"

"Your old trademark," the Doctor answered with a nod, pulling out his cigarette case. "It was under one of the benches around the Egyptian obelisk. They dusted for fingerprints and found several. There was also some blood on the thing, though it's impossible to say who or even what it came from. Much work to be done in that area of forensics, I'm afraid . . ." He lit his cigarette, then blew smoke out the open window with a troubled but fascinated look on his face. "Who the devil would kidnap the daughter of a high Spanish official and then fail to capitalize on it in some way?"

A smile crept into my face. "Then you *are* going to help them."

The Doctor sighed again. "I have a dilemma, it seems. I wouldn't want you to have to be sent away, Stevie, yet I can't be the agent of further threats to your safety." He took another long drag off his cigarette. "Tell me—what would *your* solution to such a problem be?"

"Mine?"

"Yes. How do you think I should handle it?"

I groped for words. "You should—well, you should do what you've always done. Just be my friend. Trust that I know how to handle myself. Because I do." I let out a small grunt of a laugh. "Good as the rest of you, anyway."

The Doctor smiled, then walked over to tousle my hair lightly. "True enough. And stated with your usual respect for your elders."

Then we heard the front door open and close, after which Cyrus came loping up the stairs. He paused when he saw me in the parlor, as if he thought that the conversation might be private; but the Doctor called him in.

"You may as well know, too, Cyrus," he said, putting his cigarette out in an ashtray. "We seem to be reentering the detection business—that is, if you wish."

Cyrus just nodded once. "Very much, sir."

"You'll keep an eye on our young friend here, won't you?" the Doctor added. "It seems that he's already been knocking about the city at all hours of the night with the detective sergeants." The Doctor looked up from the ashtray to Cyrus. "You wouldn't know anything about that, I suppose?"

Cyrus only smiled, crossed his hands, and glanced at the floor. "I might know something about it, yes, Doctor."

"I thought you might," the Doctor answered, heading for the stairs. "Well . . . I, for one, intend to get some sleep. It may be in short supply soon." He paused before heading upstairs and turned to us. "Do be careful—both of you. God knows where this thing will lead."

Cyrus and I mumbled solemn pledges that we'd try to watch ourselves; but when the Doctor had disappeared up the stairs and into his bedroom, there was no way on earth we could keep ourselves from smiling.

CHAPTER 9

The Doctor telephoned Miss Howard, Mr. Moore, and the detective
sergeants the next morning to inform them of his decision and to direct Miss Howard to set up a meeting with Señora Linares for that
evening at Number 808 Broadway so that he could personally interview
her. Miss Howard soon called back, saying she'd been able to schedule an
appointment for 8:30. Then the Doctor withdrew into his study, to begin
gathering his thoughts and assembling his research for the job ahead. He
issued occasional orders to Cyrus and me, dispatching one or the other of
us to various stores and libraries to track down books and journals. This
activity nearly kept me from my own urgent mission of the morning: getting bets down for myself and Mr. Moore on the first real class horse race
of the season, the Suburban handicap at the Coney Island Jockey Club's
track in Sheepshead Bay. But I juggled it all fine, and Mr. Moore and I finished the day with some very tidy winnings.

At about 7:45 in the evening, the Doctor announced that we'd better
get ready to go, as he wanted to walk downtown. He claimed that it was
on account of the fine weather, but I think he really felt much more nervous about going back to Number 808 than he'd expected to. The walk
over to Broadway and then downtown did seem to calm him, though, and
by the time we'd reached the old headquarters sunset was beginning, the
rich golden color that spread over the rooftops making it hard to imagine
that we were venturing into anything really dangerous.

Dr. Kreizler entered Number 808 much as the rest of us had two days
earlier: slowly, cautiously, letting the memories take full effect before he

made any definitive movement or statement. As the elevator carried us up to the sixth floor, silence abounded, though when the Doctor saw the sign that Miss Howard'd had painted on the door, he couldn't help but laugh once quietly and shake his head.

"Sufficiently euphemistic, I should think," he murmured. "Sara certainly knows her audience . . ."

Then it was inside, to find Miss Howard and the señora once again sitting in two of the easy chairs. Señora Linares wore the same black clothing, and her veil was up, showing that her wounds had healed only a little since the last time we saw her. She seemed very relieved to meet Dr. Kreizler, and as they spoke she opened up in a way she hadn't when Mr. Moore and the Isaacsons had examined her. As for the Doctor, he stayed intensely focused on the visitor for most of the time, though his occasional quick glances around the room tipped me off to the fact that he was thinking about other things, too: things that weren't far enough in the past yet to seem really finished.

The Doctor's examination of the señora took just over an hour and involved, of course, questions that to most people would've seemed thoroughly unrelated to the matter at hand: questions about her family, her childhood, where she'd grown up, how she'd met her husband, why she'd married him. Then there were deeper inquiries about the state of that marriage over the last couple of years. The señora willingly answered these, even though she was clearly confused about their purpose. I think the Doctor would have kept going longer if he could've, being as his subject was so compliant; but when she realized that 9:30 had come and gone, she became very anxious and agitated, saying that she hadn't had time to work out a good cover story for the meeting and needed to get back home in a hurry. Cyrus deposited her in a hansom, returning to the sixth floor just as true darkness descended on the city.

During the few minutes he was gone the Doctor started silently wandering around the room, maybe going over what he'd just heard, maybe thinking again about other, older matters, maybe doing a bit of both; whatever the case, nobody even considered interrupting him. Only the sound of the elevator's return finally brought him back out of his deep ponderings. He looked up kind of blankly, then turned to Miss Howard, who'd switched on a small electrical light and was sitting on the edge of its glow.

"Well, Sara," the Doctor said. "What's become of our board?"

Miss Howard smiled wide and fairly ran over to the Japanese screen, laying hold of the big, rolling chalkboard and dragging it out to face the desks. It had obviously been recently scrubbed clean.

The Doctor approached it, staring at its black, empty surface. Then he removed his jacket, picked up a spanking new piece of chalk, cracked it in half, and, in quick, slashing motions, wrote the words POSSIBLE POLITICAL EXPLANATIONS across the top of the board. Shaking the half piece of chalk around inside one closed hand, he turned to the rest of us.

"We begin with the futile, I'm afraid," he announced. "The first task that faces us is to explore any possible political component of this crime—though I must tell you before we go any further that I do not believe such a component exists."

Mr. Moore automatically slipped behind one of the desks as he asked, "You buy the idea that the child's identity is just a coincidence, Kreizler?"

"I 'buy' nothing, John—but I believe, as the detective sergeants have suggested, that this is a random act. And I must tell you that if our goal is to return the child to her mother—as I presume it is—then that randomness attains a very grim dimension." With a single broad stroke the Doctor drew a circle in the center of the board and then marked stations at its major points as he spoke on. "As I think even you will see, Moore, any attempt at a political explanation results in something of a logical circle, one that leads nowhere. We start here." He tapped the twelve o'clock position on the diagram. "The child has been abducted in the manner the señora says—I don't think there's any question about her telling the truth, there. She's a sound, strong person—her being here alone proves that much. Were she the sort of neurotic woman who craves sympathy and attention"—the Doctor suddenly paused, staring out the window—"and such creatures do exist . . ." He came back from wherever he'd been. "Then we would hardly do as an audience, and a fabricated story about a kidnapping, accompanied by a thorough beating, would hardly be a convenient dramatic vehicle. No. Her history, her position, her mentality—they all point toward the truth. And so—the child has been abducted and the mother struck on the head. By, if we are to accept Moore's political hypothesis, an expert."

"Who chooses a very public spot, in broad daylight," Lucius droned doubtfully, opening a little notebook to make a record of the discussion.

"Ah, my dear Detective Sergeant, I share your skepticism," the Doctor answered. "But we must not dispose of this theory through mere intuition." He quickly wrote AN ABDUCTION BY A PROFESSIONAL FOR POLITICAL PURPOSES at the top of the circle. "After all, perhaps the kidnapper was a man of rare pluck and pride who enjoys the challenge of working under unusually dangerous circumstances."

"With a piece of lead pipe," Marcus added, his voice crossing over into open sarcasm.

"With an instrument that he can easily discard, so that it will not be discovered on his person by the police, should he be detained for any reason. After all, our young friend in the windowsill"—the Doctor jerked a thumb in my direction—"carried just such a weapon for just such a reason. Isn't that so, Stevie?"

I glanced around to find each of them staring at me. "Well—yeah, I guess." They kept staring, and I started to fidget. "It ain't like I do it anymore!" I protested, which seemed to give them a chuckle.

"All right, then," the Doctor said, taking the limelight back off of me. "He's a professional. Who happens to be about the height of his victim and possesses a remarkably light touch." The Doctor moved to the right side of the circle. "But who can have hired him? Moore? You're the one who favors this interpretation—give me your candidates."

"We're not short on those," Mr. Moore answered from his desk. "There's a lot of people who'd like to see a diplomatic incident between the United States and Spain right now. We can start with the war party in this country—"

"Very well," the Doctor said, listing them as U.S. CITIZENS FAVORING WAR on the board. "Those Americans who don't care who starts the war, so long as we finish it."

"Exactly," Mr. Moore said. Then he frowned. "Though I doubt they'd want Americans to come off looking quite so brutal."

"Who else?" the Doctor demanded.

"Well, there's the Cubans," Mr. Moore replied. "The exiles here in New York. They'd be in favor of anything that started a war, too."

"The Cuban Revolutionary Party," Marcus added. "They've got an office down on Front Street, near the docks on the East Side. Moldy old building—they're up on the fourth floor. Lucius and I can roust them tomorrow, if you like."

"I submit that tonight would be more useful," Dr. Kreizler replied. "If they have the child, they are far more likely to plan its fate in the dead of night than during the day." CUBAN REVOLUTIONARIES went on the right-hand side of the circle.

"Then there's the Spaniards themselves," Mr. Moore said. "Personally, I like them best—they remove the kid and keep the mother in the dark, figuring she's not up to being part of it."

"And make no announcement of what's happened?" Miss Howard said. "Why frame our country and then fail to report the crime?"

Mr. Moore shrugged. "They may be waiting for the right moment. You know the situation in Washington, Sara—you said it yourself, McKinley's still looking for some way out of this damned war. Maybe they're waiting until he *has* no way out."

"In that case, why not remove the child later?" Miss Howard asked. "Or sooner? There was more war hysteria in the spring than there is right now."

"Perhaps they've simply mistimed their play," the Doctor offered, writing SPANISH WAR PARTY on the board. "Spain is hardly being run by geniuses at the moment. Those who favor war are either psychopathic sadists like Weyler"—by which he meant the infamous General Weyler, the governor-general of Cuba who'd begun the practice of putting Cuban peasants into what they called "concentration camps," where they couldn't help the rebels but *could* die like flies of disease and starvation— "or deluded monarchists, dreaming of the days of the *conquistadores*." The Doctor stood away from the board. "So—that completes the list of suspects. One of the groups hires a professional, he abducts the child, and it is taken into hiding. By—"

"The woman on the train," Miss Howard answered quickly. "She's the caretaker—unless you think the señora was mistaken about seeing the baby."

"A different woman might have been," the Doctor answered. "But this woman? No. She has the presence of mind to come here and discuss the affair in detail, even though she's aware of the potential consequences should her husband discover it. This is not a woman given to either delusions or hysteria. No, when she says she saw the child, I believe her." Inclining toward the bottom of the circle on the board, the Doctor wrote THE WOMAN ON THE TRAIN:, the colon showing that he intended to write more. "All right, John," he continued. "Explain this mysterious woman in a political context."

Mr. Moore looked to be at a loss. "Well, she's—she's just what Sara says. A caretaker. She was dressed like a governess, the señora said—probably another professional, hired for the job."

"A job which she undertakes on the last car of the Third Avenue Elevated in the middle of the night? It won't do, John, and you know it. Though I'm inclined to agree with you about her being a professional of some kind." He wrote the words GOVERNESS OR NURSE after the last phrase as he added, "But for entirely different reasons."

"She could've been taking the train down to the Cubans' headquarters," Mr. Moore protested.

"John," Miss Howard said, fairly condescendingly, "anyone who goes to the trouble of hiring a kidnapper and a nurse can certainly afford to pay for a *cab*."

"Have you ever met those Cuban Revolutionary fellows, Sara?" Mr. Moore answered, topping her condescension. "*I* have—they're a moth-eaten group, if ever I saw one. Whatever money Hearst is using to spread war fever, he isn't giving much of it to them."

"John's right about that much," Marcus said. "Maybe they've run out of funds."

"Which still does not explain what the devil she was doing on the train in the first place," the Doctor answered. "The general idea is to keep the child hidden, isn't it? Not parade her around before half of the city. There must be a reason why they would allow her to be seen in public, and that reason must have a political dimension."

Lucius spoke up: "Well—there's really only one."

The Doctor turned. "Yes?"

"They *wanted* the girl to be seen."

Dr. Kreizler nodded once. "Yes. Thank you, Detective Sergeant. That is, in fact, the only possibility." The words DELIBERATE DISPLAY then went up. "Someone, somewhere—perhaps even the señora—was *supposed* to see the child, so that the kidnappers could prove they actually have her and are in earnest. And the best place to do such a thing would be in a very public place. And so we arrive at our final destination . . ." The Doctor moved up to the left-hand side of the circle. "Having demonstrated that they have the child, our abductors make their demands known. Yet the señora seems to think that they have not."

"Consul Baldasano and Linares could be lying to her," Lucius said. "They may have received the demands and don't intend to meet them. They don't want a stink, so they lie to the mother."

The Doctor was busy writing DEMANDS: as he weighed this. "Yes. Again, Lucius, the only possibility, really, unless Moore is right and they're biding their time. But whether they're waiting or have been refused, what is it that each group would want? A simple kidnapping for ransom is again ruled out here, because one doubts that the Spanish would fail to meet mere monetary demands. We must stick to the political dimension—which means what?"

"Well," Mr. Moore said. "The American jingoes and the Cubans want just one thing—war. It's not really a matter of 'demands' as such."

The Doctor spun around and pointed an accusing finger at his old friend, smiling. "Precisely. Thank you, Moore, for eliminating two of your own suggested culprits." He turned round again, writing WAR under DE-MANDS:, as another lost look came over Mr. Moore's face.

"What're you talking about, Kreizler?"

"You abduct a child. Your goal is a diplomatic incident. The child's disappearance is designed to be the cause—her absence alone is important. Beyond that, she is a liability."

Miss Howard's face lit up. "Yes. And in that case—*why is the child still alive?*"

"Exactly, Sara," the Doctor answered. "For both the American war party and the Cubans, the living child is only a breathing risk—she can only contribute to their capture. If either group *were* responsible, the Linares girl would be at the bottom of one of our rivers by now, or perhaps, like the detective sergeants' discovery of Sunday night, in pieces at the bottom of several rivers. Of all the potential political culprits, only the Spanish would have any interest in keeping the child alive—yet they also have the greatest interest in keeping her out of sight and the most resources with which to make sure she stays so. And thus"—the Doctor drew a hard line back to the top of the board—"a circle. Leading nowhere. Time, as I say, may reveal it to be the correct analysis, but . . ." He paused, looking at his work; then he said, "Detective Sergeant?" and inclined his head toward Lucius.

"Doctor?"

"Have you made a copy of this diagram?"

"Yes, sir."

"Good. Keep it, in the unlikely event that we should need to refer to it again." The Doctor picked up an eraser.

"What are you saying, Dr. Kreizler?" Marcus asked.

"I am saying, Marcus," he answered, starting to wipe away what he'd written with energetic strokes, "that it is all—so—much—*poppycock!*"

When the Doctor stepped back from the board again, only two sets of words remained: AN ABDUCTION toward the top of the board and THE WOMAN ON THE TRAIN: GOVERNESS OR NURSE at the bottom. "Remove all the improbable details contained in the circle, and we are left with a far more useful geometric configuration." He proceeded to slowly and deliberately drag the chalk from the words at the top of the board to those at the bottom. "A straight line."

We all looked at the thing for a few seconds: it seemed like there was an awful lot of empty space on that board, all of a sudden.

Mr. Moore sighed, putting his feet up. "Meaning exactly what, Kreizler?"

The Doctor turned, his face darkened by genuine apprehension. "It's understandable that you seek to impose a political explanation on this crime, John, because the alternative is, in fact, far more disturbing and volatile. Yet it is also far more likely." He pulled out his cigarette case and offered its contents to Miss Howard, Marcus, and Mr. Moore in turn. I was dying for a smoke myself, but it'd have to wait. After they'd all lit their sticks, the Doctor took to pacing in his usual way, and he was still going when he announced, "I believe that the detective sergeants' analysis of the physical evidence is, as always, flawless. Señora Linares was in all probability attacked by another woman, whose use of a piece of pipe she found on the scene, as well as her willingness to strike in a public place in broad daylight, indicates spontaneity. That she did not injure the señora more seriously is a testament to blind luck and the limits of her own strength, I suspect, and not to any professional skill."

"All right," Mr. Moore answered, though he was clearly unconvinced. "In that case, Kreizler, I've got only one question, though it's a big one: why?"

"Indeed." The Doctor walked over and wrote WHY? in large letters on the left-hand side of the board. "A woman takes a child. She demands no ransom. And several days later she is observed in public, apparently caring for the girl as if—as if—" The Doctor seemed to be searching for the right words.

It was Miss Howard that gave them to him: "*As if she were her own.*"

The Doctor turned his gleaming black eyes on Miss Howard for a moment. "As always, gentlemen," he said, "Sara's unique perspective cuts to the heart of the matter. As if the child were her own. Think of it: whoever this woman is, she has managed to abduct, out of all the children in New York, one whose disappearance could cause an international crisis. Bend your mind to it, for a moment, Moore—if there is no political dimension to the abduction, what does that tell us?"

Mr. Moore scoffed. "That she didn't do her damned homework, that's what it tells us."

"Meaning?"

It was Cyrus's turn to step in: "Meaning, if you'll excuse me, Mr. Moore, that, faced with the situation she was in, she couldn't do anything but obey the impulse of the moment." He glanced around at the others, then smiled a bit and looked to the floor. "Something I know a little about . . ."

"Precisely, Cyrus," the Doctor said, starting to note things under the WHY? heading. "Thank you. It means that she was in the grip of an urge, a spontaneous urge that destroyed any possibility not only of self-control but of premeditation, of researching her victim. Of, as Moore rather caustically puts it, doing her homework. What could possibly cause such recklessness?"

"Well, I hate to state the obvious," Marcus said, "but—she apparently wanted a baby."

"True," the Doctor said with a quick nod, adding this thought to the WHY? column. Then he erased the notations at the bottom of the board and moved them up to the middle-right-hand side. There were now three general categories up top—WHY?, AN ABDUCTION, and THE WOMAN ON THE TRAIN: GOVERNESS OR NURSE—with space to the extreme right for one more.

"But not just any baby," Lucius added quickly. "Apparently, she wanted *this* baby."

"And quite desperately," Miss Howard said.

"Good," the Doctor pronounced; then he scratched THE LINARES CHILD in the top-right-hand corner of the board. "But you must all slow down—we run ahead of ourselves." He stood back, examining the board with the others. "It begins to take shape," he murmured, putting his cigarette out in an ashtray with a deeply satisfied stamp. "Yes, Detective Sergeant, she wants the Linares child. But as John has said, she cannot have known *who* the Linares child was—and your own investigation demonstrates the spontaneity of the attack. Put those elements together, and what conclusion do you reach?"

Lucius gave that matter just a few seconds' consideration: "That it's not *who* the Linares child was that mattered—it's *what* she was."

"*What* she was?" Mr. Moore said, confused and still not completely convinced of the usefulness of the entire exercise. "She was a *baby*, is what she was—and we've already said that the woman wanted one."

Miss Howard laughed. "Spoken like a truly confirmed bachelor. She wasn't just *a* baby, John—every baby is different, every one has his or her own characteristics." She turned to the board. "And so the character of the child can tell us about the character of her abductor."

"Brava!" the Doctor fairly hollered, moving to the right-hand side of the board. "Continue, Sara—you are the one to take the lead here."

Miss Howard got up and assumed the job of pacing in front of the chalkboard. "Well," she said as the Doctor stood poised with the chalk. "We know that Ana was—happy. Cheerful by nature. Noisy, perhaps, but noisy in a way that charmed people."

"Go on, go on," the Doctor said, scratching away.

"In addition, she was healthy—she'd had every advantage and seemed to embody all of them."

"Yes?"

"And bright. At a precociously early age she was amused by things that we consider great works of art but which were, to her, intriguing in an ingenuous way. There's a sensitivity there."

Mr. Moore grumbled, "You're talking about her like she's a *person,* for God's sake . . ."

"She *is* a person, John," the Doctor said, still writing. "Difficult as that may be for you to imagine. Anything else, Sara?"

"Only—only that she would have been a logical target, I'm afraid. Her gregariousness would, as I say, have attracted attention—admiring attention from most—"

"But covetous envy from one," Marcus said, letting out a big cloud of smoke that caused his brother to cough hard. "Oh. Sorry, Lucius," he said, though without much genuine concern.

"Excellent," the Doctor said. "More than enough for a good beginning. Now, then—let us turn the light of these observations onto our shadowy woman on the El. We have already determined that she did not research her victim. Rather, she experienced an apparently irresistible spontaneous urge to immediately take this child, no matter whose she was. Any other conclusions?"

"She probably hasn't got any children of her own," Marcus offered.

"Granted," the Doctor answered, noting it. "But many women don't, and they are able to restrain themselves from kidnapping."

"Perhaps she *can't* have any children of her own," Miss Howard said.

"Closer. But why not adopt one? The city abounds with unwanted children."

"Maybe she can't do that, either," Lucius said. "A legal complication—probably a criminal record, if her behavior here is any indication."

The Doctor considered it. "Even better. A woman physically incapable of childbirth, who is legally prevented from adopting an unwanted child because of a criminal record."

"But it's deeper than that," Miss Howard murmured thoughtfully. "She doesn't *want* an unwanted child. She's drawn to this child in particular, a child who could not *be* more wanted. And with good reason, given the child's healthy, vivacious character. So if we assume that all of this touches some chord . . ." She paused.

"Sara?" the Doctor asked.

Miss Howard seemed to shiver a bit. "I'm sorry. But there's—almost a sense of tragedy about it. Could she have *had* children, Doctor, and lost them—say, to disease or poor health?"

The Doctor mulled that one over. "I like it," he finally said. "It's consistent with her choice of victim. Most of us—with the exception of the likes of Moore, there—feel a certain longing when we see such a child as Ana Linares. However unconscious or remote. Could tragedy have been the experience that made this woman's longing irresistible? Is this to be the healthy, happy child she has always wanted?"

"And apparently feels entitled to," Marcus added.

"What about the clothing?" Lucius asked. "If Señora Linares is right, and she was some kind of nurse or governess—"

"Ah, Detective Sergeant, you have read my thoughts," the Doctor said. "For what have we just described, if not a woman who would be drawn toward caring for children as a profession?"

"Oh, no," Mr. Moore said, rising and backing away. "No, no, no, I smell where this is going . . ."

The Doctor laughed. "Indeed you do, Moore! But why should you be afraid of it? You proved during the Beecham case that you have a positive *talent* for such work!"

"I don't care!" Mr. Moore answered, his horror only half theatrical. "I hated every *minute* of it! I've never had to do such boring, miserable drudgery—"

"Nevertheless, it will be where the hard part of our investigation begins," the Doctor answered. "We will visit every nursing and governess service in this city, as well as every hospital, every foundling home, and every lying-in facility. The woman is *here,* with the child, and if Señora Linares's eyes are to be trusted—as I believe they are—then she holds a position in the field somewhere."

Lucius's face had screwed up into a human question mark. "But—Doctor. We don't even have a name. Just a verbal description. I mean, if we had a photograph, a picture of some kind—"

The Doctor set his chalk down, then slapped the white dust from his hands and vest. "And why shouldn't we?"

Lucius looked even more confused. "Why shouldn't we what?"

"Have a picture," the Doctor answered simply. "After all, we have an extremely vivid description." Picking his jacket up, he slipped it back on as he continued, "You gentlemen have missed the major feature of this case. What was the principal thing we lacked in the Beecham affair, the principal thing that is lacking in most crimes of this nature? An accurate description of the criminal. Yet we have one—and my guess is that, put to the test, Señora Linares's description will be even more detailed than it has been thus far."

"But how would we translate that into a visual image?" Miss Howard asked.

"*We* would not," the Doctor replied. "We would and will leave that to someone trained in the field." Pulling out his silver watch, the Doctor popped it open and squinted at it. "I should prefer someone of Sargent's ability, but he is in London and would demand an absurd fee. Eakins might do, too, but he is in Philadelphia—even that is too far, given the urgency of our task. Our opponent may flee the city at any moment—we must move quickly."

"Let me get this straight, Kreizler," Mr. Moore said, ever more dumbfounded. "You're going to commission a *portrait* of this woman, based on a *description*?"

"A sketch should be sufficient, I think," the Doctor said, tucking his watch away. "Portraiture is an immensely complex process, Moore. A good portrait painter must be something of a natural psychologist. I see no reason why, given enough time with the señora, a very reasonable likeness could not be created. The first job is to find the right artist. And I believe I know where to get a reference." He looked my way. "Stevie? Shall we pay a call on the Reverend? I believe we'll find him at home and hard at work at this hour—provided he's not out on one of his nocturnal rambles."

I brightened up. "Pinkie?" I asked, jumping out of the windowsill. "Sure thing!"

Marcus looked from me to Dr. Kreizler. " 'Pinkie'? 'The Reverend'?"

"A friend of mine," the Doctor said. "Albert Pinkham Ryder. He has many nicknames. As do most eccentrics."

"Ryder?" Mr. Moore wasn't buying this idea, either. "Ryder's no portrait painter—and it takes him years to finish a canvas."

"True, but he has a keen psychological instinct. He'll be able to recommend someone, I've no doubt. If you'd care to come along, Moore—you, too, Sara."

"Very much," Miss Howard answered. "His work is fascinating."

"Hmm, yes," the Doctor said uncertainly. "You may find his rooms and studio less so, I'm afraid."

"That's the truth," Mr. Moore threw in. "You can count me out—that place makes my skin crawl."

The Doctor shrugged. "As you wish. Detective Sergeants—I dislike asking you to perform what I fear is a useless task, but it may be worth—how did you put it?"

"Rousting the Cubans," Lucius answered, sounding like there weren't many things he'd like to do less. "Oh, *this*'ll be a treat . . . Black beans, garlic, and dogma. Well, at least I don't speak Spanish, so I won't know what they're saying."

"I do apologize," the Doctor said, "but we must, as you know, cover as many possibilities as we can. And as quickly as possible."

We all began to move for the door, Marcus bringing up the rear at a slow pace. "There's just one thing, Doctor," he murmured, taking deliberate steps as he turned something over in his head. "Señor Linares. What we're assuming—and I agree with the assumption completely—is that this is an abduction committed by someone who didn't know the identity of the baby."

"Yes, Marcus?" the Doctor said.

"In that case, why is Linares trying to conceal it?" The detective sergeant's face was full of concern. "The fact is that the woman we're describing, whatever her psychological peculiarities, is in all probability American. That would be just as useful to the Spanish government as a politically motivated kidnapping. So why aren't they using it?"

Mr. Moore turned a somewhat smug face to the Doctor. "Well, Kreizler?"

The Doctor looked at the floor and nodded a few times, smiling. "I might've known it would be you who would ask, Marcus."

"Sorry," the detective sergeant answered. "But as you say, we've got to cover all the angles."

"No need to apologize," the Doctor answered. "I was simply hoping to avoid that question. Because it's the only one I can't begin to answer. And *should* we find the answer, I fear, we will also find some rather unpleasant—and dangerous—facts. But I don't think we can allow that consideration to delay our actions."

Marcus weighed this, then signaled agreement with a small nod. "It's something we ought to keep in mind, though."

"As we shall, Marcus. As we shall . . ." The Doctor allowed himself one more slow, thoughtful lap around the room, coming to a rest at the window. "Somewhere out there, even as we speak, is a woman who unwittingly holds in her arms a child who could prove an instrument of terrible destruction—as devastating, in her innocence, as an assassin's bullet or a madman's bomb. Yet for all of that, I fear the devastation that has already occurred in the kidnapper's mind most of all. Yes, we shall be alert for the dangers of the larger world, Marcus—but we must, once again, place our greatest efforts behind knowing the mind and the identity of our antagonist. Who is she? What created her? And above all—will the savage fury that drove her to this act eventually be turned against the child? I suspect so—and sooner, rather than later." He turned to the rest of us. "Sooner, rather than later . . ."

CHAPTER 10

I t's always seemed to me that there's two types of people in this life, them what get a kick out of what might be called your odder types and them what don't; and I suppose that I, unlike Mr. Moore, have always been in the first bunch. You'd have to've been, I think, to have really enjoyed living in Dr. Kreizler's house, for the folks he had in and out of there—even the ones like Mr. Roosevelt, who were long on brains and went on to great fame and success—were some of the more peculiar characters you could possibly have met in those days. And of all those strange but noteworthy souls, none was stranger than the man I liked to call "Pinkie," Mr. Albert Pinkham Ryder.

An artist by religion in addition to profession, the tall, soft-spoken, kindly man with the big beard and searching eyes gave off the general impression of a monk or priest, which was why he was known as "the Reverend" or "Bishop Ryder" to his friends. He lived in rooms at Number 308 West Fifteenth Street and spent most of his nights either working or on long walks around the city—its streets, its parks, even its suburbs— studying the moonlight and shadows that filled so many of his paintings. He was a solitary soul, a recluse, by his own estimation, who'd grown up in the spooky old whaling town of New Bedford, Massachusetts. He'd had a Quaker for a mother and a collection of brothers for company—all of which meant that one of his more extreme peculiarities was his way of dealing with women. Oh, he was polite enough, in a way what would've seemed chivalrous if it hadn't been so damned odd. There was the time, for instance, that he heard a beautiful singing voice floating through his building and, when he found the woman who possessed it, immediately proposed marriage to her. Now, this woman was a fine singer, sure enough, but on the street and at the local precinct house she was known to be other things, too; and it was only when a group of his friends stepped in to lower the boom on the idea that poor old Pinkie was saved from what probably would've been a thorough fleecing.

He liked kids; he was kind of a big, strange boy himself, and he was always happy to see me (the same could not be said for some of the Doctor's other friends). By 1897 he was famous and successful enough, among those who understood art, to be able to live pretty much as he pleased—which was basically like a pack rat. He never threw a thing away, not a food carton or a piece of string or a pile of ashes, and his rooms really could get a little frightening at times for most people. But his gentle, quiet kindness and the definite pull of his hazy, dreamy paintings more than made up for all that, especially for me, a boy from the Lower East Side who was used to garbage piling up inside flats. That, combined with the fact that he shared my taste in food—he kept a kettle of stew always on the boil and, when out, preferred oysters, lobster, and baked beans in a waterfront restaurant—made his place a destination to which I was always happy to accompany the Doctor.

It was just the three of us—Miss Howard, the Doctor, and myself— what made the pilgrimage that night, as Cyrus (who admired Pinkie's paintings but, like Mr. Moore, didn't think much of his living habits) begged off to get a full night's sleep. Pinkie's building was just west of Eighth Avenue on Fifteenth Street, and was one of thousands like it in that neighborhood: a simple old brick row house that'd been converted into flats. We traveled by hansom, moving uptown with the thickening stream of traffic what was heading for the Tenderloin at that time of night and then branching off to find that a small kerosene lamp was burning in Pinkie's front window.

"Ah, so he's home," Dr. Kreizler said. He paid off the cabbie, then took Miss Howard's arm. "Now, Sara, I must prepare you—I know that you find courtly deference to your sex abominable, but in Ryder's case you really must make an exception. It's perfectly innocent, and perfectly genuine—he does not intend it as any veiled attempt to keep women fragile and weak, I assure you."

Miss Howard nodded in a not-completely-convinced way as we climbed up the stoop of the building. "I'll give anyone the benefit of a fair trial," she said. "But if it becomes insulting . . ."

"Fair enough," the Doctor said. "Stevie? Why don't you run ahead, so that Ryder has some warning."

I dashed inside the building and up the dark stairs to the door of Pinkie's flat, then knocked on it hard and called out to him in a loud voice. I knew that he sometimes didn't let even good friends in, if he was in a fever of creation, but I felt sure he'd respond to me. "Mr. Ryder?" I shouted. "It's Stevie Taggert, sir, come with the Doctor!"

From inside I heard the kind of rustling that squirrels make when they get into a pile of autumn leaves, and then some heavy, slow footsteps moved toward the door. The footsteps stopped, and there was a long pause, accompanied by heavy breathing that I could hear even in the hall. Finally, a deep, rich voice what was at once slow but a bit skittish asked:

"Stevie?"

"Yes, sir," I answered.

A lock was undone, and as the door was pulled away from me a large form moved in to fill the opening. I made out the beard first, then the high, glowing forehead, and finally the eyes, the color of which—light brown or blue—I could never quite figure.

I moved inside with a salute. "Hellooo, Pinkie!" I announced, marching past the piles of books, newspapers, and just plain trash in his front room toward the back of the flat, where his studio—and the kettle of stew—were located.

He smiled in his particular way, what Dr. Kreizler always called "enigmatically."

"Hello, young Stevie," he said, wiping his paint-covered hands on a rag. For all that he'd lived in New York for years, there was still much of the old-time New Englander in the way he spoke. "What brings you to these reaches at this hour?"

"The Doctor's following me up," I said, moving between walls covered with unframed canvases that, to the untrained eye, would have looked like finished pictures: beautiful golden landscapes, stormy dark seascapes (or what the art crowd called "marines"), as well as scenes from the poetry, drama, and myths what fascinated old Pinkie. He was quite a poet himself, and, like I say, his interpretations of "The Forest of Arden" or "The Tempest" would've looked to anybody else like they were ready for shipping. But it was near impossible for Pinkie to consider a painting done, ever, and he fussed and fidgeted with them, as Mr. Moore had said, for years before he'd release them to the usually exasperated patrons what had paid for them long ago.

Grabbing a wooden spoon, I helped myself to a nice scoop of Pinkie's hearty lamb stew, which he'd sweetened with some fresh apples. Then I took a turn around the studio. "Quite a crop, Pinkie," I called to him. "How many of them are sold?"

"Enough," he answered from the front room. Then I heard the Doctor's and Miss Howard's voices and raced back out, so that I could witness the ritual that Pinkie went through anytime a woman came to his hideaway.

Making a deep bow, he said, "I'm deeply honored, miss," with rumbling sincerity. Then he held out a hand. "Please . . ." Next he started to quickly clear a path through all the garbage in the room to the one easy chair he owned, a beat-up but comfortable old thing that sat by the front window. As he finished clearing the floor in front of the chair, he grabbed a small oriental throw rug and spread it out so that Miss Howard could rest her feet on it once she'd sat down, like a Bohemian queen on a throne. Ordinarily, she wouldn't have been a woman to go for such treatment; but coming from Pinkie, such things were just so sincere and so peculiar as to make anybody suspend their usual reactions.

"Well, Albert," the Doctor said cheerfully, "you look well. A bit swollen, perhaps, in spots. How is the rheumatism?"

"Always lurking about," Pinkie answered with a smile. "But I have my cures. May I offer you both something to eat? Or to drink? Beer? Water?"

"Yes, I'll have a glass of beer, Albert," the Doctor answered, looking to Miss Howard. "It's a pleasant night, though not as cool as I'd expected."

"Yes, beer would be lovely," Miss Howard said.

Pinkie held up a long finger, indicating he'd only be a moment, then started for the back of the flat. As he went, I noticed that his feet were making little squishing sounds. I looked down to see that he was wearing oversized shoes filled with straw and what appeared for all the world to be cooked oatmeal.

"Say, Pinkie," I said, following him, "I guess you know you've got oatmeal in your shoes."

"The best thing for rheumatism," he answered, fetching a few bottles of beer and running a couple of suspicious-looking glasses under a cold tap. "My walks have become a bit painful lately. Straw and cold oatmeal— that's the answer." He started back for the front room.

"O-*kaay*," I said with a shrug, still trailing him. "You oughtta know, ain't nobody in New York walks as much as you do."

Moving with little huffing sounds, Pinkie set the beer bottles and glasses down on a table made of an old wooden crate and then started to pour. "Here we are," he said, handing the glasses to the Doctor and Miss Howard. "To you, Miss Howard," he toasted, holding his glass up. " 'I look upon thy youth, fair maiden, I look upon thy youth and fancy laden,

Would that I a fairy were, That with magic wand I could deter, All evil chance, and spare thy coming years, All unwrought by rain of tears, With a rainbow bright.' "

"Well said, Albert," the Doctor replied, holding up his glass and drinking his beer. "Your own?" he asked, though I could tell that he knew it was.

Pinkie inclined his head humbly. "Poor, but my own. And fitting for your companion."

Miss Howard seemed genuinely touched—and that was no easy trick, for a member of the male sex to move her. "Thank you, Mr. Ryder," she said, holding up her glass and taking a sip. "That was lovely."

"Say, Pinkie," I tossed in, knowing that he was also a turf enthusiast, "how'd you make out in the Suburban today?"

A look of mingled disappointment and excitement came into his face. "I'm afraid I had no time to put a bet down," he said. "But it's odd that you should mention the races, Stevie . . ." He lifted the same long finger again and directed us to follow him to the studio, which we did. "A very strange coincidence, indeed! You see, I've been working on something. A picture with a story behind it, you might say. Some years ago, a waiter with whom I had a passing but convivial acquaintance wagered all of his life's savings on a horse race—and lost. Despairing, he then shot himself."

"How dreadful," Miss Howard said; but her shock could not hide the fact that she was becoming what you might call enchanted by the paintings that began to close in around her.

"Yes," Pinkie said. "It set my mind to work, I shall not tell you precisely how—but you must see the result, as I think it may have possibilities."

He took us over to a large easel in one corner of the room, on which rested a canvas of about two feet by three, covered with a light, stained piece of cloth. Pinkie lit a nearby gas lamp, turned its flame up, and then stepped to the easel.

"Mind you, it's nothing like finished," he said, "but—well . . ."

He took the cloth away.

On the easel was one of the most eerie of all his pictures that I'd ever seen. It showed a scraggly oval track, surrounded by a similarly rough horse fence. On the muddy ground in front of the track was a large, nasty-looking snake; above it, in the distance, some barren hills and a sky so gloomy that it could've been either day or night; and on the track itself, a lone rider—Death, the Reaper himself—riding bareback in the wrong direction, holding his scythe high.

Now, most of Pinkie's pictures were mysterious, but this thing was downright grim—scary, even. The Doctor and Miss Howard, however, were clearly impressed, for their eyes positively·glowed with fascination as they studied it.

"Albert," the Doctor said slowly, "it's brilliant. Harrowing, but brilliant."

Pinkie shuffled self-consciously in his oatmeal at that, and did so again when Miss Howard added, "Extraordinary. Really . . . entrancing in its way . . ."

"I've decided to call it simply 'The Race Track,' " Pinkie said.

I looked from the Doctor and Miss Howard to Pinkie and finally back to the picture. "I don't get it," I said.

Pinkie smiled at me and stroked his beard. "Now, *that's* what I like to hear. What don't you get, young Stevie?"

"What's with the snake?" I said, pointing at it.

"What does it mean to *you*?" he answered.

"Gotta be one fast snake, to keep up with that horse." Pinkie seemed to find that very satisfying. "And speaking of the horse, Pinkie, he's going the wrong direction—you oughtta know that."

"Yes," Pinkie answered, looking at the picture.

"And how about the sky?" I asked. "Is it supposed to be day or nighttime?"

"Do you know," Pinkie answered, squinting those strangely colored eyes. "I hadn't thought about it."

"Hunh," I said, giving the picture the once-over again. "Well, sorry, Pinkie, but it gives me the jitters. I'll take that one up there." I pointed to a nice, richly colored job that showed a pretty young girl with strawberry-blond hair: shadowy, yes, but comforting, not gloomy.

"Ah," Pinkie said. "My 'Little Maid of Acadie.' Yes, I rather like her, too—and she's almost finished. You've a good eye, young Stevie." He covered the unsettling picture on the easel back up. "Now, then, Laszlo, have you come just to check on my health, or for some other reason? I suspect the latter, as you are a man who always has reasons."

The Doctor looked away a little self-consciously. "Unkind, Albert," he said with a smile. "But true. I told you, Sara, that Albert could have been a psychologist if he'd wished." Pinkie shut the gas lamp off, and we started back for the front room. "The fact of the matter is, Albert, that we've come for a reference."

"A reference?"

"We need a portraitist," the Doctor said, as Miss Howard got back onto her flea-bitten throne. "One capable of doing a portrait not from life but from a detailed description."

Pinkie looked intrigued. "An unusual request, Laszlo."

"It's my request, actually, Mr. Ryder," Miss Howard said—and very wisely, too, for while Pinkie might've smelled something in the wind if the suggestion had come from a man, he'd take it as gospel coming from a woman—especially a handsome young woman. "It is—or rather was—a distant member of my family. She died rather suddenly. At sea. We've found that we have no painting, not even a photograph, to remember her by. My cousin and I—she lives in Spain, as did our dead relation—were discussing how much we wished we had some kind of an image for a keepsake, and the Doctor said it might be possible to do one from memories and descriptions." She took a very fetching little sip of her beer. "Do *you* think it might? I have only the greatest admiration for your work, and would count your opinion as definitive."

Well, sir, Pinkie walked right into it: he grabbed hold of the lapels of his worn wool jacket, got most of the usual stoop out of his stance, and started to walk the floor as if his shoes were the best patent leather, instead of filled with straw and oatmeal. "I see," he said thoughtfully. "An interesting idea, Miss Howard. Your relative was a woman, you say?"

"Yes," Miss Howard answered.

"There are many excellent portraitists in New York. Ordinarily, Chase would be the first choice—do you know him, Kreizler?"

"William Merritt Chase?" the Doctor asked. "We've only met briefly, but I know his work. And you're right, Albert, he's a superb choice—"

"Actually," Pinkie cut in, "I don't think so. If your subject is a woman . . . and if you're working from memories alone . . . I think you ought to have a woman do the job."

That brought a smile what was in no way an act to Miss Howard's face. "What an excellent idea, Mr. Ryder!" She glanced up pointedly at the Doctor. "And how refreshing . . ." The Doctor simply rolled his eyes and turned away. "Do you happen to know one?"

"I'm often taunted by my colleagues for seeing the work of as many artists as I can," Pinkie answered, "whatever their background. Or sex. I believe there is merit in almost any serious picture, no matter who the painter may be. Yes, I believe I know the very person for you. Her name is Cecilia Beaux." Miss Howard's head cocked a bit, as if in recognition. "Do you know of her, Miss Howard?" Pinkie said, ready to be impressed.

"I seem to know the name," Miss Howard answered, wrestling with it. "Does she teach, by any chance?"

"Yes, indeed. At the Pennsylvania Academy. She has a bright future there."

Miss Howard frowned. "No. That's not it . . ."

"But she also conducts a private class," Pinkie went on. "Twice a week, in New York. That is what made me think of her."

"Where is the class held?" the Doctor asked.

"At the home of Mrs. Cady Stanton."

"Of course!" Miss Howard said, brightening. "Mrs. Cady Stanton and I are old friends. I've heard her speak of Miss Beaux—and in very admiring terms."

"As well she should," Pinkie judged. "There is a quality in this woman's work—well, Laszlo, I can't do better than to say that she sees through to the very essence of the personality. She has been well appreciated in Europe, and will be here, in time. Remarkable portraits, really—particularly those of women and children. Yes, the more I think of it, Cecilia Beaux is the person for you."

"And I can reach her through Mrs. Cady Stanton," Miss Howard said, looking at the Doctor. "First thing in the morning."

"Well, then"—the Doctor lifted his beer again—"our problem is solved. I knew we were right to come to you, Albert—you are a living compendium." Pinkie flushed and smiled, then grew more serious as the Doctor said, "Now, Albert—about 'The Race Track'—is it sold?"

The two men fell to discussing the fate of the picture and drinking more beer. Pinkie hadn't yet sold his unsettling work, but he insisted to the Doctor that he wouldn't even consider doing so for a long time, as it was far from finished. (It wouldn't *be* finished, by the way, until 1913.) It was the same story he told about all his canvases, and the Doctor displayed the same frustration what most collectors did on trying to bring Pinkie into the cold world of practicalities. Finally Dr. Kreizler dropped the subject and they all fell to talking of art in general, leaving me to wander into the studio again and have a little more of the delicious stew. As I ate, I looked up at the "Little Maid of Acadie" for a while longer, realizing for the first time that, in the vague sort of way what was our host's style, it was the image of Kat.

We stayed at Pinkie's for another hour or so, everyone having a very pleasant time amidst those piles of relics, trash, and waste. A funny kind of life, that—the old boy lived just for his pictures, and was quite happy to have that much. Give him a little good, humble food, a room to work in, and the ability to take his long walks, and he was fine. Simple, you might say; to which I'd answer, yeah—so simple that only one in a million can manage it.

CHAPTER 11

The next morning Miss Howard called on the telephone to say that she'd contacted Mrs. Elizabeth Cady Stanton, the famous old crusader who'd been pushing women's rights for half a century. Miss Howard, it seemed, had known and admired Mrs. Cady Stanton (who always insisted on using her maiden name in addition to her husband's) ever since childhood; and as Mrs. Cady Stanton had blue-blood relatives in the Hudson Valley, not far from where the Howard family estate was, Miss Howard had been able to make her acquaintance early on through mutual friends. Miss Howard had warned the Doctor that there were bound to be complications with Mrs. Cady Stanton being the agent of our meeting Miss Cecilia Beaux, as the sharp old bird was well aware of Miss Howard's personal and professional connections. She'd know full well, for instance, that Miss Howard didn't have any recently deceased relative, if Miss Howard even tried to float that lie. This left our friend with the job of trying to make her hiring of a portrait painter look thoroughly innocent. But Mrs. Cady Stanton also knew that Miss Howard was a private detective, and she instantly became fascinated by what she was sure was some kind of intrigue—so much so that she flat-out asked to be present for the sketching session what Miss Howard scheduled for Thursday evening at Number 808 Broadway. Left without a graceful way to tell Mrs. Cady Stanton to mind her own business, Miss Howard was forced to agree. So it looked as if we were going to have an additional guest for the occasion.

Señora Linares, meanwhile, sent a note along to Miss Howard saying that her husband was definitely getting suspicious about her absences and that this was probably the last time she'd be able to get away: whatever we needed, we'd have to get it Thursday evening. As for the detective sergeants, their rousting of the Cubans had produced nothing except a lot of bad feeling, and they came away from the encounter convinced that nobody in the Cuban Revolutionary Party had the brains or the organizing skill to pull off anything like the kidnapping of Ana Linares. This little confirmation of his theory that the abductor was a woman acting alone sent the Doctor back into his study Wednesday afternoon, and by the following morning he still hadn't emerged; his food was taken in on trays, and he left strict orders not to be disturbed. Mr. Moore and Miss Howard dropped by at around two on Thursday to plan strategy for the sketching session. On finding the Doctor still closeted away, they asked me what was going on, to which I answered that I really didn't know, being as I hadn't seen him for twenty-four hours. It was time, however, to get things prepared for the evening to come, so together the three of us decided to go on up to the study and find out what was happening.

Mr. Moore knocked on the door and got a sharp "Go away, please!" in return. He looked to me, but all I could do was shrug.

"Kreizler?" Mr. Moore said. "What the hell's going on, you've been in there for two days—and it's time to get ready for the portrait!"

A long, exasperated groan came from inside the study, and then the door unlocked from within. The Doctor, dressed in a smoking jacket and slippers, pulled it open, his face in a book. "Yes, and I could be in here for two *years* before I'd find anything really useful." He looked up at us blankly, then, with a tilt of his head, signaled that we should follow him in.

The study was lined on three sides with mahogany shelves and paneling, while the Doctor's large desk sat in front of the window in the fourth wall. There were piles of open books everywhere, along with journals and monographs, also open. Some looked as though they'd been placed where they lay; some had clearly been thrown.

"I have been attempting," the Doctor announced, "to assemble some research with which we can make ourselves acquainted with the psychological peculiarities inherent in the woman-child relationship. And I have, not for the first time, been disappointed by my colleagues."

Mr. Moore grinned and cleared some journals off of a sofa, then plopped down onto it. "Well, that's good news," he said. "Then we don't have to do any lessons this time around, eh?"

He was referring to the Beecham case, during which the Doctor'd made everyone on the team read not only the basic psychological works of the day but also articles written by specialists what had particular application to the investigation. Cyrus and I had done most of the reading, too, just to keep up; and it had been, I don't mind saying, tough going. There can't be many people in the world what can blow wind like your average psychologists and alienists.

The Doctor just frowned at Mr. Moore. "Assuming that you have retained even a portion of what you learned last year," he said in some disgust, "then no, I don't know that there's a great deal more to be done. It's idiotic. Perfectly sound, rational men, when they reach one specific instinct—the maternal—begin to blather like idiots! Listen to the august Herr G. H. Schneider—one of James's favorites, John." (Mr. Moore had been at Harvard with the Doctor and had also studied, though very briefly, with Professor James.) " 'As soon as a wife becomes a mother her whole thought and feeling, her whole being, is altered. Until then she had only thought of her own well-being, of the satisfaction of her vanity; the whole world appeared made only for her; everything that went on about her was only noticed so far as it had personal reference to herself—now, however' "—and here a wicked kind of sarcasm came into the Doctor's voice—" 'the centre of the world is no longer herself, but her child. She does not think of her own hunger, she must first be sure that the child is fed—now, she has the greatest patience with the ugly, piping crybaby, whereas until now every discordant sound, every slightly unpleasant noise, made her nervous.' I ask you, Sara, have you ever heard such utter rot?"

Miss Howard's face took on a resigned sort of look. "That *is* the common perception, I'm afraid."

The Doctor kept ranting. "Yes, but listen to what he goes on to say: 'Thus, at least, it is in all unspoiled, naturally-bred mothers, who, alas!, seem to be growing rarer.' But does he go on to discuss the mental composition of those increasingly numerous '*un*–naturally bred' mothers? He does not!" The Doctor set the book aside.

The wheels in Miss Howard's head had started to spin during this tirade: her brow wrinkled with an idea. "Doctor—" she started.

But he wasn't finished. Picking up another book, he bellowed, "And listen to James himself: 'Parental love is an instinct stronger in woman than in man—the passionate devotion of a mother to a sick or dying child is perhaps the most simply beautiful moral spectacle that human life affords.' And there ends the discussion! How would such men react, I should like to know, were I to show them the dozens of case studies I have compiled over the years of women beating their children, starving them, throwing them into lit ovens, or simply killing them outright? It's unbelievable!"

"Yes, Doctor," Miss Howard tried again, "but I wonder—is there some usefulness in all this prejudicial thinking?"

"Only by inference, Sara," the Doctor scoffed, tossing the book he was holding onto a pile of others and then picking up the first volume again. "Just one brief comment of Schneider's offers anything like illumination: 'She'—meaning the mother—'has, in one word, transferred her entire egotism to the child.' "

"Yes, that's it—exactly," Miss Howard said. "Suppose you were one of those unnaturally bred mothers, one who'd lost her own children and couldn't have any more—wouldn't you feel the desire to somehow acquire another, if only to prove that you could adequately perform what is perceived by society to be the basic feminine function?"

The Doctor's face went blank, his hands fell to his side, and then he tossed the Schneider book onto the pile with the James. "And given the correct individual context," he said, nodding, "that urge could grow to destroy normal inhibitory power. . . . Well—where have *you* been for the last two days, my oracle of the feminine psyche?" He walked over and put his hands on Sara's shoulders. "It's taken me God knows how many hours and pages of fruitless reading to reach that very conclusion!" The Doctor walked to the door and called out into the hall, "Cyrus! Draw me a bath, if you don't mind, and lay out fresh clothes!" He turned to Miss Howard again. "The last time we worked together, Sara, we studied the known laws of psychology. This time, the biases of our society will force us to write some new ones, I suspect. You must keep careful notes and be always on hand, for yours is the perspective we most need. The rest of us cannot—"

The Doctor was interrupted by the sound of light snoring coming from the sofa; we all turned to see Mr. Moore dozing. "Well," the Doctor sighed, "let's just say that certain other points of view will be far less crucial. However, let him rest, for the time being—because with any luck, we send him out onto the streets tomorrow."

Once the Doctor'd gotten himself cleaned up and dressed, we found that the only way to rouse Mr. Moore was to offer him a late lunch at Delmonico's restaurant on Madison Square. Dr. Kreizler had been spending less time than usual at that establishment, because Mr. Charlie Delmonico, keeping pace with the steady uptown movement of fashion and money, had recently opened an additional restaurant on Forty-fourth Street; and though he swore to the Doctor that he had no plans to close the Madison Square branch, the Doctor believed that it was only a matter of time before that fate befell the place. So he'd been withholding as much as he could of his patronage (he could never have stayed away altogether) as a method of protest.

Cyrus and I walked with the rest of them up to Madison Square. Though we never actually ate with the Doctor in the restaurant—that just wouldn't have been possible in those days—we liked to go along, anyway, being as I'd been able to make friends with Mr. Ranhofer, the French head chef and bullyboy of the kitchen, and could usually net us a couple of containers of good food what we could eat in the park. We saw the Doctor and his guests to the main entrance, where Charlie Delmonico stood greeting patrons. Dr. Kreizler extended a hand what Mr. Delmonico shook, even as the Doctor announced half seriously, "I'm still not speaking to you, Charles." Then, once they were inside, I ran around the corner to the delivery station.

Winding my way through shouting men carrying crates of vegetables and fruit, as well as ice-covered wooden pallets of fish and big sides of beef and lamb, I passed through a dark hallway and soon found myself in the brick kitchen, where dozens of pots and pans hung from the vaulted ceiling. I could already hear Mr. Ranhofer's voice bouncing off the tiled walls: "No, no, no! Pig! I would not feed that to an animal! Why, why is it so impossible for you to learn?" The object of his bellowing, I soon saw, was a young dessert chef, who seemed to be taking all the insults very much to heart and looked ready to break down. Mr. Ranhofer—his huge round body wrapped in white and his big, similarly colored mustache bristling—tried to calm down a bit, then stepped over to the young man's station. "Here, come, I show you—but only once!"

Waiting for the exercise to be over, I glanced around at the enormous space, where some twenty or thirty chefs, assistant chefs, and assistant assistants were all working like mad and hollering at the top of their lungs—sometimes to nobody at all that I could see. Different-colored flames occasionally shot up from the stoves, and the hundred different smells of the place—some tasty, some just peculiar—blended together into one unidentifiable aroma. The whole joint had the general air of some of the insane asylums I'd visited with the Doctor—except that in the elegant dining rooms upstairs, people were paying top dollar for what came out of this madhouse.

Eventually I saw an opening and grabbed at Mr. Ranhofer's apron. "Say! Mr. Ranhofer!"

He turned and, after a quick smile, frowned. "Please—Stevie—go away! Not today, it is lunacy—lunacy!"

"Yeah, looks like it," I said. "What's going on?"

"He'll kill me—that Charles will kill me! Three private luncheons and then to follow a dinner for eighty! How in God's name can any human manage such things?"

"Ah, you'll do it," I said, as reassuringly as I could. "You always do, right? That's why you're top dog in the chef pack."

That got him. He smiled quickly again and called out, "Franz! Two containers—the soft-shell crab! *Now!*" He started wiping and wringing his hands as he surveyed all the activity in the place and then glanced down at me again. "Please—Stevie—take the food and go. This is no day for me to converse—" Something caught his eye. "*No!* Stop! Do not, you *imbecile,* how can you possibly—" Then he disappeared in a fat flash.

I took the containers of food from the man called Franz, who kept one eye out for his boss like he was wondering when it was going to be his turn to catch hell. On my way out I snuck two forks and a like number of napkins out of a rack, then ran back through the same hallway, which was now packed even thicker with deliverymen.

Cyrus was sitting on a bench inside Madison Square Park, beyond a long line of hansoms that were waiting for fares on Fifth Avenue. Still running, I made my way through the cabs, past the grass at the edge of the park, and then clear over the bench, handing Cyrus a container, a fork, and a napkin as I sat down on the ground beside him. We talked while we crunched on the crabs—done the way I liked them that day, just fried plain in some butter—and ate the side portions of Italian salad and rice with bananas. It was a fine meal, all the better for being free, and after I'd finished I lay on the grass and had myself a smoke.

"Cyrus," I said, looking up through the big tree boughs and branches to the sky, "how long do you figure it'll be before the Doctor gives Mrs. Leshko the sack?"

"I don't know," he answered, polishing off the last of his food. "But things can't go on forever like this."

"Yeah." I waited a moment before voicing what'd been on my mind since I'd seen Pinkie's "Little Maid of Acadie" the night before. "Cyrus?"

"Still here."

"You figure the Doctor might hire Kat? As a maid, I mean."

The long pause that followed told me clearly what Cyrus thought, but he soon gave out with the words: "Kat'd have to want the work, Stevie. She's got big ideas. Big plans for herself. I doubt she'd be interested."

"Yeah. I guess so. I just thought . . ."

"I know," he said, trying hard to be sympathetic. "You could ask the Doctor—but like I say, she'd have to want the work."

I didn't pursue the topic, and after a few silent minutes we passed on to other things. But the idea had planted itself in my head, and I meant to explore it.

It was past four by the time the Doctor, Mr. Moore, and Miss Howard came out of Delmonico's—and they didn't look happy when they did. The Doctor just strode quickly past Cyrus and me, saying "We'll walk" crisply, and the rest of us fell in with him. I started purposely dragging my steps, as did Cyrus and Miss Howard, while Mr. Moore kept up with the Doctor, talking to him. Neither Cyrus nor I needed to ask what had happened; Miss Howard could read the question in our faces.

"It was awful," she said. "Word of the investigation into the Institute's affairs has gotten all over. Even friends of his cut him dead. It was like we weren't even there. Thank God for Charlie, or it wouldn't have been tolerable."

We walked on down Broadway.

It was a predictable reaction, I suppose, from them what likes to call themselves "society," and while I knew the Doctor would make like he didn't care, I also knew that in fact it would anger him deeply. For, as Miss Howard had said, there were some few in that society crowd what the Doctor counted as his friends, and to see them retreat into rudeness with the rest . . . Well, I was just as glad that we had time to walk to Number 808 Broadway. I could only hope that Mr. Moore would be able to get the Doctor refocused on our purpose by the time we got there.

He actually managed that job, or at least as much of it as could reasonably be expected. When we reached the yellow brick building, we found the Isaacson brothers waiting for us, and the Doctor was all business with them. As we went up and into the sixth floor, the conversation turned to how we were going to present the sketching session to our guests. Miss Howard had apparently warned Señora Linares to say nothing about what was really happening, but she went on to tell us that "nothing" wasn't going to be enough to satisfy the extremely curious Mrs. Cady Stanton. Miss Howard had toyed with the idea of saying that the subject of the sketch was an old friend—or even, again, a relation—of the señora's, but that wouldn't explain the latter's bruises and cuts; and Miss Howard knew that Mrs. Cady Stanton would ask all about those, since husbands beating on their wives was a topic that she'd been lecturing on for decades. In fact, Miss Howard told us, Mrs. Cady Stanton had often been criticized by other women's rights leaders because she put as much emphasis on trying to change the conditions that caused violence in the home (drunkenness and the like) and on making it easier for women to get out of bad situations by loosening up divorce laws as she did on securing the vote for her sex. I'm bound to say that I saw her point: most of the women in my old neighborhood couldn't have cared an owl's hoot about who was president—they were too busy trying to survive the rampages of their husbands.

Anyway, Miss Howard and Mr. Moore were still playing with ideas as to just what lie they were going to present Mrs. Cady Stanton with when the Doctor said that they should just drop the subterfuge and tell the old girl the truth—or rather, most of the truth: there was no reason to say who Señora Linares was *exactly* and no reason to mention her daughter. We could just explain that she'd been attacked by another woman in Central Park and robbed; if Mrs. Cady Stanton wanted to make more out of it, let her try. Miss Howard didn't much like that idea, and only gave in when an electrical buzzing device what was connected to a button in the lobby of the building let us know that Señora Linares had arrived. As she went down to retrieve our first guest, it remained obvious that Miss Howard figured "make more out of it" was just what Mrs. Cady Stanton was likely to do.

The señora was in a bit of a state when she first got out of the elevator, convinced that she'd been followed, either by her husband or somebody else. Cyrus was sent down to scout the area but couldn't spot anyone who seemed to be keeping an eye on Number 808. This offered the señora some consolation, but not much, and it was all she could do to focus on the instructions the Doctor gave her about what she was and was not supposed to say in front of the other women. The sound of the buzzer going off again sent her back into a bit of a panic, but Mr. Moore stayed with her and got her calmed down, while Miss Howard went to fetch the promising painter and the living legend.

—

CHAPTER 12

None of us really knew what to expect when we heard the elevator rumble back up. I guess I figured some sour old battle-axe smelling of mothballs was going to come barreling in like one of the Furies. I was pretty surprised, then—and so, from the looks on their faces, was everyone else—when a very respectably but fashionably dressed lady walked gracefully through the front door, her hair carefully done up in tight curls and the delicate lace around her neck and chest decorated by a large, pretty cameo. For a minute I thought she must be the painter: based on what I'd seen of women reformers, they didn't go much for frills and jewelry. But then I saw that the hair was snow white and the skin was sagging and wrinkled, and I knew that she was too old to be the artistic comer Pinkie'd talked about. The eyes, though, had a youthful, alert look about them, which clued me in to the fact that, while this might be somebody's grandmother, it wasn't anybody you wanted to treat as such. She carried a brass-handled stick but held herself proud and upright, like the renowned veteran she was: Mrs. Elizabeth Cady Stanton, the only woman who'd had the nerve to go so far as to rewrite the Bible from the woman's point of view.

Behind her came a younger lady who might've been Miss Howard's older sister, so similar were their looks, dress, and demeanor. Miss Cecilia Beaux had features what were handsome rather than beautiful and what centered on a positively mesmerizing pair of light eyes. She wore a plain button-down blouse with a little ribbon around the neck, as well as a light linen tunic and a simple skirt to match. The common ground between her and Miss Howard seemed to be more than just superficial, too, for they were already chatting away like old friends, Miss Howard telling Miss Beaux about our trip to Pinkie's and Miss Beaux talking of a similar trip she'd made. In addition, I later learned that the pair shared like backgrounds, both coming from wealthy families (Miss Howard's, as I've said, in the Hudson Valley, Miss Beaux's in Philadelphia) that thoroughly disapproved of the young ladies' unusual styles of living.

Introductions were made all around, after which I withdrew quickly into my windowsill and didn't say a word. You could see in Mrs. Cady Stanton's face, as she looked from person to person, that she was trying to size the situation up but not getting very far. As Miss Beaux took out her sketching materials and drew up a chair next to the señora, Miss Howard gave out with the fabricated—or, as the Doctor might've preferred to call it, incomplete—explanation of what we were about and why we'd engaged Miss Beaux's services. Mrs. Cady Stanton's eyes grew narrow at Miss Howard's words, but when she spoke her voice was pleasant enough:

"You say it was another *woman*, Sara? That's unusual—and the motive was money?"

Mr. Moore cut in, trying to blunt the questions with charm: "In New York, Mrs. Cady Stanton, the motive is generally money—and there's very little in this city that can be accurately called 'unusual,' I'm afraid."

In a snap, Mrs. Cady Stanton's expression became much cooler, and she turned a stern eye on Mr. Moore. "Indeed, Mr.—Moore, is it? Well, I've lived many years in New York, on and off, Mr. Moore, and not always in the best of neighborhoods. And I think I can safely say that an attack by one woman on another in Central Park in broad daylight is not a common occurrence. Perhaps one of these policemen will confirm that." She tossed her head in the direction of the Isaacsons, who, while at a loss as to how to handle her, were clearly annoyed at being so labeled.

"Oh!" Lucius said, taking out his handkerchief to wipe his forehead, "I couldn't—that is—"

"Not common," Marcus finally said, as confidently as I imagine anyone could've in that situation. "But not unheard of, ma'am."

"Indeed?" Mrs. Cady Stanton didn't care for that answer. "I'd like someone to give me some examples."

While this little exchange was going on, Miss Howard had moved into one corner of the room with Miss Beaux and Señora Linares, and the señora had begun the actual work of telling the artist what her attacker had looked like. Seeing that the discussion was likely to keep Mrs. Cady Stanton out of this important business, the Doctor stepped in:

"If you have a day or two, Mrs. Cady Stanton, I should be happy to list any number of cases involving violent attacks committed by women."

Mrs. Cady Stanton turned on him. "*By* women *against* other women?" she said, disbelievingly.

"Against other women," the Doctor said, with a smile that warned he was in earnest. "Daughters against mothers, sisters against sisters, rivals for affection against one another—and, of course, mothers against daughters." He pulled out his cigarette case. "Do you mind if I smoke? And would you care to?"

"No. Thank you. But you go ahead." Studying the Doctor for another minute, Mrs. Cady Stanton raised a finger to point at him as he lit his stick. "I know about you, Doctor. I've read some of your work. You specialize in criminal and children's psychology."

"True," the Doctor answered.

"But not in feminine psychology," Mrs. Cady Stanton said. "Tell me, Doctor, why is it that no scientists of the mind make women their field of specialization?"

"It's odd that you should ask," the Doctor answered. "I've recently been wondering about that very question."

"Well, let me answer it for you." Shifting in her chair so that she fully faced him, Mrs. Cady Stanton started to out-and-out lecture the Doctor. "Psychologists do not study female behavior because the overwhelming majority of them are men—and if they were to undertake such a study, they would inevitably find that at the base of all such behavior as you are describing lies a man's brutal enslavement of and violence toward the woman in question." The eyes narrowed again, but this time in a friendlier way. "You've been in some fairly hot water lately, Dr. Kreizler. And I know why. You're trying to explain the actions of criminals in their—what is it you call it—their 'individual context.' But people don't want explanations. They think you're just providing excuses."

"And what do you think, Mrs. Cady Stanton?" the Doctor asked as he smoked.

"I think that no woman comes into this world with a desire to do anything but what nature intended—to create and to nurture. As mothers of the race, there is a spiritual insight, a divine creative power that belongs to women. If that power is perverted, you may rest assured that a man is involved somewhere."

"Your words are persuasive," the Doctor said, "but I find the ideas behind them a bit—difficult. Are women, then, a separate species, immune to the emotions that move other humans?"

"No, not immune, Doctor. Far from it. More deeply touched by those emotions, in fact. And by their causes. Which, I think, go far deeper than even an educated, progressive man like yourself suspects."

"Really?"

Mrs. Cady Stanton nodded, touching at her white curls in the way that your average woman will do but—oddly, for someone of her age and opinions—not at all embarrassed by the passing display of vanity. "I agree with some of what you've written, Doctor. In fact, much of it. Your only problem, so far as I can see, is that you do not take your notion of context far enough." She put both hands authoritatively on her walking stick. "What is your opinion of the effect of the prenatal period on the formation of the individual?"

"Ah, yes," the Doctor said. "A favorite topic of yours."

"So you dispute the idea?"

"Mrs. Cady Stanton—there is no clinical evidence to suggest that, beyond the impact of her physical condition, a mother has any formative effect on the fetus she carries."

"Wrong, sir! You could not *be* more wrong. During the nine months of prenatal life, mothers stamp every thought and feeling of their minds as well as their bodies on the plastic beings inside of them!"

The Doctor had started to look like General Custer must've, the moment his boys told him there were a few more Indians around than they'd originally expected. Mrs. Cady Stanton pushed him ever deeper into an argument what he'd started out thinking of as a diversion but had quickly grown into a full-scale debate. It stopped making much sense to me after about ten minutes, mainly because I wasn't really paying attention; I wanted to get around and see what the other three women were coming up with. So at a moment when I thought no one would notice, I slipped off my windowsill and around the outermost edge of the room, eventually reaching the spot where the sketch was taking form. As I approached I heard Señora Linares saying, "No . . . no, the chin was less—pronounced. And the lips slightly thinner . . . yes, so . . . ."

"I see," Miss Beaux said, her bright gaze fixed on the large sketch pad before her. "Overall, then, you'd say she had more Anglo-Saxon than Latin features. Is that right?"

Señora Linares thought it over, then nodded. "I had not thought of it in such a way, but yes, she was very American, in the way one sees in the older parts of this country—New England, perhaps."

I edged up to Miss Howard's elbow and looked at the sketch. It was still about as vague as one of Pinkie's paintings, though in spots Miss Beaux had been able to pencil in sharper, more definite lines. The face that was taking shape was, just as the señora said, an angular, chiseled one, not un-attractive but hard, like you might see in a Massachusetts or Connecticut farm town.

Miss Howard suddenly noticed my presence and smiled. "Hello, Stevie," she whispered. Then she cast an evil little glance at the center of the room, where the Doctor and Mrs. Cady Stanton were still going at it. "I'll bet you wish you had a cigarette along about now."

"Do I ever," I said, still watching Miss Beaux's delicate hands as they moved with quick precision over the pad. She'd make a stroke, then line it again or smudge it for shading, as was wanted, or erase it altogether if the señora said it wasn't right. She caught me watching her and smiled.

"Hello," she said, also whispering. "You're Stevie, aren't you?"

I could only nod; to tell the truth, I think I was a little smitten by her.

"They sound like they're having quite a time," she went on, still sketching but occasionally showing me the same delicate smile that was lit up by those remarkable eyes. "What in the world are they talking about?"

"I can't quite make it out," I answered. "But Mrs. Cady Stanton sure got the Doctor's goat—in record time, too."

Miss Beaux shook her head, still amused. "She was so anxious to meet him. . . . She's often that way with people she finds intriguing—she wants so much to exchange ideas that she ends up rushing into an argument."

"Yes," Miss Howard said. "I'm afraid I've been known to do the same thing."

"So have I!" Miss Beaux said, still in a hushed voice. "And then I spend days absolutely kicking myself about it. Particularly with men—most of them are so blasted patronizing that when you meet one that you think might be different, you overwhelm him with opinions."

"And being the pillars of strength that they are," Miss Howard agreed, "they run and hide behind a gaggle of pretty, empty-headed idiots."

"Oh! It's so irritating . . ." Miss Beaux looked to me again. "What about you, Stevie?"

"Me, miss?"

"Yes. How do you feel about young ladies—do you prefer that they be intelligent, or do you like them to model their opinions on yours?"

My hand made its way to my head and started to twist a strand of my hair in a nervous sort of way that, when I noticed it, I stopped quickly, feeling childish. "I—don't know, miss," I said, thinking of Kat. "I haven't—that is, I don't know many—"

"Stevie wouldn't put up with a fool, Cecilia," Miss Howard said, touching my arm reassuringly. "You can depend on that—he's one of the good ones."

"I never doubted it," Miss Beaux said kindly. Then she turned to the Linares woman. "Now, then, señora—the eyes. You said they were the feature that you found most arresting?"

"Yes," the señora answered. "And the only aspect of the face that was at all exotic—catlike, as I said to Miss Howard. Almost—you have seen the Egyptian antiquities at the Metropolitan Museum, Miss Beaux?"

"Certainly."

"There was something of that quality in them. I do not think that they were excessively large, but the lashes were quite heavy and dark and gave the eyes the *impression* of size. Then there was their color—glowing amber, I would say, almost a gold—"

I watched as Miss Beaux's hands went to work toward the top of the sketch—and then jerked my head up when I heard my name being called from across the room.

"Stevie! What are you up to over there?" It was the Doctor. "Mrs. Cady Stanton would like a word with you!"

"With me, Doctor?" I said, hoping it wasn't so.

"Yes, with you," he repeated with a smile, waving me over. "Come along now!"

Turning to Miss Howard and giving her a doomed man's last look, I stood up and dragged myself out to the easy chair what Mrs. Cady Stanton was sitting in. When I got there, she set her stick aside and grabbed both my hands with hers.

"Well, young man," she said, eyeing me carefully. "So you're one of Dr. Kreizler's charges, are you?"

"Yes, ma'am," I answered, as unenthusiastically as I could manage.

"He says you've had quite a time of it during your few years. Tell me"—she leaned closer, so that I could see small white hairs on her aging cheeks—"do you blame your mother?"

The question caught me a bit off guard, and I glanced at the Doctor. He just nodded in a way what said, Go ahead, tell her whatever you like.

"Do I—" I paused as I considered it. "I don't know if blame's the word, ma'am. She set me down the road to a criminal life, there's no two ways about that."

"Because some man was telling her to, no doubt," Mrs. Cady Stanton said. "Or forcing her."

"My mother had a *lot* of men, ma'am," I said quickly. "And to tell you the truth, I don't think any of them ever *forced* her to do anything. She put me to the work she did because she needed things—liquor, at first. Drugs later."

"Which men supplied to her."

I shrugged. "If you say so, ma'am."

Mrs. Cady Stanton studied me. "Don't blame her too much, Stevie. Even wealthy women have very few choices in this world. Poor women have virtually none."

"I guess," I said. "You'd know better than me. But like I say, I don't know that I blame her, exactly, ma'am. Life was just easier when I didn't have anything to do with her anymore, that's all."

The old girl studied me for a minute and nodded. "A wise statement, son." She livened up then, and shook my arms. "I'll bet you were trouble before you met the doctor. That's the way with you scoundrels. My three oldest were all boys, and no end of trouble! I had whole towns that wouldn't speak to me because of what they'd get up to." She dropped my hands then. "None of which changes my point, Dr. Kreizler . . ."

As she went on, I looked to the Doctor again. He just smiled once more and indicated with a quick jerk of his head that I could go back to what I'd been doing. Meanwhile, his conversation with Mrs. Cady Stanton soon got back up to full speed.

It took about two hours for Miss Beaux to complete her sketch, and I spent the rest of that time sitting with the women, speaking when I was spoken to but mostly just observing. It was quite a process: the words would come out of Señora Linares's mouth, enter Miss Beaux's ear, then be transformed into movements of her hands that were sometimes very true to the señora's memories and intentions, sometimes less so. Miss Beaux went through an entire India rubber eraser as she worked away, and dulled a stack of heavy, soft-lead pencils; but along toward eight o'clock a real, living face had taken shape on that page. And as we all crowded around to look at it, we fell into a kind of shocked silence, one what gave quiet confirmation to what Señora Linares had originally said: it was not a face anybody was likely to forget.

The señora'd been able to remember more details of the woman's features when presented with the ability to see her memories brought to life, just as the Doctor had thought she might, and the woman who stared back at us from the sketch pad fit every adjective that our client had used in describing her. The first thing you noticed was unquestionably the eyes, or maybe I should say the expression in the eyes: hungry, Señora Linares

had said, and hunger was unquestionably there. But that wasn't all; the fe-
line eyes had an additional expression, one what was all too familiar to me
but that I didn't want to name. I'd seen it in my mother, when she wanted
something out of me or out of one of her men; and in Kat, when she was
plying her trade; it was *seductiveness,* the unspoken statement that if you'd
just do something for this person that you knew was wrong, she'd give
you whatever attention and affection you craved in return. The rest of the
face—she looked to be about forty or so—had probably been very pretty
once, but was now kind of drawn, toughened by hard years of experience,
judging from the set of the jaw. The nose was small, but the nostrils flared
with anger; the thin lips were pursed tight, with small wrinkles at the corners of the mouth; and the high cheekbones hinted at the shape of the
skull, instantly making me think of Pinkie's painting of Death on a horse.

This was a woman what fit every speculation the Doctor and the others
had made: a hard, desperate woman who had seen too many tough things
in her time and was prepared to answer in kind. Pinkie, too, had been
right in his prediction: Miss Beaux, without ever seeing her subject, had
cut through to "the very essence of the personality."

I think everyone, including Miss Beaux, was a little shocked by what
she'd created; certainly the señora just sat in her chair nodding, seeming
like she would've wept if she'd felt free to. The silence wasn't broken until
Mrs. Cady Stanton said:

"There's the face of cold experience, gentlemen. There's a face that
man's society has hardened forever."

Miss Howard rose at that and took Mrs. Cady Stanton by the arm. "Yes.
Indeed. Well—I hadn't realized how late it's gotten. You'll want your dinner, Mrs. Cady Stanton, and you too, Cecilia." She turned to shake the
younger woman's hand. "And I meant what I said—I'd love to join your
class, or just have lunch or dinner. Whenever you're in town."

Miss Beaux brightened, somehow relieved, it seemed to me, to get
away from her own creation. "Oh. Yes, I'd like that, Sara. It's really been
fascinating."

Miss Howard started to nudge the two ladies toward the door, and
everyone made their good-byes. I was a little shy about approaching Miss
Beaux, but she walked right up and took my hand, saying she was sure
we'd meet again soon—maybe I could come to lunch with her and Miss
Howard, she said.

As they got into the elevator, Mrs. Cady Stanton turned to the Doctor.
"I trust *we'll* see each other again, too, Doctor. It's been very illuminating
for me—and, I hope, for you, too."

"Indeed," the Doctor answered politely. "I shall look forward to it. And Miss Beaux"—he brought a bank check out of his pocket—"I hope that you'll find this acceptable. Miss Howard told me your standard fee, but given the unusual circumstances, and your willingness to come to us— well . . ."

Miss Beaux's eyes went wide when she took a quick look at the check. "That's—really very generous, Doctor. I don't know that—"

"Nonsense," he said, glancing back at the sketch, which sat on a table before the señora. "No true price can be put on what you have given us."

The elevator grate clattered closed on the three women, and then the Doctor shut the inner door, listening to the machine's hum as he pondered things.

I breathed once, hard. "I ain't sorry to see the last of *that* old duck," I said, turning away.

The Doctor and the others chuckled. "What a mouth," Mr. Moore said, lying on the divan. "Like a machine."

"Yes. It's a pity." The Doctor walked back over to the señora. "If fate and our society had not forced her to narrow her thoughts with a political agenda, she could have had a truly first-class scientific mind." He knelt down next to the Linares woman. "Señora? I don't need to ask if this is the woman—your face gives me the answer. But is there anything I can get you?"

Her lips trembled as she answered, "My daughter, Doctor. You can get me my daughter." Her eyes finally broke away from the sketch, and she began to gather up her bag and hat. "I must go—it's late. I shall not be able to return." Standing up, she gave the Doctor a final pleading look. "Can it be done, Doctor? Can you do it?"

"I think," he said, taking her arm, "that we now have a good chance. Cyrus?"

Cyrus stood up, ready to escort the señora to a hansom for the last time. She murmured thanks as best she could to the rest of us, then got into the elevator with him when Miss Howard brought it back. Seeing the señora's condition, Miss Howard put her arms around her, at which the señora finally started to cry. Together, the threesome floated back down to Broadway.

The detective sergeants ambled over for another look at the sketch. "That Beaux woman has got a real future in wanted posters," Marcus mused. "If the art business doesn't work out . . ."

"It's remarkable," Lucius said. "I've seen photographs in the Rogues' Gallery at headquarters that aren't as good."

"Yes," the Doctor agreed. "And speaking of photographs, gentlemen, we shall need a dozen or so of the sketch. As soon as you can make them."

"They'll be ready by morning," Marcus said, rolling the sketch up to take with him. "And so will we."

"*I* won't!" Mr. Moore protested from the divan.

"Oh, come now, Moore," the Doctor cajoled. "This is the true labor of investigation. You are the foot soldier, the unsung hero—"

"Really?" Mr. Moore answered. "Well, I'd like to be the *sung* hero for a change, Kreizler—why can't *you* do the door-to-door work—"

He was cut off as the front door slammed wide open. Cyrus hustled in, a supporting arm around Miss Howard. She was moving under her own power but seemed very woozy. We all dashed over, and the Doctor looked at her closely.

"Cyrus!" he said. "What happened?"

"I'm—all right," Miss Howard whispered, trying to catch her breath. "Just a fright—that's all . . ."

"A fright?" said Mr. Moore. "That had to be one hell of a fright, Sara, to put *you* in this shape—what was it?"

"We'd just put the señora in a cab," Cyrus explained, reaching into his jacket pocket, "and were coming back into the lobby. This lodged in the door frame near Miss Howard's head as we were passing through."

Holding out his big hand, Cyrus displayed one of the most peculiar knives I've ever seen: leather-gripped and hilted with rough iron, it had a shining blade that curved in a series of S-shapes, like a slithering snake.

Lucius took hold of the thing, holding it up to the light. "Do you think it was intended to hit one of you?" he asked.

"Can't tell, Detective Sergeant. Not for sure, anyway. But—"

"But?" Marcus said.

"Well, from the way it hit just the right spot in the frame—I'd say no. Whoever threw it meant to come close. Nothing more."

"Or less," the Doctor said, taking the knife. "Well . . . the señora said she felt she'd been followed here."

"You didn't see anyone?" Mr. Moore asked Cyrus.

"No, sir. A young boy, running around a corner—but he couldn't have been the one. This was an expert, if you ask me."

The Doctor handed the knife back to Lucius. "An expert—sending a warning." He pointed at the knife. "A peculiar blade, Detective Sergeant. Do you recognize it?"

Lucius frowned. "I do, though I wish I didn't. It's called a *kris*. The weapon of the Manilamen—they believe it has mystical powers."

"Ah," the Doctor noised. "Then the señora was right. Her husband knows where she's been. We can only hope that he doesn't know why, and that she can invent a story that he will believe."

"Wait," I said. "How can you be so sure she's right? What is that thing, anyway? Who are the Manilamen?"

"They're pirates and mercenaries," Marcus answered. "Some of the toughest characters in the western Pacific. They take their name from the capital of the Philippine Islands."

"Yeah? So what?"

The Doctor took the knife again. "The Philippine Islands, Stevie, are one of the most important colonies in the Spanish Empire. A most valued jewel in the queen regent's crown. Well . . ." He walked toward the center of the room, still examining the knife. "It would seem that we have gained an advantage tonight—and lost one." He gave us all a very serious look. "We must *move.*"

CHAPTER 13

The strange knife from the Philippines may not have done Miss
Howard or Cyrus any harm, but it dealt a death blow to Mr. Moore's
reluctance to get started on finding the woman in our sketch. He'd known
Miss Howard since childhood (her family'd had a house on Gramercy
Park in addition to their estate in the Hudson Valley), and though she was
always quick to maintain that she didn't need any man's help to protect
herself—which was as true as true could be—Mr. Moore didn't like the
idea of crazed Filipinos following her or any of us around with *kris* at the
ready. And so, bright and early Friday morning, he marched into Number
808, carrying a long list of every agency in town that offered care for infants and children. He'd told his bosses at *The New York Times* that he
wasn't going to be around for a while, and that if they didn't like it they
could go ahead and fire him. They hadn't been much surprised by this
statement, as Mr. Moore was known to be a loose cannon around his office; but since the scoops he periodically came up with continued to make
it worth putting up with his uppity behavior, they didn't let him go but
gave him an indefinite vacation. (There were only a couple of occasions
during his years at the *Times* when he crossed the line far enough to get
the sack, and even then the exile was only temporary.)

The detective sergeants, Miss Howard, and Mr. Moore proceeded to di-
vide the list up, and then each set out with photographic copies of Miss
Beaux's sketch, ready for long days of frustrating inquiries at places that
were often run by very uncooperative people. All of us at Seventeenth
Street knew that this process would take some time, time that would pass

faster if we filled it with constructive activity. For the Doctor, that meant locking himself back up in his study and combing through more psychological texts, trying to determine a hypothetical background for the woman we were tracking. The occasional cries, curses, and execrations that came out of that room, though, indicated that he was failing to get much further than he had earlier in the week. As for Cyrus, the detective sergeants had secretly asked him to prepare a report on each member of the Doctor's staff at the Institute, since they'd have to juggle that investigation with the Linares affair. No one knew the Doctor's assistants—the teachers, matrons, even the custodians—better than Cyrus, and he took advantage of the time to put together a set of summaries what were very detailed.

As for me, I'd been struck, during the business with the Filipino knife, by my own ignorance of where and what those islands were and of their importance to the Spanish Empire. So I asked the Doctor for some books and monographs that might help me understand just what the situation regarding Spain and the United States was all about. Pleased by my genuine interest, the Doctor obliged, and I took the materials up to my room and sank into them.

So wrapped up did I become in these ruminations that by Saturday evening I was still going at it—two days of steady study, a longer time than I'd been able to manage in my two years of service with the Doctor. As night descended along with a late rainstorm that blew in from the northwest, I realized with a sudden start just how late in the week it was, and remembered that Kat had told me she planned to move out of Frankie's dive and into the Dusters' headquarters sometime during the next week. Checking to see that the Doctor was still locked up in his study, I told Cyrus that I was heading out for a while and began the long, wet walk down to my old stomping grounds near the intersection of Baxter and Worth Streets.

The dive known as Frankie's was located at Number 55 Worth, and was as dismal a place as any kid ever passed an idle hour in. It was also the location where I'd first met Kat about six months previous. Its main attractions were bloody battles between dogs and rats in a deep pit, an even younger than usual collection of girls in the back, and a drink that was a nasty mix of buttered rum, benzene, and cocaine shavings. I'd never spent much time there during my criminal days, though I knew plenty who did; but my acquaintance with Kat had, I regret to say, caused me to journey down in recent months and pass far more hours amid the violence and squalor than I probably should've.

That Kat . . . She'd arrived in the city about a year before I'd met her in the company of her father, a small-time con man who got too drunk one winter night and fell into the East River. After his death Kat had tried for months to make a legitimate living vending ears of hot roasted corn out of an old baby carriage on downtown streets, a job what wasn't in any way as simple as it might sound. Hot corn girls in New York were something of a puzzle: most of them weren't whores, but somehow the average person— particularly your run-of-the-mill out-of-towner—was always convinced otherwise. Nobody seems to know where the idea got started. The Doctor says it all had to do with "subconscious associations" that most people formed about young girls alone on the street selling something "hot" that had a general shape what the alienists call "phallic." Who knows . . . the point is that a lot of men who bought corn off those girls figured they were actually making a bargain for sexual favors; and when Kat wised up to how much more money she could make actually selling those favors, well, she took the chance. I didn't judge her for it; nobody who's ever been on the streets would've. You could get damned sick and real tired standing barefoot in the cold all day hawking corn, not even making enough money to buy yourself a bed in one of the worst flophouses in town.

In her early days of whoring, Kat found her trade on the streets. But eventually she ended up working out of Frankie's, as the kid trade was steadier, safer, and, she said, a lot less painful on her insides. I met her by chance, when I stopped in to Frankie's to see an old pal. Sad and strange, what a year on the streets and working the skin trade can do to a country girl: she'd become all brass by the time we were introduced, having seen more of the way of the world in her short piece of a life than your average citizen experiences in a full one. Maybe I fell for her the minute I saw her, I'm not sure; but if it wasn't that exact minute, it wasn't too long after. The brass was mostly an act that covered something much more decent, I could see that even then, although she would never admit it. And I think maybe, too, that I just wanted to see one of those poor kids at Frankie's make it out to a better way of life, since I'd learned that such a thing did, in fact, exist. It was all a boy's romantic foolery, of course; but there aren't many things more powerful in this life.

She made me pay for my time with her; said she had to or Frankie would get upset. But most of those nights we just went into the back and talked, her telling me about her years with her father, moving from small town to small town, one step ahead of the local law enforcement. For my part, I told her about my old lady, my underworld career, and growing up in New York in general. It was months before anything physical happened between us, and then it was only because Kat was hopped up on Frankie's doctored liquor. The whole experience was difficult for me, as I knew nothing about such ways and she was already an expert, amused by my ignorance and embarrassment. We managed the act itself, and she said it wasn't half bad; but it hadn't been what I'd dreamed about having with her. We never repeated it, but we stayed friends, even though my continued attempts to get her to quit the trade were sometimes cause for real anger on her part.

As I made my way downtown that night, I passed by many of the streets I'd once lived on, which now looked more than ever to me like what they were: some of the worst stretches of tenement hell in the city. The rain was keeping most people inside, so I didn't worry too much about getting jumped; and before I knew it, I was rounding the corner of Worth Street and closing in on Frankie's. Saturday nights were, of course, especially wild there, and when I got close I could see kids spilling up and out of the dark basement space in various states of drunkeness and drug intoxication. Making my way down the steps through this crowd and saying hello to the kids I knew, I ran into Nosy, the boy what I'd seen on the waterfront earlier in the week. He told me that the cops had held him and his friends overnight in nothing but their shorts but that they'd gotten clear the next morning and had been having good laughs all week about the reports that were continuing to pop up in the papers about the "headless body" being the work of a crazed anatomist or medical student. Even the halfwit what Nosy called Slap knew enough to say that the story was a lot of hot air.

Inside Frankie's the smoke was so thick I couldn't even see the back wall, and the sounds of kids screaming out bets, a dog barking and growling, and rats squealing clued me in to the fact that there was a hot contest going on in the pit. I didn't stop to look at it—that was one sport that truly made me sick—but kept on pushing my way through the crowd and into the back hall, eventually reaching the door of the little room that I knew Kat shared with two other girls. I gave the door a loud knock and heard some female giggling coming from inside. Then Kat's voice sang out, "Come on in, though if it's a good time you want, you're too late!" I opened the door.

Kat was standing over the room's lousy mattress, a small wicker suitcase open before her. The other two girls, who I also knew, were drinking and obviously had been for quite some time. The look in Kat's eyes said that she wasn't far behind them. A big smile came into her face when she saw me, and the other two girls started to laugh as they said hello; then Kat came over and threw her arms around my neck, reeking of benzene.

"Stevie!" she said. "You decided to come to my good-bye party! That's sweet!"

I put my arms around her awkwardly, causing one of the other girls to say, "Go ahead, Stevie, get it while you can!" Then another round of giggles broke out.

"Hey, Betty," I said to the one with the mouth, handing her a couple of bucks, "why don't you and Moll go chase yourselves around the bar?"

"For two bucks?" Betty looked at the money like it was the Federal Depository. "You got it, lover-man!" As they went out she mumbled, "Give him something special, Kat, for his last whirl!" Kat laughed, the door closed, and we were finally alone.

"I mean it," Kat said, looking drowsily into my eyes. "It's sweet of you to come, Stevie—" She caught herself, then took her arms away. "Oh, no. Wait a minute. I'm mad at you. Almost cost me that gentleman, you did, with your damned whip. What'd you go and do that for, anyway? He was old, it didn't take but a few minutes to make him happy. Easy jobs like that are tough to find, you know."

I winced inside at that, but tried not to show it. "Things'll be even tougher at the Dusters'."

"Unh-unh," she said, shaking her head. "I'm gonna have my pick of customers there. My new man says so."

"New man? And who'd that be?"

"Ding Dong, that's who." She put her hands proudly on her hips. "How do you like *that*, Mr. Errand Boy?"

If her previous remark had brought a wince, this one hit like a sledgehammer. "Ding Dong," I whispered. "Kat—you can't—"

"And why not? If you're thinkin' he's too old, the fact is he likes his ladies young—told me so. And since he's one of them what started the gang, I'll have protection all over the city. I don't service nobody without he says it's okay, neither."

I didn't say anything for a few minutes. I'd crossed paths with this Ding Dong many times during my days with Crazy Butch: he ran the kids' auxiliary of the Hudson Dusters (whose turf was the West Side and the waterfront below Fourteenth Street), and he did it through the simple but brutal trick of turning kids into cocaine fiends and then controlling their access to the stuff. The Dusters were all what we called burny blowers, addicted to snorting powdered cocaine, and a few of them even jabbed the drug: it tended to make them wild, reckless, and violent, so much so that most other gangs just steered clear of them altogether, since none of their territory was what you'd call vital. They were darlings of the moneyed Bohemian crowd, who shared their craving for cocaine and liked to come down and slum it in their headquarters, an old dive on Hudson Street; and the sickening sight of the Dusters' leader, Goo Goo Knox, having his praises sung in ditties and poems dashed off by educated but misled fools was, I'm sorry to say, not uncommon.

The blood I'd seen on Kat's glove the night we'd run into her on Christopher Street had clued me in to how she'd been enlisted by the Dusters; and if that hadn't been enough, she now sat on the bed and produced a sweets tin what was filled to the brim with the fine white powder.

"Want some?" she said, in that half-ashamed way that all drug fiends do when they can't resist going to the well in front of another person. "I can get all I want."

"I'm sure of that," I said. Then urgency set my blood afire. "Listen, Kat," I said, sitting on the bed next to her. "I've got an idea. It could get you out of all this. The Doctor needs a maid—a regular, live-in housekeeper. I think I could convince him, if you'd be willing to—"

I was interrupted by the loud sound of her snorting the burny off her wrist. Her face winced with the sting, then settled into relief. Finally she began to laugh. "A *maid*? Stevie—you ain't *serious*!"

"Why not?" I said. "It's a roof over your head, a good roof, and steady work—"

"Oh, yeah," she said, "and I can just imagine what I'd have to do for this Doctor to *keep* it."

A sudden wave of anger flashed through me, and I grabbed her wrist hard, spilling the cocaine off of it. "Don't say that," I growled through clamped teeth. "Don't ever talk about the Doctor like that. Just because you never met people like him—"

"Stevie, goddamn it!" Kat cried, trying to salvage the cocaine I'd spilt. "You never get it, do you? So I never met people like him? I got news for you, boy, I met people like him ever since I came to this town, and I'm sick of it! Old gents ready to give you something, yeah, I've met 'em—but they always want something back! And I'm *sick* of it! I want a *man*, Stevie, a man of my own, and Ding Dong's gonna be it! He ain't no boy, no silly little kid with foolish ideas—" She stopped herself there and tried to catch her breath. "Ah. I'm sorry, Stevie. I like you, you know that—always have. But I'm gonna *be* somebody—maybe, I don't know, a revue girl or an actress—and a rich man's wife, someday. But not a *maid,* for Pete's sake—I'm gonna *have* maids, plenty of maids!"

I got up and wandered toward the door. "Yeah," I mumbled. "It was just an idea . . ."

She followed me over, again putting her arms around me. "And it was a nice idea—but it ain't me, Stevie. If it's a good place for you, that's fine. But it ain't me."

I nodded. "Unh-hunh . . ."

She turned me to her and put her hands on the sides of my face. "You can come see me sometimes—but you gotta behave. Remember—I'm Ding Dong's girl, now. Okay?"

"Yeah . . . okay." I started to open the door.

"Say." When I looked back, she was smiling. "Don't I get a kiss good-bye?"

With some reluctance but more desire, I leaned over to comply; but just as my face was nearing hers, a big drop of blood ran down out of her nostril to her lip. "Dammit!" she said, turning away quickly and wiping at the blood with her sleeve. "That always happens . . ."

I couldn't take any more of it. "So long, Kat," I said, and then I ran out the door. I kept on going, through the bar, past the baiting pit, and finally out onto the street. Kids whose faces I couldn't make out called to me, but I just kept on moving, faster and faster, near to tears and not wanting anyone to see it.

By the time I stopped running, I was near the Hudson and quickly made for the waterfront, the comforting smell of the river keeping me from breaking down and crying. It was foolish, I told myself, to feel so strongly about Kat's fate, for it wasn't like anyone was holding a gun to her head and forcing her to follow the path she was taking. She'd chosen it; and sorry as I might be, it was just plain ridiculous to take it so hard. I must've repeated that statement to myself a thousand times as I watched the night boats, ferries, and ships move up, down, and across the waters of the Hudson. But it wasn't any attempt at being rational that finally mended my spirits; no, it was the sight of the river itself, which always made me feel, somehow, like there was hope. She has that quality, does the Hudson, as I imagine all great rivers do: the deep, abiding sense that those activities what take place on shore among human beings are of the moment, passing, and aren't the stories by way of which the greater tale of this planet will, in the end, be told. . . .

I finally wandered back into Dr. Kreizler's house at well past three o'clock and stumbled on up to bed. The Doctor's study door was open and that of his bedroom was closed, indicating that he might finally be getting some sleep—but then I noted that a dim light was shining out from the crack underneath the bedroom door. As I passed on up the stairs, I saw the light go out; but the Doctor never came out to ask where I'd been or why I was coming in so late. Probably Cyrus had already figured it out and told him, or maybe he was simply respecting my privacy; either way, I was grateful to be able to just get to my room, close the door, and fall onto my bed without any further words.

It wasn't many hours later that I was woken by fairly violent shaking. I was still in my clothes, and it took me several seconds to come out of a very deep sleep. Cyrus's voice became identifiable even before his face:

"Stevie! Come on, wake up, we've got to go!"

I shot upright, at that, figuring I'd overslept and forgotten to do something, though I couldn't for the life of me remember what that thing might've been. "S'okay," I said sleepily, cramming my shoes on. "I'll get the horses—"

"I already have," Cyrus answered. "Get some fresh clothes on, we've got to meet the others."

"Why?" I said, going for a new shirt in a chest of drawers. "What's happened?"

"They've found out who she is."

I dropped a handful of clothes on the floor. "You mean—the lady in the sketch?"

"That's right," Cyrus answered. "And Miss Howard says there's plenty of interesting details. We're meeting them at the museum." I was still having some trouble with my movements, and Cyrus held a shirt out for me. "Come on, boy, wake up now—you're driving!"

CHAPTER 14

As we rolled off of Fifth Avenue and into Central Park, bearing right to head onto the Metropolitan Museum's carriage path, I understood for the first time just how insane, daring, or desperate the woman we believed had snatched the Linares baby must've been. The construction site for the museum's new Fifth Avenue wing took up the full stretch of ground between Eighty-first and Eighty-third Streets, and beyond it to the west, inside the park, the square red brick mass of the museum's three older wings occupied another city block or so of territory. The Metropolitan was what the Doctor and his architectural friends always called "a mongrel of styles"—Gothic and Renaissance revivals in the first three wings, what they called "Beaux Arts" in the new Fifth Avenue hall—but, different as the various sections were in their color and concept, even the first was not that much older than the one currently being built. All of which, so far as we were concerned, meant that there'd been precious little time for any trees or shrubbery to grow in this part of the park, and a lot of what had been planted or had sprung up had been ripped away by the never-ending process of construction. So when the detective sergeants said the crime had been committed in broad daylight and in a very open public spot, they meant just that. The only object what rose to any great height was the Egyptian obelisk what sat beyond the front (soon to be the side) entrance of the museum, and Señora Linares had been struck just as she got there: like I say, the abduction had been either a very gutsy, despairing, or crazy act, depending on how you elected to see it.

The ride uptown had been as quick as I could make it, and on the way the Doctor tried to relate some information from the front page of the *Times,* telling me as I drove that the Cuban rebels had massacred a party of Havana stagecoach riders while, in a separate engagement, the Cuban government was claiming to've killed one of the main rebel leaders. (The first report turned out to be true, the second wishful thinking.) But it was tough for us to keep our minds on any subject other than the business at hand, and as I kept urging Frederick forward past the churches of upper Fifth Avenue, where the wealthy families of Mansion Row were just leaving early services, I threw a panic into some people who figured Sunday morning would be a safe time to stroll absentmindedly across the boulevard. I got some angry shouts and even a few curses from those ladies and gents for splashing horse dung and piss on their Sunday best, and I threw some feisty words back; but nothing stopped our forward motion, and we pulled up to the steps of the Metropolitan at just before eleven.

Ordinarily, the Doctor would have wanted to walk over and check what progress had been made on the new wing: the original architect, Mr. Richard Morris Hunt, who'd died a couple of years earlier, had been another old friend of his, as was Mr. Hunt's son, who'd taken over the direction of the work. But, things being what they were on this day, the Doctor just jumped out of the calash and charged up the museum's steps, passing between a large pair of iron lamp fixtures and through the square granite doorway. Cyrus followed him, leaving me with the question of what to do with the carriage. Spotting another driver nearby, I offered him four bits to watch our rig for what I said would only be a few minutes. It was above the going price for such a service—which was one that I sometimes performed myself for other drivers—and the man was glad to get the money. Then I took to the steps, glancing up at the red brick walls, the grey granite archways, and the high, peaked roof of the building, feeling the way I always did when we came to this place: like I was entering some sort of temple, whose services and rituals had once seemed as strange to me as a towel-headed Hindoo's, but what I was coming to understand better and better the longer I lived under the Doctor's roof.

The galleries just inside the entrance to the museum were full of what, for me, were the most boring objects in the place: sculptures, old (or, I should say, ancient) pottery and glass, and Egyptian artifacts. The Doctor figured that, given the señora's description of the woman who'd snatched her baby, it was in the latter hall that we'd find our friends; and so we did. Mr. Moore and Miss Howard were near one carved and painted face of an Egyptian woman, holding up Miss Beaux's sketch for a comparison and nodding, apparently agreeing that the eyes were a good match. But as they did so, Mr. Moore for some reason kept bursting into a tired, giddy kind of laughter. The detective sergeants, for their part, were going over a small stack of papers excitedly but with serious purpose. There weren't many other people in the place at that hour, and when we approached our bunch they all lit up like it was six or seven holidays boiled down to one.

"It's as positive an identification as I've ever seen anyone make," Lucius said as he moved over to meet us, trying to keep his voice under control but seeming ready to burst out of his sweaty clothes.

"Amazing," Marcus added. "From a *sketch*! Doctor, if we could ever get this idea accepted by the department, it would change the entire process of identification and pursuit."

Miss Howard and Mr. Moore rushed over next. "Well, Doctor," Miss Howard began, "it took a few days, but—"

"You won't believe it!" Mr. Moore said, chuckling in that strange way again. "It's too rich, Laszlo, you're never going to believe it, I tell you!"

The Doctor was shaking his head impatiently. "I won't if none of you tells me what the devil 'it' is! Kindly get some sort of a grip on yourself, Moore—and one of you, please, go on."

Mr. Moore just lurched away, holding his head in a kind of exhausted wonder and trying to stifle further laughter. It was up to Marcus to reveal what they'd discovered: "Suppose I were to tell you, Doctor, that last year—at the very same time that we were investigating the Beecham case together—the woman we're now looking for was working just down the street from your own house?"

I could feel my own jaw drop, and saw the Doctor's and Cyrus's do the same. But it was also plain that, though shocked by it, we all knew what Marcus was talking about:

"You mean—the hospital?" the Doctor murmured, staring off at an Egyptian mummy case without seeing it. "The Lying-in Hospital?"

Lucius smiled wide. "The New York Lying-in Hospital. Whose principal benefactor was and is—"

"Morgan," the Doctor mumbled on. "Pierpont Morgan."

"Which means," Miss Howard added, "that even as you and John were being—*entertained* in Mr. Morgan's house, this woman was, effectively, being paid by him to tend to mothers and newborns." She glanced over at Mr. Moore with a smile what indicated doubts about his current mental condition. "That's what's got *him* so tickled, you see—that and sheer fatigue. He's been that way ever since we found out, and I'm not entirely sure how to snap him out of it."

Mr. Moore's amusement was thoroughly understandable. It might have been heightened by the relief of locating our quarry, but its main source was definitely the discovery that the woman in question had once been in the employ (even if indirectly) of the great financier who had played a crucial, and at times troublesome, part in our investigation of the Beecham murders. The thing had a kind of poetic—and, yes, amusing—justice to it. You see, during that investigation Mr. Moore and the Doctor had been kidnapped and taken to J. Pierpont Morgan's house for a showdown over the effect that the case was having on the city; and while the result of that meeting had been a useful one for our cause, it'd left the pair of them with something less than the warmest feelings for the country's most powerful businessman, banker—and philanthropist.

Among his many other charitable activities, Mr. Morgan had been the main source of funding for the transfer of the New York Lying-in Hospital to a large mansion previously owned by Mr. Hamilton Fish, which stood, as Marcus had said, just half a block away from the Doctor's own house, on the corner of Seventeenth Street and Second Avenue. There were those uncharitable but knowledgeable souls what said that Morgan had made the expansion possible so that he'd have enough beds to accommodate all his mistresses. Whatever the fact, the hospital was one of the few medical facilities that worked with children what the Doctor had no contact with: partly because its concern was unwed and impoverished mothers and their newborn infants, which was out of the Doctor's area of specialization, but mostly because it was run by Dr. James W. Markoe, who happened to be Mr. Morgan's personal physician.

An amazing set of coincidences, some might say; but the born New Yorker knows what a small town this truly is, and that such things happen fairly frequently. So while it did take a good thirty seconds for the Doctor to absorb all this information, it took no longer, and he soon had his mind back on practicalities. "You say she worked there last year." His eyes focused on Marcus. "I assume, then, that she was released or resigned?"

"A bit of both," Marcus answered. "And under what might kindly be called a cloud." From the stack of papers in his hand Marcus pulled a single sheet. "Dr. Markoe wasn't at the hospital this morning, and when we contacted him at home he refused to give us any help. We could've pressed it and visited him in an official capacity, but our feeling was that a little cash spread around to the other nurses at the hospital would be more effective. It was—and here's what we found out." He indicated the paper, which was covered with notes. "To start with, every one of the nurses who was working at the hospital last year was absolutely certain of the identity of the woman in the sketch. Her name is Elspeth Hunter."

Marcus paused for a second—but it was a long second, the kind I'd come to recognize from the Beecham case. When an unknown, unnamed person you've been pursuing—without even knowing for one hundred percent sure if they exist—stops being a bundle of descriptions and theories and becomes a living individual, it produces an eerie, frightening feeling: you're suddenly certain that you're in a very-high-stakes race, and that you can't quit until you either win or get whipped.

"Any more of a background?" the Doctor asked.

"The nurses didn't know anything," Marcus answered, "but we were able to fill in some holes from her file."

Lucius looked at the Doctor with meaning: "Her file—at headquarters."

"So . . ." the Doctor breathed. "A criminal background, in fact?"

"Not so much a background as accusations," Marcus continued. Before he could go on, though, a swarm of children herded by several governesses came flying into the room, making a racket as they bolted over to look at the mummy cases.

Glancing around at them, the Doctor said, "Upstairs," quickly, at which we all made for one of the central cast-iron staircases and walked quickly up to the picture galleries. Moving through the rooms at the same fast pace, we reached one that was devoted to American paintings—and was deserted.

"All right," the Doctor said, quickly moving across the plain wood floor and taking a seat on a viewing bench in front of Mr. Leutze's enormous painting "Washington Crossing the Delaware." He glanced back the way we'd come when he heard someone approaching, but it was only the still clucking Mr. Moore. "Go ahead, Marcus," the Doctor said.

Marcus pulled out several other papers from his pile. "We—*borrowed* the file from Mulberry Street. It seems that Dr. Markoe reported Mrs. Hunter—she's married, by the way—after several of the other nurses voiced disturbing suspicions concerning the patients she'd been attending."

Mr. Moore now pulled up to us and, having heard Marcus's last words, straightened up, so quickly that it was disturbing: for a man to shift moods that fast, it seemed that something dire must be coming. "You'd better prepare yourself for this, Kreizler," he said, breathing out the last of his humor and relief in a heavy sigh.

The Doctor only held a hand up to him. "Patients?" he said. "Do you mean the mothers she attended?"

"Not the mothers," Miss Howard answered. "Their babies."

"It seems," Marcus continued, "that during the eight months she was employed by the Lying-in Hospital, Nurse Hunter attended to an inordinately high number of babies who died—most of them only a few weeks after birth."

"Died?" the Doctor echoed, quietly but with a kind of frustrated bewilderment. It was as if he'd been given a square peg of information that just didn't fit into some round hole of an idea that he'd formed in his brain. "*Died . . .*" The Doctor stared at the floor a moment. "But—*how?*"

"Difficult to say, precisely," Marcus answered. "The police report doesn't go into any real specifics. But the nurses did. They claim that the children—there were four cases that they all agreed on, as well as some others that were questionable—were perfectly healthy when they were born, but fairly quickly developed respiratory problems."

"Unexplained episodes of labored breathing," Lucius added, "resulting, uniformly, in cyanosis."

"Hunh?" I noised.

"A telltale bluish coloration of the lips, skin, and nail beds," Lucius answered. "All caused by reduced hemoglobin in the small vessels—which generally indicates some kind of suffocation." He looked to the Doctor again. "There would be two or three preliminary episodes, and then one during which the child would expire. But here's the key: every time a child *did* die, Nurse Hunter was either rushing it to a doctor on her own or alone in a wardroom with it."

Dr. Kreizler just kept looking at the floor. "Did the doctors at the hospital ever draw any connection between the events?"

"You know how things are in institutions like that," Miss Howard said. "Sometimes the mothers had already left the hospital, giving their babies up. Under those kinds of circumstances there's a high mortality rate, and nobody in authority tends to ask any questions. Dr. Markoe only went to the police because the nurses brought it to his attention—not that he's a bad man, but—"

"But when you've got a dead infant and too few beds and nurses to start with," Mr. Moore said, "it's ship the body to the old potter's field and on to the next case."

"Actually," Marcus said, "the doctors had always considered Nurse Hunter's efforts on behalf of the cyanotic infants to be quite—well, heroic, in a way. It seemed to them that she worked tirelessly to prolong the babies' lives."

"I see . . ." The Doctor stood up and walked over to stare into the eyes of one of General Washington's frozen oarsmen. "And what, then, made the nurses think that there was anything untoward?"

"Well," Marcus said, "they took note of all the similarities involved in the various incidents, and decided that they were too exact to be coincidences."

"Was Nurse Hunter particularly unpopular?" the Doctor asked.

Marcus nodded. "That's a problem—she was apparently very high-handed, very competitive, and could carry quite a grudge against anybody who crossed her."

The Doctor nodded along with the detective sergeant. "According to the other nurses, at any rate. I fear, Marcus, that these statements must be taken with a certain grain of salt—the medical profession breeds petty jealousy and infighting in *all* its branches."

"Then you're reluctant to believe the other nurses?" Miss Howard asked.

"Not reluctant," the Doctor answered. "Not precisely that. But it simply doesn't . . ." He shook his head once, hard. "Well—go on."

Marcus shrugged. "Like Sara says, the rest of the nurses made a stink with Dr. Markoe. He went to the police, and Nurse Hunter was brought in. She vehemently denied any wrongdoing—got so incensed, in fact, that she immediately resigned. And it wasn't as if these crimes—if in fact they *were* crimes—could be proved. Every one of them looked just like spontaneous infantile respiratory failure. And the way Nurse Hunter told it, she'd kept them alive for as long as they did live. Markoe was inclined to believe her, but—well, he has to worry about his funding. There can't be even a hint of scandal."

"True, Marcus," Dr. Kreizler said. Then he held up a warning finger. "But you must remember that the facts *can* be construed so as to support the assertions put forward by Nurse Hunter."

"And Dr. Markoe, as I said, apparently agreed. He didn't want to pursue the matter once Nurse Hunter had resigned, so there was nothing for the police to do. She went home a free woman."

"And do we have any idea," the Doctor breathed, "where that home is?"

"Yes—or where it *was,* at any rate," Lucius said. "It's in the police report. Ummm—" He took a piece of paper from his brother. "Number 39 Bethune Street. Down in Greenwich Village."

"Over near the river," I threw in.

"We shall have to check it," the Doctor said, "although she has, in all likelihood, moved on." He sat down again, and looked over at a whole wall of early American portraits in genuine and somewhat bitter consternation. "Died . . ." he said again, still unable to accept it. "*Disappeared,* I might have expected, but—*died* . . ."

Miss Howard sat down next to him. "Yes. It doesn't seem particularly consistent, does it?"

"It's beyond that, Sara," the Doctor answered, holding his hands up in resignation. "It's a positive paradox." There were a few moments of silence, during which we could hear the laughing, shouting children downstairs; then the Doctor roused himself. "Well, Detective Sergeants? Why, having discovered all this, have you summoned us here?"

"It seemed as good a place as any to try to make sense of it," Lucius answered. "We haven't yet had a chance to do a really thorough search of the whole area or to retrace what this Hunter woman's steps must have been. So, since it's Sunday and there's not much else we can attend to . . ."

The Doctor shrugged. "True," he said, standing up. "We may as well determine what the mechanical method has to offer. Señora Linares said the child liked to visit the sculpture gallery, isn't that correct?"

"Yes, sir," Lucius answered. "On the first floor, in the north wing."

"Well, then"—the Doctor indicated the stairs with his outstretched arm—"let's get started. Detective Sergeant, would you mind—"

"Notes for the board," Lucius said, pulling out his small pad. "Of course, Doctor."

We got back down to what the Metropolitan's operators liked to call the "sculpture galleries," but where in fact, as the Doctor'd told me on one of our first visits to the museum, most of the figures on display were plaster casts of great statues from other galleries and institutions around the world. They'd been put on display in New York for those folks what would never get the chance to travel and see the originals. This accounted for the uniform bright whiteness of many of the pieces, and for the way that they were thrown together, almost like they were in a warehouse. The sunlight what came in softly through big rectangular windows was reflected off ceilings and moldings what were also bright white, and also off the polished red marble floor. The wood paneling of the walls, by way of contrast, was dark and together with the arched doorways gave the place a kind of stately feel. But as for the sculptures themselves, they—like the stuff in the first floor of the south wing—didn't do much for me, and I doubt I would've felt much different if I'd been looking at the originals. Greek and Roman gods, goddesses, monsters, and kings (or pieces of

them, anyway); strange beasts and blank-eyed men from Babylonia; together with nudes, chalices, and vases from all over. . . . What about it
could've been so entertaining for a fourteen-month-old girl was beyond
me. But the more important question, as I listened to the others trade
ideas, seemed to be what it all might've meant to Elspeth Hunter.

"Providing, of course, that she actually spotted the señora and Ana
here," Mr. Moore said, "and not in the park."

"Why, John," Miss Howard needled, "you actually referred to the child
by her name. That's progress. But I'm afraid your suggestion doesn't seem
very likely. If we stay with our theory that it was Ana's cheerful, noisy demeanor that attracted the kidnapper's attention in the first place, then it
seems probable that the sighting occurred here—this is the place that she
liked best."

"Sara's point is sound, John," the Doctor said. "For whatever reason,
this was the Linares girl's private playground. But what would bring a disgraced nurse here, I wonder?" He gazed around at the place, which
seemed like a combination of a mausoleum and a menagerie. "What did
Elspeth Hunter find so compelling in this room?"

The question hung in the air unanswered for a good fifteen minutes,
until everybody acknowledged that they had no ideas and agreed to move
on to the next spot we knew Nurse Hunter must have visited: the construction site near Fifth Avenue, where she presumably had grabbed her
piece of lead pipe. As we got outside and wandered east I signaled to my
fellow driver to let him know we wouldn't be much longer. Then I fell in
beside the Doctor and Miss Howard, who were following the paved path
as the Isaacsons, Mr. Moore, and Cyrus fanned out and started sifting
through the grass and debris that led to the actual building site. It wasn't
much more than a big hole in the ground at that point.

"Have you seen the drawings of the new wing?" Miss Howard asked
the Doctor as we walked.

"Hmm?" he noised, his mind still fixed on other matters. "Oh. Yes, I
saw the originals before old Hunt died. And I've seen his son's latest edi-
tions, too—quite spectacular."

"Yes," Miss Howard said with a nod. "A friend of mine works in their
office. It'll really be something—a lot of statuary."

"Statuary?"

"Decorating the façade."

"Ah. Yes."

"I know it sounds like a bit of a non sequitur," Miss Howard said with
a laugh, "but there *is* a connection to what we've been discussing and

looking at, Doctor. All those symbolic statues designed for the façade—the four principal artistic disciplines, the four great ages of art—they're all to be female. Did you notice that? Only the smaller stone medallions will be male—and they'll be actual portraits of great artists."

The Doctor drew closer to her. "I do sense a point, Sara."

Miss Howard shrugged. "A tired point, I'm afraid. The symbols are all women—the people are all men. It's the same with those statues in the hall back there. The occasional goddess or some nameless ideal of beauty and womanhood who generally sprang from a man's head—those are the female forms. But the figures with names, the living humans of any historical note? Men. Tell me—what does that teach a young girl, as she grows up?"

"Nothing useful, I fear." Slipping his hand affectionately around her elbow, the Doctor smiled, a bit apologetically. "And the cumulative effect of thousands of years of it only makes matters exponentially worse. Women on pedestals . . . Change *is* coming, however, Sara—though I grant you, it approaches with glacial speed. But it will come. You shan't be idealized for ever."

"But it's *perverse* idealization!" Miss Howard said, kicking a leg out and holding her free hand up. "In fact, there's as much denigration in it as worship. Listen, Doctor, I don't mean this as a purely philosophical conversation. I'm trying to think of what brought the Hunter woman here. I mean, look at those statues in there. The Babylonians and Assyrians, with their Ishtar, mother of the earth—and, at the same time, she was the goddess of war, a cruel, punishing bitch." She gave me a quick look. "Sorry, Stevie—"

I could only laugh. "Like I ain't heard worse."

Miss Howard grinned and ranted on: "And the Greeks and Romans, with their scheming, plotting goddesses. Or the Hindoo deity Kali, their 'Divine Mother' who dispenses death and viciousness. There seem eternally to be *two* faces."

Dr. Kreizler's eyes narrowed. "You're thinking of the apparent contradictions in Elspeth Hunter's behavior?"

Miss Howard nodded, but slowly. "I think so. Though I'm not precisely sure of the connection. But—Señora Linares said that when she saw the woman on the train she seemed to be genuinely caring for Ana. Yet she also said that the woman looked like a predatory animal. Now we find out that she was a nurse, working in one of the most difficult—and admirable—areas of her profession. The doctors think she was a heroine; the nurses believe she was a murderer."

Cyrus came jogging back to us at that point, the other three men following at a walk. "Nothing of any interest here, Doctor. The detective sergeant wants to try to walk it through, though."

"All right," the Doctor said. "Tell him we're at his service." Then, to Miss Howard, he added, "Hold your thought, Sara. I, too, sense something in it, though it's vague as yet."

The Isaacsons and Mr. Moore joined us, and Lucius stood at the center of our little circle, still taking notes.

"Okay," he began, pointing at the steps of the Metropolitan. "Señora Linares comes out of the museum with Ana at about five o'clock." He next indicated the huge pit that was the construction site. "The workmen have left or are leaving. It's Thursday, and they expect to be back in the morning—so they don't take as much care cleaning up as they would for the weekend, and the site is a good deal more cluttered than we see it now." He moved over toward a collection of plumbing materials that was partly hidden by a useless wooden fence. "Nurse Hunter already knows what she's going to do—at least generally. She's searching for a weapon and spots the pile of pipe through this fence. That takes her in the opposite direction from the señora, which explains why she is never noticed by her intended victim." He started to move west, back toward the Egyptian obelisk. "She takes her time and lets the señora reach the obelisk." We all followed him as he moved toward it. "It's the only area around that has any sort of tree cover—the only chance she's going to have to strike if she's at all concerned about getting away. Now it's just past five. In another fifteen minutes to half an hour people will start to cross the park on their way home from work or simply to take in the evening air—although it looks like rain, so the second of those possibilities is probably cut down a bit. But it's spring and warm enough, and plenty of people—armed with umbrellas—will still go through the park on their way home. So she's got to make her move fast."

By now we'd near reached the octagonal group of benches around the seventy-foot obelisk. This was, in fact, the only spot in the vicinity that was at all secluded by trees, being as the red granite obelisk (or so Lucius told us) had been in place since 1881, when it'd been given to the United States by the head man of Egypt.

"The clouds are keeping people away from this spot," Lucius continued. "It's out of the way and purely recreational—you don't pass by it to get across or uptown. You only come here to while away an idle hour." Which was true—the obelisk sat up on a little hill, off the park's main paths. "Nurse Hunter knows that this is her only shot. She comes at the señora from behind, as she's getting ready to sit on a bench, and hits her once, straight across the back of the head. She grabs the child and goes—where?" The detective sergeant looked around curiously. "Back out to Fifth Avenue is quickest—but she may not want to be seen quickly. And to get back to Bethune Street, she'll need to get over to the West Side, to either the Sixth or the Ninth Avenue El, presuming that the trains are her usual method of travel."

"If she hasn't got a job anymore," Marcus added, "that argues for the trains as an economic necessity."

"Yes, but the señora saw her on the *Third* Avenue line," Mr. Moore tossed in. "That argues for her having moved from Bethune Street."

"Perhaps, John," the Doctor said slowly, staring up at the obelisk. "But Sara and I have just been discussing something which may—" The Doctor stopped, his eyes having reached the base of the obelisk. He walked slowly over to it, his eyes searching a crack at the bottom of the large block of stone. He stared into the deep crevice, lifting his hand as if he wanted to reach into it; then he pulled back and turned to Marcus and Lucius.

"Detective Sergeants?" he said, with the beginnings of excitement. "Would you come here, please? There seems to be something *in* there."

Marcus and Lucius rushed over, Marcus producing a small pair of steel tongs. He gazed into the crevice, then slowly inserted the tongs, got hold of something, and withdrew it: a tiny bundle of light cotton fabric.

He placed the balled-up bundle on the walkway near the obelisk's base, then quickly put on a pair of very light gloves. We all crowded around as he began to untangle the little ball, its yellow-and-white fabric soiled and damp. As he proceeded, the shape of the thing became identifiable.

"Looks like a—a tiny hat," Mr. Moore said.

"A baby's hat," Miss Howard said, indicating two little strands of delicate, braided cotton string what were used to tie the thing at the chin and a trim of white lace around its front.

"There's something else," Marcus said, still flattening out the fabric. He unfolded the back of the cap to reveal fine golden embroidery at its rear border: " 'A—N—A,' " he read out. The rest of us just stared at the thing as the detective sergeant looked up and out at the park. "Well . . . looks like west it was. She got rid of the hat in case somebody stopped her—probably the only identifying article on the girl."

"Don't jump to conclusions, Marcus," Lucius said. "She could have stuffed the hat in here and then gone the other direction."

"I don't know," Mr. Moore said, standing between the obelisk and the benches. "It's a good thirty or forty feet out of her way—that's time she's wasting, stuffing it in there. Plenty of other spots to hide it if she went east—starting with the construction site."

"True, Moore," Dr. Kreizler said, staring up at the obelisk. "But in addition, there is the question of *where* she chose to hide it—where *precisely* . . ."

"What do you mean, Doctor?" Marcus asked.

But the Doctor only turned to Miss Howard. "The Egyptian obelisk. It's one of a pair. The other stands in London. Do you know what they are known as, Sara?" Miss Howard just shook her head. " 'Cleopatra's Needles,' " the Doctor went on, looking back up. "An ominous title—she was quite a deadly woman, Cleopatra."

"And yet," Miss Howard continued, getting it, "the 'Mother of Egypt,' in her day. Not to mention the lover of Caesar and Antony—she even bore Caesar's child."

"Caesarion," the Doctor said with a nod.

"What the hell are you two on about?" Mr. Moore demanded.

But the Doctor just kept talking to Miss Howard. "Suppose, Sara," he asked, moving toward her, "that the apparent paradox is not a question, but the answer? Something connects the two sides of the character, the two faces of the coin. We don't know what that connecting element is yet, but the connection exists. So that what we are faced with is not an inconsistency so much as a troubled unity. Aspects of a condition—related stages in a single *process*."

Miss Howard's face darkened. "Then I'd say we're running out of time."

The Doctor gave her a quick look of agreement, then called out, "Marcus! The children Nurse Hunter attended—how long did you say the average interval between their births and their deaths was?"

"Not more than a few weeks," Marcus answered.

"Laszlo," Mr. Moore insisted, in that way he did when he felt like the mental pack was pulling away from him. "Come on, what are you two talking about?"

The Doctor continued to ignore him and counted on his fingers. "She took the child on a Thursday—that was ten days ago." He glanced at Miss Howard again. "You're right, Sara—the woman may be entering a critical phase. Stevie!" I hopped it up to him. "Can we carry everyone in the calash?"

"Not at top speed," I answered. "But I don't see any cabs around."

"I don't want a cab," the Doctor answered urgently. "We'll need the time together to explain."

"Well—traffic shouldn't be too bad," I judged. "We oughtta be able to go at a decent trot. Frederick's had a couple of days off, he'll be game."

"Then get him—now!"

As I shot off to fetch the calash, I heard Mr. Moore still asking what was going on and the Doctor telling him to hurry up and get into the carriage, that he'd explain what he and Miss Howard were thinking once they were on their way downtown. I pulled the rig around to them, and then Cyrus climbed up top with me, while Miss Howard squeezed between Lucius and the Doctor on the seat. Marcus and Mr. Moore roosted themselves as the detective sergeants had done during our commandeered cab ride, on the two iron steps on either side of the carriage.

"Where to?" I called back, though I was pretty sure of what the answer would be.

"Number 39 Bethune Street," the Doctor answered. "With any luck the Hunter woman and her husband haven't moved—and if they have, the new tenants may know where they are now!"

"It'll be fastest if I cut through the park," I said. "And use a few—short-cuts."

"Then do it, do it!" the Doctor yelled, at which I slapped the reins against Frederick's haunches and raced off down the park's East Drive, heading south.

CHAPTER 15

Frederick had just bounded at a crisp trot off of the Central Park carriage drive and onto the broad grass plain of Sheep Meadow (a questionable thing for me to ask of him, I know, but a shortcut's a shortcut) as the Doctor began to speak to his assembled colleagues:

"When we first undertook criminal investigative work together," he said, "we accepted as our starting point the idea that the criminal mind could be, medically speaking, sound, and formed like any other healthy person's—through the context of individual experience. I have seen nothing, professionally, during the last twelve months to convince me that the true incidence of mental disease among criminals is any higher than I thought then. Nor have I heard anything about this Hunter woman which would suggest that she suffers from either *dementia praecox*"—which was the term alienists used in those days for what they're now starting to call 'schizophrenia'—"or one of the lesser mental pathologies. She may be impulsive, and extremely so—but impulsiveness, like extreme anger or melancholia, does not on its own indicate a disease of the mind. The fact that she is also capable of elaborate calculation, particularly within compressed time frames, supports the notion that we are dealing with someone who is quite sane."

Mr. Moore shook his head and looked off toward Central Park West as we rejoined the carriage path. "Why do I find myself wishing we could be up against a lunatic this time?" he said with a sigh.

"You've got good cause to, John," Lucius said. "Lunatics may be dangerous sometimes, but they're a hell of a lot easier to track." The detective sergeant started scratching at his pad again. "Please go on, Doctor."

"We begin, then," the Doctor continued, "with the notion that this woman is sane—she has kidnapped a child and may well have killed others, for reasons that we *can* postulate."

"And what do we do if we catch her?" Marcus asked. "You're talking about a real sacred cow, Doctor—no matter how many women knock off kids in baby farms, no matter how many crones make fortunes running abortion parlors, no matter how many mothers kill their offspring, people don't like to get near cases that deal with women's relationships toward children being anything other than healthy and nurturing. You heard Mrs. Cady Stanton the other night. That's the majority opinion: if women are doing something bad concerning birth and kids, either they're crazy or men and the society that men have created are behind it somewhere."

The Doctor was trying to stop Marcus with an impatient hand. "I know, I know, Detective Sergeant, but it will be our job, again, to ignore popular sentiment and focus on facts. And the most salient fact is this: we are faced with a woman whose behavior embodies what appear to be two diametrically opposed attitudes and acts. The one is nurturing; the other, destructive. Perhaps even murderous. If we accept that she is sane, we must link them."

"Tough," Mr. Moore said. "Very tough."

"Why, John?" the Doctor asked as we exited the comforting greenery of the park at its southwest corner, then passed by the Riding Academy and moved through some very sparse traffic around the Columbus Monument. "Who among us can't claim to embody conflicting urges and conflicting goals at times? Take yourself. How often do you go out and ingest enormous amounts of a liquid poison, in the form of expensive alcohol, while at the same time inhaling dose after dose of a toxic alkaloid called nicotine—?"

"And who," Mr. Moore asked indignantly, "very often accompanies me?"

"You miss my point," the Doctor answered. "Sometimes, after these bouts of marginal self-destruction, you must spend hours caring for yourself, nurturing yourself, as if you were a child. Where is the consistency in *that*?"

"All right, all right," Mr. Moore said in annoyance. "But it's a long jump from mocking my bad habits to showing how a woman can be nurturing—can be a nurse in natal care, for Christ's sake—*and* harbor a desire to kill infants, *and* be sane, all at the same time."

"Has your research helped you at all, Doctor?" Lucius asked.

"I fear not," he answered with the same gloominess he'd shown on the subject for days. "As I've told Sara, there is precious little in the current psychological literature that touches on the subject. Both Krafft-Ebing and Freud are willing to discuss the sexual dimension of a mother's relationship to her children, particularly in the context of male children. And such men will even discuss the desire of children to destroy their parents, either literally or figuratively, again emphasizing boys. In addition, there are some explorations of violence by men against children, although these usually occur within broader discussions of the secondary effects of alcoholism and drug addiction. But I have searched in vain for truly meaningful discussions of women attacking children that are in their care, whether the children are their own or someone else's. The general consensus is that such cases are either extreme or delayed manifestations of postpartum psychosis or, where that cannot be made to apply, mental disease of unknown etiology. I'm afraid that legal records and explorations have been far more helpful than psychological ones, in this respect."

"Really?" Marcus said with some surprise: he'd had a fair degree of legal training before joining the force. "Progressive thinking from lawyers—that's a switch."

"Indeed," the Doctor replied. "And I don't mean to imply that there's been anything like a systematic study of the phenomenon in legal or judicial circles. But the courts are forced to acknowledge the realities that are placed before them—and those realities, all too often, include cases of mothers, governesses, and other adult women committing violence against children. Very often infants."

"But if I'm not wrong," Marcus commented, "the act of infanticide is usually laid at one of two doors in the legal system: poverty or illegitimacy."

"True, Marcus—but there have been cases, even a few celebrated ones, that could not be explained by either the mother's being too poor to support the child or her being unmarried. Nor could they be hidden under the rug with a sweeping pronouncement of some unknown kind of insanity. You will recall the case of Lydia Sherman?"

At the drop of that infamous name, which occurred just as we were making our way across Forty-second Street on Eighth Avenue, both of the Isaacsons and Miss Howard went into a kind of rapture.

"Lydia Sherman," Lucius said wistfully. " 'Queen Poisoner.' Now, *there* was a case . . ."

"We'll never know how many people she actually murdered," Marcus said in the same tone. "It could've been *dozens.*"

"And," Miss Howard added, bringing things a bit more to the point, "some of them were children—including her *own* children. And she was neither poor nor unmarried when she poisoned them."

"Exactly, Sara," the Doctor said. "She had killed the children's father, desired to marry again, and found her children to be simply, as she put it, 'in the way.' The newspaper accounts were quite abundant. But as far as the alienists of the day, as well as those of subsequent years, were concerned, the case might as well have never existed—even though many of them judged her to be perfectly sane at her trial, and that was a good twenty-five years ago."

"I hate to break up this little admiration society," Mr. Moore said, "but Lydia Sherman was no nurse—she was a lying fortune hunter."

"Yes, John," Miss Howard said, "but a living demonstration that the simple accident of being born a woman doesn't necessarily bring with it a talent for nurturing—or even an inclination toward it."

"And by using her case, along with similar examples," the Doctor added, "we can dispense with Professor James's sentimental drivel about the parental instinct being stronger in women than in men and the nobility of the mother caring for the sick child. Lydia Sherman had sick children, to be sure, but she'd *made* them sick by poisoning them with arsenic—and her noble ministrations consisted of further doses of the same poison. No, I am increasingly brought back to a single brief statement that I encountered several days ago—"

Miss Howard guessed what he was referring to: "Herr Schneider's remark about maternal egotism."

The Doctor nodded. "For the benefit of the rest of you, Schneider noted that the mother, once her baby is delivered, transfers—and I quote—'her entire egotism to the child.' "

"How's that supposed to help us?" Mr. Moore asked. "The children at the Lying-in Hospital weren't the Hunter woman's, and neither is the Linares kid."

"But the way in which she took Ana," Lucius said, "indicates that she may have felt—how did you put it, Marcus? That she felt *entitled* to the child?"

"Correct." I heard the Doctor snap his cigarette case closed. "And never forget her behavior on the train—caring for the child *as if it were her own*. Then, too, such psychological bonding often occurs between nurses and patients in general—especially where children are concerned. This is unquestionably not a woman to let something like what Sara refers to as the 'accident of birth' prevent her from feeling maternal in an intensely proprietary fashion about other people's children. That much is obvious, John."

"Oh," Mr. Moore said, lighting up a stick of his own. "Sorry I missed it, then." I could hear him letting out some smoke, and then he spoke more pointedly to the Doctor. "But you're mixing something up, Kreizler. Let's say all this is true, and she has these feelings about any kid she takes a shine to—for whatever reason, she 'transfers her egotism to them.' Fine—but unlike your very considerate example of *my* personal habits, she starts *from* a nurturing attitude and moves *toward* a destructive one. None of the kids are sick when she gets hold of them—but they end up dead. What happens? They can't be 'in the way,' like Lydia Sherman's children were—these are kids she's picked out and chosen to put herself close to. So what happens?"

"Excellent, Moore," the Doctor said. "That is the true mystery of this case. The woman invests her entire self-worth in these infants; yet she destroys them. What, indeed, happens?"

"Could it be a form of indirect suicide?" Lucius asked.

"No—too easy," Miss Howard said. "If you'll pardon my saying so, Lucius. How many times can you kill yourself, even by proxy? I think—I think we need to stay with the ideas we were discussing at the museum, Doctor. The duality—woman as creator alongside woman as destroyer."

A general sort of "Wha—?" sound came out of the others all at once, to which Miss Howard and the Doctor gave out with a brief summary of their thoughts outside the Metropolitan.

"Then you're saying that some part of this woman *identifies* with the notion of a woman having destructive power?" Marcus asked.

"Why not?" Miss Howard said simply. "Haven't you ever in your life identified with a destructive male figure, Marcus?"

"Well, of course, but—"

I didn't turn, but I could tell that Miss Howard was probably shaking her head in disappointment; I hoped she wasn't going for the derringer. "But you were a *boy*," she said, fairly bitterly. Marcus didn't answer—he didn't have to. "Which means that girls don't have destructive or angry thoughts," Miss Howard went on, "and so never dream of having the power to embody them. Correct?"

"Well," Marcus answered, a bit sheepishly, "when you say it like *that,* it sounds fairly stupid."

"Yes," Miss Howard answered, "it does."

"And it is," the Doctor added. "My apologies, Detective Sergeant. But, as Sara said to me, look at the paradoxical examples young girls are offered when growing up—they are taught, on the one hand, that theirs is the pacific, nurturing sex. No outlet is provided for their feelings of anger and aggression. Yet they are human—it is, as Sara says, no more than stupidity to believe that they don't experience anger, hatred, feelings of hostility. And as they do, they also hear different sorts of stories, from oblique sources—mythology, history, legend—of cruel goddesses and wanton queens, whose very creative or supreme power permits them to indulge in rage, revenge, and destruction. What lesson would you take from it all?"

There was a break in the talk, and then Lucius said, very softly, "The iron fist in the velvet glove . . ."

"Detective Sergeant," the Doctor said good-naturedly. "I don't believe I've ever heard you come so close to poetry. An excellent image, truly—is it your own?"

"Oh. No, I"—Lucius squirmed a bit—"I think I heard it somewhere."

"Well, it fits admirably," the Doctor said. "Deadly anger, hidden behind a veil that approximates as closely as possible our society's notion of ideal, or at least acceptable, feminine behavior."

"That's very neat," Mr. Moore said impatiently. "But it still doesn't answer the question: Why, if you're feeling all this shrouded anger, do you decide to go out and be a mother, or a natal nurse, or kidnap somebody else's kid to take care of it like it's your own? Doesn't sound very angry to me."

"We're not suggesting that it is, John," Miss Howard said. "Not at *that* stage. Taking care of the child is the manifestation of the first half of the character—the one that's acceptable, the one that's responding to the constant statement that women are supposed to be nurturing, and aren't fulfilling their basic role if they're not. That's when the transference of ego occurs."

"Okay," Mr. Moore said, now pounding one foot on the step of the carriage so that the whole thing shook. "So where the hell does all this 'evil goddess' garbage come in?!"

"Let me put a case to you, John," the Doctor said. "You are such a woman. You have perhaps had your own children, but lost them—through disease, mishap, any number of misfortunes that may or may not have been your fault, but have certainly left you feeling that your own most basic role in life and in society has been taken away. You've been left to feel utterly worthless, even to yourself. So you find other ways to care for children. You become a nurse. But something happens—something that threatens your renewed ability to fulfill your primeval function. Something that enrages you so that you feel—to use Marcus's term—*entitled* to become the wrathful, primitive goddess, the *taker* as well as the *giver* of life."

"And what is that something?" Mr. Moore asked anxiously, suspecting, now, that an answer was close.

We'd reached Twenty-third Street, and were passing, on the northwest corner, the old, decaying Grand Opera House. Bolted to its Eighth Avenue side was a huge, ugly sign composed of electrical light bulbs what spelled out the hall's current entertainment staple: VAUDEVILLE.

I heard the Doctor say, "Ah, the old Grand," in a voice that made me wonder if he was truly recalling fond memories or was just tormenting Mr. Moore. "There used to be some marvelous productions in there . . ."

"Kreizler!" Mr. Moore was reaching his limit. "*What* is that something?"

The Doctor's voice stayed quiet: "Sara?"

"There's really only one possibility," Miss Howard said. "The children don't cooperate. At least, from her point of view they don't. She tries to nurture, but they don't accept it. They cry. Develop health problems. Reject her attention and her care, no matter how much effort she puts into it. She tells herself it's their fault. She has to. Because the alternative—"

Mr. Moore finally picked it up: "The alternative—is to admit that she *has* no nurturing skills." He let out a low whistle. "My God . . . do you mean to tell me that this woman has structured her whole life around something she can't *do*?"

"Given the way that she has, in all probability, been raised," the Doctor said, "what choice has she? In the face of failure she must always try again, with another candidate and even harder."

"I wonder, John," Miss Howard added pointedly, "if you understand how truly difficult, how unbearable, it is to be a woman and acknowledge that you have no talent for maternity, in this society. In *any* society. How can most women acknowledge such a thing even to themselves? Oh, you can choose to say that you *won't* be a mother—but to have it openly displayed that you *can't*?"

Mr. Moore had to give that a minute; and when he came back to the conversation, it wasn't very gracefully. "But—well, I mean—why *can't* she? What—well, what's *wrong* with her?"

I was sure I could hear the derringer cocking at that point; but it was only Miss Howard's clicking tongue. Feeling compelled to turn around, I saw the others staring in amazement at Mr. Moore. "You really are insufferable sometimes, John," Miss Howard spat out. "That's a marvelously enlightened attitude. 'What's wrong with her?' Why, I ought to—" She balled a fist, but the Doctor stayed her hand.

"*If*, Moore," he said, "by 'what's *wrong* with her?' you in fact mean, what *context* could possibly have *produced* such a woman, then *that* is what we must determine. And the process won't be helped by presuming fault or evil on the woman's part. Remember—we must, as we did in our last case, try to see the situation through *her* eyes, understand it and experience it as *she* must have."

"Oh." Mr. Moore's voice had grown what you might call contrite. "Yes. Right."

"We've reached Fourteenth Street," Lucius announced. "Just a few blocks to Bethune."

Turning west on Fourteenth and heading for Greenwich Street, we started to make our way past the shuttered packing houses of the meat district, where the stench of blood had so completely seeped into every cobblestone and building over the years that even on a pleasant, cool Sunday afternoon it was very noticeable: not exactly a good omen for what lay in front of us. Once we were south of Horatio Street on Greenwich, the structures around us turned back into residential houses, some three and four stories tall, some just old two-story jobs with dormers what seemed almost as big as the houses themselves. Trees of varying sizes and ages lined the blocks, and some of their branches had reached clear out into the street, only to be snapped off at the ends by passing traffic.

As we moved through all this scenery, we began to discuss what strategy we should adopt once we arrived at Number 39 Bethune Street. The first move, made at the Doctor's suggestion, was for me to draw Frederick up to a halt and jump down to raise the cover over the calash's seat. Since not all of us were going to knock on the Hunters' door—that would've looked a bit ridiculous—it would be best for those what stayed behind to be out of sight. That figured to be me, Cyrus, and at least one other person; and as we got back under way, it looked like Miss Howard was the only logical choice. Everybody agreed the detective sergeants should take the lead, and that the Doctor should accompany them: if Nurse Hunter and her husband still lived at Number 39 and were at home, it would be best to let Lucius and Marcus take a strict law enforcement line, being as the Linares child would probably be somewhere in the house and fairly easy to locate. And on the chance that the child needed medical help, the Doctor should be right there.

If the Hunters still lived in the house but were *not* at home, on the other hand, the Isaacsons would question the neighbors on when the couple were likely to get back, while the rest of us kept an eye out for their approach. Finally, if the Hunters had moved on to another address, Lucius and Marcus again said that it would be best to let them flash their badges and frighten the new tenants or owners into saying where their predecessors had gone.

As there wouldn't be room for four of us to hide in the carriage while the detective sergeants and the Doctor approached the house, it was decided that Mr. Moore, too, would go along. Miss Howard was sort of miffed, at first, that she wasn't going to be in the door-knocking delegation. But the Doctor explained that, given the type of woman we were speculating that Nurse Hunter was, the presence of another female was only likely to throw sand into the wheels of progress. This was especially true given what the woman had been through with the other nurses at the Lying-in Hospital. There was no real way for Miss Howard to argue with this reasoning, so she let the matter go. By way of consolation, I told her that I'd be sure to park the calash right up close to the entrance of the house, so that even though she, Cyrus, and I would be out of sight behind the raised cover, we'd be able to monitor whatever went on when and if Nurse Hunter came to greet the others.

All in all, the thing seemed pretty straightforward; and I began to wonder, as we turned off of Greenwich Street onto Bethune and once again came within sight of the waters of the Hudson, why all the philosophical conversation had even been necessary. It seemed like the detective sergeants were just going to go in, get the kid if she was there, and then quietly return her to her mother. Open and shut, you might say.

That, I soon discovered, was what alienists meant when they talked about "delusions."

CHAPTER 16

Number 39 Bethune was a three-story, red brick job, with a few window boxes full of what looked like they were trying hard to be flowers. That should've tipped me off to the whole thing right away: it'd been a cool, moist June, but there'd been days of warmth and sun, too, and there was no reason for the plants in those boxes to look so sorry—unless, of course, somebody didn't know how to tend to them. Anyway, I drew the calash around and in front of the building, which was on the south side of the street, then pulled to a halt just past the two or three small steps that led to the front door. Mr. Moore and Marcus jumped down from their perches, allowing the Doctor and Lucius to get out. Then Cyrus and I took their places inside and, together with Miss Howard, peered out through the small plate of glass that was stitched into the back of the carriage's cover. On the sidewalk, the two detective sergeants buttoned up their jackets, got their badges ready, and tried to look their most businesslike, while the Doctor and Mr. Moore followed directly behind.

They all stepped up to the door, and Marcus gave it a sharp rap.

"Here we go . . ." Miss Howard whispered.

A few minutes went by. Marcus knocked again. We could hear the sound of a voice yelling from an upper floor: a rasping, plaintive sort of sound, which I'd've said was being made by a man somewhere in his fifties. The voice stopped; Marcus knocked again.

In a sudden, harsh sort of motion the door opened, and into its frame stepped a shapely female figure in a red patterned dress, with a grey apron tied around the neck and waist. The red of the dress ran right up to a black lace collar at the neck, and above the neck was a face we'd all come to know well:

It was the woman in Miss Beaux's sketch; it was the woman whose history we already knew peculiarly well; it was Nurse Elspeth Hunter herself.

"My Lord," Cyrus whispered next to me. I turned for an instant to see his face full of troubled wonder. "Can it really be this easy . . . ?"

Up on the small stoop, which wasn't but ten feet from us, Nurse Hunter's brilliant golden eyes flitted from face to face, taking in the men before her with a look what said her brain was working hard at a whole set of problems. She started wiping her wet hands on the lap of her apron, and just as I expected her to give out with some expression of shock or alarm, she smiled: gently, slowly, and very, very coyly.

"*Well* . . ." she said quietly, in a complicated tone what matched the face. Then her hands went up to neaten her thick, attractive chestnut hair. "*I'm* very popular all of a sudden. Is there something I can do for you—*gentlemen*?" The accent wasn't what I'd expected: there was no New England drawl, yet there was still a hint of the countryside.

Marcus stepped to the fore. "Good afternoon. Am I right in supposing that you are Mrs. Elspeth Hunter?"

"Yes," she answered slowly, eyeing Marcus up and down and curling her lips. "You suppose correctly, Mister—"

He held up his badge. "Detective Sergeant Marcus Isaacson. New York Police Department."

Nurse Hunter took in the badge without a blink; if she *was* who we were looking for, then she was as cool as any con I'd ever seen during my years in the trade.

"I see," she answered, never losing the lightly coquettish smile. "And are these your troops, Detective Sergeant?" she asked, turning the smile to Lucius and broadening it.

It was as if she knew that Lucius would start to squirm under the flirtation, as indeed he did. "I'm, uh"—he held up his badge—"I'm Detective Sergeant Lucius Isaacson. Also of the New York Police Department."

"You're not *brothers*?" Nurse Hunter said, the golden eyes dancing from one to the other. "How wonderful—and they let you work together, too! But you're not at all what I'd expect—I thought that New York policemen were all named Mahoney, and had great handlebar mustaches." The Isaacsons laughed just a little at that; it was exactly the right kind of joke to get to them with.

Nurse Hunter's manner became far less playful as she looked beyond the detective sergeants to Mr. Moore and the Doctor. "And these gentlemen?" she said. "They can't be police."

"No," Marcus answered. "They are—assisting us on a case. Mr. John Schuyler Moore and Dr. Laszlo Kreizler."

Her face straightening with what appeared to be genuine awe and humility, Nurse Hunter directed her sunlit stare into Dr. Kreizler's black eyes. "I—don't know what to say . . ." Her words seemed to come with genuine difficulty. "I know of your work, of course, Doctor. I used to be a nurse, you see, at the Lying-in Hospital, just down the street from your—"

"Yes, I know," the Doctor answered coldly, looking disturbed that the conversation was going on so long.

"I hope you won't hold that fact against me," Nurse Hunter continued. "I know that Dr. Markoe thought—well, I read some of your monographs myself, and I thought they were extremely interesting."

The Doctor only bowed a bit, and that with just his head; but even if it was plain that he *knew* she was trying to touch something in him, it was also plain that she'd in fact touched it.

As Nurse Hunter turned to Mr. Moore, her face stayed straight for a few seconds; then she displayed another flirtatious look, one that soon grew into positive ogling. "And Mr. Moore . . . ?"

He smiled back at her, then showed his cards like an amateur of the sort what he definitely was not. *"New York Times,"* he said, extending his hand.

Back inside the calash, Miss Howard let out a hiss of amazement. "I'll be damned," she whispered. "Four out of four . . . she's sharp, all right."

"What's that accent?" I said quietly. "I can't quite make it—it ain't New England, but it ain't local, either."

"No," Miss Howard whispered with a smiling shake of her head. "It's upstate—my part of the country, maybe a little farther north. Yes, I've heard *that* kind of voice before . . ."

Back on the steps, the Doctor cleared his throat. "I think, Detective Sergeant," he said, "that we had better get to the business at hand."

"Oh," Marcus answered. "Yes. Mrs. Hunter, we have reason to believe—"

"Please," she said, giving Marcus the particular kind of playful smile that she'd flashed on him before. Then she held a hand out toward the inside of the house. "Whatever it is, I'm sure we'll be more comfortable discussing it over tea."

In two mirror movements, the four men on the steps and the three of us in the carriage looked at each other in shock. We'd connived and planned so much at how to get into the place to find out if the Linares baby was there that the flat-out invitation was like a kick to the chest.

"*What?*" Miss Howard whispered, when she could.

"*Tea?*" Cyrus added, similarly shocked.

"I hope they know enough not to drink it" was all I could think to say.

Nurse Hunter stood in her doorway, waiting for an answer; finally Lucius managed to come up with "Ma'am, I don't know if you really understand the nature of—"

"Detective Sergeant," she said, in a voice what was part motherly but still kind of playful. "I have, as I suspect you know, been through enough trouble in recent years to realize that you can't be here on any pleasant business. I'm only suggesting that we make it as civilized as possible. That's all."

Bewildered, Lucius looked to the Doctor, who only weighed the matter with a stone face for a moment. Then he shrugged and nodded to the detective sergeant, in a way what seemed to say, If she wants to make it easy for us . . .

"Oh, God," Miss Howard whispered. "They're actually going in."

The four men began to file into the house, the Doctor bringing up the rear. As he stepped over the threshold, Nurse Hunter tapped his shoulder, again addressing him with what seemed very genuine respect. "Oh, um— Doctor?"

He turned, and she looked at the three of us in the carriage; not in our direction, but right *at* us.

"Wouldn't you like your other friends to come in, too? I don't want to appear rude . . ."

The Doctor glanced at us, caught off-guard for just an instant; but to catch the Doctor that way, even for an instant, was a very slick trick.

"Ah," he noised. "No. I don't think so. They are my servants, you see. They'll be fine."

With that he headed inside.

Nurse Hunter glanced once down the street toward the river and once to the east. She lifted her arm, appearing to wave at someone in the distance. Then she looked directly at those of us in the carriage again:

All her smiles and respect were gone now; and for the first time, I could see hard and even murderous cruelty in those golden eyes. That vision alone would have been enough to make me ill at ease; but when I looked down the block ahead of the carriage, curious to know who or what

Nurse Hunter had been waving at, my feeling of uneasiness suddenly turned into a deeper and much more immediate fear.

Walking toward us, with the agitated gait what marks confirmed burny blowers, were several figures, one an adult, the rest boys just a couple of years older than me. The man was of medium build, with a sort of swaggering, rugged manner, while the boys—all dressed in ragged clothes—were swinging sticks and old axe handles in a way what clearly indicated they'd been looking for trouble and believed they'd just found it. As they got closer, I made out the details of the man's face—his sick, crooked smile and deranged, gleaming eyes—and realized with a wave of dread that I knew him:

It was Ding Dong, as loaded with cocaine as I'd ever seen him. The boys who trailed behind him appeared to be in about the same shape. And, just as Nurse Hunter'd done, they were all staring right at us with expressions that promised nothing good.

I leaned back, wanting to sound an urgent alarm; but for some reason, "Aw, shit" was all I came out with.

CHAPTER 17

W ho are they?" Miss Howard said, my little spurt of vulgarity having caused her to turn away from Nurse Hunter's house.

"Friends of yours, Stevie?" Cyrus asked, his voice very calm; but even as he said the words, he slipped a set of brass knuckles he generally carried out of his jacket pocket and onto his right hand. Then he casually slid the hand out of view again.

"Not exactly," I answered. "I do know the grinning ape out front, though. He's Ding Dong—keeps charge over the boys what run with the Hudson Dusters."

"*Ding Dong?*" Miss Howard asked, smiling through her own nervousness. "That can't *really* be his name."

"It is, miss," I said. "And he's rung the chimes in enough people's skulls to've earned it."

"But what can they want with *us?*" she wondered, her hand making its way into a fold of her dress—to my great relief.

"I don't know," I replied, "but it looked to me like that Hunter woman signaled to them. Whatever's going on, Miss Howard, you'll want to keep that canister of yours handy."

The group of Dusters was getting closer, and Ding Dong's half-crazed smile—which so many ladies (Kat, it seemed, among them) found so unexplainably irresistible—only grew wider as he stared at the carriage and realized I was one of the people in it. I tried to keep my eyes off of him and on the others; and, not much liking the vicious looks the three of them were giving Frederick, I swallowed my fear just before they got to us, jumped out of the carriage, and rushed to hold the horse's bridle.

Ding Dong drew up to a halt in front of me and put his hands on his hips, as Cyrus—who'd also gotten to the ground—carefully made his way around Frederick's curbside flank.

"They told me it was true," Ding Dong laughed, his eyes just getting crazier all the time. "They told me it was true, but I never believed it—the Stevepipe, workin' as an errand boy! How do you like shovelin' this nag's shit, Stevie?"

I glanced from Ding Dong to his boys. "Better'n I'd like shovelin' yours," I said, at which a couple of the fellows with sticks made a move my way.

But Ding Dong held his arms out and laughed. "You always did talk like a top-class rabbit, Stevie," he said. "And when you had yourself a piece of pipe, you could even fight like one. I—uh—don't suppose you got one right now?"

Before I could answer, Cyrus stepped around from the other side of Frederick's head. "He doesn't need one," my friend said, his right hand still in his jacket pocket. "Suppose you tell us what you want?"

Ding Dong's smile only seemed to grow as he studied Cyrus for a second. "That's one big nigger, Stevie," he said. "What monkey house didja get *him* outta?" He and his boys laughed a little, looking like they figured Cyrus would try a move at the insult, and then seeming disappointed when he didn't.

"What do you *want,* Ding Dong?" I said.

The Dusters' smiles all started to vanish, and they took a few steps closer. "Question is, Stevepipe," Ding Dong said, "whatta *you* want? Who gave you leave to snoop around this house?"

"You *care?*" I asked. "Why?"

Ding Dong shrugged. "Duster territory—that oughtta be enough."

I eyed him close. "Yeah—but it ain't. What's your *real* reason?"

Ding Dong's grin came back. "Always was smart, you little bastard. Mebbe I wanna pay you back for almost bustin' my arm last time we met."

I ignored that, still trying to figure how they'd come to be where we were at just that moment. "You didn't know it was me in the carriage when you came down the street," I said, thinking out loud. "The lady inside, she signaled to you—how come?"

As the boys tightened their bodies and started slapping their sticks into their open hands, Ding Dong moved on me slowly. "You don't wanna have nothin' to do with that lady, Stevepipe, you hear? I'm givin' you real good advice: stay away from her and stay away from her house."

There's times when those of us born with what you might call wise mouths just can't control them. For a second I thought of Kat; then I gave Ding Dong a vicious little grin of my own. "Don't try to tell me she's one of *your* girls, Ding Dong," I said. "Only way *you'd* touch a woman over fourteen's if she was your *mother.*"

At that Ding Dong lost his grin and swung hard for my head. I ducked under Frederick and went for the whip that stood by the seat of the calash. Ding Dong pursued, and then Cyrus got in front of the other boys, waving the brass knuckles. Before any actual blows could be exchanged, though, Miss Howard jumped down from the carriage, grabbed Ding Dong by the hair, and stuck the stubby barrel of her derringer hard against his head.

"Hold on, now!" she called to the other Dusters. "All of you! Just move away, we're here on police business!"

Ding Dong had more sense than to try for the gun, but he did let out a laugh. " 'Police business'? A moll, a nigger, and a kid? I was born in the mornin', sister, but it weren't *yesterday* mornin'—"

Ding Dong grunted as Miss Howard slapped the gun across his head hard and then crammed the barrel back by his ear.

"One more word out of you, and there'll be a forty-one-caliber bullet rattling around your empty skull! Now, tell your friends to *move away!*"

Hissing in pain, Ding Dong nodded. "Okay, boys—I think we made our point. No reason to go any farther with it."

The other Dusters backtracked reluctantly, and Cyrus let his right hand drop just a bit. I kept the horsewhip held high, though, knowing these types better than my friends did and aware that we wouldn't be really safe until they were out of sight. Miss Howard pushed Ding Dong toward his pals with a rough motion, one what made him stumble and then smile again.

"Rough little bitch, ain't ya?" he said. "I'll remember that. And you remember what I told you all: stay away from this house, and don't ever—Jimmy!"

In a sudden movement what I'm sure they'd practiced many times in similar spots, one of the Dusters quickly tossed his axe handle to Ding Dong, who rushed past Cyrus and slapped the flat of the wood hard on Frederick's haunch. The gelding reared in pain and confusion, and then, in a group, the Dusters all rushed Cyrus, who was alone on Frederick's left side. Ding Dong got in one good shot with the axe handle to Cyrus's ribs, while another of the boys managed to ram him hard in the chest with his thick piece of wood. The now-unarmed kid named Jimmy paid for all this by taking the brass knuckles in the face, and then Cyrus fended off another blow from the third mug.

By now Miss Howard had gotten around to them and was threatening to shoot, while I'd darted back under the still frantic Frederick and lifted the whip, letting fly at Ding Dong's face. I cut him a nice little hole in his left cheek, causing him to go down on one knee. But before I could gloat too much, I turned to see that one of the Dusters had broken into a suicidal run at Miss Howard, making it impossible for her to take aim at the others, while another was poised to lay a vicious and maybe lethal blow to Cyrus's head with his slab of wood.

I cried out, "Cyrus!" and rushed at the Duster—but I knew it was too late. The wood was about to come down, and the crazed, bloodthirsty cackle that came out of the kid indicated how bad the hit would be. But then, in a flash what was barely comprehendable—

All the madness went out of the Duster's face, and his eyes went round. He paused, arms high in the air, and then his jaw dropped into an expression of complete confusion. He managed to yell *"Ding Dong?"*—just that way, like a question—before he crumpled to the ground.

It was such a queer thing that everyone stopped for a few seconds to watch—except for me. Alone out of the group I had a view beyond the falling Duster, and I used it to quickly take in the street around us. My head moved just in time to see a little black kid—maybe ten years old, from the size of him, bushy-haired and dressed in clothes what were too big for him—running around the corner.

Ding Dong bolted over to his fallen boy, who by now was out cold. Miss Howard got her Duster to back off, finally, with the derringer, while Cyrus made ready to let Jimmy have another quick shot with the knuckles, one what Jimmy had the sense to run from. Ding Dong rolled the unconscious Duster over, and pulled something out of the back of his leg. "What the *hell* . . . ?" he mumbled; then he looked up at me.

He was holding a plain, straight stick about ten inches long—and it was clear he figured I'd stuck his boy with it. "What the hell did you do to him, Stevie, you miserable—"

He made a run for me, but then Miss Howard fired the derringer into the air. That was enough for the Dusters, who'd rightly figured that she was mad enough by now to let one of them have her next bullet, what she quickly chambered. Like the miserable pack of crazed dogs they were, they all moved as one to pick up their unconscious pal, and then Ding Dong threw the stick down in front of me.

"I'll remember this, Stevie," he said quietly, without any grin now. "I'll remember it when I'm giving Kat a good fuck tonight!"

With those words it was my turn to make a mad rush at him; but Cyrus got his big arms around me and I couldn't do anything except watch Ding Dong laugh and disappear around the corner of Greenwich Street with his boys.

"And remember!" I heard him call from half a block away. "Stay away from that house—and that woman!"

The gunshot had brought the Isaacsons, the Doctor, and Mr. Moore out onto the street, while Nurse Hunter stood in her doorway, making like she was shocked and horrified by what was going on. We all managed to get ourselves calmed down, though in my case it was tough, and when the Doctor asked Miss Howard what had happened, she only said quietly, "Later, Doctor. I assume the child isn't inside?"

The Doctor looked at her in a little surprise. "You assume correctly. But how?"

"This whole thing's more complicated than it looks," she answered, as she directed me to pick up the stick what'd struck the Duster. "And we need to get out of here. *Now.*"

The Doctor nodded, and then the four men reapproached Nurse Hunter, who'd come out onto the curb. "Were any of your people hurt, Doctor?" she asked, still seeming very concerned. "Can I help? I have some bandaging inside—"

"No, Mrs. Hunter," he said, pretty sternly.

"There are some very dangerous types in this neighborhood, I'm afraid." Nurse Hunter's golden eyes locked onto the Doctor's for just long enough to reveal that she meant her next words sincerely. "Perhaps you should go, before they come back with friends."

The Doctor paused, studying her. "Yes," he said. "Perhaps we should."

"Let's go, everybody, *now!*" Marcus called to the rest of us. "If I know the Dusters, they *will* be back, and there'll be plenty of them."

We all started to pile back onto and into the calash—all, that is, except for the Doctor. He stood looking at Nurse Hunter, waiting for her to say something more. She never broke under his gaze; and after a few seconds she just arched one eyebrow, smiled a bit, and said:

"I'm sorry I couldn't be any help with your investigation."

The Doctor paused a second before answering. "Oh, but you have been, Mrs. Hunter. You have been." He took a step toward her—and she took a step back, for the first time looking like she wasn't in complete control of the situation. "Our visit has been very illuminating. And we shall continue our work. Rest—no—*be* assured of that."

Finally he turned and got back into the calash. As he did, I saw Nurse Hunter spin on her heel, a lethal look coming into her face, and then charge through her front door, which she closed with a slam.

Frederick was by now fairly calm, but it wouldn't have taken much to set him off again; so I didn't give him the reins as a way of telling him to move, just clicked my tongue and let him set a pace of his own choosing, knowing that such freedom would work the last of the spook out of him. For the rest of us, however, that job would be a good piece more difficult. In the space of maybe ten minutes, an awful lot had happened, though none of us yet knew just how much; nor was any of us in a condition to launch into anything more than a brief recounting of the facts, so harrowing had our various sets of experiences been.

The first real order of business, as we crossed over Hudson Street and out of Duster territory, was a more practical affair: to make sure that the blows Cyrus had taken were not serious. Because of the great affection everyone had for the man, this turned out to be an effective and calming distraction. Cyrus and Mr. Moore switched places in the carriage—Mr. Moore joining me up top—so that the Doctor could give Cyrus's ribs and chest a quick examination while the others anxiously asked him how he felt. He was bruised, all right, but unbroken, thanks to the enormous amounts of muscle that protected his bones. He'd been damned lucky— all of us out on the street had been, really, given who we'd been dealing with. As for what possible interest Ding Dong and the Hudson Dusters could have had in Elspeth Hunter or her house, that was, of course, only one of the hundred questions what had appeared unexpectedly, like ghouls, during our brief stop at Bethune Street; and it was quickly decided by the adults that they needed strong drink and perhaps some food in order to start sifting through it all. The pleasant morning had turned into a fine afternoon, with a cool north wind keeping temperatures in the low seventies. Given these conditions, we determined to make once again for the safe, inviting atmosphere of the outdoor terrace at the Café Lafayette, in order to digest some lunch along with our exploits.

CHAPTER 18

B y the time we entered the Lafayette and got to our table on the greenery-covered terrace, we'd all recovered enough to start smiling and even laughing a little at what we'd been through.

"Well!" Miss Howard said with a big, astonished sigh, as she sat and took a menu from our waiter. "I hate to be the one to start asking stupid questions, but if Ana Linares isn't in Nurse Hunter's house, where in the world *is* she?"

"I don't know," Marcus answered, "but between us we covered every inch of every floor of that place—"

"Including the basement," Lucius threw in, scanning his menu.

"—and there was no sign of a baby." Marcus let his head rest on one hand in bewildered weariness. "No sign at all."

"The only thing I can suggest," Mr. Moore said, grabbing at the wine list, "given what happened to the three of you on the street, is that the Dusters are in on it, and they've got her somewhere."

I'd sat down on the floor and started to crawl in amongst some bushy greenery what ran along the iron rail at the edge of the terrace (the good-natured waiters generally let me do that); but Mr. Moore's words made me pause. "The Dusters?" I said. "In on *this* kind of thing?"

"Why not?" Mr. Moore asked. "You think they're above kidnapping, Stevie?"

I felt a little out of my place, saying anything more, and glanced at the Doctor for reassurance; but he was only staring hard at the surface of the table. "Well," I answered uncertainly. "No, not *above* it, exactly . . . just—well—too *stupid,* really. Or too crazy."

Lucius nodded a couple of times. "Stevie has a point. Organization and plotting aren't the Dusters' strong points. That's why the other gangs leave them alone: because they don't control any operations that conflict with anyone else's or that another group would want to take over. They're blowers and thugs—they don't go planning kidnappings and blackmail."

The Doctor spoke firmly without looking up. "The child is in that woman's house. I would stake everything on it."

Mr. Moore hissed. "Kreizler, you were there—she let us go through the whole damned joint."

"And?" Miss Howard asked.

"And, the only other person who lives there is her husband. He's got to be fifteen years older than her, and he's a semi-invalid. Wounded in the Civil War when he was young, apparently, and never really recovered."

"He recovered," the Doctor said, a bit testily. "Or at least his wounds did. What the war left him with was an addiction to opiates."

Marcus looked puzzled. "But he's bedridden. And his wife said that he—"

"That woman couldn't utter a true word if her life depended on it," the Doctor shot back. "As for his being bedridden, had I been jabbed as full of morphine as he has, I should be bedridden, too. Didn't you note the marks on his arms and the odor in the bedroom?"

"Yes," Lucius said, getting an annoyed glance from his brother for his trouble. "Well, it was all perfectly plain, Marcus—the man's been jabbing morphine for years."

"With, I don't doubt, the help of his wife," Dr. Kreizler added. "The good Nurse Hunter."

"What about her?" Miss Howard asked. "What was she like when you got inside? Because I have to say, she played you all like so many piano keys when you were on the steps."

The others looked embarrassed at that, but the Doctor lost his scowl and laughed once. "True, Sara! I knew it was happening, yet even I couldn't stop it initially."

"So how does she manage it?" Miss Howard pressed. "What was her style, once she had you in her lair?"

"Well—I'll just tell you this—" Mr. Moore set both the wine list and his menu aside, ready to order his food and drink but looking, despite his outwardly certain tone and manner, a trifle unsure of what he was about to say.

"I know you hate it when men clean their language up in your presence, Sara, so I'll put it to you straight: I couldn't tell whether that woman wanted to fuck me or kill me."

At that Lucius spat some water he'd been sipping clear across to the exterior wall of the restaurant, where it hit the bricks above a table that was, fortunately, empty. Everyone broke into deep laughter, and when the waiter came it proved no easy job for him to get coherent orders out of our group. Eventually the waiter started laughing, too, without knowing why, and when he went back to the kitchen he was still going.

"My God, John," Miss Howard said, trying to calm herself. "I know I asked you all to be candid around me, but—"

"Ah, now," the Doctor said, defending Mr. Moore. "You can't have it both ways, my dear Sara. Either you receive it straight from John's shoulder, or you don't." The still chuckling Doctor put a hand on Mr. Moore's back. "Your talents really are wasted at the *Times,* Moore. A statement as colorful and unprintable as it is accurate. Elspeth Hunter is an unending string of seeming paradoxes—some of them, unquestionably, possessing deadly dimensions."

Marcus dried some amused tears out of his eyes with his napkin and said, "And you really believe that the child is in the house, Doctor? Even though we searched it thoroughly, with the Hunter woman's blessing?"

"I should not like to use a word like 'blessing' in connection with that creature, Marcus," the Doctor said, as some white wine for the adults and a bottle of Hires root beer for me arrived at the table. "And remember, we searched only as much of the house as was visible to the naked eye."

Marcus looked even more perplexed. "Meaning what?"

But the Doctor directed his next question to Lucius. "Detective Sergeant—if one suspected that Number 39 Bethune Street had recently been—structurally *modified,* in some way that we do not know and could not have seen . . . how might one confirm or eliminate the suspicion?"

Lucius shrugged, taking a sip of wine as Mr. Moore poured it. "Even if she intended, ultimately, to use the space for criminal purposes, she'd have to've gotten a building permit, if it was anything structural. Otherwise she'd have had inspectors all over her, and been shut down. So you'd go downtown and check the records. It's not complicated."

Mr. Moore chuckled once. "What are you thinking, Kreizler? That the woman's built some secret room in the house, and is keeping the baby squirreled away in it?"

The Doctor ignored this, and kept on talking to Lucius. "But would the records be specific? About the work done, I mean."

"Fairly. They'd give some kind of an indication, at least. Why, Doctor?"

At that Dr. Kreizler turned to the still smiling Mr. Moore, whose face suddenly went straight as he fixed his eyes with stubborn determination on an enormous silver platter of oysters that had been set in the middle of the table. "Don't even *try* it, Kreizler," he said. "I've *done* my legwork. I'm not tracking down some harebrained idea that you got out of installment fiction—"

"Never fear, Moore," the Doctor answered. "You shall have Sara for company." Miss Howard, who'd just picked up one of the oysters, didn't look too pleased about that, but she just sighed in resignation. "Besides," the Doctor continued, "I very much doubt that either of you would enjoy the other assignment that must be undertaken—nor do you possess the necessary emblems of office to complete it."

Lucius had just slurped down an oyster, and as I reached up to grab one for myself I saw him looking suddenly worried. "Uh-oh," he noised.

The Doctor nodded. "Another—how did you phrase it, Marcus? Another 'rousting,' I'm afraid. We must know why the Hudson Dusters take so keen an interest in the activities in and around Number 39 Bethune Street. I would suggest patrolling their neighborhood for the next few nights, and harassing one or two of the less threatening members of their gang. You needn't employ our old friend Inspector Byrnes's third-degree tactics, although the threat of such treatment might—"

"We get the picture, Doctor," Marcus answered. "Shouldn't be too difficult." He turned to his brother. "But don't forget your revolver, Lucius."

"As if I would," Lucius answered uncomfortably. "What about you, Doctor? Where will you be, doing further psychological research?"

"If I thought it would help, yes," the Doctor answered, downing an oyster and taking a sip of wine. "And there may in fact be one or two women on Blackwells Island whom it will be useful for me to visit in that context. But there is another mystery that concerns me more immediately." He turned to Cyrus, then looked down to the floor, trying to locate me. "Stevie, come up here for a moment." I followed the order, slurping the last of the sweet, salty juice from an oyster shell as I stood by Cyrus. "Where is the stick? The one that you say this Ding Dong found lodged in his stricken gang member?"

I'd clear forgotten about the thing and quickly held up a finger; then I vaulted the iron rail of the terrace, ran to the calash, and checked under the driver's seat. Luckily for me, the stick was still there. I grabbed it, jumped back over the railing, and handed the strange though simple object to the Doctor.

"We now have a most unusual coincidence," he said, examining the stick. "On the night that the Philippine knife struck the doorway of Number 808 Broadway, Cyrus says that the only person he caught sight of was a young boy, dashing around a corner."

"That's right," Cyrus said. "Looked to be maybe ten, eleven."

"And Stevie, you say you saw a boy of about the same age disappearing from Bethune Street just after the Duster fell?"

"Yeah. This kid was black, though—definitely. There was enough light to tell."

The Doctor nodded, and I grabbed another oyster before the others finished them off. "Cyrus?" Dr. Kreizler said. "Can you guess at the ethnicity of the boy you saw?"

Cyrus shook his head. "Too dark. He *could* have been black, though, I can't rule it out."

"What about his dress?"

"The usual, for a boy on the streets," Cyrus answered with a shrug. "Baggy clothes—castoffs, looked like."

"Or, as Stevie said, clothes that were too big for him?"

"You could say that."

The Doctor nodded, though there was no certainty in his face; then he examined the stick again. "Either the same child, or two, then, have appeared at crucial junctures in this investigation. The first time was during a hostile, or at least a warning, event. The second, on the contrary—" The Doctor seemed to be caught by something, and his nose started to wiggle above his mustache like a rabbit's. "What's that?"

Mr. Moore looked up and around as a waiter came to clear away the empty oyster tray. "What's what?"

"That—*odor,*" the Doctor said. He glanced around, and then his eyes returned to the stick. He held it closer to his face, waving the sharp tip of the thing under his nose. "Hmm . . . yes, unmistakably. Chloroform . . ." He smelled the thing again. "And something else . . ." Unable to place it, he handed the stick to Lucius as more plates of food arrived. "Detective Sergeant?" he said, almost skewering a nice piece of sautéed salmon that Lucius had ordered. "Can you identify it?"

Lucius took the stick and held it a careful distance from his fish, green beans, and potatoes. Then he moved his nose to its tip. "Yes," he said, thinking it over, "I get the chloroform, all right. And the other . . ." His face suddenly brightened, then changed to a look of excited concern. "Stevie, would you say that the Duster was dead when they took him away?"

"Dead?" I answered, taking a dish of my favorite food—plain-grilled steak and salty fried potatoes—from the waiter and then making for my little green cave again. "No. Out cold, yeah, but—he was breathing, all right."

Lucius smelled the stick once more and then handed it to his brother. "In that case—assuming he *keeps* breathing—whoever used this is as much of an expert as our knife man was."

Marcus smiled a bit in recognition as he, too, sniffed the stick. "St. Ignatius bean," he mumbled, his own face so intrigued that he ignored the broiled baby chicken in tarragon sauce that was steaming in front of him.

"*What?*" Miss Howard said, leaning over and looking at the stick in shock.

"Which explains the chloroform," Lucius added, as he started to eat.

Mr. Moore, who seconds before had been looking very happy about the brook trout in almond sauce what the waiter had brought him, now dropped his fork and knife in frustration. "All right. Here I go again, the moron of the group." He braced himself. "What *are* you people talking about, please?"

"St. Ignatius bean," Miss Howard answered, as if the first mug what you might've buttonholed on the sidewalk outside the terrace would've known what she meant. "It's one of the plants in which strychnine occurs naturally."

"That's it!" the Doctor said with a snap of his fingers. "Strychnine! I was certain I recognized it."

"It's soluble in water, sparingly soluble in alcohol, and very soluble in chloroform," Lucius said. "Presuming the intent here was to disable and not to kill, our man knew exactly what proportions to use. And that's no mean trick."

"How come?" I asked, tearing into my steak and gulping down my root beer.

"Because strychnine's more powerful than other drugs used for similar purposes," Marcus said, handing the stick to Miss Howard and finally starting in on his chicken. "Curare, for instance, is a blend of ingredients—strychnine's one of them—and that blending makes it easier to control. But in its pure form, strychnine is very tricky stuff. That's why people use it when they've got severe vermin problems. Better than arsenic, really."

"But can you really be so sure that it *is* pure strychnine?" the Doctor asked.

"The odor's fairly distinctive," Lucius answered. "And the presence of chloroform as a solvent would seem to confirm it. But I'll take it home if you like, and run some tests. Fairly simple. Little sulfuric acid, some potassium dichromate—"

"Oh, sure," Mr. Moore said, now devouring his trout. "I do it all the time . . ."

"Very well," the Doctor said. "But let us, for the moment, assume you are correct, Detective Sergeant. Can you say who would possess such knowledge, offhand?"

"Well," Lucius answered, "the stick appears to be some sort of aboriginal dart or arrow."

"Yes," the Doctor said. "That was my thought."

"But as for who uses pure strychnine in hunting, or even warfare—there you've got me."

"And there," the Doctor said, setting to work on a plate of crab cakes, "I also find my own assignment for tomorrow."

"Ah-ha!" Mr. Moore said, holding up his fork. "At last, a cryptic comment that I can decipher—you're going to see Boas!"

"Exactly, Moore. Boas. I'm sure he'll be delighted to render his services once again."

Dr. Franz Boas was another of the Doctor's close scientific friends, the head of the Department of Anthropology at the Museum of Natural History and a man who'd helped our team gain some important tips at a crucial point during the Beecham investigation the year before. Like Dr. Kreizler, Boas was a German by birth, though he'd come to this country later in life than the Doctor. He'd studied psychology before moving on to anthropology and the United States, so he and the Doctor had no trouble communicating on a whole batch of levels; and whenever he came to the house the dining room was pretty certain to be the scene of lively talks and occasional arguments, during which Dr. Boas would sometimes slip into German and Dr. Kreizler would fall right in with him, making it impossible for me to tell what in the world they were hollering about. But he was a kindly man, was Dr. Boas, and like most of your genuine geniuses he didn't let his brains turn him into what you might call an intellectual snob.

"I shall take him both the knife and this projectile," Dr. Kreizler said, "and tell him the story of the child or children that we have spotted on the occasions that the weapons have been used. It may be that he can supply some insight, or that someone on his staff can. I confess, the entire matter mystifies me."

A general noise of chewing agreement came out of the rest of us, show-ing that we'd pretty much reached the limits of what we could make out of the morning's activities. For a while we just ate and drank, letting our nerves and our spirits piece themselves back together. But the silence was eventually broken by Miss Howard.

"For a woman whose original action seems to have been so impulsive," she said slowly, sipping her wine and playing with a dish of fresh straw-berries and hot chocolate sauce that had arrived for dessert, "this one seems to have planned how to elude capture awfully well." She gently bit into a dripping strawberry. "Another paradox, I suppose, Doctor?"

"Indeed, Sara," the Doctor answered, rolling a strawberry of his own in the chocolate. "But remember—all of you, remember—these paradoxes must not be considered contradictory. They are part of a single process. As a snake propels itself forward by pushing sideways across the sand, first to the left and then to the right, so does Nurse Hunter pursue her desperate goals. She is impulsive, then calculating. Flattering and promiscuous, then suddenly and mortally threatening. An apparently respectable woman with a bedridden husband, who nonetheless seems to have some important con-nection to one of the most degenerate, senselessly violent gangs in the city. By comparison, more outwardly excessive criminal behavior seems quite comprehensible. Even so obsessive a murderer as John Beecham moved along a course that almost appears linear and coherent—even though it was fatal—when held up against this woman. We find ourselves, in many ways, in an even stranger land when we face Elspeth Hunter. And with fewer maps . . ."

The meal soon came to an end, and—it being Sunday and all the places what Dr. Kreizler had mentioned as possible sources of information being closed—everyone agreed to go home, take care of what few details they could, and try to get some rest. As we left the Café Lafayette the Isaacsons hailed a hansom, while the Doctor offered to drop Mr. Moore and Miss Howard off. Then it was back to Seventeenth Street and, for me, into the carriage house, to take care of the calash and put a little balm on the spot on Frederick's haunch where he'd been struck by Ding Dong.

The blow hadn't left much of a mark, but I could tell as I applied the balm that it still stung Frederick a bit, and I made some calming noises and fed him a bit of sugar as I rubbed the medicine in. It made me all the madder to think that a man I'd always counted as one of the worst I knew—and, since visiting Kat the night before, had come to hate even more—had caused Frederick such pain and confusion, and as I worked on the animal's haunch I quietly assured him that I'd see that the wound was taken back out of Ding Dong's hide, one day. With interest, too . . .

Caught up in these bitter thoughts, I barely noticed Cyrus slipping into the carriage house. He came over and stroked Frederick's neck, looking straight into the gelding's eyes and giving him some words of sympathy. Then he spoke to me:

"He okay?"

"Yeah," I said, holding up Frederick's left hind leg and scraping some hard mud out of his shoe. "Not much of a welt. Scared him worse than anything."

"He's a tough old boy," Cyrus said, patting the horse's snout lightly. Then he came round and stood by me. I got the feeling he had something on his mind.

"Miss Howard didn't hear. What Ding Dong said about Kat, I mean."

My heart jumped a little, but I kept on scraping. "No?"

"She was too far away. And she had her hands full." Cyrus crouched down beside me. In a quick glance I saw some inquisitiveness in his broad face, but more sympathy. "*I* heard it, though."

"Oh," was all I could answer.

"You want to talk about it, Stevie?"

I tried to summon up a light, dismissive kind of a laugh, but came up far short. "Not much to say. She's gone to be his girl." I almost choked on the words. "I told her—you know, about the idea of her working here. But you were right. She's got other plans . . ."

Cyrus just made a small sound that said he got the picture. Then he put a hand on my shoulder. "You need anything?"

"Nah," I said, still staring at the horse's hoof. "I'll be okay. Just gotta finish up out here, that's all."

"Well . . . there isn't any reason for the Doctor to know this part of the story. Doesn't have anything to do with the case that I can tell."

"Right." I finally managed to give my friend another quick look. "Thanks, Cyrus."

He just nodded, stood up, and left the carriage house slowly.

I stayed at my work for several more minutes, the caked mud in Frederick's shoe coming away quicker as it mixed with my silent tears.

CHAPTER 19

It's a peculiar thing, how you can go to bed one night convinced of a fact and wake up the next morning to find yourself faced with its opposite. . . .

When I drifted off soon after sunset on that Sunday evening, I was dead certain that I would never see Kat again: even if my heart could have stood visiting her at the Dusters' joint, things had so fallen out with Ding Dong during our jaunt to Bethune Street as to make even an attempt at such a visit worth my life. The realization that the door on my strange relationship with her seemed to have suddenly swung shut alternately angered and saddened me all through Sunday afternoon and evening. So black and blue did my mood become, in fact, that the Doctor—preoccupied as he was with the case—felt the need to visit me in my room and ask whether I was feeling all right. I didn't tell him the true story, and he, of course, sensed that I was holding something back; but he didn't press it, just told me to get some extra sleep and see how things looked in the morning.

I woke at just past 8:30 on Monday to find the Doctor and Cyrus getting ready to head up to the Museum of Natural History. Mrs. Leshko was, not for the first time, late, and Cyrus was seeing to the preparation of coffee, a task what he could accomplish with far happier results than could our Russian cook. The three of us sat in the kitchen and had big mugs of a fine South American brew, the Doctor trying to cheer me up by reading aloud the details of a lead story in the *Times* that concerned new developments in the "mystery of the headless body." It seemed that the

lower torso of the still unidentified corpse (wrapped in the same red oilcloth what Cyrus and I had seen at the Cunard pier) had washed up at the
watery edge of the woods near Undercliff Avenue, all the way on the
north side of Manhattan. The police—whose theory of a crazed anatomist
or medical student had been dismissed even by the coroner they themselves had engaged, after the man had found about a dozen stab wounds
and a couple of .32-caliber bullet holes in various parts of the body—had
changed their theory, and were now trying to drum up panic and excitement by saying the body belonged to one of two lunatics who'd escaped
from the State Asylum at King's Park, Long Island, a couple of weeks earlier. This story, we all knew, was as likely to prove true as the first; but
whatever the real identity of the unfortunate soul whose body'd been dis-
tributed all over town, the attention that the case continued to receive
could only help us to go about our work more easily.

The Doctor and Cyrus headed off at a little before nine, and though a
visit to the Museum of Natural History would ordinarily have been my
sort of fare, the morning was a cool, grey one, and my spirits were such
that I found the idea of staying home alone somewhat comforting. And,
of course, it was advisable that someone stick around and try to determine
what in the world had become of Mrs. Leshko. So I walked the pair of
them out to the calash and saw them off, pausing to glance up at the misty
sky before heading back to the house.

I'd just gotten the door open when a voice whispered to me:

"Stevie!"

It was coming from beyond some hedges on the east side of the Doctor's small front yard. Carefully closing the front door again, I crept over
to the hedge, looked up and over it, and found—

Kat. She was crouched down low and huddling by the side of the building next door, her clothes looking very wrinkled, her hair undone, and her
face a picture of exhaustion. I couldn't've been more surprised if she'd
been a ghost or one of those mythical sirens, so resigned had I become
during the last twelve hours to never seeing her again.

"Kat?" I said, keeping my own voice low. Then I rushed around the
hedge to her. "What the hell're you doing? How long you been here?"

"Since about four," she said, glancing up and down the block, more so
she wouldn't have to look me in the eye than because she was trying to locate anything. "I think." Her eyes turned watery, she began to sniffle hard
and painfully; and when she wiped at her nose with a filthy old handkerchief, it came away bloody.

"But why?"

She shrugged miserably. "Had to get out of there—he was like a maniac last night. In fact, I ain't so sure he *ain't* a maniac, sometimes . . ."

"Ding Dong?" I said, to which she nodded. My eyes fell to the ground. "It's my fault, ain't it. . . ."

She shook her head quickly, the tears thickening in those blue eyes that still refused to look into mine. "That wasn't it. Wasn't *most* of it, anyway . . ." She finally sobbed once. "Stevie, he's got three other regular girls—*three*! And I'm the *oldest*! He never told me that!"

I had no idea what to say; the information didn't surprise me, of course, but I wasn't about to tell her so. "So," I tried, "did—did you two have an argument or something?"

"We had a *fight,* is what we had!" she said. "I told him I don't play second fiddle to no twelve-year-old piece of trash—" She slammed her fist against the side of her forehead. "But now all my things are down there . . ."

I smiled a little. "All your things? Kat, you got two dresses, one coat, and a shawl—"

"And my papa's old wallet!" she protested. "The one with my mother's picture in it—that's there, too!"

I gave her a straight look. "But that ain't what's makin' this hard, right?" I touched her elbow, trying to get her to look at me. "He won't give you any burny, will he?"

"Bastard!" she grunted, sobbing again. "He *knows* how much I need it now, he *swore* he'd never cut me off!" She finally glanced once into my eyes, real pathetically, then threw herself against me hard. "Stevie, I'm just about going out of my skull, I'm hurtin' for it so bad."

I put my arms around her shivering shoulders. "Come on," I said. "Let's get inside—a little strong coffee'll take some of the edge off of it."

I got her up and half carried her to the front door of the Doctor's house, where she paused once fearfully.

"They're—all gone, right?" she said, looking up at the parlor windows. "I waited for 'em to go, I don't want you gettin' into no trouble—"

"They're gone," I said as reassuringly as I knew how. "But there wouldn't be any trouble, anyway. The Doctor ain't that way."

She let out a doubtful little noise as we went inside.

I guided her to the kitchen and a mug of Cyrus's coffee. Her eyes got wider as she began drinking it and taking the house in; and I'll confess that, seeing the look in those eyes, my notion of bringing her to work for the Doctor resurfaced in my thoughts. So I took her on up to the parlor, to let her get the full effect of the place. Strengthened by the strong coffee, she began to move around more bravely and even smiled, amazed at all the wondrous and beautiful things the Doctor owned—and even more amazed that I lived in such a place.

"He must work you to the bone," she said, opening the silver cigarette case on the marble mantle.

"It ain't the work that's tough," I said, sitting in the Doctor's chair like I was lord of the house. "He makes me study."

"*Study?*" Kat said, her face filling with near disgust. "What the hell *for?*"

I shrugged. "Says if I ever want to live in a house like this, that's what's gonna get me there."

"Who's *he* kiddin'?" she answered. "I bet it wasn't studyin' that got *him* here."

I just shrugged again, not wanting to admit that the Doctor came from money.

"I can see why you like it so much, though," Kat went on, looking around. "Beats hell out of Hudson Street, that's for sure."

At the sound of those words a thought suddenly occurred to me, a thought that maybe should've jumped into my head as soon as I saw Kat, if only worrying about her hadn't, as usual, scrambled my mind up so much.

"Kat," I said slowly, considering the thing, "how long you been spending time at the Dusters' joint?"

She sat down in the big easy chair across from me, holding her arms into her like she was cold and then shrugging as she sipped at her coffee. "Dunno—maybe a month or so. First met Ding Dong about then, anyways."

"You know pretty much who comes in and outta there, then, I guess, right?"

She shrugged again. "The regulars, sure. But you know that place, Stevie, they got swells from all over town slummin' every night. Half the city's been through there at some point or other."

"But the regulars—you *would* recognize them?"

"Probably. Why do you wanna know?" She got up and moved over to me. "What's that look on your face, Stevie? You're actin' so odd all of a sudden."

I just stared at the carpet for a few seconds, then grabbed her hand. "Come on with me."

Making for the staircase, I half dragged Kat up to the Doctor's office. The drapes were still drawn in the dark-paneled room, and it was hard to make anything out clearly. I tripped a couple of times on my way to the window, and when I gave the drapery cord a good tug I saw that it was still more piles of books what had waylaid me: the study was an even bigger mess than it'd been the previous week.

Kat glanced around, frowning and wiping at her nose. "*This* room don't do much for me," she said, mystified and put off. "What's he want with so many damned books, anyway?"

I didn't answer; I was too busy going through papers on the Doctor's desk, looking for something, hoping that the detective sergeants had left at least one copy—

I found it lying underneath a thick book by Dr. Krafft-Ebing: one of the photographed copies of the sketch that Miss Beaux had done of Nurse Hunter.

Moving it closer to the light that came in through the sheer white curtains that still covered the windows, I signaled to Kat that she should join me.

"You ever seen this lady?" I asked, showing her the picture.

Her face filled with recognition right away. "Sure," she said. "That's Libby."

"Libby?"

"Libby Hatch. One of Goo Goo's molls," she went on, referring to Goo Goo Knox, the leader of the Dusters. Kat's face twisted up in that way it did when she didn't understand something, like her nose'd been attached to a drill bit. "What the hell's your doctor pal doin' with a picture of Libby? A good one, too."

"Libby Hatch," I said quietly, looking out the window for a few seconds—enough time to realize that, as Miss Howard had said the day before, this whole thing was a lot more complicated than it'd originally looked.

Again I grabbed Kat's hand. "Come on!"

She flew along behind me like a rag doll as I ran back for the door, then spun round again and headed back to the desk, slapping open a leather-bound book of addresses and telephone numbers what the Doctor kept on it. "Stevie!" Kat said. "Do you think you could quit yanking me around like that? I ain't exactly feeling athletic, you know!"

"Sorry," I said, opening the book to the "I" section with one hand, finding a number, and then charging back to the door with Kat still in tow.

"Ow!" she cried. "Stevie, are you listening to me at *all*?"

I didn't answer as we shot back down to the kitchen, then through to the pantry. Finally letting go of Kat's hand, I grabbed hold of the telephone's receiver and mouthpiece. In a couple of seconds I had an operator on the line, and I gave her the number of the detective sergeants' house, or rather, their parents' house, what was located down on Second Street between First and Second Avenues, next to the old Marble Cemetery and not far from two or three synagogues.

The 'phone on the other end rang, and a woman's voice answered, yelling into the thing the way people who still considered it a fantastic invention were like to do.

"Hallo?" the woman said, through a thick accent. "Who ist da?"

"Yes," I answered, "I'd like to speak to one of the detective sergeants, please."

Kat took a step back, looking worried. "Stevie—you ain't callin' the cops on me?" As usual, her first calculation was that anything what happened had something to do with her.

"Relax," I said, shaking my head. "It's—business." I liked the feeling of being able to tell her that. "Go get yourself some more coffee. We got an icebox, too, if you want—"

I stopped when I realized that the woman on the 'phone was yelling at me. "Detective sergeant—vat vun? Lucius or Marcus?"

"Hunh? Oh. Either, it don't—it doesn't matter."

"Marcus iss not here! Headqvarters! I get Lucius! Who ist—*whom* ist calling?"

"Just tell him it's Stevie."

"Stevie?" she repeated, not sounding too impressed. "Stevie who? Stevie vat?"

I was getting a little impatient. "*Doctor* Stevie!" I said, raising a small laugh out of Kat, who'd gone to investigate the food in the new icebox.

"*Business,*" she said, giving me a cunning little sideways glance. "Sure . . ."

"Oh, ah, *Doctor* Stevie!" the woman on the line said, satisfied. "Only just ein moment, please!"

She set the 'phone down with a crash that echoed into my ear and made me pull my receiver away. "Jesus Christ!" I said, hoping my eardrum wasn't busted. "Whole damned family's nuts . . ."

In a few seconds the 'phone on the other end rattled around again, and I heard Detective Sergeant Lucius speaking, though not into it. "No, Mama, Stevie isn't a doctor, he just—please, Mama, go!" There were some unidentifiable protests from the woman, then Lucius again: "Mama! *Go!*" He took a deep breath and spoke into the phone. "Stevie?"

"Right here."

"I'm sorry about that. She still doesn't really understand this thing, and I don't know that she ever will. What's going on?"

"I got some news, and I think it'll save you and Detective Sergeant Marcus some work. Can you collect him and get over here?"

"*I* can come," Lucius answered. "I've been doing the chemical analysis of the sample I took from the tip of that stick, but I just finished. It is strychnine, by the way. But Marcus is poking around down at headquarters, then going on to the Doctor's Institute. Why?"

"I think you'd better tell him to come up," I said. "What I've found, it—I think it's important."

"Where's the Doctor?"

"Him and Cyrus went to the museum already. They shouldn't be too long, though. Can you make it?"

"I'll get a cab now, and try to intercept Marcus at the Insititute." He yelled away from the telephone again: "No, Mama, that's the chemicals you're smelling, there's nothing to clean—" His voice came back to me. "I've got to go before my mother sets herself on fire. See you in half an hour." The line clicked, and I hung the receiver up.

Wandering back into the kitchen, I found Kat had scared up some eggs and a few herring and was getting ready to fry them in a big skillet. "So," she said with a smile. "How's 'business'?"

I was too amazed by what she was doing to hear the question. "Kat—you can *cook*?"

"Don't gimme that kinda air," she answered playfully. "You think me and Papa had servants, Mr. Stuyvesant Park? I cooked for him all the time. Eggs and herring, now *that's* a breakfast." She tried to crack an egg into the pan, but her hand shook badly; and as it did, she lost her smile and took a deep breath. "Say—Stevie," she said quietly, again without looking at me. "Does your doctor friend have—well, you know, does he see any patients here?"

"Unh-unh," I said, shaking my head and knowing full well what she meant by the question. "None of that, Kat."

"It's just—" Her hand shook again, and her eyes filled with those sickly, desperate tears. "I don't know if I can crack the eggs . . ."

My mind seemed to grab hold of a thought, something the Doctor'd said when I'd been at the Institute and he'd dealt with a kid who was in even worse shape than Kat: something about what a cold cutoff of drugs could do to the human body. I knew that in fact he might have some cocaine stashed in the small examination room he maintained toward the front of the house on the ground floor, but I wasn't going to let Kat have it. When she suddenly let out a little cry, though, then grabbed at her gut and sat down quick on a chair, I figured I'd better do something; so I ran

to the examination room and opened a little glass case what held a series
of bottles. Looking them over quick, I came across some paregoric tinc-
ture. I knew that people gave it to colicky babies, and such being the case
I figured it couldn't do Kat any harm. I ran back out into the hall and then
to her, crouching down.

"Here," I said, handing her the bottle. "Try some of this."

She kept one hand on her stomach and moaned as she took a deep pull
off the bottle. Then she held the thing away from her and stuck her
tongue out. "Ugh! What the hell is that?"

"Just something to calm your gut down."

"I need burny!" she answered, with a little stamp of her foot.

"Kat, there ain't any here. Just try to stay calm. Take another shot of
this—" I held the bottle to her head as she shook it, trying to avoid the
foul-tasting medicine; but after another swig, her nerves did seem to calm
down some. "Better?" I asked.

She nodded slowly. "Kinda. Whoo . . ." She finally took her hand away
from her stomach, got a deep breath into her lungs, and stood up. "Yeah.
That *is* better."

"Maybe some food now, hunh?" I walked her to the stove. "I still ain't
so sure I buy this cooking business outta you . . ."

Kat was able to laugh a little at that; and when she picked up another
egg, her hands were steady. "You wait, boy," she said, cracking the little
brown shell on the lip of the skillet with practiced skill. "You're gonna
wish you had this breakfast every day." She winced once, then turned to
the table. "Gimme a little more of that stuff, will you? Tastes awful, but it
helps."

As she labored over the eggs and herring Kat took not one but several
more shots of the paregoric, and her mood brightened considerably. The
next half an hour or so was one of the happiest times I can remember
spending with her, just making breakfast and eating in the kitchen like two
ordinary types, chatting, laughing, forgetting, for the time being, what
had driven her to the Doctor's house. She began to talk about the day
when she'd have a big, beautiful house of her own, and though I didn't
believe that whoring would ever lead her to such a place, I didn't say anything to interfere with the daydream, so chipper and healthy did it make
her seem.

In fact, I was a little sorry when the front door bell finally rang at a little past ten o'clock. I had just set to washing our dishes and Kat had lit up
a smoke, still romancing away about her future and even joking, at one
point, about how she'd hire me to work in her house. I'd never thought

of that idea before, me and Kat under one roof as adults, not even in my own moments of dreaming; nor could I conjure it up that morning, so outside the realm of possibility did it seem. Her imagination, I suppose, was a lot better than mine; had to've been, when I think about it.

Drying my hands on a kitchen towel, I started running for the front door, Kat joking about my being her butler and telling me to send whoever it was away, as she was not "receiving" that morning. She straightened right up, though, when I came into the kitchen with the two detective sergeants—she still wasn't completely sure that their visit didn't have anything to do with her. I introduced them to Kat, and together the four of us went on up to the parlor, where they all sat down. For my part, I ran further on to the Doctor's study to fetch the picture of Nurse Hunter. When I brought it back down, I found the Isaacsons arguing—in their usual testy, childish way—over the exact ratio of chemicals that was supposed to be used in the test what Lucius had conducted that morning. Kat was sitting on the edge of the same easy chair she'd been in before, glancing over at the two men and wondering, I'm certain, what in the world kind of cops behaved in such a way.

"Here we go," I said, taking the picture to Kat as she stood up. "Kat, tell the detective sergeants who this woman is."

She just stared around at the three of us for a second, then mumbled to me, "But I already told *you*."

"Yeah," I whispered back, "but tell *them*. Don't worry, it ain't gonna get you in any trouble."

"I heard *that* before," Kat answered. Then she spoke aloud: "Her name's Libby Hatch. She's—well, her and Goo Goo—"

"Goo Goo Knox?" Marcus asked. "Chief of the Hudson Dusters?"

"That's right," Kat said. "She's his girl. Well, she's one of 'em, anyway. They all got plenty, the sons of—" Kat caught herself and cut her fuming short. "But she's his favorite right now."

"*Libby Hatch?*" Lucius said, taking the picture. "You're sure?"

"Sure I'm sure—I got eyes, ain't I?"

Lucius gave Kat a careful squint. "You wouldn't happen to know where this 'Libby Hatch' lives, would you?"

Kat nodded quickly. "Right around the corner from the Dusters' headquarters. Bethune Street. She's married to some old geezer, but he's half dead, anyway, so she has to look out for herself. Goo Goo's got their house under the gang's protection—anybody gets caught even casing the place, they'll end up in the river. And they won't be swimmin', if you take my meaning."

Lucius was about to say more, but then Marcus held up a finger. "Miss Devlin? I'm sorry—would you excuse the three of us for a moment?"

"Sure," Kat said, looking ever more confused and then turning to me. "Stevie, maybe I could go downstairs, have a little more of that medicine?"

"Yeah, sure, Kat," I said. "It's right where we left it."

She tried to smile at the detective sergeants. "Just a little stomach complaint. I'll be right back."

Lucius and Marcus watched her go, Lucius looking very excited about the news we'd received. He was about to express that excitement when Marcus stepped in again. "Stevie, how do we know that this girl can be trusted?"

The question took me a little off guard. "How—well . . . because. She's a friend of mine. I've known her for—well, for a long time. Why shouldn't you be able to trust her?"

Marcus looked me straight in the eye. "Because she's a prostitute and a cocaine fiend."

My pride got ruffled for just an instant; but it was clear from Marcus's look that he didn't mean to cause any injury, he just wanted to be sure that we weren't, in fact, getting taken. I looked to the floor as I answered, "Neither of them things makes her a liar, Detective Sergeant. I'll answer for Kat."

"The cocaine fiend I understand," Lucius said to his brother, looking puzzled. "The indications are fairly clear. But why do you assume she's a prostitute, Marcus?"

"A girl that age? Living at the Dusters'? It's not a mission house, Lucius, for God's sake."

"Hmm," Lucius said grimly. "True. But she *does* know where the Hunter woman lives. And what could she possibly gain from telling us all this? I say we believe her—not least because it could make all our lives a lot easier."

"How so?" Marcus asked.

But it was me that Lucius spoke to next: "Stevie, do you think this girl might do us a—favor?"

I shook my head. "A favor, probably not. We—*I* got her into a little hot water yesterday. Anyway, Kat's life hasn't made her one for favors. But if there was something in it for her—then yeah, I think we might ask her." I looked at them both earnestly. "But only if it ain't dangerous."

"It shouldn't be," Lucius answered eagerly.

"What are you cooking up, Lucius?" Marcus asked.

But at that moment Kat came running up the stairs and back into the room. "Stevie, there's people coming into the house!"

"Don't worry," I said, going to the stairway. "Probably just the house-keeper. I been wondering when she'd turn up."

"No, it's a couple of men," Kat answered quickly, following me. "Stevie, it's your doctor! I shouldn't be here, he'll take it outta your hide!"

Looking down the stairs, I saw that the new arrivals were, in fact, the Doctor and Cyrus. Putting a quick hand on Kat's arm, I squeezed it gently. "Don't worry," I said, half amused by her fear. "I told you, it'll be fine, he ain't that way."

"But we been eatin' his food, and the medicine—"

"Calm down," I said, as the Doctor started up the stairs at a jaunt. "Go inside. It'll be fine, I'm telling you."

Kat nodded reluctant agreement but didn't move; and as the Doctor reached the top of the stairs she drew back behind my shoulder, her eyes going big as she took in his long, dark hair, his black eyes, and the clothes that matched those eyes, even in summer. I smiled; I'd flat-out forgotten how imposing—even scary—he could look when you first met him.

"Stevie!" the Doctor said, seeming satisfied. "We have returned, though rather more quickly than I'd hoped. Apparently this area of anthropology is just developing—it took half of Boas's staff, in addition to several students from Columbia, to analyze the arrow, and their explanation was only partial. The weapon does, indeed, originate in the islands of the southwestern Pacific, though there remains some confusion over—" He stopped suddenly when he made out Kat's little form hiding behind me. "Well." The Doctor smiled genuinely, but slowed his approach. "I didn't know you had company, Stevie. My apologies for bursting in so rudely."

Cyrus came lumbering up the stairs, calling out to me, "Stevie? You feeling all right? There's a half-empty bottle of paregoric on the kitchen—" Then he, too, caught sight of Kat. "Oh," he said, scrutinizing her. He smiled just a bit and bowed his head. "Hello, Kat," he said, courteously but not exactly warmly.

"Mr. Montrose," Kat noised from behind me, without moving.

The detective sergeants came out of the parlor, and the Doctor looked past me and Kat to them. "Ah! The detective sergeants as well—good. This will save some time." He turned the careful smile my way again. "Stevie? Am I not to be introduced?"

"Oh," I said. "No. I mean, yes. I mean—"

Kat jumped out from behind me ever so briefly and extended a hand, looking like she thought the Doctor might bite it off. "Katharine Devlin, sir," she said. The Doctor had just touched the hand when Kat snatched it back and got behind me again. "Stevie didn't invite me, sir. I just come of my own."

"Friends of Stevie's are always welcome," the Doctor answered simply. "Though I think we'll all be much more comfortable in the parlor, don't you?"

I could feel Kat's small breasts rising and falling quickly as she pressed herself against my back. "I think I should go," she said anxiously.

But I held her back. "Kat, it's o-*kay*," I insisted again. "Come on, I want you to tell the Doctor what you told the rest of us. And the detective sergeant's got something he wants to ask you."

Very reluctantly, Kat moved with our group back into the parlor, though she never came out from behind me as we went. Her blue eyes stayed fixed on the Doctor: she'd convinced herself a long time ago that he wasn't on the level, and his kind attitude was only making her more edgy and suspicious. The Doctor went to the mantle and got himself a smoke, offering one to Marcus, then lit up and sat in his chair.

"Please," he said, indicating an old (or, I should say, antique) French settee what was near me and Kat. "Won't you sit down?" He seemed almost as amused by her attitude as I was, but he very decently kept that amusement to himself.

She just nodded once, then sat and fairly broke my arm and neck as she yanked my shirt hard and forced me onto the settee beside her. Shoving up against my side, she let her panicky stare leave the Doctor only long enough to see what the detective sergeants were up to.

"Miss Devlin has brought us some very useful information," Lucius said, handing the photograph to the Doctor. "It seems that she has some acquaintance with Elspeth Hunter."

The Doctor's politeness suddenly grew mixed with excitement, in a way what made his eyes glow hot—which only caused Kat to grow even more nervous when he looked back at her. "Really, Miss Devlin? You know the woman?"

"I don't know what *he's* talkin' about," she answered, giving Lucius a quick jerk of her head. "But if *you* mean Libby Hatch, then yeah, I know her."

"Kat spends some of her time at the Dusters' place," I added, not wanting her to have to explain it. "She says they know Nurse Hunter as 'Libby Hatch' and that she's one of Goo Goo Knox's girls."

"Goo Goo—?" the Doctor said, confused. "Ah, yes! Knox, the strongman of the Dusters. I must say, one can only speculate as to the amount of cocaine that the members of that gang must abuse in order to invent these absurd names."

Kat gave out with a sudden sound that I thought might be alarm, but when I turned to her I found that she was smiling and that the noise had been something like a laugh. For the first time, she looked as though she might be buying that the Doctor was okay.

The Doctor laughed along with her, very encouragingly. "So, Miss Devlin," he said (and I could see that Kat liked being referred to that way), "you say that the woman in this picture is on romantic terms with Knox?"

"She's his special moll just at the moment," Kat answered.

"Indeed?" the Doctor replied.

"And," Lucius added pointedly, "Knox has her home under his personal protection."

"Does he really?" The Doctor looked to Kat again. "For any particular reason that you can think of, Miss Devlin?"

Kat shrugged, and loosened her grip on my arm a bit. "He's a wild one, is that Goo Goo—and from what I seen, so's Libby. They spend a lot of time upstairs in his room. I hear it gets a little crazy sometimes. I also hear that she—well, she—*dances* for him."

" 'Dances'?" the Doctor echoed, a bit confused.

Glancing out the window in some embarrassment, Kat nodded. "You know, sir—*dances*. He'll have the band come up, and play outside his door. And she—dances."

It finally dawned on the Doctor that Kat was talking about something what was known in those days by a number of different terms, but which we now refer to by what it is: the striptease. "I see," the Doctor said quietly. "Do excuse my ignorance, Miss Devlin. I don't mean to be thick-headed."

"Oh, no, sir," she answered, very respectfully. "Ain't no reason why you *should* know. Anyway, like I say, at the moment she's the one of his girls that can really keep up with him—even more than the younger ones. She *works* at it, does that Libby."

"Libby," the Doctor repeated softly, bouncing the knuckle of his fore-finger against his mouth as he weighed it. "Libby . . ." He turned to the detective sergeants. "An alias?"

Marcus considered it with a little shrug. " 'Libby' could be a diminutive version of 'Elspeth'—it's likely she had or has one, as 'Elspeth' is fairly ar-chaic."

"Hatch could be her maiden name," Lucius added. "She's using it in sit-uations where she doesn't want to be identified. You're not going to get many nursing jobs if it gets around that you're—*dancing* for Goo Goo Knox. But there's a more important consideration here, Doctor." Lucius approached him, glancing briefly at Kat. "There are two things we need to do at this juncture, forensically. We need to prove that the child is in Nurse Hunter's home, and we need to demonstrate that Nurse Hunter was in fact responsible for the attack in Central Park." He gave Kat another look and a very friendly smile. "I believe that Miss Devlin can help us with both things."

Kat turned to me, speaking quietly. "*Stevie* . . . you said there wasn't gonna be no trouble . . ."

"There ain't, Kat," I answered quickly. "Not for you."

"Then what's all this about a kid, and an 'attack'?"

" 'All this' is nothing in which you need fear you will be implicated, Miss Devlin," the Doctor tossed in from his chair. "The detective sergeants are investigating a case. We are providing them with some help. Our motives are that simple."

Grunting a little as she turned back to the Doctor, Kat took on a defiant look. "I don't want to get mixed up in any police investigation," she said. "Especially not if it's got to do with Goo Goo. He'd as soon beat somebody half to death as look at 'em, even when he *ain't* blowin' the burny."

"There might," Marcus said, what you could call delicately, "be a rather substantial consideration involved, Miss Devlin."

Kat squinted at him. "You mean—like money?" Marcus nodded. "Money don't do you much good in the hospital. And not when you're at the bottom of the river, neither."

"And if it were enough money to ensure that you never had to return to Hudson Street again?" the Doctor asked.

Kat's face went blank. "How could that be? If I cross the Dusters, even just one tiny bit, there won't be a place in this city I can hide."

The Doctor shrugged. "Are you so attached to life in this city? Perhaps you have family in some other part of the country?"

"And I assure you, we wouldn't be asking you to do anything dangerous," Lucius said.

"*Everything*'s dangerous, when you're dealing with that bunch," Kat answered quickly. Then she eyed the Doctor again. "I got an aunt. Lives in San Francisco—she's an opera singer."

"Really?" the Doctor said enthusiastically. "They have a most promising company. Is she a soprano? A mezzo?"

"An *opera singer*, is what she is," Kat answered, not knowing what in the world the Doctor was talking about, and looking it. "She sent me a letter once, after my papa died, saying she could get me work as a singer, too. I can sing—Stevie's heard me."

Kat turned to me, expecting some support. I just nodded hard and said, "Oh, yeah, she can sing, all right," even though I'd never thought that much of her voice. But I got a tin ear, and always have had; so I can't say, maybe she *could* sing.

"Well, then," the Doctor said, "one ticket to San Francisco—by rail or by sea, whichever you choose—and, say, a few hundred dollars to—*acclimate* yourself." I'd never seen Kat's eyes grow so big. "All in exchange for—" The Doctor suddenly stopped and turned to Lucius in confusion. "Detective Sergeant, what the devil *is* all that in exchange for?"

Lucius turned to Kat again, maintaining his smile. "A garment with buttons," was all he said.

Kat stared at him, her mouth hanging open. "A garment? You mean, like *clothes*?"

"Clothes might do," Lucius answered. "An outer garment would be best, though. Something she would be sure to wear in her own house, as well as at the Dusters'. And on the street, too, if possible. A coat or jacket of some kind would really be ideal."

"I get it," Marcus said, slapping his forehead. "Of course!"

Kat looked at the pair of them like they were even crazier than she'd first thought. "A coat or jacket," she said.

"With buttons," Lucius answered, nodding.

"With buttons," Kat said, nodding along. "Any particular *kind* of buttons?"

"Large ones would be best. The larger the better."

"And flat, if possible," Marcus added.

"Yes," Lucius agreed. "Exactly."

Kat stared at them for a few seconds, then opened her mouth to speak. Unable to find words right away, she turned to me, then back to them; and the blue eyes narrowed as her mouth curled into a slight smile. "Let me see if I'm gettin' this. You want me to lift one of Libby Hatch's jackets or coats. One with big, flat buttons. And for that, you'll give me a ticket to San Francisco and a few hundred bucks to set myself up?"

"That," the Doctor said, himself looking a bit uneasily at the Isaacsons, "*is* apparently what *we* are offering."

Kat turned to me again. "They serious, Stevie?"

"Generally," I answered with a smile. The thought of Kat leaving town didn't set me up much, that was true; but the idea of her getting away from Ding Dong, the Dusters, and all that went with that life outweighed any other consideration. "Come on, Kat," I urged. "Lifting a *coat*? You could do it in your sleep."

She slapped my leg hard. "Ain't no reason to tell the *world* that, Stevie Taggert," she scolded quietly. Then she looked back to the others and stood up. "All right, boys—uh, gentlemen. You got yourselves a deal. It may take me a day or two—"

"The sooner the better," Dr. Kreizler answered, standing and extending a hand. "But a day or two should be fine."

Kat shook his hand, much less skittishly this time, then smiled wide. "Well!" she said. "I'd best get about it, then!" Turning to me, she took on a bit of a coy air, playacting like she had in the kitchen. "Stevie—will you—" She stopped, realizing she didn't know the words.

"Show you out," I finished for her. "Yeah, sure."

The Doctor pulled out a few dollars and handed them to me. "See her to a hansom on the corner, Stevie." He bowed to Kat. "It's been a pleasure meeting you, Miss Devlin. And I look forward to the successful conclusion of our business together." He glanced at Lucius once more. "Whatever that business may turn out to be . . ."

I took Kat's arm, and we headed out of the house.

Once on the sidewalk and moving toward Second Avenue, she began to jump around like a four-year-old. "Stevie!" she near screamed. "I'm goin' to California! Can you believe it? Can you imagine it? *Me,* in San Francisco!"

"You really got an aunt's an opera singer?" I asked, as she came close to strangling me by throwing her arms around my neck.

"Well, practically," Kat answered. "She works in the opera house, anyways. And she'll *be* a singer someday, she told me."

"Unh-hunh," I said, not completely convinced. "She ain't no floozy, is she, Kat?"

"No, she ain't no floozy, thank you, Stevie," Kat answered. "And I ain't gonna be either—not no more! My life's gonna change, Stevie, *change*—and alls I gotta do is steal a jacket from Libby Hatch! Steal a jacket from a woman what has trouble keepin' her clothes *on,* from all I can tell!"

We'd reached the corner—directly across the avenue from the New York Lying-in Hospital, I noted—and as I hailed a hansom, Kat's face screwed up one more time. "Whatta you suppose they want such a thing for, Stevie? The Doctor and them two fellas? They's strange birds, those two, for cops."

"I don't know," I said, suddenly realizing that in fact I *didn't* know. "But I'm gonna go find out." I turned to her as she opened the little door of the hansom. "You'll be okay, Kat? I mean, about Ding Dong and all?"

"*Him?*" she answered. "He'll be lucky if he even *sees* me before I pull this off. Let him have his little twelve-year-olds—I'm goin' to California!"

"You'd better write to your aunt first," I advised. "Make sure she's still there, and that it's all okay."

"I already thought of that," Kat answered, stepping off the curb. "I'm gonna do it tonight." She paused before boarding the hansom to give me a hug. "Thanks, Stevie," she whispered into my ear. "You're a friend, and that's the truth." Pulling back, she glanced at the Doctor's house once more. "And you was right about your boss—he's a decent soul, sure enough. Though he *looks* like one of the Devil's own, that I *will* say!"

I wanted badly to kiss her, but she hopped into the cab, waving the few dollars I'd passed along to her up at the driver. "Hudson Street, cabbie—and take your blasted time, I wanna enjoy the ride!"

The cabbie cracked his whip, Kat gave me a little wave, and then she turned around to take in the avenue. She looked for all the world like she owned the city—and that made me smile.

I turned and ran back to the house as the cab disappeared, wanting to know what in the world the detective sergeants had been talking about.

CHAPTER 20

C oming back into the house, I almost ran headlong into Dr. Kreizler, who was standing outside his small examination room holding the paregoric bottle what I'd left in the kitchen. He launched into a bit of a lecture about my taking it on myself to dispense narcotics: it seemed that paregoric was an opiate, which explained why it was so effective on both colicky babies and the desperate Kat. I told him I had no idea it was so strong, being as anybody could buy it just about anywhere. He answered that he understood why I'd been driven to make use of it, given Kat's condition (which he, like the detective sergeants, had quickly detected); still, he didn't want me taking any more medicines out of the examination room without his permission, as he didn't much like the thought that he'd have to start locking stuff up.

This deserved but no less unpleasant lecture was cut short by the sound of the doorbell. Its two tones, produced by a small electricity-driven hammer striking a pair of long pipes in the vestibule, were particularly loud, given as we were so close, and they startled both myself and the Doctor. He sealed up the paregoric bottle tight, then put it into his examination room and said only, "I hope we understand each other, Stevie." I assured him that we did, and then he headed for the vestibule.

Before he'd even opened the front door, I could hear Miss Howard's protesting voice coming through its thick wood. She was answered by a couple of low, mumbling words from Mr. Moore, and then Miss Howard broke into protests again. When the Doctor opened the front door, she dashed through the vestibule and into the hall, looking flushed and annoyed but smiling a bit despite herself.

"Stop it, John, the job's done. You don't have to go on."

Mr. Moore came loping in, giving Miss Howard a lusty look what seemed to be only half serious. "I don't care," he said. "Two hours in that hole, I'm going to make you pay—"

The Doctor looked at them both in bewilderment. "It's a bit late for spring fever, Moore. What the devil are you up to?"

"You don't have a sedative, do you, Doctor?" Miss Howard said. "Apparently John decided this morning that if he behaved like a disgusting pig while we were at the Hall of Records he might be released from his assignment. He's been at me all morning—"

"Oh, I haven't even started," Mr. Moore said, making a move at Miss Howard. "You don't know what disgusting *is* yet, Sara . . ."

"Moore," the Doctor said, grabbing his friend lightly by the collar, "I should have thought such idiocy beneath even you. Kindly pull yourself together. We've had important developments, and now that you're here, we can all go down to Number 808 and review them together."

"All right," Mr. Moore said, his eyes fixed on Miss Howard. "I can wait."

She just turned and looked into the big mirror that hung in the front hall, securing her hair more tightly at the back of her head as she did. "I'm afraid I really will have to shoot you one day, John. Do you still have the diagram?"

"Yes, yes," Mr. Moore answered, finally dropping the act and standing up straight. He produced a folded piece of paper from inside his jacket. "Two hours, Kreizler, in that musty old tomb—did you know they used to keep prisoners there during the Revolution? And all we come away with is a blasted pencil sketch. Still—I suppose it might've taken us two *days*."

"Then you found something," the Doctor said, ignoring Mr. Moore's whining. "Records?"

"Only a copy of the permit," Mr. Moore answered. "The plans themselves have—quite mysteriously, of course—disappeared."

The Doctor looked from Mr. Moore to me, his satisfaction and excitement obvious. "Well—interesting developments on all fronts!" He rushed over to the staircase, calling up, "Detective Sergeants! Cyrus! Downtown!" Then he turned to me. "Stevie, will you tend to Gwendolyn and then follow along behind us? We'll walk down Broadway to Number 808, so that the detective sergeants and I can tell these two about your discoveries of this morning."

"Okay," I said, moving to the door to follow the order. "But I want to hear why the detective sergeants want that jacket!"

Miss Howard looked confused. "Jacket?"

The detective sergeants and Cyrus had reached the bottom of the stairs. "Back to Number 808, I take it?" Marcus asked.

"Indeed," the Doctor said. "And quickly."

They all began to file out as I went to the calash, Mr. Moore bringing up the rear at a slow pace. "I don't suppose it's lunchtime yet," I heard him mumble pathetically. "God, I never would've believed that detective work could give you such an appetite. It's no damned wonder so many cops are fat . . ."

I gave Gwendolyn a lighter-than-usual brushing down and stowed the harness and gear without bothering to clean it all, telling myself I'd tend to the job later. Then it was back outside, making sure the carriage house was securely locked, and on down Seventeenth Street toward Broadway, scanning the crowds of Monday-morning workers and shoppers for my friends. I finally caught up to them as they crossed Fourteenth Street from Union Square. My timing was a little slow, though: the Doctor and the detective sergeants had finished telling Kat's story a couple of blocks earlier, and I'd just missed Miss Howard's summary of what she and Mr. Moore had found downtown. She, however, very decently fell out of the pack to give me a quick repetition.

Some two years previous, Elspeth Hunter and her husband, Micah, had indeed applied for and received a permit to do some fairly extensive work on their house, most of it in the basement. But being as the actual records concerning the construction were missing and the copy of the permit didn't go beyond generalities, that was all that we could determine (and lucky to have that much, too). But Miss Howard had sat Mr. Moore down after they learned this and forced him to remember everything he could about said basement, which he'd actually been encouraged by Nurse Hunter to search. Miss Howard figured there had to be some kind of a clue in the area somewhere, so she'd sketched and noted its dimensions and everything that Mr. Moore could remember it containing. Nothing about the place had jumped out at them so far, but it was possible they were overlooking or misinterpreting something what the detective sergeants might think was important.

We'd reached Number 808 Broadway before Lucius began to explain what he wanted with Elspeth Hunter's (or Libby Hatch's) jacket with the

big buttons, and the Doctor decided that we should wait until we got upstairs to grill him about it. Lucius wasn't what you'd call a flamboyant or
vain type of person, but like his brother'd said that night we fetched them
from the Cunard pier, he did enjoy his occasional moment of intellectual
grandstanding; and as we rode up in the elevator, the big smile on his face
made it plain that he was pleased with the fact that none of us (except for
Marcus, of course) had figured out what his plan was. For all that I was
curious, I kind of admired Marcus for not spilling the beans and for giving his kid brother a moment to shine: it was an unusual outward demonstration that, underneath it all, the brothers really were deeply attached to
each other, as they would've had to've been, to have survived their years
of struggling together up through the ranks of the police force.

We got upstairs, and through the front windows of the office I could
see that the clouds beyond the Hudson to the west were thickening, loading up with what looked like might turn into real rain. Everybody
grabbed a seat, and Lucius stood by the big chalkboard, picking up a nib
of chalk and shaking it around in his closed hand just the way the Doctor
liked to do: Lucius had the greatest admiration for Dr. Kreizler, in a kind
of boyish way that sometimes made him seem to want to emulate the man
in small ways as well as big.

Repeating, for Mr. Moore and Miss Howard's benefit, his belief that
what we now required above all was proof that Nurse Hunter had the
Linares baby and had actually attacked the señora in the Park, Lucius proceeded to explain why so simple a garment as a jacket with buttons could
provide such proof. The bit about the buttons, once I'd heard it, was
pretty obvious, and I felt a little like kicking myself for not having thought
of it: the detective sergeants had been able to get a good set of fingerprints
off of the piece of lead pipe they'd found by the Egyptian obelisk, and
they needed a set of Nurse Hunter's for comparison. They hadn't wanted
to actually steal anything from her house, being as she seemed like the
type that would notice if even the smallest trinket was missing. And given
that the Hunter house had turned out to be under Goo Goo Knox's personal protection, it seemed a lucky thing they'd made the choice they had;
but we still needed something that they could lift prints from for comparison. An article of clothing with buttons would suit best, as there weren't
likely to be any prints on the fasteners save her own; and big, flat buttons
would be spacious enough to provide complete images of multiple fin-
gertips.

That left the question of why Lucius wanted a jacket or a coat, something that Nurse Hunter was likely to wear at home and outside. This

question in turn brought us into what was, for the rest of our group, a mysterious new world: hair identification. It seemed that forensic science had progressed to the point where a microscope could be used to determine if a given hair was human or animal and, if it was human, whether it had come from a particular person—provided a sample of the particular person's hair was available for comparison. Now, the little hat what the Doctor'd spotted at the base of the Egyptian obelisk had contained what Lucius was sure were a few of Ana Linares's hairs: baby hair was, it seemed, the easiest kind to identify, being, in Lucius's words, "short in length, rudimentary in character, and possessed of extremely fine pigmentation." So what we needed now was another sample of Ana's hair—one taken directly from an article of Nurse Hunter's clothing—what could be put into the detective sergeant's "comparison microscope," a kind of double-barreled job that would let him study the two samples side by side and make an exact match.

But why, we all wanted to know, had Lucius decided on a jacket or a coat as the best garment to try to collect such a sample from? Didn't it make more sense to try to grab a shirt, or maybe something even a little more intimate? The detective sergeant's answer was clever and worthy of the man. We already knew that Nurse Hunter had taken the baby out, bold as brass, in public; figuring that no one was ever going to nail her for the kidnapping (being as she had no interest in a ransom), she probably enjoyed every chance she got to make the world think that she was capable of having a happy, healthy child of her own. Shirts, skirts, undergarments—all those she wore inside at the Dusters' and God-only-knew where else. And as we now knew that she wasn't exactly put off by close physical contact with a variety of types, those garments would likely contain a large number of hair samples what'd take a lot of time to sort out. And time was pressing us harder: if her experiences at the Lying-in Hospital were any measure, it wouldn't be long before Nurse Hunter's proven inability to give infants effective care began to show itself. At that point even a baby like Ana Linares was likely to become a lot more cranky than usual, a condition what would only deteriorate. If Nurse Hunter held the kid responsible for the failure of their relationship (as Dr. Kreizler believed she had in the past and would again), it was only a matter of time before little Ana, too, started having unexplained episodes of labored breathing, the final one of which would result in her death.

And so a coat or, as was more likely during even that comparatively cool June, a jacket: a garment what would immediately be removed whenever Nurse Hunter entered a place where other people congregated, thereby cutting down on the number of hair samples that'd be present, but what she would wear when carrying the baby as she'd done on the Third Avenue El: tight, close to her bosom.

It was a slick piece of reasoning; and as Detective Sergeant Lucius finished it up, we all, including his brother, gave him a little round of applause. The others were anxious about whether or not Kat would be able to get the article of clothing in question, but I quieted all that nervousness down: without saying as much, I let them know that there wasn't much in the run of everyday items that Kat couldn't lift if she had a good reason.

Then came the question of what to do about Nurse Hunter's basement. Miss Howard posted the diagram she'd made on the wall, and the rest of us went over it closely. The others proceeded to pound Mr. Moore with detailed questions, most of which he couldn't come close to answering, even though he'd had free access to the space.

"I was looking for a baby, for God's sake!" he protested after someone asked him if he'd noticed any areas of concrete or masonry that appeared newer than the rest. "I didn't know I was supposed to be making an archaeological survey. It was a typical basement—it had a furnace, it had some cabinets, some garden tools, and a dirt floor. I think there was a rack of preserves, too, though I wouldn't swear to it. And the usual, you know, artifacts of domestic living: old pieces of furniture, a few picture frames . . ."

"And this was the arrangement of it all?" the Doctor asked, studying the diagram.

"That's it."

The Doctor made a noise of disappointment. "There's certainly nothing remarkable in any of that. The key, I should think, will be to find the contractor who did the work."

"Oh." Miss Howard looked up, her eyes going wide like maybe something'd gotten by her that she hadn't realized she'd missed. "But—he's dead. We asked."

The Doctor spun on her. "He's *what*?"

"Dead," Mr. Moore threw in simply. "Died right after the job was finished. Apparently, he was a friend of the clerk we spoke to at the Hall of Records. Did a lot of research work down there."

The Doctor began to rub his temples. "Did the clerk happen to say what he died *of*?"

"He did," Mr. Moore answered, absentmindedly rummaging through his pockets and coming out with an old piece of wrapped butterscotch. "Ahh—sustenance!"

"Moore," the Doctor said impatiently.

"Hmm? Oh, right. The contractor. Got his name right here—it was on the permit." He pulled out a scrap of paper as he sucked noisily on the butterscotch. "Henry—Bates. His office was in Brooklyn. Anyway, he had a massive heart attack a couple of days after he finished the Hunter job. And I don't blame him. Working for that lady'd give me a heart attack, too."

The Doctor just shook his head in his hand, sighing. Miss Howard grew ever more nervous as she watched him. "Do you think it's important, Doctor?"

He lifted his head, pulling at the skin under his eyes with his fingers. "It does strike me as an odd coincidence, yes."

"We've already had one coincidence on this case," Mr. Moore announced, waving a careless hand. "You can't take stock in *too* many of them."

"I shouldn't take stock in *any* of them, Moore," the Doctor thundered back, "were they in fact coincidences! Marcus, I suggest that you find out what you can about a contractor named Henry Bates in Brooklyn. It may well be that he had a family."

"And they'll know his medical history," Marcus said, noting the name on a pad with a nod.

Miss Howard clutched at her forehead. "Of course. Dammit . . ."

"What the hell are you all getting so worked up about?" Mr. Moore asked; and I'm bound to say that even *I* thought he was being a little dim at that point. "So the man had a heart attack. So what?"

"Moore," the Doctor said, trying to be as patient as possible. "Do you happen to remember Dr. H. H. Holmes, the mass murderer whose existence caused your grandmother so much distress last year?"

"Of course I do," he said. "Who doesn't? Killed who knows how many people in that 'torture castle' of his."

"Precisely," the Doctor answered. "The 'torture castle.' A seemingly unending maze of secret rooms and chambers, each designed by Holmes himself to serve some horrendously sadistic purpose."

"Well?" Mr. Moore asked. "What's that got to do with this?"

"Do you know the first thing that Holmes did once the castle was completed?"

Mr. Moore's face stayed simple. "Killed somebody, I'd imagine."

"Correct. He killed the one person on earth besides himself who knew the exact plans of the place."

Finally, Mr. Moore's noisy smacking of the butterscotch came to an end. "Uh-oh . . ." He looked up slowly. "That wouldn't have been—"

"Yes," the Doctor answered quietly. "His contractor."

Glancing from one of our faces to the next, Mr. Moore suddenly stood up. "I'm going to Brooklyn," he said, racing toward the front door before any real abuse could be shoveled onto him.

"I'm going with you," Marcus said, following. "The badge may come in handy."

"We need the *exact* cause of death!" the Doctor called after them as they closed the elevator grate. "As well as any details of the job that he may have shared with his family, should he have had one!"

The front door banged closed, and the rest of us were left to listen as the Doctor mumbled in discouragement, "I ought to've known better. It's hard enough to keep John's mind focused in the cold weather, but in the summer . . ." He paused, and looked at the diagram on the wall again. "The basement," he repeated softly. "The basement . . ."

Miss Howard came over to stand by him. "I really am sorry, Doctor. I was the one who should have thought of it."

The Doctor attempted to be gracious. "I doubt that it's cost us too much time, Sara," he said. "And even if we do discover some terrible secret about the construction of this basement, the question remains, what can we do about it? A direct approach by the police, given Señor Linares's attitude, is ruled out, not only because of the danger to the señora but because of diplomatic privilege, as well. The denizens of Mulberry Street, even if we could convince them to investigate the matter, would never defy the wishes of a foreign dignitary. And the dangers to our own group of returning to the house are now clearly evident—one word from Elspeth Hunter, and we should find ourselves, as Miss Devlin said, at the bottom of the river. And then there is the question of our unidentified friend with his arrows and knives . . ."

"Were you able to discover anything about all that?" Lucius asked.

"I received pieces of an answer," the Doctor said. "To which it is necessary to add a conjecture—a rather bizarre conjecture—in order to obtain a likely answer. We are presented with two weapons. The first, as you said, Detective Sergeant, is the well-known trademark of the pirates, mercenaries, and simple thieves who haunt the Manila waterfront. The second is more obscure—an aboriginal weapon, as we surmised, one which, if judged by its small size alone, we could do no more than identify as originating with one of the pygmy tribes of either the southwestern Pacific, Africa, or South America. It is the strychnine that permits us to be more specific—it is known to be used in this way only by the natives of Java."

"Java?" Lucius said. "But Java's in the Dutch East Indies—far to the southwest of the Philippines. It wouldn't seem to match with the *kris*."

"True, Detective Sergeant," the Doctor answered. "But you must bear in mind what the waterfront of Manila is—a stewpot of everything violent and criminal from as far away as Europe, San Francisco, and China. An habitué of the place is likely to become familiar with weaponry from much farther away than Java—and if he is ethnically predisposed toward a particular weapon, the chances are all the greater that he will adopt it."

"What do you mean?" Miss Howard asked.

The Doctor finally turned and walked away from the diagram. "In certain isolated parts of the Philippines—the northern part of the island of Luzon, for instance, and the Bataan Peninsula—there exist small groups of aboriginal pygmies. The Spanish and Filipinos call them 'Negritos'; their own tribal name is 'Aëtas.' They are the oldest residents of the islands, thought to have crossed over from the Asian mainland when there was still an ice bridge over that part of the Pacific. They are quite negroid in their features"—the Doctor looked to me and Cyrus—"and their average height is about four and a half feet. Which might make them appear, at a distance—"

Cyrus nodded. "To look like a ten-year-old boy, in this country."

"Precisely."

Miss Howard suddenly gave out with a gasp. "My God," she whispered.

The Doctor turned to her. "Sara? You have, I suspect, recalled something from one of your conversations with Señora Linares?"

"Yes," she answered blankly, not bothering to ask how the Doctor'd guessed. "Her husband—he comes from an old diplomatic family. When he was a young man, his father was posted to the governor-general's office—in *Manila* . . ."

The Doctor only nodded. "On the island of Luzon. There *had* to be a connection. The Aëtas are outcasts in Filipino society. If one of them should, for whatever reason, have found himself in Manila, virtually the only place where his presence would have been tolerated would have been on the waterfront. He would have brought with him the aboriginal hunting and warring skills of his people—and, in all likelihood, picked up other methods of combat necessary for his survival. At the same time, like many aborigines, the Aëtas place a high premium on loyalty. Should such a man ever have been employed or befriended by someone in a position of power . . ." He turned to Miss Howard. "It will be for you, Sara, to contact Señora Linares somehow, and determine whether or not her husband ever had such a man in his employ."

"It won't be easy," Miss Howard said. "She's being watched very carefully, day and night."

"Then we must be creative," the Doctor answered. "But we must know. This mysterious little man's behavior has been marked by two apparently contradictory intentions—we must find out why, so that we can determine when or if we are likely to encounter him again." As he crossed back to the sketch on the wall, his voice grew discouraged again. "None of which, I fear, solves the problem of this bloody basement. . . . How do we get in? And once in, how do we discover what she's created there, and if, in fact, she is keeping the child within it?"

Lucius grunted. "There aren't many times that I'd advocate the department's usual methods," he mumbled. "But in this case—what I wouldn't give to break the door in and get down there with a good old-fashioned bloodhound, to smell the baby out."

Everyone fell silent for a minute or two. I just sat there in my windowsill, knees tucked up under my chin, waiting for one of them to come up with a more practical idea. In such a state of mind, it took a few minutes for me to notice a small noise: Cyrus, gently clearing his throat in, it seemed, my direction. I looked over to find him staring at me, raising his eyebrows in an expression that appeared to say, "*Well . . . ?*" I had no idea what he meant by the look, and I wrinkled my eyebrows and hunched my shoulders to tell him so. At that point he looked to the others, making sure they were still staring at the diagram, and then wandered over to me, leaning on the window frame and looking outside so that what he said couldn't be seen or overheard.

"You still know that boy downtown?" he mumbled, casually putting an arm on the window frame and a hand across his mouth. "The one with the animal?"

For a minute I was bewildered, and even when I realized who he was talking about, it didn't clear much up for me. "Hickie the Hun?" I said. "Sure, I still know him, but—"

"And you've seen the woman's house," Cyrus said. "Figure you could crack it?"

It was a little shocking to be asked such a thing—I mean, I was supposed to have forgotten all about such matters. "*That* joint?" I finally answered. "Yeah, of course, but—"

Cyrus finally looked dead at me. "This is *your* play, Stevie. If you want to make it . . ."

He wandered away again, leaving me a little stunned. I whispered, "But, Cyrus—" after him urgently; urgently enough to cause the Doctor to turn around.

"Stevie?" he said. "Do you have something to contribute?"

Turning quickly, I shook my head innocently. "No, sir."

Cyrus mumbled, "Yes, you do," toward the wall.

"No, I *don't*," I said out of the side of my mouth.

"Okay," he answered. "If that's how you want it . . ."

"What is it?" the Doctor asked, perplexed. "Stevie, if you have some notion of how to break this deadlock, then please . . ." He held his hand toward the diagram.

I didn't move right away, just sat there and ran the thing through my head. Then I groaned and stood up. There wasn't much else to do. After all, I'd played a part in talking the Doctor into trying to save the Linares baby; and I figured, as I dragged myself across the room, that if I did know a way to take the next step, I owed it to the man to come across. So, shooting Cyrus a little look that said "Thanks for nothing"—to which he only smiled wide—I joined the other three at the diagram.

"Uhh," I noised, not sure just where to start. "You—uh—might not have to do it the way Detective Sergeant Lucius says. I mean, you might be able to get the same job done without all the noise." I pointed to the diagram. "If what you're saying is that the baby's scent oughtta be detectable in the basement, even if we don't know just where the Hunter woman's got her locked up—well, then, you might not have to bust in with cops and a bloodhound to find out. Did anybody notice what was on the back windows of the house?"

"Yes," Lucius said. "I made a special note. They've had bars installed. Not too thick, but spaced at narrow intervals."

"So you'd need a spreader," I answered.

Lucius nodded. "Yes, but even if you had one, it'd be hard to create an opening big enough for a person."

"You mean, for an *adult* person," I said. "That's how they generally set them bars. But . . ."

The Doctor looked at me, and it seemed like he couldn't decide whether to be excited or stern. "Stevie—are you suggesting that *you* could get inside?"

I nodded with what you might call extreme reluctance. "There's some stables right next door to the house. I noticed that much. Good place to hide out and then move from. Spread the bars, get inside, and go check out the basement. If we find the kid, I can bring her out."

"And what would you find her *with*?" Lucius asked.

Shrugging, I answered, "I got a friend—" I felt the Doctor's eyes on me. "I *had* a friend, anyway. Kid who does second-story jobs, like I used to. We call him Hickie the Hun, 'cause he claims his family were German aristocrats, way back. They weren't, though—Dutch, something like that. Anyways, he's got this trained ferret. Name's Mike. Hickie keeps him in a sack on jobs. Mike can get through all kinds of narrow openings." I pointed at the diagram again. "And I could get him in there. Got a hell of a nose, does that animal."

"But how does it know what it's looking for?" Miss Howard asked.

"Hickie's got this trick," I told her. "He puts something that either looks or smells like what he's trying to lift into Mike's cage and don't feed him until he learns to fetch it. It don't take too long, generally. A few days."

Lucius pondered the matter for a minute, then looked to Dr. Kreizler. "Doctor," he said, his voice making it clear that he understood the risk but was excited, anyway. "This could work."

"Wouldn't we have to find a way to get the Hunters out of the house, though?" Miss Howard asked.

"Just the wife," I answered. "And if she's spending time with Goo Goo Knox, well . . . all we gotta do is wait for her to leave some night. I don't guess her husband takes care of the kid, if he's as bad off as you all say. So she probably stows the baby while she's out. I'd go in through the ground floor—the kitchen, probably. After that, straight to the basement. They sleep on the top floor, right? We heard the husband while we were outside."

"That's right," Lucius said quickly.

"So it'd be pretty simple to pull it off while he was there. I done that kind of thing plenty of times. Not with a kid, maybe, but how much different than a sack of goods can a kid be?"

There wasn't much more to say about the actual job, so I knew what was coming next: the Doctor said, "Would you both excuse us, please?" and took me by the shoulder toward the back of the room. There he folded his arms and looked at me for a second; then he turned away and stared out the window.

"Stevie, there is a great deal about this plan that makes me uncomfortable."

"Me, too," I said. "You got another idea, I'm all for it."

"That's just the problem," he answered. "We don't. And you know that."

"Yeah. But *I* didn't think of it to start with, Cyrus did. Anyway, it don't—it doesn't have to be such a big deal. You give me one of the detective sergeants to keep watch, and if we've got the calash ready in the stable, we oughtta be fine. A gun and a badge'll take care of anybody but the Dusters, and by the time they find out what's going on, if they ever do, we'll be long gone."

There wasn't any way, of course, that the Doctor was ever going to be happy about me either putting myself in danger or going back to my old thieving ways; but he knew, to judge from the look on his face, that we didn't have any choice. The fact that Miss Howard and Detective Sergeant Lucius were all for the idea only put the icing on the thing. And so by two o'clock I found myself once again heading down into my old neighborhood, to try to locate Hickie the Hun and his ferret, Mike.

CHAPTER 21

I figured to find Hickie swimming somewhere down by the East River waterfront, even on what was, for New York, a cool summer's afternoon: the kid was as fond of water as a fish. On top of that, where there were ships there was cargo, and the best way to case the docks was to take an innocent swim and see what they had to offer. Not that shipping freight was Hickie's usual target; like I've said, he was a second-story man, a housebreaker, good enough at his trade to operate independent of any single gang, but respected enough to be able to join forces with whichever group suited him for a given job. All in all, he was a bit of a loner, was Hickie—except when it came to animals. He lived in an abandoned basement on Monroe Street, north of the Brooklyn Bridge, with a whole collection of dogs, cats, squirrels, snakes, raccoons, and nobody-ever-knew what else. The only animal he wouldn't keep was a rat, and he trained his other pets to keep his house clear of them, too. You see, when he was just two or three years old, Hickie's mother and father, who'd been immigrant cigar makers in a tenement on Eldridge Street, had been robbed and shot to death, and it had been more than twenty-four hours before anyone had discovered the crime and the young boy who'd survived it: plenty of time for the rats to set to work on the bodies. Seeing his own folks get halfway eaten by the things was enough to set Hickie on a lifelong campaign to kill every rat he saw—which, in a city like New York, meant that he was never at a loss for something to do.

Sure enough, that afternoon Hickie was down behind the Fulton Fish Market—a big, clapboarded building with three little towers what they called "cupolas"—swimming naked with a few other boys. A couple of cargo schooners and a paddle steamer were docked in the river near the swimmers, along with the Fulton Ferry, the station of which stood next to the fish market. A couple of the littler kids were taking dives off the bowsprits of the schooners, and coming within an ace of breaking their necks on the docks, too. But nobody seemed to care, least of all Hickie, who oftentimes told me that so far as he was concerned, any kid left to swim unattended in a river with currents as dangerous as them in the East was qualified to decide when and where he'd bust his own head open.

I made my way through all the smelly, noisy huckstering that was going on outside the fish market, then crawled down around the bottom of the building to where the kids were splashing in and out of the eternally shadowy, roiling waters below.

"Hey, Hickie!" I called, seeing his head bobbing up from under the surface. "You wanna die of pneumonia, you found the right way to do it!"

He gave me a grin, showing a big gap in his front teeth what had been left by two cops. "What're ya thayin', Thtevie?" he answered, his *s*'s getting lost in the gap. "Ith a *perfeck* day for a thwim!"

"Come on out," I answered. "I got a business proposition for you!"

Whipping his black hair back on his head, he began to swim, quickly and expertly, over to where I was sitting. "Well, there'th thwimmin', and then there'th buthineth," he said, shooting up out of the water in a pale white flash and running over to his little pile of clothes. He dried himself off with a rag that might've been a towel once, then got dressed in a hurry. "How've you been, Thtevie? I ain't theed you round for a bit."

"Ain't *been* around," I said, noticing that Hickie's voice had gotten lower. He was probably a year or two older than me, but small for his age. "Workin'. The legitimate life, you know, it tends to keep you busy."

"And becauth of *that,* I thtay away from it," Hickie said, now covered up in an old shirt, wool trousers, and suspenders. He pulled on a beat-up pair of shoes and shook hands with me, then slipped a miner's cap onto his head so that it slouched over one eye. "If I couldn't walk away for a thwim whenever I felt the urge, I wouldn't thee the thenth in life. Whath on your mind, old thon?"

I picked up a few rocks and started tossing them into the river. "You still got Mike?"

"Mike?" Hickie said, like I just mentioned a member of his family. "Thure, I got Mike! Couldn't get rid o' Mike, Thtevie, he's my boy—born rat-killer, ith that Mike."

"You ever hire him out?"

"Hire him out?" Hickie folded his arms, put his hand to his chin, and touched a finger to his nose as he considered it. "No . . . no, I don't believe I ever have conthidered it. Don't know ath I'd feel right about it, thomehow. Mike'th hith own man, you know."

He was dead serious; and there was no sense in anybody trying to tell Hickie that animals were just animals. "Well, I could use his services," I said. "For a week, maybe. And the pay'd be top dollar."

Hickie's finger kept tapping at his nose. "A week? Well . . ." He suddenly brightened up. "What thay we go an' athk him? If Mike taketh to you, Thtevie, that'll be a thign that he wanth the work—and thuch bein' the cathe, far be it from me to thtand in hith way!"

I watched Hickie start to march off in the direction of the hovel he called home, like the pint-sized captain of criminal industry he was; and as I fell in alongside him, I allowed as the kid would enjoy a brilliant future, so long as he could stay one step ahead of the long arm.

We caught up on each other's doings during the walk to Hickie's home on Monroe Street, which was in one of the oldest and worst sections of shantytown in the city. Hickie's building, like most around it, was a decrepit wooden deal, a leftover from the last century or thereabouts; and what he called a "basement" was really more like a cave. We reached it by going round to a back alley—which was thick with ash heaps and laundry that'd been hung out to dry—and then heading down an old set of stone steps into a dirt-floored space below. The joint was dark, save for the barely detectable light of a high, filthy window at the front—but that didn't stop a collection of dogs from starting to bark as soon as they heard us coming. Once we were inside, Hickie lit a kerosene lamp, and as soon as he did, the place jumped to life: not only dogs yapping and leaping around, but cats scurrying away from the dogs and hissing at them, and dozens of other, smaller animals moving around in ways what made it seem like the walls themselves were alive. Hickie greeted them all with great enthusiasm, a process that took some time, while I just waited cautiously, not sure which of the beasts were dangerous to outsiders and which were okay.

Past the few pieces of furniture that Hickie owned there was an old sink with a bucket of garbage underneath it, the contents of which had been strewn around the room—and out of which soon appeared a medium-sized raccoon, what gave Hickey a very guilty look.

"Willy!" Hickie shouted, moving for the garbage pail at a speed that made it tough (but not impossible) for the raccoon to escape up the sink's single water pipe. "How many timeth doth I got to tell you, no more garbage!" He looked up the pipe to the blinking, clinging animal. "You act like you don't ever get fed, you ungrateful little—"

I had to laugh. "Hickie, he's a raccoon, for Pete's sake, what do you expect?"

Hickie's hands went to his hips, and he continued to stare the animal down. "I exthpect him to act with a little common courtethy and gratitude, or he'll find himthelf thleeping in the alleyway—*that'th* what I exthpect!" He went farther toward the front of the room and lit another lamp, carrying it with him. "I named him after the Kaither Wilhelm, that one, but he don't wathte any time bein' imperial, he don't . . ." Hickie signaled for me to join him; and as I noticed that a sizable snake was making for my feet, I decided to brave the other animals and enter the deeper reaches of the room. "Now, then," Hickie said, climbing up onto a huge pile of old trunks, "come and thay hello to Mike."

In the darkness I could make out a large, framed structure on top of the trunks, and when Hickie held the lamp up I could see that it was a cage, made out of some old two-by-twos and chicken wire. Inside the cage a long, lean shadow was whipping around in agitated motions, with an equally long, fluffy tail following behind. "Mike!" Hickie finally got high enough to set the lamp down and then sit on one of the trunks next to the cage. "Mike, I've brought an old friend to pay hith rethepecth and offer you a propothithun—why, *Mike*!" Hickie's face suddenly cracked into a big grin, the gap in his teeth standing out all the more. "Thtevie! Willya look at thith!"

Off of the top of the cage, Hickie lifted a dead rat by its tail. There were bite and claw marks all over the thing, and a big tear in its throat. "What'd I tell you?" Hickie shouted, overjoyed. "Got the bathtard clear through the wire, he did! There'th none to compare to old Mike, when it cometh to rat-killin'!" Overjoyed past words, Hickie threw the rat to the floor, opened the cage, and reached inside, bringing out the two-foot-long, grey-and-white ferret. The animal's little black eyes locked on Hickie's face with what seemed like recognition: he rolled onto his back in Hickie's lap, and then shot up and around his master's shoulders in one long, streaking movement, like he'd been poured out of a bottle. Hickie laughed out loud, and then the ferret jumped back into his lap, scratching behind his rounded ears and at his pointed nose with his short front paws. The animal looked my way, the little daggers of his sharp upper teeth showing over the fur of his lower jaw. "Tickle *me,* willya, Mike, my boy?" Hickie shouted, rubbing the ferret's stomach with real affection and enthusiasm.

"Then I'll return the favor!" But the ferret only seemed to enjoy the rubbing, and after a few seconds he grew calm enough for Hickie to pick him up. "Come on, Thtevie, come on up and get to know Mike proper!" He looked into the ferret's eyes. "Now, Mike, thith ith Thtevie Taggert, who you've theen before, though you've never been properly introduthed. Thtevie—Mike." And before I knew it, he'd placed the animal against my chest, causing me to clutch him close. "What do you think, Mike?"

The ferret stared up at me for just a second, then suddenly flipped over and scurried up my arm, his sharp claws piercing my shirt and pricking lightly into my skin. It was a disturbing feeling, at first—not really painful, but strange; and in just a few seconds, the ferret's quick movements around my neck and shoulders lightened up to the point where they did, in fact, tickle.

"What—what's he doing, Hickie?" I asked, starting to laugh.

"Why, he'th gettin' to know you, Thtevie. He'th a thtrict judge of character, ith Mike, and he'll thoon dethide how he feelth about you!"

Mike ran down my other arm, jumped off onto one of the trunks for a second, then scurried back into my lap. Sniffing at my shirt with his ever-twitching nose, he stuck his head between two of my buttons—and then suddenly vanished inside. I took a deep breath of shock as I felt warm fur and cold claws against my bare skin. "Hickie!" I said, half amused and half afraid.

"Oh, thith ith rare, ith what thith ith," Hickie said. "That'th hith mark of deepetht affeckthun. I'd thay you've found yourthelf a partner, Thtevie, old thon!" Hickie clapped his hands and then rubbed them on his legs, obviously pleased as could be that Mike should've taken such a quick liking to me. When the ferret reappeared from inside my shirt, I began to stroke his back with my hand and felt how quickly his heart was beating: like a little steam engine, so fast it seemed it'd explode. Then Mike turned onto his back, allowing me to rub his stomach the way Hickie'd done.

"Mike, Mike, Mike," Hickie said, pretending to disapprove. "I'll not have you playin' cheap, now—remember your dignity, young man!" Laughing at himself, Hickie looked up at me. "You work around hortheth, do you, Thtevie?"

"Yeah," I answered. "We have two, a mare and a gelding. Why, can you smell 'em?"

"No," Hickie said, shaking his head. Then he nodded at Mike. "But he can. Loveth the thmell of hortheth, doth that one. And he'th thure taken to you. Well, then, Thtevie—what'th thith job you mentioned?"

I didn't know just how much of the story to tell Hickie, but I had to let him have the basic details, as I'd need his instructions on how to train Mike for the specific task ahead. So I just mentioned that my employer and I were trying to track down somebody what we had reason to believe was being held in a certain house against their will, inside a locked room. Would Mike be able to detect if the person was in fact in the house, and find the right room? Indeed he would, Hickie said; in fact, it would be a breeze, compared to some of the jobs Mike'd handled in the past. Then I asked about the training, and was surprised to learn how simple it would be: all I'd need would be a piece of clothing from the person I was look- ing for, the more intimate the better, as it would be that much more steeped in the person's scent. Mike was already so well trained that when he began to connect a particular object or smell with his feeding, he quickly got the idea that he was supposed to find something that looked or smelled the same; only a couple of days would be needed to get him ready. It'd be best if I took him to my place for that time, Hickie said, so's he could get fully used to me. I said that I couldn't imagine where that would be any problem, and then asked exactly what I should feed the ac- tive little fellow.

"He'th a car-nee-vore, ith Mike," Hickie said, with the attitude of an ex- pert, "but don't you go thpoilin' him on me. No porterhouth nor lamb chopth—just catch him a few mithe if you can, or, if not, thome jackrab- bit'll do. Three or four timeth a day, during trainin', to let him know what you're drivin' at."

"Do I take him in the cage?"

"Thure, thure," Hickie said, pulling the contraption off the trunks and climbing down with it. "We'll jutht find a bit of cloth to cover it with, for he don't much like the thight of thity traffic." Hickie began to root around in the many piles of junk in his room.

"And what about the money, Hickie? Top dollar, like I said."

Finding himself a piece of an old tarpaulin, Hickie had to battle one of his dogs, a midsized mastiff, for possession of it. "The money? Hmm . . . lemme think—go on, Beauregard, let go a that damned thing!" He finally pulled the tarpaulin away from the dog, and as he came back over to the cage I climbed down with Mike. "Thith ith a firtht, thith ith." Hickie care- fully took Mike out of my arms and held him up to look into his eyes. "You do a good job and keep yerthelf thafe, now, do you hear that?" He kissed the top of Mike's head and slipped him into the cage, then covered it. "Lemme thee . . . he meanth an awful lot to me, doth Mike . . ."

It was pretty obvious Hickie was waiting for me to make him an offer, and I pulled what seemed like a big number out of the air. "How about fifty bucks? For the week?"

Hickie got that glow bargainers sometimes do, when they've been offered more than they expected and figure that because they have, maybe they can do even better. "Make it theventy, Thtevie—thimply to keep my thoul at retht, mind you—and I'll know you to truly be the gentleman what I'd alwayth taken you for."

I nodded once, and we shook on it. "You'll have to come with me, though, to pick up the money," I said. "I ain't got that kind of cash on me."

"And I wouldn't let Mike go without theein' where you're takin' him," Hickie answered. He picked up the cage and indicated the door. "Lead the way, old thon!"

We got back outside and made our way out of the shantytown and over to Park Row, where it was an easy job to catch a hansom uptown. It was a jolly ride, with Hickie full of stories about old friends of ours, Mike the ferret going wild inside the covered cage as he smelled the horse in front of us, and the cabbie wondering what in the world two characters like ourselves could be up to—not to mention what we might be carrying in the strange crate that sat on Hickie's lap.

When we reached the Seventeenth Street house, we found that the Doctor, Cyrus, and Miss Howard had returned—though there was still no sign of Mrs. Leshko, a fact what was beginning to make the Doctor wonder if he shouldn't call the police. (He didn't; and at about 5:30 the woman finally did stumble in, ranting something about Cossacks, the Russian tsar, and her husband. The Doctor just told her to go home and come back in the morning.) Hickie was more than a little impressed at where I'd ended up after all my years of thieving and conning, and I think for a few seconds the sight of the Doctor's house made him wonder if there wasn't some sense to the legitimate life, after all. He made quite an impression on the others, particularly the Doctor, who took an extreme interest in Hickie's homegrown methods of animal training.

"It's really rather remarkable," the Doctor said, after Hickie'd made his good-byes to Mike in my room and then headed back downtown. "Do you know, Stevie, there is a brilliant Russian physiologist and psychologist— Pavlov is his name—whom I met during my trip to St. Petersburg. He is working along similar lines as this 'Hickie'—the causes of animal behavior. I believe he would benefit greatly from a conversation with your friend."

"Not likely," I answered. "Hickie don't much like leaving the old neighborhood, even on jobs—and I don't think he can read *or* write."

Chuckling a bit, the Doctor put an arm on my shoulder. "I was," he said, "speaking rather hypothetically, Stevie . . ."

Mike the ferret's taking up residence in my room presented me with a situation the likes of which I'd never before experienced. Suddenly I had a pet, a roommate, and for the next few days my own activities were pretty well dictated by the need to train and feed the animal. He was a living responsibility, an idea what had never before appealed to me; and yet I found that I didn't half mind it, once I was actually in the situation. In fact, Mike became the center of my attention and—given his lively, affectionate manner—my joy and amusement, too. It ended up taking Miss Howard better than a day to get in touch with Señora Linares, and another day to lay hands on a piece of little Ana's bedclothing; and I spent most of that time either romping around my room with Mike, trying to locate mice in our basement for him, or chatting away to the animal as if I expected answers. I'd seen people behave that way with pets before, but never having had one I'd never understood such conduct; suddenly the appeal was very clear, and as the time went by I found myself deliberately putting thoughts of Mike's departure out of my head.

There were plenty of developments to take my mind off of that prospect. Detective Sergeant Marcus and Mr. Moore did eventually locate the widow of the contractor Henry Bates, and the news they brought back from Brooklyn was disturbing: Bates's wife declared that he'd never had a sick day in his life, and that his heart had been as strong as an ox's. On top of that, he hadn't died a day or two after completing his job for Nurse Hunter—he'd died that very day, some six months ago, and *at* Number 39 Bethune Street. He'd been struck just after taking a cup of tea—fortified with some whiskey—what'd been offered by the mistress of the house. Nurse Hunter herself had apparently reported all this to the coroner, and had gone on to say that Bates's attack had occurred as he picked up a heavy sack of tools on his way out of the house. The coroner had told Mrs. Bates that such things did happen, and that Bates could have had some hidden heart defect that didn't make itself known until the very end. He'd asked Mrs. Bates if she wanted him to do an autopsy to confirm this; but she was a superstitious and fanatically religious woman, who had some strange notions about what would happen to her husband's soul if his heart was removed from his dead body.

This slightly demented attitude made it tougher for Mr. Moore and Marcus to buy the next theory what Mrs. Bates shared with them—that her husband had been seduced by Nurse Hunter—even though they wanted very much to. Her statement that Mr. Bates had been directed by his boss at Number 39 Bethune Street to hire and fire construction crews on a regular basis, on the other hand, seemed to make sense: Nurse Hunter would want as few people as possible to know the complete details of what she was building. The only man who wound up with such knowledge was Mr. Bates; and it was the Doctor and Detective Sergeant Lucius's belief that if we checked around the Hunter household carefully enough, we'd probably find some dried purple foxglove. Nurse Hunter might even have it growing in her yard; wherever she obtained it, the flower—source of the powerful drug digitalis, what could stop even the strongest man's heart—could easily have been mixed into that last fatal cup of tea, and any unusual odor covered up by the smell of whiskey.

This might seem to've been so much of what the Doctor called "hypothetical" thinking—and so, in fact, it was. But nobody who'd ever seen the cold glare that could come into Elspeth Hunter's golden eyes would've doubted for a second that she was capable of such an act. Still, the thought that we were up against somebody we now had good reason to believe had killed not only a whole group of infants but at least one full-grown adult male was more than a little frightening. In fact, it seemed like every day or two we were coming across some new revelation about the woman what proved her to be dangerous in a way we hadn't anticipated. Such didn't make preparing for our break-in to her house any easier. But other than carrying more and bigger firearms, there really wasn't much of a way to improve on the plan itself; and when Miss Howard showed up on Thursday morning with one of Ana Linares's little nightgowns, my part in that plan became more pressing: I now had to spend long hours making sure Mike was properly trained, being as an awful lot was riding on his nose.

Along with the nightgown, Miss Howard brought confirmation of what the Doctor had speculated about during and after his trip to the Museum of Natural History: Señor Linares did in fact have a Filipino aborigine in his employ. He was a spooky little character who gave the señora goose bumps and who she wouldn't allow to sleep in their house, forcing the little man instead to pass his nights out in the yard. The pygmy, known only as "El Niño," had been a Linares family servant for many years, but the señora was unclear about exactly what his duties were—though when Miss Howard told her about our encounters with the man, she was able to put together a much better idea. Miss Howard's revealing this information had only put another strain on the Linares's marriage, which, it seemed, was close to falling apart: the señora'd told Miss Howard that if she hadn't been a good Catholic, she would've already left her husband.

To top all this off, we had the now-daily headlines in the *Times* about the "mystery of the headless body," following the case as it began to dissolve, before the Police Department's helpless eyes, into the kind of boring domestic murder what Detective Sergeant Lucius had originally predicted it would turn out to be. By Tuesday the theory that the victim was one of the escaped lunatics from Long Island had been pretty well exploded, and the police were instead putting up the idea that the deed had been done by the same crazy butcher who had similarly killed and dismembered a young girl, Susie Martin, in a famous case a few years back. This theory, handed to the cops like a Christmas present by the pathologist who'd investigated the Martin case, took all of about two minutes to fall apart: various people with missing loved ones had shown up at the morgue to view the headless body parts, and by Wednesday no fewer than nine of these visitors had positively identified the things as being the remains of one William Guldensuppe, a masseur at the Murray Hill Turkish Baths.

The cops had (reluctantly, I was betting) pursued this lead, and by Thursday they had discovered not only that Guldensuppe had been living for a long time with a lady friend, a certain Mrs. Nack, in a house in Hell's Kitchen, but that said lady friend had recently developed an attachment to another man in their building, Martin Thorn. Guldensuppe, Nack, and Thorn had been seen and heard by other residents of their neighborhood openly fighting about the situation. Mrs. Nack was quickly found by the bulls and given a dose of the old third degree: she confessed, after twenty-four straight hours of brutal treatment, that she and Thorn had killed Guldensuppe together and then chopped up his remains. Thorn, however, was nowhere to be found, and the only way for the police to keep the matter interesting was to set up checkpoints at railroad stations and shipping piers all over the city, and to call for first a cross-country and then an international manhunt.

"He's still here," was Detective Sergeant Lucius's reaction to all the noise coming out of Mulberry Street. "You mark my words, Stevie, the man never left and never will leave this city." Only time, again, would tell; but I wasn't betting against the detective sergeant, that was for sure.

Friday brought word from Kat, saying that she'd secured one of Libby Hatch's jackets and was ready to turn it over; but she had a feeling that maybe Ding Dong knew that she was up to something, so she wanted to make the delivery somewhere other than at the Seventeenth Street house: apparently the Dusters knew I lived and worked there. I told her to bring the jacket that night to Number 808 Broadway, where the detective sergeants had set up their equipment and were ready to perform their tests—tests what would tell us, once and for all, whether Nurse Hunter had taken Ana Linares and was holding her in some deep recess of Number 39 Bethune Street.

CHAPTER 22

Kat showed up just after nightfall, and I went down in the big elevator to fetch her. She was shuffling from foot to foot on the marble floor of the building's lobby, humming a little tune and jerking her body around in time to it. At the elevator's approach she spun to face me, and even from that distance I could tell that she'd been at the burny again.

"Stevie!" she called, with a big, disturbing sort of smile. "I got the goods!" She held up a medium-sized parcel, plain brown paper tied with some twine.

As I dragged the grate open, she jumped inside and threw herself against me, laughing out loud at nothing at all. "Kat," I said, trying not to sound as disappointed—even angry—as I felt, "get a grip on yourself, okay? This is serious."

She frowned, mocking me. "Oh. Sorry, Inspector." Then I closed the grate, and as we started up in the near darkness she threw her arms around me, moving her lips close to my ear. "Want to have another go, Stevie? Right here in the elevator? Been a long time . . ."

I slammed the control handle of the machine into the STOP position, so hard that Kat was jerked away from me. She gave out a little squeal as she fell backward.

"Kat!" I said, still trying to control myself. "Why the hell did you have to show up in this kind of condition?"

The blue eyes turned mean, a meanness made all the worse by the cocaine. "Don't you take that tone with me, Stevie Taggert! Ain't I spent the whole week risking my neck to get you and your friends what you wanted? If I allow myself to celebrate a little, now that it's over, then I hope I can be forgiven by your high-minded self!"

Letting out a frustrated burst of air, I nodded at the package. "Maybe you should just let me take it," I said. "I'll meet you later, bring you the money and the ticket."

"Oh, no," Kat shot back, holding the package away from me. "I know *that* deal! I'm gettin' paid now, and I'm gettin' paid in person! If you're so damned embarrassed by me, don't worry, I won't stick around long! Who'd want to? Bunch of mighty strange types, is what you all are, and I mean to celebrate my good fortune tonight with them what knows how!"

I grabbed the elevator handle and threw the thing back into motion. "All right," I said, "if that's how you want it."

"How *I* want it? That's what *you* want, ain't it?" She faced the elevator grate and tried to fix her hair. "Damn me . . . the airs some people take on, just because they find themselves on the other side of the tracks . . ."

The rest of Kat's visit didn't go much better. Her anger made her keep her words to a minimum, but it was still obvious to me—and, I'm sure, to everybody else—that she was loaded with burny and that hers was no chippy (which is to say, irregular) habit. Oh, she had the goods she'd promised, all right: we opened the parcel up on the billiard table next to the detective sergeants' vials of fingerprint powder and their comparison microscope, and found that it contained one tight-fitting, bloodred satin jacket—with, to order, large, flat black buttons. Kat wanted to get paid right there and then, and her temper wasn't improved when the Doctor said that she'd have to wait for the detective sergeants to verify that the jacket belonged to the woman we knew as Elspeth Hunter. Kat declared that she'd wait for the fingerprinting to be done, but no longer—she couldn't imagine what else we wanted the thing for, and she wasn't going to wait to find out. The deal she'd struck required her to show up with one jacket belonging to Libby Hatch, she said; after we'd all agreed that she'd lived up to her side of the bargain, she'd take her leave. Having said this, she threw herself sullenly into one of the big easy chairs.

The process of lifting the prints didn't take long. The buttons being black, Marcus used a camel's-hair paintbrush to dust them with some fine, grey-white aluminum powder, which he then blew away, revealing a clear set of waving lines what he held up against a photograph of the lead pipe they'd found in Central Park for comparison. Nodding to the Doctor, Marcus said only, "It's a match," at which point Kat, figuring that was her cue, got to her feet and marched up to the Doctor.

"We all square?" she said to him, a little frantically.

The Doctor—who, I could see, was worried by both Kat's physical state and her attitude—attempted to be cordial. "We are indeed all square, Miss Devlin. Can we offer you anything by way of thanks? Some coffee, or tea, perhaps—"

"My money and my ticket," Kat said, holding out a hand. Then she thought to add, "Thank you very much, sir." Looking my way, she narrowed her eyes and spat out, "I wouldn't want to overstay my welcome, or make anybody uncomfortable."

The Doctor glanced from her to me and back again. I think he was on the verge of saying something more, but finally he just nodded and took an envelope from his breast pocket. "Three hundred dollars in cash," he said with a smile, "and one ticket to San Francisco. Valid at any time during the next six months. Oh," he added, as Kat near grabbed the envelope, "and the ticket is for a first-class compartment. To show our appreciation."

That melted her a bit, toward him if not me. "That's—very decent of you, sir. Thank you." She glanced at the envelope and smiled just a little. "I ain't never traveled first class. My papa, he used to say—" Seeming to catch herself, she went rigid again. "I'll be on my way now, sir. If that's all."

The Doctor nodded. "I'm sorry you can't stay." She'd just turned when he added, "Miss Devlin—" He took a business card from another pocket of his jacket and handed it to her. "I operate a—*school,* of sorts, downtown. For young people who want or need to make a change in their lives. Here is the address and the telephone number. Should you ever find yourself in New York again and be interested in such—assistance, please do not hesitate to telephone or stop by."

Kat looked at the card, and her face went wicked again; but she forced herself to smile. "Yeah. I heard about your place, Doctor." She looked up at him. "I heard you ain't runnin' it no more, is what I heard."

At that I stepped in fast. "Kat, come on," I said, pushing her toward the door.

"So who's to say, Doctor," she called over her shoulder, "which one of us needs the—*assistance?*"

I got her wriggling form back into the elevator, slammed the door shut, and closed the grate with a bang. Fairly tearing the control handle off, I started us back down. "You had no call to talk that way," I said through my teeth. "He was only tryin' to help, dammit all, Kat. What's wrong with you? Can't you ever let anybody help?"

"*I don't want nobody's help!*" she hollered back. "I want to take care of *myself*, if that's all right with you!"

"Yeah? Well, you're doin' a hell of a job!"

"Maybe you don't think so—but I ain't no servant, and I ain't yet fallen into the river dead stinkin' drunk! So just leave me alone, can't you, Stevie? Leave me be!" She turned away again, and choked back some tears as she tried to catch her breath. Glancing down at the envelope in her hands, she tore it open. "I'm countin' this," she said, just looking for more ways to sting me. She scooped out the envelope's contents, coming first across the train ticket. "Hunh. First class. Hell, I could sell this and buy *three* tickets . . ." Her eyes made out some small print at the edge of the thing. "What's this—'non . . . transferable . . . non . . . refundable.' What's all that mean?"

I was still pretty hot myself, so I just laid it out: "It means you can't sell it to anybody else and you can't cash it in, that's what it means."

The words were meant to hurt, and it was clear they did. "You mean, if I was lyin' all along about my aunt and just wanted some more money for burny, is that it?"

We'd reached the ground floor. I grabbed the handle of the grate, but before opening it I remembered one last detail. "We need to know when the woman's gonna be at the Dusters'. At night, and for sure."

"All right," Kat answered quietly, her own teeth grinding. "Since that's all you care about. They're havin' a big to-do tomorrow night. It's Goo Goo's birthday. She'll be there. I won't. Can I go now?"

I pulled the grate open for her without answering. She just looked at me and shook her head for a moment, then stormed on out. "Good-bye, Stevie," she said, still fuming quietly.

Ordinarily, I would've run after her; but that night I just didn't have it in me. There were a lot of reasons why, some of which I'd come to understand in the near future, some of which would take me years to really get. But to this day I still wonder how things might've turned out if I *had* gone . . .

I gave myself a few minutes and then headed back upstairs. Miss Howard was waiting for me when I stepped out of the elevator, and while the others were all clustered around the billiard table, watching Detective Sergeant Lucius as he peered through the comparison microscope, she pulled me over to the front window.

"Stevie," she said quietly, "is everything all right?"

Struggling to keep down a rush of irritation at the thought that everyone in the room had been let in on my personal dealings, I just threw up my hands, then wiped sweat from my forehead. "Yes, miss," I said. "Will be, anyway . . ."

Being as I kept my eyes to the floor, I couldn't swear to it, but I felt that Miss Howard was searching my face. "I was right about you," she said, causing me to look up and find her smiling. "You wouldn't fall for a fool."

"No, miss," I answered. "Too busy *being* one, I guess."

"Don't," Miss Howard answered quickly, touching my arm. "How she behaves doesn't make you a fool. She's a clever girl, your Kat—clever and independent in a world that wants her to be stupid and submissive. And pretty, too. Pretty enough to be able to take serious risks, trying to make a life for herself—and clever enough to think that she can manage the dangers that come with those risks. But she can't. No one can. And so her schemes end up hurting her worst of all—much as they may hurt you, too."

I knocked my fist against the window frame and, out of sheer frustration, asked a question I already knew the answer to: "But—she could choose another way to go if she wanted to, couldn't she?"

"Theoretically, yes," Miss Howard said with a nod. "But ask yourself this, Stevie: If the Doctor hadn't offered you another way, would you have *chosen* one?"

I looked away, not wanting to give an honest answer but not knowing what else to say. Fortunately, Detective Sergeant Lucius made further conversation unnecessary:

"Yes," he said in a loud voice, from his seat across the room. "Yes, that's it . . . that's it! A perfect match!" Miss Howard and I turned to see him look up from the twin brass eyepieces of the comparison microscope, his sweaty face beaming like a kid's. "She's there—without question, the girl is *in that house!*"

Marcus fairly tore his brother out of the chair so he could get a look into the microscope, while Cyrus and the Doctor shook hands with Lucius. Miss Howard and I ran over to do the same, and then waited our turns to take a look into the contraption on the billiard table. When I finally sat to get my glimpse, I'll admit that I was a bit disappointed, as all I was able to see were what looked like two hazy pieces of the same length of string, or rope; but to the trained eye, I was assured, what I was looking at, magnified many times over, was two hairs off of the same baby's head: Ana Linares's head.

And so we finally had our proof, and along with it an open road to direct action; and, scared as that prospect had made me during recent days, at that particular moment the prospect of putting everything else aside and rolling the dice on the break-in made me feel just fine.

"All we lack now," the Doctor said, heading over to review the notes on the chalkboard and make a few additions, "is a time when we can be certain the woman will be out of the house."

"But—we've got it." Barely aware that I'd said the words out loud, I looked around to find everyone staring at me. "Tomorrow night," I went on. "It's Goo Goo Knox's birthday—she's sure to be at the Dusters'."

The Doctor gave me what you might call a searching look, then nodded slowly. "Well, then," he said, "tomorrow night." He began to toss his piece of chalk up and down lightly. "Tomorrow night she assumes her second personality—and in so doing gives us a chance to peer into her first. The woman of two names, two faces, two lives has—quite unconsciously—set the two halves of herself to work, each against the other. We must pray our job is finished before that conflict comes to an end." The Doctor fixed his black eyes on the board. "We must interrupt the work of the savior, before the destroyer has her way . . ."

CHAPTER 23

Twenty-four hours later, all was darkness.

I was lying in the bed of the calash, along with Detective Sergeant Marcus and Mike the ferret, who was squirming around in a satchel what I'd slung around my neck and over my shoulder. The three of us were covered by a tarpaulin, which sealed out what little light came through the windows of the stables next door to Number 39 Bethune Street—and sealed the stale July heat in. Detective Sergeant Lucius had driven the rig in about twenty minutes earlier, telling the attendant that he had business in the neighborhood and reckoned to be back sometime before midnight. Then he'd strapped a bag of oats onto Frederick's snout and departed, while the attendant had gone back to standing on the sidewalk and watching some fireworks that were being set off over the Hudson: the one thing we'd all forgotten, in the midst of our planning, was that the night we'd chosen for the break-in was the eve of July Fourth, and the city was full of drunken revelers setting off firecrackers and generally raising hell. This, we'd decided when we finally remembered it, would only work to our advantage, as the attention of the police and everyone else in town—including the stable attendant—would be directed toward either participating in or controlling the revelry: all in all, a good night to go housebreaking.

The day had been spent in last-minute coaching, of Mike by me and of me by the others. I had no doubts about Mike: he'd reached the point where he had thoroughly connected the idea of getting fed with the smell of Ana Linares's nightgown. (The fact that I'd disobeyed Hickie's orders and started feeding the animal prime cuts of meat from the local butcher had notched his already considerable enthusiasm up to positive mania.) As for myself, I was confident about the breaking-and-entering part of the plan; the only thing that worried me was the Doctor's hope that I'd not only be able to grab the Linares baby but at the same time make careful mental notes of anything I saw that might help him understand Nurse Hunter's behavior on the deepest level. I understood his desire for such information, and as I say, I was anxious not to disappoint him. But he plain didn't know—and I didn't think I could explain to him—what it was like when you stepped across the line and invaded somebody else's territory: mental activity of the more intellectual variety did not tend to be high on your list of priorities.

Finally, night did fall, and the detective sergeants and I loaded into the calash. I could still read great misgiving in the Doctor's face as we left, and some of the same in Cyrus's features; but Miss Howard and Mr. Moore were there to keep their spirits on track, and by the time we rattled away from Seventeenth Street they were full of genuine encouragement. Our arrival at the stable had gone without a hitch—or at least, so it seemed to Marcus and me under our tarpaulin—and that had made the first period of hiding and waiting considerably easier. The plan from there on in was for Lucius—who was toting a .32-caliber New Service Revolver, the very latest thing to come out of Mr. Samuel Colt's arms factory—to watch the Hunter house from the cover of a factory doorway across Washington Street and, when he saw Nurse Hunter depart, to return to the stables, explaining that he'd forgotten something. He'd then let us know we were clear to get under way, and afterward resume his post. At 11:45 he'd come back again, giving us something like an hour and a half to complete the job—more than enough time, if everything went off right.

Marcus and I lay in the calash, like I say, for about twenty uncomfortably warm minutes after Lucius's first departure. We heard the occasional sound of a carriage or a horse coming or going, but we didn't move barely a muscle until we finally heard a little rap on the side of our rig. Without taking the tarp off of us, Lucius began to root around inside the bed of the carriage, taking out a small case that he'd left positioned under the driver's seat. It contained a twelve-gauge Holland and Holland shotgun, along with a box of shells: while he waited for us, Lucius figured to be the most heavily armed man in the area—and in that neighborhood in those days, that was saying something.

"Okay," he whispered to us through the tarpaulin. "She just left. Light's gone out on the third floor, looks like she already put her husband to bed. She's wearing an awful lot of makeup, and—"

Even in the darkness under the tarp, I thought I could make out Marcus's hot scowl. "Lucius!" he whispered back.

"Hmm?" his brother noised.

"Shut up and get the hell out of here, will you, please?"

"Oh. Right. The attendant's still out front. I think he's been drinking."

"Will you *go*?"

"Okay, okay . . ."

We heard footsteps fading away from us, and then there was silence, except for the faraway rattle of firecrackers and the boom of bigger fireworks over the river.

"All right, Stevie," Marcus whispered after a few minutes, pulling the tarpaulin back a bit. "I'm just going to have a look . . ." He poked his head out and up, then ducked back under. "All clear—let's move!"

With almost no sound we got out of the calash. The night was hot, but the most miserable of the summer heat still hadn't arrived yet—and that made the dark clothes we were wearing less of a burden. I had a simple pair of light leather moccasins on my feet, while Marcus was in just his socks for the moment. Around his neck was a satchel similar to the one Mike was wiggling around in, but bigger: in it he was lugging a pair of studded climbing shoes, a bar spreader, a coil of heavy rope, a crowbar, and a hefty hammer. He had a holster strapped to his hip, and in it was a pistol identical to his brother's, but with a .38-caliber barrel and chamber, to provide a little extra punch if things got ugly. In my own pocket I was carrying Miss Howard's Colt Number One derringer, half a dozen .41-caliber bullets—and a nice eight-inch piece of lead pipe.

When we got out of the calash, we found that Lucius had been able to park it right next to one of the rear windows of the stable, as far as possible from the entryway and the attendant. Because of that, it was no big job for us to get the window open and move into the alleyway behind the place; but when we completed our quiet run along the back of the building, we found ourselves face to face with a ten-foot brick wall around the Hunters' backyard. It looked like it'd been built pretty recently, certainly in the last couple of years.

"Well," I said, eyeballing the thing, "looks like *somebody* don't wanna be seen doin' *something* . . ."

Marcus nodded, going for his coil of rope and climbing shoes. "I'll boost you over and keep hold of this end of the rope. You take the other end, let yourself down, and find a spot to anchor it over there."

"Just get your shoes on," I answered, taking my end of the rope in my teeth and grabbing at the gaps in the stone blocks what made up the corner of the stables. "If I can't scale this wall without bein' boosted," I went on, through a scratchy mouthful of hemp, "then I been outta the business too long."

Using the gaps in the stable's stone corner along with a pretty solid drain gutter, I got on top of the brick wall in just a couple of minutes. I could've done it faster, too, if I hadn't been trying so hard to keep Mike from banging into anything: not a bad piece of work for somebody who hadn't been at it in many years. From my perch I had a good view of the houses that backed onto the alley and the Hunters' yard from Bank Street to the south. Only a couple of windows were lit, and those just dimly. But there was no telling when somebody with good enough eyes might glance out and catch sight of us, so we had to move quicker here than at any other time.

Knowing this, Marcus had gotten into his studded boots fast, and by the time I got up top of the wall he had a good grip on the rope and was ready for me to descend. I looped the thing around my waist, then started to walk backward down the Hunters' side of the partition. Once on the ground, I shot over to one of the back windows of the house, testing the bars: they were solid, all right, but now we would use that fact to our advantage. I looped the rope in and out of the three-quarter-inch iron strips, then tied it off and gave it a few good tugs: the bars'd stand Marcus's weight easily. I went back over to the wall and snapped my fingers a few times.

It'd been Marcus who'd identified the murderer John Beecham as an expert mountain climber during that case, and in the process he'd become pretty good at the sport himself. So I wasn't all that surprised when he made barely a sound getting to the top of the brick wall, then lowered himself down and dropped into a flower bed—one what was mostly dirt—just as quietly. Neither of us paused too long to catch our breath or examine the backyard; but even rushed as we were, we couldn't help but be a little struck by the barren feel of the place. It was the height of the growing season, but that yard—made up of flagstone walkways and a few flower and herb patches, along with some struggling ivy on the brick wall—formed a picture what was straight out of early March.

"It ain't natural," I whispered. "There oughtta be weeds, anyway . . ."

Marcus made a noise of agreement, then shivered once and touched my arm. He nodded toward the window, getting the bar spreader out of his satchel and handing it to me. It was made up of two metal mounts driven by steel rods geared to a big central screw, one what was driven by placing the crowbar through a steel eye at its end and turning it. I got the thing into position nice and snug and gave it the first few turns, watching the bars on the window start to move apart; but once the first set of iron rails hit those outside them (the gaps between each were just five or six inches) Marcus had to step in and give the crowbar a few good cranks.

"You're breaking the law, you know, Detective Sergeant," I whispered with a small smile.

"I know," he answered, returning the quick grin. "But there are laws and there are laws . . ."

The bars made a few painful creaks that sounded awfully loud in that quiet, dead yard; but then some firecrackers went off about a half a block to the west, so loud that I realized we still weren't making any real noise. Another twenty seconds, and there was an opening big enough for me to get my head and shoulders through. That was all I needed.

"Okay," I whispered, and before Marcus had even laid the spreader on the ground I was halfway into the house. I stopped, though, when he touched my shoulder.

"Remember, don't go upstairs, but anything you can find that looks interesting—"

"Yeah. I know."

"Oh, and don't forget the secretary in the front room—it was covered when we were there."

"Detective Sergeant—we been over all this."

Marcus drew a heavy breath, nodded, and then retreated into a shadowy corner nearby. As he did, I finished squeezing through the bars, then brought Mike along carefully behind me. Finally, I turned to find myself standing in Elspeth Hunter's kitchen.

The first thing I noticed was the smell: a stale, slightly rotten odor, not strong enough to be sickening, but disturbing just the same. Unhealthy, you might say—a general air of uncleanliness, such as even many of the poorest immigrant mothers I'd known on the Lower East Side wouldn't have allowed. A bucket filled with garbage, uncovered, stood in one corner, insects flying around it even in the near-darkness. Passing by the stained sink, I looked up at some pots and pans that hung over it, then reached up to touch them. Each was covered with a thin layer of grease—again, not dirty, exactly, but not clean, either. Wiping my fingers on my pants, I kept on going.

The others had told me that there was a narrow hallway between the kitchen and the front room, with a doorway cut under the front staircase: that figured to be the way down to the basement. I made my way to the front room, which was furnished with just a few old items: an easy chair, a sofa, and a rocker. A beat-up wooden mantelpiece stood over the small fireplace, and a dusty, stained rug covered the floor. Just to the left of the doorway I'd entered through was the secretary Marcus had mentioned, a cheaply veneered job scarred with chips and scratches. But it wasn't covered up, and I could see in the half-light of the street lamps what filtered through from outside that behind the glass-paned doors of its top half were a few books, along with some old photographs: faded daguerreotype portraits of a wrinkled man and woman, along with a batch of newer, neatly framed prints of young children. Some of these last were individual pictures of infants, while one was a group portrait of three older kids.

None of them was smiling.

I pulled at the lid of the lower half of the secretary but found that it was locked. The skeleton keyhole at the top of the lid was inviting—it wouldn't have taken but a minute to pick—but I figured I'd better get to the more serious business first. Across the room were the front stairs, and underneath them a doorway: the entrance to the basement. I stepped lightly over to the staircase, glancing up to make sure that all was quiet, and then pulled a small vial of machine oil out of my shirt pocket. Coating the basement door's hinges, I put the vial back into my pocket, wiped my hands once again on my pants, then grabbed the doorknob, turned it, and pulled the door back without a sound.

The stairs stretched away into darkness before me. I hadn't wanted to bring a bulky lamp along, as Mike was trouble enough, though I did have a candle and matches; but we'd noted that the light over the front doorway on the outside of the house was electrical, and figured that the whole structure, being so small, was probably wired, too. So I put one hand to the wall and slowly made my way down into the blackness, my eyes steadily adjusting and searching for any lighting fixtures. About halfway down I spotted one: right by the stairs and screwed into the basement's ceiling, easy to reach from where I was standing. Moving back up to shut the door, I bent down and switched the light on, then kept going to the bottom of the stairs.

I'd scarcely hit the dirty floor before Mike's movements inside the satchel became more agitated and he began to make little squeaking sounds.

"Okay, Mike," I whispered, "just gimme a minute."

Glancing around I saw that Mr. Moore's sketch of the basement had been pretty well on the money: about the only things to be seen were a furnace, which stood behind a load-bearing brick dividing wall; some cabinets containing what looked like old cans of paint; a few garden tools (rusty ones, which came as no big surprise); some chairs and a table what were in even worse shape than the ones upstairs; a small collection of picture frames, all empty; and a big wooden rack full of jars of preserves. The only thing he'd gotten wrong was the floor, and his mistake was easy to understand: though the thing was concrete, it was covered in a layer of soot and dirt so thick that it could easily have been mistaken for bare earth.

But there was no sign of any baby, and no indication that one'd ever been there.

Mike was by now pitching a positive fit in the satchel, and I looked down to see his snout pushing out from between two buckled fasteners. "Okay, Mike, okay, this is your time, son," I said, moving to undo the buckles on the satchel. I'd only managed to get one open before he shot out of the thing and onto the floor, moving as he'd done the first time I'd seen him: like he was made out of liquid. He got down my leg and onto the floor, held his nose up above his spread-out forepaws, then raced once around the big furnace. Pausing for just a second, he got up on his hind legs, the little dark eyes taking in the whole room in just a second or two. Then he shot behind and around the pieces of furniture, through the picture frames, and up the side of one old cabinet.

I wrinkled my brow at him. "What's going on, Mike?" I asked, but he only did another lap around the room, looking like the proverbial blind dog in a butcher shop: he could smell it, but he couldn't find it. Then he reached the rack of preserves that stood against the brick dividing wall next to the furnace, and I thought he was going to turn apoplectic on me. He leapt up and into one of the shelves, then ducked behind a few jars, reappeared, and moved up to the next shelf in a clawing, lightning-fast streak. But just like that he was on his way back down to the floor again, and around to the side of the thing.

And all the while he was sniffing and clawing, sniffing and clawing, trying to find, it seemed, some way to move the rack.

How long it took me to understand what I was looking at I'm not sure; but however long, it was *too* long, because I should've gotten the point as soon as I saw that rack. After all, I'd had enough clues: the flower boxes on Sunday; the dismal backyard; the unhealthy kitchen; the spare front room, as hospitable as the barracks in the Boys' House of Refuge; not to mention all the conversations about Nurse Hunter's character what I'd been privy to. They were all part of a pattern, and so was that rack of preserves—but it took a half-crazed ferret to drive the idea home in my head:

"Wait a minute," I mumbled, as I walked over to the rack. "*Preserves?* Who's she trying to kid?"

I grabbed one of the jars off the rack and unscrewed the rubber-lined tin lid: looking down, I saw a thick layer of mold across the top of the contents. Making a sour face, I quickly screwed the top back on and tried another jar, only to find the same thing inside. I tried two more jars from different parts of the rack, and when I found them to be in similar shape, I just stood back for a second, pondering it. Then I looked down at Mike: he was still scratching away at the bottom of the rack, first in front, than around to one side, then to the other, never getting anywhere what with the concrete, but desperate to all the same.

"Unh-*hunh*," I noised, stepping forward again. "Well, then . . ." I took a deep breath, laid hold of the corner of the rack, strained to move it away from the dividing wall, and—.

And nothing. I tried again, putting my full weight into the attempt but gaining no greater result. I might as well have been trying to move the house. Looking around, I caught sight of the rusty garden tools and ran over to grab an old hoe. I tried to slide the lip of its blade into a narrow crevice between the back of the rack and the bricks. It wouldn't go. I used the heel of my hand to jam it in and finally got a small purchase; but when I laid hold of the end of the hoe's wooden handle and pulled it so that the blade would push the rack away from the wall, the tool snapped into two pieces. And it wasn't the wooden handle that broke: it was the metal stem of the blade, half an inched of forged steel.

"What in *hell* . . . ?" I mumbled, staring at the thing.

It was odd, all right; but I'd taken part in enough robberies in my life to know that when you were faced with a safe you didn't have the tools to crack, you didn't stick around to wonder why. I scooped up the still clawing Mike, who seemed to sense that he hadn't done the job he'd been hired for and fought against me as I stuffed him back into the satchel and fastened it up good and tight. Going back to the stairs, I got halfway up them when—

Gunshots. I froze, already trying to figure how I was going to explain my presence in the basement. Then I realized: they weren't gunshots but firecrackers, out on the street. They must have been *right* out on the street, too, judging by their volume. Sighing with relief and able to move again, I reached over to shut off the basement light, then carefully moved on up to the door and opened it, the oiled hinges swinging silently.

Once in the front room again, I could hear the laughter of a bunch of kids out on the street. Then a few more firecrackers went off, their sound sharp and startling against the distant, dull thunder of the bigger fireworks over the river. I looked around quickly. We weren't going to get the baby out that night, I knew that much, but I couldn't bring myself to leave empty-handed. There had to be *something* . . .

I glanced at the secretary, and remembered what Marcus had said: if the Hunter woman had thought to cover the thing before she'd asked them in, it stood to reason that there was something that'd be of use to us in it. I grabbed my collection of picks out of my pants pocket and dashed over to it, getting the lock in the lid undone faster than even *I'd* thought I could've.

When I pulled the lid down and open, my first reaction was disappointment: there wasn't anything but some letters in the desk's little wooden slots, and a stack of papers on a worn-out blotter in front of them. Before locking the thing up again, though, I decided to overrule my thief's instinct that such items were worthless, and picked some of the papers up to read—wisely, as it turned out.

At first they made no sense to me. The items on top were written on stationery from St. Luke's Hospital: they were addressed to Elspeth Hatch, and they seemed to be a bunch of advisories concerning the condition of a child named Jonathan. Below these were a series of hospital admitting forms what seemed to pertain to the same child. And finally, there were a couple of old newspapers, all folded up and dating from two years before. I flipped back to the hospital admitting forms, not knowing what I was looking at or for, exactly: they were all too full of unreadable handwriting, all too complicated—

But then I made out a few words that stopped me cold. At the bottom of one form appeared the pretyped word DIAGNOSIS:—and next to it somebody had scrawled RESPIRATORY FAILURE, CYANOSIS.

That was enough for me. I took the whole stack of papers, stuffed them inside my shirt, and closed the secretary. I was sure that I'd found something, sure that I hadn't wasted—

"Don't you move, you little bastard!"

I did just as I was told. I'd been nailed before, and when you got a command like that it was generally best to follow it until you'd had a chance to see who and what you were up against. Putting my hands halfway into the air, I turned slowly toward where the growling, desperate, and somehow familiar voice had come from: the front stairs.

On them stood what must've been Micah Hunter. He looked to be in his fifties, and he was wearing a badly faded white nightshirt. Two bony white legs stuck out from its hem, and his grey, grizzled face—with a similarly colored, unkempt mustache—plainly bore the mad, foggy expression of a morphine jabber in full binge. He held what looked like a rifled musket unsteadily in his hands, and as I turned he stared at me in wild disbelief.

"*You!*" he said. Then he started to glance around nervously, and little whimpering sounds came out of his throat. "*You . . . ?*" he repeated with less energy this time. "Where—where's Libby? *Libby!*" He looked at me again, very afraid. "It can't be—it *can't* be you. . . . This ain't the right house . . ." His voice got stronger, though no less frightened. "This ain't the right house—and *I already killed you!*"

CHAPTER 24

I've had a lot of peculiar things said to me in my life, but none to top
that. The poor old fool genuinely believed that he had killed me, too,
that much was plain from the desperate fear that was all over his drug-
ridden face. But why he should have believed such a thing, I had no idea.

Then another batch of firecrackers went off out in the street, and Micah
Hunter spun round, holding his musket toward the front door. "So!" he
said, determination replacing some of his fear. "You ain't alone, reb!" He
shouldered the musket, looking ready to do battle with whoever came
through the door. "Well, come on, you bastards—"

"Hunter!"

Both Hunter and I snapped our heads round to the hallway, out of
which had boomed Detective Sergeant Marcus's voice. "Hunter!" Marcus
called again through the kitchen window, causing the old man to grow
fearful once more. "Stand down, soldier! That's an order!"

"Captain?" Hunter mumbled. "Captain Griggs?"

"I told you to stand down, man! You're wounded—unfit! We don't
need you, soldier—back to the hospital!"

"I—don't understand . . ." Hunter glanced at me again, then around
the house quickly. "Where's Libby? I ain't well!"

"Go on!" Marcus insisted. "Put down the weapon and get back to the
hospital!"

"But I . . ." Hunter let the gun drift to his side—

And that was all I needed. Like a shot I was back into the hallway, racing toward the kitchen window. Old man Hunter screamed something

after me that I couldn't make out, but nothing could've stopped me from slipping back through those bars like so much water. Marcus helped me through, and then cupped his hands to give me a boost back up onto the brick wall: I was a ways beyond professional pride, at that point. I used the rope to get back down into the alleyway, then grabbed the end that was still on that side of the wall. Looking around quickly, I found a water pipe with a spigot standing nearby. I tied the rope off onto it, then whispered "Go!" Marcus's boots scratched against the wall as he climbed up top, and then he pretty much just let himself fall to ground on the other side, the studs on the boots hitting the concrete alleyway hard and, to judge by the look on his face, painfully.

"Pull it over!" he said, from which I took it that he'd untied the other end of the rope. I gave it a yank, and it came over with a whipping sound. Coiling it up around my arm quickly as we ran back to the open rear window of the stables, I handed the thing to Marcus, who stuffed it away in his satchel. Then we got through the window, closed it, and jumped back into the calash and under the tarpaulin, both of us breathing as hard as little Mike.

"What do we do?" I asked, the quick heaving of my chest making it hard to whisper.

"Shh!" Marcus answered. For a long few seconds we just lay there listening. Some dogs were barking in the yards behind the stables, and in the far distance we could hear Micah Hunter yelling away, though his exact words were still impossible to make out.

"I think we'll be all right," Marcus finally said. "The people around here must be used to that kind of thing from him. We can't panic." He pulled out a watch and checked it. "Lucius should be here within half an hour. Just catch your breath and try not to move."

I followed the order, taking in deep gulps of air as I stroked the confused Mike through the leather of the satchel. "Shit," I finally said, when I could do it quietly. "I think the old maniac really might've shot me."

"It was the fireworks," Marcus said. "And the morphine. My bet is, she gives him a hell of a dose before she leaves at night. If you get woken up during the first couple of hours after a strong injection like that, you're generally pretty delusional. He seemed to think he was back in the war—and you were some Confederate kid he'd shot, somewhere along the line." Marcus paused to take in air. "What about the baby?"

"Long story," I said. "She's down there, all right—I don't think we're wrong about that. But getting to her's going to be tough. Maybe impossible. The rack of preserves is some kind of mechanical doorway, and it won't give. I found some other stuff, though—"

I clammed right up when I heard a soft tapping on the side of the calash. "Stevie? Marcus?" It was Detective Sergeant Lucius. "Are you in there?"

"Yes," Marcus answered. "And we're all right."

"I heard shouting," Lucius said. "From inside. What happened?"

"Later," Marcus whispered. "Get us out of here!"

"What about the girl? Did you find her?"

"Lucius! Get us out of here—*now!*"

In a few seconds the calash started to roll out toward the front of the stables. Lucius paused to pay the attendant, and then it was out onto the street, turning left: he'd rightly decided to head uptown along the river, as far from the Dusters' joint as possible. Within half a block he had Frederick up to a nice clip, and when we felt the carriage turn right, Marcus and I figured it was safe to come out from under the tarpaulin.

The sky above the Hudson was still blazing with fireworks, and there were groups of people all along the waterfront watching them. But we didn't pause for any sightseeing, just kept cantering forward toward Number 808 Broadway. Lucius was full of questions, but Marcus told him to hold them all 'til we got there. I undid my satchel to see if Mike was okay, and found him peering up at me, still very agitated but otherwise fine. With that, I took a deep breath and leaned back on the seat of the calash. Bringing the stolen papers out from inside my shirt, I handed them to Marcus, then lit up a cigarette and offered him one.

We were both bitterly disappointed about how things had worked out; and because of this, the warm welcome we received from the others— whose disappointment could not have been much less than ours—when we got back to Number 808 was all the more appreciated. I think that both Marcus and I, in mulling over what had happened, had forgotten just how much *more* wrong things could have gone. But the relief what was clear in the faces of all our friends served as a reminder. Miss Howard offered me a big hug that lifted me clear off the ground, while the Doctor put an arm around my shoulders and near squeezed them through to each other, smiling all the while. The fact that we hadn't succeeded was obviously far less important than the fact that we'd survived—and seeing that thought reflected in all their faces, in turn, made it much easier to talk about the break-in.

The Doctor'd ordered supper from Mr. Delmonico and had it brought down to our headquarters, a fact what put the joy of life back into Marcus. As for me, I was deeply grateful that the Doctor had not only ordered me a plain-grilled steak and fried potatoes but'd had Mr.

Ranhofer send along a few fillets of raw beef for Mike, too. Mr. Moore'd set all the food out on the billiard table, buffet style: there were olives and celery, anchovies on toast, pheasant and guinea fowl (complete with ornamental feathers), foie gras aspic, lamb chops, lobster and shrimp salad, rice pudding, small meringues with fruit, Neapolitan iced cream, and, of course, bottles of champagne, wine, and beer, along with root beer for me. As the adults all got platefuls of their luxurious fare, I retreated into my windowsill with my steak, the beef fillets, and Mike, who proved to be almost as hungry as yours truly. One by one the others made their way over to the big chairs and desks with their suppers and drinks, and as they did we all started to go over the strange events that Marcus and I had just been through, a process what began with the two of us laying out the basic facts and ended with Marcus handing the papers I'd lifted over to the Doctor. As he did, I saw for the first time a bit of a cloud float into Dr. Kreizler's features.

"What's wrong, Doctor?" Marcus said, opening up some windows to let the warm evening breeze come into the place, along with the sounds of celebration from the street. "From what I could see, those documents may be the evidence we need to demonstrate a pattern in this woman's behavior."

"That may be, Marcus," the Doctor said, going over the papers. "I cannot yet tell. But what they most certainly *will* do—or rather, what their *absence* will do—is let Nurse Hunter know who broke into her house, and why."

"Well, come on, Kreizler," Mr. Moore said, carefully setting an overloaded plate onto an arm of one of the easy chairs. "If our visit on Sunday wasn't an open declaration of hostilities, I don't know what *would* be."

"It is not hostility toward *us* that concerns me, Moore," the Doctor answered, still reading the hospital reports. "It is the possibility that our attempts to rescue the child may eventually be interpreted, in Nurse Hunter's mind, as the child's fault. That is her peculiar ability, to turn responsibility for all that goes wrong—in her own life as well as the lives of the children she touches—back onto the children themselves."

The Doctor turned to a new sheet of paper as the rest of us absorbed that disturbing notion; then his eyes suddenly went very big. "My God . . ." He quickly set his plate aside so that he could tear into the stack of documents faster. "My God . . ." he repeated.

"What have you found, Doctor?" Miss Howard asked for all of us.

But the Doctor only looked to Marcus. "How many of these letters did you read?"

Marcus shrugged, gnawing on a lamb chop. "Just enough to get the general idea: a child named 'Jonathan' was in her care, and went through several cyanotic episodes. The last one was fatal."

The Doctor pounded a finger on the stack of papers. "Yes. But the relationship was not that of nurse to patient. This last admitting form reveals the child's family name: 'Hatch.' He was *Jonathan Hatch. Her own son.*"

Even *my* jaw dropped at that one, and I thought right away about the series of photographs of babies and children that I'd seen in the secretary at Number 39 Bethune Street.

"She was not a *nurse* at St. Luke's," the Doctor went on. "She brought the child in as a *patient*. Three times."

Marcus just sat there, the lamb chop bone dangling from his hand. "But—I just assumed . . ."

The Doctor waved him off, the motion of his hand saying "Of course, of course" as clearly as his voice could have. He kept on reading and digging. Then his voice went shocked again. "Good *Lord*—she lists her place of employment as One West Fifty-seventh Street."

Mr. Moore's wineglass hit the floor with a crash. "Christ!" he said in shock. "That's Corneil Vanderbilt's house!"

Cyrus was still struggling with the first bit of new information. "But I thought we'd decided that the woman was incapable of having children."

The Doctor just kept waving his hand. "True, Cyrus. And there's nothing to say that she—wait. Here." He'd grabbed the newspapers that were at the bottom of the pile and handed them to Cyrus. "See what sense you can make of these."

His mouth full of pheasant, Cyrus picked up his plate with one hand and took the papers with the other, moving to one of the desks, where he could both read and eat.

The Doctor kept his eyes on the hospital reports. "Each of the events conforms precisely to the pattern described by the nurses at the Lying-in Hospital. Every time that the woman—described here as '*Mrs. Elspeth Hatch*'—arrived at the hospital, the child Jonathan, eighteen months old, was already choking and cyanotic. Each incident occurred in the middle of the night—the mother claimed to have been awoken by the sound of his gasping, and rushed to find him unable to breathe. The first two letters are quite dramatic: 'Had you, Mrs. Hatch, displayed any less alacrity in bringing the child into professional hands,' writes the attending physician in the initial communication, 'he should most certainly have expired. Your anguish as you waited to learn of his fate was, according to our staff, most touching to behold.' Who in God's name wrote that?" As Dr. Kreizler read on, I remembered that he'd often worked with colleagues who were attending physicians at St. Luke's. "Hmm . . . 'Dr. J. Langham.' I don't know him."

"He should go into dime novels," Mr. Moore said, wiping up the wine and broken glass that covered the floor by his chair with a napkin. "Does it say anything more about Vanderbilt?"

"No," the Doctor answered. "But she was apparently living in a flat near Fifty-seventh Street—that's why she took the child to St. Luke's. The hospital was still located on Fifty-fourth Street at the time. Here are some more statistics. Under 'Age,' she writes 'Thirty-seven.' 'Occupation: Day maid.' 'Place of birth: Stillwater, New York.'" The Doctor looked up. "Anyone?"

"Upstate?" Lucius tried.

"There isn't a great deal of 'downstate' from here, Lucius," Miss Howard said with a smile. "I know the town, Doctor. It's on the upper Hudson, near Saratoga." She cleared her throat proudly and took a small bite of food. "Exactly, if anyone cares to remember, the area in which I placed her by her accent."

"Congratulations, Sara," the Doctor said. "Let's hope you are as successful with the next set of mysteries. Cyrus? Any luck with those newspapers?"

Cyrus didn't answer. He'd stopped eating altogether, though he was only halfway done with his food; and he was staring at the old, yellowing newsprint as if he were reading about his own death.

"Cyrus?" the Doctor repeated. When he turned and saw the look on the man's face, he immediately got out of his chair and rushed over to him. "What is it? What have you found?"

Looking up slowly, Cyrus seemed to stare right through the Doctor. "She's done it before . . ."

Mr. Moore asked, "What do you mean? Done what?" But the rest of us were silent, having gotten the point of what Cyrus was saying, though not wanting to.

Cyrus touched the papers and turned to Mr. Moore. "There's four clippings here. The first three are from the *Journal* and the *World*. They all contain stories about a kidnapping, in May 1895. A couple named Johannsen—they owned a grocery store on East Fifty-fifth Street, and had a son, Peter. Sixteen months old. The mother was attacked on a side street, when she was bringing the baby home alone. The boy was taken, and no ransom note was ever received."

As Cyrus said all of this, the Doctor grabbed the newspapers hungrily and began to scan them. "And the last paper?" he asked.

"A copy of the *Times*," Cyrus answered. "Two months later. It lists a death notice—for Jonathan Hatch. Age, eighteen months. Survived by his loving mother . . ."

"*Libby,*" the Doctor finished. Then he waved an arm at Lucius. "Detective Sergeant—on those forms there should be a physical description of the child—"

Lucius ran over and picked up the hospital forms. "Description, description . . ." he mumbled, going through the things. "Here we are, description."

"What do you have for hair and eye coloring?" the Doctor asked.

"Let me see—length—weight—ah! yes. Eyes: Blue. Hair: Blond."

"Typical Scandinavian coloring," the Doctor murmured. "Not that it's conclusive, at such an age, but—" He slapped his hand down. "*Why* does she keep these? As trophies? Or as mementos?"

Holding a little more raw beef in front of Mike's mouth and watching him grab it away and then rip into it, I said quietly, "She's got his picture . . ."

The Doctor looked my way. "Indeed, Stevie?"

I turned to him and nodded. "It was in the secretary. Little blond boy. Blue eyes. Picture looked pretty recent. I mean, compared to—"

I stopped, suddenly realizing what you might call the implications of what I was about to say.

"Yes, Stevie?" the Doctor asked quietly.

"Compared to the others," I answered, looking out the window to the dark churchyard below and suddenly feeling cold. "She's got more. A couple of individual kids—babies, like the Linares girl and this one. Then there's a picture of three other kids, all together. They were older."

Again, there was silence for a second; then Mr. Moore mumbled, "You don't think—not *all* of them . . ."

"I don't *think* anything," the Doctor answered, walking to the chalkboard.

"But that—" Mr. Moore went for another drink. "I mean, the whole idea, it's—"

"Unnatural." Marcus had said the word, and I turned to find him looking at me. He was remembering, I was sure, that moment when we'd first found ourselves in the dead, dismal yard at Number 39 Bethune Street.

"I really do urge you to dispense with that word," the Doctor replied quietly. "All of you. It isn't worth the breath its utterance requires, and it distracts us from the more important result of this encounter. We have opened one door, only to find ourselves faced with many more." Picking up a piece of chalk, the Doctor set to work on the board. "We have a host of new leads—and, quite probably, new crimes—to pursue. The worst of this business, I fear, lies ahead of us."

Everybody's appetite seemed to slack off quite a bit with that realization—everybody's but Mike's. Slowly becoming aware of his noisy chewing, I looked down to see him sitting in my lap, gnawing away, happy as he probably knew how to be. I put my finger behind his ear and scratched at his soft fur.

"Next time you get to feeling sorry you're a ferret and not a person, Mike," I muttered, "I want you to remember all this . . ."

The Doctor turned around to find a collection of blank, depressed faces, and, sensing that motivation was dwindling away, he marched back over to his plate of food and his wine and picked them up.

"Come, come," he said, maybe more cheerfully than he felt. "This meal is entirely too good to waste, and none of you will be able to work on an empty stomach."

Mr. Moore looked up in bleary confusion. "Work?"

"Certainly, Moore," the Doctor answered, eating a bit of foie gras on a toast point and taking a sip of wine. "We have now catalogued the information we gained from this little escapade. It remains to be interpreted. When our adversary returns home, she will doubtless realize what we have been about and adjust her movements and actions to it. Time therefore presses, now more than ever."

"But, Kreizler," Mr. Moore said, unconvinced. "What's there to interpret? We can't get the Linares kid out, not without tearing the house apart. We still can't go to the cops. And once this woman, whatever the hell name she's using, tells Goo Goo Knox what's happened, we'll all have to spend our nights ducking attacks from the damned Hudson Dusters! Now, what the hell do you think we're going to do that's going to change any of that?"

Lucius was holding his face in his hands, and it was sinking between them. "The woman *has* covered herself awfully well, Doctor. Just as Sara said the other day." He lifted his head and pulled out a handkerchief, starting to wipe sweat from his brow but soon giving up. "I realize this point's been made before, but . . . the Beecham case was so much more—*direct*. He was *challenging* us, and there were things that we could grab onto, points that we could proceed to and from, with some kind of logic. But this . . . every time you think you're getting somewhere, you find out something new that changes the entire picture."

"I know, Detective Sergeant, I know," the Doctor answered quickly. "But remember one essential difference between this case and our last: some hidden part of Beecham desperately *wanted* to be stopped."

"The sane part of him," Mr. Moore said. "So are you saying this Libby Hatch is *insane*? Because if she is—"

"Not insane, John." The Doctor went to the board and wrote the word SANE under the woman's names, then underlined it. "But characterized by so severe a lack of self-knowledge, of self-awareness, that her behavior becomes incoherent enough to *seem* insane, sometimes. On the other hand, she can often be quite coherent—as you have all pointed out, this time she has managed to shield her actions very well."

Marcus looked up. "*This* time?" he echoed.

"Mmm, yes," the Doctor answered as he sipped his wine. "*This* time." He drew a large box under the section of the board labeled THE WOMAN ON THE TRAIN and proceeded to label the box PAST CRIMES. Then he wrote the numbers 1 through 6 underneath the label. Next to the number 1 he scratched PETER JOHANNSEN, 1895: KIDNAPPED, MAY, BECAME JONATHAN HATCH; DIED ST. LUKE'S HOSPITAL, JULY. SUFFOCATED. "And indeed," the Doctor went on, stepping back, "why should she *not* have been ready this time? She has certainly had enough practice. If we are interpreting the elements presented to us correctly, I think we can assume that all of the children that Stevie saw in the photographs—at least six, by my count, and perhaps more—were believed by the Hatch woman to be her own—either because they in fact were, or by way of still more kidnappings. And we can be just as certain that they were her victims."

"She keeps pictures of children she's *murdered* in her *house*?" Mr. Moore said.

"Don't sound so shocked, Moore. After all, we have already posited that she does not hold herself responsible for their deaths—her mind will not allow it. In her view, they die *despite* her, not *because* of her—they are wanton, imperfect, defective children who defy her tireless maternal efforts to nurture them."

"We've granted all that, Doctor," Miss Howard said, herself sounding a little downcast; and she was always the last person to show flagging spirits. "But how can it help us here? I mean, practically speaking? How can we use it to rescue a child whose father has no interest in rescuing her—who, in fact, dispatches his macabre family servant to warn us *against* rescuing her?"

The Doctor turned to her quickly. "And so what should we do, Sara? Drop the case? When we know that the girl will die, and soon? And when we have no idea what the political repercussions of that death may be?"

"No." Miss Howard spoke quickly, battling herself as much as the Doctor. "But I just can't see any way *into* the thing anymore."

Moving over to crouch by her, the Doctor took Miss Howard's head in his hands. "That's because you're thinking like *yourself,* Sara—directly, in a straight, linear fashion. Think like *her.* Be indirect. Oblique. Even devious." He picked up her plate and handed it to her. "But above all, eat."

"Doctor—" Marcus, who had managed to finish his dinner, stood up, pointing at the board with his bottle of beer. "I think I understand. We— Stevie and I—when we were at their house, we saw things. And we started to *understand* things. About her, I mean. She may have planned this crime well, but—that doesn't change the fact that she's *not* the most capable of women, in many other ways."

"I'll say," I threw in. "You shoulda seen their kitchen—I wouldn't eat in it for love or money. And the yard—it's like a cemetery."

"Go on," the Doctor said, encouraged.

"Well"—Marcus took a deep pull off his bottle—"It seems inconceivable that a woman like that could pull off six separate crimes as effectively as this one. And we also have to remember that part of what seems like her 'skill' here was just luck. If she had no idea who Ana Linares was, then she couldn't have known that the child's father would refuse to look for her or go to the police. So, in fact, she *has* made mistakes—we just can't do anything about them. But that doesn't stop us from pursuing her elsewhere— in the past, I mean."

"Oh, this is perfect," Mr. Moore moaned. "The case has fallen to pieces, and now Marcus thinks he's H. G. Wells. Well, when you build your little time machine, Marcus, we'll all pile in and—"

"No. Wait, John." Miss Howard's green eyes had gotten their usual glitter back, and she sat up. "He's right. She must have slipped up somewhere in the past—it's just that no one was looking for it, at the time. If we hold off on the Linares case for now, and dig around in some of these other deaths—then we can come at her from a blind side."

"After all, Moore," the Doctor agreed, "look at the new leads we have obtained. We now know where the woman comes from. That is crucial, and must be explored—for all such killers manifest some sort of aberrant behavior early in life. And we are nearly certain of the crime she committed before the Linares kidnapping. It was dismissed as a natural occurrence at the time, but if we interview the doctors involved, and review the matter in light of what we now know, we have a very good chance of changing that interpretation."

Mr. Moore had been listening to all this carefully, and I could see he wanted to keep arguing; but something seemed to come into his head. "Sara—did you say that her hometown's near Saratoga?"

Miss Howard's face screwed up at the disconnected nature of the question. "Stillwater? Yes, it's about fifteen miles southeast of the Springs, more or less. Right on the river. Why, John?"

Mr. Moore thought about it for a second, then held up a finger. "I've got a friend. He used to work in the Manhattan district attorney's office. But he grew up near Saratoga. A few years back he had to leave New York, and he's now working in the D.A.'s office up there. Ballston Spa's still the county seat, isn't it?"

"Yes, that's right," Miss Howard answered with a nod.

"Well," Mr. Moore went on, "if this Hatch woman did cross any legal lines up there, Kreizler—then Rupert Picton is the man for us to talk to. A born prosecutor, *loves* to dig up dirt."

"There, you see, John?" The Doctor lifted his glass. "How difficult was that? And let's not forget—we have established a link between the woman and the Vanderbilts at the time of the last murder. It must be investigated."

At the mention of the great family's name, Mr. Moore's face turned evilly gleeful, like a boy with a box of matches. "Yes, and I want in on that one," he said. "Corneil Vanderbilt, that pious, pompous old—I want to be there when we tell him his day maid spent her off-hours kidnapping kids and suffocating them!"

"Let's not flat-out jump to conclusions, gentlemen," Lucius said. "We have just one *possible* homicide, at this point, along with two definite kidnappings."

"Oh, *I* know that and *you* know that, Lucius," Mr. Moore said. "But *Vanderbilt* doesn't. I want to tweak his nose, that—"

"You've made your point, John," the Doctor interrupted, "and you shall be there when Vanderbilt is interviewed. One final question remains." Starting his normal pacing of the floor—a signal, somehow, that we'd beaten back the moment of doubt and were going to proceed with the job—the Doctor took to shaking his chalk in his free hand. "We know that Libby Hatch—as I think we should now refer to her—almost certainly will reach a fatal crisis with Ana Linares. I also believe, after hearing Stevie and Marcus's story about the condition of her husband, that she is slowly killing him with morphine, in such a way that his death will be viewed as a result of his own degeneracy—thus gaining her the kind of sympathy and admiration she seems, from all accounts, to crave. There are collateral benefits to his demise, as well—inheritance of both his pension

and what I suspect is *his* house, not to mention the removal of any ob-
struction to her activities with Knox. The pressing question is, how can
we forestall these events? If we continue to conceal ourselves from her, she
will believe we are beaten. If, on the other hand, we make her aware that
we are investigating her past—"

"Then she won't feel safe to murder again," Miss Howard finished. "At
least, not until we *have* left her alone."

"Are you talking about a direct statement to her, Doctor?" Lucius said.
"I've got to remind you of what John said about the Dusters: if she knows
we're after her, she'll tell Knox to turn them loose on us."

"Which is why *you* shall make the declaration, Detective Sergeant. You
and Marcus. And not in our name—in that of your department. We may
in fact be prevented from making this an official inquiry, but there's no
reason why *she* should know that, is there? You need not present any war-
rants or indictments, only the simple statement that the department is
aware of her past actions and will be watching her future movements. If
you create the impression that you are speaking in an official capacity, she
will pass that impression on to Knox. The Hudson Dusters, while violent,
are neither ambitious nor suicidal. One very much doubts that they will
jeopardize either their freedom, their access to cocaine, or their status as
romantic Bohemian idols for anyone's sake, including that of Knox's *para-
mour du jour*."

Marcus looked to his brother. "He's got a point."

"Far more than a point," the Doctor answered, collecting the newspapers and hospital documents and holding them up. "We now have her
past. Or pieces of it, at any rate. That is what we have been missing—some
hint of what lies behind the current behavior, some 'way in,' as Sara puts
it. Until now we have been crippled, primarily by the lack of any guidance
from my own profession, which, like the rest of our society, suffers from a
myopia which prevents us from seeing that a woman, a mother, can be capable of such crimes. And so we have moved haltingly, unsteadily, trying
to know things about this particular woman that each of us, in some recess of our own minds, wishes was unknowable and untrue. Oh, we may
have had her physical image, and evidence of her most recent destructive
behavior, but how much could we truly read into that? Now, however, we
have specific details of her past—*keys*. And we must not hesitate before
using them."

"Except, perhaps, Doctor"—Miss Howard suddenly rose and looked
my way—"to take a moment to acknowledge the person whose bravery
got us here."

She held her wineglass up—to *me*. I shifted uneasily as the others then turned. Discouragement was gone from their faces and had been replaced by confidence, readiness—and smiles. One by one, they each held up their glasses and bottles; and I don't mind saying, it made me nervous as hell.

But I was smiling a little, too.

"To Stevie," Miss Howard went on. "Who's done what none of us could have done," she continued, "because he's lived what none of us have lived."

The rest of them all said, "To Stevie!" together, took big sips of their drinks, and then came at me in a wave.

I just looked at Mike and then out the window, as uncomfortable and as pleased as I can ever remember being.

"Okay, okay," I said, shielding myself with my hands from their displays of affection and appreciation. "We got work to do, remember . . ."

CHAPTER 25

On Sunday, Mike the ferret went home with Hickie, and I no longer had a companion to help me forget how badly I'd left things with Kat. But Monday morning saw our investigation pick up pace, and I was soon too busy carting the Doctor and the others around town to think much about where she might be or what she might be doing. I knew that she'd written to her aunt, and was waiting for a reply before heading to California; and I could only hope that she'd see her way clear to contacting me before then. But hoping was a step up from worrying, and as Kat had her money and her ticket now, I figured it was safe to put my fears for her aside, regardless of whether or not I heard from her.

The Doctor, Mr. Moore, and I started out Monday morning on the long trip up to St. Luke's Hospital, which had moved the year before from its old home on Fifty-fourth Street to five new buildings between Amsterdam Avenue and Morningside Drive at 114th Street. I saw the Doctor and Mr. Moore as far as the entrance to one of the pavilions—by coincidence, the Vanderbilt Pavilion—where nurses in long, sky-blue dresses and white aprons were trying to keep little white caps perched on their heads as they shuffled quickly up and down a spiral steel staircase what surrounded a small elevator. The Doctor and Mr. Moore got into the elevator and headed to an upper floor, while I went back to the calash and drove down to Morningside Heights, to spend the next few hours smoking a batch of cigarettes and looking down the steep rocks into the wide stretch of Harlem below.

The visit didn't go as well as the Doctor'd hoped: those physicians, surgeons, and nurses on the hospital staff what had attended to Mrs. Libby Hatch and her "son" two years earlier were horrified by the suggestion that she might've done the boy in, and the Doctor had been forced to appeal to higher authorities in order to get access to official records. And those records hadn't revealed anything new about Mrs. Hatch's visits to the hospital: like the documents I'd stolen from her house, they all said that she'd acted with speed and courage, and kept herself composed throughout the ordeal in a way what had only inspired the admiration and sympathy of the staff of St. Luke's.

This last bit interested the Doctor particularly, he told me and Mr. Moore during the ride downtown. It seemed that in Germany there were a batch of alienists, psychologists, and nerve specialists (what they called "neurologists"), who, while studying the subject of female hysteria, had found that their patients could sometimes become as addicted to the attention of medical professionals as any morphine jabber or burny blower was to drugs. If Libby Hatch shared this need, the Doctor said, she might've been using the illnesses of the children what she took care of (or failed to take care of) to satisfy it. It was two birds with one stone, you might say: she would've been covering up her maternal inabilities *and* getting attention and praise from doctors and nurses in the process. We'd know for sure if she did have such a craving when we got more information about her past, as it was a characteristic that would've formed early in life and showed up over and over. The day might even come when we could use the need against her somehow, being as, like any fiending behavior, it was at bottom a severe weakness and handicap, one what could betray and even destroy the person afflicted with it.

Mr. Moore, after considering all this, flew the idea that such a craving could've been the reason why Libby Hatch, or Mrs. Hunter, had treated Dr. Kreizler in a very different way than she'd approached either himself or the detective sergeants. True, she'd come at each man in a fashion designed to appeal to his weakness or vanity; but maybe there was something more in her very respectful treatment of the Doctor. Maybe she hadn't figured on such a person taking part in the investigation of the abduction, and maybe, when she'd tried to be cordial to him as we were all leaving, she'd felt a real need for him to respond in kind, to believe that she was innocent. Certainly, that would help explain the furious way she'd reacted when he'd rejected her attempts to be cordial. And, Mr. Moore continued, if she did harbor some sneaking desire to be approved of by the Doctor, the fact that he was going to stay on the case with the cops might be something the detective sergeants would want to include in their warning to her: a little worm to plant in her brain, so to speak, just to help keep her off balance. When we met up with Marcus and Lucius that night at Seventeenth Street, they agreed with this line of reasoning wholeheartedly, and decided to make it a part of their presentation.

That event would not take place, though, until after they, with the help of Miss Howard, had further investigated the deaths of the babies at the Lying-in Hospital, being as they wanted to be loaded with as much ammunition as possible when they faced our opponent. But this side investigation proved especially tricky, being as it was difficult if not impossible to even locate most of the mothers of said babies, much less get them to talk. The Lying-in Hospital, like I've said, catered to unwed and poor mothers, and a lot of them didn't give their right names when they checked in. This was true, in particular, of the more well-to-do women who were in the Hospital to cover the results of adultery or who'd enjoyed the advantages of matrimony before actually bothering with its formalities. It took the detective sergeants and Miss Howard days to find even a single woman who'd acknowledge that one of the dead babies had been hers; and when they did find that lone mother and told her about their suspicions, the woman showed them out in a hurry, smelling legal trouble and wanting no part of it. So they were forced to press on with their search.

The Doctor and Mr. Moore, meanwhile, went about their next task: getting in to see the honorable Mr. Cornelius Vanderbilt II, him what Mr. Moore had referred to as "Corneil." (The name distinguished him from his grandfather, the larcenous old coot who'd put the family on the map, and also from his own son, Cornelius III, who was called "Neily.") He was a generous man when it came to charities, was Mr. Cornelius II, but he was also about the most holier-than-thou customer in New York; and he certainly had no interest in meeting with someone as questionable as Dr. Kreizler. If any of our team was going to be admitted to the enormous mansion—which was known to architectural types as a "French Renaissance château"—that took up the whole end of the block of Fifth Avenue between Fifty-seventh and Fifty-eighth Streets, favors were going to have to be asked of third parties: specifically, Mr. Moore would have to seek the help of his parents, something he genuinely despised doing. And, though they did fix an audience up for Thursday afternoon, they also told Mr. Moore that, whatever his business was, he'd better make sure he didn't bring up the subject of Mr. Vanderbilt's son Neily, whose existence the old gent wasn't currently recognizing.

Apparently, young Neily'd had the nerve to go and marry somebody he actually loved, but who his family considered socially below him. The battle over the marriage had become so hot that Cornelius II had actually had a stroke, and pretty well written his oldest son out of his will. The young man himself had gone through with the marriage, then high-tailed it to Europe with his bride. They'd only recently returned, though the city'd been buzzing with word of their doings the whole while. The yellow press, of course, had jumped into the thing, and all on the side of love, the better to sell papers. Most of high society was likewise sympathetic to the young couple, since *really* old New York families, like Mr. Moore's and Miss Howard's, considered the recently rich Vanderbilts gate-crashers at their long-running party in the first place. The affair had continued to wear on Cornelius II (who was now migrating between his palace in New York and his even more ridiculously elaborate joint in Newport, Rhode Island), and by that summer he'd grown so bitter and self-righteous that it was actually killing him. Seventy million dollars and the New York Central railroad system all his own to play with, and the man was going to let two young people's romantic escapades drive him into the ground: there was and is no figuring rich people sometimes . . .

Anyway, Thursday afternoon arrived and we drove uptown in the covered calash. The average daily temperature had been steadily going up as we dragged deeper into July, and by the eighth it was rising so fast that it was causing that depressing type of warm summer rain that always fails to cool or cleanse the city. Sloshing our way through particularly nasty-smelling horse waste, we rolled over Murray Hill and then entered the mansion district in the Fifties, eventually passing the other Vanderbilt palaces, what had all been built within a few blocks of Cornelius II's. The main purpose of each of those mansions, it'd always seemed to me, was nothing more than to outdo the rest, even if that meant piling on so many details and extras that the structures themselves crossed over into what you might call laughable, or just plain unsightly.

This was true of One West Fifty-seventh Street most of all: the bright red color of the bricks against the whiteness of the limestone used for the window frames and detailing may've been supposed to re-create the look of the French Renaissance; but for my money it came a lot closer to a circus tent. The addition that'd been built onto the back of the house by Mr. Richard Morris Hunt—him what had designed the new wing of the Metropolitan Museum—was much easier on the eyes, and could even be con-

sidered handsome, if looked at apart from the rest. But the effect of the
front of the house, when you came at it from downtown, was to make you
think that you were on your way to see some kind of high-class joker.
Which, of course, you were; it was just too bad that Cornelius II himself
didn't get the gag.

About half a block south of Fifty-seventh Street the noise of our carriage, along with those around us, suddenly died: huge sheets of some
kind of padding—it looked like tree bark—had been laid down on the
blocks around One West Fifty-seventh, so that the ailing Mr. Vanderbilt
wouldn't be disturbed by the sounds of passing horses and rigs. It might
seem unbelievable, nowadays, to think that whole city blocks would be
repaved just to let one man rest easier; but Cornelius II was that important to the city, mostly because of his philanthropic work. Of course, it
wasn't noise that was making him sick, as the Doctor pointed out: you
could've put the man into a room lined with concrete and lead, and, so
long as he had the thought of how little control he'd been able to exercise over his son to keep him company, his body would've continued to
deteriorate.

When we got to One West Fifty-seventh, the Doctor informed Mr.
Moore that, especially as the interview had been so tough to obtain, he
was not to enter it intending to tweak Mr. Vanderbilt's nose, as he'd said
he wanted to. They'd just tell the sorry old invalid that they were trying
to trace Mrs. Hatch's movments in order to contact her, being as they
thought she could be of some assistance with a case the Doctor was
working on; nothing else. Mr. Moore reluctantly agreed, and then they
walked on up the front steps to the big, arched limestone doorway. Mr.
Moore rang the doorbell and a footman answered, saying that they were
expected by Mr. Vanderbilt in the "Moorish room" at the back of the
house. Knowing enough to realize that he was talking about a smoking
room what probably looked like a plate illustration for *A Thousand and
One Nights*—such rooms being all the rage among rich people in those
days—I got down off the calash's driver's seat and, when the footman returned, asked him if he wouldn't mind keeping an eye on the carriage for
a minute, as I had an errand I had to run for the Doctor a few blocks uptown. The man very decently obliged, and I tore off to and around the
corner of Fifth Avenue. When I reached the back of the house, near the
handsome porte cochere what Mr. Hunt had designed, I found that a
fairly high cast-iron fence separated me from the backyard. I wouldn't
have any trouble getting over the thing, of course, but there were a few

strollers around, even on that wet afternoon, and so a bit of caginess was called for.

I tried an old trick: looking to the high roof of the mansion across the street, which was only a bit less luxurious than Mr. Vanderbilt's, I pointed up and screamed:

"He's going to jump!"

This, of course, is the single statement guaranteed to get any and all New Yorkers to stop whatever they're doing and turn to search the direction indicated. The strollers out on Fifth Avenue that afternoon were no exceptions, and in the few seconds it took them to realize that I'd been putting them on I got over the Vanderbilts' fence and ran to hide behind one of the square columns of the porte cochere. Scanning the back of the house, I soon caught sight of an open bay window on the western end, out of which were drifting voices. I could easily hide on the far side of the bay, and did, allowing myself just one peek inside the room.

If there's one word to describe the Vanderbilt family's taste, I'm not in possession of it. You could, I suppose, just say that they liked "more": more stone with their stone, more frills with their frills, more artwork with their artwork, more food with their food. The "Moorish room" that I peered into that day was a very good example of all this. It wasn't enough that the wood of the walls—fully two stories high—was as expensive as possible or that it was carved in more complicated patterns than the Arabian models what it'd been based on; no, the walls also had to be inlaid with other precious substances, including, if you can believe it, mother-of-pearl. Mother-of-pearl in your walls . . . if you can order that kind of nonsensical detail—and order it from no less a designer than Mr. Louis Comfort Tiffany—then it's no wonder, I suppose, that you'd have a stroke when your own kid refused to do what you told him. Hanging from the high ceiling was a gigantic, bulbous Tiffany lamp, with smaller lamps, also of Tiffany glass, suspended in a circle from the top of this central fixture. Below that conglomeration, set in front of a marble Moorish fireplace and on top of several enormous, thick Persian carpets, were some straight-backed velvet chairs. In two of these sat the Doctor and Mr. Moore, seeming very small in that room; and opposite them—covered, in spite of the July heat, by a rich fur blanket—was Mr. Vanderbilt, looking like what he was: a man on a slow but steady course to death. His long face and glaring eyes, which once could intimidate most men even from a good distance, were now full of a beaten sadness, and his voice was rough.

"And what reason can you possibly have to come to me for such information?" he was asking.

I ducked back down to hide and listen as Mr. Moore responded, "The woman was a servant of yours, Mr. Vanderbilt, for a time—at least, she listed you as her employer on some hospital forms we've seen."

"What of it?" Mr. Vanderbilt answered, in a tone what you might politely call condescending. "Yes, she was employed here. But as to her private dealings—they were precisely that, and respected as such. Elspeth Hatch was a trusted servant. She had been since her arrival in the city."

"And that was—" the Doctor asked.

I heard a hoarse sigh of exasperation come out of their host, causing Mr. Moore to add, "If the matter weren't so urgent, Mr. Vanderbilt—"

"Urgent?" old man Vanderbilt cut in. "Urgent, yet you will not tell me what it is?"

"The confidentiality of patient and physician," the Doctor replied. "I'm sure you understand."

"And we really wouldn't impose on you," Mr. Moore said, "if we had any choice."

"Well," Mr. Vanderbilt grunted. "At the very least you recognize that it *is* an imposition. Had I any less regard for your family, Mr. Moore—"

"Yes, sir," Mr. Moore answered. "Quite."

Another irritated sigh got out of Mr. Vanderbilt. "We engaged Elspeth Hatch in—I should say it was in the summer of 1894. Very soon after the tragedy. We had heard of her misfortune from friends upstate, and my wife thought that offering her a position—we needed a maid in any case— would offer her a chance to leave her home and put the past behind her. Mrs. Vanderbilt is a woman of uncommon compassion." He grunted again. "*And* breeding . . ."

There followed a few more silent moments, during which I figured that the Doctor and Mr. Moore were glancing at each other, trying to come up with a way to find out what the "tragedy" Mr. Vanderbilt had mentioned was. Given his attitude, it didn't seem likely he'd share any information about his former servant's personal misfortune if he thought his visitors weren't already aware of it.

"That was indeed uncommonly compassionate of your wife, sir," the Doctor finally said. "And no doubt it helped Mrs. Hatch recover. A change of locale is often the only effective antidote to such an unfortunate experience."

" 'Unfortunate experience'?" Mr. Vanderbilt rumbled back. "Seeing your own children shot down before you by a madman? Are you a disciple of understatement, Doctor, or have you simply become inured to tragedy through your work?"

That statement caused my eyes to pop a bit; and I could only think of how hard the Doctor and Mr. Moore must've been working to hide a like reaction.

"I—certainly didn't mean to sound callous, sir," the Doctor finally said. "Perhaps my work sometimes does prevent me from treating—*murder*"— he said the word carefully, as if he half expected a contradiction; but none came—"with the proper consideration," he finished.

Mr. Vanderbilt huffed, rather than grunted, this time. "I suppose that's to be expected. At any rate, she arrived here just two or three months later. And she worked with uncommon diligence, considering that the fate of her eldest daughter remained so uncertain."

"Ah. Yes, of course," Mr. Moore said. "And she left your employ, you said . . . ?"

"I did *not* say, Mr. Moore. But she departed from our service the following May, when she was remarried and her nephew was left in her care. I offered her a recommendation, and it would have been an unqualified one, but she said that she wished to pursue a career in nursing. I told her that if I could be of any service in that regard, she should not hesitate to contact me. She never did. And that, gentlemen, is really all I can tell you."

I heard the sound of a door opening, and then a careful little voice said, "Excuse me, sir, but the missus says it's time for you to rest."

"Yes," Mr. Vanderbilt answered, "I'm coming. Well, gentlemen. I must obey the orders of my physician. I hope you will be able to locate Mrs. Hatch—although I suppose her name must have changed."

"Yes," Mr. Moore said. "Thank you, Mr. Vanderbilt, for seeing us. You have been exceptionally gracious—and helpful. Will you be leaving for Newport soon?"

"Tomorrow, in fact. Which is why I must gather my strength. I'll have someone show you out."

"Please, sir," the Doctor said, "do not trouble yourself. We are quite capable. And thank you, once again."

There were some general sounds of movement, and that was my cue: waiting 'til just a few people were passing by on the avenue, I ran full out for the iron fence, threw myself up and over it, then landed on the sidewalk and walked breezily away, ignoring the stares of a couple what were strolling by and trying to look like I jumped millionaires' fences every day, twice on Sundays.

I got back to the calash a few seconds after the Doctor and Mr. Moore had reached it, making it necessary for me to explain where I'd been. This had the advantage of making it *un*necessary for them to tell me about their conversation with Mr. Vanderbilt, though my second act of trespassing in a week didn't please the Doctor much. But the shock of what they'd heard inside overrode any other considerations.

"I hate this!" Mr. Moore said as we started the drive back downtown. "I *hate* it! It's *exactly* as Lucius said: every time we think we're getting somewhere, slap!, some new piece of information crops up that changes the whole picture."

"And what makes you so sure that the picture has changed, Moore?" the Doctor asked.

"You heard what he said, Kreizler!" Mr. Moore shouted in frustration. "The woman's children were 'shot down in front of her by a madman'! What the hell was *that* all about?"

The Doctor shrugged. "Any number of things. It may be true. It may also have been a fantasy she created."

"Kreizler," Mr. Moore answered, banging one hand against the door of the calash in annoyance, "he said he was told about it by friends. What's she doing, going all over the *state* making up stories about dead children to gain people's sympathy?"

"Not all over the state. The event occurred near the town where she was born, apparently. So if there's any truth to it at all, your friend in the district attorney's office should be able to tell us about it. Have you been able to contact him yet?"

"I wrote on Monday," Mr. Moore answered glumly, settling into a mood that matched the hot, humid weather. "And sent a telegram on Tuesday. But I suppose now I'd better wire him again, or try to get him on the telephone. Let him know about this." He roused himself just once more. "And what did he mean about her 'nephew' being left in her care, anyway?"

"That," the Doctor said, "was almost *certainly* a fantasy. Or, to be more explicit, a lie. She had to create some story to explain the sudden appearance of the Johannsen boy in her life."

"Oh. Yes." Mr. Moore's understanding of this detail didn't cheer him up any. "Christ, it's like trying to keep up with the machinations of three different people."

"True," the Doctor replied. "Layers upon layers . . ."

On hearing that statement, Mr. Moore gave up on trying to make any more sense out of the strange things Mr. Vanderbilt had said and just took to smoking cigarettes and knocking his feet against the wall of the carriage every few minutes, saying "I *hate* this!" over and over, like we hadn't gotten the point. Dr. Kreizler tried to get his friend's mind off the thing by going over the front page of the *Times*. But the news there wasn't such as would cheer any of us up. The police had finally captured Martin Thorn, the suspected culprit in the "mystery of the headless body," and, true to Detective Sergeant Lucius's prediction, he'd never left the city during the whole time the manhunt for him had been going on. We had some reason to believe that the distraction of the case would continue a bit longer—though a confession had been gotten out of Thorn, it conflicted with all the "evidence" and theories the police had assembled—but at best the case would be resolved in a matter of days. An even greater worry was the fact that Senator Henry Cabot Lodge, Mr. Roosevelt's closest friend and po-litical ally in Washington, was openly urging President McKinley to take stronger action against the Spanish Empire in all contested matters: the American war party was getting impatient, and though we didn't know just what that would mean for our investigation, it didn't seem to indicate anything good. Finally, there was a report of more personal importance to both the Doctor and Mr. Moore: Madame Lillian Nordica, one of their fa-vorite singers from the Metropolitan Opera, was critically ill in London. The *Times* made it seem like she was at death's door, though we eventually found out that the report was exaggerated; but even the possibility of such a loss was enough to cause the Doctor to join Mr. Moore in downhearted silence.

The rain didn't let up much as we drove downtown, and neither did the stench on the street, which was a very bad sign: weather of that variety, coming at that time of year, could take quite a while to blow on out of town. As it turned out, that day did indeed mark the start of the first really dangerous period of the summer, the kind of natural phenomenon what the papers had taken to calling a "heat wave." For the next week, average temperatures would not fall below the eighties; and even at night, the humid air and lack of wind would make sleep just about impossible. This situation was not helped by the fact that our investigation soon narrowed down to the tedious business of continuing the search for a talkative member of the group of women whose kids had been under Nurse Hunter's care at the Lying-in Hospital (a job what had me driving the de-tective sergeants and Miss Howard to dismal parts of the city or, worse yet, out to the suburbs, over the next few days), as well as waiting for Mr. Moore to hear from his old pal up in Ballston Spa. By the following Mon-day, some of us were beginning to doubt the existence of this person. Mr. Moore had sent not one but two cables to the man, telling him what we were up to, but he'd had no reply. Such didn't necessarily mean anything, one way or the other; but it was, given our circumstances and the weather, cause for much frustration.

Add fear to that mix, and you had a truly rocky time. This last emotion came first in the form of occasional appearances in the Stuyvesant Park area by members of the Hudson Dusters. They made no threatening moves, being as they weren't interested in getting into a scrape so far outside their territory; but it was clear that they wanted to remind us that they were around, and that—cops or no cops—we'd be better off minding our own business. Unsettling as these visits were, they didn't compare to the several sightings by some members of our team—including me—of El Niño, the Filipino pygmy employed by Señor Linares. Like the Dusters, this little man made no attempt to attack or even threaten any of us; but he was there and watching, knives and arrows at the ready should our investigation actually start to move forward in some kind of dramatic way.

As all of this was happening, the detective sergeants also had to pursue their investigation of affairs at the Doctor's Institute. They hadn't reported their progress on this matter to anyone in our group; hadn't said anything about it at all, in fact, excepting the time they'd requested information from Cyrus concerning the staff of the place, and another occasion when they'd asked me if I'd seen anything in Paulie McPherson's behavior that might help explain his suicide. I'd told them I hadn't; and from the disappointed way they nodded at me in reply, I took it that they hadn't been having much better luck digging information up anywhere else.

Then, on Monday the twelfth, the detective sergeants showed up at Seventeenth Street looking pretty grim. It was late in the afternoon, and the heat wave was still going strong: in fact, the weather claimed its first victim that day, a small child who was struck down by sunstroke and taken to the Hudson Street Hospital (not far, I immediately thought when I heard the news, from the house where Libby Hatch lived her life as Nurse Elspeth Hunter). The Doctor was in his study working, Cyrus was out in the carriage house tending to the horses, and I was in the kitchen, helping Mrs. Leshko clean up half a dozen plates what she'd smashed to bits with the end of a mop during a moment of typically vigorous but destructive cleaning.

When the doorbell rang, I ran to answer it, leaving a wailing Mrs. Leshko to the last of the sweeping up. The detective sergeants were all business when they came in, immediately asking where the Doctor was. I told them he was in his study, and they marched right upstairs, looking like they'd been hoping to avoid this moment but were now resigned to it. There wasn't any way I was going to miss what came next: I let them get a floor or so ahead of me, then followed on up at the same distance, finally dashing to the study door when I heard it close. Creeping carefully, I made my way to the thing, then lay on the carpeted floor and peered through the narrow crack underneath it, seeing several pairs of feet along with the bottoms of many piles of books and papers.

"We're sorry to bother you, Doctor," I heard Marcus say, as his feet came to rest in front of the legs of one of the chairs near the Doctor's desk. "But we thought we'd better let you know what's going on with the— other matter."

There was a pause, and Lucius's feet started tapping nervously between the legs of the sofa. "The news isn't bad, exactly—but we can't really say it's good, either."

The Doctor drew a heavy breath. "Well, gentlemen?"

"So far as we can tell," Marcus said, "there's no reason to believe that the McPherson boy's suicide was prompted by anything or anyone at your Institute. We've questioned and requestioned the entire staff, and put to-gether a general chronology of events from the time the boy arrived to the time he died. There's simply nothing that suggests he was treated in a way that would have sparked self-destructive tendencies."

"Even members of the staff who don't particularly like each other," Lu-cius added carefully, "—not that there are more than two or three of them—can't find fault with each other's behavior toward the boy. As for family—assuming he was going by his right name, we really can't find any relations at all."

"I tried myself," the Doctor added quietly. "Without success."

"We checked out the cord he used," Marcus said, trying to sound more optimistic, "and it doesn't match the materials found in any of the drap-ery or curtain mechanisms in the building. Which means he must've brought it in with him—"

"Which suggests that he'd been contemplating the act before he got there," Lucius said.

"And *that*," Marcus continued, "will be useful in court, I think. Now— about that court date . . ." There was another pause before Marcus went on. "Judge Reinhart, who was in charge of your initial hearing, neglected to inform anyone that he's retiring at the end of this month. His caseload has been farmed out to a series of other magistrates. You, I'm afraid, have drawn Judge Samuel Welles." I heard a hiss come out of the Doctor. "Yes. You've crossed paths with him before, we understand," Marcus said.

"Several times," the Doctor answered quietly.

"We don't know him," Lucius said, "but we hear that he's fairly stern."

"That's not my main concern," replied the Doctor. "He can be stern, yes, but I've seen him be lenient, as well. And *that* is the difficulty. He is utterly unpredictable. I've never been able to anticipate his reactions precisely enough to structure my testimony accordingly. In addition, he is not a man who requires extensive evidence of wrongdoing in matters such as these. If the state chooses to make a case that throws serious moral opprobrium on the Institute—"

"Which it will almost certainly do," Marcus said.

"—then the mere fact that the McPherson boy died while in my care may be enough for Welles."

"Yes." Lucius's voice was a strange mixture of hope and gloominess. "That's why we thought we'd better come—to let you know that it's really going to ride on the hearing itself. It's been delayed a bit, by the way. Apparently, Welles will be on vacation until the first week of September, and—"

The sudden sound of people entering the house and loud voices echoing up the staircase made me stop listening and jerk my head around; then, realizing that the Doctor and the detective sergeants could probably hear it, too, I got to my feet and started downstairs, not wanting to get caught eavesdropping. Looking down between the banisters, I could just see Mr. Moore, Miss Howard, and Cyrus pounding up the stairs.

"Well, then, where the hell *is* he?" Mr. Moore was asking, in a loud, breathless voice.

"I believe that the Doctor is in his study, Mr. Moore," Cyrus explained in a baffled and not altogether pleased tone. "If you'll just tell me—"

"No, no," Mr. Moore answered. "We'll tell him—we'll *all* tell him! Come on, Cyrus, you're part of this, too, you'd better hear about it!"

They kept on coming up at the same fast pace, Mr. Moore taking the stairs two at a time and, when he saw me, just about falling in a faint at my feet.

"Stevie!" he breathed. "Is he up there? My God, I've run across half the damned city—"

"Oh, really, John," Miss Howard said. She was a little out of breath, too, but nothing to match Mr. Moore. "From your house to my house to Seventeenth Street hardly constitutes half the city. If you'd just get some blasted exercise occasionally—"

"It is—a well-known fact," Mr. Moore panted, "that—too much exercise—is not good for you. And I'm living proof, just at the moment. . . . Well, Stevie?"

I indicated the study with a nod. "He's in there. With the detective sergeants."

That got Mr. Moore right back up. "Excellent," he said. "Saves any more running around." He made for the study door, the rest of us behind him; and I was surprised when he didn't bother knocking, but just burst on in.

The Doctor looked up from his desk, a little shocked and, like Cyrus, a little miffed at the lack of courtesy. The detective sergeants got to their feet, also looking surprised, as Mr. Moore leaned on the doorknob and kept on panting.

Then he held up an envelope. "This just arrived . . . special delivery . . . from Rupert Picton." He took another deep breath. "I really do *hate* this case . . ."

CHAPTER 26

Mr. Moore opened the envelope as Cyrus, Miss Howard, and I filed into the study with the others. Unfolding the letter inside, our exhausted friend took a deep breath and tried to start reading it; but he'd only gotten as far as the salutation—"Moore, you swine!"—before he fell to his knees, still trying to catch his breath. Handing the letter to Miss Howard, he said, "Sara, you read it," then crawled over to the sofa and pulled himself up onto it.

"What the devil's the matter with him, Sara?" the Doctor asked. "Is he drunk, or has he merely been shot?"

"Worse," Miss Howard answered. "He's been running. But he's right about the letter, Doctor. Listen to this, it's dated yesterday: 'Moore, you swine! I would take the time to elaborate on what a mud-dwelling, feculent—'"

"You don't have to read that part!" Mr. Moore protested from the sofa.

Miss Howard only smiled and went on: "'—but the communications from you which I found heaped on my desk when I returned from the Adirondacks today actually must take precedence. All joking aside, John, listen to me—if you have indeed, in your infinite wisdom, managed to get yourself mixed up in a private investigation that is directed at the woman who was known in this town as Libby Hatch, then be as careful as you know how to be. The story you heard from Mr. Vanderbilt is indeed true, or rather, is the commonly accepted explanation of a horrendous crime that occurred here just over three years ago. Her three children were shot, supposedly by an itinerant Negro lunatic—who was never seen by anyone but Mrs. Hatch. Two of the children died. The third survived but has been mute ever since. An extensive search failed to produce any sign of the Negro, or of anyone who'd even gotten so much as a glimpse of the man—nevertheless, the case never got past a coroner's inquest, so effective was Mrs. Hatch's inventiveness, and so scarce the support for any other interpretation. I had my own ideas—and having been through what you have, I'm sure you can guess what they were.

" 'As to the other matters you say you are looking into, I am appalled but not surprised to learn of them. The woman is, I believe, one of the most dangerous persons alive. It's a pity I couldn't ever convince anyone else of that. You indicate that your investigation in New York is at a bit of a standstill. If this is true, I advise you to take it as a sign. Make no more direct moves against Libby Hatch yourself, and, if the people you're working with are even semicapable investigators, waste no time getting up here with them. Dr. Kreizler I of course know by his writings and reputation, and I should be delighted to make his acquaintance.

" 'Wire me if and when you're coming. I am in deadly earnest, John— don't try to beat this woman with an informal investigation. Even if you had the entire Police Department on it with you, I should worry—she'd find a way to con them all and kill you, if it came to that. Either leave the thing be, or get up here and we'll see what we can do together. Any other course will be disastrous.

" 'Your friend, Rupert Picton.' "

Miss Howard folded up the sheet of paper and replaced it in the envelope. "That's all," she said.

The Doctor just sat still for a moment, then looked over to the sofa, where Mr. Moore appeared to have recovered. "He seems quite a colorful fellow, this friend of yours, Moore."

"Don't let the banter fool you," Mr. Moore answered, going for a box of cigarettes that sat on the Doctor's desk. "He's got one of the sharpest legal minds I've ever run across. He could have had any job in the state, but like the fool he is he decided to play it straight instead—cried bloody murder to the legislature about corruption in the city D.A.'s office, and got run out of town on a rail. There were rumors about some kind of a mental breakdown after that." Mr. Moore lit his cigarette. "I never really got the details."

Cyrus spoke up, in a slightly perplexed voice: "Then he's saying that *she* shot the children?"

"Yes," Miss Howard answered. "He seems quite certain of it."

"More victims to add to the roster," Lucius said.

"They could've been the ones in the picture," I threw in. "The photograph I saw in the desk, of the three older kids together."

"It would make sense," Lucius answered. "You can't exactly induce cyanosis in three children who're old enough to struggle—and to talk, if they survive."

"But it doesn't really fit the pattern, does it?" Cyrus asked, still unclear. "She's only killed infants, that we know of—because she's had trouble with them during that stage of life."

"It's a wrinkle, Cyrus, to be sure," the Doctor answered, toying with a pen on his desk. "But the overriding similarity remains—the children *were* attacked, and the attacker's intention was clearly to kill them all."

Marcus let out a stunned kind of sigh. "If this whole thing weren't so horrifying, I'd say it was getting ridiculous . . ."

"Far from it, Marcus," the Doctor answered. "This news only confirms the entrenched nature of her tendencies. Her past is at one with her present behavior." The Doctor's voice grew quieter as he mouthed the words that were the closest thing he had to a motto: "The keys are in the details . . ." He stood up, and turned to look out the window of his study at the small garden behind the house. "And those details are upstate—not here. If we wish true progress, then we must go."

"Is that smart?" Lucius asked. "If we leave, she may think we've given her the field—and God knows what'll happen then."

"We shall not leave before the two of you confront her, Detective Sergeant," the Doctor replied. "And now you can include our awareness of this incident in your statement. We can only hope that such awareness will make her act with even greater caution. Because if we stay here, we will remain stymied. The past is our way in—we must follow it."

Marcus spoke again, very carefully: "And the other matter, Doctor? How do you feel about leaving with your own affairs—unresolved?"

The Doctor shrugged. "As you both have said, Marcus, there is little I can do before the hearing. If there had been any secrets to unearth, I know that you would have found them. Whether I stay or go is of little consequence." Watching him, I saw something that seemed almost like bitterness enter his face. "And I confess," he continued, again softly, "that I have never been so weary of this city. Or its citizens . . ." He shook the moment off and turned to face us. "Getting away may be the best thing, all the way round."

"No question about that," Mr. Moore said cheerfully. "Especially given the destination. Saratoga's absolute heaven at this time of year. And when you add the—*diversions* . . ."

Everyone else in the room smiled and groaned, and Miss Howard picked up a book to fling at Mr. Moore. "Yes, we all know why *you* want to go, John—but you'll have precious little time for your usual pursuits."

"I'm just talking about our off-hours!" Mr. Moore protested, shielding himself. "We can't work day and night, you know! And let's face it, Saratoga—"

"Saratoga is a vulgar, disgusting *sty,*" Miss Howard finished for him, "where fat, wealthy men gamble, lie to their wives, and make panderers and prostitutes rich." The harshness of the words made it clear that she sincerely meant what she said.

"Oh, you sound like your friend Nellie Bly," Mr. Moore replied with a wave of his cigarette. "Besides, I'm not married—or fat."

"Give yourself time," Miss Howard returned. "And as for Nellie, everything she wrote about that wretched place in the *World* was true, and it took great courage to say it."

"Yes," Mr. Moore countered. "Almost as much courage as it took to marry that seventy-five-year-old millionaire of hers."

Miss Howard's eyes went thin, and she poised herself to strike. "Mr. Seaman is *not* seventy-five."

"No. He's seventy." Marcus had said the words absentmindedly; but a glance from Miss Howard was all it took to make him regret it. "Well, I'm sorry, Sara, but he *is*—"

"My God, it's a miracle the human species still exists," Miss Howard seethed, "with apes like you carrying it forward!"

"Children, children!" The Doctor clapped his hands. "We have far more pressing matters to deal with. It's now Monday evening. How soon can we all be ready to depart?"

"Tomorrow," Mr. Moore answered quickly, obviously dying to get up to the great American resort town of Saratoga Springs, where, as Miss Howard had said, gambling, whoring, and philandering had long ago pushed taking the waters out of the way to become the chief pastimes.

"Marcus and I'll need a bit longer," Lucius threw in. "I don't think we'll have any trouble selling Captain O'Brien on the idea that we're going along to watch your movements, Doctor, but it may take a couple of days to tie everything up—and, of course, there's that little visit to Bethune Street to make."

"Very well," the Doctor answered. "Shall we say Thursday morning?" There was general agreement to this idea, and the Doctor grabbed for his copy of the *Times.* "We can take one of the paddle steamers as far as Troy, and from there the train to Ballston Spa. Moore, as for going on to Saratoga, you'll have to arrange that yourself."

Mr. Moore grinned wide. "That won't be any trouble—they've put in an electric trolley from Ballston to the center of Saratoga. Fifteen or twenty minutes, and I can be standing in front of Canfield's Casino."

"I'm delighted for you," Miss Howard mumbled, what you might call acidly. Mr. Moore just grinned at her.

"Stevie?" the Doctor said, and I snapped to it. "In the morning you'll go down to the Twenty-second Street pier—see what embarks Thursday morning. Try for the *Mary Powell,* if she's available—I prefer her private parlors, and she's generally less crowded than the other day lines."

"Right," I said. "How many parlors?"

"We should need only one," the Doctor said. "But get two in the event that the rain doesn't subside. As to packing, I should recommend planning on a month's stay, to be safe. Moore, I leave the hotel accommodations to you and Sara. All right, then, everyone—let's waste no more time."

At that we all left the room, and split up to start packing and preparing. The prospect of getting out of New York in midsummer quickly began producing its usual effect—relief and a giddy sort of joy—despite the disturbing things we'd learned from Mr. Rupert Picton: if we had to pursue the miserable case of Libby Hatch, it would be a sight more pleasant to do so in the green wilds of upstate New York than in the sweltering heat of Manhattan.

That, anyway, was what we thought at the time.

CHAPTER 27

Things were humming on Seventeenth Street for the next couple of days. We not only had to pack our things but board the horses and close up the house itself for what might be an extended absence. And then there was the job of finding somebody to look in on the place occasionally, somebody less destructive—and, hopefully, with a better command of English—than Mrs. Leshko. The Doctor eventually snuck an offer, through Cyrus, to one of the custodians at his Institute, a fellow he knew could use some extra money; and through the same agent, the man agreed. Luck was with us all the way around on this score, because when we told Mrs. Leshko we'd be leaving and that she wouldn't be needed while we were gone, she said—or at least, as best we could tell she said—that such was just as well, being as she wasn't going to be able to work for us anymore. It seemed that she and her husband had decided to head out west to try their luck opening a restaurant in a silver-mining town in Nevada. The Doctor, relieved that she'd spared him the job of firing her, gave her two weeks' salary and a nice-sized bonus, to boot. But none of us was what you might call optimistic about the prospects of her actually selling her cooking. We tended to doubt that even miners got that hungry.

As it turned out, the *Mary Powell* was indeed making a day run up the Hudson on Thursday, and I was able to book us two private parlors. It continued to look like this was a wise precaution, being as the rain didn't let up all through Tuesday. That afternoon Mr. Moore and Miss Howard—still bickering about the morality of the wild activities of Saratoga—came to the house at Seventeenth Street to wait with us for the detective sergeants, who'd gone downtown a little earlier to put Libby Hatch on notice as to what we knew about her. It was a nervous few hours that we spent in the parlor, with Cyrus trying to keep everybody calm by playing the piano softly. But despite his efforts, the building wind and rain outside seemed to say that some kind of calamity was on its way.

That particular fear, however, turned out to be uncalled for. The detective sergeants showed up at about five, in very relieved and slightly tipsy spirits. Their visit had gone as well as they could've hoped for: the mistress of Number 39 Bethune Street had once more tried to play coy and seductive with them, and had even invited them inside again—but they'd stood their ground and said their piece right there on the doorstep, with the rain and the runoff from the roof pouring down on them. They'd listed every important point that we'd devised, both false and true, starting with the declaration that the Police Department was aware of what she was doing and then moving on to our knowledge of her secret "hideaway" in the basement and the Doctor's continuing to serve as a special consultant on the case. They'd wound up with the announcement that they'd figured out what'd happened in Ballston Spa three years ago and were on their way to confirm their suspicions. If anything happened to her husband in the meantime, they said, or if a baby answering Ana Linares's description turned up dead somewhere, she could look forward to a date with the electrical chair at Sing Sing. It was true that few women got executed in the United States, they'd told her; but someone with her murderous record could definitely count on gaining entry into that select group.

Lucius described the woman's reaction to all this. She'd gone from playing the coy temptress to forcing some tears and protesting her innocence, then moved on to saying that the detective sergeants just didn't understand the "extenuating circumstances" of what she'd done (such being Lucius's phrase, not hers). Finally, pure malevolence had made its way into those golden eyes. That was the only moment, both the brothers said, when they'd become truly unsure of what they'd started. They were, after all, in the heart of Hudson Duster territory and open to attack from the gang, assuming that Libby Hatch felt like having her boyfriend's thugs tend to the matter and didn't just shoot the pair herself. But the Isaacsons had warned her that plenty of people in the department knew where they were and what they were doing, and if they didn't make it back to headquarters, nobody'd have any trouble figuring out why. When he and Lucius walked back to the cab they had waiting, Marcus said, he could feel the pure hatred coming from the doorway of Number 39, like bright sunshine on bare skin; then as they left they'd heard a loud slam of the door and a small cry of rage from inside. But they'd made it out of the neighborhood without any trouble, and had stopped on their way to the Doctor's house only long enough to calm themselves down with a quick shot of rye and a short beer—a rare thing for Lucius—at the Old Town Bar on Eighteenth Street and Park Avenue.

And so, as Mr. Moore put it, war had been declared, and directly to our enemy's face. But the Doctor was quick to remind him that, while we could be happy that all had gone well and the detective sergeants were safe, thinking of Libby Hatch as our "enemy" was not going to help our cause. We were on our way upstate not only to learn exactly *what* she'd done, but *why;* and while it might be tough, given all the things we knew about her, to try to see things as she'd seen them during her years of growing up and becoming a mother, it was more important than ever that we do so. Talk about "enemies" and a "war" wasn't going to help that process: if we were ever going to understand what had driven the woman to her past and current acts of violence enough to guess at her next moves, we were going to have to let go of the image of her as the Devil's handmaiden. She was a person, one who'd been made capable of unspeakable things by unknown events what we would never really appreciate if we couldn't see them through the eyes of first the girl and then the young woman she'd once been.

This was all sensible talk, and I'd heard similar from the Doctor many times before; and maybe if the weather had calmed down at all on Wednesday, it would've been easier for me to stay equally reasonable. But dawn that morning saw the sky black and every window in the house starting to rattle in its frame. By noon a howling gale had roared up from the southwest to slam into not just the city but the whole eastern part of the state, as well. Up in Matteawan, we later learned, the rain was so heavy that a whole set of dams burst, and eight people were killed in the flood that followed. Maybe it's true that what goes on in the sky is just weather and doesn't signify anything more; but the notion that we'd stirred the wrath of some powerful being somewhere flitted into and out of my head all day long as we made our final preparations for departure the next morning.

By late Wednesday evening the storm was still raging, and I still hadn't seen or heard anything from Kat. As the night wore away, I realized with ever more misgiving that she would likely end up leaving for California while we were upstate and, lacking any way to contact me there, would think I had no interest in what had become of her. Caught up in such thoughts, my mind was tormented for several hours with the question of whether I should make a quick circuit of her usual haunts. When she'd been at the Doctor's house, she'd left me with the notion that she wouldn't be going back to the Dusters'; but the amount of cocaine what had clearly been in her body when she'd come to Number 808 Broadway had made me doubt that she'd kept completely clear of the place. And as I sat in my room and watched the lightning, thunder, and rain throw branches of the trees in Stuyvesant Park first one way and then another, my doubts only multiplied. Did she have a flop, I wondered, on a night like this? She had the money to afford someplace decent, that was certain—or had she already spent it on a burny binge? Had Ding Dong found out about her good fortune, and forced her to fork it over? Could she count on anybody besides me to care enough to find out? I hoped so. Because no matter how fretful I got that night, I found that I just couldn't head out the door. I told myself it was the high winds and the rain; but a voice inside me answered that I'd spent plenty of time wandering the streets in weather like that. Then I protested that it was her place to come to me for once, if she needed help; but I knew that, mad as she'd been when we parted, she never would. The plain truth was that I didn't know why I couldn't go out to look for her. I was worried whether I'd ever hear from her again, I was worried about where she was and what she was doing, but I simply couldn't go after her and I couldn't say why.

I woke the next morning to find that the great storm had blown out to sea. Sunshine and a light breeze were quickly drying the city, while the temperature had finally dropped into the seventies. There were a few branches on the grass and walkways of Stuyvesant Park, but other than that the tempest didn't seem to've left any permanent scars on our neighborhood. It wasn't yet 7:30, but the carriage the Doctor'd engaged to take our bags and ourselves down to the Twenty-second Street pier would arrive in just half an hour, and the *Mary Powell* was due to get under way at nine; so I dressed and cleaned up quickly, sitting on the lids of the big suitcase and small valise the Doctor'd given me so that the things would close, and then banging my way downstairs with them.

Cyrus and the Doctor were both awake, the Doctor in his study packing books and papers and Cyrus in the kitchen, once again making coffee. By the time it was ready, the three of us were, too: we'd stacked our bags and trunks by the front door and had nothing left to do but drink Cyrus's strong coffee and grow ever more anxious to get on the boat, the first of which activities only aggravated the second. I made a last round of the back door, the yard, and the carriage house, sneaking myself a smoke as I made sure everything was locked down tight. Then, finally, the hired rig appeared. The driver, an old German who the Doctor spoke to in his native language, helped us get the bags aboard, and then we turned to say our good-byes to the house, not knowing just when we'd pass through the little iron gateway to the front yard again.

The weather only improved as we made for the Hudson, the breeze remaining mild and the sky marked by just a few large, quick-moving clouds. When we reached Ninth Avenue and Twenty-second Street, I stuck my head out of the carriage and looked ahead to the pier: the *Mary Powell* was docked and surrounded by a large crowd. We crossed over Tenth and then Eleventh Avenues, and as we did the number of people and rigs making for the pier steadily increased. The smell of the river and the prospect of going someplace new and exciting were making my blood positively race, but I didn't know how agitated my movements had become 'til the Doctor threw a playful arm round my head, telling me it was the only way he could think of to keep my skull from exploding.

Our fellow passengers at the pier seemed to be as excited and relieved by the sudden change in the weather as we were. Most of them weren't near as laden down with baggage, though—ships like the *Mary Powell* catered mostly to day cruisers—and we didn't have any trouble finding a porter to help us with the bags. I told the Doctor that I'd help the man get them off the carriage and on board the ship if he and Cyrus wanted to go ahead and check our parlors to see which other members of our party had arrived. This they did, and I quickly commenced moving the luggage onto the amiable Italian porter's hand truck with the assistance of our big German driver. I didn't understand a word what either man said, but that didn't matter; the sight of the river steamer all decked out and ready for the voyage, her twin stacks and big side paddles signifying confidence and power, together with the excitement that was coursing through the merry collection of people both aboard the ship and on the pier, kept me moving in a happy, spirited, and sure fashion.

Strange, what little things can change your mood faster than spit: a sound, maybe, or even just a smell can sometimes twist your thoughts and feelings worse than hours of conversation or days of experience. For me, that morning, it was a sight—just a glimpse, really—of the person I least wanted to see in the world:

Ding Dong. He was sitting about thirty yards away, atop a big pile of freight on the wharf—but his eyes were honed right in on me. His vicious features were twisted by the same evil, idiot grin that was generally in evidence; and as soon as he knew I'd caught sight of him, he jumped to the ground, grinned even wider, and made a vigorous, obscene movement with his hands and his pelvis.

I got the message, all right: Kat had gone back to him.

It hit me hard, forcing my eyes to the ground and my jaw to fall open. Then a voice sounded from somewhere inside my own head: *Of course she went back to him,* it said. *She didn't have anywhere else to go, thanks to you . . .*

By the time I looked back up, Ding Dong had vanished into the crowd. Most likely he'd trailed us from the Doctor's house and, satisfied to see us leaving town, just wanted to send me off with a personal message that'd make my heart as sore as I'd made his face. He'd succeeded, all right. I dropped the suitcase I had in my hand and just kind of collapsed onto it, so dazed that I barely heard a familiar voice—this one definitely outside me—calling.

"Stevie!" It was Mr. Moore, moving my way with a suitcase of his own in hand. A porter carrying a trunk was trailing behind him. "Stevie," he said again as he reached me. Then he crouched down. "What is it, kid, what's going on? Where's the Doctor?"

"They—" I shook myself hard, trying to get rid of the shock. "They—went aboard already. I'm bringin' our stuff—with the porters."

Mr. Moore put a firm hand on my shoulder. "Stevie, has something happened? You look like you've seen a ghost."

"Not a ghost." I couldn't go into a full explanation, but a piece of one was called for. "Dusters. Must've followed us here."

Spinning to search the wharf, Mr. Moore squinted. "They didn't get on the boat, did they?"

"Nah," I said. "They're gone. Just letting me—*us*—know they're still watching."

"Unh-hunh," Mr. Moore answered. "Well, come on. With any luck, we'll be out of town long enough for the Dusters to forget all about us." I got back up and moved with him toward the gangplank of the *Mary Powell,* our porters following close behind. "It's not like you to let them rattle you this way, Stevie," Mr. Moore said, punching my shoulder lightly. "Though after that brawl, I guess I can understand it."

I didn't answer, just nodded and tried to get my breathing back to some kind of regular pace. By the time we got on board, I'd almost managed that much, too; but the burning rock of guilt in the pit of my gut wasn't going anywhere.

Once on the ship, Mr. Moore and I let our porters lead the way to our private parlors. Located amidships on the portside upper deck, they were handsome rooms indeed, with trimmed wood paneling, rich furnishings, and windows that would offer us views not only of the Palisades cliffs soon after our departure but the Catskills and other handsome mountains along the way. For the moment, though, all such pleasures and advantages were lost on me. Once I'd seen the bags safely into the rooms, where the Doctor, Cyrus, Miss Howard, and the detective sergeants were already lounging and exploring happily, I mumbled something about wanting to get a look around the ship and left quickly.

Down on the main deck, just forward of the large dining rooms, I found a public men's room and entered it, getting a bit of a skeptical glance from the old attendant as I did. Locking myself into one of the toilet stalls, I leaned against the tiled wall on one side and lit up a smoke, trying to drive away the devilish thoughts and feelings what were tearing at my insides. I hadn't made much progress before I heard the attendant outside the stall:

He cleared his voice with purpose and said, "This washroom is for *gentlemen.*"

Which was not the kind of attitude to take with somebody in my condition. "This *toilet* is for *passengers,* mug," I snapped back. "So go chase yourself, unless you wanna finish this trip with a busted arm." I heard the man take a deep, angry, and insulted breath, but he didn't say anything; and as I took another deep drag off my smoke, I remembered that he was just doing his job. "Don't worry, pal," I said, quietly now. "I'll be gone in a second." I allowed myself another minute or two's smoking, then dropped my butt into the toilet and headed out without looking at the attendant.

As I headed back up the wooden steps to the upper deck, a huge bellow came out of the ship's main whistle: we were getting under way. Not yet ready to return to the others, I went on up to the promenade deck and got as far forward as I could, cramming myself into the narrow little corner of space between the outer railing and the steering house. I was on the starboard side of the ship, away from the pier so that I couldn't see the crowd ashore. Then the *Mary Powell* started to slowly move out and away from the waterfront. Before long we'd eased out to the middle of the river, where the big side paddles engaged with a loud rumble and rush; not loud enough, though, to quiet that same voice in my head.

She ain't like you, it said. *She didn't grow up in this town; she's never understood it, really, no matter what she says; and you stood there and let her wander right back off into what you knew was trouble, just because she embarrassed you—*

Lost in all this bitter thinking, I pretty near jumped clear of the deck when I heard the Doctor's voice behind me:

"You won't see very much from this side," he said, joining me at the rail. "Or did you want to watch the city fade behind us?"

I turned back to look at the waterfront of Hell's Kitchen as we moved steadily past it. "Something like that" was all I could say.

The Doctor nodded, and for a few more silent moments, we just stood there. "We'll be coming up on the Palisades soon," he finally said. "Shall we go to the other side?"

"Sure." I peeled myself off the rail and followed him round the back of the wheelhouse.

On the ship's port side the distant view before us changed as dramatically as if we'd stepped into another world. On our left were the small, quaint houses of Weehawken, New Jersey, while in front of us the sparse outskirts of other towns formed a picture what was similarly humble and peaceful. Soon greenery closed in completely on the river, not to be interrupted again until we reached those giant brown-and-grey slabs of rock that rise hundreds of feet into the air for miles on end and are known as the Palisades. The cliffs were the first of many remarkable natural wonders what the Hudson had to offer the day traveler, and their effect—like the river's itself—was to reassuringly remove a person from the immediate cares of the human world.

As we stared at those rocks, the Doctor took in a deep breath, then let it out in what seemed to me a peculiar combination of relief and consternation. "This is a strange case, Stevie," he murmured. "Strange and disorienting. The human mind does not readily accept such events and possibilities." Continuing to look out at the Palisades, he held up a hand. "And do you know, I cannot help but think of my *own* mother, when considering it. Is that odd, do you think?"

"I—don't really know," I answered. "Depends on what brings her to mind, I guess."

"A simple realization, really. I have always been unable to understand why, when things between my father and myself were at their worst, my mother never intervened. Even when I was only three or four years old, and utterly unable to defend myself, she never involved herself." His eyes seemed to be questioning the water, forest, and rocks before us, as if they might offer him some clue to the matter he was contemplating. There wasn't any sense of self-pity in the look, for the Doctor despised and avoided such tendencies. It was just a kind of honest, sad questioning—and he was entitled to wonder.

From the time Dr. Kreizler'd arrived on this earth, it seemed, the people closest to him had been either a vexation or a heartache, and sometimes both. His father, a rich German publisher who'd come to America after the European revolutions of 1848 went bust, had had it in for his son right from the start. Though in society circles the old man was a popular and admired character, at home he was a boozy tyrant, who treated his Hungarian wife and his two kids (for the Doctor had a sister who currently lived in England) to the backs as well as the fronts of his hands—fists, too. I didn't know just what had made the Doctor bring the subject up that day, but I was grateful to think and talk about anything other than Kat.

"Maybe she didn't know what was happening," I said with a shrug. "Or maybe she was afraid he'd lay into her even worse than usual if she did anything."

The Doctor's face filled with a look that said he'd considered such suggestions many times. "As to her not knowing," he said, "that seems unlikely, if not impossible, given her own violent relationship with the man. And as to her not wishing to incur his wrath—she did so deliberately far too often for me to accept that proposition. I have always known that his violence toward her gratified some perverse part of her psyche. But the violence toward my sister and myself? I don't think she relished that." He squinted a bit, and seemed to be struggling with an idea. "No, since we began this case, another possibility has presented itself to me—the thought that, although my mother cared for her children, their welfare was simply not her first priority. And the real question is not why that should have been so, but why it should have been such a difficult theory to either formulate or accept—why, indeed, it should have taken a murder case to make me think of it. After all, a man who makes his children of secondary or even minor importance, though he may be criticized by some, is hardly held to be unusual. Why should we believe any differently of a woman?"

"Well," I found myself saying, simply and automatically, "*because* . . . she's your *mother.* It's only natural."

The Doctor chuckled. "That answer from *you,* Stevie?"

I realized the stupidity of what I'd said, and tried to cheat my way out of it: "Well—it's not like we're talking about *my* mother—"

"No. In such discussions we never seem to be talking about *anyone's* mother. We seem to be talking about what Sara would call an abstract—a myth." The Doctor took out his cigarette case. "Have I ever told you about Frances Blake?"

"The woman you almost married when you were at Harvard?" I asked.

"The very same. She would have surprised you. Wealthy, a gadabout—fairly intelligent, but too personally ambitious to take the time to develop her insights. Just ask Moore. He quite disliked her." Lighting his cigarette, the Doctor chuckled. "As *I* grew to, eventually." He blew out some smoke, and his face took on a puzzled look. "She was not unlike my mother, in many ways . . ."

"So what was the attraction?" I asked.

"Well—in addition to some more obvious factors, she had a rather vulnerable side, one that seemed to allow her to understand the destructive foolishness of much of what she did. In my youthful naïveté, I believed I could nurture that side of her until it became dominant."

"So—you wanted to change her?"

"Do I detect censure in your voice, Stevie?" the Doctor asked, laughing quietly again. "Well, you're right to put it there. I behaved idiotically. . . . Imagine, contemplating marriage to a woman simply because you perceive her as vulnerable to change. She wasn't, of course. As pigheaded as . . . well. Set in her ways, shall we say."

I looked down at the waters of the Hudson as they churned away from the bow of the steamer. "Unh-hunh," I said, jabbing a finger on the rail in front of me and thinking about my own life as much as about the story I was listening to.

A big gust of cool wind hit the ship, and the Doctor drew his jacket tighter. "It was all unconscious, of course," he said. "But then, one can be as foolish unconsciously as consciously, eh?" He took another drag off his stick and turned his back to the wind. "And then, as I grew older, I realized that my actions had embodied something more sinister than a simple desire to change Frances. I had actually believed that if she failed to change and continued on to the life for which her own silly desires had destined her, it would somehow be my fault."

"*Yours?*" I said, looking up at him. "How did you figure that?"

He shrugged. "I didn't 'figure' it. I felt it. I was an inexperienced young man, Stevie, one whose relationship to his own mother had failed in some central way. I couldn't help but take the responsibility for that failure on myself—precisely because of all the things we've talked about. It's 'unnatural' to hold your own mother accountable for terrible wrongs. So I buried such feelings, and looked for some other woman whose behavior I could alter. The only blessing is that another, equally primitive part of my mind told me I couldn't sacrifice my entire life to such an endeavor. And so I said farewell to Frances." He shook once in the wind. "Still, it's an interesting technique—leaving one person behind in order to find her or him somewhere else. And *in* someone else."

"Yeah," I said, quietly amazed that—as usual—he'd been able to speak to exactly what was troubling me without ever mentioning my life at all.

Then I had a constructive thought of my own: "It's kinda like what we're doing on this job."

"Indeed?"

I nodded. "We're leaving Nurse Hunter in New York to go and find Libby Hatch upstate. Only difference is, they're not *like* each other—they *are* each other. So maybe this time, that kind of technique can actually work—since it's aimed at the right target."

The Doctor considered that as he finished off his cigarette. "You know—you may have a talent for this sort of work, Stevie." He glanced around, then stuck the butt of his cigarette into a nearby bucket of sand. "Well, this wind is stiffening. We've ordered breakfast. Steak and eggs for you. Come down when you're ready."

He gave me the quickest of glances, along with that fast but reassuring smile of his. Then, clapping his hands together, he walked back to the stairs—a bit unsteadily in that swelling, tidal portion of the lower Hudson—and vanished below.

I turned and looked back at the Palisades, feeling for the packet of cigarettes in my pocket; but then I decided against having another one. The horizon before me was beautiful, but it would be beautiful from our parlor, too, and I suddenly realized that my mood was changing, and I didn't want to be alone anymore.

"Well, Libby Hatch," I said, looking ahead at the long, wide stretch of the Hudson and then drumming my fingers on the rail as I turned away from it. "You got no place left to hide . . ."

I bounded down the stairs that the Doctor'd taken without ever glancing at the waters behind us.

If I had taken a peek in that direction, I would've seen a small steam launch what was trailing behind the *Mary Powell* as fast as its small engine would permit. And if, having caught sight of said vessel, I'd squinted and looked hard, it's possible I would've made out a small figure standing in its prow: a figure whose dark features, bushy hair, and suit of baggy clothes I would've recognized. But no matter how hard I'd looked, I wouldn't have seen the arsenal of strange weapons from the Orient what the mysterious little character was carrying—for those he kept hidden from view, until he was ready to strike.

CHAPTER 28

When I'd first come to live with the Doctor and undertaken to study, among many other things, the history of my own country, he'd figured that the best place for me to start was close to home. And so my earliest voyages into what was, for me, a great darkness—the story of the world before my arrival in it—had been made up of books about the history of New York City and New York State. I'd also been on a few trips up north with the Doctor, when he'd had calls to pay on the penitentiaries and lunatic asylums what were located throughout the Hudson Valley, or when he went to Albany to give testimony to some commission or other about how the state should handle its mentally deranged citizens. So I was no stranger to the beautiful—if slightly spooky—landscape that surrounded us on our very pleasant voyage aboard the Mary Powell that day; all the same, a queer sort of feeling crept into me as we headed upriver, one that I'd never experienced on any of those earlier trips. I found that I was much more aware, not just of the misty mountains and green fields that lay beyond the riverbanks (the usual objects of study for the sightseer) but of the towns that were cut into the countryside, and the many factory works what had been built over the years (and were still being built) along the river itself. In other words, the growing presence of people—in what I knew had been, just a hundred years earlier, a wild wilderness—was for some reason weighing heavy on my mind.

All through breakfast I wondered what could be making me see things so differently than I ever had before; and I got worried as to whether the change might not be permanent. It wasn't until I went up onto the promenade deck with Miss Howard after breakfast to have a smoke that I started to comprehend my own feelings a little better: it was our recent discovery that Libby Hatch had been born and raised in similar surroundings that was changing my view of the country we were passing through, and the people in it, so much. This wasn't some quiet, simple region where people lived close to nature and far from the ugliness and violence of cities like New York, I began to see; this was just a string of smaller New Yorks, where certain people engaged in the same kind of disheartening, and in some cases sickening, behavior that so many folks in the big city did. As this grim realization started to really sink in, I was surprised to find myself making a kind of wish: a wish that the great wilderness what still dominated up on mountains like the purple Catskills—standing in the distance to my left that afternoon—would spread back down over the earth and swallow up the ugly little nests of human beings what'd sprung up in the river valley. It was a wish that, true to my original fear, has never really gone away in all the years since.

And it certainly wasn't altered any that day when we hit the middle stretch of the Hudson, where the manor houses of the old Dutch and English river families began to dot the hillsides to our right. Mr. Moore came up to join us, and both he and Miss Howard grew very quiet as they stared out toward those heights. I knew that each of them had real cause for sadness, being as they'd both spent much of their bittersweet childhoods there. In Mr. Moore the scenery obviously brought back memories of the brother whose death had saddened him so and caused such a breach with the rest of his family (Mr. Moore having contended that they'd driven his brother to morphine and drink with their strict Dutch ways). Miss Howard, on the other hand, was clearly thinking about the many summers and autumns she'd spent hunting, shooting, and generally living a boy's life with her beloved father, who'd had no son (nor any other child besides his one daughter) to share his sporting pursuits with. Said father had died in a mysterious hunting accident in amongst those woods some years back, and there'd been talk of suicide. But Miss Howard—who'd taken the death so hard that she'd had to retreat to a sanitarium for a time—had always denied such rumors. Considering all this, it wasn't too surprising to see the pair's spirits sag beyond melancholy as they watched the high hills and the stately houses pass by. And though we eventually went below again to consume a very tasty lunch, and even managed to play a few silly but diverting deck sports afterwards, the general mood among our party remained what you might call reserved.

The *Mary Powell* stopped only briefly in Albany, a bustling city with many factories, railroad tracks, and workers' houses lining its riverfront: not the kind of scenery that was going to put me or anyone else in a more cheerful state of mind. Many of the steamer's passengers debarked at the state's capital, leaving just them what were finishing off the round trip to New York, along with those of us who were going on through a dredged upper section of the river to Troy. Only a few miles of the riverside between Albany and Troy were still unpopulated, and the fiery, smoky factories that we passed, along with the large groups of dirty, miserable workers who were coming out of them, served to underline the notion that the countryside was becoming ever more infected by mankind's petty but brutal desires.

As for the city of Troy, it was a prosperous but dreary place, its dozens of brick manufacturing works and cargo steamships fouling the river just so's to make the latest laundry, gardening, and locomotive machinery available to the rest of the world. By the time we left the *Mary Powell*, a beautiful sunset had begun to appear above the western portion of the city, making me anxious to strike out into the country, toward that fiery sinking ball and away from the city; so it came as a great disapppointment to discover, when we reached the Union Depot and the offices of the Delaware and Hudson Canal Railroad Company, that the previous day's great gale had struck this portion of the state, too, and caused a bad derailment on the line between Troy and Ballston Spa. We'd have to wait until morning to finish our journey, which meant spending a night in the nearby Union Hotel: not a terrible joint, by any means, but still discouraging for a young man who was chafing to get away from civilization and out into the wilderness.

The train ride the next morning offered me some relief, being as once we'd left Troy and its environs behind, we did start to pass through patches of countryside what hinted at how magical that part of the state must've been before civilization hit it like a runaway streetcar. There were long stretches of what seemed like ancient woodlands, and we passed by a couple of big silver lakes; but each time we'd quickly move on to some cluster of farms or past a bustling little town, all of which hammered home the point that the old forest was losing its fight for control of the landscape. Before long the conductor on our train was announcing our approach to Ballston Spa, and when we arrived at the town's outskirts I found that my mood of the day before had returned, and maybe even gotten worse; though such was not a bad outlook to have, I quickly discovered, when you were entering the seat of Saratoga County.

Cyrus had brought along a little guidebook to the towns of the northern Hudson area, and he read from it as we chugged slowly toward the end of our journey. Ballston Spa, I learned, had once been famous for its string of quiet little health retreats, but over the last century things had changed pretty drastically: many of the mineral springs had dried up, and the spas had been replaced by a collection of mills. In their early days these large brickworks had produced wool, cotten, linens, and a peculiar battle-axe what looked like a Turkish scimitar (this last for the Union Army during the Civil War). But even the mills had fallen on hard times by 1897. Most of them had been built along a rushing creek what ran through the town, the Kayaderosseras (an old Iroquois word what meant something to the effect of "stream of the crooked waters"), but in the years that followed so much lumbering had been done around the stream's watershed that the Kayaderosseras itself had been reduced to a trickling little creek what couldn't power anything of consequence. So now the black smoke of furnaces poured from the chimneys of the mills, which, though they still made some farm tools, were currently known mostly for paper products.

Cyrus's guidebook tried to relate all this information in what you might call a positive fashion, but there wasn't much way to avoid the conclusion that—because of their own shortsightedness and in the space of just a century—the citizens of Ballston Spa had gone from operating the best health retreats in the North to boasting that their town was home to "the world's finest paper bags." The old resort hotels, which couldn't compete with a string of gigantic, luxurious competitors what'd opened in nearby Saratoga Springs, had either been converted to boardinghouses for factory workers or burned down. Still, nobody ever though to rename the town, even though, by 1897, there wasn't much about Ballston that brought the word "spa" to mind.

The train depot sat just below a hill what separated the industrial parts of the town from the homes of the local swells. On top of said hill ran what some imaginative mug had named High Street, where most of the town's churches, along with the county offices, were located. The station building itself wasn't much to look at, just a long, low structure of the type you generally find in such places; and the few people who were standing out on the platform waiting for our train to pull in seemed made to match. All, that is, except for one of them:

He was all the way out on the easternmost end of the platform, as if he knew that Mr. Moore liked sitting at the back of trains and would've convinced us all to do likewise (which, in fact, he had). Smoking a pipe like his life depended on it, the short, ginger-haired man was also by turns pulling on a neatly clipped beard and mustache and running a hand through his similarly cut hair, all the while looking in every direction and walking round the platform as if the thing was on fire. His eyes, which I later determined were a very light grey, seemed a sort of silvery color from a distance, and they carried an expression that was both determined and a little wild. He pulled his watch out no less than three times while our train was slowing to a stop—just why I couldn't say, seeing as we'd already arrived—and each time he tucked it away with a look of worry, then smoked and paced some more. I lost sight of the fellow as we made our way to the door of our car; but somehow I knew this was the man we'd come to see.

Mr. Moore turned to the rest of us as the train groaned and squeaked into the station. "All right, listen, all of you," he said, his voice urgent. "Especially you, Kreizler. There's one thing I neglected to mention about Rupert, because I didn't want to discourage you from trusting the case to him. He truly is brilliant, but—well, the fact of the matter is, he can't shut up."

The rest of us looked at each other with expressions what indicated a shared belief that this must be some kind of gag.

"What do you mean, Moore?" the Doctor asked. "If he's excessively ver-bal—"

"No," Mr. Moore answered. "I mean he *can't* shut up."

Marcus laughed. "Of course he can't. He's a *lawyer*, for God's sake—"

"*No,*" Mr. Moore said again. "It's something more—something physi-cal. He's been to doctors about it. Some kind of—compulsion or some-thing, I forget what they call it."

"Pressured speech?" the Doctor guessed, looking intrigued.

Mr. Moore snapped his fingers. "That's it. Anyway, it works wonders in court, but in conversation it can be a little much—" Banging into the closed front door of our car as the train came to a halt, Mr. Moore started for the steps. "I just wanted to warn you—he's as nice a person as you'll ever meet, but thoughts just come into his head and shoot right out of his mouth. So don't take anything he says too personally, all right?" Checking each of our faces, Mr. Moore nodded once, and then we followed him out onto the platform.

Mr. Rupert Picton was still pacing and smoking, those big silver eyes looking very anxious. When Mr. Moore saw the sight, he grinned in a heartfelt way.

"Picton!" he called, walking toward his friend on the platform. "Good God, man, you look like you're going to have kittens!"

"Your train's late!" answered Mr. Picton, smiling through what he seemed to realize was very obvious nervousness. "They're always late, these days—we can talk about going to war with Spain, but we can't make our trains run on time! How are you, John?"

"Fine, fine," Mr. Moore answered, as the rest of us joined him. "Let me introduce you to the others. This is Miss Sara Howard—"

"Hello, Mr. Picton," Miss Howard said, extending a hand. "I'm afraid I'm the one who started all this unfortunate business."

"Nonsense, Miss Howard," Mr. Picton answered, shaking her hand vigorously and talking not only a lot, but at a very fast pace. "You mustn't think that way. You didn't start it—Libby Hatch did, when she first drew innocent blood and found that she had a taste for it! What *you* have started is an end to her sinister tale, and you should be proud that—ah! And here's Dr. Kreizler!" The active little hand shot out again. "I recognize you from the pictures that have appeared with your monographs, sir—fascinating work, yours is, fascinating!"

"Thank you, Mr. Picton. It's kind of you to—"

But Mr. Picton had already turned to Lucius and Marcus; he grinned and grabbed each of their hands in turn. "And I assume that you gentlemen are the Detective Sergeants Isaacson?"

Marcus smiled, and had just managed to say, "Why, yes—" before he was cut off.

"Don't go crediting me with any powers of detection," Mr. Picton said. "None greater than smell, at any rate. There is a vague aroma of sulfuric acid—"

Lucius cast his brother a hard glance as he took his turn shaking Mr. Picton's hand. "I'm sorry about that, sir. If *someone* hadn't made me perform that strychnine test *again* before we left New York . . ."

"I hope you've brought all your chemicals and devices along," Mr. Picton answered, nodding encouragingly. "We'll need them. Now, then, let's get your things together—"

Cyrus and I, having found a porter to help us tend to the baggage as we watched all this, now approached the group from behind our host. Cyrus cleared his throat just once—but once was enough to make Mr. Picton, who hadn't seen us coming, shoot into the air.

"Great jumping cats!" he cried, spinning on Cyrus. "Who're you? Ah! Don't tell me—John wrote about you. You're Dr. Kreizler's man, correct? Mr.—ah—ah—"

"May I present Mr. Cyrus Montrose," the Doctor said, at which Mr. Picton shook Cyrus's big hand. "As well as Master Stevie Taggert. Both associates of mine."

Mr. Picton turned his hand in my direction, and I stuck my own out to receive his jolting shake. "Master Taggert! Good to meet you! Well—" He stood back and put his hands to his hips, taking us in. "So this is the group that has actually put fear into that murderess's heart, eh? I admire you for it, I must say! Libby Hatch certainly never had anything to be nervous about in *this* county, I can tell you. Let's get your bags onto my rig, and get over to my place. We need to get to business as soon as we can! Porter—follow me!"

"Your place?" Mr. Moore said. "But Rupert, I made reservations at the Eagle Hotel—"

"And I canceled them," Mr. Picton answered. "I've got a house big enough for a regiment, John, with just me and the housekeeper. I won't hear of you staying anywhere else!"

"But," Mr. Moore said carefully, as we made for an old surrey what was standing outside the station, "are you sure you're up to it, Rupert? I mean, I heard you weren't well—"

"Not well?!" Mr. Picton thundered back. "Why, I'm as sound as a dollar—in fact, I'm even *sounder,* given the current strength of our currency. Oh, I know what they said in New York before I left, John, and I'll admit that I needed a rest at the time. You know my disposition—high-strung I am, certainly, you'll get no argument from me. But those rumors about my suffering a breakdown were just further attempts to discredit what I was saying."

"Mmm, yes, I'm acquainted with that phenomenon," the Doctor said, as Mr. Picton began to lob our luggage from the porter's truck into his surrey, smoking furiously all the while.

"Yes, I understand you are, Dr. Kreizler!" our host answered. "I understand you are! And so you probably know the weariness it breeds—trying to stop what was going on in the district attorney's office fairly well exhausted me, as I say, and wore my nerves positively raw. But that's a far cry from madness, don't you think?"

"Well—" the Doctor answered slowly; too slowly, it turned out, for Mr. Picton.

"Exactly my point!" he said. "It's a funny world we're living in, Dr. Kreizler—and I don't mean funny in the amusing sense—where a man can be labeled mad simply for trying to expose egregious corruption! Ah, well, no matter . . ." Tossing the last of our bags into the surrey, Mr. Picton made for the driver's bench. "Climb aboard, everyone. Mr. Montrose, perhaps you and Master Taggert might not mind riding on the steps, there. You can get a grip on the canopy, and we're not going far."

"Fine with me!" I said happily, finding that I was starting to enjoy Mr. Picton's slightly crazy way of saying and doing things.

"Of course, sir," Cyrus said, also taking an outside perch after the others had climbed aboard.

"Good men!" Mr. Picton said with a grin, saluting us with his pipe. "Hang on, now—here we go!" The surrey began to roll, but we hadn't even gotten out of the station yard before Mr. Picton had started in again. "As I say, Doctor, it doesn't matter, really, all that business in New York, and what those people may have said about me—doesn't matter at all, not in the long term. The world is going to Hell in a hack, and New York will be one of the first places to arrive; if it hasn't already, and I could make a case for it having done so. That's one of the reasons I came back to Ballston—it's actually possible to do an occasional bit of good here without having to worry about the magnates and the bosses." He let out a few more smokestack blasts with his pipe as he steered his horse along a street that ran west below the steepled hill. "But don't let's get drawn too far into this sort of talk—we have other matters that are pressing." He took out his watch and checked it again. "Pressing, indeed! You must all get settled in and fed—Mrs. Hastings will see to that. My housekeeper." He shook his head as we rattled our way toward the western edge of town. "Terrible case. She and her husband ran a dry-goods store together for most of their lives. Then, a couple of years ago, three local toughs—not all that much older than you, Master Taggert—robbed the place while she was out. Beat her husband to death with a shovel. I prosecuted the case, and afterwards she came to work for me—as much out of gratitude as anything else, I think."

"Gratitude?" Miss Howard asked. "Because you helped her through a difficult time?"

"Because I made sure those three boys went to the electrical chair!" Mr. Picton answered. "Ah! There's my house now—at the end of the street."

Mr. Picton had a mansion-sized place at the juncture of Charlton and High Streets, not too far from the courthouse and close to the old Aldridge Spa (currently a boardinghouse) and the Iron Railing Spring, the pair of which were the last real remains of the town's salad days as a health resort. To judge by the four big turrets what formed the corners of Mr. Picton's house, along with the wide porch what was wrapped around the whole structure, it wasn't as old as many of the residences we'd seen

and passed. But the size alone was enough to give it kind of an eerie quality, and I wondered why a man would choose to live alone with his housekeeper in such a building. The front and rear gardens were full of climbing
roses and ivy that'd gone a little berserk, along with a couple of elm trees
what must've been considerably older than the house itself—all of which
only added to the feeling that this was a very ghostly dwelling indeed.

"My father built it for my mother," Mr. Picton explained as we neared
the house. "And thirty-five years ago it was considered the height of Vic-
torian Gothic style. Nowadays, well—fashion has never mattered much to
me, so I've left it more or less as it was. Mrs. Hastings is constantly after
me to redecorate, but—oh, there she is now!" A round, kindly-looking
woman of about sixty or so, wearing a blue dress with a white apron,
came out the front door of the house just as we pulled into the yard. Mr.
Picton drew the surrey to a stop and then smiled as he waved to his housekeeper. "Mrs. Hastings! You see, I managed to find them without any
trouble. I trust the turret rooms are all ready?"

"Oh, yes, your honor," Mrs. Hastings answered, wiping her flour- and
food-coated hands on her apron and smiling warmly. "And lunch is waiting for you all. Welcome, welcome, it'll be a real breath of fresh air, it will,
having guests!"

Mr. Picton made the introductions, and then the others started toward
the house while Cyrus and I hung back to unload the bags.

"Well?" I said quietly to my big friend. "What do you think?"

Cyrus shook his head once. "He's a character, all right. Mr. Moore sure
wasn't exaggerating about that talking business."

"I like him," I said, starting toward the front door with a batch of suitcases. Looking up at the high walls and dark turrets before me, I paused
for a minute. "The house looks like it might have a ghost or two, though,"
I whispered over my shoulder.

Cyrus smiled and shook his head again. "You always like the odd ones,"
he said. Then his face went straight. "But I don't want to hear any more
about *ghosts.*"

The ground floor of Mr. Picton's house had a reception room what
might've served as a convention hall. Stocked to overflowing with heavy,
velvet-upholstered furniture that was centered around a carved stone fireplace you could've walked right into, it also contained the usual recreational items, like a piano and a big card table. At the center of the house
was a staircase made out of heavy, polished oak, and then, mirroring the
reception room on the other side of the stairs, there was an enormous dining room crammed full of chairs, sideboards, and a table what were all in

the same style as the things in the living room. The bedrooms on the upper floors—located, as Mr. Picton'd said, in the four corner turrets—were of similarly huge dimensions, each with its own big fireplace and most with their own baths. By the time I got upstairs, the others were roaming around shopping for rooms, and I could hear Mr. Picton saying:

"Oh, good choice, Miss Howard—that's really the best room in the house! You get a splendid view of the garden and the stream."

On the third floor I could hear the detective sergeants arguing over another bedroom, but I couldn't make out what'd become of the Doctor and Mr. Moore, whose suitcases I was carrying. Then the sound of low conversation came from down one long hall, and I followed it to find the two of them in yet another bedroom.

"Kreizler, I swear to you, I don't know," Mr. Moore was saying as I reached the door. "And I don't think *he* does either, or at least he's never told me—"

"There are several manias that could account for it," the Doctor said carefully. "And some of them are degenerative." He gave Mr. Moore what you might call an uncertain look. "We're risking a great deal on this man, John."

"Laszlo, listen to me. It has *never* impaired his work. It used to be a bit of a joke in social situations, but in the courtroom it's a genuine boon. He can absolutely overwhelm defense lawyers when he gets going—" Mr. Moore stopped as he caught sight of me at the door; then he smiled, thankful for a way, I think, to end his conversation with the Doctor. "Hello, Stevie. Got my things, by any chance?"

Ignoring the question, I just shrugged, looked to the Doctor, and repeated what I'd said to Cyrus: "I like him."

"There you are," Mr. Moore announced, taking two of the suitcases from me. "What is it they say about children and dogs being the best judges of character, Kreizler? I don't remember alienists elbowing their way onto the list anytime recently."

"I assure you both, my concern in no way reflects on the man's character," the Doctor said. "He seems entirely straightforward and likable—and that's not a bad bit of work for a lawyer. Nor am I saying that his difficulty is without doubt mental or emotional in origin—there are several physical pathologies that could easily be responsible."

Mr. Moore nodded once. "All right, then. Let's drop this business for now."

"For now," the Doctor agreed, taking his suitcases from me and then examining my neck and hands. "Good Lord, Stevie," he said, with a combination of a scowl and a laugh. "What have you been doing? Make certain you find a washroom before lunch, young man."

Once Cyrus and I had all the bags inside, I took a bedroom up on the third floor with the detective sergeants and went into the bathroom to wash up before lunch. The noise of the running water bounced off the marble and tiles of the big chamber, to the point where it sounded as though I might be standing by a waterfall: everything in that house, it seemed, was unusually large—cavernous, even—and as I dried my face, neck, and hands I began to wonder who would've built such a place, and what had become of them. But, funnily enough, there was no longer any fear in the wondering: huge and mysterious as the house might be, I found that Mr. Picton filled it with a feverish but friendly kind of activity, and that I'd stopped feeling like I might be in a dangerous spot.

Starting back down toward the ground floor and the dining room, where the others were already collected, I ran my hand along the fat banister of the staircase and suddenly realized that it would be just the thing for sliding. I didn't know why the thought should've occurred to me, I only knew that it was the first really amusing idea that I'd had in days. So I looked down, scouted the ground-floor hallway, and, not seeing anyone, decided to give the banister a try. Feeling ever more playful and relaxed, I climbed aboard on the second-floor landing and gave myself a little push-off—

And in about a second and a half found myself sprawled on the floor in the front hall. The banister had been even more suitable—which is to say slippery—than I'd figured, and after flying off of it I'd hit the hallway carpet at high speed, sliding across the polished floor and into the front door with a crash. That brought the others out of the dining room, and produced a look of shock on the Doctor's face.

"Stevie!" he said. "What in the world—"

"Ha!" Mr. Picton bellowed, snatching his pipe out of his mouth and leaning back to have a good laugh. Then he came over to help me up. "More slippery than it looks, eh, Master Taggert? Don't be embarrassed—the same thing happened to me the first time I tried it, and that was just a few years ago! Nothing broken, I hope?" I shook my head, feeling my face go red; but Mr. Picton's open confession of similar foolery made me feel much better about it. "Good!" he went on. "Then come in and have some lunch. Afterwards, I'll show you a few tricks that'll keep your speed down—and your backside intact!"

I followed the others into the dining room, getting another perplexed look from the Doctor as I went.

Mr. Picton insisted on escorting each of us to our seats and further insisted that the Doctor take the head of the table. "I'm perfectly happy at the foot," he said, when the Doctor protested, "and this is *your* investigation, Doctor—I don't want you to think for a minute that I don't understand that. We'll have a great deal to discuss at this table, and I want you to consider me simply your latest ally—and pupil."

"That is gracious indeed, Mr. Picton," the Doctor said in an even tone, as he carefully and curiously studied our host.

Mr. Picton took his seat at the foot of the table and rang a small bell, at which Mrs. Hastings appeared through a swinging door what led through to the kitchen. She was carrying the first of many platters of food. "All from the farms and streams of our own county," Mr. Picton explained. "And, though simply prepared, no less appetizing for its humility. John, there's some decent claret on the side table there, if you wouldn't mind pouring." As Mr. Moore eagerly moved to follow the order, Mr. Picton looked my way. "And we have a full case of root beer in the kitchen for you, Master Taggert—Mrs. Hastings will bring you a bottle. John tells me you are a devotee, and I confess, I have a weakness for the stuff myself." Glancing around the table as the rest of us started heaping chicken, brook trout, sweet peas, baby carrots, and mashed potatoes onto our plates, Mr. Picton held up his glass. "And so—welcome, all of you!" He took a deep drink, and then his silvery eyes opened wide. "Now, then—let me tell you what I know about Libby Hatch . . ."

CHAPTER 29

S he arrived here," Mr. Picton began, as he put some food onto his own plate, "just over ten years ago, as near as I can tell. From Stillwater."

"Yes," Miss Howard said. "She listed it as her place of birth on one of the hospital forms we saw."

"Did she?" Mr. Picton answered. "Well, that was just another lie, I'm afraid. I've checked the birth records of every town in this county. There's no listing for an 'Elspeth Fraser,' which was her name back then. She *did*, however, *live* in Stillwater for a time—though just how long, I don't know."

"And you never ascertained where she actually *was* born during your investigation?" the Doctor asked, a little surprised.

"You proceed from the assumption that I was allowed to *conduct* an investigation, Doctor. The case of Libby Hatch, her assaulted children, and the phantom Negro never got past a coroner's inquest—my superior at the time could find no justification for either the effort or the expense of a formal investigation, and neither could the sheriff."

"There's nothing unusual in that, unfortunately," Marcus said. "I doubt if there's one case in twenty involving dead children that gets past a coroner's inquest. The crimes are too private—it's just too damned difficult to figure out who did what."

Mr. Picton looked up with some interest. "I get the feeling you've had some legal training, Detective."

Marcus had just filled his mouth with some of the sweet, buttery peas, so it was Lucius who answered: "Marcus was on his way to becoming a lawyer, when we got involved in police work instead. I was slated for medicine."

"I see," Mr. Picton said, smiling and looking very interested. "Well, your analysis is correct, though I'd say your numbers are a little low. I'd be surprised if one child's death in a *hundred* is really investigated. And when a white woman claims that a colored man is responsible—I'm sure Mr. Montrose is aware that racial bias is very much alive in the North." Cyrus just bent his head a little, as if to say he was only too aware of that fact. "So I wasn't really surprised that the district attorney and the sheriff were so willing to accept Libby's version of events. As for me, I confess I wasn't yet aware of what bearing the woman's background might've had on the matter. You see, Dr. Kreizler, I hadn't yet encountered your writings—your theory of 'context'—and I was fairly focused on the circumstantial evidence."

The Doctor gave a polite little shrug to that. "Circumstantial and forensic evidence are invaluable, Mr. Picton—that is why we depend so much on the detective sergeants. But there are crimes that offer few such clues, and that cannot be solved if the personal lives of the participants are not studied in depth."

"Oh, I completely agree with you *now*," Mr. Picton answered, eating his food in quick little movements, like an animal or a bird. "But *then,* as I say, I hadn't really been exposed to the concept. The only thing I thought might prove or disprove Mrs. Hatch's claim was the apprehension of the mysterious Negro, and I unofficially pressed that search as hard and for as long as I could. But after a time, the district attorney ordered me to give up the hunt, and forget the affair. Now, however, I can see that the few facts I did assemble about Mrs. Hatch during that brief time may be relevant, somehow."

"Very much so," the Doctor answered. "Detective Sergeant?"

Lucius already had his small pad out. "Yes, sir. I'm on it."

"Oh. And Mr. Picton"—the Doctor paused to take a sip of his wine—"is there a store in town where we might purchase a chalkboard?"

"A chalkboard?" Mr. Picton repeated. "How large?"

"As large as possible. And as soon as possible."

Mr. Picton thought the matter over. "No . . . I can't think . . ." Then his face brightened. "Wait a minute. Mrs. Hastings!" The housekeeper appeared almost immediately. "Mrs. Hastings, would you mind telephoning over to the high school? Tell Mr. Quinn that I'd like to borrow one of his largest chalkboards."

"A *chalkboard*?" Mrs. Hastings repeated, moving around the table to re-fill the wineglasses. "What in heaven's name would your honor want with a chalkboard? And where would we *put* such a thing?"

"Mrs. Hastings, please, the matter is very urgent," Mr. Picton said. "And I don't know how many times I have to tell you, I'm an assistant district attorney at home, not a judge in a courtroom—you really don't need to address me as 'your honor.'"

"Hmm!" Mrs. Hastings grunted, turning and making for the kitchen again. "As if that fool jury would've convicted those boys without your driving them to it!" She pounded her way back through the swinging door.

Our host smiled in his nervous, quick way, tugging at his beard and then his hair. "I think we can find something that will suit your needs, Doctor. . . . And so! We return to the facts of Libby Hatch's background. Or at least, to what bits and pieces I eventually assembled. Libby Fraser, as I say, was her name when she arrived here. She tried to get all sorts of employment in town, but nothing worked out—she was too headstrong to follow the rules of conduct at the telephone exchange, expressed too many opinions about customers' tastes to hold a sales position in the ladies' clothing department of Mosher's store, and had no real education of any kind, which narrowed her remaining choices down to various domestic positions. Yet she seemed to find *that* work more objectionable than anything else—she took and lost three positions as a maid in as many months."

"And yet Vanderbilt had only high praise for her," Mr. Moore said.

"Yes, I noted that in your last telegram, John," Mr. Picton replied. "It's curious. She may have been putting on an act, or she may simply have let the less aggressive side of her nature take over, for a time. After all, most people who knew the woman in her early Ballston days didn't think she was a wicked person, really—just entirely too determined to do and have things her own way. Everyone expected that those qualities would be knocked out of her, though, when she accepted a post as housekeeper to old Daniel Hatch. He was the local miser—most of these villages have a character like him. Lived in a big, ramshackle house outside town, alone, except for his servants. Dressed in rags, never bathed—and was rumored to have cash stuffed and sewn into every wall and cushion in his place. As mean as a snake, too, and went through housekeepers as if he were keeping score. But Libby took him on—and the shocks just kept coming, for the next several years."

"Shocks?" the Doctor asked.

"Indeed, Dr. Kreizler. Shocks! Within a few months the old miser and his housekeeper were engaged to be married. The wedding followed a few weeks later. That in itself should not, perhaps, have come as such a sur- prise—even though she had just turned thirty, Libby Fraser was a youth- ful, handsome woman. Lovely, in some ways, despite her impulsive manner. And Hatch, though a shriveled old goat, did have a great deal of money. But when a *child* followed, just nine months after the mar- riage. . . . Well, Hatch *was* seventy-three at the time. And when that first daughter was followed within thirty months by two sons—as you can imagine, it set tongues wagging all over town. Some saw the hand of God in it, and some the work of the Devil. And then there were those few of us who chose to look a little closer to home in trying to determine if Libby Hatch had evil intentions."

"*Evil* intentions?" the Doctor repeated, his eyebrows arching a bit.

Mr. Picton laughed and then pushed away from the table, having eaten only half the food what was on his plate. "Oh, dear," he said, getting up and checking his watch again as he took his pipe out of his jacket pocket. "That's right, you object to that word, don't you, Dr. Kreizler?"

The Doctor shrugged. "I don't know that I object to it," he said. "I sim- ply find it an ambiguous concept—one that I've never had a great deal of use for."

"Because you feel it contradicts your theory of context," Mr. Picton an- swered with a nod, as he began to pace around the table, chewing on his pipe. "But it may surprise you to learn that I disagree with you on that score, Doctor."

"Indeed?"

"Yes, indeed! I accept your proposition that a human being's actions cannot be fully understood until one has studied the context of his or her entire life. But what if that context has produced a person who is, quite simply, evil? Wicked, pernicious, threatening—to use just a few of Mr. Webster's definitions."

"Well," the Doctor answered, "I'm not at all sure that—"

"I'm not making a mere academic point, Dr. Kreizler—believe me, it will be crucial, if we ever get our day in court!" Stopping to study each of our plates, his head snapping around on his neck like a scared rodent's, Mr. Pic- ton asked, "Everyone finished eating? Mind if I smoke? No? Good!" He lit a match against his pants and then drew on his pipe in that quick, violent sort of way. "As I was saying—I know that what you seek are explanations for criminal behavior, Doctor, and not excuses for it. And as I say, I admire your quest. But in a case such as this, and a town such as this, we must be especially careful to frame our explanations so that they do not cause either the populace or the jury to view her sympathetically. Because believe me, they will already be inclined to do so, given what will surely be their reluctance to accept our charges against her. Any psychological explanations must only underline the idea that her nature is evil."

"You seem quite certain that evil does exist, Mr. Picton," the Doctor said.

"In this case? I have no doubt of it! And when I show you certain things—well, I think that you will believe it, too." Taking out his watch and checking the time yet again, even though no more than a few minutes had passed since the last time he had, Mr. Picton nodded in satisfaction. "Well! We'll need to hurry! No time for dessert, I fear—sweets for you later, Master Taggert, along with a lesson on the banister!" In a quick move, he pulled my chair out from the table, and then went around to do the same thing—though more gently—for Miss Howard. Holding one arm toward the door, he looked to the others. "We'll walk up to the court house, and after that drive out to the eastern outskirts of town." His eyes came to rest on the head of the table. "And there, Dr. Kreizler, you will see and hear some surprising things. About how a lone woman can cast first a sinister and then a sympathetic spell over an entire town. And when you've heard and seen the details—not to mention the effects—of her technique and her actions, I daresay you may change your opinions concerning the existence of evil."

Our curiosity most definitely roused, we all got up to follow Mr. Picton to the front door; and as we went, I noted that his agitated manner had a sort of infectious quality, being as we were all starting to move and talk in a much quicker and jumpier way. All of us, that is, except the Doctor, who moved steadily and curiously through the front hall, his mind clearly focused on the matter of Libby Hatch but possessing enough spare energy to try to figure the riddle of our host, too.

It was pretty apparent from the size of the houses on Ballston Spa's High Street that it had been favored by the gentry of the town for many generations. There were joints that were even bigger than Mr. Picton's place; and those what were smaller generally made up for the deficiency by being very old and bringing to mind, with their simpler but still refined styles, the days when white men had first put the power of the Kayaderosseras behind their moneymaking schemes. Some of the trees around the newer houses were young, but there were enough thick, shady old-timers to give testimony to the age of the land that the town was built on; and as I studied those stout maples, oaks, and elms, I again began to feel very sorry that what must've once been a beautiful stretch of land-scape should've been turned into a homely little mill town. Yet that same feeling of sadness and waste made the place a peculiarly fitting spot in which to be talking about a woman like Libby Hatch.

"Until shortly before the birth of her second child," Mr. Picton said as we left his front yard, "Libby was the same mercurial woman the town had come to know over time. But then, suddenly, she changed—drasti-cally. She seemed to become nothing short of a loving mother and doting wife, happy in a situation that most women wouldn't have wished on their worst enemy."

"Isn't it possible," Miss Howard said, "that she might have been just what she seemed, Mr. Picton? No one ever knows the intimate facts of a marriage except the couple themselves, after all. Perhaps she really had learned to care for the old man."

"Don't listen to her, Rupert," Mr. Moore threw in. "She's just trying to rationalize her pal Nellie Bly's marriage to that old fossil Seaman."

If we'd all known Mr. Picton a little better, I'm sure that Miss Howard would've belted Mr. Moore right then; as it was, she gave him one of her more deadly looks.

Mr. Picton chuckled a bit. "To tell you the truth, there's a part of me that would like to agree with you, Miss Howard."

"Sara," Miss Howard said, her look changing with typical speed to a very engaging smile. "Please."

Though caught up in his story, Mr. Picton flushed and stuttered a bit. "Why, I—I'm honored!" he said. "And you must call me Rupert, Sara—unless of course you dislike the name. Some people do. I'll answer to al-most anything, as Moore will confirm. However, I digress! Yes, Sara, if I could believe that Libby Hatch had ever actually cared, on the deepest level, about either her husband or her children, I would be far less haunted by this case. But you tell me what you think of the facts that follow. About two and a half years after her second son was born, Libby's mood *again* changed overnight. One day she was the same pleasant, engaging citizen whom people had gradually grown to accept; the next, she had reverted to her old self. Worse, really: she became a scowling, seemingly desperate ball of nerves. No one could explain it—until word got around that Daniel Hatch was mortally ill."

"Did that come as a surprise?" the Doctor asked. "He must have been close to eighty by then."

"True," Mr. Picton answered. "And as a result, it did *not* come as a sur-prise, but rather served to explain why Libby's behavior had become so agitated. She was, apparently, deeply distressed over the fate of the old miser that she and she alone had found a way to love."

"If anybody feels a little moist," Mr. Moore said, "that'll be Rupert's sarcasm."

Laughing once, Mr. Picton nodded. "All right, I confess, I was and remain utterly skeptical. But I later learned that I had reason to be. You see, old Hatch suffered through a prolonged illness, punctuated by two severe attacks. Yet when I came to assemble a chronology of the period, I discovered that Libby's pronounced change in mood had *preceded* the onset of the illness. So it was not concern for his health that rattled her so badly."

"Mr. Picton," Marcus said, asking the question that was in all our heads, "just what kind of 'attacks' were they that Mr. Hatch suffered?"

Mr. Picton smiled. "Yes, Detective. They were *heart* attacks." As the rest of us received this news silently, our host stopped walking and reached into his jacket pocket. "After I got your messages, John, I went out to the old Hatch place. It's falling down, now, and the garden's terribly overgrown. But I was able to find this. . . ."

Out of his pocket Mr. Picton brought a withered but still very distinctive-looking flower.

"*Digitalis purpurea*," Lucius announced quietly. "Purple foxglove."

"Oh, it wasn't *easy* to kill him!" Mr. Picton said, in a tone that you might almost call excited. "Hatch was a strong old coot, and as I'm sure you know, Detective, digitalis induces many toxic side effects if given in doses that are insufficient to produce fatal overstimulation of the heart."

Lucius nodded as we all started walking again. "Nausea, vomiting, blurred vision . . ."

"He held on to life almost as tightly as he'd held on to his money," Mr. Picton went on, in the same energetic tone. "Lasted some three months, before she could finally get enough of the stuff into him without any of the servants noticing." At the sound of his own words, Mr. Picton's smile shrank up and his voice grew quieter. "The poor, unpleasant old soul. No one should have to go like that."

"There was never any suspicion cast on Mrs. Hatch?" the Doctor asked.

Mr. Picton shook his head. "No. Not given the way she'd always acted toward her husband. But as it turned out, Hatch had been less fooled by his wife than had most of the town. She received virtually nothing in his will."

"Who'd he leave it all to?" Mr. Moore asked. "The children?"

"Just so," Mr. Picton said. "In trust, until they achieved their majority. And he named the local justice of the peace—*not* his wife—as trustee.

Libby was to receive only enough money to support the family. Apparently, Hatch had become quite bitter about something toward the end. But his actions were foolish, because the arrangement of the estate only put the children at terrible risk."

"Meaning that if anything happened to them," Miss Howard said, "the fortune would pass to her?"

"Yes," Mr. Picton answered. "And, bitter as he obviously was, I don't think even Hatch knew what his wife was really capable of—ah! Here we are."

We'd reached the front of what Mr. Picton later told us was called the "new" court house, being as it'd been occupied for less than ten years. It wasn't a particularly interesting-looking building, just a big, gabled mass of stone with a square tower rising out of one corner; but my guess was that, whatever the architectural types might think of its design, as a jail it was probably top of the line: the walls were ponderously thick, and the bars across the cell windows in the basement were strong enough to contain even a seasoned escape artist.

"Well, with any luck at all, this will be our battleground before long!" Mr. Picton announced, looking up at one of the four clock faces what were set into each side of the tower's roof and pulling out his watch to check it against the bigger time piece. Then his silvery eyes moved steadily around our group, taking, it seemed to me, the measure of each of us in turn. After that he smiled. "I very much wonder if you know what you've gotten yourselves into . . ."

Mr. Picton walked up the court house's few steps, then held the big door open for us; and as we all filed in without a word, he kept on smiling, without ever telling us why.

The inside of the Ballston court house more than made up for the place's run-of-the-mill exterior. The walls in the main hall were constructed of alternating types and colors of stone, set in pleasing patterns, and the double-height windows were framed in deep oak what was kept richly polished, as were the big mahogany doors to the main courtroom, located at the far end, and the smaller hearing room on the left. Sunlight was thrown across the marble floor from a few different directions, and the marble stairs what led up to the offices had a beautiful semicircular window at their first landing, along with a series of expertly made iron lighting fixtures running along the banisters. There was a guard's post to one side of the large space, and Mr. Picton called out to a big man who was standing at it, reading a copy of the town paper, the *Ballston Weekly Journal.*

"Afternoon, Henry," he said.

"Afternoon, Mr. Picton," the man answered, without looking up.

"Did Aggie bring those files from the clerk's office?" Mr. Picton asked, leading us to the stairs.

"Yeah," the man answered. "She said it looks like you're gonna try to go after that nigger ag—" The man stopped suddenly when he looked up and saw Cyrus standing near Mr. Picton; his small eyes grew as big as they could, and he rubbed the top of his narrow head in confusion. "That—uh—that fellow who shot Mrs. Hatch's kids. She said it—looks like you're gonna go after him again."

Mr. Picton brought himself to a stop at the bottom of the marble staircase. It looked like he might get hot for a second, but then he just stopped, sighed, and said, "Henry?"

"Yes, sir, Mr. Picton?" the guard answered.

"Mr. Montrose, here, is going to be working with me for a bit."

"That so, Mr. Picton?"

"Yes. So, Henry—find another word. I doubt that you'd appreciate my coming in here every day and saying, 'Good morning, Henry, you pin-headed shanty trash'!"

The guard's face sagged like a kicked dog's. "No, sir. I would not."

"I didn't think so," Mr. Picton said, turning and continuing to lead the way upstairs. Once we were on the second floor, he turned to Cyrus.

"I *am* sorry, Mr. Montrose," he said.

"It's nothing unusual, sir," Cyrus answered.

"Yes, and not very helpful to our cause, in its commonness," Mr. Picton said with another deep sigh. "Such a *quaint-looking* little town, too, isn't it?"

The hallway on the second floor was less grand than the big entryway downstairs, but just as pleasant to look at. There was a series of polished oak doors leading back toward an entrance to the gallery of the main courtroom. We grabbed a quick look inside this last chamber, as court was not in session that day; and though it had less frills than most of the court-rooms in New York I'd frequented, it was still handsome, with fruitwood pews for the spectators on the main floor and in the gallery, and a high judge's bench made out of the same fine material. Looking down at the room, I began to realize that this might actually be the place where we would bring the golden-eyed woman with many names to some kind of justice for murdering God-only-knew how many children; and as my nerves started to flutter with this thought, I began to understand why Mr. Picton had wondered if we were really ready for all the things that might happen during what was sure to be a controversial and probably very un-popular trial.

Mr. Picton's office was located across and down the hall from the gallery doorway, around a corner from the district attorney's much grander suite. As only an assistant D.A., he had just two rooms, one a small space for a secretary (though he preferred to work without one), the other, beyond a thick oak door, a larger office that looked out over the railroad tracks and the train depot what lay down the hill. The office had a big rolltop desk and the usual endless quantity of law books and files that could be found in any lawyer's office, all of them scattered around in what seemed a very disorganized way. But as soon as we were inside, Mr. Picton began to retrieve things in a fashion what showed that the clutter made perfect sense to him.

"Just clear a space for yourselves wherever you can," he said to the rest of us. "I fear that I'm too ardent a disciple of the philosophy that an orderly office indicates a disorderly mind. And vice versa."

"Amen to that," Mr. Moore said, quickly dumping some books off of a big leather chair, then sinking down into it before anyone else had a chance.

As he continued to go through some files on his desk with fast motions what made him look like a second-story man at work, Mr. Picton caught sight of Miss Howard still standing, and then pointed with some embarrassment to the outer office. "Oh, I am sorry, Sara. There are more chairs outside. Moore, you swine, get out of there and let Sara sit down!"

"You don't know her yet, Rupert," Mr. Moore answered, settling in further. "Sara despises deference to her sex."

Cyrus had snatched an oak desk chair from outside. "Here you are, Miss Howard," he said, setting it near her.

"Thank you, Cyrus," she answered, sitting down and giving Mr. Moore a sharp kick in the shin as she did.

He let out a yelp and bolted upright. "Dammit, Sara! I will *not* take any more abuse! I mean it! I'll go to Saratoga and start gambling right now, and you and your señora can go hang!"

"As you can see, Mr. Picton," the Doctor said, shooting Mr. Moore a warning with his eyes, "ours is a rather unusual investigative style. But please, if you would return to your story?"

"Certainly, Doctor." Mr. Picton handed a file across to him. "Here is the sheriff's report on the incident—Sheriff Jones was his name. Since retired."

The Doctor began to read the document quickly as Mr. Picton related its contents to the rest of us in a way what was not only agitated, but hinted at the kind of dramatics the man might be capable of in a court-room.

"Mrs. Hatch claimed that on the night of May thirty-first, 1894, she was driving her family's depot wagon home after spending the afternoon buying groceries and gardening supplies in town and then taking her children over to Lake Saratoga to watch the sunset. At what she guessed to be about ten-thirty P.M., out on the Charlton road about half a mile shy of her house, a colored man armed with a revolver jumped out of a stand of bushes and demanded that she come down off the wagon. She refused, and tried to drive quickly on. But the man leapt onto the driver's seat and forced her to stop. Then, seeing the children, he said that if Mrs. Hatch did not do everything he told her to, he would shoot all three of them. At that point, although close to hysteria, she agreed to follow the man's orders.

"He told her to get down off the wagon and remove her clothes. She followed the command. But as she was removing her undergarments she stumbled, apparently making the man think that she was trying to either flee or go for a weapon. The man shouted, 'Lousy white bitch—this'll be on *your* head!' and shot each of the children. Thomas and Matthew—ages three and four, respectively—died instantly. Clara, aged five and a half, survived, though she was comatose. The man, after firing the shots, jumped down from the wagon and fled back into the woods, leaving the now-distraught Mrs. Hatch to first try to tend to her children and then, when she realized how dire the situation actually was, to make for home as quickly as possible. Dr. Lawrence, one of our medical men who doubles as the town's coroner, was summoned. However, he could do nothing. Clara Hatch survived, but did not regain consciousness for quite some time. When she did, it was found that she had lost the ability to speak, along with the use of her right arm and hand."

There were some quiet expressions of sadness in the room (though none of surprise), along with the scratching sound of Lucius taking notes. Then the Doctor asked, "Was the little girl shot in the head?"

Mr. Picton looked very happy with the question. "No, Doctor, she was not. The bullet entered the upper chest and traveled at an upward angle, passing out through the neck."

"But—that doesn't make sense," Lucius said softly.

"Nor do a great many other things, Detective," Mr. Picton answered. "Our next chapter"—he handed the Doctor another file—"is Dr. Lawrence's report. By the time he arrived, Mrs. Hatch and her housekeeper had moved the children inside. Mrs. Hatch was in a state of hysterical distraction, alternately trying to revive the boys and racing through the house—through *every room* in the house, including her dead husband's—screaming incoherently. Lawrence quickly determined that Thomas and Matthew were dead and that Clara was in a desperate state. He informed Mrs. Hatch of all this, sending her off into an even greater fit. She told Dr. Lawrence—and I'd like the detectives to note this, particularly—that her husband had kept a revolver under his pillow all his life, and that she had never removed it after his death. But now, she said, she was afraid that she might seize the gun and do herself harm, so great was her grief and guilt at allowing her children to be attacked. Lawrence immediately administered laudanum to get the woman under some kind of control, and told the housekeeper—Mrs. Louisa Wright, a widow woman who'd taken on the housekeeping chores after Libby and Daniel Hatch were married—to retrieve the gun from Mr. Hatch's room and dispose of it. He then did what he could for Clara and sent to Saratoga for a surgical specialist."

"And did he make a report on the particulars of the wounds themselves?" Lucius asked, still scribbling away.

"He did," Mr. Picton answered, handing over another file. "Each child had been shot in the chest. The boys' bullets had struck their hearts, while Clara's, again, had passed at an angle through the upper chest and neck, grazing the spine as it exited."

"And the range," Marcus said. "Did he hazard a guess at that?"

"Yes," Mr. Picton answered, again pleased that the right questions were being asked. "Point-blank. There were powder burns on both the clothing and the skin."

"And where exactly were the children when the attack occurred?" Miss Howard said.

"That, Lawrence did not bother to ask," Mr. Picton replied, picking up another file. "Nor did Sheriff Jones. They were, you see, accepting the story completely at face value. But Jones had telephoned me at home, and asked me to come out—thoroughly expecting that I, too, would buy into Mrs. Hatch's tale."

"And you did not?" the Doctor asked.

"No, no," Mr. Picton said. "You see, I had—*encountered* Libby Hatch several times since my return to Ballston Spa. That's the Presbyterian Church you can see across Bath Street, there"—he pointed to his window, and we all looked out to get a glimpse of a fair-sized, steepled structure, older and less luxurious than the other churches along High Street—"where she and Hatch were married and attended services. I would sometimes go walking on Sunday morning when church let out, and eventually we were introduced by mutual acquaintances." Mr. Picton paused, looking to the men in the room. "I don't have to tell you what meeting Libby is like."

"No, you do not," Mr. Moore answered, a shiver running through his body. "But what could she have wanted from *you,* Rupert?"

"I shall ignore the insult implied in that question, John," Mr. Picton answered, "and say only that I was baffled by her flirtatious, seductive manner myself. But looking back, I realize that she was hoping to buy herself some safety when the inevitable crisis came."

"Crisis?" Marcus asked.

"Hatch's death. She was planning, I think, even then to kill him, and she was covering her bets—trying to cultivate a friendly ear in the district attorney's office, aware that we would have to at least look into the death, when it happened. And her method was, I'm bound to say, well conceived—at least objectively. She divided her conversation with me between inquiries about affairs in the district attorney's office and those coy, seductive remarks with which she attempted to charm you gentlemen." Mr. Picton paused, staring out his window and down at the church. "But she'd miscalculated, in my case . . ."

"Had she?" the Doctor asked, sensing that he was about to get a useful little nugget of information concerning Mr. Picton. "And why is that?"

"Well, Doctor," Mr. Picton said, turning back to us, "I'm quite beyond such things, you see. Quite beyond them." For just an instant, his attention seemed to wander. "Seen a lot of such behavior . . ." He shook himself hard. "As has anyone who's ever worked in the New York City office. Yes, I'm afraid that I was in a position to detect Libby Hatch's true nature from the beginning!"

I could see that the Doctor believed this last statement, but I could also see that he wasn't buying that it was a complete explanation of Mr. Picton's suspicions. But Mr. Picton didn't know the Doctor well enough yet to recognize such things himself, so he just went on with his story.

"I'd had my doubts about Daniel Hatch's death, when it finally had occurred, but there really hadn't been any way to pursue them. Dr. Lawrence had cited some sort of unexplained heart disease as the cause, despite the old man's lack of any history of such a disorder. And that, so far as the district attorney was concerned, was that. But when the children were attacked—well. I wanted to be particularly careful that we got all the facts. So I went out to the Hatch place myself, to make inquiries. It was an ugly scene, I can tell you—blood everywhere, and poor little Clara—but Libby'd been calmed by the laudanum, so I decided to get a few details. According to her, the children had been riding in the bed of the wagon with the gardening supplies. Their backs had been to the driver's seat and front wall of the bed, and Clara'd been holding little Thomas. Libby claimed that she'd told them to stay where they were when the attacker appeared, and that they'd obeyed."

"Which means," Marcus announced, "that the 'attacker' had to've had some mighty long arms."

"Yes," Mr. Picton agreed. "Either she was mistaken, or she was lying. No one could reach all the way around from the driver's seat of such a wagon and fire point-blank into the chests of three children who were below him in the bed and whose bodies were facing in the opposite direction. And even if he *had* managed the angle, surely one of the other children would have moved after the first shot, preventing point-blank execution of all three. Then there was the question of why the man hadn't shot Libby, too—she was, after all, the one who'd seen his face clearly. Her explanation was that he must've been crazy, and that there's no accounting for what crazy people do—not the kind of reply that inspires a great deal of confidence. Most disturbing of all, though, was her attitude toward Clara. She seemed to have no trouble mourning over the bodies of the boys, embracing them, kissing them—but she could barely approach her daughter, and her constant questions to Dr. Lawrence about whether or not the girl would regain consciousness seemed to stem out of a variety of emotions. Grief wasn't necessarily the strongest of them, to my way of thinking. Guilt was very evident, too, though that could perhaps be laid to her failure to protect her children. But there was fear, it seemed to me, as well."

"Did the sheriff organize a search?" Mr. Moore asked.

"Immediately. Volunteers were easy to raise, and the area was combed with dogs throughout the night and the following days. Inquiries were made in all the surrounding towns, and men who knew the hills well— men who ordinarily would've been reluctant to get involved in such matters—were persuaded to check any and all hiding places in the high ground. The case aroused that much emotion. But no trace of the man, as I've told you, was ever found."

"What about the money?" Miss Howard said. "Surely someone other than you considered the fact that Mrs. Hatch stood to gain from her children's deaths?"

"You would think so, Sara, wouldn't you?" Mr. Picton answered. "But I'm afraid you'd be wrong. I brought the subject up exactly once, to the district attorney. He informed me that if I wanted to commit professional suicide by pursuing such a line of inquiry, I could go ahead—but I'd get no help from him or anyone else in the office! I did what I could in the months that followed—checked, as I've told you, the county records, wrote some letters. . . . But Libby left Ballston within a matter of weeks, to take the job with the Vanderbilts in New York. She had, after all, no real prospects here—none to suit a woman of her restless and ambitious nature, at any rate. Just a small stipend, a decrepit old house, and a daughter whose recovery would be a long and painful one, requiring constant and careful attention."

"Concerning that," the Doctor said, "the daughter was left in whose care?"

"A couple who live out on the Malta road," Mr. Picton answered, producing his watch again and looking at it. "They've taken in a couple of orphans, over the years, and were more than willing to look after Clara. They're expecting us shortly."

The Doctor seemed slightly surprised at that, but pleased, too. "It's completely consistent, of course," he said, "that Mrs. Hatch would want to avoid caring for the child herself. But tell me: when she left, had the doctors assured her that Clara would never speak again?"

"Oh, yes, indeed!" Mr. Picton answered. "They thought it impossible, though even *I* questioned why a wound to the cervical spine should impair the power of speech. But the doctors in this area are not what one might term brilliant—or even, in some cases, competent." Mr. Picton snapped his watch closed and tucked it away. "But we really should be on our way," he said, starting toward the door. "I'm afraid that the Westons— that's the couple—don't want Clara to be overwhelmed by visitors, so I told them I'd just be bringing you, Doctor. The girl is still quite fragile, emotionally, and extremely shy of strangers—of people in general, really. I hope you all don't mind."

"No," Miss Howard said, "it's perfectly understandable."

"We'll just go back to my house and get the surrey," Mr. Picton said to the Doctor. "As for the rest of you, there is a livery stable quite close by, and they hire rigs for very reasonable prices. There are a great many other things for you to do and see, after all."

"There certainly are," Lucius said. "Any chance of getting that chalkboard today?"

"It should arrive by this evening at the latest," Mr. Picton answered.

"And what about the old Hatch place?" Marcus asked. "Not to mention the wagon, and Hatch's gun—what happened to them?"

"The house and grounds are available for our inspection," Mr. Picton said. "Mr. Wooley, at the stable, can give you directions on getting there—

it's quite easy. The wagon is still in the barn, though I'm afraid it's falling apart. As for the gun, that's a bit more complicated. Yes, indeed, a bit more complicated. Mrs. Wright told me that she wrapped it up and dropped it down a dry well, which you'll find about a hundred yards down a hill, behind the garden. You'll probably want to take the files"— he handed the stack over to Marcus—"so you can go over the details during your ride."

"Just one more thing before we go," Miss Howard said. "The children—do you happen to know if they were looked after by a wet nurse when they were babies?"

"A wet nurse?" Mr. Picton answered. "No, I don't know. It shouldn't be too hard to find out, though—Mrs. Wright still lives here in town. Why, Sara?"

"I'm just trying to explain the ages of the children. If they lived past infancy, there's got to be a reason."

Dr. Kreizler nodded to this, and followed Mr. Picton out into the hall. "Sound reasoning. I'm sure Mrs. Hastings can tell you how to contact the housekeeper, Sara. Now, Mr. Picton—concerning this visit of ours. I certainly understand the delicacy of the situation, but I should nonetheless like both Cyrus and Stevie to accompany us. If you don't mind."

Mr. Picton stopped at the top of the marble staircase, glancing from Cyrus to the Doctor uncomfortably. "Dr. Kreizler—Mr. Montrose—I don't wish to appear rude, but—surely you understand the risk—"

"I do," the Doctor answered. "And in the unlikely event that Mrs. Hatch's story should prove true, I shall have a great deal to answer for."

"Well . . ." Mr. Picton started down the stairs at what, for him, was a ponderous pace, though it was still faster than the rest of us were moving. "All right, but—" He turned to me and Cyrus. "I warn you both, the situation really is very delicate. I must respect the Westons' feelings, you see, and Clara's, too—she and I have become quite good friends, the poor girl—and I would hate for you to make the trip and then be forced to wait in the carriage—"

The Doctor caught up with Mr. Picton and put a hand to his shoulder. "Calm yourself, Mr. Picton," he said with a small smile. "I don't think that will be necessary." The Doctor thought about the matter for another instant, then proceeded farther down the stairs. "No, I don't think that will be necessary at all."

CHAPTER 30

After getting back to Mr. Picton's house and aboard his surrey, we began our trip to the Westons' farm by heading over to the east side of town, where Cyrus (who'd volunteered to do the driving) followed Mr. Picton's directions and steered us onto Malta Avenue, so named because it eventually turned into a road what led to a town of the same name. Just as soon as we were safely on this thoroughfare, Mr. Picton started asking for details about the Linares case and all the things we'd been through during the past few weeks in New York. It was all the Doctor could do to keep up with this rush of questions, especially as, in spite of their mad pace, they all cut right to the heart of the case.

Once we got back out of town, farms and woods took over the countryside around us again; and as I watched them go by in the late-afternoon light, I tried to imagine the scene of robbery and murder that Libby Hatch claimed had taken place on a road what couldn't have been much different than the one we were traveling along. It was a beautiful setting, one what glowed gold and green the way the Hudson Valley will do during July; but all the same, it wasn't hard to imagine violence scarring such a place, for they were lonely roads, those dirt tracks that led from small town to small town, with nothing but the occasional farmhouse for civilization. A clever criminal could've made quite a living off of them. Yet there were details of Libby Hatch's story that just didn't fit with the idea of a clever criminal. Even granting the isolated quality of the setting, things about the supposed attack just didn't make sense, particularly not to anybody who'd spent time around murderers, thieves, and rapists, as I had.

Why did the "attacker" give up his assault, for instance, once he knew Mrs. Hatch didn't actually have a weapon? And why kill the kids, but not the woman who could've identified him? And if he *was* so stupid or deranged as to be capable of such things, how could he suddenly become smart enough to escape a whole series of search parties what'd kept after him for days on end? No, it was obvious even to me that Libby Hatch had been banking on emotions and not reason taking over when her fellow townspeople heard her tale; and she'd been right, too, so far. But so far was only so far . . .

The Westons' farm was a humble but successful enterprise located right off the Malta road about a mile and a half from Ballston Spa. They kept dairy cows and chickens, and grew vegetables to sell during the summer and fall. Mr. Picton told us that the couple'd never been able to have children of their own, and that when a pair of tragedies in town—one a train wreck, the other an illegitimate birth—had left two kids without families, the Westons'd taken them in. They'd done such a good and kindly job of raising them that Mr. Picton'd thought of a similar solution right away when it began to look like Libby Hatch wasn't going to stick around to take care of little Clara. As we drew closer to the drive that led off the main road and up to the Westons' rectangular, clapboarded farmhouse, Mr. Picton told us that while we could speak freely around Mr. and Mrs. Weston, we'd have to be careful what we said in front of their kids: they weren't aware of all of Mr. Picton's suspicions concerning the Hatch case, and, given the nature of how rumors and news traveled in so small a town, we couldn't risk them finding anything out until we were ready for it to become common knowledge.

Following this warning, Mr. Picton anxiously inquired as to why the Doctor'd been so determined to have me come along on the visit. "You'll forgive my asking, I hope, Doctor," he said. "And you, too, Stevie. I understand, of course, how crucial Clara's reactions to Mr. Montrose may be—"

"Provided," the Doctor interrupted, "that the Westons have not prejudiced her mind in that area."

"Oh, no, not at all," Mr. Picton answered quickly. "I come out to visit Clara fairly regularly. The Westons, as I say, are aware of my suspicions about Libby, and though they've never said as much, I think that their years of taking care of her daughter have planted doubts about the woman's honesty in their minds." He paused, glancing at me. "But Stevie—what is *his* role to be?"

The Doctor looked at me with a smile. "Stevie, although he would be loath to admit it, has a unique and reassuring effect on troubled children. I've observed it many times at my Institute. And bringing at least one person who is not an adult will make us appear far less threatening, I suspect."

"I see . . ." Mr. Picton replied.

"But tell me," the Doctor went on, "has she really not uttered a word since the attack? Not a sound?"

"Sounds, occasionally, yes," Mr. Picton answered. "But no words."

"And what of written communications?"

"Again, no luck. We know that she has the ability—Mrs. Wright, the housekeeper, taught her the basics of both reading and writing. But Clara's done neither since the attack. Doctor Lawrence and his colleagues attribute it to the spinal damage. You may not believe it, Doctor, but they actually told me that the injury must have had some kind of indirect effect on her entire nervous system!"

The Doctor almost spat in disgust. "Idiots."

"Yes," Mr. Picton said. "Yes, I must say, they never seemed to pursue the matter very energetically. Not that I've been able to do much better. I've tried every way I can think of to get her to tell me something, *anything,* about what happened. But no luck. I hope you have some experience getting people with such afflictions to communicate, Doctor—because this little girl is a hard case."

Cyrus and I glanced at each other quickly, and then I turned around to stare straight ahead. Mr. Picton, of course, had no way of knowing what he'd just said, no way of knowing exactly what kind of bittersweet experience the Doctor *did* in fact have with getting through to people—and to one person in particular—who'd been written off as unable to communicate with the rest of the world. For the Doctor's lost love, Mary Palmer, had suffered from just such an affliction, and his efforts to find a way to communicate with her had formed the beginnings of the bond between them that had endured right up to her death,

"I . . . believe I know some techniques that may prove effective," was all the Doctor said.

"I hoped you would," Mr. Picton answered. "Indeed, I hoped you would. Oh, and one more request, Doctor: when you meet Clara, make a note of her coloring."

"Her coloring?" the Doctor repeated.

"Her hair, eyes, and skin," Mr. Picton went on with a nod. "I'll tell you something you'll find very interesting about it, on our way home . . ."

As we rolled up the Westons' long drive, we caught sight of a thick-armed, middle-aged man and a boy who looked a little older than me standing on the edge of a piece of pastureland what was located between the house and a stream that ran at the base of a high wooded hill behind it. They were wrestling and struggling with a section of barbed wire, trying to mend it. On the other side of the house was a big vegetable garden, where a girl in her late teens and an older woman were weeding and tending to produce. Like the man and the boy, they were dressed in worn farm clothes and were going about their business with a kind of determination what was enthusiastic and a little frustrated at the same time. It was the sort of attitude I've seen in a lot of similar farmers, over the years: the manner of people who have to fight against everything that Nature and human society can throw at them just to get by, but who still have a strange love for a life lived so close to the land.

There was a fifth member of this little family, too, a girl who, I already knew, was just shy of nine years old, and who didn't fit into the peaceful scene around her quite so comfortably as the others. Her dress wasn't made for working: even with two good arms and hands, a kid her age wouldn't have been able to do a whole lot of the kind of physical labor a place like that required, and it was obvious even from far off that this little girl couldn't use but one of her upper limbs. She just sat at the edge of the garden with a doll and what looked like a big pad of paper in her lap, her good left hand going over the paper again and again with some kind of writing or drawing utensil.

The smell of manure started to hit us about fifty yards from the house, which was set close to a big brick-red barn. When they saw our rig drawing up, all five of the residents came ambling in from their chores, the little girl moving the slowest and most cautiously and needing to be nudged along by the woman. As they got closer, I could see that the Westons themselves looked to be in their forties or fifties, the deep creases in their leathery skin and the greying of their hair making any more exact guess impossible. They had broad, kindly faces, but that didn't mean much to me: some of the worst people I'd ever come across in my life had been kindly looking foster parents—not a few of them farmers—who took in poor kids from the city and treated them like slaves, or even worse. But the two teenage kids looked happy and healthy enough, so I wasn't too suspicious to start out with.

As Mr. Weston—Josiah, we discovered his name was—approached Mr. Picton, he glanced at me and Cyrus with a kind of concern that caused the pair of us to hang back a bit, away from the others.

"I took it as understood that there weren't to be but one visitor, Mr. Picton, sir," he said.

"Yes, Josiah," Mr. Picton answered. "That being Dr. Kreizler, here." Mr. Weston wiped his hand to shake the Doctor's. "But the other gentleman and the boy are associates of his, and he feels that he may need them in order to accurately assess the situation."

Josiah Weston nodded, not happily, exactly, but not in a hostile way, either. Then his wife spoke up: "I'm Ruth Weston, Doctor, and these are our children, Peter and Kate. And hiding somewhere around here," she went on, pretending to search the area behind her skirt where Clara was hiding, "is another young lady . . ."

Clara didn't make any move to reveal herself yet; and seeing this, Peter smiled and said, "We'll get what we can finished while there's light, Papa. Come on, Katie, and give me a hand."

The pair of them went back off to the chore of mending the wire fence. They looked pretty cheerful as they did, and from this I figured that they had in fact been treated well during their years with Josiah and Ruth Weston. Once they were gone, little Clara started to appear from behind Mrs. Weston slowly, her pad of paper and doll tucked under her left arm and a bunch of pencils held tight in her left hand.

"Well!" Mr. Picton said, merrily but gently. He'd caught sight of Clara, but was glancing around as if he hadn't. "Where *is* my little girl? I'd hate to think I came all the way out here only to find that she's disappeared . . . no sign of her? All right, then—thank you, anyway, Ruth, but I suppose we'll just head back to town."

Mr. Picton started to walk back toward the surrey, and then Clara rushed out from her hiding place to tug at the tail of his jacket with those parts of her thumb and forefinger what weren't engaged in holding the pencils. As she did, I got my first really good look at her (though in fact it was my second overall, since I'd seen her likeness in the group photograph hidden in the secretary at Number 39 Bethune Street); she was a skinny little thing, with light brown hair gathered into one big, wide braid at the back of her head; eyes of a color similar to the hair (though, I noted uneasily, a touch more golden); and pale skin with very rosy cheeks. Like most kids who've seen things at an early age that nobody should ever have to, Clara's skittish movements were echoed by the pitiable nervousness of her silent face.

Turning around in mock surprise, Mr. Picton smiled wide. "Why, there she is! She appears out of nowhere, does this one, Doctor, and never *will* teach me the trick! Come and meet a friend of mine, Clara." Still clutching the tail of Mr. Picton's jacket, the little girl followed him over to the Doctor. "Dr. Kreizler, this is Clara. Clara, Dr. Kreizler works with hundreds and hundreds of children in New York, the city that I've told you I once lived in. And he's come all this way—"

"All this way," the Doctor interrupted, giving a meaningful smile to Mr. Picton that said he'd take it from here, "to see your drawings." He knelt down to look her in the face. "You like to draw very much, don't you, Clara?"

The girl nodded; but it was much more than just a nod, we could all see that. It was a kind of request, too: a wish, you might say, that the Doctor would ask her more. And the funny thing was that, though Cyrus and I were continuing to stand back, we understood the moment better than either the Westons or Mr. Picton did: for we'd seen the Doctor use the trick on many other kids at his Institute. Drawing, painting, molding clay, they were all some of the quickest ways to get a little girl or boy who'd survived something that they plain and simple couldn't speak about to begin to communicate. That was why the Doctor kept so many kinds of artistic materials in his consulting room at the Institute.

"Yes, I thought you might," the Doctor went on, slowly lifting a finger to point at Clara's clenched little fist. "Because you have so many pencils. But no *colored* pencils." He put on a troubled look, then brightened. "Did you know that there are such things as colored pencils, Clara?"

The light brown eyes went very big, and Clara shook her head to make it pretty obvious that, though she hadn't known there were such things, she'd certainly like to have some.

"Oh, yes. All the colors you can imagine," the Doctor answered. "Tomorrow I'll bring you some from town—because you really *do* need colored pencils to draw things as they actually are, don't you?" Clara nodded. "My friends and I sometimes draw, too," the Doctor said, indicating Cyrus and me. "Would you like to meet them?" More nods followed, and then the Doctor signaled us over. "This is my friend Stevie," he said, pointing to me.

"Hey, Clara," I said, smiling down at her. "Does your friend draw, too?" I pointed at her doll, to which Clara shook her head hard and thumped her pencils against her chest. "Oh, I get it—drawing's *your* game. Let her find her own way to have fun." Clara's shoulders began to move up and down; and then a scratchy sound what could've passed for a small laugh got out of her throat.

Finally, it was time for the big test: the Doctor pointed at Cyrus. "And this is my friend Mr. Montrose," he said.

For about fifteen seconds, Clara stared up at Cyrus with a face what was plain impossible to read. *Something* was going on in that head of hers, that much was clear—and while none of us could yet say just what said thing was, it was obvious from the way that Clara stood her ground calmly that it was *not* terror. But it should have been: if any piece of Libby Hatch's complicated story was true, if anything like the infamous attack by the mysterious black man out on the Charlton road really had happened, then when that little girl looked up at Cyrus, she should've taken off for the hills, or at the least for the safety of her foster mother's skirts.

But she didn't.

Finally Cyrus smiled kindly and bowed. "Hello, Clara," he said, his voice sounding especially deep and soothing. "You know, when *I* was a little boy, I drew a picture of a wonderful house." He knelt down to look into her eyes. "And do you know what the strange part of it is?" Clara studied Cyrus's face hard and then shook her head slowly. "The strange part is that I *live* in that house now—it's the *Doctor's* house." Clara pondered that for a few more seconds; then she held her drawing pad up to Cyrus.

On it was scratched a rough picture of the Westons' farmhouse. Cyrus grinned, and Clara once again let that strange little noise out of her throat. "Well, well," Cyrus said quietly. "So it's happened to *you,* too."

None of us ever found out whether Cyrus had caught a glimpse of what was on Clara Hatch's pad of paper before he said what he did to her, being as, in that slightly amused, slightly mischievous manner that he sometimes exhibited, he always refused to tell us. But it really didn't matter. The important thing was that, at the moment he told Clara his little story, you could just feel trust start to flow out of the girl: sticking her pencils under her arm with her other belongings, Clara turned away from Cyrus and took the Doctor by the hand, a move what caused Ruth Weston to gasp and Josiah Weston to put a hand to his mouth in amazement. The girl then led him over to Mr. Picton, put the Doctor's fingers to her doll's chest very carefully, and glanced up to give Mr. Picton a questioning look.

Mr. Picton slowly started to smile. "Why, yes," he said quietly. "Yes, Clara. I'm sure that the Doctor will know how to make your little girl feel much better. That's his job, you see, to make children feel better. Perhaps you should take him inside, and show him what's wrong."

The girl took the Doctor's hand again, but before going anywhere she looked up to Mrs. Weston.

"Of course," the woman said, reading another question in the little face. "I'll go with you. Maybe some of your other friends could use the Doctor's help, too."

The three of them walked toward and then into the house.

"That's the damndest thing," Mr. Weston said quietly, scratching his head. "Three years she's been here, and I've never seen her take to a stranger that way."

"As I told you, Josiah," Mr. Picton answered. "Dr. Kreizler is no ordinary visitor! Alone in his field, you might say—and his field is made up of cases like Clara's. Well, then—Stevie? Cyrus? Shall we go inside, too?"

Cyrus nodded and began to move toward the door with Mr. Picton and Mr. Weston. But I stayed where I was. "If you don't mind, sir," I said, "I think I've pretty well served my purpose here. Unless there's anything else, I'd like to get out to the old Hatch place and see what the detective sergeants are up to."

Mr. Picton gave me a slightly puzzled look. "It's over three miles from here, Stevie."

"Yes, sir. But I'm used to walking. I can find my way."

Mr. Picton nodded. "All right. We'll see you back at my house, then."

I looked to Cyrus, who signaled the okay to me with a little nod. Starting to run down the drive, I suddenly remembered what manners I had, and turned to call, "Nice to meet you, Mr. Weston!"

"What?" the man answered, still sort of stunned by what he'd witnessed. "Oh—yes, and you, too, son!" he called with a small wave, as he continued to guide Mr. Picton and Cyrus toward the house. Once they were inside I took off at top speed, waiting 'til I was well out of sight of the farm to light up a cigarette.

CHAPTER 31

I hadn't got halfway back to town before I began to wonder just how bright an idea my walking three or four miles alone on those shady country roads had been. The sun was starting to edge ever closer to the treetops, but even at high noon the strange, scurrying sounds that came out of those forests would've been worrisome. So when I found myself on the edge of Ballston Spa again, a peculiar mixture of relief and disappointment at being back in "civilization" came into me. I kept moving quickly, onto Charlton Street, which road, like Malta Avenue, took its name from the town that it eventually led to. Before long I was back out among the farms and the woods again, moving south and west through country that was even less inhabited than those stretches what lay to the east of Ballston Spa. I had close to two miles to cover, and I was determined to enjoy the adventure and not let myself get wrapped up in fear again; but I have to admit that it took the sound of exactly one hooting owl to kick me from a fast walk into a solid run, and by the time I finally began to hear familiar human voices in the distance, I'd grown nervous enough that I actually broke out into a grin, and felt a few tears of relief come into my eyes.

The sight of the old Hatch house, though, when I finally reached it, was enough to send a shiver of lonely fear back through me, and I found myself again wondering if maybe I shouldn't've stayed at the Westons' farmhouse. For if that latter happy spot had a reverse image, it was the joint I was now approaching, no question about it. There was no paint at all on the outside walls of the old two-story building, just some dark shingling that over time had turned a blackish shade of brown, what made it look almost as if the whole house had been consumed by fire without actually being destroyed. There were big, wild hedges growing both outside and inside the busted windows on the bottom floor of the place. In the back-yard loomed a huge dead oak tree, under which were a few old, worn headstones inside a rusty iron fence. The front yard, meanwhile, had pretty well turned into a hayfield, and you could hardly see the collapsing barn for a stand of maple saplings and creeping vines that had sprung up in front of it. There was evidence of some kind of life spilling out the front door and onto the grounds—broken bottles, rusted cans, yellowing cham-ber pots, and washbowls—but they were all scattered in a way that indi-cated the place had turned into nothing more than a popular spot for local kids in a troublemaking mood. A big rectangular space what figured to've once been the garden made up the far side of the yard: bushes, weeds, and time itself were making short work of the fence what had once run around it. Finally, beyond this last sign of human industry was the line of the woods, a line that was doing its best to creep back up and take over the whole area again.

The well, I remembered hearing Mr. Picton say, was down behind the garden, so I began to wade through the overgrown grass and bushes in the front yard until I came to the top of a high hill at the edge of the woods. I still couldn't see the others, though I could hear them, so I cupped my hands in front of my mouth. "Detective Sergeants? Mr. Moore?"

"Stevie?" I heard Mr. Moore answer. "We're down here!"

"Where's 'here'?"

"Bear left as you come down the hill!" he answered. "We're just behind a stand of pine trees!" I started to follow the instructions, then heard Mr. Moore's voice again: "Oh, dammit, Lucius, I don't *care* what kind of pine trees they are!"

About halfway down the hill I did in fact catch sight of Mr. Moore and Marcus, who were standing in their shirtsleeves over a collapsed collection of heavy rocks, in the center of which was a hole what was just big enough for a man to negotiate. A wooden cover for the hole lay to one side of the rocks. Mr. Moore and Marcus'd placed a strong tree limb across the hole, and were slowly pulling a thick rope up through the opening. From the sounds that echoed out of the blackness below, I figured that Lucius was actually down in the well.

"Ow!" he shouted. "Will you please be careful, dammit?"

"Oh, for once in your life stop whining!" Marcus answered.

"Whining?" Lucius shot back. "I like *that*! I'm down here in this filth, exposing myself to God-knows-how-many diseases . . . !"

As I arrived at the well, the top of Lucius's balding head began to appear through it. I gave Mr. Moore and Marcus a hand pulling the rope, and once Lucius was out he rolled over on the ground to catch his breath.

In his arms, he was cradling an old brown paper parcel.

"Is that it?" I said. "Is that the gun?"

"It's *a* gun," Marcus answered, starting to coil his rope. "And we've removed the pieces of the wagon that might have bullets lodged in them— the front wall of the bed and the driver's bench."

I nodded, then glanced around, noticing that someone was missing. "Where's Miss Howard?"

"Took the rig back to town," Mr. Moore answered. "She wanted to find that Wright woman—the Hatches' housekeeper—and ask her a few questions. What about the Westons' farm? How did it go? Oh, and you haven't got a cigarette, have you, Stevie?"

Sighing at the question (he always asked it, even though he always knew the answer), I took out my packet and handed him a stick, then offered one to Marcus, too. "Maybe the smoke'll keep some of these black-flies away," Marcus said, swiping at the tiny insects what were starting to swarm around our sweaty heads. Then he lit up off a match I'd struck, blowing out a big cloud of smoke that did seem to send some of the bugs scurrying. "Did the Doctor meet the little girl?"

I nodded quickly. "It went good—I think Mr. Picton was surprised by *how* good. The Doctor had the kid holding his hand inside of five minutes."

"Hmm," Mr. Moore noised uncertainly as he smoked. "Holding hands isn't talking, though—any sign her condition is psychological, rather than physical?"

"Well, she does make some little grunting noises," I answered. "And she can laugh, or something close to it."

Marcus looked encouraged by that fact. "But that's conclusive—at least, I think it is." He turned to his brother, who was still resting on the ground. "What about it, Lucius?"

"Well," Lucius answered slowly, as he sat up, "grunts and laughter argue against physical trauma or some other pathology making her incapable of talking. Assuming, that is, that the bullet didn't hit any of the throat organs associated with speech. There definitely wasn't any brain damage, according to Dr. Lawrence's report, and that would be the usual physical cause of the kind of muteness they were talking about at the time."

"So if it's not physical pathology or trauma," Marcus said, "then it's psychological."

"And if it's psychological," Mr. Moore chimed in, "there's a good chance Kreizler can break through."

Nodding and then glancing up the hill, Marcus took a drag off his stick. "Let's have another look at those pieces of the wagon," he said, as he started back up.

Mr. Moore, Lucius, and I trailed behind him. "What are we looking for, exactly?" I asked.

"A bullet," Marcus answered, his city shoes slipping a bit on the many years' worth of dead and decaying leaves what coated the hillside. "Or, if we get very lucky, bul-*lets*. You see, Stevie, Dr. Lawrence's report mentions only the point of *entry* for the two shots that killed Thomas and Matthew Hatch. They were dead when he arrived at the house, so he didn't think to go into any more detail. He did trace the path of the bullet that struck Clara a little more carefully, since she was still alive. It had been traveling at an upward angle, but may still have embedded somewhere in the wagon—probably the underside of the seat."

"But," I said, scrambling to keep up, "can't we just *ask* Dr. Lawrence about the bullets what killed the boys?"

"We did," Mr. Moore answered, "on our way out here. But Lawrence has been coroner since '84—seen a lot of dead bodies in those years. And like Marcus says, his attention in this case was pretty well focused on the little girl. He really can't say whether there were exit wounds in the boys' backs."

"Which leaves us with two options," Marcus continued, "one just tedious, the other next to impossible. We can either tear the appropriate parts of the wagon into tiny pieces to see if a bullet lodged in the wood somewhere, or . . ."

"Or?"

Marcus sighed. "Or we try to get a court order allowing us to exhume Thomas and Matthew."

"The problem there being," Mr. Moore added, "that any judge is going to want to consult with the mother before ordering an exhumation." He looked at me and smiled. "Care to post some odds on what Libby Hatch's reaction to that kind of request would be, Stevie?"

I just shook my head. "Wouldn't be worth the trouble of figuring them."

Leaning against one big tree in the front yard was a four-by-three-foot slab of ash wood along with an old, moth-eaten driver's seat. The bunch of us collected around the things and stared at them.

"But I still don't understand," Mr. Moore said. "If Libby was the one who shot the kids, wouldn't she have made some effort to get rid of the wagon, and any stray bullets along with it?"

"Ballistics is an infant science, John, even among experts," Marcus answered. "Also, Dr. Lawrence admits that he never examined the boys for exit wounds, since they were already dead—so he never would've mentioned such wounds while he was in the house, which meant that she wouldn't have thought of them, either. Lawrence would, of course, have made a fuss over the wound in the back of Clara's neck, which must have been pretty awful, given the range."

"She keeps her hair in a fat braid at the back," I said, feeling a sudden sadness that I hadn't when I'd noticed the girl's hair at the Westons' farm. "Probably to cover the scar."

Marcus cocked his head in a way what said this fact fit in with his theory. "But it's doubtful," he went on, "that Libby was educated enough about firearms to go speculating about exit trajectories."

Just then we heard the sound of a rig coming our way, and we all turned to look down the overgrown drive. Heading up it was Miss Howard, sitting on top of a hired buckboard and steering a feisty-looking Morgan stallion. She wrangled the compact, muscular animal to a stop near us, then brushed a few stray wisps of hair out of her face and jumped to the ground.

"Found her!" she called, smiling wide and marching over to us. "Mrs. Louisa Wright, of Beach Street—she lives in a house behind Schafer's commercial greenhouses. She worked for the Hatches for seven years— and there is, apparently, *nothing* that she won't talk about!" She pointed down the hill. "What about the gun? Any luck?"

"Hopefully," Lucius answered, holding up his moldy old package.

"Yes," Miss Howard said when she saw it. "Mrs. Wright told me that she wrapped it in a brown paper bag before dumping it. Well, then, we'd better get back, there's a lot to do!"

As we all gathered around to pile the pieces of the Hatches' wagon onto our buckboard, Marcus asked Miss Howard what else she'd been able to find out during her visit with Daniel Hatch's former housekeeper.

"I'll tell you on the way," Miss Howard answered, climbing back up to do the driving. "She was, as I say, very talkative. But one thing stands out: she suspects that only *one* of Daniel Hatch's children was shot that night."

"What do you mean, Sara?" Mr. Moore said, as the rest of us got aboard.

But Miss Howard looked to me. "You saw Clara, did you, Stevie?" I nodded. "Fine, light brown hair, eyes a similar shade? Pale-skinned?" I nodded again. "Well, that's not what the two boys looked like, apparently."

I right away thought back to Mr. Picton's request during our approach to the Weston farm that Dr. Kreizler make a note of Clara Hatch's coloring. "So *that's* what he meant," I said.

"What who meant?" Mr. Moore said.

But before I could answer, Miss Howard had cracked the reins against the Morgan's haunches and we were under way.

I wasn't sorry to say good-bye to the old Hatch place, and was glad to see Miss Howard continue to make liberal use of the reins to get us away quickly. Mr. Moore and I sat up on the seat with her, while the detective sergeants rode in the bed with the ash plank, the driver's seat, and the gun, the last of which items they didn't plan on unwrapping until we got back to Mr. Picton's house. For the moment they were full of questions about Mrs. Louisa Wright, questions what Miss Howard tried to answer as fast and thoroughly as she could; and each little bit of information she revealed made it plain that the old housekeeper was going to be a very important player in our case against Libby Hatch.

She hadn't had much use for Libby during her years with her, Mrs. Wright hadn't; but fortunately she'd felt the same about Daniel Hatch, which meant that her observations about what went on in the house wouldn't look to a jury like she was nursing a grudge against the handsome younger woman who'd been her boss. When Marcus asked why, if Mrs. Wright disliked the Hatches so much, she'd stayed on with them for so long, Miss Howard explained that the tough, take-no-nonsense widow'd been the only woman in town who'd been willing to serve the couple; because of that, the family'd grown more and more dependent on her over the years. As they did, Mrs. Wright eventually reached a point where she could pretty well name her fee from old Daniel: over time she'd squeezed enough money out of her tightfisted boss to be able to buy a decent house of her own in town, something that no other job in Ballston Spa what was available to a woman would've put her in a position to do. Mrs. Wright hadn't shed much of a tear when Hatch died, being as he'd left her nothing in his will; and when Libby asked her to stay on at the house the housekeeper'd insisted on her regular salary, which Libby'd agreed to pay, rather than go to the trouble of trying to find and break in somebody new. In other words, emotional considerations hadn't warped Mrs. Wright's opinions any; so what she'd seen and was now reporting to us could be pretty well relied on.

Which wasn't to say that she'd felt nothing for the Hatch kids, who, Mrs. Wright'd told Miss Howard, were caught in a strange and mixed-up situation that kept them in a constant state of skittishness. They'd all spent their early months, as Miss Howard had suspected, with a wet nurse, a setup what'd stopped them from becoming living demonstrations of Libby Hatch's maternal shortcomings—and was, because of that, the only reason why they'd survived their infancies at all. But life after those early months had still been pretty rocky for them. Clara'd had things the best, being as Daniel Hatch was as sure as he could be that she was his child. But the arrival of first Matthew and then Thomas had caused trouble, being as by then Hatch had begun to suspect his wife of being unfaithful. The fact that the two boys had thick, curly black hair, deep brown eyes, and olive skin (unlike either of their parents or their sister) was taken by Hatch as proof that they'd been fathered by another man; and even though he was never able to say who that man was, he grew more and more hostile to Libby as time went by, and lost interest in Thomas and Matthew altogether.

Strangely enough, Mrs. Wright said, all this hadn't been just an old man's ravings: Libby *had* been cheating on her husband, though with a man that her husband never would have suspected of the crime. It seemed that the minister who'd married the Hatches, one Reverend Clayton Parker, had the same coloring as young Matthew and Thomas, and paid regular visits to the Hatch homestead, where old Daniel entertained him to the best of his curmudgeonly ability. Apparently Mrs. Wright had more than once seen Parker and Libby locked in steamy embrace in the woods beyond the Hatch house, and Libby's sudden relapse into moody agitation in the summer of 1893 had occurred, coincidentally, right after Parker'd told his superiors that his spiritual talents were being wasted in Ballston Spa, and he'd been dispatched to do good works in that modern-day Babylon, New York City.

"A *minister?*" Marcus said, when he heard all this. "What the hell did a minister have to offer a woman who was married to one of the richest men in town?"

"Youth, good looks, and charm, for openers," Miss Howard answered. "Though I think Mrs. Wright is correct when she says that Libby wouldn't be satisfied with just those qualities. No, it was something else, too. A kind of—respectability, in a way. No, more than that. Redemption, maybe."

"Redemption?" Lucius said.

"An inside track to God?" I threw in.

"Yes, that's closer to it, Stevie," Miss Howard answered, urging the little black Morgan along toward Mr. Picton's house. "I'm not exactly clear—I want to get the Doctor's opinion . . ."

We'd reached the section of our route where the Charlton road became Charlton Street. Standing up to try to peer ahead through the dimming light of the evening, I soon caught sight of the four turrets of Mr. Picton's house—and I also saw the surrey standing horseless by the porch.

"Well, it looks like you'll get your chance," I said to Miss Howard. "They're back from the Westons'."

After we'd pulled up to the house, we put the section of boarding and the driver's seat from the Hatches' wagon up on the porch and went inside, entering the living room to find Cyrus at Mr. Picton's piano and our host standing in the far corner, where the Doctor was transferring notes onto a large chalkboard what had appeared. The thing was well on its way to becoming a duplicate of the one at Number 808 Broadway, and Mr. Picton was clearly fascinated by the process.

"Now, this," Miss Howard said with a smile, making them all aware of our entrance. "is a homey little scene, isn't it?"

Cyrus stopped playing, and the Doctor and Mr. Picton came over to us quickly. "At last!" the Doctor said. "What news from the Hatch house? Our new board awaits!"

The next hour or so was one of those jumbled times, as everybody tried to explain to everybody else what progress had been made during our first day in town. Things between the Doctor and Clara Hatch had continued to go very well after I'd left the Westons' farm, and though the girl still hadn't given out with any actual words, the Doctor was sure that he could eventually coax her to do so. It wouldn't be easy: Clara was in a state of what the Doctor called "protracted hysterical disassociation," meaning that what she'd seen was too terrible to make any sense of, either to herself or to anybody else. But Mr. Picton made it clear that we had to get her to talk: he didn't have a ghost of a chance of getting his boss, District Attorney Oakley Pearson, to agree to summon a grand jury to consider an indictment against Libby Hatch unless Clara was prepared to say flat out that her mother had shot her. We could assemble all the physical evidence in the world, but none of it would count for much in a case that had aroused so much emotion—and would surely fire up a new kind of outrage when we announced our theory of the crime—if the girl didn't talk. Though he went on for quite a while explaining all this to us, Mr. Picton's basic point was simple: if you were going to accuse a woman of murdering her own kids, you'd better be damned sure you had not only motive, opportunity, and means, but a witness, too.

Motive, opportunity, and means would still, though, play their parts, and these were things that we could pursue while the Doctor went about the process of trying to get Clara Hatch to communicate. The subject that seemed the most open to investigation that evening was means, being as Lucius had, we hoped, brought the instrument of attack up out of the old well. Asking Mrs. Hastings for a piece of oilcloth what he proceeded to drape over the piano, Lucius carefully positioned his damp brown parcel on the thing, then slowly began to unfold and pull away the paper bag with a couple of his steel medical probes.

"I asked Mrs. Wright if she'd noticed anything unusual about the gun before she dropped it down the well," Miss Howard said, as we all crowded around Lucius. "Anything that might indicate that it'd been moved or fired. But she said she'd been far too upset to take any notice of those kind of details."

"Understandable," Marcus said, watching his brother straighten out the bag, its hidden contents still bulging outward. "Did she say how old the thing was?"

"Hatch told Mrs. Wright he'd always kept it under his pillow," Miss Howard said. "He didn't fight in the Civil War himself—he paid a substitute—so that eliminates the possibility of it being a weapon he picked up in the army."

"Yes," Marcus answered. "It's probably one of the more common store-bought brands. And given his age, along with the likelihood that he hadn't fired guns very often, he probably wanted something easy to use."

"Right," Miss Howard continued. "Something like a Colt Peace-maker—it looks like one, from the silhouette. An early edition, too. The first Single Action Army models came out when, in '71? The timing would be about right."

"But is it a weapon that would be easy for a woman to use?" the Doctor asked.

It was the kind of question what Marcus or Lucius would ordinarily have answered; but Miss Howard enjoyed the limelight, and the two brothers knew enough to stay out of her way. "I don't see why not," she said with a shrug. "A forty-five-caliber pistol might not seem like a woman's weapon, on the surface, but the Single Action Army used metal cartridges, and had very smooth action. A fairly simple, serviceable piece, really. Add the fact that even the longer-barreled models didn't weigh much more than three pounds, and she would've been fine, even if she didn't have much experience with guns."

I saw Mr. Picton give Miss Howard a surprised look, and then turn to Mr. Moore. "Do *not*," Mr. Moore said, "push your luck with this girl, Rupert."

Lucius suddenly looked troubled. "I don't think I can get the bag off in one piece."

"Any reason why you need to?" Mr. Moore said.

"If we can prove that the wrapping was manufactured locally," Marcus explained for his brother, "then it argues against the possibility that this was some other gun dumped more recently by someone else."

"Well, you don't need to keep it in one piece to do that," Mr. Picton said. "Look at the bottom of the thing, Detective—you should find the words 'West Bags, Ballston Spa, New York' in small black print."

Lucius focused his attention on the part of the bag what was draped around the mouth of the gun barrel; then he brightened up. "You're right, Mr. Picton—it's there! Let me just cut it loose—" He pulled a surgical scalpel from his pocket and made four neat little slits in the bottom of the bag, then pulled away a rectangular piece of the brown paper and laid it out carefully on the sheet. "There we go. And now we can . . ."

With slightly faster strokes, Lucius began to peel away strips of the remaining brown paper, revealing a plain, single-action revolver, of the type seen in your standard Western magazine illustrations. Its dark brown grips were dusted with light green mold, and its blue steel chamber and barrel were red with rust. None of the rest of us knew quite what to think until Lucius picked up the gun by slipping one of his probes through the trigger guard, examined it with his brother, and then smiled.

"Thank you, Mr. West," he sighed.

"You mean it's in good shape?" Mr. Moore said.

"Let's just say this," Lucius answered. "Ballston Spa *is*, in fact, the home of the world's finest paper bags."

Marcus nodded confidently as he took his turn examining the pistol. "Hmm, yes," he said, trying to control his enthusiasm. "With a little work we should be able to actually fire it again."

"And that means—" Mr. Moore asked.

"That means," Miss Howard answered, herself smiling, "a ballistics test."

Mr. Moore's face went blank. "A what?"

"Provided," Lucius said, putting down the gun and holding up a finger, "that we can find a bullet in those pieces of the wagon for comparison."

"Whoa, slow down, here," Mr. Moore said.

"What about it, Mr. Picton?" Marcus asked. "How are your judges on the subject of ballistics analysis?"

Mr. Picton shrugged. "They're aware of the field, of course. But to my knowledge we haven't yet had a case where it's been used to convict. On the other hand, I can't think of one where it's been specifically excluded, either. And our judges don't tend to be absolutely primitive about such matters—they don't mind setting a precedent every now and then. If we come up with something convincing—especially if it's in conjunction with other evidence—I think I can run it up the pole and get a salute."

"Run what up the pole?" Mr. Moore said. "What the hell are you people talking about?"

I was in a pretty confused state myself, and I could see that the Doctor and Cyrus weren't doing much better. But we preferred to let Mr. Moore keep asking the dumb questions, being as—and I say this with all due respect to the man's more admirable qualities—it came so natural to him.

"Assuming we can make it work," Lucius said to Mr. Picton, still ignoring Mr. Moore, "we'll need to set up a firing range of some kind."

"Well," Mr. Picton answered happily, indicating the back of the house, "my yard is yours, Detective! There's nothing but a large cornfield beyond it. If you'll tell me what you need—"

"Not much," Lucius answered. "Just a few bales of cotton."

"Easily done," Mr. Picton answered. "Mrs. Hastings! We—" He turned to find his housekeeper already standing at the doorway, watching us with a blank, dumbfounded look. "Ah! Mrs. Hastings. Call Mr. Burke, if you would, and tell him—"

"Yes, sir," Mrs. Hastings answered, turning away and throwing up her arms. "A few bales of cotton, sir, so's you can shoot up the backyard!"

"This should be ideal," Miss Howard said, still staring at the gun.

"Oh, yes," Mr. Moore chimed in, his voice taking that turn toward whining it generally did at such moments. "Ideal. Don't bother to explain it to the rest of us, though, whatever you do."

Mr. Picton laughed at that, then turned to his old friend. "I'm sorry, John, we're being a bit rude, aren't we? How about this, to make amends—we've taken care of just about everything we can for today. In fact, I'd say it's been a particularly successful afternoon! What about hopping on the trolley and heading up to Canfield's? We can talk more about it over dinner—then some roulette, maybe a few hands of cards—"

"Silence!" Mr. Moore commanded, holding up a hand and suddenly looking eager and excited. "Everyone upstairs and into your dinner clothes, before there's any more discussion or Rupert changes his mind! Go, all of you, go!"

"And if we don't want to go?" Miss Howard protested, as Mr. Moore pushed her toward the stairs. "I'm not interested in—"

"Then you can simply eat and come right home," Mr. Moore said, cutting her off. "Leave the rest of us to lose our wanton souls!"

I'd jumped for the stairs quickly, but then, remembering something, I turned to Mr. Moore. "You'll lay my bets for me? They don't let kids play in that place, I hear."

"Have no fear, Stevie," Mr. Moore answered. "I'll follow your instructions to the letter. But all the same, you're going to have to put on the monkey suit, just to get into the dining room."

I nodded back at him and smiled. "That's why I brought it—only thing that could get me to wear the thing's an honest game!"

Charging on up the stairs, I shot into my room, closed the door, and tore open the big mahogany armoire where I'd stuck a set of evening clothes what the Doctor'd bought for me a year or so back. I think he'd been hoping, in those days, that I might develop some kind of a taste for opera and get to the point where I'd actually enjoy tagging along with him and Cyrus to the Metropolitan;ᵥbut so far I'd been in the Doctor's box at said house—and had said suit of evening clothes on—exactly once, and then only because it'd been important to the Beecham investigation. But this time around I was happy to cram myself into the stiff, starched white shirt and the black jacket and pants, if it meant that I could get some bets down on a reliable roulette wheel, which I'd always heard could be found at Richard Canfield's famous gaming house and restaurant in Saratoga, known throughout most of the country as just "the Casino."

Still, desire to get the clothes on wasn't any substitute for experience at doing it: I huffed and cursed as I stuffed and belted and pulled my way into the things, finally leaving the tie for somebody else to take care of. By the time I got downstairs all the others were ready to go, and Mr. Moore grumbled impatiently as Miss Howard very decently did up the band of white silk what was dangling around my neck. Finally, we left the house and strolled down in the warm darkness to Ballston Spa's electric trolley station, where we boarded a small, open car in high spirits—never suspecting for a moment that our host intended this little trip as something more than just recreation.

CHAPTER 32

The Ballston-Saratoga trolley system was only a year old, and looked it: the car that we boarded had polished railings and clean appointments, and it was set on top of a shining set of narrow tracks. The thing moved at a good clip through the four or five miles of countryside what separated Ballston Spa from Saratoga's main street, Broadway, and the breeze that hit us in our seats at the front of the car was refreshing and even exciting, given where we were going. It was the kind of air what heightens anticipation, you might say; and though the trip lasted only fifteen minutes or so, it seemed to my young soul to go on forever.

When the car finally did slip into America's greatest recreational center, it did so by way of the southern end of Broadway. From that spot we got an excellent view down into the heart of the town; and I've got to say, it was a wonder to behold. Lined by spreading, beautiful elm trees, Saratoga's Broadway, taken as just a street, would've been a credit to any town anywhere; but behind the trees, the well-tended sidewalks, and the streetlamps stood the blazing lights of countless shops and the city's massive hotels, all of which promised excitement of every stripe and gave the lie to the town's outdated label of "resort." There was no sign that retreat and relaxation were prized goods (or even possibilities) in Saratoga: the old days, when political men, scholars, and artists from all over the world had met to "take the waters" together and talk of lofty things were definitely gone by 1897, and the place was a full-blown pleasure market.

Canfield's Casino was a square, mansionlike building located down in a green, shady park where the Congress Spring (one of the town's many old

mineral water fountains) had formerly been the main attraction. The
Casino had actually been built by another famous gambler, John Morrissey, a burly Irish prizefighter and Tammany tough who'd made use of his
winnings to set himself up in the gaming room and horse track businesses
(Morrissey'd also built Saratoga's first track). During the construction in
1870–1871 of what'd then been known as "the Club House," Morrissey'd
pumped every Italianate luxury he could think of into the place, and it'd
done a booming business from the start. It hadn't been enough, though,
to net Morrissey the prize he wanted most: acceptance by the society
types who came to fritter their dollars away by the thousands in his establishment. He'd died in 1878, and ownership of the joint had passed
around to various second-rate operators for a time, until it was bought
and refurbished in 1894 by its current owner, Richard Canfield.

Canfield, like Morrissey, had made a personal fortune in the gambling
trade, though he didn't have the thug's past what'd kept Morrissey from
ever being treated like a true gentleman. Having run gaming houses in
Providence, Rhode Island, and then in New York, Canfield had spent his
spare time (and a short prison term) turning himself into a kind of self-
taught scholar and art critic. When he took over Morrissey's Club House,
he put all his learning to work, filling the joint with top-of-the-line furniture and art, building a big new gourmet dining room, and hiring one of
the most famous French chefs in the world to cook for his patrons. And
by refusing to allow women and kids to play at his tables, he'd even out-
smarted the reformers who, for a short time during his early days of operation, had tried to shake things up in Saratoga and had actually succeeded
in getting a lot of other, smaller houses closed down. At the same time,
though, Canfield had built said women and children a nice big lounge
where they could amuse themselves with ices and entertainments—and
tell their husbands and fathers what bets to put down for them.

The park around the Casino was a suitable setting for all this luxurious
recreation, with its fountains, pools, statues, and handsome trees lining
the walkway to the ivy-covered walls of the three-story Casino. We entered the building that night through the front door, the detective
sergeants noting with relief that Mr. Canfield was one of the few gaming
house and hotel operators in Saratoga who didn't hang a "Jewish Patronage Not Solicited" sign outside his establishment. Once in, we found ourselves in a large, crowded, and thickly carpeted lobby what was just
outside the public gaming room. Inside this room the stakes were low
(white chips went for a dollar, red for five, blue for ten, yellow for a hun-

dred, and brown for a thousand) compared to what went on in the private rooms upstairs, where everything was multiplied by a hundred.

Antsy as I was to start playing, I have to confess that I was even more anxious, that night, to meet the man who was famous everywhere as "the Prince of Gamblers." I didn't have long to wait: as soon as we walked in I caught sight of a fleshy but knowledgeable-looking soul, clean-shaven, with dark eyes that took in everything what was going on around him. (The face was so fascinating that it eventually snagged the interest of no less a painter than Mr. J.A.M. Whistler, who reproduced it on canvas.) When said face observed Mr. Picton's entrance, it and the rest of the man hurried on over, putting a hand out in happy greeting.

"Well, Mr. Picton!" Mr. Canfield said. "Feeling up to a night at the tables, are you? Or is it just Columbin's cooking that brings you up?"

"Canfield!" Mr. Picton said, with heartfelt good cheer. "No, I have some houseguests for a time, and I told them they couldn't leave the county without seeing our greatest contribution to modern American culture!" Mr. Picton made a quick round of introductions, and Mr. Canfield greeted us all in the smooth way what marks the successful gambling magnate. But there was something more in it, too; it seemed like the simple fact that we were Mr. Picton's guests meant that we'd get some kind of special treatment.

"Mr. Picton was a big help at a particularly dicey time," Mr. Canfield explained, as if he could hear the thought what was in my head. "During the town's nasty little reform fit, he argued to the county that Saratoga could shut down all the smaller houses it wanted to, but that it had to let 'establishments of quality' like the Casino stay open—unless it wanted to go back to depending on mineral water for its livelihood."

"I don't know that I was *quite* so instrumental, Canfield," Mr. Picton said. "Even the staunchest of the reformers eventually saw that they were cutting their own throats. How's the crowd tonight?"

"Oh, they're all here," Mr. Canfield answered, starting to walk us toward the dining room. "Brady, Miss Russell, Jesse Lewisohn—and Gates is upstairs, still determined to set a record."

This lineup had me speechless: the names of Diamond Jim Brady, the railroad supply magnate with a stomach six times normal size and an appetite for food that was almost as big as his lust for precious stones, and Miss Lillian Russell, the famous entertainer and Brady's constant companion, were, of course, well known to the world at large back then, as they still are; but in gambling circles, the names of Jesse Lewisohn—"the sporting banker"—and Mr. John Gates (who'd soon earn the nickname "Bet-a-Million" for losing and then winning back almost that sum—all in one day—at Saratoga) were just as legendary, and cause for even greater excitement.

"Brady's in the dining room, of course," Mr. Canfield went on. "Been through half of Columbin's stock already, and he's calling for more. I'll get you a table away from him—even with the diamonds, he doesn't do much for other people's appetites at moments like this." Signaling to a waiter at the entrance to the dining room, Mr. Canfield shook Mr. Picton's hand again. "Albert'll take care of you all—I'll see you in the gaming room. I assume you won't want any action upstairs?"

Mr. Picton shook his head with a smile. "On my salary? Not a prayer, Canfield. We can injure ourselves quite sufficiently in the public room, thanks."

Mr. Canfield paid his respects to the rest of us and then started to disappear back into the crowd; but then, seeming to remember something, he stopped.

"Oh, by the way, Picton. Word's going around that you're going to reopen that case—the one where the kids got shot?"

The rest of us couldn't do much to hide our surprise; but Mr. Picton just smiled and shook his head.

"All right, Canfield," he said. "I'll try to keep you posted."

"You know how it is," Mr. Canfield answered with a respectful shrug. "People in this town'll bet on anything, and do—there's bound to be a line on the manhunt and the trial. I'd just like to be able to set some reasonable odds."

"Two to one on the manhunt, for now," Mr. Picton answered. "As for the trial, I'll let you know."

Mr. Canfield gave that what you might call an appreciative look. "Two to one? Confident."

"Confident," Mr. Picton said. "Though who we actually arrest may surprise you."

Mr. Canfield nodded, turned, and, with another signal of departure, went back to his business of making suckers happy.

"And that, my friends," Mr. Picton said, "is what I mean about word traveling fast in these towns."

"Do you mean to say they're going to *bet* on this case?" the Doctor asked, taking in the wealthy crowd and starting to look a little revolted.

"Unquestionably. But you can get that gleam out of your eye, Moore," Mr. Picton said, glancing at his friend. "Canfield didn't get where he is by letting people with inside information fleece him." Mr. Picton began to walk toward the far end of the lobby. "Well, then—let's eat, shall we?"

Our table in the dining room might've been far away from Diamond Jim Brady's and Miss Lillian Russell's, like Mr. Canfield said, but we still had to pass by that famous pair to get to our seats; and such was not exactly a heartening experience. Not that we had any actual contact with the couple or their party; but I quickly found out just by watching their antics that what makes an amusing legend can sometimes amount to a pretty depressing reality. I knew all about Diamond Jim's famous sets of jewelry pieces, the sum of what totaled some twenty thousand diamonds. And of course, I knew about his appetite. But none of those stories prepared me for the sight of a hog-faced man—whose famous girth was stuffed inside clothes what vanity dictated be two sizes too small—going about his usual mealtime trick: starting with his diamond-studded belly about a foot from the table and refusing to stop eating until it touched the edge of the thing. At the particular moment we walked by, he was doing his worst to a whole family of lobsters, and had a bib tied around his pricey white suit and his precious diamonds. He was loud, too; loud, foul-mouthed, and very easy with what he said to his ladies, knowing full well that, given his millions and their own lack of any talent other than being pretty, they'd not only have to put up with it, but smile and laugh too.

Next to Diamond Jim was Miss Lillian Russell, whose face, of course, I'd seen on billboards in New York—though it occurred to me, when I saw her in the flesh for the first time, that they'd been damned flattering billboards. She, too, was lapping up Brady's loud vulgarity like a cat going at a dish of milk. Now, I don't mean to sound prudish: God knows, my mouth wasn't then and still isn't what it ought to be. But there's a difference between certain ripe choices in vocabulary and downright obnoxious behavior, and Brady was what you might call that difference made flesh. We all knew the rumor that Miss Russell didn't actually grant her sexual favors to Brady (it didn't seem possible that anybody could actually perform the physical act with that tub of excess) but was rolling in the hay with Brady's pal Jesse Lewisohn. That night, though, I figured that Mr. Lewisohn wasn't getting such a hot deal: Miss Russell might've been a famous performer, but she also had a figure what showed she'd done some damage at many a dinner table herself. Whatever poor team of maidservants had to stuff her into the kind of tight-waisted gown she was wearing that evening earned their pay as sure as any coal miner, that much was certain.

The rest of the activity in that dining room—which was a beautiful, long hall, with small stained-glass windows set into the ceiling and a polished

oak floor—tended along the lines set at the Brady table: all the other patrons in the place were stuffing themselves, drinking like fish, talking way
too loud, and "flirting" in ways that would've earned the average streetwalker in New York a night in the local precinct. These were respectable
people, too, in their ordinary lives: people who, when they went back
down the Hudson, were responsible for big business and government decisions, and for the lives of millions of ordinary people into the bargain. It
was a good thing we'd come for the gambling, I began to think: if we'd
had to do any socializing, I don't think I could've stood it.

I wasn't alone, either: by the end of our meal the general mood at our
table had grown pretty disgusted—and as we walked out I discovered that
such was exactly why the devious Mr. Picton had brought us to this spot.
"Get a good last look, all of you," he said. "Because if we succeed in bringing Libby Hatch to trial, it won't be just the outrage of the humble citizens in towns like Ballston Spa that we'll have to deal with. No, no—all
the mighty weight of this sparkling society will come crashing down on
our heads, too. For it's the essence of hypocrisy, isn't it, Doctor, that it requires masks to hide behind? And the masks of the idyllic home and the
sanctity of motherhood are the first and most untouchable of all. Yes, if
I'm right, you can expect to see some of these same faces sitting in the galleries of the Ballston court house in the weeks to come."

Which wasn't exactly the most charitable thought to offer at a moment
when some of us were trying to fix our sights on recreation. Miss
Howard, for her part, had seen all she could stand in the dining room, and
elected to head back to Mr. Picton's house on the trolley right away. The
Doctor, Cyrus, and the detective sergeants—none of them possessing
much real sporting blood—all agreed to accompany her, clearing the field
for the true enthusiasts. Mr. Moore and Mr. Picton had a couple of quick
drinks while I gave them a brief summary of my roulette strategy, and by
the time they headed into the public room they were looking and sounding like they'd managed to drown their repulsion with the crowd. As for
me, barred from actually watching the games, I was left to pick between
heading into the ladies' and children's lounge and going outside for a
smoke: not what you'd call a tough choice.

Wandering in amongst the long branches of a weeping willow what
hung over one of the little pools of water in the park outside the Casino,
I pulled at my starched collar and tie with an annoyed groan, wishing I
could just take the things off. Then I lit a stick and began to think, not
about what my earnings might amount to if all went well inside, but
about what Mr. Picton had said in the dining room. It wasn't what you'd

call comforting, to think that by prosecuting Libby Hatch we'd be ril-ing—and maybe even threatening—all those rich, powerful hypocrites and philanderers; and at first I thought it was just the unpleasant notion of what lay ahead that was starting to give me a distinctly nervous sensa-tion. But soon I realized that the ripples in my stomach had a more im-mediate cause, something to do with the area right around me at that moment. I couldn't say just what the uneasiness was, at first, but after a couple of minutes I put my finger on it:

I was being watched.

Spinning around, I stepped deeper into the branches of the willow and searched the darkness all around me; but there wasn't a soul to be seen anywhere in that part of the park. All the same, I grew more convinced moment by moment that somebody somewhere was observing every move I was making. Pulling at my tie and collar again as I broke into a cold sweat, I started to shift from foot to foot, breathing very fast. Finally I called out, to what seemed like nothing but empty darkness:

"Who's there? What do you want?" Realizing that I was being a bit un-reasonable but unable to prevent myself, I shoved one hand into my pants pocket. "I've got a gun!" I called out. "And I'll use it, I'm telling you—"

Suddenly a dark blur passed in front of me: dropping down, it seemed, from the sky came a fast-moving shadow, one what hit the ground softly but nonetheless caused me to shriek and jump back. Only by grabbing the trunk of the willow did I keep from falling into the pool; and though I heard fast footsteps moving away from me, by the time I looked up the person who'd made them was gone.

As I caught my breath I realized that I was now definitely alone: I felt that as certainly as I'd sensed the stranger's presence. Whoever'd been hid-ing in the tree—probably some kid, I stupidly figured—must've been ter-rified by my mention of a gun, and had lit out, more scared of me than I'd been of him. Realizing that I'd dropped my cigarette, I lit up another and then started back for the Casino, laughing at my own foolishness and never realizing what a close brush I'd had with real danger.

I'd learn, though: for in a matter of hours, I'd confront that danger again, and see its face.

———

CHAPTER 33

M r. Moore, Mr. Picton, and I didn't do half bad at the tables that night, and as a result we woke up Saturday morning with what you might call a rosy outlook on the tasks what lay ahead of us. The Doctor and Cyrus had already gotten themselves together and headed back out to the Westons' farm in a small hired gig; and Marcus and Miss Howard were in the backyard of Mr. Picton's place, wrangling with three big bales of raw cotton what had been delivered earlier. Lucius, meanwhile, had set up shop on the back porch and was carefully examining every part of Daniel Hatch's Colt and dusting the thing for fingerprints before he went about the business of dismantling and refurbishing it. With everyone so usefully employed, it seemed safe for Mr. Picton to head up to his office at the court house and continue doing his research into cases what bore some resemblance to ours (what the legal types called "precedents"), while Mr. Moore and I headed into the dining room to have some of Mrs. Hasting's excellent breakfast.

After we'd eaten, it was our turn to be pressed into labor: Lucius gave us a pair of magnifying lenses, a medical probe, and a couple of very sharp pocket knives, and told us to get to work on the section of planking and the driver's seat from the Hatches' wagon, which the detective sergeants had dragged around to the back of the house. We were supposed to go over every inch of these two items and, when we found something that looked like it might be a bullet hole, use the medical probe to see if there was in fact a metal object lodged inside. If there was, we were most definitely *not* supposed to try to pry it out: instead, we'd use the knives we'd been given to cut away all the wood around the thing, in order to keep it intact. Mr. Moore and I listened to these instructions with a noticeable lack of enthusiasm, since it was clear that if we followed this procedure, it would take quite a while to free a bullet from the wood, even if we got lucky and stumbled onto one quickly. But we tried to keep the grumbling to a minimum, and before long we were wrapped up in the job.

It took about an hour to come across the first likely candidate for a bullet hole. I found a small opening in one corner of the section of board and was very excited to discover that when I stuck the medical probe into it I made contact with something what was most definitely metal. I called the detective sergeants over to get their opinions, and they agreed that what I'd found might indeed be a bullet. The important thing now was to make sure that while I was cutting the wood around the object away, I didn't touch the thing with the blade of my knife; a consideration that I, in the heat of my enthusiasm, confessed to not really understanding. If the bullet was recognizable as such, what did it matter if it had a couple of knife marks on it?

That, of course, was not the sort of question you generally wanted to ask Marcus or Lucius, unless you were in the mood for a very long lecture on some budding branch of forensic science. In this particular case, Mr. Moore and I were treated to forty-five uninterrupted minutes on the new field of ballistics, a clinic made all the more complete by Miss Howard's participation. Put simply, ballistics seemed to amount to the firearms equivalent of fingerprinting: earlier in the century, an Englishman had discovered that bullets, when they passed through the barrel of a gun, were marked by whatever distinctive defects (nicks in the metal and the like) characterized said barrel. By 1897, when almost all pistols and long arms had rifled barrels, it'd been found that bullets were also marked by the rifling itself, which was made up of what were called "grooves and lands." The grooves were the spiral tracks what were carved on the inside of the barrel (rotating toward either the right or the left) to make the bullet spin as it came out of the muzzle and thereby fly much straighter through the air; the lands were the spaces between these grooves. Bullets propelled through said grooves and lands were marked by lines that exactly reflected the specific rifling of the particular barrel. This system of identification had already claimed some success, though not in the United States: some years earlier, a French colleague of the detective sergeants', one Monsieur Lacassagne, had matched the number, spacing, and twist of grooves on a bullet taken from a dead man to the barrel of a gun owned by a suspect. The man was afterward convicted, mostly on the strength of the ballistic evidence.

Now, this judgment had, the detective sergeants admitted, been a little premature, seeing as the lands and grooves of guns had never been catalogued even by manufacturer or model, much less by the individual characteristics of specific pieces; so it was possible that somebody else in France had owned a weapon with the same arrangement of lands and grooves as the gun what belonged to the fellow who'd been convicted. But the fact remained that there were now three ways to try to determine if a given bullet had come from a particular firearm: first, obviously, there was the caliber size; then there were particular marks left by defects in the barrel (not that every gun necessarily had such defects, but many did); and finally, there were the number and twists of the lands and grooves. Convincing as all this might've seemed, though, even a match between a bullet and a gun on all three counts couldn't yet be considered the last word on identification, being as, again, there was no central authority that required gun manufacturers to register the individual specifications of each of their models: the possibility still existed that a given bullet what matched a given gun according to caliber, defects, and grooves and lands had actually been fired by some unknown matching weapon. Oh, sure, ballistic experts like the detective sergeants could protest that the chances of any two guns having exactly the same specifications were somewhere in the neighborhood of a million to one; but even a million to one left room for doubt, and so, while ballistic evidence had become what you might call mighty handy to modern-thinking investigators, it still wasn't accepted as legally conclusive.

By the time the Isaacsons and Miss Howard had finished explaining this bit of business to Mr. Moore and me, I'd pretty well finished the job of getting my bit of metal free of the board; but my spirits, which had started to race at the prospect of actually being able to put a bullet to the ballistics test, sank considerably when I realized that I'd spent the better part of an hour carefully preserving an old nail head. Such discouragement, though, was common to detective work, I knew that much: so I picked up my magnifying lens and continued going over the surface of the wood, looking for another likely hole.

Lucius, Marcus, and Miss Howard, meanwhile, continued their lecture, explaining what the younger Isaacson brother was up to with Daniel Hatch's Colt: for ballistics didn't begin and end, it seemed, with the matching of bullets to barrels. Lucius also had to carefully try to determine, based on the amount of rust and powder buildup on the Peacemaker, how recently it'd been fired, and how many times. The second question seemed easy enough to answer: there were three cartridges still in the six-shooter, giving the impression that three shots had been fired. This came as no big surprise: three was the number of bullets we'd expected to be involved in the shooting of Libby Hatch's children. But, as usual when you were dealing with forensic science, things weren't as simple as they appeared.

It was general practice, Miss Howard explained, for people who kept pistols in their homes to leave one chamber empty at the top position, so that if something or someone accidentally happened to catch the hammer without cocking it, the firing pin wouldn't slam back down on anything but air. And as Lucius's examination went on, the three of them became ever more convinced that Daniel Hatch had followed this procedure. Three chambers of his gun were, like I say, still loaded; but of the remaining three, only two had the kind of powder deposits that would indicate they'd been fired since the gun's last cleaning. On top of that, the third empty chamber had a larger buildup of rust than the other two, indicating it'd been vacant longer. And as for the unlikely chance that somebody had found the gun, shot it, reloaded it, and dumped it back down the well, Marcus and Lucius felt they could rule that out by the measurement they took of the amount of rust in the barrel: the gun hadn't been fired in years.

This was all very disturbing. For our theory that Libby Hatch had herself shot her three children to work out, we appeared to need three shots to've been fired; but only two had been discharged from the Colt. This gap perplexed Marcus and Lucius mightily, and as they continued to dust the gun for fingerprints, their faces grew as knotted as the old trees out in the yard. They did find several prints that matched Libby's on both the gun's grips and its trigger; and there was a partial print on the hammer what they felt comfortable labeling as hers, too; but there was no sign that she'd ever touched the cylinder, which appeared to rule out the possibility that she'd reloaded and refired the thing at any point. We knew that one bullet had traveled clear through Clara Hatch's neck (and hopefully lodged in some part of the wagon, probably the underside of the driver's bench); but if only *one* other shot had been fired, how could we account for *two* dead boys?

Their mood getting nothing but more glum, Marcus and Lucius carefully recorded all their opening findings on the condition of the gun, and then began to disassemble the thing to get it ready for the test firing. It was Miss Howard who brought hope back into the picture by coming up with a possible solution to the riddle of two bullets and three victims. Going for the stack of Mr. Picton's files on the shooting, which were lying inside on the piano, she pulled out Dr. Lawrence's postmortem report on the two Hatch boys, reminding us that nowhere in the thing was there any reference to exit wounds on either Thomas's or Matthew's body. And while Lawrence did say that there were powder burns on the children, he didn't specifically state *which* children: Mr. Picton had assumed he'd meant all three, being as they'd all died of gunshot wounds. But that might not've been the case. As for Libby Hatch's statements about what positions the kids'd been in when they were shot, we couldn't accept those any more than we could believe anything else the woman had said. So we were free, inside of certain limits, to imagine an entirely different sequence of events from the one that Mr. Picton had dreamed up on the basis of the reports.

Suppose, Miss Howard said, that little Thomas had, in fact, been sitting in Clara's lap when the rig stopped. The girl had been shot in the chest, and there was no way that *anybody* could have shot her in that region without first moving Thomas out of the way. So, Miss Howard said, we had to figure that Libby had taken Thomas and stuck him somewhere else— probably in *Matthew's* lap. Libby'd then shot Clara, an act what almost certainly would've made Thomas very upset, causing Libby to shoot him quickly. Now, the Colt .45 Peacemaker was a powerful gun: the bullet what'd struck Clara had traveled clear through her chest and neck. So the bullet what'd hit little Thomas would definitely have gone straight through him and into whatever was behind him—or *whoever* was behind him, if we now accepted the idea that he'd actually been sitting in front of Matthew.

This thought got Marcus's and Lucius's eyes twinkling again. Was Miss Howard suggesting, they asked, that the two boys had been killed by *one* bullet? To be sure, she answered; nothing else made any sense, given the state of the Colt. But before anybody went getting too happy, Miss Howard continued, we had to remember one thing: the single bullet might not have been traveling with enough power to make it through both bodies and into the front of the wagon's wooden bed. If that was the case, we were in trouble; for among the many things Dr. Lawrence's report didn't mention was his having taken any bullets out of the dead boys. In other words, if the missing bullet wasn't in the hunk of wood in front of us, then it'd been buried with Matthew Hatch in Ballston's town cemetery (which was, it turned out, just around the corner from Mr. Picton's house). This realization wiped the smiles right back off the detective sergeants' faces, and also lit a new fire under me and Mr. Moore—joined, now, by Miss Howard—to tear the piece of planking and the driver's seat into toothpicks in an effort to find the second deadly missile; because without it, we had no way of even suggesting that Daniel Hatch's Colt had been involved in the shootings.

As we madly pursued our work, Marcus and Lucius went back to working on the gun. Mr. Picton eventually returned to his house for lunch, and over that meal we told him about our morning's work, which he found intriguing but also very unsettling. Once he'd set back out for his office, we went to work again with even more determination; but the early hours of the afternoon went by without anyone making any discoveries.

The approach of evening brought the return of Dr. Kreizler and Cyrus, who took up positions next to us and joined in the search. Still, though, there were no hopeful sightings. We were beginning to run out of places to look, and it was Mr. Moore who first realized the dreadful implications of that fact. Along toward cocktail time his brow had become positively creased by discouragement; but when Mr. Picton came home and suggested that everyone quit working and have a drink before dinner, Mr. Moore forced himself to put on a cheery face, and urged the detective sergeants—whose eyes had gone bloodshot from a full day of very close work—to accept Mr. Picton's invitation. The rest of us would be along, he said, in a minute, to which Marcus and Lucius nodded wearily and headed on into the house.

As soon as they were safely out of earshot, Mr. Moore's face filled with urgency. "All right," he said, putting his magnifying lens down. "That's it for tonight. Everybody knock off."

"But why, John?" Miss Howard said. "There's still some daylight, and not that much left to do—"

"That's exactly the point," Mr. Moore answered. "We're going to need some part of this thing to be intact in the morning."

I was still confused; but Cyrus had begun to nod in understanding. "It's not here, is it, Mr. Moore?"

"The odds are against it," Mr. Moore answered. "A forty-five-caliber bullet would've left a big enough mark that *one* of us would've seen it by now."

"So why save *some* of the thing?" I asked.

"Because I don't want Rupert to have to outright lie in court, or Marcus and Lucius to have to perjure themselves. There's only one place that bullet can be—and we're going to get it. Then, tomorrow morning, we'll put it in what's left of this thing and let them find it. None of *us* are going to be called to testify in this particular area, so we don't need to worry about lying—and so far as the rest of them will know, they'll be telling the truth."

The Doctor's eyebrows arched a bit. "John—you realize that you're suggesting—"

"Yes, I know what I'm suggesting, Kreizler," Mr. Moore said, moving away from the table. "But there's no other option. We all know we'd never get a judge to order something like this without the mother's permission. Not based on the little evidence we've gathered so far." He paused, waiting for arguments; but none came. "I'll check in the basement for a shovel," Mr. Moore went on. "We'll do the job tonight."

Miss Howard, Cyrus, and I looked at one another in a little shock; but the Doctor summed up all our deeper feelings by saying, "Moore's right. It's the only way we can be sure."

All five of our heads started nodding slowly; but much as we may have agreed that Mr. Moore's plan was the only way to both get what we needed and look out for Mr. Picton's and the detective sergeants' legal and ethical positions, that didn't change the fact that we were contemplating a grisly, frightening, and illegal action, one what had gotten many people hanged—or worse—over the centuries. It took, you might say, a little adjusting to.

Mr. Moore did manage to find a shovel in the basement, along with a couple of lengths of strong rope, and he put them all outside the kitchen door while the rest of us were in the living room. Then we all went in to dinner, the prospect of what we were about to undertake keeping most of us pretty quiet through the better part of the meal. Mr. Picton, fortunately, filled up the silence with a stream of talk about the cases he'd been studying; then it was back into the living room for a little more of the music what Cyrus had been playing the day before. Finally, the time came to head upstairs. We'd have to wait for Mr. Picton and the detective sergeants to go to bed, at which point the rest of us would leave the house separately, to meet up around the corner on Ballston Avenue. From there we'd head down to the cemetery.

CHAPTER 34

The house finally grew completely quiet at just past one o'clock. I left my room carefully and got outside, almost running headlong into Mr. Moore on the front lawn as he made his way around from the kitchen with his shovel and rope. We didn't see any sign of the rest of our fellow ghouls until we arrived at the appointed meeting spot around the corner. The Doctor and Miss Howard were sharing a cigarette, with Cyrus peering anxiously around at the darkened houses on either side of the street. He could've saved himself some sweat, the way I saw it, even given what we were up to: Ballston Spa was obviously the kind of town what shut down early and stayed shut down, even on a Saturday night.

"All right, now, remember," the Doctor murmured, as Mr. Moore and I reached them. "What we are about to undertake is a serious criminal offense. Moore and I will therefore be the only ones to actually participate. Stevie, you'll stand watch at this end of the street. Cyrus, you'll go an equal distance in the opposite direction. Sara will be our last line of defense—she'll guard the cemetery gate."

"With the artillery," she said, producing the weapon what she used on really special occasions: a .45-caliber Colt revolver of her own, one with a short barrel and pearl grips. She checked its chamber with the quick moves of an expert as the Doctor went on:

"If you encounter *anyone, any* of you, you must claim complete ignorance. You're a guest of Mr. Picton's, and you're out taking the air on a lovely night. Understood? Very well, then . . ."

Mr. Moore started to move farther up the block with Miss Howard and Cyrus. "Why don't you stay here with Stevie until I've got the hole dug, Kreizler? The fewer people inside at one time the better, and it's not like—" Mr. Moore cut himself off quickly, though he'd already glanced at the Doctor's bad left arm.

"Yes," the Doctor said, following Mr. Moore's eyes down to his slightly withered limb. "I take your point, Moore—I wouldn't be much use to you in the digging. Very well. Signal when you're ready."

Nodding and looking a bit sorry for what he'd said, even though he'd clearly meant no offense, Mr. Moore hustled off with the other two.

The Doctor and I just stood there for a few minutes, myself not knowing exactly what to say to break the awkward moment brought on by the subject of his arm. But he soon made that job unnecessary by himself glancing down at the thing again, and then laughing once, quietly.

"It's strange," he whispered, "I never thought it might actually serve some purpose . . ."

"Hunh?" was all I could say.

"My arm," the Doctor whispered back. "I've been so used to seeing it as a source of pain and a reminder of the past that I never imagined it could be anything else."

I knew what he was talking about with that "reminder of the past" business: when he was only eight, the Doctor's left arm had been smashed by his own father during the worst of their many fights. The older man had then kicked his son clear down a flight of stairs, aggravating the injury and making sure that the arm would never heal properly. The recurring pain in the scarred bones and muscle, along with the underdeveloped state of the arm, served to keep the trials what the Doctor'd been through during his childhood pretty constantly in his mind. But as for what he meant by the arm "serving some purpose," I couldn't tell, and I said so.

"I was referring to Clara Hatch," he said, taking his eyes off the arm and glancing up and down the street. "From our first meeting, I naturally felt some empathy with her having lost the use of her right arm, quite probably because of an attack by her own mother."

We both turned when we started to hear the quiet sounds of a shovel digging into dirt; but it'd been a wet summer, and as the shovel reached deeper, softer ground, the sound died away altogether. The Doctor continued his story:

"Today I decided to use the coincidence of our injuries in my effort to make her feel safe enough in my presence to start to allow images of what happened to reenter her thoughts."

"Images?" I asked. "You mean, she doesn't remember the whole story?"

"A part of her mind does," the Doctor answered. "But the greater portion of her mental activity is directed at avoiding and erasing such memories. You must understand, Stevie, that she is emotionally hobbled by the fact that her experience makes no apparent sense—how could her mother, who should have been the source of all safety and succor, possibly turn into a mortal threat? Then, too, she knows that Libby is still alive and could return to strike again. But the combination, today, of the set of colored pencils I gave her and the story I told her about my father and my injury seemed to at least plant the idea in her mind that she might begin to confront such confusions and fears, and perhaps even share them with another person."

I smiled. "She really went for the pencils, hunh?"

The Doctor shrugged. "You've seen such things at the Institute. It's remarkable, what seemingly mundane objects can achieve in such situations. A toy, a game—a colored pencil. Not surprisingly, the first one she reached for was red."

"Blood?" I asked quietly, figuring that, in her position, I probably would've made the same choice.

"Yes," the Doctor answered, shaking his head and hissing. "Imagine the savagery of that scene, Stevie. . . . It's no wonder she can't speak of it, that even its memory has been exiled to the farthest corners of her conscious mind. And yet from that corner it presses—it *cries*—for release, but only if that release will be safe for her." The Doctor paused, thinking the matter over. "A red stream . . . you remember the picture of the Westons' house that she showed Cyrus? There's a brook that runs behind it, and she added that brook to the picture today. But she drew it in red—gushing torrents of red. And beside the stream she drew a dead tree, a tree whose roots reached down into the red water." The Doctor shook his head, then held up his left hand, clenching it into a fist. "I tell you, Stevie, if we do no more while we are here than help to mend that poor girl's mind, the trip shall not have been wasted."

I thought about that for a few minutes, and then asked, "How long do you figure it'll take before she can start to communicate with you about it?"

"Actually, I'm fairly optimistic, based on her behavior this afternoon. It should only be a matter of days before we can discuss the incident through pictures and simple questions. But as for getting her to speak—for that I will have to come up with some new strategies."

We didn't say much more, for a while. I guess I was just absorbing the idea of little Clara living out there on that farm, among people who'd once been strangers, trying desperately day and night not to think about why she should have to live with them, but at the same time wanting so badly to understand why. How could her brain operate, when it was given two sets of orders that were so opposite and so urgent? How could she ever get a moment's sleep, or even peace, with all those voices screaming inside her skull, telling her to do different things? It was a miserable thought; and I began to be grateful, standing there on that street corner, that when I'd been a young boy in New York I'd at least been clear about who my enemies were, and what it would take for me to survive. Badly as she'd behaved, I didn't think my mother'd ever wanted me actually, literally *dead*; and for the first time I saw that as, if not a blessing, at least one of the better on a long list of bad choices.

Suddenly there came the sound of approaching footsteps. The Doctor and I withdrew into the shadow of an elm tree and waited: but it was only Miss Howard, come to tell us that Mr. Moore was ready for the Doctor.

"Things are pretty quiet up there," she said, indicating the cemetery. "So he had Cyrus give him a hand lifting the coffin out of the ground. Not that it's all that heavy . . ."

The Doctor gave her a grim nod, then turned to me. "All right, Stevie," he said. "You'll be on your own for a few minutes. Stay alert."

The two of them moved back down Ballston Avenue, and I stayed under the elm tree, staring at the shadows that were being thrown by the moon. A warm wind soon began to kick up, and that played hell with my vision—and my imagination. All those shadows what surrounded me were turned into ghostly, man-shaped silhouettes, the whole collection of which was moving and dancing and, I became more and more convinced, getting ready to pounce on me. Oh, sure, I *told* myself it was the wind, and that I didn't have anything to worry about; they were all tricks of the light and my eyes, just a lot of—

Then I noticed something: one of those manlike silhouettes—a small one underneath a tree across the street—wasn't moving. Not only wasn't it moving, but it wasn't where it should've been, given the position of the moon. There were a couple of twinkling spots, too, right at about eye level—

And for a shadow, it was doing something that was awfully close to smiling at me.

I froze up tight, scared and bewildered. The more I stared at the thing, the more I grew convinced that "it" was an actual person; but at the same time, all that staring had started to make my vision go slightly crazy. I knew that I wasn't going to be able to figure anything out unless I could find a way to make the thing come out from under its tree and into the moonlight; but that might wind up being a very dangerous proposition. Whoever or whatever it was that I was watching, though, didn't seem to be sending up any alarm or making any hostile move; so I figured I'd be okay if I just took a few steps out from under my own tree and tried to get a better look.

I started to walk. Then I shivered once, mightily, when the shadowy thing across the street mirrored the move. As soon as we were clear of all the shadows, I could see plainly who it was:

El Niño, Señor Linares's little Filipino aborigine. He was dressed in those same clothes what were four sizes too big for him—and for whatever reason, he was, in fact, smiling at me. Slowly lifting an arm, he seemed to try to signal to me in some way, and for a minute I grew less fearful. The attempt at communication and the smile combined with his appealing round features to make him look something other than threatening. But then he made a different sort of move: lifting his head, he reached up with one hand and ran a finger around his neck. Now, in most parts of the world what I know of, that only means one thing; but he was still smiling, so I gave him the benefit of the doubt for another few seconds, on the off-chance that I was reading him wrong. But what came next was in no way reassuring: still grinning, he put his hand around his throat in a kind of choke hold, as if he meant to strangle someone—in this case, pretty apparently, yours truly.

Shivering violently again, I turned and bolted up the street toward the cemetery, fully believing that the little man who I figured for some kind of assassin was going to follow me and that I was in a race for my life. I didn't look back—I'd seen how quick El Niño was, and I didn't want to slow down for even a second. When I hit the northern edge of the fenced-in cemetery, I got within sight of Miss Howard, who had her back to me. Not wanting to scream for help, I just picked up my pace, hoping that she'd catch the sound of my feet. She soon did, and when I was about thirty feet from her and she could see the look on my face, she pulled out her revolver, holding and aiming it with practiced skill at the area behind me. Much relieved, I kept on running toward her; but then, when I saw her face go blank and her arms drop to her sides in confusion, I slowed down. She just looked at me and shrugged, and I stopped altogether, gasping for air and finally glancing behind me.

The little aborigine was nowhere to be seen.

Miss Howard walked quickly over to join me as I leaned down, hands on my knees, to take in some big gulps of air and spit into the street.

"Stevie," she said quietly, "what's happened?"

"That servant of Señor Linares'," I answered. "El Niño—he was down there!"

In a flash Miss Howard brought her pistol up again, though only as far as her hip this time. "What was he doing?"

"Just—*watching* me," I answered, finally getting my breathing under control. "And he made a sign with his hands—Miss Howard, I think he meant to kill me. But it was strange—he was *smiling,* too, the whole time."

With her free hand she grabbed my right arm and pulled me toward the cemetery gate. "Come on," she said. "The Doctor'll want to know about this."

I've never counted myself a religious man, really; but when we got to the gate I looked inside the graveyard and saw a scene what struck me as so unholy that I stopped dead in my tracks. The area directly ahead of us was lit partly by the moon, but also by the faint glow of a pair of arc streetlamps what stood just outside the back fence of the cemetery. Together, these sources of light made it pretty impossible to mistake what was going on: the Doctor was crouched over a small coffin, his jacket off and his shirtsleeves rolled up. The lid of the coffin lay to one side, along with a pile of dirt from a nearby open grave. In the Doctor's gloved hands were a scalpel and a pair of steel forceps: he was working quickly but carefully, like a man carving a turkey at a table full of hungry people. Mr. Moore was standing to one side and looking away, a handkerchief over his mouth. It was pretty apparent that he'd been sick in the last few minutes.

"Wait," was all I could say as Miss Howard started into the cemetery. "It ain't—it ain't worth interrupting him. We can tell him when he comes out."

Miss Howard gave me the once-over in a way what said she completely understood my reluctance. "You stay here and keep watch," she said. "But I've got to tell him—the aborigine may not have been alone. Do you want my revolver?"

I looked down at the thing, but just shook my head in reply; like I've said, guns were never my style. Miss Howard walked quickly in to Mr. Moore and the Doctor, and though I couldn't hear what they said, I could see looks of extreme alarm register on both their faces. But we'd come too far to break the thing off now, even I knew that; so the two men just sent Miss Howard back to the gate, and then the Doctor returned to his work with even more energy. I looked farther down Ballston Avenue and saw

Cyrus, who was peering back toward us, obviously wanting to know what the hell was going on.

I thought to run up and tell him; but then I heard a satisfied sound—one what was maybe just a little too loud, given the situation—come from the Doctor's direction. Turning, I saw him holding something up between his gloved fingers: it had to be the bullet. Mr. Moore looked at the thing and patted the Doctor's back with a smile of relief. Then they quickly started to get the lid back onto the coffin. Looking over to me and Miss Howard, Mr. Moore hissed, "Stevie!" as loud as he felt it was safe to do; and, with the part of my stomach what hadn't gone into my throat at the sight of El Niño now starting to rise and join the rest, I ran inside to them.

The smell of dirt and decay hit me from about ten yards away, though thankfully, by the time I got to the grave site, they'd refastened the lid of the little coffin. Then it was up to me and Mr. Moore, using the lengths of rope, to maneuver the thing back into the hole he'd dug, which we managed to do without too much trouble. This task kept me busy enough to avoid really taking in where I was—along with what I was doing—but once the coffin was down and we'd started to first refill the grave with dirt and then re-cover it with large sections of sod what Mr. Moore'd carefully cut away, I had a chance to glance around at all the headstones and monuments what were surrounding me.

With a start I suddenly realized that I was actually standing on little Thomas Hatch's grave. Moving quickly to do my job from another angle, I glanced at Thomas's and Matthew's headstones. The pair of them were identical, except for the words what were carved into each. In the upper portions they displayed the boys' names and years of life, and under each name was the phrase "Loving Son of Daniel and Elspeth." But under these words were two different quotes. Thomas's read, "A lamb gone too soon to the Lamb," while Matthew's said, "He that believeth in Me shall not Die." At the bottom of each stone, in lettering what was less stodgy and more flowing than the rest, was a message: "Love always, from Mama."

Maybe I was just looking for something to fix my mind on as a way of calming down, but it occurred to me to ask, "How come they're buried here, and not at the Hatch place? There's a cemetery out there, behind the house."

"Many cities and towns now require burial in a designated public cemetery," the Doctor answered, holding the small object he'd found up above his head and studying it. "For reasons of public health. I'm sure Mrs. Hatch didn't object—she must have realized that the chances of anyone attempting just what we're doing now were far more remote in a public graveyard."

"Yes, and she had good reason to think so," Mr. Moore said, getting the last of the sod into place and trying to cover the remaining visible cuts in the ground by pulling up clumps of loose grass and sprinkling them over the cuts. "It's a lot easier to get caught in a place like this." He stood up, examined his work, and then nodded once in satisfaction. "Okay. Let's get the hell out of here."

The Doctor moved quickly for the gate, but I lagged behind with Mr. Moore, who was struggling to get his jacket back on as he dragged the shovel and bits of rope. Taking these last items from him, I asked, "So you found it? The bullet, I mean."

"Looks like it," he answered, not wanting to get too hopeful before he was sure he had reason. "In very good condition, too. But as for whether or not it's *the* bullet—only tomorrow will tell. I hear you had a little run-in with our Filipino friend."

I shook my head and let out a sigh of relief. "I thought I was dead for sure."

"I doubt he meant anything like that," Mr. Moore answered. "You've seen him work—if he wanted to kill you, it's a safe bet you never would've heard or seen a thing."

"Hunh." I paused at the gate, realizing that Mr. Moore was right. "But then," I said, as Cyrus came running down to join us, "what did he want?"

"That we do not know," the Doctor answered, having figured out who and what I was talking about. "Though we must try to find out. However, what's most vital right now, Stevie, is that you not mention the encounter to either the detective sergeants or Mr. Picton. As far as they're concerned—as far as we're all concerned"—he glanced once more into the cemetery, and then we all started to walk away—"none of this ever happened."

"You won't get any argument out of *me*," Mr. Moore answered, taking a cigarette the Doctor offered him. "I'm not too proud of this little escapade."

"Do you think Matthew Hatch will reach out from the grave, Moore?" the Doctor needled. "To rebuke you for disturbing his eternal rest?"

"Maybe," Mr. Moore answered. "Something like that. *You* don't seem too damned troubled along those lines, Kreizler, I must say."

"Perhaps I have a different understanding of what we've just done," the Doctor answered, his voice growing more serious. "Perhaps I believe that Matthew Hatch's soul has not yet *known* peace, eternal or otherwise—and that we represent his only chance of attaining it." Lighting first Mr. Moore's cigarette and then one of his own, the Doctor took a drag and got more animated. "What I don't understand," he said, his mind jumping from subject to subject as nimbly as usual, "is what the devil they want. The man sends us a warning at Number 808—saves Cyrus's life on Bethune Street—and now *here,* in another part of the *state,* he evidently attempts to deliver some sort of deadly message to Stevie. What can it mean?"

"Señor Linares," Miss Howard answered, following the Doctor's wandering thoughts, "evidently wants us to know that he's aware of our movements—and our actions."

Mr. Moore nodded. "It seems like as long as we're not associating with his wife or trying to find the girl, we're all right. But if we cross those lines . . ."

"Is that what the aborigine's signals to Stevie meant?" the Doctor wondered. "That we can do what we like to and about Libby Hatch, so long as we leave the Linares family out of it?"

"Maybe," Mr. Moore answered with a shrug.

"Well, then, why doesn't the man just *tell* us as much?" the Doctor asked, his frustration growing. "Why all these cryptic messages, sent through a mysterious go-between?"

I was shaking my head. "I don't think that's what he meant . . ."

"Stevie?" the Doctor said.

"I don't know," I answered, puzzling with the thing. "It's just that— well, that wasn't the look on his face. El Niño, I mean. I was scared at the time, sure, but—looking back on it, I don't think he was threatening me or warning me. It was almost like . . . like he *wanted* something."

"The aborigine?" the Doctor said, as we approached Mr. Picton's house. "What could he possibly want from us?"

"Like I say, I don't know." I brought my voice down to a very low whisper as we formed into a stealthy file to move back inside. "But something tells me he'll let us know before too long."

CHAPTER 35

W̲e couldn't have asked for the rest of our plan to play out any closer to its design. When we got back to Mr. Picton's house, Mr. Moore carefully inserted the bullet into an empty gap in the planking we'd taken from the Hatches' wagon, and the following morning we were all woken by the sound of Lucius's wild shouting. He'd gotten up early to have a go at the examination himself, thinking that maybe the rest of us had missed something—which it now looked like we had. Poking around in the small hole with one of the medical probes, Lucius announced that he'd found an object inside what was definitely made out of some kind of soft metal; and while the rest of us got dressed and had breakfast, he and Marcus went about freeing the thing from the wood. It was an anxious time for the two brothers, and for Mr. Picton, too; and the rest of us tried to make it appear that we were also on edge. But to this day I don't know how convincing we were.

Cheers went up from all sides when the last chips of wood gave way to the detective sergeants' patient knife work, and revealed a large, almost intact, and very recognizable bullet. Marcus took the slug inside to the card table and set it down on the green felt surface for the rest of us to look at. I'd seen more than a few such missiles in my time, but I hadn't ever taken the time to really study one as closely as I now did through one of the magnifying lenses. I was trying to get a glimpse of the identifying marks what Marcus and Lucius had told us about the day before; and they were there, all right, plain enough for anybody to see, or at least the grooves and lands were. As for any defects produced by the Peacemaker's barrel, we'd have to judge that from a comparison bullet—which it was now time to obtain by heading into the backyard and putting the cotton bales to the test.

With the moves of an expert, Lucius fired the three bullets what he'd found in the pistol (and had slightly refurbished) into the cotton from across the yard. Only one of the cartridges showed the effects of time by failing to go off; the others ignited admirably, after which it was up to the rest of us to scour the cotton for the slugs, which we located inside of twenty minutes. Marcus and Lucius assured us that they were both in very good shape, so it was now time for the comparison work; but that, they warned, could take many hours. We all went back inside the house, where Marcus had set up the double-barreled microscope on the card table. Going on the assumption that we would eventually get a match on the bullets, we began to plan what other moves we'd need to make over the coming days in order to get a grand jury indictment.

Ordinarily, said indictment would've been a sure bet, grand juries generally being the stooges of district attorneys; but, as we all knew only too well, we had some special circumstances working against us in this case, and they demanded that we do more than just the usual homework. For Mr. Picton, that meant more long days in his office, continuing to go back over all the information on the case and putting together as many precedents as he could, along with determining what witnesses (expert, eye-, and otherwise) should be called to testify. For Marcus and Mr. Moore, meanwhile, it meant going back down to New York to perform a whole batch of crucial jobs. First, they'd have to officially notify Libby Hatch that she was going to be the subject of a grand jury investigation, just in case she wanted to appear at the proceedings and testify, as was her right. (Mr. Picton figured to make Marcus a special officer of the court, temporarily, so's he could handle the notification.) Second, the pair had to try to find the Reverend Clayton Parker, a potentially crucial witness whose last known address in New York Mr. Moore would try to discover by heading over to the Presbyterian church that afternoon. Finally, if Libby Hatch decided not to have anything to do with the grand jury (as we figured would likely be the case), Marcus and Mr. Moore would have to stay in the city and try to watch her movements without getting their skulls broken by the Hudson Dusters.

For their part, Lucius and Cyrus were teamed up for the job of going back to the old Hatch place on Monday and turning the house upside down in a search for any additional clues. Miss Howard and I drew the assignment of trying to learn everything we could about the facts of Libby

Hatch's mysterious past, a journey what would begin with another visit to Mrs. Louisa Wright, move on to the little town of Stillwater (where we knew Libby'd lived for a time), and then take us God-only-knew where. As for the Doctor, he would, of course, continue to work with Clara Hatch: we couldn't hope for an indictment, Mr. Picton repeated, unless the girl could be made to answer at least simple yes-or-no questions before the grand jury.

The Doctor and Cyrus left for the Westons' farm that afternoon just after lunch, while Mr. Moore walked down to the Presbyterian church and Mr. Picton returned to his office. They'd all returned, though, before there was any sign of progress from the card table in the parlor. Hour after dreary hour ticked by with no indication of success; but then, at about six-thirty, Lucius finally shot out of his chair and started to scream like a mad-man, a move what the rest of us decided to take as a hopeful sign.

Collecting around the card table, we soon learned that our hopes were well grounded. Not only did the spacing of the bullets' grooves and lands (there were seven of each, spiraling to the left) match the barrel of the Colt perfectly, but at the same spot on each of the slugs there was another mark, so small that it'd taken hours to identify. It turned out to've been left there, said Marcus, by a tiny nick in the steel of the pistol's barrel, just inside the muzzle. This mark would make the ballistic testimony what the detective sergeants (or anybody else) gave carry that not-conclusive-but-still-million-to-one weight we'd been looking for: even if you accepted the idea that another Colt .45-caliber Single Action Army model might have the exact same pattern of grooves and lands as ours did, the notion that it would also have exactly the same defect in the barrel was pretty hard to swallow. So it looked like a very big corner had been turned, and the jaws of our complicated trap were starting to close tighter.

Mr. Picton was so confident, in fact, that he announced that he in-tended to schedule the grand jury hearing for the following Friday; only five days away. As we discovered the next morning, however, our host's boss, District Attorney Pearson, didn't share his assistant's confidence: when Mr. Picton told him about his plan, Mr. Pearson declared that he now intended to move his vacation, which he'd been planning to take in two weeks anyway, up a week—and that he wouldn't be back until the whole "unnatural" business of the Hatch case was over. Mr. Picton, for his part, didn't seem at all concerned about this: he merrily said good-bye to Mr. Moore and Marcus (who were set to leave for New York at noon) and then withdrew into his office, at which point the rest of us split off to pursue our separate tasks.

For Miss Howard and myself, the first order of business was a visit to Mrs. Louisa Wright's house over on Beach Street. It was an odd place, located so near the Schafer greenhouses that it existed in a sort of continuous daylight, being as there wasn't an hour of the night when some part of the giant floral plant wasn't artificially lit up. Because of this Mrs. Wright—a pleasant-looking but tough-talking lady in her fifties whose husband had died during the Civil War, when she was still young—had her windows covered with particularly heavy curtains and drapes, what made the house as quiet as the grave. A clock on her parlor mantle was the main source of noise, its steady ticking seeming to cry out that life was slipping by. The many pictures of Louisa Wright's young husband what decorated the house completed the funeral home feel of the joint.

Mrs. Wright served us tea and sandwiches in the parlor, very content, it seemed to me, to get even further involved in our pursuit of Libby Hatch—and when she heard that she was going to be called as a witness before a grand jury investigating the matter, her contentment seemed to grow into positive satisfaction. As will (with any luck) become clear soon enough, what the old girl had to say about Libby Hatch, Reverend Parker, the Hatch kids, and the death of old Daniel was very revealing, and reinforced all the things she'd originally told Miss Howard about the case. Because of this, when Miss Howard and I left the house at about three to head over to the livery stable and hire a rig for our trip to Stillwater, we were in very optimistic spirits.

We engaged the same buckboard—pulled by the same little Morgan stallion—what had brought us back from the old Hatch place on Friday, and the first part of our ride east and south, while not exactly luxurious, was made quick and easy by the steady-spirited horse. Unfortunately, the rig itself proved a lot less reliable: just after we turned onto the road what ran alongside the Hudson, we threw a rear wheel with a jarring, nasty crash, and while the collapse didn't damage either the wheel or the rig, it did mean that we were stuck on the side of the road for a couple of hours, until a passing farmer who was carrying some heavy rope offered to give us a hand raising the buckboard and getting the wheel back on. This process took another couple of hours, and then we had to slowly follow our Good Samaritan back to his farm, where he had the tools to make sure that the wheel stayed in place. Miss Howard gave the amiable if not very talkative man five dollars for his help, and then we decided that, being as we were slightly closer to Stillwater than we were to Ballston Spa (though we were a good distance from both places), we'd keep heading south and try to at least begin our second assignment of the day.

By the time we pulled into Stillwater, the sun was setting on the small town, which didn't consist of a whole lot more than a couple of industrial works on the river and several blocks of houses running inland from the waterfront. The town was considerably more depressing than most of the places we'd seen in the area: it was tough to say just what those factories produced, but there was a general feel of dirtiness and degradation all over the village, of the variety what was usually associated with bigger cities. Even the Hudson, usually clear and inviting this far north, seemed to bear a film of filth in this stretch of its run. The fact that nobody was out on the streets didn't do much to improve the cold, forbidding air of the town; and as the sun began to set much faster very soon after our arrival, both Miss Howard and I began to wonder out loud if we'd made the right decision about which way to turn after getting our wheel fixed. Of course, the fact that we knew Libby Hatch had once lived in this dismal little backwater didn't improve our impression of it any, either.

I drew the buckboard to a halt in a spot what looked like it might be the center of town (though there was still not a soul to be seen), and then we got down and started to wander about, figuring that eventually we'd bump into *someone* who could tell us something about the place. Finally, after failing to spot any activity for some ten minutes, we heard a door open across the street from one of the riverfront factories, and saw a man come out of one of the small, shacklike houses what lined the block. Miss Howard called, "Excuse me?" to this character, at which all of his heavy, six-foot frame seemed to jump about a foot into the air. We walked quickly over to where he was standing, and as we got nearer he looked around anxiously and straightened himself up a bit, like maybe he thought we were either the law or religious types.

"Excuse me," Miss Howard said again as we reached the man, "but we're looking for some information about someone who used to live here. Is there anyone we could talk to? I know it's late, but—"

"They'll be down to the tavern," the man answered quickly, taking a couple of steps back from us. "Anyone who ain't home, that is. They'll all be down there." He nodded at the general area near the riverfront some three or four blocks behind us.

"Oh." Miss Howard turned to try to locate the tavern the man was talking about, then nodded. "I see . . ." She turned back round again. "I don't suppose *you* could help us, by any chance? It was a long time ago, so—"

"I been here my whole life, ma'am," the man said. "If it was someone who lived in *this* town, I'll know better than those dagos and micks who've come up to work the mills."

Miss Howard paused, studying the man and then smiling just a bit. "I see. Well, then—we're looking for information about a woman. When she lived here, her name was Libby Fraser, although since then—"

"*Libby Fraser?*" The man's face did an odd little dance: in quick, panicky ripples it went from shock to fear and finally to hatred. "What the hell d'you wanna know about *her* for?"

"Well, you see, we're involved in an investigation—"

"Ain't nobody that's going to want to talk to you about Libby Fraser. Not in this town. Ain't nobody that's got nothing to say." The man's eyes stared out from his dirty face like he was getting more scared and angry by the second. "Understand? *Nobody.* She went away from here a long time ago. You want to ask questions about Libby Fraser, you find out where she went after she left and go there." He spat into the dusty street. "That'd be the smart thing to do." Tucking his shirt into his pants more tightly as if to make it clear that he was serious, the man turned—and walked straight back into the house he'd just come out of.

Both Miss Howard and I watched him go with what you might call blank faces. "Well," Miss Howard finally said, "you've got to hand it to the woman, she inspires strong reactions wherever she goes."

Looking back down the street, I saw a sign hanging outside one of the buildings on the riverside, past the factory works. I couldn't read just what it said in the near darkness, but it was pretty obvious what the general message was. "You figure we ought to try that tavern?" I asked, pointing.

"I suppose we have to," Miss Howard answered. "We've come this far."

We didn't bother to get back into the buckboard, but walked the three blocks or so to the building with the sign, which did in fact reveal that an establishment what could get away with calling itself a "tavern" in that town (but that in New York wouldn't have amounted to more than a cheap dive) was located inside. I wasn't at all sure how smart it was for a woman and a kid to head into a place like that alone, and I think Miss Howard could read the worry in my face: she pulled out her pearl-handled revolver and let me get a glimpse of it.

"Ready?" was all she said, as she slipped the gun back amongst the folds of her dress.

I nodded to her, though I was still plenty nervous. "Okay," I said, and then I pulled open the screen door of the old clapboarded building.

The room inside reeked of all the usual stenches—beer, booze, smoke, urine—but, being as it also sat on top of a nice dead part of the Hudson, rotten river water got into the mixture, too. There was a long bar and a pocket billiard table, and the joint was lit (or something like it) by a half-dozen kerosene lamps. About twenty men were scattered around, only a few of them talking or doing anything at all, other than staring at the walls and out the windows with the dead eyes of hardworking characters engaging in the only recreation they'd ever known or were ever likely to know: sitting and nursing a stiff drink. As'll happen in such places in such towns, they all turned toward the door at the same time when we entered; and it was a bit of a surprise for us to see, standing at the corner of the bar, the same man we'd been talking to not three minutes earlier. Whatever Libby Fraser'd done and been in that town, it was powerful enough to make a big, tired man run a long, roundabout route at what must've been a flat-out pace so's to be able to warn his pals that there were strangers in town asking questions about her.

Miss Howard nodded in the man's direction. "Hello," she said quietly; but the man just turned back to the bar like he'd never seen us before. Not sure of her next move, Miss Howard looked to me.

I waited for the low mumbling in the room to start up again before I said, "The bartender," very quietly. We found an empty space at the far end of the bar, then waited for the thin, sour-faced man behind it to come our way. He didn't say anything, just looked at Miss Howard coldly.

"Good evening," she said, trying the common pleasantries again. But they didn't work any better this time around: the man just kept staring at her. "We're trying to find out some information—"

"Don't sell it," the bartender answered. "Got drinks. That's all."

"Ah." Miss Howard considered that for a second, then said, "Well, in that case, I'll have a whiskey. And a root beer for my friend."

"Got lemonade," the man answered, turning the cold stare to me for a second.

"Okay, so lemonade," I said, not wanting the mug to know he was making me nervous.

It took the bartender only a few seconds to fetch the drinks, and as Miss Howard laid down some money, she said, "We don't expect the information to be free . . ."

But that just seemed to frost the bartender even more: his eyes got thin, and he leaned over the bar to her. "Now, you listen to me, missy—" All of a sudden every man in the place was staring at us again. "You already been told that there ain't nobody in this town that's going to talk to you about Libby Fraser. She ain't the smartest person in the world for *anybody* to talk about—including strangers."

Miss Howard glanced around the dark, dirty room quickly, then asked, "I don't understand. What is it that you're all so afraid of?"

A flutter of dread went through me: we weren't in the kind of place where you wanted to go accusing men of being cowards. But oddly, the bartender didn't leap straight down Miss Howard's throat, nor did anybody else who'd heard the question. They just kept staring steadily, and finally the bartender, in a hushed voice, answered, "Fear's nothing but common sense sometimes. So's keeping your mouth shut. And after what happened to the Muhlenbergs—"

"The Muhlenbergs?" Miss Howard repeated; but the bartender caught himself, realizing he'd said too much.

"Just finish up your drinks and get out of here," he said, walking down to the other end of the bar.

"Can't you at least tell us where these people live?" Miss Howard asked, pushing our luck. "I don't think you understand, we're conducting an investigation that may result in the woman's being brought up on serious criminal charges."

Everybody in the room just stayed silent. Then one mug in a corner whose face we couldn't see said, "They live in the old yellow house at the south end of town."

"You shut the hell up, Joe!" the bartender growled.

"What for?" the man in the corner said. "If they're gonna go after the bitch—"

"Yeah?" said the man we'd spoken to on the street. "And what if they don't get her, and she finds out you were part of their trying?"

"Oh . . ." It wasn't much more than a scared whisper; but it was the last we heard from the fellow in the shadows.

"I ain't gonna tell you again," the bartender said. "Finish your drinks and *leave.*"

The smart move seemed to be to follow the order, being as the atmosphere in the place was becoming very uncomfortable. Fear was having its usual effect on ignorant people, making them antsy and prone to violence; and I figured that we'd best be getting back outside, and maybe back out of town altogether. Miss Howard, unfortunately, saw things differently. When I tapped her shoulder and then started toward the door, she did follow; but as we reached the end of the bar, she paused one more time to look at the collection of faces in the room.

"Is every man in this *town* afraid of her?" she asked.

Knowing that she was now definitely going beyond what those boys would accept quietly, I fairly pushed Miss Howard out the door and then on toward the buckboard, though she wasn't very happy about it: she wasn't a woman to back down in the face of male bullying or threats, and the behavior of the men in the bar had only made her more determined to stick around Stillwater and find something out. Because of that, we didn't end up moving north and out of town again when we got back on our rig, but kept going south, until we rolled up to an old, run-down house. The place *might* have been yellow at some point in time, but now it was just a mass of dead climbing plants and peeling paint. The faint light of a lantern could be seen through one window, and once or twice the silhouette of a person passed in front of it.

"We going in?" I asked, hoping that maybe there was still some way Miss Howard would change her mind.

"Of course we're going in," she answered quietly. "I want to know what the hell happened here."

Nodding in what you might call resignation, I got down off the buck-board, then followed Miss Howard past the broken-down little fence what ran around the overgrown front yard. We got to the front door, and Miss Howard was about to knock; then I made out something in the darkness away to the side of the house.

"Miss," I said, nudging her with my elbow and then pointing. "Maybe you want to look over there . . ."

Turning, Miss Howard followed my finger to take in the sight of some black ruins in the lot next door. They were obviously the remains of an-other house, being as two crumbling chimneys stood at either end; and even by the faint light of the moon we could see a couple of cast-iron stoves and some bathroom fixtures—a tub and a sink—lying in the rubble. There were young trees and shrubs growing in the midst of it all, indicat-ing that the fire what had destroyed the place hadn't occurred any time re-cently.

All in all, the scene called to mind the old Hatch place in Ballston Spa very quickly.

"So . . ." Miss Howard whispered, taking a couple of steps away from the door and studying the grim wreckage. It seemed to me like we were both thinking the same thing: maybe those boys in the tavern had been right to be so fearful.

"Wouldn't want to've been in *that* house," I said quietly. "Fire like that'd be pretty tough to survive."

"Impossible, I'd think," Miss Howard answered, nodding.

But as it turned out, she was wrong: something *had* survived that fire. Not just *something* but *someone*—and we were about to meet her.

CHAPTER 36

All we ever saw of that dark little house on the south edge of Stillwater was the front hall and the sitting room; but the memory of those spaces is burned so deep in my brain that I could probably re-create them right down to the thousand tiny cracks that were spread out through the walls like so many dying blood vessels. For the purposes of this story, though, it'll be enough to say that we were let into the place, after knocking, by an old Negro woman, who looked us over with an expression what said that they didn't get many callers in that house, and that such a state of affairs suited them just fine.

"Hello," Miss Howard said to the woman, as we stepped inside the door. "I know it's late, but I was wondering if either Mr. or Mrs. Muhlenberg might be home?"

The old black lady gave my companion a hard, slightly shocked look. "Who are you?" she asked. But before Miss Howard could answer the question, she took care of it herself: "Must be strangers hereabouts—there *ain't* no Mr. Muhlenberg. Hasn't been these ten years or more."

Miss Howard took in that information with a slightly embarrassed look, then said, "My name is Sara Howard, and this is"—pointing to me, she tried to find an explanation what would wash in the situation—"my driver. I'm working for the Saratoga County district attorney's office, investigating a case that involves a woman who once lived in this town. Her name then was Libby Fraser. We were told that the Muhlenbergs had some contact with her—"

The old woman's eyes went wide and she held up an arm, trying to herd us back outside. "No," she said quickly, shaking her head. "Unh-unh! Are you crazy? Comin' around here, askin' questions about—you just get out!"

But before she could shoo us back into the night, a voice drifted out from the sitting room. "Who is it, Emmeline?" a woman asked, her voice cracking roughly. "I thought I heard someone say . . . Emmeline! Who is it?"

"Nothin' but some lady askin' questions, ma'am," the old woman answered. "I'm sendin' her away, though, don't worry!"

"What kind of questions?" the voice answered—and as it did, I took note of what the Doctor would've called a paradoxical quality in the thing: the sound itself indicated someone of about the black woman's age, but the tone and pacing of the words were very sharp, and seemed to come from someone much younger.

The woman at the door filled up with dread as she sighed and called out, "About Libby Fraser, ma'am."

There was a long silence, and then the voice from the living room spoke much more quietly: "Yes. That's what I thought I heard. . . . Did she say she's from the district attorney's office?"

"Yes, ma'am."

"Then show her in, Emmeline. Show her in."

Reluctantly, the black woman stepped aside to let me and Miss Howard wander down the cavelike hall and into the sitting room.

You couldn't have put a color to the cracked walls in that chamber, or to the patches of ancient paper what still clung to a few small spots on them. The furniture what was clustered around the heavy table that held the lamp was also in a state of decrepitude. The dim yellow light of the lamp's small, smoky flame spread toward but not into the corners of the room; and it was in one of those corners that our "hostess" sat on a ratty old divan, a handmade comforter covering her legs and most of her body. She was holding an old fan in front of her face, slowly moving it to cool herself; at least, that was what I thought she was doing. And so far as it was possible to tell, there wasn't another soul in the house.

"Mrs. Muhlenberg?" Miss Howard asked quietly, looking into the dark corner.

"I didn't know," the scratchy voice answered, "that the district attorney had taken to employing women. Who are you?"

"My name is Sara Howard."

The head behind the fan nodded. "And the boy?"

"My driver," Miss Howard said, smiling to me. "And my bodyguard." She turned back to Mrs. Muhlenberg. "It seems I need one, in this town."

The shadowy head just kept nodding. "You're asking about Libby Fraser. She's a dangerous subject . . ." In a sudden rush, Mrs. Muhlenberg took in a big gulp of air with a moan what would've raised the hackles on a dead man. "Please," she went on after a few seconds, "sit . . ."

We found two straight-backed chairs that looked a little sturdier than the other items in the room, and tried to settle in.

"Mrs. Muhlenberg," Miss Howard said. "I confess that I'm a little puzzled. We—I—certainly didn't come here looking for trouble. Or with the intention of offending anyone. But it seems that the mere mention of Libby Fraser's name—"

"You saw what's left of the house next door?" Mrs. Muhlenberg cut in. "That used to be *my* house. My husband's, actually. We lived there with our son. The people of this town don't want to see their own places reduced to charred brick and ashes."

Miss Howard absorbed that for a few seconds. "You mean—*she* did that? Libby Fraser?"

The head started to nod again. "Not that I could ever have proved it. Any more than I could've proved that she killed my child. She's much too clever . . ."

The mention of another dead kid, coming in a town and a house like that, had me ready to dive through the sitting room window, get onto the buckboard, and whip our little Morgan until we were all the way back to New York. But Miss Howard never flinched.

"I see," she said, in a low but firm tone. "I think you ought to know, Mrs. Muhlenberg, that Assistant District Attorney Picton is preparing an indictment against the woman you knew as Libby Fraser for murder—the murder of her own children."

That brought another one of those pitiable gasps from behind the fan, and one foot at the end of the divan began to shake noticeably. "Her own—" The foot suddenly grew still. "When? Where?"

"Three years ago—in Ballston Spa."

Still another gasp floated our way. "Not the shooting—the one they said was a Negro?"

"Yes," Miss Howard answered. "You know about it?"

"We heard rumors," Mrs. Muhlenberg said. "And a party of men searched the town. Those were *Libby's* children?"

"They were. And we believe she killed them. Along with several others in New York City."

A different sort of sound now came from behind the fan; and after a few seconds I made it out as hoarse sobbing. "But why should I be shocked?"

Mrs. Muhlenberg finally said quietly. "If any woman could do such a thing, it would be Libby."

Leaning forward, Miss Howard put all the sympathy she was capable of—which was a very great deal, especially when she was dealing with a member of her own sex—into her next question: "Can you tell me what happened here, Mrs. Muhlenberg? It may help us in our effort to prosecute her."

There was another pause, and then the soft sobbing stopped; but the foot started twitching again. "Will she be executed?"

Miss Howard nodded. "It's very possible."

Mrs. Muhlenberg's voice now filled with a kind of relief, maybe even excitement. "If she can die—if you can bring that about—then yes, Miss Howard. I'll tell you what happened."

Very quietly and carefully, Miss Howard produced a pad and a pencil, ready to take notes. As Mrs. Muhlenberg launched into her tale, the old black woman left the room shaking her head, as if listening to the story was more than she could stand.

"It was a long time ago," Mrs. Muhlenberg began. "Or maybe it wasn't, to most people's way of thinking. The late summer—1886. That's when she came to us. My husband's family owned one of the mills here in town. We moved into the house next door right after our marriage. It had been his grandmother's. Oh, it was a beautiful place, with wonderful gardens leading down to the river. . . . The caretaker of the estate lived in this house then. That summer our first child was born. Our only child. I was unable to nurse him, and we advertised for a wet nurse. Libby Fraser was the first applicant, and we both found her charming." The small gasp of a dead laugh punctuated the statement. "Charming . . . I always thought, to tell you the truth, that my husband found her a little *too* charming. But she was desperate for the work, desperate to please—desperate in every way. And I sympathized with that. I sympathized . . ."

After a long pause, Miss Howard gambled a question: "And how soon did your son begin to have problems with his health?"

Mrs. Muhlenberg nodded her head again, slowly. "So. You *do* know about Libby. . . . Yes, he got sick. Colicky, we all thought at first, nothing more than that. *I* could calm him, and did, as much as possible—but I couldn't feed him, and being with Libby always seemed to make him worse. Hour after hour of crying, for days on end. . . . But we didn't want to let the girl go—she really had been so desperate for the work, and she was trying so hard. But before long there was no choice. Michael—my son—just didn't respond to her care. We decided that we had to find someone else."

"How did Libby take the news?" Miss Howard asked.

"If only she *had* taken the news!" Mrs. Muhlenberg answered, her voice still soft, but passionate and heartbroken, too. "If only we'd *made* her take it, and forced her to go. . . . But she was so crushed when we told her, and begged so earnestly for one more chance, that we couldn't help giving it to her. And things did change, after that. Things did change. . . . Michael's health took a turn—for the better, we thought at first. His fits of crying and colic calmed, and it seemed as if he was accepting Libby's care. But it was an evil calm—a sign of illness, not happiness. A slow, wasting illness. He lost color and weight, and Libby's milk passed through him like water. But it wasn't water. It wasn't water . . ."

Things were quiet for so long that I thought that maybe Mrs. Muhlenberg had fallen asleep. Finally, Miss Howard glanced at me with a question in her face, but all I could do was shrug, in a way what I hoped showed her how much I wanted to get the hell out of that house. Miss Howard was after something, though, and I knew we weren't going anywhere 'til she got it.

"Mrs. Muhlenberg?" she said quietly.

"Mmm? Yes?" the woman answered.

"You were saying . . ."

"I was saying?"

"You were saying that it wasn't water—Libby's milk."

"No. Not water." We heard another sigh. "*Poison* . . ."

I shifted in my chair nervously at the word, but Miss Howard just kept pressing: "Poison?"

The dark head rocked up and down. "We had the doctor in many times, but he couldn't explain what was happening. Michael was ill—terribly ill. And then Libby's health began to suffer, too. That made the doctor think it must've been a fever, some kind of infectious illness that my son had passed on to her. How could we have guessed . . ." Her foot started to move nervously again. "I was suspicious. Call it a mother's instinct, but I couldn't believe that my son was infecting Libby. No—I was convinced that *she* was doing something to *him*. My husband said that I was so careworn I was becoming unbalanced. He said that Libby was exposing herself to danger to help Michael. He made her sound heroic, and the doctor did, too. But I grew more convinced every day. I didn't know how she was doing it. I didn't know why. But I began to sit with them when she fed him, and soon I refused to leave him alone with her—ever. But he never got any stronger. The illness grew worse. He was wasting away, and she was getting weaker, too. . . ."

"Finally, I went into her room one day when she was out taking the air. I found two packets in her dresser. The first contained a white powder, the second a black one. I didn't know what they might be, but I took them to my husband. He didn't know what the black powder was, but he had no doubts about the other." Mrs. Muhlenberg seemed scared to go on, but finally she got the word out: "Arsenic."

Miss Howard seemed to guess that I was ready to bolt, and she put a hand to my arm to hold me where I was.

"Arsenic?" she said. "Was she feeding it to your son?"

"If you know about Libby," Mrs. Muhlenberg said with a small hiss, "you know that she's too smart to've done anything so bold as give it to him directly. And I was watching her whenever she was with him. Whenever she was with him—but not when she was *alone*. And that was my mistake. . . . My husband asked Libby why she had the arsenic. She said that she'd been woken one night by a rat in her room. As if we ever had rats. . . . But we couldn't think of any other explanation." Trying to hold down more sobs, Mrs. Muhlenberg gasped out, "Michael died soon after that. Libby played at being grief-stricken very well, and for days. It was only when we were burying my son that the truth came to me. Libby was standing there weeping, and I realized that her own health was returning. Suddenly, I saw everything clearly—so clearly. . . . She *had* poisoned him—she'd eaten the arsenic herself, and *it had passed to him through her milk*. Not enough to kill a grown woman, but enough to kill a baby. Satan himself couldn't have been more clever."

That was about it for me. "Miss Howard—" I whispered.

But she just tightened her grip on my arm, her eyes never leaving the dark corner across the room. "Did you confront her?" she asked.

"Of course," Mrs. Muhlenberg answered. "I couldn't prove anything, I knew that. But I wanted her to know that *I* knew she'd done it. And I wanted to know why. Why kill my son? What had he done to her?" The tears started to come again. "What could a baby boy do to a grown woman to make her want to kill him?"

I thought for a minute that Miss Howard might try to explain the theory of Libby Hatch's mind what we'd worked out over the last few weeks, but she didn't; wisely, I figured, being as even if Mrs. Muhlenberg could've grasped the ideas, she was in no emotional shape to bear them.

"She denied it all, of course," Mrs. Muhlenberg went on. "But that very night . . ." One of her hands went up, pointing in the direction of the ruins next door. "The fire . . . my husband was killed. I barely survived. And Libby was gone . . ."

Another pause followed, and I prayed that the story was over. It turned out that it was, but Miss Howard wasn't ready to let matters go at that. "Mrs. Muhlenberg," she said, "would you be prepared to go before a jury and talk about your experiences with Libby? It might help."

That awful, piteous moan floated across the room again. "No—no! Why? You can tell them—someone else can tell them! I can't prove anything—you don't need me—"

"I *could* tell them," Miss Howard said, "but it won't carry any weight. If they hear it from you, and see your face—"

At that the moan became another hoarse, terrible laugh. "But that's what's impossible, Miss Howard: they can't see my face. Even *I* can't see my face." There was a terribly still pause, and with a sudden chill I realized what the fan was for: "*I have no face*. It was lost in the fire. Along with my husband—and my life . . ." The shadow of her head began to shake. "I won't parade this mass of scars in a courtroom. I won't give Libby Fraser that last satisfaction. I hope that my story can help you, Miss Howard. But I won't—I can't . . ."

Miss Howard took a deep breath. "I understand," she said. "But perhaps you can help in another way. We've been unable to determine just where Libby came from. Did she ever mention her home to you?"

"Not exactly," Mrs. Muhlenberg answered. "She talked many times about towns across the river, in Washington County. It was always my impression that she came from there. But I can't be sure."

Miss Howard nodded and, finally letting go of my arm, stood up. "I see. Well—thank you, Mrs. Muhlenberg."

The old black woman had reappeared at the doorway to show us out. As we started toward the front hall, Mrs. Muhlenberg said, "Miss Howard?" We both turned. "Look at your boy's face. Do you see the terror in his eyes? You may think it's just his imagination. But you're wrong—what was once my face is worse than anything his mind is conjuring up. Do you know what it's like to terrify people that way? I'm sorry I can't do more—and I hope you truly do understand . . ."

Miss Howard just nodded once, and then we moved on back outside, the Negro woman closing the door on us silently.

I moved for the buckboard as fast as I could, and was surprised when Miss Howard didn't do the same. She was staring in the direction of the river and puzzling with something.

"Didn't we pass a ferry station on our way into town?" she asked quietly, wandering toward the rig.

"Oh, no," I answered quickly, fear making me a bit uppity. "I ain't crossing that river tonight, Miss Howard—no, ma'am." Then I remembered myself as I fumbled for my packet of cigarettes: "I'm sorry, but there just ain't no way—"

Suddenly, I heard a very disturbing sound: footsteps, plenty of them, shuffling through the dry dust of the road. Both Miss Howard and I stepped away from the rig and stared into the darkness to the north, which soon belched out about ten of the men from the tavern. They were moving our way—and they did not, to put it mildly, look like they were interested in talking.

"Aw, shit," I said (my general reaction to such situations); then I glanced around quickly, trying to figure out what to do. "We can still get away to the south," I decided, not seeing anything in that direction what would indicate trouble. "If we move fast enough—"

The sound of a spinning revolver cylinder caused me to jerk my head back around. Miss Howard had her Colt out, and was checking the chambers with a look what said she meant business. "Don't worry, Stevie," she said quietly, as she hid the gun behind her back. "I have no intention of letting people like that push us around."

I looked at the approaching band of drunken, sullen men, then at Miss Howard again, and realized I was on the verge of watching something truly ugly take place. "Miss Howard," I said, "there ain't no reason for this—"

But it was too late: the locals had reached us, and fanned out in a line across the road. The man we'd spoken to when we first hit town stepped out front.

"We *figured* maybe you didn't get our point," he said, stepping closer to Miss Howard.

"What's there to get?" Miss Howard answered. "You're a mob of grown men, afraid of a single woman."

"You're not just dealing with us, lady," the man answered. "When it comes to Libby Fraser, you're dealing with this whole *town*. She's done enough damage here. Nobody wants to have anything to do with her, nor with nobody that's got any interest in her. And if that ain't clear enough . . ."

The whole bunch of them took a few steps closer. I don't know what it was that they intended to do to us, but they didn't get the chance: Miss Howard produced her revolver, and leveled it at the lead man.

"You just back up, mister," she said, her teeth clenched. "I warn you, I will have absolutely no difficulty putting a bullet in your leg—or something more vital, if you force me to."

For the first time, the man smiled. "Oh, you're gonna shoot me, are you?" He turned to his friends. "She's gonna shoot me, boys!" he said, getting the usual variety of stupid laughs from his pals. Then he looked at Miss Howard again. "You ever shot anybody before, missy?"

Miss Howard just stared at him hard for a few seconds, then said, very quietly, "Yes. I have." As if to punctuate the statement, she pulled the hammer of her Colt back quickly.

The sincerity of the words and the cocking of the gun were enough to wipe the smile off the man's face, and I think he was about to turn around and call the whole confrontation off. But then a small, hissing sound cut through the stillness, and the man cried out, clutching at his leg. Yanking something out of his hamstring, he looked back up at Miss Howard, then slowly crumpled to his knees. His eyes rolled up into his head, and he keeled over onto one side, his hand out in front of him.

In it was a plain, ten-inch stick, what was sharpened at one end.

CHAPTER 37

M iss Howard and I gave each other quick looks of what you might call horrified recognition, as the rest of the men hustled to their friend.

"What the hell've you done to him?" one of the men shouted: a question I'd heard before, and under similar circumstances.

I could only get out the words "Believe me, it wasn't us—" before the men picked up their friend and began to hustle him away in terror.

"You get the hell out of here!" one of them called. "And you *stay* the hell out!" With that they disappeared back in the direction of the tavern.

Miss Howard kept hold of her revolver, as we both spun to look all around. "Where is he?" Miss Howard asked in a whisper.

"In this darkness?" I said, also whispering. "He could be *anywhere.*" We didn't move for another minute, but kept listening and waiting, expecting some move out of our small enemy—if in fact he *was* our enemy, which I was beginning to doubt. But there was no trace of any activity on the road or in the shadowy trees and shrubs what lined it, and that was good enough for me. "Come on," I said to Miss Howard, taking her arm.

She didn't need much persuasion, by that point, and in another half minute we were aboard our rig and heading north again, the little Morgan stallion moving at a nice trot. As we passed by the tavern, I could see a few pairs of angry eyes following us, and the body of the man who'd been struck by the aborigine's arrow was laid out on the bar: how long he'd be unconscious, or if in fact he was dead, I didn't know, and I certainly couldn't have said why Señor Linares's servant had once again come to our assistance. The first time, during our bout with the Dusters, might've

been laid off to his arrow finding the wrong mark; but this second incident made it clear that the strange little man who'd seemed to threaten me
with death on Saturday night was trying to keep us alive.

"Maybe he just wants to kill us himself," I said, once we'd gotten half a
mile or so out of Stillwater.

"He's had more than enough opportunities to do that," Miss Howard
answered, shaking her head. "None of it makes any sense . . ." She finally
shoved her revolver back into its hiding place, then took a deep breath.
"You don't have a cigarette, do you, Stevie?"

I shook my head with a small laugh, feeling relieved that we'd made
good our escape. "You'd think people would get tired of asking me that
question," I said, going for my pants pocket with one hand as I let the
reins slack a bit with the other. Pulling out the packet of smokes, I handed
them to her. "Light me one, too, if you would, miss." She put a match to
two cigarettes, then handed one over. After taking a few deep drags off
her own, she put her head between her hands and began to rub her temples. "You got pretty hot back there," I said.

She managed a chuckle. "I'm sorry, Stevie. I hope you know I wouldn't
put you in danger deliberately. But that kind of insufferable idiocy—"

"World's full of men like that, Miss Howard. Can't go telling them *all*
where they get off, and not expect a few to get riled."

"I know, I know," she said. "But there are certain times. . . . Still, I *do*
hope you know that we were never in any real danger."

"Sure," I answered; then I took a few seconds to study my companion.
"You really would've shot him, wouldn't you?"

"If he'd touched either one of us?" she said. "Absolutely. Nothing like a
bullet in the leg to make men mind their manners."

I chuckled again, although I knew that she was perfectly serious. There
probably wasn't another woman in the world who was as comfortable with
guns—or, for that matter, with shooting people—as Miss Howard. She
had some very personal reasons for being that way, and it isn't my place to
recite those reasons here; she'll take care of that job one day herself, if she's
so inclined. All that mattered to me that particular night was that when she
said she would've shot a man to protect me, she meant it; and that knowledge allowed my nervous system to grow ever more calm, and my mind
ever more inquisitive, as we traveled along the moonlit river road.

"How can she do it, Miss Howard?" I eventually asked, after smoking
the better portion of my stick.

Miss Howard answered with a long, deep sigh. "I don't know, Stevie.
It's the nature of people who are racked by feelings of powerlessness, I

suppose, to try to exert power over whoever or whatever's weaker than they are—and God help those weaker beings if they don't play along. Drunken, frustrated men beat and kill women, women desperate to prove they can control *something* beat and kill children, and those children, in turn, torment animals. . . . Remember, too, babies may look charming to those of us who haven't got any, but there are plenty of mothers who lose patience with all the noise, the sleeplessness, and the plain and simple *work* of nurturing."

I was shaking my head. "No, that's not what I meant. The actual killing, that part of it I've begun to understand. I think. But the way she makes other people act. How does she pull *that* off? I mean, look at what we've heard—and seen, too. Some people who worked with her in New York thought she was a saint; other people, *in the same joint,* thought she was a murderer. That poor fool husband of hers treats her like she's his sole salvation—but then she goes around the corner and gets the likes of Goo Goo Knox more lathered up than any moll or streetwalker what's ever been through the Dusters' front door. Then we come up here and find out that in Ballston Spa people first thought she was a hussy, then a good woman—and then she got ranked as a hussy again. *Now,* we go to *this* damned place—Stillwater—and find out that the whole *town's* scared to death of her! How the hell does one person pull it all off?"

"Well," Miss Howard answered, with a slight smile, "I'm afraid *that* question's a little more complicated." She held her cigarette up and puzzled with a thought. "Try to think about all the things you've just mentioned, Stevie—what's the one quality that they have in common?"

"Miss Howard," I said, "if I knew that—"

"All right, all right. Consider this, then: none of those personalities, those different ways that people see her, are complete. None of them is a description of an actual person—they're all simplifications, exaggerations. Symbols, really. The ministering angel—the fiendish killer. The devoted wife and mother—the wanton harlot and brazen hussy. They all sound like characters out of a story or a play."

"Like the—whatever—the 'myths' you talked about? That day outside the museum?"

"Exactly. And like those myths, what's amazing isn't that someone can come up with such characters—anyone crazy or just imaginative enough could do that. It's that so many people—not just the citizens of towns like Stillwater but whole societies—actually accept and believe in them. And I'm afraid all *that* gets back to something that may be a little difficult for you to understand." Miss Howard must've read something like injured pride in my face, because she put a quick hand to my arm. "Oh, I don't mean because you're not educated enough or smart enough, Stevie. You're one of the smartest males I've ever known. But you *are* male."

"Yeah?" I said. "And what's that got to do with the discussion?"

"Everything, I'm afraid," Miss Howard answered with a shrug. "It isn't really possible for men to understand how much the world doesn't *want* women to be complete people. The most important thing a woman can be, in our society—more important, even, than honest or decent—is *identifiable*. Even when Libby's evil—perhaps most of all when she's evil—she's easy to categorize, to stick to a board with a pin like some scientific specimen. Those men in Stillwater are terrified of her because being terrified lets them know who she is—it keeps them safe. Imagine how much harder it would be to say, yes, she's a woman capable of terrible anger and violence, but she's *also* someone who's tried desperately to be a nurturer, to be a good and constructive human being. If you accept all that, if you allow that inside she's not just one or the other, but both, what does that say about all the *other* women in town? How will you ever be able to tell what's actually going on in *their* hearts—and heads? Life in the simple village would suddenly become immensely complicated. And so, to keep that from happening, they separate things. The normal, ordinary woman is defined as nurturing and loving, docile and compliant. Any female who defies that categorization must be so completely evil that she's got to be feared, feared even more than the average criminal—she's got to be invested with the powers of the Devil himself. A witch, they probably would have called her in the old days. Because she's not just breaking the law, she's defying the order of things."

I turned to give Miss Howard an uncertain little smile. "You want to watch it—you're starting to sound like you look up to her a little bit."

Miss Howard started to smile back, but stopped quickly. "Sometimes it seems that way, even to me," she admitted. "And then I remember that picture of Ana Linares, and realize how desperately unaware of her own true motives—and therefore dangerous—Libby really is."

"Okay," I answered, trying to get Miss Howard perked back up by continuing our discussion. "So what about somebody like Goo Goo Knox? He knows Libby's married to Micah Hunter and is playing the good wife to him, *nurturing* him—but he still wants to carry on with her."

Miss Howard nodded vigorously. "It's the same thing. Knox may be a gang boss, but he's still a man—he still wants to slip women into convenient categories, to keep them from causing any problems. He doesn't believe that Libby actually *cares* about Hunter. He assumes that in the deep-est part of her soul she's a libertine, a whore, and that when she performs for him, and with him, he's seeing the real Libby. Yet what have we found out? That she's persuaded Knox to place her home under his gang's pro-tection. His thugs are keeping watch over the very house where she's con-structed some sort of hiding place for the babies she's still trying desperately to prove that she can care for. So for all we know, she *loathes* spending time at the Dusters', but does it to facilitate her attempts to nur-ture."

My hand went to my forehead, as if rubbing it would make my mind work harder. "So—then—she's not the whore that Knox thinks she is?"

"She might be," Miss Howard answered, confusing me again.

"But you just said she was doing it to take care of the kids—"

"She's doing that, too."

"So which one is the actual *her?*" I almost yelled, starting to feel a little dim and not much liking it.

"None of them, Stevie," Miss Howard explained, slowing down a bit for me. "The actual *her* was broken to pieces a long time ago. And that's what the different characters she assumes are—the broken pieces, separate from each other, no longer coherent. We don't yet know the specific child-hood context that made Libby into the killer she is. But we do know this much, especially given what we've seen and been through since we got up here: ever since she was just a girl, she was almost certainly told that there was only one way for her to be a full, complete woman."

"To be a mother," I said with a nod. "Which she wasn't any good at."

"Or which she may not, deep down, have even *wanted* to be," Miss Howard said. "We don't know. Again, all we *do* know is that the message girls get when they're growing up—especially in corners of the world like this one—is that if you want to do something with your life other than raise children, not only will your road be difficult, but you'll never really be a *woman.* You'll just be a *female,* of some indefinite and not very ap-pealing type. A harlot, maybe. Or perhaps a servant. Or, if you join a pro-fession, a detached functionary. Whatever the case, underneath it all you'll be a cold, unfeeling aberration." With an angry flick of her finger, Miss Howard showered the road below us with sparks from the burning tip of her cigarette. "Unless you want to be a nun, of course—and even they don't always get away with it. . . . A man can be a bachelor, and still be a man—because of his mind, his character, his work. But a woman without children? She's a *spinster,* Stevie—and a spinster is always something less than a woman."

"Well," I said, my brain working too hard at keeping up with her thoughts to worry about being tactful, "what about *you*, then?"

Miss Howard's green eyes slid slowly sideways to give me a glance what said I'd better make my meaning a bit clearer.

"What I'm saying," I added in a hurry, knowing how fast her temper could flare, "is that none of that business really goes for you. You're not married, you don't have any kids, but you're—" I looked away, suddenly embarrassed. "Well—you're as much of a woman as any mother *I* ever knew. If you see what I mean."

That brought her hand gently to my arm again, and allowed the green eyes to open wider. "That's the most decent thing anyone's said to me in a long time. Thank you, Stevie. But remember, too, you're still young."

"Oh," I said, grabbing at my own chance to get huffy, "so my opinions don't count? Or they'll change, just because I'll get older?"

It was Miss Howard's turn to squirm a bit. "Well," she noised, "it does happen sometimes . . ."

"Okay," I pressed. "What about the others, then? The Doctor and the detective sergeants and Cyrus—even Mr. Moore? They all feel the same way."

Miss Howard shot me a doubtful look. "Hardly an average selection of American men. I'm sorry, Stevie. Of course I value and respect how you and the others feel—you may never know how much. But to the rest of our world I'll probably always be that strange Sara Howard, the spinster detective lady—unless and until I have a family. Not that part of me wouldn't like to, someday. If I ever feel like I've really made a difference with my work, I might consider children—it's just that I object to the notion that I won't be *whole* until I do. It's a cruel standard—especially to the women who can't achieve it. Libby couldn't, and the failure broke her. Yes . . . for all her cleverness, she's terribly broken. A little like your friend Kat, in that way. Clever, yet lost. Lost, and somehow—somehow—"

Suddenly Miss Howard's face, so passionate while giving voice to ideas what I knew were as important to her as any in the world, went completely blank. Her words fell off with a quickness what let me know she'd caught sight of something—and there was only one "something" it could be.

"Where?" I said, whipping my head from side to side. "Where is he?"

Miss Howard put a steadying hand to my shoulder. "Just slow down, Stevie," she whispered. "If I'm not mistaken, he's right in front of us . . ."

I searched the dark road ahead; and there, to be sure, was the silhouette of a small person, the bagginess of the clothes and the bushiness of the hair giving away his identity. El Niño wasn't moving, either away from or toward us; he seemed to be waiting for our rig to reach him, and as we got closer I began to make out that damned smile again.

"What the hell . . ." I mumbled. "Is he *real,* even? The mug gets around quicker than spit."

"Oh, he's real, all right," Miss Howard answered. "The question is, what does he want?"

"Figure we should stop?"

She shook her head. "No. Keep going at a walk." She pulled out her revolver and placed it in her lap. "Let's see what happens."

CHAPTER 38

I followed the order. The aborigine didn't move, just stood there smiling until we were about twenty feet from him. Then, very deliberately, he put his hands into the air. I drew the Morgan to a halt, and we waited. Lowering one arm, the aborigine pointed to the ground.

"I don't hurt you," he said, his smile getting wider. Following his finger, we could see that there was a small bow, a couple more of the plain little arrows, and another wave-bladed *kris* on the road. "And you don't shoot me," he went on, putting his arm back up. "Yes?"

Miss Howard nodded; but she kept the gun right where it was. "All right," she said. "What is it you want?"

"I to help you!" the aborigine answered. "Sure—can help you, yes! Sometimes, I help you already."

"But you're Señor Linares's man," Miss Howard answered. "Why do you help us?"

The aborigine moved to pick up his weapons, prompting Miss Howard to pull back the hammer of her Colt. The little man's eyes went very wide, and then he threw up his hands again. "Is okay—I no hurt you, lady, and you no shoot me! I *help* you!"

"Suppose you just tell me why you help us, before you pick those things up," Miss Howard ordered.

El Niño's appealing smile returned and then his round features began to display what you might call theatrical disgust. "Oh, is not for me, to work for the señor—no more! He beat me—beat his wife—beat everybody, with fists like—like—" Looking around quickly, the aborigine grabbed a big stone from the side of the road, then held it up to Miss Howard.

"Like rocks," she said.

"Yes, is true, like rocks!" El Niño answered. "Give me one suit of clothes—" He held his arms up, displaying the rolled-up cuffs of his jacket, and then pointed down at his trousers, what were cut off roughly at the ankles. "Too big! Is not for me. First, one time, I work for father—old señor—"

"For Señor Linares's father?" Miss Howard asked.

"Yes, lady. He different man. Good man. This son—not the same. Beat everybody with fists, think he great man—because his mama love him too much!"

I burst out laughing at that, and got myself a sharp elbow from Miss Howard for it; but she, too, was having trouble containing her amusement at the little fellow. "And so what do you want from *us*?" she asked, lowering the Colt.

El Niño shrugged. "I to work for you, I think. Yes, I think so. I watch you—see you try to find baby Ana. Is good. The señor, he not want you to find her. But she a baby! I think you find her, because you good people. I work for you, I think—sure."

Miss Howard and I exchanged shocked looks. What were we supposed to say? The idea seemed so strange as to be out of the question, but neither of us particularly wanted to tell *him* that. Not with that arsenal lying in the road, and knowing that he'd been keeping track of every move we'd made for weeks now. There was also the fact that we'd both identified something likable in the little fellow—likable and decent. So maybe it wasn't so peculiar a notion after all.

"But," Miss Howard said, "what do you mean, 'work' for us? What would you do?"

The aborigine was about to answer, but first he eyed his possessions on the road. "I can pick up?" he said to Miss Howard carefully.

She nodded, looking at him like he was a naughty kid. "*Slowly*," she said.

He followed the instruction, and tucked all the pieces of his arsenal into big pockets what'd been sewn special inside his jacket. Then he started to approach us, swaggering like a man twice his size. "Many things I do!" he declared. "Protect you from enemies—kill them, or make them sleep! Cook, too!" He pointed at the landscape around us. "Snake, dog—sometimes rat, if you *very* hungry!" Both Miss Howard and I let moans of disgust out through the smiles that had settled in on our faces. "See things—find things out! If you have El Niño to work for you, you have eyes *everywhere!*" He passed an arm out across the horizon again.

"And what," Miss Howard asked, "would be your salary for all this?"

"My sa—?" the aborigine noised, puzzled.

"What would we have to pay you?"

"Oh, pay, yes!" he answered, filling his chest with air proudly. "El Niño *Manilaman*—Manilamen work only for pay! The señor pay me with nothing—with shit!" I let out another loud laugh, and Miss Howard didn't even try to stop me; in fact, she joined in, and so did El Niño, who was pleased with our reaction. "With *shit* he pay me!" he went on. "Bad clothes—food after others have eaten it—and the señora make me to sleep outside, even in wintertime! You can give me good food—bed to sleep in, yes? House has many beds. And you—" He pointed at me and then he did the little dance around his neck with one hand again, causing my grin to shrink suddenly.

"Whoa, now, don't start that!" I said. "I don't want any trouble with you—"

"No, no!" he answered. "Not trouble! Clothes! Your clothes—three nights past from here—you do not like your clothes, yes?"

Counting the nights on my fingers and trying to get some idea of what he was talking about, I remembered the trip to Saratoga; and then, in a rush, I recalled my encounter with what I'd taken for a kid in the gardens of the Casino. "So that was *you!*" I said. "You saw me in the monkey suit!"

"Monkey suit?" El Niño asked, puzzled. "Not for monkeys—fine clothes for fine man—fit me! You do not like them," he said, putting the finger to his neck again. Then I got it: he'd seen me straining at the white tie, and figured out that I hated wearing the thing.

"Stevie," Miss Howard said, "what does he mean?"

"He saw me at the Casino—saw that I don't like wearing them clothes. I think he wants them." I spoke louder to our new friend: "You want those clothes, is that the deal?"

"Fine clothes for fine man!" he answered, slapping his chest. "You give them to El Niño, he work for you!"

I shook my head. "But you can't wear them *all* the time—"

"Why not?" Miss Howard asked, turning to me. "Frankly, Stevie, I think this fellow can do just about as he pleases."

I gave that a second's thought, then nodded. "Yeah, you've got a point there, all right. But what the hell's the Doctor going to say?"

"When we tell him that we've brought one of our main opponents over to our side?" Miss Howard countered with a smile. "What do you *think* he's going to say?"

I kept nodding, and then thought about our host in Ballston Spa. "And Mr. Picton?" I didn't even have to wait for the words; Miss Howard just gave me a look, and I smiled. "Yeah, you're right. He'll laugh himself sick—and this guy'll give him a run for his money in the gab department, that's a fact. Well, then . . ."

Miss Howard turned to the aborigine. "All right," she said, indicating the bed of the buckboard. "Climb aboard—and tell us what we should call you."

"Call me El Niño!" he said, slapping his chest again. Then his face grew more cautious. "I work for you?" he asked, as if he didn't quite believe it.

"You work for us," Miss Howard answered. "Now get in."

"No, no! It is not right so—El Niño can walk, while the lady rides."

Miss Howard sighed. "No, El Niño, *that* is not right. If you work for us, you're one of us. And that means you ride with us."

Looking about ready to bust, the aborigine did a little piece of a dance in the roadway, then sprang onto the bed of the buckboard with the speed of a jungle cat. He stood up on the bed behind us, grinning from ear to ear. "With El Niño to work for you," he declared, "you *find* baby Ana! Sure!"

Not quite believing or understanding what we'd gotten ourselves into, I gave the Morgan the reins and we headed for home.

We got the full story of El Niño's life on that trip, one what we relayed to the others once we'd reached Mr. Picton's house. It seemed that as a boy in the jungles of the Philippines' Luzon Island, the aborigine had been out hunting with the men of his tribe one day when they'd been set upon by a party of Spaniards. The older Aëtas had been killed for sport; the younger ones had been taken to Manila and sold into a lifetime of bondage. El Niño had escaped his first master after several years, then spent his early manhood haunting the waterfront and becoming a roving mercenary. He'd done time as a pirate, fought in small wars all over the South China Sea, and finally found his way back to Manila, where he'd been arrested for petty thievery. Brought before a Spanish magistrate, he'd been sentenced to life at hard labor—which was when the older Señor Linares, a diplomatic official, had stepped in and given him a chance to work off his "debt" to the Spanish Empire as a household servant. I couldn't help, when I heard all this, but think of my own experiences with

Dr. Kreizler; and this common background quickly formed a bond between me and our new partner.

He was a character, there was no denying that much: everybody in Mr. Picton's house found his strange mixture of manly posturing and gentle, almost childlike kindness to be both amusing and touching. When he met Cyrus in particular, he behaved in a way what was very affecting yet still kind of comical. He bowed in a deep, respectful manner, and was amazed when the bigger man—who he seemed to think was some kind of oracle—actually offered him his hand. The fact that "Mr. Mont-*rose*" (as El Niño would always pronounce it) lived among whites as a trusted equal—wearing the same clothes they did, eating the same food, and sleeping in the same quality of accommodations—seemed to the aborigine to mean that he had attained a high level of secret knowledge; and El Niño set out to model his behavior on that of my big, quiet friend. Such, of course, was no easy task, for such a chatty, active little fellow.

None of this, though, gave us any better idea of what we were going to *do* with with our new ally. We didn't particularly need anybody followed or rendered unconscious, at the moment, and he was bound to cause comment wherever he went in Ballston Spa—especially after I gave him the evening clothes I'd promised, which he put on right away. Strutting around like a peacock (he'd been right in supposing that the clothes would fit him), he looked ready to take on the world; but we all wondered if the world would be similarly prepared for him. Thinking for the moment of practicalities, a confused Mrs. Hastings put El Niño to work washing up the dinner dishes, a job what he took to with great good spirits.

As for the information Miss Howard and I brought back from Stillwater, it was duly posted on the chalkboard in Mr. Picton's living room. Then we moved out onto the back porch to talk over the importance of the tale. It was no surprise to anybody that Mrs. Muhlenberg hadn't known the full details of the Hatch case, being as she lived in a different township, which meant a different sheriff's department—and small-town sheriffs were generally even less cooperative and communicative with each other than New York City police precincts. As for the poor woman's refusal to testify, Mr. Picton informed us that such was no great loss, being as Saratoga County's resident Solomon, Judge Charles H. Brown, was a stickler for trying every case on its own merits, and almost certainly wouldn't have allowed any unproven allegations about something what'd happened ten years ago to reach a jury's ear. The same held true for all the work we'd done in New York, which, our host firmly reminded us, hadn't even resulted in an official police investigation. The case of Libby Hatch's murdered children would have to be confined to just that; the only purpose Mrs. Muhlenberg's story could serve would be to help us better understand the character of the woman we were dealing with.

What it offered us along these lines was further proof (not that we needed any) of just how clever our opponent was. The Doctor told us that Mrs. Muhlenberg's little theory of how Libby'd killed her son, Michael, a tale what some might've written off as the ramblings of a woman driven half mad by grief, was very likely the truth: such substances as poison, taken by a nursing woman, can in fact pass on through her milk into whatever baby she's feeding. As for the packet of black powder Mrs. Muhlenberg had found in Libby's room along with the arsenic, the Doctor suspected that it'd been, to use his term, *carbo animalis purificatus,* Latin for "purified animal charcoal." The rest of the world knows the stuff as "bone black," and it's commonly used as an antidote for many poisons— including arsenic. Libby'd probably kept it handy just in case she got impatient with her plan and took too high a dose of the arsenic herself. As for *why* she'd done what she'd done, we all knew the answer to that one by now: little Michael Muhlenberg had committed the lethal mistake of making it obvious that Libby didn't have much in the way of maternal talents, and instead of just admitting as much and trying to find something else to do with her life, the murderess had concocted a situation in which she came off looking like a hero for her efforts to save a kid she was actually killing. It was the same pattern we'd identified in the cases of Libby's "adopted" children, along with the babies at the Lying-in Hospital: the woman had been at her grim work far longer than any of us—except, of course, the Doctor—had suspected, or likely would've believed.

There *was* one bit of information what passed for a helpful clue contained in Mrs. Muhlenberg's sorry tale: if Libby Hatch had been hiring herself out as a wet nurse, it meant that she had to've given birth to a child of her own, at some point. If Libby hadn't been lying on the hospital forms we'd seen, and was now thirty-nine, then in 1886 she would've been twenty-eight, and said kid could've been anywhere from an infant to my age—although the fact that she'd shown up at the Muhlenbergs' alone indicated that the child was probably dead (which came as no big surprise to any of us). But dead or alive, there had to be some evidence of his or her existence somewhere.

So Miss Howard and I would now be looking for more than just Libby's parents, over on the east side of the Hudson: most probably, another child's grave awaited us, too. The interview with Mrs. Muhlenberg had given us only a general idea of where to start our search—there was a whole string of small towns on the opposite bank of the river—and because of that we needed to get started as soon as possible. I think Miss Howard would've been just as happy to leave that night, but there was no way I was going anywhere in the dark again; besides, we owed El Niño his first night in the bed we'd promised him. Mr. Picton showed him to a room up on the top floor of the house, the two of them chatting like old chums as they went up the stairs: we'd been right in thinking that their vocal natures would make them friends from the start. As for what in the world would become of El Niño once the case was over, Mr. Picton said he wouldn't at all mind keeping him on as a servant; it'd certainly give the citizens of Ballston Spa something to talk about. His fate happily decided in this manner, the aborigine dove into the moderately sized bed in his room like it was an ocean, pausing in his wild celebration only when Mr. Picton told him that Mrs. Hastings wouldn't appreciate his rolling around in the bedding with my dress shoes on.

The Doctor decided that our new partner would continue to work with Miss Howard and me for the immediate future: it was impossible to predict what kind of new trouble our search for Libby Hatch's origins would stir up, but it was safe to say that if we did run into more danger, El Niño's talents would come in handy. This was an easy enough consideration to see and accept; what wasn't so obvious, but would prove pleasantly true over the next two days, was just how amusing our companion would continue to be. As we scrounged around those villages on the east bank of the Hudson, with Miss Howard asking anybody and everybody she could find about the Fraser family, El Niño and I became better and better friends, clowning, laughing, and telling any troublesome or resentful locals we ran into just where they could take their small-town hostility. The aborigine's fierce loyalty—now enthusiastically transferred to us, after years of being reluctantly given to the mean-spirited son of his original benefactor—caused Miss Howard to develop her own attachment to him, in a way what wouldn't have been possible with your average American white male: there was no condescension or attempt at chivalry in El Niño's approach to her, just simple respect for someone who'd done him a good turn.

We needed all the bright spirits we could muster during that first day of our search, for it produced nothing but negative answers to Miss Howard's questions, and more moody, distrustful stares from the local population. The fact that we were pursuing a murderer didn't seem to cut much ice with those people: we were, first and foremost, strangers, and no constructive goal of ours could remove that barrier. Wednesday night found us back at Mr. Picton's with nothing to show for our efforts, but we got up before dawn on Thursday and headed out again, trying not to let frustration get to us. When sunrise did come, we were crossing the river on a small ferry, heading directly into the bright, harsh morning glare. It was a state of affairs what would've been sickening if it hadn't been for El Niño, who lay in the back of the buckboard sharpening his *kris* and happily singing some song in his native tongue what he informed me was about morning in the tropical jungles that'd once been his home.

The rest of *our* morning was filled with more disappointment, as was our afternoon. Town after town, tavern after tavern, postal office after postal office went by, with Miss Howard diligently dragging herself into every establishment and asking the same set of questions about a family named Fraser. By the time the light started to turn golden, I for one was more than willing to acknowledge the hopelessness of our finding anything out before the grand jury convened: we didn't even know, after all, if Fraser had been Libby Hatch's original name, an alias, or the handle what the father of her first child had gone by. All we felt sure of was that somewhere—maybe in a completely different state—there was a grave with that first kid's name on it; and as late afternoon wound on into early evening Miss Howard, too, began to think that maybe such was all we really needed to know, at least for the time being. If Mr. Picton found that he required more specifics concerning that portion of the woman's life for the actual trial (assuming we got that far), we could keep trying to find them—and he could grill Libby about such matters on the stand, too. But more and more Miss Howard was starting to feel that Libby's violence was as much a result of having been born a girl in an oppressive, hypocritical society as it was of any possible irregularities in her family life; and our fruitless, pressured search was starting to seem like a waste of time as a result. Needless to say, Miss Howard wasn't one to put up with such a feeling for very long.

And so, when the court house clock in Ballston Spa tolled out seven o'clock that evening, we found ourselves in a position to hear it, having made our way back into town along the Malta road. We wound through Ballston's closed shops and quiet houses, then around the train depot and up Bath Street, passing beneath Mr. Picton's window. El Niño was sleeping in the bed of the wagon, Miss Howard was deep in her own thoughts as she rode next to me, and I was having a tough time keeping my eyes open, as my mind was lulled into relaxation by the slow, steady clatter of our faithful Morgan's hooves.

Which, of course, was exactly the sort of moment when all hell was bound to break loose.

"Stevie!" I half thought the voice was in my head, part of some dream I was slipping into. "Stevie! Sara! Dammit, can't you hear me?"

Miss Howard roused me, and together we turned to look at the quiet blocks around us, failing to see a single soul; but when the voice called out to us again, I marked it as Mr. Picton's, and realized it was coming from his office window.

"Up here!" he said, at which point we glanced up to see him hanging almost half out of the court house, waving his pipe in one hand and a piece of paper in the other, trying desperately to get our attention. "Listen, Stevie," he went on, "you've got to get out to the Westons' and bring the Doctor back here! They don't have a blasted telephone, and we need to talk! He was going to be back by nine, but I've just had a wire from John—we've got to go over it *now!*"

"But the hearing's in the morning," Miss Howard tried to answer, "and he's still got to—"

"That doesn't matter—all taken care of!" Mr. Picton shouted, confusing the hell out of both Miss Howard and me. "Sara, you'd better take my surrey and go fetch Lucius and Cyrus—but Stevie, you've *got* to get the Doctor, as fast as you can!"

In one quick move Miss Howard jumped to the ground, starting toward High Street and the court house steps at a run. She turned around when she was about halfway there to tell me, "Wake El Niño up, Stevie—he can keep you from drifting off again!"

"Like that's gonna happen!" I said, full of new energy. "I wanna know what the hell's going on!"

Miss Howard smiled, gathered her skirt together, and turned to keep running. Thinking the matter over, I figured I could in fact use some company to break the monotony of a drive back along the road we'd just come in on, so I gave my companion on the bed of the wagon a good shake, causing him to bolt upright, produce his *kris,* and ready himself to throw it, all in one lightning move.

"Take it easy, son," I said, patting the driver's bench where Miss Howard had been sitting. "Come on up here and grab ahold of something—the ride's about to get a little rough!" With a gleeful laugh at the idea of being graduated to the bench, El Niño jumped up beside me and got ready to roll as I turned the wagon around and slapped the reins against the Morgan's backside. We wouldn't be able to travel full speed until we got outside town again, but once we did the little stallion showed he was no worse for the day's work, and as we barreled along we raised such a cloud of dust—not to mention such an unholy racket—that El Niño couldn't resist breaking into another song, what he told me he'd picked up during his pirating days in the South China Sea.

It was still fully light out when we reached the Westons' farm, a testament as much to the durability of our horse as to my driving talents. Josiah Weston, though taken off guard by the sight of the aborigine in my evening clothes, told me that the Doctor and Clara Hatch were somewhere down by the stream behind the house, once again drawing. This didn't surprise me; the Doctor had amazing patience when it came to these things, and if a given kid responded to a certain form of treatment or communication, he could stay with it for days on end. Telling El Niño to get some feed and water for our horse, I took off down toward the stream at a run.

Shooting around the big vegetable garden, then through a cornfield and down along the banks of the loud, clear brook, I found myself getting more and more excited, about just what I had no idea. I jumped and bolted over the rocks and muddy grass of the streambank, searching for the Doctor and Clara but not finding them right off; and, even though I knew that they wouldn't be able to hear me over the noise of the rushing water, I called out their names a couple of times, never pausing to listen for an answer. Finally, after some five minutes of dashing and leaping, I caught sight of the Doctor's back about half a mile upstream from the house. He was sitting underneath a large maple tree, one whose roots had grown out to form a kind of platform over the streambed. Clara was sitting quietly across from him, sketching away.

When I finally did get within earshot of the Doctor, I slowed down a bit. The part of the stream where the two of them were sitting was a little bend where the water spread out into an undisturbed pool, and grew quiet enough for me to hear the Doctor's gentle voice as he spoke with Clara. He was obviously at a critical juncture in his effort to reach the girl, based on what I could hear of his words:

". . . and so you see, Clara, I began to understand that what had happened was not my fault—and that if I only told others the truth about what had happened, it would help. It would help me to stay safe, and it would help my father to stop doing such things."

This was all fairly predictable: again, I'd heard its like before, from the Doctor, and though I knew enough to approach quietly, I also calculated that a pause in the conversation—brought on by Clara's silent attempt to wrap her troubled young mind around his last thought—would follow. I waited for it, figuring that at said point I could gracefully step in and break the news that we were urgently needed back in town.

What happened instead was that my jaw dropped at the sound of Clara answering the Doctor in a soft, slightly hoarse, but still amazingly clear voice:

"And did your papa get better?"

I could see the Doctor nod slowly. "He was a very sick man. Like your mama. But yes, he got better, eventually. So will she."

"But only if I tell the truth . . ." Clara said, quietly and with real fear.

There was no doubt about it: they were having a conversation.

CHAPTER 39

I did my damndest not to interrupt the scene, knowing that what was happening was crucial; but the sogginess of the streambank below me prevented the attempt. Standing there holding my breath, I began to feel my foot sinking into a deep patch of grassy mud. Letting out a little holler, I yanked my leg up, a move what produced a loud and slightly humorous sound. The pair of these noises caused the Doctor and Clara to spin round quickly and get to their feet. The little girl rushed to hide behind the Doctor's leg, though when she saw it was only me—and then that the bottom of my leg was covered in a thick sludge—she began to laugh some, in that hoarse little way of hers. The Doctor smiled, too; as for me, I could feel my own face going red.

"Sorry," I said, shaking chunks of clay and mud off my boot. "I didn't mean to barge in, but—" I just looked down at my foot, and then the two of them laughed even harder.

"Well, Clara," the Doctor said, "I think that someone's been trying to sneak up on us. What do *you* think?" The girl's laugh shrank to a smile as she looked at me; then she reached her head up, wanting to whisper into the Doctor's ear. He bent down to listen, then laughed again. "No, he certainly is *not* very good at it!" Giving me a meaningful look what said if my business wasn't important I'd best beat it, the Doctor went on, "And so, Stevie, what brings you?"

I tried to keep my voice casual, not knowing just what might upset Clara. "It's Mr. Picton, sir. He says maybe it's time to call it a day." I let my tone get a little more pointed. "Seems he's had a telegram—from Mr. Moore."

The Doctor's eyes did a little dance, but he kept his emotions under control. "I see." He glanced down at Clara, then back at me. "All right. I'll meet you at the house. Five minutes."

I nodded and departed, the Doctor turning to have a serious heart-to-heart with his young patient as I went.

By the time I got back to the house, the mud on my foot and leg had started to dry, but it was still sufficiently stupid-looking for El Niño to get a big damned howl out of it. He kept going as I removed my boot and tried to get myself cleaned up, but when the Doctor and Clara appeared he snapped to attention and became all respectful business. The girl found the aborigine a strange sight, but not, it seemed, a threatening one; and she whispered a few remarks into the Doctor's ear again once she'd fully sized him up. The Doctor smiled and then put a hand on Clara's head, telling her that El Niño's size was normal for people like him.

"He comes from the other side of the world," the Doctor explained. "There are *many* unusual things there. You might see them someday, if you like." He then crouched down to look her in the eye. "I'll be back in the morning to take you to the court house, Clara. And I'll stay in the room there with you, just as I promised. Only Mr. Picton will ask you any questions—so you see, there's really nothing to be afraid of. It *will* help—the truth will help *everyone*."

Clara nodded, trying hard to believe the Doctor's words as Josiah Weston came over to put an arm around her. Obviously very much aware that we were on the eve of Clara's first big test, Mr. Weston shook the Doctor's hand with what seemed like confidence; but at the same time I thought I could see a bit of lingering doubt in his eyes about whether they were doing the right thing. But as the Doctor turned to board his hired gig, Clara rushed over and threw herself around the Doctor's leg, the way I'd seen many kids at the Institute do; and I think that convinced Mr. Weston more than any words could have that they had truly started down the only path what would ever lead to any kind of real peace for her.

As we rolled back along the Westons' drive, I pulled over to one side to let the Doctor bring the gig up beside us, and then gave him a quick version of the situation in town, or what little I knew about it. As to what Mr. Picton had meant by the Doctor's business at the Westons' being "all taken care of," it seemed that Clara had actually started talking that morning, and that the Doctor had dispatched Peter Weston to town with the news immediately, so that Mr. Picton would know that he could count on having the last weapon in his arsenal at the ready when he went before the grand jury. After telling me this, the Doctor slowed the gig, got behind our wagon again, and then put his mind to the task of keeping up with me: the rest of our ride back was as fast and rough as the trip out'd been. When we reached the court house, the Morgan stallion finally made it clear through a series of heavy sighs that he'd done all the running he was going to that day; and I told El Niño, as he led the two horses and rigs back to the livery stable, to make sure that Mr. Wooley gave the remarkable animal an especially good meal and brushing down for his efforts.

The sight of Mr. Picton's surrey outside the court house clued the Doctor and me in to the fact that Miss Howard had beaten us back with her charges, and the thought that the three of them might be upstairs coercing whatever mysterious news had arrived from New York out of Mr. Picton before our arrival caused us to charge into the court house and toward the marble steps at high speed. The big guard by the door, the one Mr. Picton had called Henry, called out to us resentfully, saying that we couldn't just go tearing around the place like we owned it, that there were rules what had to be followed; but we paid him no mind. Observing similarly few formalities when we reached Mr. Picton's offices, we just barged on in, to find the others waiting.

"At last!" Mr. Picton said, smoking and gnawing on his pipe like one of the more nerve-racked types I'd occasionally seen during the Doctor's visits to Bellevue Hospital's Insane Pavilion in New York. "I was afraid that if you didn't arrive soon these three were going to physically assault me and *take* the telegram! But fair is fair, that's what I told them—the Doctor and Stevie deserve to hear the news at the same time as everyone else!"

"Please," the Doctor said breathlessly, ignoring Mr. Picton's kindly consideration, "go ahead . . ."

"The wire arrived at just past six," Mr. Picton said, setting his pipe aside for the moment and adjusting himself nervously in his chair. "And it's my hope that together we can make more sense of it than I've been able to do alone. I'll just read it to you—" He unfolded the thing with a loud flutter, then cleared his smoky throat and proceeded:

"MR. RUPERT PICTON, BALLSTON SPA COURT HOUSE, BALLSTON SPA. *URGENT*. L.H. DECLINES RIGHT TO APPEAR BEFORE G. JURY, REFERS STATE TO HER AFFIDAVIT AT TIME OF CRIME. NOTHING MORE TO ADD. LOCATED REV. PARKER YESTERDAY. ALIVE, THOUGH NOT UNDAMAGED. WILL TESTIFY IF GUARANTEED PROTECTION. MICAH HUNTER DIED YESTERDAY OF MORPHINE OVERDOSE. CORONER SAYS SELF-INFLICTED, BUT CAT IS NOW OUT OF BAG. TWO LOCAL COPS ACCOMPANIED CORONER, L.H. KNOWS THERE IS NO OFFICIAL POLICE INVESTIGATION INTO HER ACTIVITIES. DUSTERS NOW TOO

DANGEROUS FOR US TO REMAIN ON WATCH. ALMOST KILLED TAILING HER
AS SHE MOVED A.L. TO THEIR PLACE. TRYING TO ARRANGE FOR EYES ON THE
INSIDE. VANDERBILT BACK IN TOWN. L.H. WENT TO HIM IN FULL MOURN-
ING. V. HAS ENGAGED CHICAGO LAWYER TO ASSIST IN HER DEFENSE. MAR-
CUS DEPARTED LAST NIGHT TO FIND OUT WHO MAN IS. I RETURN BY NEXT
AVAILABLE TRAIN. WOULD APPRECIATE TRANSPORT AND LARGE WHISKEY
AT STATION. MOORE.

"And that, my friends," Mr. Picton said, taking his pipe back up, "is the
sum of things. I've checked the timetables—John should be arriving at
about eleven, though of course there'll be delays. Which gives us several
hours in which to figure out just what he's talking about." Mr. Picton
waved the telegram above his head. "Some of it's obvious, of course, and
none too surprising—I didn't honestly expect Libby to show up for the
grand jury proceedings, for instance. But there are other elements that are
quite confusing."

The Doctor got up and reached toward the telegram. "May I?"

"Oh, yes, of course, Doctor," Mr. Picton answered, handing the thing
over. "You've known John far longer than I have, after all, so perhaps
you'll do better with some of his vague references—starting with the statement that Reverend Parker is 'alive but not undamaged.'"

"Either Moore was simply demonstrating his usual clarity of language,"
the Doctor answered in what you might call a dry tone of voice, scanning
the piece of paper, "or he didn't want to take the chance that anyone might
get hold of a copy of the message. Vanderbilt's reappearance, looked at in
such a light, *is* somewhat sinister."

"Yes," Lucius agreed. "There's not a lot his people wouldn't be able to
find out, if they had a mind to."

"I'd be willing to bet," Miss Howard said, "that the business about
Parker means that Libby *did* sic the Dusters on him at some point. If John
and Marcus could find him, *she* must've been able to also. And God knows
what shape he ended up in."

Cyrus shook his head. "Bad enough to make his life a genuine misery, I
expect, miss," he said quietly. "Maybe bad enough to make him wish he
was dead. It might be that she'd take more satisfaction from that than from
actually having him killed."

Miss Howard gave Cyrus a grim look what indicated she agreed with
him; the Doctor, too, nodded. "Yes," he said, still studying the telegram,
"but a more permanent solution was apparently necessary for Micah
Hunter. That, too, is understandable. He probably never knew anything

about what happened up here before he married Libby—but when Marcus brought the news about the grand jury, Hunter doubtless began to suspect the truth. And it wouldn't have been much work, even for his drug-ridden brain, to draw the obvious inferences about the ill-fated children his wife had been 'attending to' in New York."

Mr. Picton cocked his head, with something that almost looked like respect in his face. "Killing him's a clever tactic for the trial, too. Libby'll now arrive in the clothing of a recent widow who spent years nursing a Civil War veteran." His look of strange admiration suddenly turned into a wince. "My God, what a depressing thought. Judges, juries, and the public are prone enough to side with a woman during a trial—but the grieving widow of a Union soldier . . . nothing like a black dress and the flag to bring out sympathy. But tell me, Doctor—what does Moore mean when he says he's 'trying to arrange for eyes on the inside'?"

"It relates to yet another clever move on our antagonist's part, I'm afraid," the Doctor replied. "I had hoped that, if summoned to Ballston Spa, she would arrange for some temporary caretaker to look after Ana in her house."

"And why would that have helped our cause?" Mr. Picton asked.

"It wouldn't," the Doctor answered. "Not in terms of the trial, at any rate. But in the event that we fail, and she's acquitted—"

"Then she'd have to get rid of that caretaker on returning to New York," Lucius finished for him with a nod, grabbing hold of the idea. "And with any luck, we could've been there to catch her in the act and prevent it."

"Or if we failed in that attempt, we would at least have had—and I do not mean to sound excessively callous, here—another murder which we might have attempted to lay at her door," the Doctor said. "Now, however, knowing that the police are *not* in fact investigating her, she can be far bolder—Moore says that they actually *saw* her transferring the child to the Dusters' headquarters, a place the police do not frequent without the strongest of motivations." Pausing, the Doctor focused his eyes more sharply on the telegram. "I'd say that John is endeavoring to find someone within, or at least close to, the Dusters who will be willing to keep watch over Ana—for if we should succeed in convicting Libby, the child's fate will be sealed unless we have inside help."

"But—who could he possibly contact?" Lucius said. "I mean, even *approaching* anybody who's known to frequent that place would get him a broken skull."

At that point I became aware of a pair of eyes fixing on mine, and looked over to see Cyrus staring at me. "Not necessarily," he said gently;

and as he did, my own heart sank with the realization of what—or *who*—
he was talking about.

"What do you mean, Cyrus?" Miss Howard asked. "Who could he possibly—" Following Cyrus's gaze and looking at me, Miss Howard suddenly caught on. The Doctor and Lucius also glanced my way, knowingly
and uncomfortably.

All of this attention caused me to start shifting my feet. "But—" I said
quietly. "But—she's gone." My heart beating faster by the second, I soon
found it impossible to keep my voice down. "She's *gone*! She went to California—"

"We don't know that, Stevie," the Doctor said evenly. "And there
doesn't seem to be anyone else that Moore could possibly be referring to."

I'd started to shake my head even before he'd finished talking. "No," I
said, in an effort to convince myself, as much as anyone else. "She *left*,
she's gone!" But then I remembered the glimpse of Ding Dong I'd caught
on the Twenty-second Street pier before our departure from the city, and
my voice died away as I realized that my argument wasn't worth the air it
took to voice it.

"I'm afraid I'm a bit behind, here," Mr. Picton said, puffing on his pipe
and seeming to sense that the moment was a tricky one. "It may, of
course, be none of my business, but—who are you all talking about?"

The Doctor—once he saw that, though I was still upset, I was starting
to get myself under some kind of control—turned to Mr. Picton. "It is the
friend of Stevie's of whom you've heard us speak—Miss Devlin. We had
thought that she'd left the city for California." He glanced my way once
more. "It would appear that we were mistaken."

"But that's splendid!" Mr. Picton's warm, loud words threw me and
everybody else in the room off kilter for a second; I looked up to give him
a very puzzled stare. "Well, I mean," he went on, with warmhearted sincerity, "the girl's been a great help with the case so far, Stevie. If she's still
in New York, what better person to continue to ask for assistance?"

The thought, one what none of us who actually knew Kat would have
come up with, was strangely comforting, and I found that it had the effect of calming the pounding in my head and my chest, to the extent that
I could even nod a bit.

"That's true, Stevie," Miss Howard said, in her most encouraging tone.
"We don't have any reason to believe that Kat won't do what's right. She
has so far, after all. Whatever her flashes of temper."

Even Cyrus, who knew best of all of them how open to question Kat's
participation would probably be, tried to be positive about the notion:

"They've got a point, Stevie—she's a tough girl, and Lord knows she's unpredictable. But she's done right by us at every turn."

"Yeah," I said softly. "I guess that's so . . ." But I wasn't going to buy into the thing fully until I saw a look of certainty in the Doctor's face.

I turned—but the look wasn't there. "We have to hope, Stevie," he said, one of his eyebrows arched. He'd never lied to me in the past, and I think he knew I wouldn't've wanted him to start at that point. "It's all we can do. But it won't be blind hope—that much, at least, is the truth. She *has* truly been a help to us in this business."

I just nodded again, swallowing hard and ready to move on to some other subject, being as I wouldn't be able to begin to come to real terms with the question of Kat 'til later, when I could have a few smokes on my own.

Thankfully, the Doctor moved everyone's attention on to other matters by going back to the telegram. "The final question, then—and I fear the most perplexing—is who the devil this 'Chicago lawyer' Moore mentions may be."

"Perplexing, indeed!" Mr. Picton said, standing up and heading over to his window. He glanced out it and started to tug at the bristly ginger hair on his head so hard I thought the stuff might start coming out in clumps. "Chicago . . . why in God's name Chicago? New York has the best criminal trial attorneys in the country—and with Vanderbilt behind her Libby could have any one of them!"

"Maybe Vanderbilt's got some special contact in Chicago," Lucius said. "He must have some reason for going that far afield for help. After all, he's no fool."

"No," Mr. Picton agreed, kicking at a pile of papers on the floor. "But he *is* a railroad man. The only people he'd have any reason to be well acquainted with in Chicago would be corporation lawyers. I can't see where one of *them* would—"

At that moment we all turned at the sound of a knock on the outer office door. It was quickly followed by the voice of the guard from downstairs: "Mr. Picton? Mr. Picton, sir?"

"It's all right, Henry!" Mr. Picton shouted. "Come in!"

The big guard opened the outer door slowly, then cautiously made his way inside, slouching over slightly in what looked to me like some kind of automatic deference at being in one of the offices. He was holding an envelope.

"This just came for you, sir," he said, handing the item over as Mr. Picton crossed the room to receive it. "From the Western Union office. I told 'em to bill the D.A.'s account."

"Well—that was quick thinking, Henry," Mr. Picton said, as he started to open the envelope. The guard frowned, not knowing whether Mr. Picton was serious or mocking him. But the shorter man's next comment made his attitude pretty clear: "Do you know everyone, Henry?" he said, looking up into the guard's pasty, small-eyed face and then indicating the rest of us. "Or shall I make introductions?"

The man scowled down at Mr. Picton. "No, sir," he said glumly. Then he turned the dumb, injured look on the rest of us. "I guess I know 'em all right, sir."

"Well, then," Mr. Picton said, "if you're waiting for a tip, I can only remind you that's it's against county policy. Good evening, Henry."

Not knowing how to respond to that, the guard simply nodded and then lumbered moodily back out the door.

"Idiot," Mr. Picton mumbled once he'd gone. "To think that someone with a *mind* might actually make use of all the food and oxygen it takes to keep that sort of—" He stopped as he got the envelope open. "Well! News from Marcus." Scanning the thing quickly, Mr. Picton shrugged and then handed it to the Doctor, crossing back to his desk. "Though precious little! He seems to have learned the name of the lawyer Vanderbilt's engaged. He's trying to assemble a case record on the man, and talk to some people who have dealt with him. There's a possibility that he can get an interview with the fellow himself, too."

"All that *could* be helpful," Lucius commented with a shrug.

"What's his name, Rupert?" Miss Howard asked. "Do you recognize it?"

Mr. Picton was gazing out his window, pulling at his hair again. "Hmm? Oh! Darrow. Clarence Darrow. I can't quite place it—but there is something . . ."

"*I've* no knowledge of him, certainly," the Doctor said simply, dropping the telegram onto the desk.

Mr. Picton kept struggling, then threw up his hands. "Nor, it appears, do I," he said, his face twisting unhappily. Then it straightened out. "Or do I? There was something—wait a minute!" Bolting across the room, he gathered a stack of law journals what were piled on the floor up into his arms, then threw them onto his desk. "*Somewhere,* there's *something* . . ." Going through the journals in his usual style—which meant hurling them around the room so that the rest of us had to occasionally duck to keep from taking one of them in the mouth—Mr. Picton eventually grabbed the particular number he'd been looking for. "Ah-ha!" he said, collapsing into his chair. "Yes, here it is! A piece that mentions Clarence Darrow—who *is,* in fact, on the payroll of the Chicago and Northwestern Railway, though it's only a part-time retainer. But he used to be their corporation counsel, and that's no doubt where Vanderbilt first heard of him."

"But I still don't understand," the Doctor said. "Why hire a corporate attorney for a criminal case?"

"Well," Mr. Picton answered, holding up a finger, "there are some interesting details that may provide an answer. You remember the Pullman strike, back in '94?" There were general mumblings in the affirmative, as we all thought back to the infamous time when the American Railway Union had struck against the Pullman Car Company in Chicago. The battles what'd taken place during the action had been so infamous and so bloody that even *I'd* heard them mentioned, among those labor-minded enthusiasts what made up the most loudmouthed portion of the population in my old neighborhood. "Well, despite the fact that he was still a consulting attorney for the Chicago and Northwestern, Clarence Darrow agreed to represent Eugene Debs and several other officers of the railway workers' union. It wasn't a criminal trial—Debs and the others were only charged with inciting the workers to strike, which is technically an antitrust matter. But Darrow managed to argue the thing all the way to the Supreme Court, just the same." Mr. Picton flipped a few more pages of the journal, growing silent.

"And?" Miss Howard asked.

"*And,* he lost, of course," Mr. Picton answered. "But it was quite a good fight. And, more importantly, while Debs and the others were serving several months in jail for the civil violations, they were indicted on a more serious criminal charge: attempting to obstruct the mails by way of the railway strike. Darrow took the case again, and won by default—the government eventually dropped the charges. So while he lost the less serious civil case, Darrow won the more important criminal one."

"Which doesn't tell us," Lucius said, "why Mr. Vanderbilt thinks that a man who splits his time between working for railroad corporations and workers' unions—a combination that strikes me as awfully odd, by the way—is the ideal candidate to come in on a murder case."

"No," Mr. Picton answered, his mood brightening. "No, it doesn't. But I'll tell you, Detective—I'm relieved! Whatever Darrow's talents may be, Vanderbilt could, as I say, have brought some very big guns up from New York, once he chose to get involved."

"Perhaps that's the point," the Doctor said. "Perhaps Mr. Vanderbilt senses that there may be something untoward about this case, and doesn't want his name connected to it in any New York circles."

Mr. Picton considered that, then nodded. "I suspect you're right, Doctor—I suspect you're absolutely right! Doubtless Marcus can confirm the theory for us when he gets back. But for now"—Mr. Picton clamped his pipe between his teeth and put his hands on his hips—"I vote that we go home and have ourselves a pleasant dinner. Things are starting to look up, I daresay!"

Feeling much relieved by this turn of events, as well as by Mr. Picton's confidence, we all started to head for the office door, hungry and more than ready to take his advice regarding a relaxing evening at home. True, we had the grand jury to wrangle with in the morning; but with Clara Hatch now talking, there seemed little reason to think that we wouldn't proceed easily past that obstacle to the criminal trial what lay beyond, where, we happily assured ourselves, we'd be faced by a lawyer inexperienced in such cases, who wouldn't be able to put up much of a fight against two men as seasoned in these sorts of contests as the Doctor and Mr. Picton.

It was one of the worst errors of judgment we made during the entire case.

CHAPTER 40

Mr. Moore arrived that night, looking bedraggled and persecuted, and rightfully so: he'd had a pretty devilish week in the city, and had barely gotten back out with all of his organs and limbs intact. And even when he and Marcus hadn't been in situations where their lives were in immediate danger—like when they'd gone to interview the Reverend Clayton Parker—violence had been a topic of conversation: apparently the reverend had been set on about six months earlier by several men who we could reasonably assume to've been Hudson Dusters, and'd had both of his knee caps shattered with baseball bats, along with one of his ears cut off. Even as he retold the story to us, Mr. Moore got so jittery that he needed a couple of stiff belts of Mr. Picton's best whiskey to calm his nerves. But the news that we were ready to face the grand jury the next morning cheered him up considerably, as did the leftovers from our dinner, with which he stuffed himself 'til fairly late in Mr. Picton's kitchen. By the time he retired, he'd taken in enough encouraging intelligence—along with enough whiskey—to be able to sleep as soundly as the rest of us.

Before I could let him go to the rest he so richly deserved, though, I had to find out whether he'd actually been in touch with Kat and, if he had, what the outcome'd been. As he was unsteadily scrubbing his teeth in his bathroom after pouring half a tin of Sozodont powder over his brush and into the sink, I snuck on in and put the questions. His mouth foaming like a mad dog's, Mr. Moore told me that yes, he'd met up with Kat outside Duster territory and informed her about our predicament, then asked if she'd be willing to keep a watchful eye on Ana Linares. Kat'd demanded money for her services, making it seem certain to me that all we'd given her, and probably the train ticket too, had gone to Ding Dong; but Mr. Moore said that such wasn't the case, that Kat'd shown him the ticket and told him that she was just waiting for word from her aunt before setting out for California. When I asked Mr. Moore if he thought Kat was still blowing the burny, he answered that he hadn't been able to tell, in a nervous way what made it plain he was lying; but I decided that all I had time or energy to do was take heart from the fact that Kat still had the train ticket and was still willing to work for us. The rest I'd have to cope with when we got back to New York.

Mr. Picton had prepared us for the possibility that some of the townsfolk of Ballston Spa would take an interest in the activities of the deliberative body what was slated to convene on Friday morning at eleven in the smaller wing chamber of the county court house; but we weren't at all ready (and I don't think he was, either) for the sight that greeted us when we rolled up to the building in the surrey. There must've been a hundred people of every age, size, and description on the steps and lawn of the place, milling around like so many hungry chickens. The guard Henry was at the top of the steps barring the entrance, being as the activities of grand juries are not open to the public (a fact what many of those would-be spectators were obviously unaware of). But the big, horse-faced Henry seemed to be talking sympathetically with the crowd as much as holding them at bay. And the closer we got, the clearer it became that the general mood among all of them—Henry included—was not a happy one.

"Oh, good," Mr. Picton said, as he reined his horse to a halt. Then he huffed in an irritated manner, causing his pipe to shoot sparks upward. "I was *so* hoping that my fellow citizens would take an interest in the proceedings—nothing like the public getting involved in the affairs of government, especially when they're too ignorant to know at what point they're not allowed to *be* involved!" He brought the surrey to a halt and, picking up one of the several big stacks of books and files what were sitting on the floor under the driver's bench, jumped down to the street. "I'd advise you not to fetch Clara alone, Dr. Kreizler," he said, as the Doctor moved up from the back to the front seat. "God knows how many more of these people have come out to offer their opinions in other parts of town."

"Cyrus and Stevie will accompany me," the Doctor answered with a nod as I moved on up to take the reins.

"And El Niño, too!" the aborigine said, swinging around toward us from his perch on the outside of the rig. "If you have El Niño to guard you, there will be no trouble for the Señor Doctor!" He flashed a grin, one that the Doctor, even in that uncertain situation, couldn't help but return.

"Very well, El Niño," he said. "You shall come along, too. But don't be too quick to reach for the tools of your trade." The Doctor glanced at the crowd in front of the court house. "People such as these are to be feared more for their ignorance than for their daring."

"Yes, Señor Doctor!" El Niño said, jumping onto the back seat beside Cyrus as Mr. Moore vacated the spot. "Is true!"

"You don't want me to come along, too, Laszlo?" Mr. Moore said, still looking sleepy after his first decent night's rest in five days.

"I think we're an impressive enough little escort, John," the Doctor said, eyeing those of us what were still in the surrey. "And someone's got to get Mr. Picton through that crowd. Someone, that is"—the doctor gave Miss Howard a quick smile—"who won't reach *immediately* for a firearm."

"Oh, *my* hands will be full," Miss Howard answered, smiling as she picked up another pile of books and files. "Fortunately for these people."

"It's all very well to joke," Lucius said, wiping his forehead, which was shining bright in the hot morning sun. "But you will be careful, Doctor? The girl is the key to our case, after all."

"Yes, Detective Sergeant," the Doctor answered. "And a good deal more than that. No harm will come to her or to anyone else, I pledge you that."

"And so does El Niño!" declared the aborigine, at which I smiled to the detective sergeant.

"And so does El Niño," I said, clicking my tongue at Mr. Picton's horse and starting us slowly on our way.

As we drove, we turned to keep an eye on the other four as they made their way through the crowd in front of the court house, Mr. Picton's pipe still blazing like the smokestack of a forge as he greeted faces he recognized with a cheeriness what couldn't have been more phony. "Ah, Mr. Grose, I *am* relieved to see a representative of our *Weekly Journal*—and the editor himself! This is truly gratifying! A man in my line of work rarely experiences such an exhibition of support!"

We began to drift out of earshot just as an irritated voice replied to Mr. Picton, "The *Ballston Weekly Journal* most definitely does *not* intend to support you, sir, if you are truly seeking an indictment against the unfortunate Mrs. Hatch!"

The last piece of this conversation we heard was Mr. Picton's reply: "Ah! What a pity! Sheriff Dunning, you *will* remind these people—including friend Grose, here—that these proceedings are closed to the public, won't you? Good man . . ."

A heavy sigh came out of the Doctor, and I turned to him. "Bloody hell," he whispered, turning away from the scene in front of the court house and then rubbing his bad arm with his right hand. "It begins already . . ."

When we reached the Westons' farm, we found the whole family out in front of the house and gathered around their carriage, a simple but dignified rig what bore a shiny new coat of black paint. They looked like they were ready for church, scrubbed and dressed in the kind of somber, formal clothing what they most likely only brought out for Sundays, weddings, and funerals. The Doctor boarded the carriage with them, sitting next to Clara on one seat while Mr. and Mrs. Weston took the other and Kate climbed onto the driver's bench with Peter, who had the reins.

Clara was a picture of nervousness and confusion, of course, her golden eyes as round and skittish as a spooked Thoroughbred's. Almost as soon as the Doctor was in the carriage, he got her to open her sketch pad and start working with her pencils: the best way, he obviously figured, to keep her mind off where she was going and why. As Peter started down the drive, I pulled the surrey in behind him, and all the way back to town Cyrus, El Niño, and I kept a careful lookout for any curious or hostile faces what might appear by the road.

We didn't catch sight of any 'til we were back on the edge of Ballston Spa; but the cold stares we started to receive at that point indicated that word about what was going on at the court house had spread all through the village. The general reaction seemed to be the same as the one exhibited by those brave souls who'd marched up to the court house steps in a pack. It wasn't exactly a mob mentality—I'd seen mobs at work, and this was something different. The citizens of Ballston Spa seemed mostly bewildered: their faces were disturbed and furrowed and plainly displayed the wish that we would disappear back to the evil city what had disgorged us.

"It is strange, Señorito Stevie," El Niño remarked at one point. "These people—they do not wish for baby Ana to be found?"

"They don't really get the connection," I answered, as we rolled by the Eagle Hotel and netted a whole slew of new glares. "And we can't tell them, because the señor says so. It's a secret, if you get my meaning."

"So," El Nino answered with a nod, "that is why they look this way. If they know the story of baby Ana, they feel different. Sure."

I hoped like hell that the aborigine was right.

Back up at the court house the scene hadn't changed much; and as our two rigs moved along High Street, one heavyset man with a thick gray mustache, wearing a wide-brimmed straw hat and a badge on the lapel of his jacket, approached us.

"Josiah," he said in a polite but serious tone of voice, signaling to Mr. Weston.

"Sheriff Dunning," Mr. Weston answered with a nod, his voice betraying no emotion. "A few folks here."

"Yessir," Sheriff Dunning answered, looking a little uneasily at the crowd. "Nothing serious—but you'll want to take your rig around back, maybe. Come in through the ground floor. Be easier on everybody." He glanced once at Clara. "Hello, there, little miss," he said with a smile. "Come to visit the court house, have you?" As an answer Clara hid herself behind the Doctor's arm, at which point the sheriff turned his gaze up to meet the Doctor's. The man's smile vanished in the process. "Anyway, Josiah," Sheriff Dunning said. "I just figure that'll be the easier way to go about it."

Mr. Weston nodded, then turned his rig onto Bath Street and rolled down the hill toward the back entrance to the court house. I made a move to follow with the surrey, but Cyrus reached up to grab my arm.

"No, Stevie," he said. "The front door. Let's make sure those folks don't follow them down."

I knew what he meant: between Cyrus and El Niño the focus of the crowd's attention was likely to stay on our carriage, wherever it went; and if we just pulled up in front of the court house and brassed it out by heading in at the main entrance, we were likely to make certain that Clara and the Westons would get inside without any trouble.

So I slapped Mr. Picton's horse into a nice high step and made as much of a deal as I could out of the half block that we had left to cover. True to Cyrus's reasoning, every eye in the crowd turned on us as we got down off the surrey and made our way toward the steps. There were a few laughs, but more clicks of the tongue and mild curses; and of course, the occasional mumbling of "damned niggers" and the like were heard, all of them designed to get some kind of a reaction out of Cyrus and El Niño. But those bright souls what gave voice to the slurs didn't know who they were dealing with; for El Niño, if he heard them, didn't register any awareness of what they meant, while Cyrus had long since learned to hold his emotions down when such labels were flung at him.

At the front door we came face to face with the guard Henry, who, seeming to care quite a bit about what the crowd would think of his next move, took to biting at the nails of one hand.

"What's this, Henry?" said one pompous-looking man in a suit, whose voice I recognized as belonging to the editor of the *Ballston Weekly Journal,* Mr. Grose. "Are respected citizens of this community and members of the press to be denied entry to these proceedings, while children and—well"—Mr. Grose's eyes went from Cyrus to El Niño—"*savages* are to be allowed in?"

Plainly not knowing what to do, Henry obeyed the instincts of the true follower: he crossed his arms, widened his stance, and then looked Cyrus in the eye. "Sorry," he said, "the grand jury's de—the de—"

" 'Deliberations,' " Cyrus supplied with a straight face.

The guard's eyes filled with resentment. "The *deliberations* are closed to the public."

"Sir," Cyrus answered quietly. "You know that we're investigators in the employ of Assistant District Attorney Picton. And we know you know it. So you can either let us through now—or you can play up to this crowd and explain your decision to Mr. Picton later. He's your superior." Cyrus nodded toward the general area behind him. "These people aren't."

Somebody behind me mumbled "Smart-ass nigger," and then I saw a hand appear from out of the closing swarm of bodies to grab Cyrus's shoulder. The arm connected to the hand tried to pull my friend backward, and the face on the owner of the arm was filled with a resentment obviously fortified by a few morning drinks. But whoever the fellow was, he'd let liquor lead him to a bad decision: Cyrus just grabbed the fingers what were fixed on his shoulder in his own hand, and then held them up an inch or so. Keeping his eyes fixed on the guard Henry's face, Cyrus began to squeeze—and as beads of sweat appeared on Henry's face, Cyrus started to squeeze very hard.

Now, Cyrus has always had a grip that's got a lot in common with your average steel vise; and after about twenty seconds or so you could hear the man who'd grabbed him starting to whimper. Then came the sound of bones crunching, at which the man started to plain howl.

"All right, all right!" Henry said, stepping away from the door. "Get inside, the three of you—but I'm telling Mr. Picton about this!"

Cyrus assured Henry that he'd also be letting Mr. Picton know exactly what had happened. Then we slipped through the door, slamming it closed as the crowd outside started to make louder and angrier noises.

Inside the main hall we saw Mr. Moore, Miss Howard, and Lucius anxiously pacing outside the doorway to the small hearing room, which was over on the left-hand side of the space.

"What the hell was all that about?" Mr. Moore said, as we moved quickly over to them.

"Seems like tempers are getting pretty hot already," I answered. "One of those mugs tried to start something with Cyrus."

"Are you all right?" Miss Howard said, looking up at Cyrus's barely rattled features.

"He is all right—sure!" El Niño answered, staring up at Cyrus in awe. "He is *el maestro*—not all of those pigs outside can challenge Mr. Montrose!"

A little embarrassed, Cyrus just nodded to Miss Howard. "Nothing out of the ordinary, miss. Have they begun the proceedings?"

"I think so," she answered. "They let the family go in with Clara, thank God—she was as pale as a sheet by the time she actually got up here."

"Well," I said, trying to sneak a peek through the crack between the sliding mahogany doors of the hearing room but unable to see anything. "Looks like it's a waiting game for a while." I held up my hands. "And yes, before anybody asks, I've got plenty of cigarettes . . ."

It was an anxious time, those next couple of hours, with nowhere to go (a walk outside being pretty effectively ruled out) and nothing to do but smoke and worry. Whoever'd built the doors in that court house had turned in some solid work, for along with being unable to spot anything through the cracks, we never heard any sound clearer than vague mumbling coming from inside—and precious little of that. Mr. Moore remarked that such was a good sign; but good or not, it was strange and not a little disturbing to be standing outside a courtroom without ever hearing the usual sounds of argument. We didn't even get the occasional echo of a banging gavel, for a grand jury proceeding, like I've said, was and is the district attorney's show (or, in this case, the assistant D.A.'s), and there was no judge inside that chamber to go messing with the way things were conducted. There was just Mr. Picton, his evidence and witnesses, and the jury itself. Given such an arrangement and the limited amount of noise what bled out through the door, there did seem to be good reason for us to believe that things were going pretty well; and as the time dragged on, each one of us tried harder and harder to accept that idea.

For once, our assumptions turned out to match the facts. At about one-thirty we heard the sounds of chairs and feet moving around inside the hearing room, and then the mahogany doors slid open, an officer of the court manning each slab. The Doctor and the Westons were the first ones out of the room, the Doctor speaking with some feeling to the still pale Clara; but as he passed by the rest of us, he managed a small, sure nod, saying in no uncertain terms that they'd gotten the indictment. There was a quick moment of mutual congratulation among the rest of us, but it was cut short by the sight of the Weston family coming out of the hearing room: old Josiah looked like he'd been through a battle, and his wife, Ruth, was very pale and wan—in fact, she would've collapsed to the floor, I think, if Peter and Kate hadn't been holding her up by the arms. As they passed by, any joy we felt was doused by the cold realization both of what had just happened and what remained to be done—and of how much danger they all might be in once Libby Hatch was brought back to Ballston Spa.

The members of the grand jury stayed milling around inside the hearing room, as if they were afraid to come out; and when Mr. Picton eventually emerged with Sheriff Dunning, the lawman looked so rattled and confused that it was easy to tell that the town of Ballston Spa, which had spent the morning being so confused and hostile, was about to get a shake-up what would magnify those feelings many times over. Mr. Picton had his pipe out, and he was sticking it in the sheriff's face like a pistol as he lectured him:

". . . and I *mean* it, Dunning—whatever your personal opinions about this matter, due process has been served, and I expect you and every other officer of the court and the law in this county to respect and uphold the grand jury's findings. That *includes* extending your protection to whatever persons my office may choose to work with, as well as anyone else I think may need it. District Attorney Pearson will be absent for the duration of this affair, so I'll be in charge. I hope I'm not the only one who realizes that—and I hope I make myself clear."

The sheriff held up a hand. "Mr. Picton, sir, you can spare the effort. I'll admit, I wasn't in favor of this investigation, nor of this hearing, before today—but after what I seen and heard in there . . ." The man's suncreased eyes wandered to Clara Hatch; and it seemed to me like maybe a tear or two might come out of them. "Well, sir," he went on, stroking his big gray mustache, "I'm man enough to admit when I've been wrong. And I've been wrong about this one." He turned the tough eyes to Mr. Picton again. "We'll get the woman up here, sir, provided the New York cops give us a hand. and all I can say concerning what comes after that is"—Sheriff Dunning held out a hand—"I hope the Lord stays with you, Mr. Picton. Because you're doing his work."

Mr. Picton, who might've been expected to at least show *some* gratitude or emotion in response to this pretty earnest eating of crow, just shook the sheriff's hand quickly and nodded, making it clear that praise and damnation from such people were all one and the same to him. "Well, the Lord's work right now involves me talking to that crowd outside," he said with a flick of his head. "So if you and your deputies will just clear me a spot on the steps . . ."

"Yes, sir," the sheriff answered quickly. "Right away. Abe! Gully! Let's go, boys!"

The three men moved toward the front door, what was still tightly closed, while the rest of us fell in behind them. A strange kind of thrill—exciting, but frightening and maybe a little sad, at the same time—was beginning to course through me, and I think that all the other members of our team felt the same way. As for the Weston family, the only parts of said emotion they shared were the fear and the sadness, that much was pretty obvious: they clustered around Clara like a human wall, as if they thought someone might try to snatch her right out of their midst. Given the mood outside the courthouse, such didn't seem an unreasonable attitude, either.

As the door cracked open, the same angry mumbling what we'd left outside two and a half hours ago started up again, and Sheriff Dunning and his boys had to do a little coaxing—and finally some straight-out pushing and shoving—to clear a little place at the top of the steps for Mr. Picton. Stepping out and putting a match to his pipe, Mr. Picton looked out over the bobbing, grousing heads with an expression of what you might call extreme disdain. After he'd let them shout at him for two or three minutes, he held his hands up.

"All right, all right, get yourselves under some kind of control, now, if that's possible!" he shouted. "Neither the sheriff nor I have any desire to declare this an illegal assembly, but I've got to ask that you listen to what I have to say *very carefully*!" The general level of noise died down, and then Mr. Picton scanned the faces in front of him more closely. "Is Mr. Grose still here?"

"I am!" came the voice of the newspaper editor in return. He moved up to the front of the crowd. "Though I'm not too happy about standing in the midday July sun for hours on end, sir, I will say!"

"Quite understandable," Mr. Picton answered. "But the wages of rabble-rousing have never been just, have they, Mr. Grose? At any rate, I'd like you to get the following details straight, so I don't have to repeat them endlessly during the coming weeks. The grand jury has met, and it has made its decision—and we all owe that decision our respect."

"Indeed we do!" Mr. Grose said, looking around with a smile. "I hope *you're* prepared to respect it, Mr. Picton!"

"Oh, I am, Mr. Grose," Mr. Picton answered, delighted to discover that the editor was assuming that the state'd lost its bid. "I am. At this moment an indictment is being prepared against Mrs. Elspeth Hunter of New York City, formerly Mrs. Elspeth Hatch of Ballston Spa, formerly Miss Elspeth Fraser of Stillwater, New York. She is charged with the first-degree murder of Thomas Hatch and Matthew Hatch, as well as the attempted murder of Clara Hatch. All on the night of the thirty-first of May, 1894."

I'll admit that I'd thought the crowd might break out into a good old-fashioned riot at this news. So I was surprised—as was Mr. Picton, from the look of him—when the sounds what came out of those citizens were ones of hushed horror, as if some ghost had just wandered across their collective path.

"What—what are you saying?" Mr. Grose asked. Then he looked to Sheriff Dunning. "Phil, does he mean—?"

The sheriff just gave Mr. Grose a long and serious stare. "I'd let him finish, if I were you, Horace."

As the crowd quieted, Mr. Picton—no longer quite so testy as he'd been—finished his statement: "We have physical evidence that will demonstrate the woman's guilt, we have a powerful motive that will be supported by witnesses, and we have an eyewitness to the shooting. This office would not take action on a matter like this with anything less."

Mr. Picton paused, still looking like he expected some kind of an outburst from the crowd; but all he got was a sudden cry of "Jesus H. Christ!" from one man at the back of the herd, who immediately turned and started running down toward the trolley station. As he went, I caught enough of a glimpse of his face to be able to identify him:

It was the waiter who'd taken care of us at Canfield's Casino. It didn't take a genius to figure out that he'd been sent by his boss to find out the latest developments in the case, so that odds on the trial could be posted at the Casino for those of Mr. Canfield's clients who didn't get enough satisfaction out of roulette, poker, and faro. But the man obviously hadn't been ready for what he'd heard, and judging by how fast he beat it to the trolley station, I guessed that Saratoga's true gamesmen were going to be able to get some very long odds on a conviction from Mr. Canfield starting that night.

As for the rest of the crowd, they just continued to stand and stare blankly at Mr. Picton, in the same sort of way that people all over town had stared at us when we'd brought Clara to the court house that morning: they were still resentful, all right, but added to the resentment now was the kind of confusion that an angry cow feels when it's been smacked in the forehead with a shovel. It didn't seem like most of them even knew what to do with themselves, until Sheriff Dunning stepped out in front of Mr. Picton.

"That all, sir?" the sheriff asked.

"Yes, Dunning," Mr. Picton answered. "You'd better break them up—there's nothing more to say."

"Nothing more to say?" It was Mr. Grose, his voice now very different than it had been before: the pompous arrogance was all gone. "Picton," he went on quietly, "do you realize what you've *already* said?"

Mr. Picton nodded, very seriously. "Yes. I do, Horace. And I'd be grateful if you'd print it in full in tomorrow's edition." His silver eyes moved out over the crowd as he smoked. "This isn't a matter for sidewalk debate, ladies and gentlemen. The town of Ballston Spa and the county of Saratoga will be forced to search their souls, in the days to come. Let's hope we can live with what we find."

With that Mr. Picton turned and came back inside, while Sheriff Dunning and his men gently started to break the crowd up. Closing the court house door slowly, Mr. Picton then approached the Doctor.

"Well," he said, "as you suspected, Doctor, we'll have no disturbances—yet."

The Doctor nodded. "The sinister phenomena implied by this crime resonate far deeper in the human soul than anyone can immediately grasp. You've been struggling with them for years now, Mr. Picton—the rest of us, for weeks. And the townspeople? Simple anger wasn't to be expected, at this point. Confusion will dominate for a time—perhaps a great deal of time. That will work to our advantage. For there is much to do before our antagonist arrives. And when she does, we may find that popular confusion will give way to something distinctly uglier . . ."

The Doctor led us over to join the Westons, and then we set out as a group—minus only Mr. Picton, who had a lot of paperwork to take care of—to make sure that the family got home safe.

On our drive back to town from the Westons' farm, the Doctor told us about what had happened during the grand jury's proceedings. Though an emotional tale, it wasn't a particularly complicated one: Mr. Picton had carefully laid out most of the physical evidence we'd assembled, and then gone on to paint, with Mrs. Louisa Wright's help, a picture of Libby Hatch as a fortune hunter and a libertine, a willful, wanton character who, if she hadn't been directly responsible for her husband's death, had certainly expected that she was going to profit by it. When it had become clear that her children stood in the way of that profit, Mr. Picton'd stated flatly, Libby had attempted to eliminate them. The Doctor told us that Mr. Picton's language had been so persuasive—and, true to Mr. Moore's prediction, so fast and overwhelming—that it'd seemed like many members of the jury were convinced of his argument even before Clara Hatch had been called to testify. And when the girl *had* taken the stand, Mr. Picton'd asked her only four questions:

"Were you in your family's wagon with your mother and your brothers on the night of May thirty-first, 1894?" The answer had been a not-so-easy "Yes."

"Did you see anyone else during your ride home?" Answer: a firm "No."

"Then you were shot by someone in the wagon?" To this Clara'd just nodded.

"Clara, was that person your mother?" A good minute had gone by before the girl could cope with that one; but steady looks of reassurance from the Doctor, and of love and support from Josiah and Ruth Weston, had given her courage, and finally she'd whispered, "Yes."

No one in the hearing room had made a sound as the girl stepped down. The members of the jury, the Doctor said, had looked just the same as the crowd outside the courthouse had when they'd gotten the news about the indictment: as if they'd all been hit with one enormous brick. Mr. Picton had wrapped up his business pretty quickly after that, and the jury's assent to an indictment on two counts of first-degree murder and one of attempted murder had been very quick.

It wasn't the kind of story what would make anybody overjoyed or triumphant; and to be sure, all of us in the surrey—having seen what the day had done to little Clara—felt a deep sense of regret and sadness as we clattered back to Mr. Picton's house. But underneath said emotions of the moment, for all of us, was something what maybe went even deeper: what you might call an unspoken feeling that we were, as a group, finally on something what my dice-throwing pals downtown would've called "a roll." Our investigation, it appeared, had been transformed into a sort of quiet locomotive—and that locomotive was bearing down unstoppably, it seemed, on the woman who'd been committing so much mayhem for so many years. Evidence and testimony—hard won by hard work—were the ropes we were using to strap the golden-eyed killer onto the tracks. True, our responsibilities to Clara, to the Westons, to little Ana, and to our own safety were considerable—but our responsibility to keeping our engine running was the most important of all. And on that Friday evening, we appeared to have a full head of steam, and the way ahead looked good and clear.

That was before Marcus came back from Chicago.

CHAPTER 41

The Doctor'd been right in supposing that the general state of what he called "moral confusion" what took hold of Ballston Spa during the days after the indictment of Libby Hatch would make our work easier. It wasn't that we were suddenly looked on any kindlier by the townsfolk; it was just that they were too busy trying to make sense of the affair—and its long, horrible history—to pay us much mind. The fact that people like Sheriff Dunning had been so convinced of Libby's guilt by what they'd heard during the grand jury hearing made it impossible for those vexed citizens to just write the upcoming trial off as the work of ungodly troublemakers from New York City; and it was hard for even them what hung on most stubbornly to the tale of the mysterious Negro to get around the fact that an eight-year-old girl who'd suffered years of physical pain and spiritual torment had stood up before a panel of adults and stated flat out that it'd been her own mother who'd in fact been the agent of it all.

Libby Hatch—or, as she was labeled in the grand jury indictment, Mrs. Elspeth Hunter—was arrested at Number 39 Bethune Street in New York on Tuesday afternoon. Sheriff Dunning had gotten in touch with the New York City police on Friday, and had been referred to the Bureau of Detectives. Together with officers of the Ninth Precinct, the bureau had put Mrs. Hunter under surveillance right away, and reported that she didn't seem to be making any moves toward beating it out of town. (During the time they were watching her, the city cops apparently didn't experience any interference from the Dusters, which we took as a further demonstration that Libby didn't intend to avoid capture.) Sheriff Dunning directed the Ninth's detectives not to make any moves toward actually arresting the woman before his arrival, unless it suddenly started to look like she was going to bolt; then, on Monday, he took the train down to the city with two of his deputies.

This slightly leisurely way of going about capturing a murderess had those of us on the Doctor's team a little confused; but Mr. Picton explained that the longer we delayed Libby Hatch's arrival in Ballston Spa, the longer we could take advantage of the eerie, spooked calm what'd descended on the town. So when he saw Sheriff Dunning and his boys off at the train depot, he didn't urge them to go about their business *too* hastily, an instruction what Dunning took to mean that he and his deputies were free to enjoy a night in the big city before returning home with their prisoner. They were met at Grand Central Terminal by a couple of the detectives from the bureau, who proceeded to take them down to the Ninth Precinct's station house on Charles Street. (Being unaware that any New York City detectives had been involved in Mr. Picton's investigation, Sheriff Dunning spared himself the cold reception he almost definitely would've received if he'd dropped the Isaacsons' names.) Together the lawmen decided to wait until Tuesday morning to actually clap the irons on Mrs. Hunter; and we were left to imagine what the sheriff and his deputies got up to that night, since it would've been tough to come up with anybody better suited to showing them a good time in the big city than the men of the Ninth. The fact that Dunning waited until Tuesday afternoon to pinch Mrs. Hunter seemed proof positive that he and his boys had taken full advantage of the cultural "resources" of New York. But as things worked out, a hangover wouldn't have been much of a disadvantage to them on Tuesday: when they arrived at Bethune Street, they found Mrs. Hunter packed and ready to go—almost, Sheriff Dunning told Mr. Picton when he called from Grand Central Terminal before boarding the train north, like she was anxious for the trial to begin. Dunning went on to report that, barring delays, he and his deputies would be arriving with their prisoner at midnight.

All through that Tuesday, the citizens of Ballston Spa had continued to stew over what Mr. Moore, true to form, insisted on calling the "moral implications" of the case. They had no choice but to stick with that activity on into the evening, as everyone began to anticipate Libby's return in irons; in fact, it was starting to feel like brooding would keep the town occupied indefinitely, or at least until somebody came up with an explanation for the killings what would let their society (which, if it hadn't actually produced Libby Hatch, had certainly believed her lies) off the hook. Of course, if they'd known that one of the only men in the entire country who was capable of coming up with such an explanation was at that point packing his bags in Chicago and getting ready to journey to their town, their mood might've been considerably different.

But, fortunately for us, the only person who was as yet aware of the movements of Mr. Clarence Darrow was Marcus; and late on Tuesday afternoon, he returned from Chicago in advance of the mysterious midwestern lawyer. After exchanging warm greetings with the rest of our group at the depot, Marcus handed me his suitcase (which El Niño immediately grabbed, refusing to allow me to carry it), and then we all started walking up Bath Street toward the court house. We'd been ordered to bring the detective sergeant to said building just as soon as his train got in, being as even though Mr. Picton had many pressing matters to attend to in his office (the trial was slated to open on the following Tuesday, August 3rd), he said there was nothing more important than learning about the background and tactics of the hired legal gun who was being brought in from so far away to face him. I figured that Marcus could've done with a hot bath and a good meal, after his long journey, but orders were orders. Besides, the discoveries that Marcus had made about Mr. Darrow were such that he himself was very anxious to share them with the rest of us. Because of this, the Doctor had cut his day with Clara Hatch short (he was still working with her as hard as ever) and joined us at the train station, ready to give Marcus his own version of the third degree: a version what included a box of the Doctor's best custom-rolled smokes instead of bright lights, and a flask of Mr. Picton's excellent whiskey in place of brass knuckles.

Once settled into the big old leather chair in Mr. Picton's office, whiskey in one hand and a cigarette in the other, Marcus began his report.

"The vital statistics were easy enough to lay hands on, or at least most of them were," he said, taking a drink from the flask, setting it aside, and pulling out a small notebook. "He's either thirty-nine or forty—I couldn't get the exact date of birth. Parents: a Unitarian minister who gave up the pulpit to become a furniture maker and a New England suffragist. He seems to take after the father, for the most part—the old man never lost the crusading spirit. Darrow himself has had a lifelong fascination with Darwin, Spencer, Thomas Huxley—considers himself quite a rationalist. Oh, and he knows about your work, too, Dr. Kreizler."

"Does he?" the Doctor asked, surprised. "And how did you find that out?"

"I asked him," Marcus answered simply. "Got in to see him yesterday evening—told him I was a publisher from New York who wanted him to defend an anarchist who's up for building bombs in New York. The last part of the story's true, too—you remember Jochen Dietrich, Lucius? That idiot downtown who kept blowing up tenements because he couldn't get his timing devices to work?"

"Oh, yes," Lucius said, recalling the name. "The Seventh Precinct boys picked him up just before we left town, didn't they?"

"That's right," Marcus answered, slowly running one of his big hands through his thick black hair and then rubbing his tired brown eyes. "Anyway, one of the Chicago cops I talked to said that Darrow's got a soft spot for anarchists—fancies himself to be a bit of one, intellectually. So he agreed to see me." Marcus shook his head and took a big drag off of his cigarette. "He's a strange sort of character—not at all what you'd expect from a man who's made a pretty decent living off the corporate payroll. He seems to have a careless attitude toward his appearance—clothes are slightly rumpled, hair's cut rough and hangs in his face. But there's something very self-conscious about it all—calculated, even. It's like he's *trying* to play the homespun hero, the plain prairie lawyer. His style of speaking's the same: he's got the outward manner of the lonely cynic, but he makes sure you can hear the heart of an idealistic romantic, too. Just how much of it's genuine, or which parts, I certainly couldn't tell you." Marcus flipped a page in his notebook. "There's some other minor details: he's a baseball fanatic and an agnostic—"

"Well, of course he's an agnostic," Mr. Picton said. "He's a defense lawyer. There's only room for one supreme savior in this world, and defense lawyers like to play that role themselves."

"Now, now, Rupert," Mr. Moore scolded, "don't be bitter."

"He likes Russian literature—poetry and philosophy, too," Marcus went on. "He has a sort of salon of like-minded souls out there—reads aloud to them at their little gatherings. All in all, a very theatrical and very manipulative character, for all his talk about social justice. Even his own people say so. I talked to a woman who's a partner in his firm—"

"He's got a *woman* in his firm?" Miss Howard said. "An actual *partner?*"

"That's right," Marcus answered.

"Just to show off to his suffragist friends?" Miss Howard continued. "Or does she actually do something?"

"Actually, that's the interesting part," Marcus answered. "He's not much of an advocate of women's rights himself—doesn't really consider them an 'oppressed' part of society. Not like, say, labor men or blacks."

"Well," the Doctor said, "perhaps we'll be spared the usual lectures on maternal sanctity, then."

"Oh, I think we will," Marcus replied quickly. "But I think what he'll come at us with instead will be more dangerous—much more dangerous." Taking a pull off the flask, Marcus hissed and turned to our host. "Mr. Picton, how much of a history were you able to compile on Darrow?"

"I found a piece on the Debs trial," Mr. Picton answered with a shrug. "It mentioned his background with the railway, but there wasn't much more than that."

"Nothing on the Prendergast case?" Marcus asked.

"The Prendergast case?" Mr. Picton said, sitting bolt upright. "Great jumping cats, was he involved in *that*?"

"I'm afraid so," Marcus answered. "Heavily involved."

"Well, well, well," Mr. Picton said. "I assume you remember the affair, Doctor."

The Doctor was already nodding gloomily. "Indeed. A more ludicrous example of perverting justice to please the public has rarely been seen."

Marcus laughed a bit. "Oddly enough, Doctor, that's exactly how Darrow saw it."

Mr. Moore was trying hard to catch up, knocking a fist against his head. "Prendergast, Prendergast . . ." His face lit up. "Not the fellow who shot the mayor of Chicago?"

"The same," Marcus answered. "On the last day of the Exposition of 1893—the first assassination in the city's history. Eugene Patrick Prendergast turned himself in, along with a four-dollar revolver, and claimed that he'd killed Mayor Carter Harrison because his honor hadn't lived up to a pledge to put Prendergast in charge of building the city's new elevated track lines. The claim was a fantasy, of course, and the man was obviously a lunatic. But, well, Harrison *had* been shot at the Exposition, which made for some *very* bad international press—"

"And so the state of Illinois," the Doctor continued bitterly, looking at those of us what didn't already know the story, "decided to entrust the assessment of his sanity to the chief *physician* of the Cook County Jail—a man with no special training in mental pathologies. Yet even this hand-picked flunky had absolutely no trouble declaring that Prendergast was a raging psychotic."

"Not that it mattered," Mr. Picton finished. "Prendergast was quickly declared sane by a jury. He was sentenced to hang—and he *did* hang, didn't he, Detective?"

"There's more to the story than that," Marcus answered. "After the conclusion of the first trial, Darrow—whose personal opposition to the death penalty has always been almost fanatical—offered to help Prendergast's lawyer try to get a new sanity hearing. This second proceeding began on January twentieth of '94, and it was very revealing, especially for our purposes." Flipping further through his notes, Marcus took another pull from the flask. "Darrow took the lead in arguing the defense's case. And his tactics, according to several people who witnessed them, represented a whole new kind of lawyering. From the start, he shifted the focus *off* of Prendergast, and *onto* the jury: he told them that the prosecution was asking them to violate their sacred oath to weigh the case on its merits in order to satisfy society's desire for revenge. Now, word had gotten around that Darrow was an expert at manipulating juries, so this group was at least somewhat ready for him. But it turned out that he *knew* they'd been prepared, and instead of crying foul he used that fact to his advantage. In his opening remarks he addressed the rumors that he was going to try to bamboozle them with a lot of technicalities and theatrics. He solemnly pledged that he wouldn't, because if he tried such trickery and failed, he said, the responsibility—and that's a key ploy in Darrow's arguments, *responsibility*—for Prendergast's death would rest with him. And he refused, he said, in his plainspoken, humble way, to assume such a moral burden. So he promised that he'd be perfectly straightforward in his arguments—and if the jury decided that his honest attempts weren't good enough, the responsibility for sending a lunatic to his death would rest with them—not him."

"Clever," Mr. Picton said, smiling slowly. "Very clever . . ."

"And complete nonsense, of course," Marcus added. "I mean, in reality he used every trick he could think of, during the trial. He wept—actually *wept*—over the dead mayor, and the cruelty of a world that could produce a creature like Prendergast, and he *begged* the jury to let their humanity prevail. And most importantly, so far as we're concerned, he went after the prosecution team *personally.* He turned what was supposed to be the trial of an assassin into an eloquent, sarcastic—the man has wit, there's no doubting that—and relentless examination of the motives of the state and its men in prosecuting lunatics, even murderous lunatics. Any unlucky soul the prosecutors called as a witness was badgered and tainted with whatever kind of suspicion Darrow could dream up, so that the questioning became about them and their beliefs, not about Prendergast. By arguing constantly in the negative, instead of advocating his client's cause, he turned the whole trial topsy-turvy."

I turned to look at the Doctor, who was staring at the floor and pulling at the patch of hair under his lower lip. "But it didn't work," he said.

"No, not in the end," Marcus answered. "The jury withstood the pressure, and upheld the earlier sanity verdict. But the important thing is that he made a close race out of what looked like it was going to be the pure and simple railroading of a lunatic."

The Doctor sat back and sighed. "Unfortunate methods," he judged quietly. "But I can't say that I disapprove of his goal."

"Maybe not in that case," Marcus said. "But if I'm right about what he'll try to do *here,* you may feel differently, Doctor."

"Yes," the Doctor answered with a small smile, "I suspect you're right, Marcus."

"I don't understand," Lucius said. "What can he try to do here? I mean, he can certainly find forensics experts who'll argue our findings, and maybe even personal acquaintances of Mrs. Hatch's who'll disagree with our interpretation of her motives. But what about Clara? How can he argue with an eyewitness?"

"By attacking the man who's *behind* the eyewitness," Marcus said, still looking to the Doctor. "Or at least, the man he'll *paint* as being behind her."

"Yes," Mr. Picton said, "I begin to get your point, Detective. And we can't depend on Clara's testimony alone to fend off such an attack. Young children—especially if they're as fragile as Clara—are not the most reliable witnesses. They're too easy to bully or cajole. That's why it's been so important that the Doctor continue working with Clara—so that she can learn to provide *detailed* explanations of her story that won't fall to pieces the first time the defense goes after her."

"The point is," Marcus continued, "our roles will, in a very strange but potentially damaging way, be reversed in this trial: Darrow will be arguing the *negative,* knowing that no one wants to believe what we're saying about Libby Hatch, and it will be up to us to *advocate* our cause. As you've surmised, Doctor, the man's not going to come in with a lot of pious arguments about the sanctity of womanhood and maternity—he's going to attack, not defend, and try to get us back on our heels before we know what's happening. And the logical place to start any attack is at the weak point—which, in the public mind, I'm afraid, is—"

"Me," the Doctor finished for him.

Refilling his pipe from a pouch in his pocket, Mr. Picton struck a match on his chair as the rest of us pondered that. "So!" he said, firing up his pipe and showing that enthusiasm in the face of trouble what was his best quality. "The question becomes, how do we defend against such a line of attack, and thereby preserve the integrity of Clara's testimony?" Drawing hard on his pipe, Mr. Picton considered the matter for a moment. "I had hoped, as you know, to keep any discussion of psychological theory to a minimum in this case, Doctor. But if Darrow attacks with it, you must be prepared to strike back. In kind, and with the superior force which you, as an expert, possess!"

The Doctor stood up, pacing slowly in what little free floor space the room offered. "It is not a position with which I am unfamiliar," he said, rubbing his bad arm. "Though I confess that I hoped taking this case would mean that for once I'd be on the offensive. Perhaps that is destined never to happen."

"Oh, but it *must* happen!" Mr. Picton bellowed, gripping his pipe and swinging it through the air. "That's just what I mean about you 'striking back.' I don't want you to *defend* yourself from behind an intellectual barricade—I want to see you *counterattack,* on the open field of ideas, where the jury can see you! Draw blood from this man—*first* blood, if you can! To back you up, I'll go over every shred of personal information about Darrow that Marcus has been able to assemble—and I won't hesitate to use it. We are *not* going to let this trial get away from us." Mr. Picton banged a fist on his desk, hard. "Darrow may represent some new breed of lawyer, but dammit all, we'll match him trick for trick!"

"Señor Doctor?" El Niño, who'd been sitting cross-legged on the floor, got up to approach the Doctor with cautious respect. "This man—he is dangerous to you? You wish El Niño to kill him?"

The statement, coming at the somewhat difficult moment it did, served admirably to break the thickening ice: after staring at the aborigine in amazement for a few seconds, we all began to laugh out loud, and the Doctor put his right arm around his small defender's shoulders.

"No, El Niño," he said. "The man is not a danger in that way. He does not intend to injure me—physically."

"But if he is to interfere with finding baby Ana," El Niño said, smiling at our laughter without really knowing what it was about, "then we should kill him, yes?"

"I think," Miss Howard said, getting up and moving over to the Doctor and the aborigine, "that this may be the moment to call a break for dinner. Let's go, El Niño. On the way home I'll try to explain to you why killing this man is *not* the best way to deal with the situation." As she guided El Nino to the door, Miss Howard cocked her head. "Assuming, of course, that it really isn't."

As the Isaacsons followed the other two out of the office, Mr. Moore, Cyrus, and I went up to the Doctor. "You going to be all right with all this, Laszlo?" Mr. Moore said.

"It's not myself I'm worried about," the Doctor answered. "It's Clara. This trial was already going to be excruciating for her—but now, to be targeted by a lawyer who uses the kind of tactics Marcus has told us about . . . Still," he went on, throwing his hands up with a sigh. "I suppose I'll just have to make that much more certain that I prepare her adequately. As long as she doesn't encounter her mother before giving testimony, I think she'll have a fighting chance at coming through it well—or at least intact."

"What about it, Rupert?" Mr. Moore said to Mr. Picton, who was stuffing a batch of files into a soft leather briefcase to take home with him. "Is Judge Brown the type we can count on to post a reasonably high bail, in a case like this?"

"I hate to try to predict anything about Judge Brown," Mr. Picton answered. "But the brilliant Mr. Darrow is not yet here, and apparently *someone* has retained Irving W. Maxon to be Libby's local counsel. Maxon's quite good, and has a lot of connections down in the city, but I don't think he'll be able to win an argument for moderate bail on his own. Remember, though: if Vanderbilt *is* secretly bankrolling this thing, we can't safely assume that *any* bail, however high, would be prohibitive. I'll have to go for an out-and-out denial, and that's never a certainty. And then there's the question of the arraignment and the plea tomorrow."

"What about them, sir?" Cyrus asked, puzzled.

"Well, Cyrus," Mr. Picton answered, fastening his case and then looking up. "If Darrow *should* get here before the arraignment, there's always the possibility that he'll try to balance his personal books by entering another insanity plea—redress the wrong of the Prendergast case by getting Libby Hatch freed on the basis of mental incompetence, that sort of thing. Lawyers carry grudges like everyone else—maybe even more. I'm not worried about *my* end of the matter, so far as that goes—I have enough motives and scheming on Libby's part to demonstrate cold premeditation. But it's another area where he might go after *you,* Doctor. Can you successfully argue that a woman who has killed her own children can nonetheless be mentally sound?"

The Doctor breathed deeply. "I should feel more confident, of course, if we'd discovered more details of her youth—on a hypothetical basis, it becomes much harder. Still, there are precedents—and as you say, Mr. Picton, the presence of cold, even clever, premeditation eliminates the possibility of any clearly demonstrable mental pathology, such as *dementia praecox,* or of any sufficiently severe brain trauma. To argue that she was mad, Darrow would have to return to the idea of 'moral insanity'—the notion that a person can be morally but not intellectually deranged. It's a concept that has been almost universally repudiated. Then, too, there's always the chance that our diligent workers"—here he gave my hair a tousle—"will manage to find out more about the woman's past before the trial begins."

"Well, then!" Mr. Picton said, snatching up his briefcase. "We have cause for cautious optimism. Particularly, I will say, when you consider our position at the moment: the woman's in custody, she's on her way here, and she's going to stand trial. I confess that I wasn't at all sure we'd ever get this far! So let's not sink into pessimism—it's bad for the appetite, and Mrs. Hastings will have been cooking all afternoon. Mustn't disappoint her!"

With our host continuing to encourage us, we wandered out into the hallway, there joining the others for the walk down the marble stairs to the first floor of the court house. Mr. Picton paused to make sure that the guard Henry had prepared one of the cells in the basement: Libby Hatch would be spending at least one night in jail, since her arraignment wasn't scheduled to take place 'til the next day. The guard said that yes, one of the cells was ready, and then we all began to file outside for the walk down High Street.

Just before passing through the front door, I stopped and looked around at the big stone chamber, what was lit up by the soft, straw-colored light of a July evening.

"What is it, Stevie?" Mr. Picton said, noticing me pause.

I shrugged. "Last time we'll see it this quiet for a while, I guess," I said. "Gonna be a lot of action after tomorrow."

"And, provided we can get bail denied," Mr. Picton answered with a nod, "there'll be a new tenant—for the next couple of weeks, at any rate. Henry won't like that. None of the guards will, eh, Henry?" Mr. Picton smiled as he taunted the man. "You boys'll actually have something to do for a change!"

Chuckling to himself, Mr. Picton clamped his pipe in his mouth and headed outside; and just as I followed, I saw a gleam of resentment enter the guard's eyes.

We all talked and laughed a lot at dinner, though not much was said about the case. It was as if, knowing what was scheduled to happen later that night, we didn't want to put a hex on things by acting as if Libby Hatch was already safely arrived and locked up in her cell. Mr. Moore went into a bit of a fit halfway through the meal when he realized the date: July 27th, which meant that he'd missed the opening day of the season at the Saratoga Racing Association. In an attempt to make him feel better, Miss Howard suggested a game of poker after dinner. This seemed to fill the bill not only for the purposes of getting Mr. Moore to stop whining, but also for taking our minds off of more pressing concerns.

Heading into the reception room after we'd laid waste to one of Mrs. Hastings's excellent pies, everyone except Cyrus and Lucius gathered around the card table. The younger Isaacson brother was too nervous to sit still for cards, while Cyrus preferred to pass the time playing Mr. Picton's piano. The rest of us, though, threw ourselves into our small-stakes gambling with genuine enthusiasm. The contest grew pretty heated as the evening wore on, and it wasn't until Mrs. Hastings came down from her room to tell us that we needed to get going if we wanted to be sure of meeting the midnight train that we realized how late it'd gotten. When we did, I think everybody's heart did a kind of fluttering jig; at least, there was a lot of pointless running around what preceded our actually getting out the door, the kind of activity that generally marks people who've reached some long-dreamed-of but still, in a way, unexpected point.

Our walk down to the depot was quiet enough, but I marked that there were a lot of faces at a lot of dimly lit windows watching as we passed, a very unusual state of affairs in a town that, as I've said, generally bedded down early. It wasn't hard to explain the unusual behavior: the feeling that the whole community was on the eve of something that might change the way they thought about a lot of things—not least themselves—was thicker than it had been at any point during the previous five days; thicker, even, than when Mr. Picton had announced the indictment; and when we first heard the distant whistle of the midnight train echoing up from many miles to the southeast, I was sure that we couldn't have been the only people in town who felt our bodies shiver mightily.

There were only a few other people on the train platform when we got there: the guard Henry, who'd been told by Sheriff Dunning to meet the train, along with Mr. Grose of the *Ballston Weekly Journal* and a couple of his employees. As for the mayor of the town, he'd been on vacation since before we came to the place, and after hearing about the indictment, he'd decided to extend his holiday: like District Attorney Pearson, he figured there was no political gain to be had from this case, only damage, and maybe considerable damage. Mr. Grose didn't say much to any of our party, and Mr. Picton didn't offer him anything fresh for his newspaper. Not that Mr. Grose would've printed such; in fact, I think he was just there on the off-chance that Dunning would show up empty-handed, or that a calamity of some kind might take place at the depot. My bet was that if everything went smoothly, the evening's activities wouldn't get more than a few lines in the following Saturday's edition of the weekly paper.

Midnight came and went, causing Mr. Picton to remark that he hoped the Spanish government and people were even worse at keeping to timetables than Americans were, if our country really intended to go to war with Madrid. Finally, at about 12:15, the train's whistle sounded again, much closer this time. El Niño hopped down and did the old Indian trick of putting his ear to the tracks, then nodded eagerly as he rejoined us on the platform. The actual noise of the train's engine reached our ears just as a light flashed through a break in the buildings beyond the depot; and in a few more seconds the steaming locomotive and its four nearly empty cars stormed in, causing us all to take a few steps back toward the station.

Sheriff Dunning was the first man off the forward car, and even in the near darkness his face looked plainly exhausted. One of his deputies followed, and then there was a long pause. Finally, *she* appeared.

The very shapely body was draped in a fine black silk dress, a stiff crinoline undergarment keeping the skirt in perfect order. The hands were cuffed together with old-style manacles. A small hat with a jet-black rooster feather sat forward on the head, holding a black veil in place; but the weave of the veil was an open one, and the golden eyes were plainly visible as they caught the light of the gas lantern on the platform and threw it back in our faces.

"*Well,*" Libby Hatch said, just the same way she had the first time we'd ever heard her speak: in a tone what was open to a half-dozen interpretations, and what made me think of Miss Howard's words about Libby's personality being broken into pieces. Then, seeing past us to Mr. Grose and the others, Libby put on a more melancholy air. "Mr. Picton," she said, slowly coming down the steps of the car and getting a hand from Sheriff Dunning, "I never expected to see you again—certainly not under such circumstances as these."

"Really?" Mr. Picton said quietly, not able to keep a small grin off his face. "How odd—since I always suspected we might meet again, and under *precisely* these circumstances."

The golden eyes flashed on the rest of us with a quick glare of hate, and then softened as they came to rest on Mr. Grose. "Is that you, Mr. Grose?"

"Yes, Mrs. Hatch," the man answered, a little surprised. "You remember me?"

"We only met once or twice," Libby answered with a gentle little nod. "But of course I remember." Golden tears began to well up under the veil. "How is my baby—my Clara? They tell me she can finally speak again. But I can't believe that she'd—that she'd—" Her shoulders began to heave, and the sound of gentle sobbing escaped her tightly pursed mouth.

Mr. Grose, who looked very confused but very emotional, too, was about to answer, but the Doctor stepped between them quickly. "Mr. Picton," he said, quietly but firmly, "may I suggest . . ."

"Of course," Mr. Picton answered, getting the point right away. "Dunning, you and I will take Mrs. *Hunter*, as she is now known, to the court house. There's a cell waiting. You brought a rig, Henry?"

The guard, who also seemed moved by what he'd seen, stepped forward. "Yes, sir," he said.

"Then we'll be on our way, madam," Mr. Picton finished, indicating the station yard. "If you wish to speak to the press, or they to you, requests can be submitted to my office."

Sheriff Dunning got behind the woman. "Come along, ma'am," he said. "Best to do what Mr. Picton says."

Libby Hatch kept sobbing for a few more seconds; but when she saw that it wasn't going to buy her anything, she turned on the Doctor, the sadness disappearing with frightening speed. "This is *your* doing, Doctor. Don't think I don't know that. But I don't care *what* you've said to my daughter or made her believe—once she sees me, she'll know what to do. I'm her *mother*." Mr. Picton took a firm hold of Libby's right arm, and indicated to Sheriff Dunning that he should do the same on her left: together, they got her moving. "Do you hear, me, Doctor?" she called over her shoulder. "I'm her *mother!* I know that doesn't mean anything to you, but it will to her—and to *anyone* with a heart! Whatever else you may have done, you can't change that!" Sobbing again, the woman passed out into the yard with her escort, the deputies and the courthouse guard following behind.

The rest of us wandered out to watch them all get aboard a big, plain wagon with three bench seats what was drawn by two horses. With its lone female occupant still in tears, the rig rolled away; and as it did, Mr. Grose turned to give the Doctor a silent scowl. Then he nodded to his people, and turned to silently march off toward the low end of Bath Street, where the offices of the *Journal* were located.

"Well, Kreizler," Mr. Moore said, as we stood there in the silent yard. "I guess that's really the question, isn't it?"

The Doctor turned to him, his mind very far away. "The question?" he asked softly.

"She's Clara's mother," Mr. Moore said, with a grim but curious look on his face. "*Can* you change that?"

The Doctor just shook his head, his eyes going wide. "No. But we may, perhaps, be able to change what that *means*."

CHAPTER 42

The arraignment was set for ten o'clock the next morning, and by fifteen minutes to the hour we were all gathered in the main courtroom.
Mr. Picton was seated at one long table on the right side of the big chamber, beyond a low, carved oak railing what separated the gallery from the
officers of the court. At a similar job on the left-hand side of the room
were Libby Hatch and a well-dressed, dark-haired man who wore gold-
rimmed pince-nez perched on top of his long, thin nose. No fancy glasses
or expensive suit, though, could keep a look of genuine uncertainty out of
Irving W. Maxon's eyes: he kept glancing around the room like a nervous
bird, as if he wasn't sure how he'd landed in his current predicament or
just what he was supposed to do about it. Libby Hatch, on the other
hand—still wearing her black silk dress, but not the hat or veil—was a picture of confidence, staring at the high fruitwood bench in front of her
with a face what seemed forever on the verge of breaking into the coquettish smile it so often displayed.

As for Mr. Picton, he had his watch open on the table in front of him
and was staring at it, more calm than he'd been at any time since we'd met
him.

The Doctor, Mr. Moore, the detective sergeants, and Miss Howard
were all sitting in the first row of gallery chairs behind Mr. Picton's table
and the wooden railing; Cyrus, El Niño, and I were right behind them.
We'd gotten the aborigine scrubbed down pretty good for the event, and
the combination of his cleanliness and my evening clothes made him one
of the most presentable people in the galleries, which since nine o'clock

had been crammed full of a ragtag collection of townspeople, along with some sharper-looking visitors who'd come down from Saratoga. Sheriff Dunning was sitting at a small table just to the right of Mr. Picton, and beyond him, against the right-hand wall, was the jury box, its twelve seats empty. There was a guard standing on the other side of the room, and in front of him was the court stenographer, a proper-looking lady who went by the peculiar name of Iphegeneia Blaylock. The bailiff's desk in front of the bench was empty, and on either side of the bench itself were two iron lamp fixtures and a like number of flags, one the American, the other the state banner of New York. Back by the front door, keeping a careful eye on who came into and out of the place and how they behaved, were the guard Henry and a slightly shorter (but, to judge by the look of him, no less powerful) uniformed man.

It was a strange experience for me, to be observing all the details of the situation from someplace other than the defendant's chair; but the strangeness soon gave way to a feeling of relief and even excitement, as I realized that this was the place where all our recent labors would reach some kind of a conclusion in the days to come. It was like standing under the wire at the track and waiting for the horses to get out of the starter's gate: I found myself tapping and banging my feet and hands and wishing the thing would just *start*. To judge by the noises around me, I wasn't alone in said feeling, either: the talking, mumbling, and skittish laughing in the courtroom rose as every second of waiting went by, until by three minutes to ten I found I almost had to yell to make myself heard by Mr. Moore.

"*What?*" he called back to me, touching his ear.

"I *said*, have you heard anything from Canfield's about the *odds?*" I shouted back.

He nodded. "Fifty to one—and I'm sure it'd be higher if someone other than Rupert were arguing the state's case!"

I whistled, glancing at the floor; then, as an idea hit me, I looked back up. "You don't suppose we could get any bets down through a third party, do you?"

Mr. Moore smiled but shook his head. "I already thought of that, but I promised Rupert we wouldn't! He's superstitious—thinks it'll put the Jonah on his chances!"

I smiled back and nodded: any gambling soul would've understood exactly how Mr. Picton felt.

Just then a door in the back wall of the big room opened and the bailiff walked in, looking like he was ready to take on any and every person in the room what might have thoughts about trying to turn his court into a circus. He was another big fellow, was Jack Coffey, with the kind of steely eyes what you might've expected to find in a frontier barroom instead of an eastern court house; but when I caught sight of Judge Brown, I began to understand why he'd retained the services of such a beefy bailiff. So small he almost disappeared behind the bench as he walked up the little flight of stairs to take his seat behind it, Charles H. Brown had big ears what stuck out like a monkey's, a short but full dusting of pure white hair over his head, and plenty of wrinkles in his aged clean-shaven face. But his eyes matched the bailiff's in their determination and their open warning that he would put up with absolutely no nonsense, while the firm set of his thin, wrinkled lips and square jaw told of just how much justice he'd dealt out, over his years.

I was even more glad, looking at him, that it wasn't me sitting in Libby Hatch's chair.

"All rise!" boomed Bailiff Coffey from deep in his barrel chest, bringing everyone to their feet and instant silence to the room; and as he went on to announce the exact number of that session of the court, he kept glancing up at the crowd, still looking for some wise mug what might think he wasn't in the presence of the full power of the state of New York. Holding a clipboard up in front of him, Coffey next announced the first order of business for that day: "The People of Saratoga County versus Mrs. Elspeth Hunter of New York City, formerly Mrs. Elspeth Hatch of Ballston Spa, formerly Miss Elspeth Fraser of Stillwater—on the charge that she did, on or about the thirty-first day of May, eighteen hundred and ninety-four, willfully and with premeditation murder Thomas Hatch, three years old, and Matthew Hatch, four years old, and that at the same time she did willfully and with premeditation attempt to murder Clara Hatch, five years old, all in the township of Ballston Spa."

The charge sent a ripple of mumbling through the room, one what Judge Brown brought to an end with a sudden, savage rap of his gavel. From his cushioned leather chair—which, high as it was, still only raised him clear of the bench from the chest up—Judge Brown scowled around the courtroom.

"The court," he eventually said, in a tough, gravelly voice, "would like to make it clear from the start that it is aware of the amount of interest the public takes in this case. But the court has never allowed public interest to interfere with the pursuit of justice, and it is not about to start at this late date. I would therefore remind those of you in the galleries that you are the guests of this court, and warn you that if you behave as anything else you will feel the court's boot in your collective backside." There were a lot of smiles at that, but only one man at the back of the room actually threw out a laugh—and he soon regretted taking the liberty. Judge Brown's eyes fixed on the fellow quicker than spit, as his wrinkled, thin hand brought the gavel up and pointed it. "Remove that individual," the judge said, "and make certain he does not again attend these proceedings."

The guard Henry grabbed the man by the collar and, before the stunned victim had a chance to protest, got him out through the big mahogany doors.

"Now, then," the judge went on, looking around to be sure he'd made his point. "Is the accused present?"

"She is, Your Honor," replied Irving W. Maxon, his voice a little shaky.

"You have heard the state's charge," the judge went on, looking to Libby Hatch. "How do you plead?"

"If it please the court," Mr. Maxon answered, before Libby could say anything. "We beg a few moments' indulgence, as we are awaiting—"

Judge Brown cut him off with a big, loud sigh, one what turned into a groan as he rubbed a hand over the short white hairs on his head. "We are all of us awaiting *something*, counselor. I myself have spent my *life* awaiting a trial that is free of unnecessary delays." The old eyes bore in on Mr. Maxon. "I am *still* awaiting."

"Yes, Your Honor," Mr. Maxon replied, his nervousness growing under the ancient stare what showered down from the bench. "If you'll only allow me to explain—"

Just then the gentle clap of the mahogany doors closing was heard, and Mr. Maxon turned along with the rest of us to get a look at the newcomer who'd produced the sound:

Even from a distance, I could tell that it had to be Clarence Darrow, being as he so completely matched Marcus's description of the man. Unlike lawyer Maxon, Mr. Darrow's clothes were of an ordinary variety—just a plain, light brown suit and white shirt, with a simple tie knotted carelessly at the neck—and they looked as if he'd slept in them on the train. Though not as thoroughly sloppy as it would one day become (Mr. Darrow had only begun to establish a disheveled appearance as one of his trademarks), this look was still very different from that of the other officers of the court, as was his way of walking: slow and stooped over, a kind of loping movement what was especially noticeable given his considerable size. His hair, as Marcus had told us, was uncombed, and a lock of it hung over his forehead. The face wasn't as wrinkled, naturally, as it would become during his years of greater fame, but it was still weathered and rugged; and the eyes had the same light color and sad, searching expression that would also become so legendary in the future. The soft mouth was pursed in a way what matched a pair of big circles under the eyes: a way what seemed to speak about the high price of wisdom bought by too much exposure to man's inhumanity to his fellow man. As he moved down the center aisle, Mr. Darrow took in the crowd with a steady, strong gaze what was different from Judge Brown's, but produced just as much of an effect: by the time he'd reached the railing, every eye in the place was locked on him.

It was a performance, of course; but I'd been in a lot of courtrooms, and it was one of the best I'd ever seen—good enough to let me know right away that we were in more trouble than we'd figured on being.

Clutching an old, beaten-up briefcase, Mr. Darrow signaled to Mr. Maxon, who said, "If the court will excuse me for one moment," and rushed over. Judge Brown didn't look happy about that, but he sat back with another sigh and waited as Mr. Maxon opened the railing of the gate and let Mr. Darrow over into the business side of the room, where he quickly shook hands with Libby Hatch.

"If it please the court," Mr. Maxon said, smiling now. "I—"

"It does *not* please the court, counselor," Judge Brown said, sitting forward again. "Just what are you about, sir?"

"Your Honor," Mr. Maxon went on quickly, "I should like to introduce Mr. Clarence Darrow, attorney-at-law from the state of Illinois. It is the defense's request that the court allow him to appear, *pro hac vice,* as the defendant's primary counsel."

"Darrow, eh?" Judge Brown said. "Yes, I've had some communications about you, Mr. Darrow. From downstate."

Mr. Darrow smiled humbly and chuckled. "I hope," he said, in a deep, soothing sort of voice, "that those communications haven't prejudiced Your Honor against me."

The people in the galleries liked that; and so, in his own way, did Judge Brown. "It certainly doesn't help," he said, producing some chuckles in the crowd that he let go. "If the defendant wishes to retain out-of-state counsel, that is her prerogative. But this court does not require advice from *anyone* in New York City on how to conduct its affairs."

"I understand, Your Honor," Mr. Darrow answered, smiling in a way what I had to admit was charming. "We feel the same way about New York City in Chicago."

The crowd laughed again, but got the gavel and a scowl for it. "If it is the defendant's true request," the judge said, turning to the defense table again, "then the court will be pleased to allow Mr. Darrow to practice in this state, *pro hac vice.*" The judge then looked to Libby Hatch, who stood up and widened her glowing eyes innocently.

"I'm sorry, Your Honor," she said, her lips curling up a little as she did. "I'm afraid I never had any Latin."

Little whispers to the effect of "Me, neither" and "Well, of course she didn't" circulated through the crowd, bringing another rap of the gavel.

"*Pro hac vice,*" the judge explained, as gently as I'd guess he was capable of, "simply means 'for this occasion,' Mrs. Hunter. It grants Mr. Darrow the right to practice in New York, but only for this case. Is that your wish?"

Libby nodded gently, then sat back down.

"And does the state have any objection?" the judge asked.

Mr. Picton smiled gamely, tucked his thumbs into the vest of the crisp gray suit he was wearing, and stood up. "Not at all, Your Honor," he said, moving out beside his table and seeming even shorter, more wiry, and quicker up against Mr. Darrow. "The court knows of Mr. Darrow by reputation, and if the defense contends that adequate counsel cannot be found in Saratoga County, then, while we may not share their assessment of our native talent, neither can we think of any reason why Mr. Darrow should not be permitted to serve."

The audience wasn't in much of a mood to find anything Mr. Picton said funny—but they couldn't help a few proud, satisfied smiles at his statement.

Mr. Darrow also smiled, in a gracious sort of way; but his face went straight when, looking over toward Mr. Picton, he caught sight of Marcus. Quickly recovering, he made a quick motion what said he took his cap off to the detective sergeant for his clever bit of research work. Marcus smiled and saluted back as Mr. Darrow said, "I thank the honorable district attorney. And I must say I'm impressed by his efforts to learn all about my—reputation."

Mr. Picton, having seen the little exchange what'd taken place between Mr. Darrow and Marcus, grinned. "Mr. Darrow inflates me, Your Honor. He is perhaps unaware that I am only an *assistant* county prosecutor, District Attorney Pearson being, as yet, unwilling to quit his very fine suite of offices."

Putting on a puzzled face what was so extreme as to make it plain that he actually knew exactly what Mr. Picton's rank was, Mr. Darrow scratched at his head. "An assistant? Well, I beg the state's pardon, I'm sure, Your Honor—I'd assumed that in a capital case as fraught with importance as this one the state would've wanted its senior officer to represent the people."

"As Your Honor knows, here in Ballston we enjoy as few temperate weeks as do the citizens of Chicago," Mr. Picton answered. "And we did not wish to deprive Mr. Pearson of any of them. Since I was the investigating officer in this case, we felt safe entrusting it to my meager talents."

Judge Brown was nodding his head and looking a little annoyed. "If you two gentlemen are finished needling each other," he said, "I'd like to see if we can't get a plea in this matter before noon. Mr. Darrow, the state having no objection, you are permitted to serve as primary counsel for your client in this court. I hope you don't regret the trip. Now, then, Mrs. Hunter, you have heard the very grave charges against you. How do you plead?"

Looking to Libby Hatch, who was staring up at him anxiously, Mr. Darrow nodded. Then Libby stood again, folded her hands before her, and said, "Not guilty, Your Honor."

A wave of whispers went through the courtroom, bringing a bang from Judge Brown's gavel. "Very well," he said, scowling around the room again. "Now, Mr. Picton, as to the matter of—" The judge paused as he noticed Mr. Picton staring at Mr. Darrow with a puzzled face, one what was about as genuine as the bigger man's had been just a few seconds earlier. "Mr. Picton? Are you mesmerized, sir, by the learned counsel from Illinois?"

Shaking himself, Mr. Picton turned to the bench. "Hmm? Oh! I *am* sorry, Your Honor. I confess I wasn't aware that the defense had completed its plea."

"You find their plea inadequate, Mr. Picton?" the Judge asked.

"It isn't for *me* to find it so, Your Honor," Mr. Picton answered. "I only thought that some sort of—defining phrase might be attached to it. 'By reason of something-or-other'—that sort of thing."

The judge stared down hard at him. "Mr. Picton—you and I have done too much business in this room over the last few years for me to be unaware of what you're up to. But there's no jury here for you to vex with your suggestions yet, and I won't tolerate any playing to the galleries. Mr. Darrow is a qualified attorney who does not appear to suffer from any impediments of speech. If he wished to qualify the defendant's plea in any way, I'm sure he would have. Do you wish to so qualify the plea, Mr. Darrow?"

"Certainly not, Your Honor," Mr. Darrow said, in dark earnest. "The plea is a simple, straightforward, and absolute 'Not guilty.' "

"Clear enough," Judge Brown replied. "In future, Mr. Picton, the state can keep its assumptions, as well as its hopes, to itself." Mr. Picton just smiled and bowed. "Now," the judge continued, "as to the matter of bail—"

"*Bail?*" Mr. Picton blurted out, getting a groan and another scowl from the judge.

"Yes, Mr. Picton," the old man said. "Bail. You are familiar with the practice?"

"In a case like this, I fear I am not, Your Honor," Mr. Picton replied. "The defendant is accused of the worst sort of violent assault on her own children, one of whom barely escaped with her life and is currently the state's principal witness. Does the court seriously intend that the state should, even for a moment, countenance the possibility of *bail* in this matter?"

"The court intends that the state should follow the rules of criminal procedure, *whatever* the offense!" Judge Brown bellowed back. "I warn you, Mr. Picton—do not make any more efforts to get on my bad side so early in this trial! As you well know, it's a big place, my bad side, and once on it you may have trouble finding your way back over again!"

Mr. Picton tried not to smile, and nodded with what you might call pronounced respect. "Yes, Your Honor. I ask the court's pardon. The state earnestly directs the court's attention to the severity of the crime with which the defendant is accused, and the danger that might be posed to the state's principal witness should the defendant be freed. We ask that bail in any amount be denied."

"Your Honor," Mr. Darrow countered, looking shocked, "my client is a respectable woman who endured the greatest tragedy that can be inflicted on a member of her sex: the savage murder, before her eyes, of two of her own children, and the attempted murder of a third—"

"I beg the learned counsel's pardon," Mr. Picton answered, with a hefty dose of sarcasm. "I was not aware that the issue had already been decided so conclusively. I thought that we were gathered together in this room to *determine* what, in fact, happened to the defendant's children."

Still scowling, Judge Brown nodded. "I'm afraid I must agree with the state here, Mr. Darrow. The burden may be on them to prove their allegations, but until they've failed, I cannot accept your assertion that Mrs. Hunter has endured any such tragedy, and I must ask you not to further inflame what is already a very emotional matter by making such statements. You have a request regarding bail?"

"We do, Your Honor," Mr. Darrow answered. "If, indeed, my client is guilty of violence against children, it'll be the first that this or any other state knows about it. Besides being a devoted mother, she's been a governess and a nurse to many children other than her own, and in that capacity has often behaved as heroically as she did on the night in question. We ask that you recognize that she is no threat either to the state's witnesses or to the community and that, given the delicacy of both her sex and her nature, you post a reasonable bail, to prevent her languishing in the county jail for the duration of what may be a protracted proceeding."

With the crowd—and those of us in the first two rows especially—waiting anxiously, Judge Brown rocked back in his chair, almost disappearing behind the bench. He stayed there for a minute or so before sitting forward again.

"The court appreciates Mr. Darrow's remarks concerning the gender and character of the defendant," he said slowly. "But it also notes that she is charged with a capital crime of a particularly violent and passionate nature. We regret any discomfort it may cause, and shall instruct Sheriff Dunning to make every possible provision to ensure that Mrs. Hunter's stay in this building will be, if not a pleasant, then at least a bearable one. But bail itself is denied."

That set the crowd mumbling again, and the judge went to work with the gavel. "I remind our guests of my earlier remarks!" he said. "And I assure them that they were in earnest!" With quiet restored, Judge Brown looked at the two tables below him. "We will reconvene on Tuesday morning at nine o'clock for the purpose of beginning jury selection. But before we go, let me once more emphasize something to both sides in this case: the court is aware of the feelings aroused by this matter, and urges both of you to refrain from any blatant appeals to emotion or popular sentiment. It won't do either cause any good, and may injure your purposes beyond repair. Court is adjourned!"

Another bang of the gavel, and we all got to our feet, as Judge Brown made his way back down to the door behind the bench and then disappeared through it. As soon as he was gone, the room roared to life with conversation and comment again, particularly once Sheriff Dunning and Bailiff Coffey had guided Libby Hatch out through a side door what led directly down to the cells in the basement of the building. Mr. Darrow gave her some words of encouragement on her way out, and she did her very best to look humble and grateful; but in her eyes, again, was that flirtatious, seductive glitter what she seemed unable to keep from flashing at men she'd only just met. After she'd gone, Mr. Darrow began to talk with Mr. Maxon, a conversation what Mr. Picton interrupted by marching himself straight over to their table and loudly declaring, "Well,

Maxon! So you've got yourself some help. I'm not sure how I'd take that if I were you, though I suppose when the assistance comes from a man as thoroughly acqainted with as many areas of the law as Mr. Darrow, you can't object!" He thrust out his hand. "Mr. Darrow, my name's Picton."

"Yes, I know," Mr. Darrow answered, shaking Mr. Picton's hand with a noticeable lack of enthusiasm and eyeing him in a way what was more than a little condescending. "You see, I've heard about you, too, Mr. Picton, though I've got to say that my information came through slightly more"—he cast an eye over at Marcus—"straightforward channels."

"Well, great men do as they will, lesser men do as they must," Mr. Picton answered lightly. "Where has Vanderbilt got you staying, Darrow? Somewhere comfortable, I trust—not that Ballston has many luxuries to offer. But perhaps you'll let me provide you with the odd meal at my house, if you find you need it."

At the mention of Mr. Vanderbilt, Mr. Darrow looked at Mr. Picton in a way what went past condescension toward outright annoyance. "I *will* hand it to you, Mr. Picton, there don't seem to be many aspects of this situation that've escaped your attention. Or does all of Ballston Spa know the details of Mrs. Hunter's arrangements for her defense?"

"Oh, good God, no!" Mr. Picton answered with a laugh. "And I wouldn't tell them if I were you. Judge Brown's attitude toward the citizens of our downstate metropolis is, I assure you, quite typical of the residents of this county. But you don't have to worry about *me* telling anyone—wouldn't be sporting, would it?"

It was pretty easy to see that Mr. Picton was doing his best to irritate Mr. Darrow, and that he was succeeding. "I'm not sure 'sporting' is a word I'd care to use in connection with a case as tragic as this one," Mr. Darrow mumbled back. "And I'm afraid I won't be able to take you up on your offer, as I'll be staying at the Grand Union Hotel in Saratoga. We'll be organizing our efforts from there."

Mr. Picton frowned at that one. "Hmm," he noised. "Well, I wouldn't let *that* bit get out, either—people in Ballston don't have much more use for Saratoga than they do for New York. They figure it's just a playground for rich strangers and their hired hands." Mr. Darrow's eyes went wide with shock at that slap, but Mr. Picton just kept chattering away. "I hope you don't mind my being so free with advice, but I really do want to make sure that we keep the field as level as possible. Well, good-bye, Maxon—best of luck. And Darrow, if you change your mind about that meal, you *will* let me know, won't you?"

By way of reply Mr. Darrow rumbled something under his breath as he walked out through the gate in the railing with Mr. Maxon. Passing by our rows of seats, Mr. Darrow took our group in with a cold glare; but then, recognizing the Doctor's face, he caught himself and turned around to approach the front row of chairs with a more friendly air.

"It's Dr. Kreizler, isn't it?" he said, the deep voice now becoming very genial. The Doctor shook the hand what Mr. Darrow offered. "I'm a great admirer of your work, Doctor, if you'll permit me to say so."

"I will," the Doctor answered, studying the lawyer as he smiled engagingly. "Thank you, Mr. Darrow."

"Tell me, sir," Mr. Darrow went on, "is it true that you're acting as an adviser to the prosecution in this case?"

"That fact surprises you?" the Doctor asked.

"I'll admit that it does," Mr. Darrow answered. "I wouldn't have thought you the kind of man to get involved in satisfying the state's desire to punish whatever person they could actually catch, just so that they can write an end to this mysterious tragedy."

"Is that my motivation, Mr. Darrow?"

Shrugging his big shoulders, Mr. Darrow said, "I can't think of any other. And I've got to say, such behavior doesn't sound like you. But maybe I've formed a wrong impression. Or maybe you've got your own reasons for doing business with the state of New York." Seeing the Doctor's eyes go a little wider at this barely disguised reference to the investgation into the Kreizler Institute's affairs what was still going on in New York, Mr. Darrow smiled. "Whatever the case, I hope we'll get a chance to talk at some point. Outside of court, I mean. I'm being wholly honest when I say that I admire what you do. What you—*generally* do. Good morning."

The Doctor nodded once, still smiling. "Good morning to you, sir."

Mr. Darrow followed Mr. Maxon to the mahogany doors, where they were immediately buttonholed by Mr. Grose and a few other newspapermen who'd come down from Saratoga.

"Clever man," the Doctor said, watching Mr. Darrow hold court with the journalists in a way what showed that the Chicago lawyer was very at home with the process.

"Oh, yes," Mr. Picton said, coming over to join us. "A clever, sanctimonious prig, wrapped up in the broadcloth of the people." Turning to pack up his briefcase, Mr. Picton laughed once, hard. "One of the easiest kinds of people to irk!"

"You were certainly doing your best, Rupert," Mr. Moore said, with a shake of his head. "Do you *want* to spend this trial bickering with the man?"

"I'm sure the Doctor will agree, John," Mr. Picton answered, sticking his unlit pipe into his mouth. "That when a man is perpetually irritated he's far more likely to make errors of judgment than might otherwise be the case."

"Yes, I thought that was your purpose, Mr. Picton," the Doctor answered. "And you achieved it admirably."

"Oh, nothing to it," Mr. Picton answered, tucking his briefcase under his arm. "Lawyers like that, as I've told you, generally think they have nothing to learn from Jesus Christ himself when it comes to being saviors with a mission. Annoying them is like falling off of a log, really. Well! The opening's gone well, but I'd like to regroup and go over our next set of steps, if it's all right with you, Doctor." Taking out his watch again, Mr. Picton checked it. "We can talk in my office, if you like."

"Of course," the Doctor answered, leading the way up the aisle and around the little group of newspapermen who were still throwing questions at Mr. Darrow and Mr. Maxon. They tried to pull Mr. Picton aside, too, with questions what were pretty predictable: wasn't the state's charging Libby Hatch an act of desperation, what possible motive could a mother have for killing her own kids, wouldn't such a woman have to be insane—all that sort of stuff. But Mr. Picton was ready for it, and very handily talked his way through the group without saying anything of importance, all the while referring them back to Mr. Darrow, who, he was sure, would have much more interesting things to say than any humble assistant county prosecutor.

Once up in his office Mr. Picton told the rest of us that his main concern at that point in the affair was to figure out just what kind of citizens would make the best jurors for the case, and to assemble a set of questions what would separate such people from the rest of the candidates who would be called in. He asked the Doctor's opinion on this matter, and got a quick answer: poor men, the Doctor advised, preferably farmers, would be the best prospects—men who led tough lives, and whose families were well acquainted with hard times. Such characters would best know just how easily personal conflicts and money concerns can lead to violence, even in a family what seems happy and peaceful on the outside: they likely would've seen or at least heard of women going after their own kids when things got especially discouraging or frustrating, and wouldn't have your more well-to-do man's opinions about the purity of female motives and actions. Mr. Picton said that he was relieved to hear all this, as it matched his own opinions perfectly; the trick now would be to find ways to identify such men without tipping Mr. Darrow off to the fact that he was doing it.

As for the Doctor, his main concern was still preparing Clara Hatch for what was to come: now that we'd actually met Mr. Darrow, it was easy to see that he'd be clever enough to find many ways to trip Clara up and make her seem not so much a liar as a confused little girl who didn't actually remember the real facts of what'd happened to her, but had been fed a story by the prosecution. It was likely, the Doctor said, that Mr. Darrow would make this attempt in the kindest and friendliest manner possible, and that Clara would be tempted to play along with him as a result. So she would have to be carefully taught that even a person who seems pleasant and respectful might be out to lay traps for you: a fact what she certainly knew from experience, but might not have fully developed in what the Doctor called her "conscious mind."

The Doctor would be doing double duty through the weekend and on into Monday, for while he'd spend his days getting Clara ready, he'd spend his nights interviewing Libby Hatch and assessing her mental condition. Having been through this procedure with the Doctor myself, and having watched him perform it on others, I knew generally what would take place in Libby's basement cell: there'd be few or no straight inquiries about the murders, just a series of random questions about the woman's childhood, her family, and her personal life. Libby was required by law to cooperate with him, though such didn't mean that she couldn't at least try to manipulate her answers so as to confuse the Doctor. But I'd seen much more hardened criminals try the same thing with him and fail pretty badly: it didn't seem that Libby'd stand much of a chance, even with all her cleverness. Still, I knew it would be a pretty interesting little set of encounters, and I hoped that I'd have time to listen in on some of it.

Such seemed unlikely, though, seeing as the rest of us weren't going to be exactly idle in the few days left before the start of the trial. The Isaacsons—joined, now, by Mr. Moore, who'd use any excuse to get back up to the gaming tables in Saratoga—put themselves to the job of finding out what witnesses and experts Mr. Darrow was planning on calling, along with trying to predict as much of his trial strategy as they could. Miss Howard was still determined to find somebody who, if not actually related to Libby Hatch, knew about her childhood, and it looked like I'd have to continue to give her a hand with the search, at least until Tuesday. This fact didn't exactly set me up, as it seemed to me that by now we were definitely chasing ghosts. I would've much preferred to go along to Saratoga with Mr. Moore; but I knew how important Miss Howard's task was, and I tried to accept the assignment with as much good humor as El

Niño showed at the prospect of continuing to play bodyguard to "the lady" who'd been his original benefactor in our group.

But good intentions and keeping your nose to the grindstone don't always pay off, and by the weekend we hadn't turned up anything what would've passed for useful information. It began to look almost as if there'd been some deliberate attempt to wipe away any trace of Libby's existence. Our travels eventually took us pretty far north, around the southern shores of Lake George and into the edge of the Adirondack forest; and though the countryside got nothing but more beautiful, the towns also got nothing but smaller and less frequent, until it took the better part of the day just to reach them and most of the evening to get back home. One thing, at least, was for sure: if Libby Hatch had truly been born and raised in a town in Washington County, then neither she nor her family had gotten out and around much—assuming, of course, that she hadn't killed the lot of them off years ago, an idea what began to haunt my thoughts more and more on those long, useless trips from village to village. For her part, Miss Howard didn't seem to like the idea of continuing to look for a needle what might not even be in our assigned haystack any more than I did; and I knew that she also shared my desire to sit in on some of the Doctor's interviews with Libby Hatch. But she kept me and El Niño on the job, knowing that any clue to Libby's past what might be used in court would mean a lot more than our being entertained by the battle of wits what was taking place under the Ballston court house.

We did get nightly reports about those meetings, though, as we sat around Mr. Picton's dining room table for what, given all our activities, usually turned out to be very late suppers. During the first of these meals the Doctor explained that Libby's attitude toward him had been typically changeable: she'd started with expressions of deep injury, as if the Doctor—someone whom Libby'd expressed admiration for when they first met—had done her some kind of deliberate hurt by trying to lay not just the Linares kidnapping but the deaths of the kids she'd had care of in New York and the murders of her own children at her door. Such was a smart position for her to start from, the Doctor told us: whether consciously or unconsciously, Libby was trading on every person's secret horror of accusing a mother of horrible crimes toward the children she is supposed to watch over, and on society's hopeful belief that what Miss Howard called the "myth of maternal nurturing" was in fact as solid and reliable as the Rocky Mountains. But once it became clear that the Doctor wasn't going to let his own uneasiness overrule his intellect, Libby had quickly moved

on to what was, for her, an equally familiar role: the seducer. She'd begun
to coyly tease the Doctor about what secret longings and desires must be
hidden underneath his detached, disciplined exterior. This, of course, also
got her nowhere, and so in the end she'd been forced to rely on the last of
her most accustomed behaviors: anger. Throwing the victim and temptress
acts aside, she'd become the punisher, and sat petulantly in her cell, giving
the Doctor short, resentful answers to his questions—many of them, he
could tell, outright lies—and punctuating the statements by telling him
how sorry he'd be one day for ever tangling with her. But what she didn't
realize was that this change in attitude itself gave the Doctor just what he
was looking for: Libby's ability to analyze what he was trying to do and
come up with a series of different but carefully planned responses was evidence that, as he'd always suspected, no serious mental disease or brain disorder was dominating her behavior. The very fact that she knew enough to
come up with wily, dishonest answers to his inquiries—all of them designed to serve a larger purpose—was proof that she was as sane as anyone.

This was all very interesting stuff, and Miss Howard and I continued to
wish that we could've been there to see some of it; but no one envied the
Doctor's becoming the specific object of Libby's hatred, given how many
examples we'd uncovered of how she dealt with people—young or old—
who frustrated her designs. I'll confess that the more I heard about the assessment process, the more I began to worry about the Doctor, until I
finally asked him if he was making sure that there was somebody present
during the interviews who could prevent the woman from doing him any
sudden, unexpected physical harm. He answered that yes, the guard
Henry was outside Libby's cell every minute that he was inside it, paying
careful attention to all what went on.

As for the detective sergeants and Mr. Moore, their attempts to find
out what Mr. Darrow was up to in Saratoga were about as fruitful as our
group's efforts to learn about Libby's past—until Saturday, that is. That
night, as the rest of us sat in Mr. Picton's dining room listening to the
Doctor talk about his most recent interview with Libby, the three of
them showed up later than usual, their mood considerably better than it
had been when they'd left the house that morning. It seemed that they'd
finally gotten a break, in the form of a private investigator who'd been
working for Mr. Darrow in New York: Lucius knew the investigator,
and when the man had shown up at the Grand Union Hotel to give his
report to Mr. Darrow, the detective sergeant had intercepted him and
pumped him for quite a bit of information—without, of course, saying
that he was working for the opposing side. Though the investigator

hadn't offered a lot of specifics, his general comments had been enough to confirm that Mr. Darrow was indeed trying to find out everything he could about the Doctor's current activities and situation in the city, including the troubles he'd run into after Paulie McPherson's suicide. None of this was all that shocking: we'd guessed from the beginning that Mr. Darrow would use the Doctor as his way of attacking our case against Libby Hatch. But what you might call a passing reference what Lucius made to something else that the investigator'd told him caused the Doctor considerably more concern.

"Oh, by the way," Lucius said, smiling up at Mrs. Hastings as she put a big plate of food down in front of him. "He's got an alienist of his own coming to do an assessment of Libby."

Mr. Picton suddenly looked puzzled. "Really? I wonder why. He's already made it fairly clear that he doesn't intend to pursue an insanity defense."

"True," the Doctor said, "but when the prosecution plans to bring in testimony about someone's mental condition in a case like this, the defense generally feels the need to answer in some way. In all likelihood Darrow will use the opportunity to show just how distressing the deaths of the children were to Libby, while at the same time demonstrating that she's a fully competent person, balanced enough to look after not only her own children, but those of strangers, as well. Your colleague didn't happen to mention the alienist's name, did he, Lucius?"

"Mmm, yes," Lucius answered, as he attacked the home cooking what we'd all grown very devoted to since our arrival in Ballston Spa. He began to search his pockets with one hand, refusing to put down his fork. "I wrote it down somewhere . . . ah." He pulled a small piece of paper from his inside his jacket. "Here—White. William White."

The Doctor stopped chewing his food suddenly, and looked up at Lucius with concern. "William *Alanson* White?" he asked.

Lucius checked the paper again. "Yes, that's right."

"What's the matter, Kreizler?" Mr. Moore said. "Do you know the man?"

"Indeed," the Doctor answered, pushing his plate aside. Then he slowly got to his feet and picked up a glass of wine.

"A problem?" Mr. Picton asked.

The Doctor's black eyes turned to the window and stared out into the night. "A mystery, certainly. *White* . . ." Giving the matter a few more seconds thought, the Doctor finally shook himself and came back to the conversation. "He's one of the best of the younger generation—a brilliant mind, and highly imaginative. He's been working at the State Hospital at Binghamton and has done some fascinating work concerning the criminal mind—the criminal unconscious, in particular. He's become a skilled expert witness, too, despite his comparative youth."

"Is he an enemy of yours?" Marcus asked.

"Quite the contrary," the Doctor replied. "We've met many times, and correspond frequently."

"That's strange," Miss Howard said. "You'd think that Darrow would want to get someone openly hostile to your theories, if he's bothering to bring in anybody at all."

"Yes," the Doctor answered with a nod, "but that's not the strangest part, Sara. White and I do tend to share low opinions about this country's penal system and its methods of discouraging crime and caring for the mentally diseased. But we generally disagree on the definition of mental disease itself. His classifications tend to be far broader than mine, and he includes more criminal behavior in his categorization of 'insane acts' than I could ever do. Because of this, when he serves as an expert witness it is almost always for the purpose of demonstrating that a given defendant is somehow unbalanced, and therefore not legally responsible for his—or her—actions."

"Hmm," Mr. Picton noised. "Which would seem to lead back to the idea that Darrow may be holding on to some sort of an insanity card, in case he needs to play it later. Although I wouldn't think him so stupid."

"Nor would I," the Doctor agreed. "The insanity defense, when introduced midway through a trial, is rarely effective—few juries fail to recognize a change in plea as an act of desperation."

"Well, then," Mr. Moore said, looking blankly from the Doctor to Mr. Picton, "what do you suppose Darrow's up to?"

The Doctor just shook his head slowly. "I don't know—and that fact disturbs me. Indeed, there is much about our opponent that disturbs me." Pacing by the window, the Doctor rolled his wineglass in his hands. "Did you discover when White is to arrive?"

"Tuesday night," Lucius said. "After the trial's begun."

"Leaving me little time to confer with him," the Doctor answered, nodding again. "Yes, it's the smart move. But what in God's name is it that Darrow wants him to say?"

We'd learn the answer to that question soon enough; and it, like almost everything else about Mr. Darrow, made it easy to understand just why he would one day become the greatest criminal defense lawyer the country has ever seen.

CHAPTER 43

Our education began on Tuesday morning, when men called in from fields, shop counters, and parlor rooms all over Saratoga County crowded into the Ballston Spa court house to find out whether they'd spend the next couple of weeks as jury members in what was becoming popularly known as "the Hatch trial."

From the beginning of this process, Mr. Darrow showed that he knew exactly what Mr. Picton was up to, and that he intended to frustrate him at every turn. Both sides were given twenty of what they called "peremptory challenges"—the right to refuse a jury candidate for no stated reason—and the first ten of Mr. Darrow's were exercised on men who couldn't have fit the Doctor's and Mr. Picton's description of an ideal juror any better. Each man was poor but sharp, with a kind of wisdom about the world what didn't seem to fit with the fact that most of them had never been out of the county, much less the state. When his turn came to question these fellows, Mr. Darrow was nice enough to them—he cared too much about working the crowd in the galleries not to be. He'd strike up a pleasant conversation about the state of business in town or about how the wet, cool weather that summer was affecting the local crops; but the minute any man mentioned, say, the fact that he'd grown up in a one-room farmhouse or, worse yet, that his mother, grandmother, aunt, or sister had on occasion been given to violent behavior, he found himself dismissed with a friendly "Thank you" (but no word of explanation) from the counsel for the defense.

Mr. Picton, for his part, wasn't fooled by the seemingly innocent, humble way that Mr. Darrow questioned the better-off, more educated jury candidates about the "natural state" of men and women, and whether or not human society could've deteriorated to the point where the most basic attachments between members of the species—"the natural law of human society," as Mr. Darrow put it—might be broken without any cause. Mr. Darrow didn't say outright that the bond between a mother and her children was part of said "natural law"; he didn't have to. It was clear that most of the people in the courtroom silently believed such to be the case. But in the same way that Mr. Darrow had dismissed any potential juror who spoke openly about female violence, so did Mr. Picton give the axe to any man who voiced a belief in such "natural" or "fundamental" attachments. Mr. Darrow eventually protested that Mr. Picton seemed to be throwing out the "entire concept of natural law," a notion what he declared was the foundation of the American Constitution and the Declaration of Independence. Mr. Picton answered that it wasn't the business of the court to get into such philosophical discussions—they were concerned with criminal, not natural, law. It was an attitude that, while it didn't earn him any affection from Judge Brown, was perfectly proper and within his rights, and many candidates what Mr. Darrow clearly preferred were duly sent packing.

By noon each man had used up the better portion of his peremptory challenges, and had rejected a few jurors for specific cause, to boot, so that when the midday recess was called only half the jury had been selected. It looked like the afternoon session might get a little testier than the morning had been, for when one or the other of the lawyers ran out of peremptories it meant that he'd have to start coming up with full sets of reasons for rejecting a given candidate. By three o'clock the peremptories on both sides were gone, with five jurors still to be selected; and while Mr. Picton figured that most of the men already in the box were characters that he could probably persuade to see things his way, he also suspected that Judge Brown was a lot more likely to be sympathetic to Mr. Darrow's stated reasons for rejecting candidates than he would be to the prosecution's. This suspicion proved justified. Mr. Darrow just kept repeating the idea that "natural law" was the mainstay of all of American government and society: if any man accepted the idea that the "bonds of nature" could be "capriciously broken," Mr. Darrow said, he was basically saying that the United States itself was a seriously flawed concept—and if he felt that way, said man had no business serving on an American jury.

It was, as the Doctor put it, "ludicrous but singularly effective logic," expressed by Mr. Darrow as if it were a deeply held conviction but more likely created for the particular case and town he found himself working. (This idea seemed confirmed when we found out that Judge Brown had served as an officer in the Civil War—a fact what Mr. Darrow had most likely discovered.) Mr. Picton had no similarly simple philosophical justification for rejecting jury candidates; in fact, he had no reason at all that appealed to Judge Brown's old-school patriotism. He could only keep protesting that people's personal feelings about politics, philosophy, or even religion shouldn't be allowed to influence their judgment in a criminal proceeding, where guilt or innocence were determined by evidence, not beliefs. Such thinking was a little bloodless for the likes of Judge Brown, and as the shadows grew longer on the courtroom floor it began to wear on him pretty clearly, while Mr. Darrow's deliberate attempts to appeal to the old man's deepest sentiments—voiced, as they were, in the "plain" midwestern oratory what Mr. Darrow had obviously mastered—only seemed to grow more colorful and persuasive.

By the time all twelve seats in the jury box had been filled, there was no real way to determine which side had the upper hand in terms of the personal inclinations of the men in the chairs. But if I'd been forced to bet on it, I would've said that the balance was leaning in Mr. Darrow's favor—and the fact that Mr. Moore brought word back from the Casino that night that the odds against a conviction had gone up to sixty to one seemed to bear this feeling out. For Mr. Picton, the battle would start out as an uphill one.

Still, we did have witnesses and evidence in our favor, and there wasn't any real reason yet to believe that these wouldn't change the opinions of even those jurors what were privately inclined to view the charges against Libby Hatch with some doubt; after all, Sheriff Dunning had started out skeptical about the prosecution's case, but'd had his mind thoroughly changed by the grand jury proceedings. Knowing all this, Mr. Picton stayed in his office very late on Monday night, going over his opening statement (to be delivered the next morning) and also the schedule according to which he planned to reveal circumstantial evidence and call witnesses. Mrs. Hastings asked me to take some food up to the court house at about midnight, and I found Mr. Picton still going like a madman, smoking, reading, rehearsing, and once again having at the hair on his face and head like he was intent on doing himself some injury. The sight made me marvel all the more at how he was able to come across so cool and collected in the actual courtroom: I knew that there was no telling where a particular person might feel the most at ease with the world, but the difference in this case between the anxious, slightly peculiar man we knew outside the courtroom and the steady, brilliant lawyer we saw pursue the case against Libby Hatch was so extreme as to be confusing.

But confusing or not, Mr. Picton *was* always impressive in court, especially the following morning, when he opened the case against Libby Hatch. At ten o'clock Judge Brown gaveled the proceedings to order, and Iphegeneia Blaylock got her quick hands ready to record Mr. Picton's statement. When the assistant district attorney rose to address the jury, there was no sign on his face of the devilish smile what had been in evidence throughout the arraignment and the jury selection: he was all seriousness, knowing, it seemed to me, that his change in mood would cause the jury to sit up and take special notice from the start. Wearing a dark suit what seemed to reinforce the idea that he'd come before them on business what he had no personal wish to pursue, Mr. Picton paced in front of the jury box for a minute or so before speaking; only when he saw the faces of the twelve men inside that box grow completely attentive and what you might call receptive did he open his mouth.

"Gentlemen," he began, in a much slower and more melancholy way than was his habit, "you have heard the state's charges against the defendant. But there are facts outside the indictment of which you should be aware." Mr. Picton lifted a hand toward the defense table without looking over at Libby Hatch. "This woman has recently been deprived of her husband, a man of great bravery who earlier in life sacrificed his health to the noble causes of Union and emancipation. You must none of you think that the state is unaware of this fact, or that it would, as the counsel for the defense has intimated in the local press, disturb the mourning of such a woman simply for the sake of solving an old and troubling crime. I tell you honestly, we would not do it. Even had we the time to pursue such private, perverse agendas, the memory of a man who was one of his country's many heroes at a critical hour would block our path, as surely as the felling of a mighty tree would block the passage of traffic on the Charlton road."

I was leaning forward in my chair, not only to make sure I heard everything Mr. Picton said, but also to catch the Doctor's reactions to it all. At the mention of poor old Micah Hunter, the Doctor started to nod, working hard to keep the expression on his face absolutely still. "Good," he whispered. "Good—don't let Darrow *possess* that subject."

Mr. Picton paused, staring up at the ceiling. "The Charlton road . . ." He turned to the jury again. "We are here—reluctantly, gentlemen, never doubt it—because something unspeakable occurred three years ago on the Charlton road. An event of a kind that we, as a community, pray never to see repeated—and would, perhaps, like to forget. But we cannot. There are two graves in the Ballston Avenue Cemetery that will not let us forget it, and there is a little girl—half paralyzed and, until several days ago, stricken dumb with terror—who will not let us forget it. Her very existence has been a reminder, for these three years, of the horror that took place that night. Yet now, suddenly, she can offer us more than simply her poignant presence. Finally, after three long years during which she has endured a private torment that is beyond the imagination even of those brave men who survived the carnage of our great Civil War, finally, little Clara Hatch can speak! And can anyone believe, gentlemen, that when she at last feels safe enough to give voice to her terrible memories, such a child could be persuaded to *lie*? Can any of you seriously believe that after all she has endured, this eight-year-old girl could be approached by agents of the state and persuaded to *fabricate* a history of what occurred on the Charlton road, where her two brothers were shot to death and she herself received a wound that her assailant clearly hoped was mortal?"

Taking a moment to stare at the jury, Mr. Picton made a visible effort to get his passions under control—an effort what I could already tell, knowing him as well as I did, was going to fail.

"The defense would have you believe so," he went on, nodding. "Indeed, the defense would have you believe many things. They will refer you to the sworn affidavit of the woman who was then known as Mrs. Libby Hatch, and will call her to the stand to again tell her strange, unsupported story concerning a mysterious Negro assailant who attacked her children but not herself and then vanished into the night, never to be seen or detected again despite the most vigorous of searches. But the facts as the only other witness to the events of that night tells them are too simple and too clear, even in all their horror, for you to be further led down any fantastic garden paths by the defense. I am sure of that—sure, because I have heard little Clara's version of the events from her own lips. And it is only because I *have* heard that fateful tale that the state brings these charges against the former Mrs. Hatch. Do not doubt that, gentlemen. Do not doubt that if Clara Hatch had not stated—in this very building, under oath and before all the frightening power of a court of law—that it was her own *mother* who did the infamous deed, who coldly put the muzzle of a forty-five-caliber revolver against those three small chests and deliberately pulled the trigger not once but repeatedly, until she was convinced that all her children were dead—I tell you, do not *doubt* that if anyone but Clara Hatch had made such an assertion, the state would never have had the temerity to bring this awful charge against this woman! No, gentlemen! We serve no ulterior motive here. We would not trifle with the mental composure, with the very *sanity*, of a child, simply to close the books on an unsolved crime. Better a *hundred* crimes go unsolved than that the state engage in such behavior! We—*you*—are here for a single reason: because the only person who witnessed what happened on the Charlton road that May night three years ago has come forward to tell her story. And when such a horrifying account is presented to the state, it has no choice but to reluctantly—I say it again, gentlemen, reluctantly!—to *reluctantly* set the machinery of justice into motion, no matter how much the ensuing events may disrupt the peace of the community, as well as the peace of each of its citizens."

At that point Mr. Picton paused again to draw a deep breath, rubbing his forehead as if it did indeed pain him to speak about the case.

"Smart," Marcus whispered to the Doctor. "He's taking on Darrow's criticisms before Darrow's even stated them."

"Yes," the Doctor answered. "But watch Darrow. He has a nimble mind, and is manufacturing new avenues of attack even as Picton closes the old ones down."

Glancing at Mr. Darrow, I could see what the Doctor meant: though he was holding himself in a pose of slouching carelessness, his face showed that his mind was working like a dynamo.

"In a moment, gentlemen," Mr. Picton continued, "you will hear just what evidence the state will present and what witnesses it will call, along with what you may expect to learn about this matter as a result. But as you listen, a question will linger in the back of your minds. And lest that question cause your attention to the details of evidence to wander, I feel I must address it now. All the evidence and all the witnesses in the world will not stop you from wondering how—how could a woman be guilty of such a crime? Surely she would have to be mad to commit such an act. But the woman before you has no history of madness, nor does the defense seek to portray her as being mad. Neither were her children born out of wedlock, the other explanation most commonly cited for 'prolicide,' the murder of one's own offspring. No. Thomas, Matthew, and Clara Hatch had a home, a father whose name they bore, and a mother whose mind was and is wholly sound. And so, you will ask yourselves, how could this happen? Time and the rules of procedure prevent me from arguing the state's theory of how at this juncture—the evidence must do that. I ask now only that you be aware of the reluctance of your own minds to countenance even the possibility that such an argument may be proved true. For only if you confront your prejudices, just as those of us who have investigated this case have reluctantly—yes, I repeat it again, *reluctantly!*—confronted ours can justice be served." Pausing once more to make sure the jury'd gotten this point, Mr. Picton sighed deeply and then went on. "As to the matters of means and opportunity, the evidence will show . . ."

Here our friend launched into a detailed but quick-paced review of every bit of circumstantial evidence we'd collected, moving from that recital into a discussion of what his other two principal witnesses—Mrs. Louisa Wright and the Reverend Clayton Parker—would have to say about Libby Hatch's possible motives for committing the crime.

"Well, Moore," the Doctor whispered as all this was going on, "He's doing quite a job. Even *I* almost believe he's reluctant to pursue the case."

"I told you," Mr. Moore answered, nodding as he watched Mr. Picton, "he was *born* for this kind of thing."

"It's a strange reversal," Miss Howard added. "He sounds more like an advocate than a prosecutor."

"That's the trick," Marcus said. "He knows Darrow's going to argue in the negative, so he assumes the positive. He's *defending* his witnesses and his case, even before they're attacked. Very smart—should take a lot of the wind out of Darrow's sails."

"I wish I believed that," the Doctor whispered.

We all turned our attention forward again as Mr. Picton brought his discussion about the evidence what the prosecution would present to a close. He returned to his table, almost as if he was getting ready to sit down; but then, pausing like he'd just thought of something he wasn't sure he should bring up, he held a finger to his lips and approached the jury box again.

"There is one more thing, gentlemen. The court and the state have raised no objection to the accused's being represented by out-of-state counsel. It is her right, and the counsel for the defense is an accomplished attorney. I should like you to remember that. A *very* accomplished attorney. In his years of practice he has represented the interests of clients humble and mighty, of great corporations and lunatic assassins. What brings him, you might reasonably ask, to our little town, so far from the teeming city of Chicago, and to this case in particular? The state cannot pretend that there are not forces at work here—for the accused, during her years of residence in New York City, found employment with some of the most powerful people in that metropolis. And they, perhaps naturally, seek to aid her in this, her hour of need. And so they have reached out of state for the assistance of, as I say, a very accomplished attorney. That is their affair. But you should be aware of this much: in the process of becoming so accomplished, the counsel for the defense has learned a thing or two about juries. He has learned about how they think, how they feel, and how they view the terrible responsibility of deciding a fellow human being's fate in a capital case. Yes, you will doubtless hear a great deal about *your* responsibility, when the counsel for the defense makes his opening remarks."

For the first time Mr. Picton smiled, ever so briefly, at the twelve faces before him. "But what *is* your responsibility, gentlemen?" he asked, his face going straight again. "To weigh the evidence and the testimony which will be presented to you by the state, as well as the defense. Nothing less—and nothing more. The counsel for the defense will ask you to believe that he does not intend to work upon your emotions or your natural sympathies, only that he wishes to present to you as clear and honest an argument as possible, so that if you decide that this woman is guilty the responsibility will be yours and yours alone. But, gentlemen, our jury system has been centuries perfecting a means of ensuring that no one man would ever feel that he held the fate of another in his hands in imitation of the Almighty. Your responsibility is only to weigh what is presented to you. It is the responsibility of the counsel for the defense and the responsibility of the state to adequately prepare and communicate their arguments. If you find the accused not guilty, then the responsibility is not yours—it belongs to the state. To *me,* gentlemen. And what is true of one side is true of the other. You are not the Inquisition of old, commissioned and empowered to arbitrarily decide the fate of a fellow human being. If you were, then indeed, you should bear the responsibility for what happens here. But that is not your commission. Your task is simply to listen— to the evidence, the witnesses, and the voice of doubt that is inside each of you. If I cannot silence that voice to a reasonable extent, then you must decide against the state. And believe me, gentlemen, it is the *state* that will bear that responsibility." Mr. Picton turned and glanced at Mr. Darrow as he added, "That, at any rate, is the way things are done in the state of New York."

Returning to his table, Mr. Picton sat down with a heavy breath, then took out his watch, placed it before him, and fixed his eyes on it.

Judge Brown studied Mr. Picton for a few seconds, with a look that combined annoyance with what you might call grudging respect; then he turned to the table on the other side of the room. "Mr. Darrow? Would the defense care to make its introductory remarks now, or will it wait until the opening of its own case?"

Mr. Darrow stood up slowly, giving the judge a small smile as the usual lock of hair fell over his forehead. "I've just been considering that question, Your Honor," he said, his voice sounding deeper and smoother than ever. "I don't suppose you've got any advice for me?"

The crowd chuckled quietly, causing Judge Brown to grab his gavel; but they got themselves settled before he had to start rapping it.

"This doesn't seem quite the time for levity, Counselor," the judge said sternly.

Mr. Darrow's smile disappeared, and all the lines in his face seemed to grow deeper with worry. "No—no, it isn't, Your Honor, and I apologize for sounding that way. The defense will go ahead and open now, with your permission." Slowly moving out from behind his table, Mr. Darrow walked at a very slow pace over toward the jury box, his shoulders hunched like those of a man what's carrying a painful burden. "My apology was sincere, gentlemen—sometimes confusion can cause inappropriate behavior. And I'll admit that the state has confused me mightily, and not just about this case. Mr. Picton seems to know an awful lot about me—seems to know just what it is that I have to say to you, and what words I'll use to say it. I know I'm not a young man anymore, but I didn't think I'd gotten *quite* so old and set in my ways." The men in the jury box smiled out to Mr. Darrow, who returned the look briefly. "He makes me sound like a pretty dangerous character, doesn't he? Why, if I were in your spot right now I'd be good and on my guard, ready for the big-city lawyer who's going to—how did the state put it? To 'work upon your emotions and your natural sympathies.' Quite a job, to get twelve grown men to dance like puppets all at once—and I'll admit to you, gentlemen, I'm not up to it. Especially not when I'm so confused . . ."

Putting a hand to his neck, Mr. Darrow rubbed it hard, squinting his eyes as he did. "You see, the state seems to want you to believe that they would just as soon've let this case alone—that there they were, going about their own business, when suddenly along comes a little girl, along comes Clara Hatch, bursting at the seams to tell her story of what happened on the Charlton road on May the thirty-first, 1894. Well, gentlemen, the truth is a little different. The truth is that after the—the *nightmare,* the unimaginable *tragedy* on the Charlton road, my client, Clara Hatch's mother, was left in such a devastated state that she knew she couldn't care for a girl whose needs would be as extreme as Clara's. So what did she do? She agreed to let two good, kind citizens of this town, Josiah and Ruth Weston—most of you know them—care for her daughter while she went off to secure a new future for the both of them, so that they might escape the horrors of the past. She fully intended to return for Clara, when the day came that she was well enough to leave the Westons'. Until recently, she thought that day was still a long way off. And then she received word that Clara had recovered the ability to speak—received it from Sheriff Dunning, who'd come to New York to arrest her. For what, apparently, was the first thing that little Clara said, after her three years of torturous silence? That her own mother had shot her. This tormented, terrified girl one day resumes communicating with the world—a momentous enough event on its own—and *without urging,* she *offers* the state an explanation of her tragic experience, one that doesn't match a single detail of the story that was accepted by everyone in this county as true three years ago, but that *does* happen to name a culprit for the crime that the state can easily lay its hands on!"

Mr. Darrow took his hand from his neck and shrugged in a big, exaggerated motion. "Dramatic stuff, gentleman. And, if it were true, very hard to contest. But the fact is, the story isn't true. Clara Hatch didn't just wake up one morning ready to tell her tale, and insistent on doing so—she was carefully coached, coached and *prodded* back into the speaking world. And by whom? By the same man who now sits behind the state's attorney." Mr. Darrow didn't look to the Doctor at that point; but everybody else in the courtroom did. "A man who's spent his life working with children who have been the victims of tragedy and violence. And a man who happens to have spent the last *week* assessing the mental condition of my client, and who will be called to the witness stand to speak on that subject—by the *state.*" Finally, Mr. Darrow looked our way. "Dr. Laszlo Kreizler. The name may not be familiar to you, gentlemen, or to the citizens of Saratoga County generally. But it's very well known in New York City. Very well known. Respected, by some. Others . . ." Mr. Darrow shrugged again. "Gentlemen, you may well wonder what and who has brought me here from Chicago to defend my client. But *I* wonder what and who has brought this stranger, this *alienist,* here from the madhouses of New York City, to coax a young girl into telling the world that her own mother shot her. That's what's got *me* confused, gentlemen. That's what troubles the 'very accomplished attorney,' to the point where I just can't gather my wits enough to be able to 'work on your sympathies.' Whatever *that* means . . ."

Those of us in the two rows behind Mr. Picton shot each other wide, anxious glances—for while Mr. Picton had spoken eloquently to the jury, Mr. Darrow was speaking their own language, and we all knew it.

Rubbing his neck wearily again, Mr. Darrow pulled out a handkerchief and started to wipe away beads of sweat that, as noon got closer, were starting to form faster and faster on his face. "Your Honor," he said, his voice going very soft and sad, "gentlemen of the jury—life presents us with many events that go unexplained. Some of them are wondrous, and some of them are terrifying. A simple enough thought, maybe, but, like so many simple things, full of implications. Because the mind tends to reject what it can't explain—reject, fear, and revile it. So it's been with this case, especially for the men whose job it is to solve crimes and mete out justice for the state. The assistant district attorney calls my client's explanation of what happened that night a 'fantastic' tale. Well . . . maybe it is. But that doesn't make it false. That doesn't even make it complicated. Look at what she's said—that while she was driving her children home after a long day spent enjoying each other's company in town and at the lakeshore, she was set upon by an apparently lunatic Negro, who attempted to assault her and threatened her children when she hesitated to surrender herself. The man was wild, crazed, desperate—and when my client made a sudden movement that this man interpreted as resistance, he shot the children and fled."

Thrusting his hands into the pockets of his pants, Mr. Darrow returned to the jury box. "You don't get a lot of behavior like that up here in Saratoga County, I know. But that doesn't mean it can't happen. It happens every week in Chicago. Maybe we should ask Dr. Kreizler—who's a man in a position to know, gentlemen—how many times a *day* it happens in New York City. Is it 'fantastic' there, too? Or just *here,* because this is a quiet, pleasant little town? The state's going to tell you that the fact that no one besides my client ever saw hide nor hair of the crazed lunatic means that he didn't exist. But remember, gentlemen—it was *hours* before my client was coherent enough to tell anyone exactly what had happened on the Charlton road. More than enough time for such a man to make his way to the train depot and hide aboard a freight car, or to sneak unnoticed into the back of a shipping truck, and find himself the next morning somewhere far from the search parties in Ballston Spa. Maybe he showed up in Chicago. Maybe in New York. He would've had time. Maybe he was picked up, raving about some white children he'd shot, by the New York City police, who, after failing to find that any white children had been shot in their jurisdiction, figured he was crazy and sent him over to the famous Bellevue Hospital Insane Pavilion. And maybe Dr. Kreizler—who does a lot of work in that hospital—was called in to, as the alienists say, 'assess' the man's mental condition. Maybe he thought the fellow was having delusions. Maybe the miserable creature's still there, rotting away in a cell, tortured by dreams of those three children in the wagon . . ."

By now Mr. Darrow was staring at the floor, and a faraway, wandering tone had come into his voice. His brows then furrowed suddenly over his eyes, and he shook himself. "The point, gentlemen," he continued, "is that we may never know. This case, and thousands like it every year, go unsolved and become open wounds in the soul of our society. We want to close those wounds—of course we do. Who wants to go through his everyday business with the knowledge that at any moment a lunatic may spring from the roadside and rob him of the things—or, more horribly, the people—he values most? None of us. And so we look for solutions, for safeguards, and every time we find one we tell ourselves that we're that much closer to being perfectly safe, perfectly secure. But it's an illusion, gentlemen—an illusion to which I have no intention of seeing my client sacrificed. The state may rest easier, thinking that it has brought the murderer of Thomas and Matthew Hatch to justice, and so may the citizens of this community. But that won't make these charges any more true, or any more believable to those who have the courage to stand back and look at the thing in the cold light of reason. The state has told you what evidence it will introduce, and what witnesses it will call to prove its allegations. And I tell you now that on every one of these points the defense will enter the testimony of witnesses—expert and otherwise—that will refute the prosecution point by point."

Lifting a heavy finger and pointing it in Mr. Picton's direction, Mr. Darrow started to pound away: "They'll tell you that they have physical evidence, supported by 'experts,' that the gun used to shoot the Hatch children belonged to their father, and was fired by their mother. But that entire theory is based on forensic 'science,' which, as the defense's expert witnesses will explain to you, isn't worthy of the name. The prosecution will then tell you that my client had financial and romantic reasons for wanting her children dead. But, gentlemen—household gossip is not evidence!" His blood getting hot, Mr. Darrow spun round to look at the galleries, the first really quick movement he'd made. "Finally, they'll tell you that my client is sane, and that, being sane, she deserves to be taken to a terrible little room in the state penitentiary and strapped into a chair that would've had more place in the dungeon of some blood-crazed medieval tyrant than it does in the United States, and that she should then be assaulted by the vicious power of electricity until she's dead—all so that the state can declare the case closed and its citizens can have their 'peace' restored!'"

Stopping himself suddenly and catching his breath, Mr. Darrow dropped his hands helplessly. "Well, that's really the point, isn't it, gentlemen? Yes, my client's sane. And in the days to come you'll hear, from people who have a long experience with these matters, that no sane woman could or would commit such violence against her own children. Oh, the prosecution will give you precedents—they'll tell you a lot of ghastly tales about women who've committed such crimes in the past, and were found sane by courts of law, and were locked away forever or hanged as punishment. But, gentlemen—prior injustices should not make you feel any better about committing an injustice *here*. Yes, there have been such women. But you will hear—again, from people who've studied these matters carefully—that those women, too, were suffering from terrible mental disorders, and that they were sacrificed to the same craving that drives the state in this case. The craving, not for justice, but for revenge—revenge and, even more urgently, an end to the uneasiness, the *fear*, that is engendered by a horrible crime that admits of no solution."

Wandering in front of the jury box, Mr. Darrow went back to work on his neck again. "Gentlemen, I can't tell you why this happened. I can't tell you a lot of things. I can't tell you why babies are born dead and deformed, why lightning and cyclones destroy lives and homes in an instant and without warning, or why disease eats away at some good but unfortunate souls, while letting others lead long and useless lives. But I know that these things happen. And I wonder . . . if a bolt of lightning *had* flashed down out of the sky that night and put an end to those three poor children—just as the prosecution now seeks to put an end to their mother—would the district attorney's office have tried to coax an explanation out of the sky, so that the citizens of this county and this state could rest easier? Because in the end, that's the only place you're probably going to get an explanation for what happened out on the Charlton road on May the thirty-first, 1894—from above. If you try to provide an answer here, in this courtroom, you will only compound the horror. And for that you—yes, *you*, and I, and the state's attorney, and everyone else involved—will bear the responsibility. Chance terror killed Mrs. Hatch's children, but *her* death would be something very different. Something very different, indeed . . ."

With that Mr. Darrow wandered solemnly back over to his table and sat down. He never turned to Libby Hatch, but she did glance at him; and in her eyes was a light of hope, one what quickly became a frightening gleam of triumph when she looked beyond Mr. Darrow to all of us who were sitting behind Mr. Picton. It was pretty plain that she figured she was going to get off; and as I looked around at the faces of the jury and the people in the galleries, I couldn't honestly say that I thought she was mistaken. Strange, the effect what that thought had on me: suddenly all I could think of was of the little Linares girl and Kat, and what would happen to them both if Libby was allowed to walk out of that court house a free woman—a possibility what had never seemed so likely before.

To judge by the looks on both the Doctor's and Mr. Picton's faces, they also realized how much damage had been done. The jury and the crowd, who likely would have bought even a poor defense of Libby Hatch, had taken Mr. Darrow's cagy, expert, and passionate words straight to heart. The evidence and the testimony, now more than ever, were our only hope. And that afternoon, the process of introducing them started with a bang, when Clara Hatch was called to the stand.

CHAPTER 44

The frightened little girl and her family arrived at the court house during the midday recess, escorted by Sheriff Dunning and a gang of specially appointed deputies. The Doctor made sure he was at the back door to greet Clara, and judging by the look on her face when she saw the crowd what was waiting for her, it was a good thing he did: even during my old days downtown, I'd rarely seen a kid what looked so confused, so lost, and so desperate. Searching through the jungle of faces and bodies what swarmed around her family's carriage, Clara appeared to calm down only when her golden-brown eyes locked onto the Doctor; and she fairly flew down to the ground in her rush to get to him. Some nearby newspapermen took particular interest in that fact, for reasons I didn't quite understand until I forced myself to look at the case from the opposition's point of view: if you were disposed to think that the Doctor was controlling and engineering what Clara said and did, then her plainly urgent need to be close to him might've looked sinister, indeed.

As the Westons followed Clara and the Doctor into the courthouse, Sheriff Dunning's men strung themselves out across the back doorway, keeping the curious crowd outside. Then we all went up to the second floor of the building, where we sat in Mr. Picton's office and ate some sandwiches what Cyrus had picked up from Mrs. Hastings. We tried to be as merry as we could, given the circumstances, and nobody said anything about the case; but none of it seemed to make Clara any easier in her mind. She didn't eat anything, just sipped on a glass of lemonade what Cyrus gave her; and each time she set the glass down, her one good hand, sticky with lemon juice and sugar, wandered to either Mrs. Weston or the Doctor, who were sitting on either side of her. Not seeming to hear any of the light conversation or strained jokes what floated around the room, she just stared at each of our faces kind of blankly until it was near time for us to return to court; and then, when she thought no one was paying attention, she looked up at the Doctor.

"Is my mama here?" she asked, very quietly.

The Doctor nodded, with a gentle smile but a very serious look in his eyes. "Yes. She's downstairs."

Clara began to kick her feet against the legs of her chair and turned her head down to stare into her lap. "This is my Sunday dress," she said, carefully straightening the flowery, light blue fabric with her good hand. "I just didn't want to eat so's it wouldn't get it messy."

Mrs. Weston smiled down at her. "Clara, honey, don't worry about that. If you're hungry—"

But Clara just shook her head, hard enough to bring the big braid in her hair round front and reveal some of the nasty scar on the back of her neck.

The Doctor lifted a hand to touch the top of her head. "Very sensible. I wish you could teach Stevie to be so sensible. His clothes are an infernal mess most of the time."

Clara looked up at me quickly and smiled.

"Yeah," I said, nodding. "I'm just a pig in a sty, nothing I can do about it." By way of emphasis, I let a piece of roast beef from my sandwich fall onto my shirt, a move what got a scratchy little laugh out of our witness. Then she turned away, quickly and shyly.

By two o'clock we were back in our seats in the main courtroom, while the Westons waited outside with Clara. Mr. Picton had elected to open his case with testimony from the former sheriff, Morton Jones, a grizzled, tough old type who looked like he'd spent the better part of his retirement on a bar seat. Jones told of what he'd found when he'd arrived at the Hatch house on the night of May 31st, 1894, and what steps he'd taken to address the situation, including telephoning Mr. Picton. This summary acquainted the jury with the basic facts of the case, facts what Mr. Darrow did nothing to challenge; when his turn came to cross-examine the witness, he turned the opportunity down.

Next onto the stand was Dr. Benjamin Lawrence, the sometime coroner. He told about how, when he'd arrived in the Hatch house, he'd found Mrs. Hatch in a state of extreme hysteria and the bloodied children laid out on sofas and a table in the sitting room. He'd given the mother laudanum to quiet her down, then set to work on the kids, quickly determining that Matthew and Thomas were dead. But Clara was still alive, though Libby and the housekeeper, Mrs. Wright, thought otherwise. Testifying that her pulse had been very faint but still detectable, Dr. Lawrence went on to say that he'd given the girl half a nitroglycerin tablet and then injected brandy into her arm to get her heart moving faster. After that, he set to work stopping her bleeding. But the wound itself was beyond his capabilities, and he'd phoned up to Saratoga to ask Dr. Jacob Jenkins, a surgical specialist, to come down as quickly as possible. Jenkins was set to follow Lawrence to the stand, but before he was through with the first medical witness Mr. Picton made sure to ask whether Libby Hatch's hysterical state had immobilized her in any way. Not at all, Dr. Lawrence answered; when he'd gotten to the house, Mrs. Hatch had been running through each and every room at a high speed.

"Almost as if she had some purpose, would you say?" Mr. Picton asked.

Dr. Lawrence was about to agree, but Mr. Darrow shot up. "I must object to that, Your Honor. The question calls for a speculative answer from the witness, who cannot have known what was in or on the former Mrs. Hatch's mind."

"Agreed," Judge Brown said with a nod. "I've warned you, Mr. Picton—no suggestions. The jury will ignore the state's question."

Sitting forward again, I heard Dr. Kreizler mumble, "As if they could." Then I saw him hide a smile with his hand.

Mr. Picton had a few final questions for Dr. Lawrence: had he been in attendance at the Hatch house when Mrs. Hatch had given birth to her three children? Dr. Lawrence answered that he had indeed. And what had been Mrs. Hatch's condition after her third labor? Revealing a bit of information designed to prepare the jury for Mr. Picton's intended claim that Libby in fact resented her kids (and one what also matched our speculations from early in the case), Dr. Lawrence said that young Tommy's birth had been difficult, and left his mother unable to bear any more children. Mr. Darrow challenged the relevance of this information and by way of reply Mr. Picton sat down, turning the witness over to his opponent. But once again, the counsel for the defense passed up his chance at cross-examination.

He did the same with Dr. Jenkins: after Mr. Picton had gone over said witness's recollections of treating Clara Hatch—taking special care to make the jury understand that there was no connection between the bullet wound the girl had received and the fact that she hadn't spoken in three years—it was time for the defense to take over. But Mr. Darrow just stood briefly, said, "We have no questions at this time, Your Honor," and then sat back down.

A few comments made their way through the galleries at that, and Judge Brown began to rub the white hair on his head, looking a bit disturbed. "Mr. Darrow," he said slowly, "I realize that you have a different way of doing things out west—but I trust you still follow the same basic rules of procedure in a criminal trial?"

Mr. Darrow smiled and stood back up, chuckling what you might call self-consciously. "I thank the court for its concern. The simple fact is, Your Honor, that the defense has no argument with the state concerning what happened immediately *after* the shootings. At least, not so far as *these* witnesses are concerned."

The crowd seemed to find that information reassuring; as for Judge Brown, he nodded a few times and said, "Very well, Counselor. Just so long as you're aware of what's happening."

"I do my best, Your Honor," Mr. Darrow replied, sitting again.

The Judge turned to Mr. Picton. "The state may call its next witness."

Mr. Picton stood up and took a deep breath; and I could see the Doctor's hand tighten on the arm of his chair until his knuckles went white.

"Your Honor," Mr. Picton said, "the state has an unusual request to make at this time."

Judge Brown's little eyes did their best to open wide. "Indeed?"

"Yes, Your Honor. The state's next witness is Clara Hatch. Clara is just eight years old, and, she has not seen her mother—her *blood* mother, that is—in more than three years. The citizens of Ballston Spa"—here Mr. Picton threw a look around the room that I could've wished'd had a little more of what they call the *common touch*—"are as charitable and considerate in such matters as those of any community, I have no doubt. But given these special considerations, the state would like to ask that the galleries be cleared for the duration of Clara Hatch's testimony."

"Hmm," Judge Brown noised, tugging at one of his monkey ears. "Ordinarily I don't care for closed trial sessions, Mr. Picton. They smack of the Old World to me. But I do concede that you may have a point. What about it, Mr. Darrow?"

Standing up even slower than was his usual practice, Mr. Darrow began knotting his forehead up. "Your Honor," he said, as though it was very difficult for him. "Like the court, we do concede that this is a special witness, who needs to be treated carefully. But—and I say this with very mixed feelings—the prosecution has already stated that this little girl is its primary witness. And she has already appeared before one closed court, that being the grand jury. Now, as I say, I'm sympathetic to the sensibilities of a child, but—Your Honor, my client is on trial for her *life*. Whatever her age, if this girl's words are going to put her mother in the electrical chair, well, then, I think she ought to be able to say them in front of the same audience and under the same duress as every other witness who's going to appear here."

The galleries, for their own selfish reasons as much as anything else, began to rumble in agreement; but the judge didn't hesitate, this time, to let them have it with his gavel. "The court is aware," he said, looking around coldly, "of our audience's prejudice in this regard—so let's have no more comment, or I *will* clear this room, and quickly, too!" Pausing to see how long it took the people in the galleries to obey him (only a few seconds), the judge then looked to Mr. Picton again.

"The court appreciates the state's concerns," he said. "And I can assure you that, if I so much as hear a pin drop in the galleries while this girl is testifying, I will satisfy the state's request. But until that happens, I'm afraid consideration toward the defense must remain paramount. The girl is understandably nervous—but I daresay the accused is nervous, too. Bring on your witness, Mr. Picton."

Mr. Picton frowned and held out his hands. "But, Your Honor—"

"Your *witness*, sir," the judge repeated, sitting back in his chair.

Sighing once, Mr. Picton dropped his arms. "Very well. But I will feel free to remind the court of its pledge regarding the behavior of the galleries, should that behavior interfere with my witness's composure."

Judge Brown nodded. "If you can find fault with our guests' behavior before I do, Mr. Picton, I should be very surprised. But please feel free to let me know if it happens. Now—get on with it."

With another deep breath, Mr. Picton looked over at Iphegeneia Blaylock. "The state calls Clara Hatch."

Turning to the big mahogany doors, Mr. Picton nodded to the guard Henry, who opened one door and said, "Clara Hatch," in a low but firm voice.

And in they came: the little girl in the simple summer dress, her left hand holding her right, followed by Mr. and Mrs. Weston, who looked like they were being scorched by the burning stares of every pair of eyes in the room. The folks in the galleries were mostly people the Westons had known for years; but at moments like that, years of knowledge and friendship can be knocked down and trampled by the greater pressures of confusion, suspicion, and plain and simple fear.

Once again, Clara searched out the crowd before her with quick turns of her little head; and when she found the Doctor's face she stayed locked on it, as if he were a lighthouse that might guide the little ship of her life back into safe port after it'd weathered the storm what lay beyond the oak rail at the end of the aisle. And as she looked at the Doctor, I turned to look at Libby Hatch: the girl's mother—her "blood mother," as Mr. Picton had cleverly put it—saw that Clara's eyes were fixed on the Doctor, and the pleading, loving expression what the woman had managed to shoehorn into her features in hopes of appealing to Clara quickly soured into an expression of jealousy—and hate. But once the little girl was guided onto the other side of the rail by the bailiff, Libby managed to get her face rearranged yet again; and though it wasn't quite as affectionate as it had been before, it was still closer to that mark than anything I'd ever seen her exhibit to date.

About halfway to the stand Clara stopped walking, as if she could feel the pair of golden eyes boring into the back of her head; then she slowly turned to take in the woman in the black dress, who smiled gently at her before suddenly putting her hands to her mouth with a gasp and sobbing just once. Looking strangely calm, little Clara said three simple words—"Don't cry, Mama"—in a voice what couldn't have been more grown up or more considerate; and the sound of those words struck every person in the galleries as dumb as the witness herself had been for the last three years.

Turning again, Clara climbed on into the witness box and held up her good left hand, following the procedure what the Doctor had spent long hours preparing her for. Bailiff Coffey, having been alerted by Mr. Picton, took the girl's lifeless right hand and placed it on his Bible.

"Do you solemnly swear," he said, softer than was his habit, "that the testimony you are about to give in this court—"

"I do," Clara said, jumping the gun in her first outright show of nerves.

Bailiff Coffey just held up a finger, telling her to wait. "—shall be the truth, the whole truth, and nothing but the truth, so help you God?"

"I do," Clara repeated, her face going a little red.

"State your full name, please," Bailiff Coffey said.

"Clara Jessica Hatch," she answered softly. Then, at a signal from Coffey, she sat down. Clara glanced at her mother quickly again, but just as quickly turned away to look at the Doctor once more. He gave her a firm little nod, to let her know that she was doing just fine. Finally, Mr. Picton stood up to approach the witness box.

"Hello, Clara," he said, in a careful but still chipper sort of way. The girl opened her mouth to respond, but only managed a nod, as she pulled her right hand up onto her lap. "Clara," Mr. Picton continued, "I'd like you to tell these gentlemen"—he held a hand up to the jury box—"—everything that happened on the night of May the thirty-first, three years ago. In your own words. Can you do that for me, Clara?" The girl paused, trying hard now not to look at her mother. After a few seconds she nodded. "Then please," Mr. Picton continued, "go ahead."

As she took a deep breath, the fingers of Clara's left hand locked onto her numb right forearm, gripping it hard. Letting the air out of her lungs, she began her story, in that same scratchy but brave voice.

"We went to town, to buy some things. And then to the lake—"

"Lake Saratoga?" Mr. Picton asked.

"Yes. Sometimes we'd go there in the summer. To watch the sun go down. And sometimes they have fireworks. But Tommy was getting sleepy before the fireworks started. And Matthew's tummy wasn't so good, on account of because he ate so many butterscotches. So Mama said we'd better go on home."

" 'Mama?' " Mr. Picton asked. "Clara, do you see your mama anywhere right now?" The girl nodded quickly. "Can you point to her, please?" Glancing up ever so briefly, Clara stole a look at Libby, and then bent her head back down as she pointed toward the defense table. "Let the record state," Mr. Picton said, "that the witness recognizes the accused, Mrs. Elspeth Hunter, as being her mother, the former Mrs. Elspeth Hatch, more commonly known as Libby Hatch." Mr. Picton drew closer to the witness box and softened his voice again. "All right, Clara. Tell me, did you *want* to leave the lake that night?"

The girl shook her head, being careful to keep her braid behind her. "No, sir—I wanted to see the rockets."

"And your mama—did she want to see the rockets, too?"

"Yes. But she said we had to get Tommy and Matthew home."

"Was she happy about that?"

"No, sir. She was kind of—mad. She got kind of mad, sometimes."

"Did she say anything that let you know she was kind of mad?"

Clara nodded once again, though reluctantly. "She said what she wanted didn't matter—didn't ever matter. That she always had to take care of us instead of doing what she liked."

"Did she tell you what she would've 'liked,' exactly?"

Clara shrugged—or at least, her one good shoulder did. "I figured she meant seeing the rockets."

Letting the girl take a few breaths to steady herself, Mr. Picton waited before saying, "Now, then, Clara—you got into your wagon to go home?"

"Yes, sir."

"Did your mother *do* anything, being as she was so angry?"

Clara's face went puzzled. "She didn't spank us or anything, if that's what you mean. She just told me to get the boys into the wagon, and then we left."

"Told *you?*" Mr. Picton asked, moving over to the jury and plastering a look of surprise on his face. "*She* didn't put the boys into the wagon?"

"She tried," Clara answered. "But Matthew started to cry. So she just told me to do it, and went down to the water to wash her face."

Mr. Picton looked at the jury what you might call meaningfully. "Did she often ask you to take care of the boys?"

Nodding, Clara looked down at her hands again. "Mm-hmm. It was my job."

Mr. Picton nodded, still studying the jury, who were starting to look as wide-eyed and confused as Sheriff Dunning had when he'd come out of the grand jury hearing. "I see," Mr. Picton said. "That was *your* job . . . and once the boys were in the wagon?"

"Then Mama came up from the water, and we started to drive home," Clara answered; but the words weren't as strong as they had been to that point.

Mr. Picton, hearing the change, came back over to her, and stood so that his body blocked Clara's view of Libby, and vice versa. "But you didn't *get* home, did you, Clara?"

Seeming relieved that her mother was out of sight, Clara shook her head with more certainty. "No, sir."

"And why not?"

Another deep breath and another look at the Doctor, and Clara went on; "We drove back through town, and we were on the road home—"

"The Charlton road?" Mr. Picton asked.

Clara nodded. "All of a sudden Mama drove the wagon over under a big tree, off the road. It was dark by then, and I didn't know why she stopped. It was scary, on that road."

"And where were you sitting, at that time?"

"I was in the back, holding on to Tommy so's he didn't bother Matthew—he was asleep by then."

"Matthew was?"

"Yes, sir. And I didn't want Tommy to wake him up so's he'd start crying about his stomach again. It bothered Mama. I asked her why we stopped. She didn't say anything for a few minutes, just sat up on the bench, staring at the road. I asked her again, and then she got down and came around to the back of the wagon. She had her bag in her hand. She said she had something important she needed to tell us."

Hearing Clara's voice start to trail off again, Mr. Picton said, "It's all right, Clara. What did she tell you?"

"She said that she'd stopped . . . she'd stopped . . ."

"Clara?"

The girl's eyes'd gone glassy, and for a minute my heart sank, thinking that she'd shrunk back into the horrified silence what'd gripped her for so long. I saw the Doctor's jaw set hard, and I knew that he was worrying about the same thing. We both started breathing again, though, when Clara near-whispered:

"She said that she'd seen our dada."

Judge Brown leaned over, cupping one of his big ears with his hand. "I'm afraid you'll have to speak up a little, young lady, if you can," he said.

Looking up at him and swallowing hard, Clara repeated, "She said that she'd seen our dada. She said he told her he was with God. She said that he told her God wanted us to be with Him, too."

Mr. Picton nodded grimly, glancing to the jury box. "For the jury's information, Clara's father, Daniel Hatch, passed away on December the twenty-ninth, 1893—approximately six months before the night in question. The cause was a sudden"—here Mr. Picton turned around to look at Libby—"a *very* sudden, and unexplained, attack of heart disease."

"Your Honor," Mr. Darrow said, standing up as quick as he could, "this kind of innuendo—"

"Mr. Picton," the judge agreed, nodding to Mr. Darrow and then looking at the assistant district attorney, "I've warned you—"

"Your Honor, I suggest nothing," Mr. Picton said, his eyes going wide and innocent. "The plain truth is that every medical man in Ballston Spa examined Daniel Hatch during his illness, and could find no explanation for his condition."

"Then *say* that," Judge Brown replied. "Half-truths are not better than lies, sir. Continue with your questions."

Mr. Picton turned to Clara once more, letting his voice go soft again. "And what did you think that your mama meant, when she said that your dada told her that God wanted you to be with Him?"

Clara's left shoulder shrugged again. "I didn't know. I thought she meant that—that *someday*—but . . ."

Nodding, Mr. Picton said, "But that wasn't what she meant, was it?"

Clara shook her head, this time hard enough to move the braid; and as the scar on the back of her neck became visible, I noted that one or two of the jurors caught sight of it, and silently pointed it out to the others. "She opened her bag," Clara said. "And she took out dada's gun."

"Dada's gun?" Mr. Picton asked. "How did you know it was your dada's gun?"

"He kept it under his pillow," Clara answered, "and he showed it to me once. He told me never to touch it, unless somebody bad was in the house. Somebody who was stealing, or . . . Mama left it there after he died."

The girl's voice trailed off, and her face began to get frightened: frightened in a way what even looking to the Doctor didn't seem to help. Knowing that he'd reached a very dangerous point, Mr. Picton moved in closer to ask, "What happened then, Clara?"

"Mama, she—" Clara's head began to shiver a little, and the left side of her body followed. Wrapping her good arm around herself, she worked hard to go on: "Mama came up into the wagon. She woke up Matthew and told me to give Tommy to him. So I did. Then she looked at me again. She told me it was time to go see Dada and God. That it would be a better place, and we had to do what God wanted." Tears filled the girl's eyes and started to roll down her face, but she never really cried as such, just grabbed herself tighter and tried to keep going. "She touched me with the gun—"

"Where did she touch you, Clara?" Mr. Picton asked. The girl pointed to her upper chest, finally letting out just one choking sob. "And then?"

"I remember she pulled the trigger, and there was a big bang—but that's all," Clara answered, getting a better hold of herself. "I don't remember anything more. Not until I was in my bed at home."

Mr. Picton nodded, letting out a deep breath of his own. "All right, Clara. It's all right. We can talk about something else now, if you want."

Clara wiped her face with her hand and said, "Okay."

After giving her a couple of minutes, Mr. Picton asked, in a louder voice, "Clara—do you remember Reverend Parker?"

"He—he gave the services at our church. And he came out to visit Mama and Dada sometimes."

"And what did he do when he came out to visit?"

"He'd come to dinner," Clara answered. "And sometimes he'd go for walks with Mama. Dada didn't like to go. He said the air was bad for him."

"Did your mama ever take you or the boys along?"

Clara shook her head. "She said it wasn't our place."

Mr. Picton reached into the box to touch the girl's left arm, looking very relieved. "Thank you, Clara," he said. Then he added, not caring whether it was loud enough for anybody else to hear him, "You've been a very brave young lady." Turning to walk back to his table, Mr. Picton then stood and looked at the judge and the jury. "The state has no more questions for this witness, Your Honor." He sat down, leaving Clara exposed to the full power of her mother's eyes.

Libby had reacted to her daughter's testimony very much the way that the Doctor had predicted she would: first she'd tried quiet tears and hand-wringing, then she'd bobbed her head around, trying to get Clara to look at her. Then, when Mr. Picton stepped in to make sure Clara couldn't see her, the tears and head bobbing had stopped, and she'd settled into still silence, while her eyes filled again with that cold, hateful glare.

But had the jury been able to see that? Or was it only the few of us what knew her full history who'd been able to read Libby's face?

Looking terribly alone without Mr. Picton nearby, Clara turned her eyes downward once more, and started moving her lips silently. Seeing the near desperation on the girl's face, the judge leaned over toward her. "Clara?" he said. "Are you able to go on now?"

With a start Clara looked up at him. "Go on?" she asked softly.

"The defense must question you now," the judge answered, with just about the only smile I ever saw him exhibit during the trial.

"Oh," Clara answered, like maybe she'd forgotten. "Yes. I can go on, sir."

The judge sat back, looking to the defense table. "All right, Mr. Darrow."

During the whole of Mr. Picton's examination of Clara, Mr. Darrow's hands'd been folded in front of his face, so that it'd been pretty tough to tell what he was thinking or how he was reacting. But when he stood up for his cross-examination, all the deep worry and occasional outrage what we'd seen him exhibit to this point seemed gone, and his features became open and relaxed in a way what Clara pretty obviously considered a relief.

"Thank you, Your Honor," Mr. Darrow said, gently smiling and moving toward the witness box. But he moved at an angle what made it impossible for Clara to get any more looks at the Doctor: life is never more tit-for-tat than when you're in a courtroom. "Hello, Clara," he said as he got closer to her. "I know this isn't easy, so I'm going to try to get you out of here as soon as I can." Clara just dropped her eyes as an answer. "Clara, you say the next thing you remember is waking up in your house, is that right?" At another nod from the girl, Mr. Darrow went on, "But I don't guess you thought you'd had a bad dream, did you?"

"No," Clara answered. "I was—hurt . . ."

"Yes," Mr. Darrow said, fairly oozing sympathy. "You were hurt pretty bad. And you'd been asleep for a long time, did you know that?"

"They told me later—the doctors did."

"A long sleep can make people confused sometimes. I know if I sleep too long, I sometimes don't even know where I am or how I got there, when I wake up."

"I knew where I was," Clara said, softly but firmly. "I was at home."

"Good girl," the Doctor whispered, craning his neck in an effort to get a look at her but not wanting to be obvious about it.

"Of course you were," Mr. Darrow said. "But did you know everything else? I mean, as soon as you woke up, did you remember everything else?"

As if she couldn't help herself, Clara again glanced over at her mother, who had her hands folded on the defense table like she was pleading for something, while her eyes'd filled with tears. Seeing this, Clara bobbed her head back down like she'd been jerked with a rope, and said, "I remember Mama screaming. And crying. She said that Matthew and Tommy were dead. I didn't understand. I tried to get up and ask her, but the Doctor gave me some medicine. I went back to sleep."

"And when you woke up the second time?"

"Mama was next to my bed. With the doctors."

"Did your mama tell you anything?"

"She said that we'd all been attacked—by a man. A crazy man. She said he'd killed Matthew and Tommy." Tears now slowly streaming down her face again, Clara added, "I started to cry. I wanted to see my brothers, but Mama said—I couldn't ever. Ever again . . ."

"I see," Mr. Darrow told her. Then he pulled a handkerchief—one what was a lot neater than the clothes it'd been concealed in—out of his breast pocket. "Would you like to use this?" Clara took the white piece of linen and wiped her face. "Clara, how long after that did your mama go away?"

"Soon. I think. I don't know, not for sure."

"But was she with you all that time before she left?"

Clara nodded. "Her and Louisa—our housekeeper. The doctors, sometimes, too. And Mr. Picton visited."

"I'm sure he did," Mr. Darrow said, looking over at the jury. "And what did your mama tell you before she went away?"

Stealing another look at Libby, Clara answered, "That she had to go find us a new place to live. So we didn't have to live in that house. It was too sad, she said—Dada was dead, and Tommy and Matthew, too. She told me she'd find a new place, and come back to take me away when she did."

"And did you believe her?"

"Yes."

"Did you usually believe your mama?"

"Yes. Except—"

"Except—?"

"Except when she got mad sometimes. Then, sometimes, she would say things that—I didn't believe her. I don't think she meant them, though."

"I see," Mr. Darrow said, turning his body away from her without moving from his spot on the floor. "So—the last things you now remember about that night on the Charlton road are your mama touching you with a gun, then pulling the trigger—and after that there was a loud noise?"

"Yes."

"But you didn't remember it when you woke up?" Clara shook her head. "And you can't remember anything about what happened to Tommy and Matthew?"

"I didn't—I didn't *see*—what happened."

"You're sure?"

"Yes."

"And so your mama went away, and you went to live with Mr. and Mrs. Weston—is that right?" Clara nodded. "And did you remember anything about what happened that night during the time you lived with them?"

"Not—" Here Clara worked very hard, pretty obviously to remember something. "Not so's I could talk about it. Or show it. Only so's I could see it. In my head."

Mr. Darrow spun quickly to the girl, causing her to start a bit and try, without success, to look at the Doctor. "That's quite a mouthful, for a little girl. *Not so's you could talk about it or show it, but so's you could see it in your head.* You think of that all by yourself?"

Clara looked down quickly. "It's the way it was."

"Did you think of that all by yourself, Clara?" Mr. Darrow repeated. Then, without waiting for an answer, he moved in closer. "Or isn't it in fact true that Dr. Kreizler led you to see it that way, and told you to use those words when it came time to tell the story in court?"

Mr. Picton was out of his chair like the seat was lined with hot coals. "Your Honor, the state protests! We asked for special treatment of this witness, and what do we get? Leading and badgering!"

Before the judge could answer, Mr. Darrow was holding up a hand. "I will withdraw the question, Your Honor, and try to make my questions more palatable to the state." Again smiling at the witness, Mr. Darrow asked, "Clara, when did you first start to remember what happened that night? I mean, remember it so that you could talk about it?"

Clara shrugged, her face looking even more worried after the short but sharp exchange between the lawyers. "Not too long ago, I guess."

"*Before* you met Dr. Kreizler?" Clara reluctantly shook her head. "*After* you met Dr. Kreizler?" Clara didn't move. "Or was it *when* you met Dr. Kreizler?"

Mr. Picton was up again. "Your Honor, with all due respect, which question does the learned counsel from Illinois wish the witness to answer?"

"Sit down, Mr. Picton," Judge Brown replied. "The counsel for the defense is within his rights."

"Thank you, Your Honor," Mr. Darrow said. "Well, Clara?"

"I never forgot," the girl answered, more tears coming as she did. "I never forgot, not really."

"And what didn't you forget? You never knew what happened to Tommy and Matthew, that's fine, you've told us that. So you couldn't and don't remember it. But what *did* you know that you *didn't* forget?"

"I never—" Looking up at the bench pleadingly, Clara said, "I don't know what he means."

"I *mean*, Clara," Mr. Darrow went on, being a little firmer now, "what was it that you know that you never forgot, and what was it that you know that you forgot and only remembered not too long ago?"

Her body shaking once, Clara finally let out a sob as she looked from the judge to Mr. Darrow, and then tried to peer around the lawyer at the Doctor, who, for his part, was also desperately attempting to get himself into position to be seen by her.

"What the devil?" the Doctor whispered. "He's deliberately attempting to confuse her—"

"I don't understand!" Clara said again, openly crying now.

"Clara," Mr. Darrow went on, "it's very simple—"

"It's not!" the girl cried. "I don't understand—"

"Which is which?" Mr. Darrow said, surprising everyone in the room by letting his voice get stern, even a bit harsh. "What did you always know, and what did you forget but remember not too long ago, perhaps at about the time that you met Dr. Kreizler—and perhaps *when* you met Dr. Kreizler? Clara! You must—"

"*Stop it!*" a voice called out, silencing both the lawyer and the mumbling what had started in the galleries. The entire room turned to the defense table, where Libby Hatch was, like her daughter, in tears. "Leave her alone!" she shouted at Darrow. "You can't treat her like this, not with what she's been through. If she doesn't remember, then she doesn't! Stop browbeating my child! Stop it—stop!" Throwing her face into her hands, Libby collapsed onto the table as the crowd started to hum like a hive again, causing Judge Brown to smash his gavel down.

"The defendant will get herself under control!" he ordered. "And so will the galleries! Mr. Darrow—the court would like to know—"

"If it please the court, Your Honor," Mr. Darrow said quickly. "The defense will forgo the remainder of its questions to this witness. Under the circumstances, we ask for an adjournment until tomorrow morning."

The noise of the crowd grew louder at that, and the judge set to rapping away. "Silence! I won't have another sound!" As his order began to take effect, the judge set his gavel aside, looking very displeased. "The witness is excused," he called. "And court is adjourned until ten o'clock tomorrow morning—at which time I'd better see some radically different behavior, or I *will* close these proceedings!" A final rap, and Bailiff Coffey moved to help Clara—who was weeping heavily now—down out of the witness box. Mr. Picton rushed over to lend a hand, but the little girl's tormented eyes were fixed on her apparently devastated mother.

"Don't cry, Mama!" Clara called once more as she was led away. But her tone was very different, now: all the grown-up quality was gone, and the desperation in her words was underlined by the weight of her sobs. "Don't cry, it's going to help you! It's supposed to help you, they told me—"

Libby Hatch never looked up. Sensing what was happening, the Doctor moved quickly for the gate in the railing; but when Clara saw him, her anguish only appeared to get worse, and she ran past him down the center aisle to Mr. and Mrs. Weston, who rushed her out of first the room and then the building.

The judge had already departed; and as the jury moved to do the same, Mr. Darrow got Libby to her feet and moved her in the direction of the side door down to her cell. But before either she or jury had exited, she began to wail, "She doesn't remember! She doesn't remember, how can you expect her to, she's just a child! Oh, my poor Clara, my poor baby!"

At that Mr. Darrow turned to the jury box, looking uneasy; but the sight of their confused faces seemed to reassure him, and he gave the guard who'd been standing behind Iphegeneia Blaylock the okay to take his client on downstairs.

With things finally settling down, Mr. Picton made his way over to the Doctor. The look what they exchanged indicated nothing good, and I certainly didn't have any trouble understanding why. The rest of our group crowded round, also looking deeply troubled; only Mr. Moore was scratching his head.

"Well," he said, "if you ask me, Vanderbilt's throwing his money away. Imagine trying to bully an eight-year-old girl like that! Darrow must be crazy! Hell, even her own *mother*—" Then he suddenly stopped: watching the rest of our faces, he finally realized what we'd already grasped. "Dammit!" he seethed quietly, with a stamp of his foot. "I *hate* being the last one to get these things! He planned the whole scene, didn't he?"

"Son of a bitch," Marcus said, more amazed than angry. "He took an unmitigated disaster for his client and turned it into a possible advantage."

"And she played her part perfectly," Mr. Picton said regretfully. Then he turned to Mr. Moore. "Men like Vanderbilt do not maintain their stations in life by making stupid choices, John." He hissed once and slapped at the railing. "What the hell does Darrow care if people think *he's* callous, if at the same time he can make the jury believe that Libby genuinely loves her daughter, and wouldn't do anything to hurt her?"

I looked up at the Doctor, whose face had gone a little pale. He turned to stare at the mahogany doors, as if he thought Clara might come back into the room; but all he saw, all any of us saw, was the crowd filing out, some of them turning back to give our group what might politely be called very unsympathetic glances. Feeling for his chair, the Doctor swayed back and then sat on it, his features suddenly going very ashen: the kind of ashen they'd gone, I realized with some dread, when he'd gotten the news about Paulie McPherson.

As I stood there watching him, I felt a little tug at my arm, and turned to find El Niño giving me a grave look.

"Señorito Stevie," he said, trying not to be heard by the others, "this is not a good thing."

"No," I answered, "it ain't."

The aborigine considered that, and then nodded, straightened his white silk tie, and put his hands to his hips. "This man Darrow—you are *certain* I should not kill him?"

"Actually," I answered, shaking my head, "I'm beginning to wonder . . ."

CHAPTER 45

Spirits were very depressed around Mr. Picton's house that night, all the more so because at the start of the day we'd figured that the afternoon's events would put us pretty firmly in control of the case. Instead, the clever Mr. Darrow had battled us to what amounted to a draw, or maybe worse: he'd made Clara look unsure and confused, and he'd planted the idea that her confidence and maybe even her story had been the Doctor's work, not her own. True, the facts as she'd recalled them worked to our favor; but as anybody who's ever been involved with the law will tell you, facts aren't always or even usually what decides a case. And so we didn't talk much during dinner, the adults putting most of their energy into making another good-sized dent in Mr. Picton's wine cellar. After the meal Marcus and Mr. Moore took the trolley on up to Saratoga to try to get an idea of what the general public's reaction to Clara's testimony'd been—though the answer to that question seemed pretty obvious.

As for me, I found that nightfall brought more worries about Kat. Ana Linares was still on my mind, too, as she was on everybody else's; but the thought of what would happen if Libby got off, went back to New York, and found Kat trying to protect the baby tugged at my heart and my stomach in a way what I found I just couldn't control. After dinner I went for a long walk, and when I came back I just sat out on the front porch of the house, still trying to think my way out of what I was feeling by telling myself that Kat should've already left New York, that she only had herself to blame for her new predicament. But it didn't really work. The more I considered the problem, the more it brought me to a state of mind what was typical, when it came to my dealings with Kat: a kind of frustrated sadness, and underneath it a sense that somehow I was to blame for at least part of the situation.

Wrapped up in such cogitations and emotions, I barely noticed the sound of the screen door opening behind me. I knew it was the Doctor: he'd been able to read my worried face at dinner, and it would've been like him to want to make sure I was all right. I didn't feel much like talking— as usual, the subject of Kat only made me feel stupid when I discussed it with other people—and so I was grateful when he just sat beside me and didn't say a thing. We listened to the crickets for a time, and traded a few short comments about a swarm of fireflies what were giving a good imitation of the starry sky above us out on Mr. Picton's front lawn. Other than that, though, we stayed wrapped up in our separate worries.

It was plain what the Doctor was thinking: the moment when Clara Hatch'd run past him and out the door of the courtroom had been a terrible one, and'd caused him to wonder whether he'd done right by the little girl, or if he hadn't, in fact, been using her for his own purposes instead of helping her. There wasn't anything I could tell him—I honestly didn't know how I felt about it. Maybe silence and forgetting would've been better, part of me thought, for somebody like Clara Hatch; maybe facing the devils of your past, especially at such a young age, was just a painful waste; maybe the key to life, despite everything the Doctor believed and'd spent his life working on, was to just put the ugliness what you encounter—what *every* person encounters—behind you, and get on with things. Maybe memory was just a wicked curse, and the kind of mind what could wipe out painful recollections a blessing. Maybe . . .

We were still sitting there on the porch when Mr. Moore and Marcus came wandering up. Catching sight of them, the Doctor stood and called out, "Did you see White?"

Mr. Moore nodded, holding up a small envelope. "We saw him." They reached the steps, and Mr. Moore handed the envelope to the Doctor. "He didn't have much to say, though."

"There's more," Marcus added, as the rest of our group, drawn by the returning men's voices, came out onto the porch. "Several other guests arrived at the Grand Union today—courtesy of Mr. Vanderbilt."

"Defense witnesses?" Miss Howard asked.

Marcus nodded, then looked to his brother. "They're bringing in Hamilton, Lucius."

The younger Isaacson's eyes went wide. "*Hamilton?* You're joking!"

Marcus shook his head as Mr. Picton asked, "And who is 'Hamilton'?"

"*Doctor* Albert Hamilton, of Auburn, New York," Marcus said. "Though there's no proof that he actually has a doctorate of any kind. He used to sell patent medicine. Now he passes himself off as an expert in everything from ballistics to toxicology to anatomy. A complete charlatan—but he's made quite a name for himself as a legal expert, and he's fooled a lot of smart people. Sent a lot of innocent ones to the gallows, too."

"And Darrow's engaged him?" Mr. Picton asked.

Marcus nodded. "My guess is, you'll get a request for the gun and the bullets first thing in the morning, so Hamilton can run his own 'tests' on them."

"But that's ridiculous!" Lucius said. "Hamilton will say anything the people paying him *want* him to say!"

"Which is the easiest way to become a successful expert witness," Mr. Picton grunted. "Anybody else?"

"Yes," Mr. Moore answered. "And I do not like the possibilities involved with this one. Darrow wants somebody he can present as an expert on feminine psychology and character—someone fairly local, who the crowd'll be familiar with and maybe even sympathetic to." He turned to Miss Howard. "It's your friend Mrs. Cady Stanton, Sara."

"*Mrs. Cady Stanton?*" Miss Howard repeated.

"But she was *there*," Cyrus commented, looking worried. "When we had the sketch made—she knows we've been after the woman."

"Exactly why Darrow wants her, I suspect," Marcus said. "He'll try to paint this as a witch-hunt on the Doctor's part."

"He won't get far," Mr. Picton pledged firmly. "Your earlier meeting with Mrs. Cady Stanton relates to another case, an unproved case that has yet to be officially investigated, and I can use that to our advantage here. If Darrow evens *hints* at what you were up to in New York, I'll get Judge Brown to slap him down for going outside the merits of this case."

"Yes," Miss Howard said, "but the fact that she knows we've been after Libby for so long is likely to make Mrs. Cady Stanton hostile—and she can be very persuasive when her blood's up." Considering the possibility, Miss Howard kicked at one of the posts that held up the roof of the porch. "*Damn it*, that man's clever."

The Doctor had heard all of this, but hadn't commented on it: he was too busy reading his note from Dr. White, which seemed to cause him much concern.

"More good news, Kreizler?" Mr. Moore asked, seeing the worried look on the Doctor's face.

"It's certainly not what I was hoping for," the Doctor answered with a shrug. "White says that, given the circumstances, he doesn't think it would be a good idea for us to meet before he's given his testimony. It's not the sort of attitude he would typically take."

"Maybe not," Mr. Picton said. "But it's consistent—Darrow's keeping a tight lid on everything and everyone connected to his case. I think he's been a little surprised by how prepared we've been, and wants to make sure he can offer some surprises of his own in return. That's certainly what we saw today."

"Well, surprisingly enough, it seems that we don't need to overreact to what happened today," Marcus advised, heading inside. "At least, not according to the betting line at Canfield's."

"Where does it stand now?" Cyrus asked, following Marcus into the house.

"No change," Mr. Moore called after them. "Still sixty to one against a conviction—and Canfield's finding a lot of takers, even at those odds."

Without moving his eyes from the note he'd received, the Doctor asked, "And how much did you lose while ascertaining that information, Moore?"

Mr. Moore headed for the screen door. "It could've been worse," he said as he entered the house, in an embarrassed way what led me to believe that it couldn't have been very *much* worse.

Still, expensive as it might've been, the news that them what were paying the most attention to the case—the heavy gamblers—didn't think our cause had been hurt by Mr. Darrow's antics of the afternoon was encouraging, and we were all able to sleep a little sounder, I think, because of it. Lucius was the last to turn in: he was due on the stand to talk about the circumstantial case against Libby Hatch the next morning, and he wanted to make sure he had all his ducks in a row before he let himself drift off. He was up early, too, and when I came downstairs I found him neatly dressed and pacing around the backyard, mumbling to himself and already sweating. Always cool as ice when it came to the business of investigation and scientific testing, he (much like myself) hated any kind of direct attention from crowds of strangers, and I think we all would've felt a little better if his much more diplomatic brother had been the one who was going to handle the testimony. But putting Marcus on the stand would've given Mr. Darrow the chance to hint, if not flat-out declare, that he'd been personally scouted by the prosecution prior to the trial, a fact that, while it certainly didn't amount to anything illegal, might've been represented in a way what would've made us look desperate.

And so it was Lucius who, at just past ten, took the oath and sat in the witness chair, ready to reveal all the details about Daniel Hatch's gun that he and his brother had put together during our stay in Ballston Spa. The courtroom had a different feel to it, now, one brought on by the new faces what were visible behind the defense table: Dr. William Alanson White, a young, short man with spectacles; Mrs. Elizabeth Cady Stanton, looking her best; and finally a peculiar-looking mug what tried to make up for his unimpressive size by puffing himself up like a rooster: "Dr." Albert Hamilton, the well-known ballistics "expert." Dr. White and Mrs. Cady Stanton only offered the most formal of greetings to those members of our party they knew, making it clear from the outset that they didn't agree with what we were up to; and I don't think the strained nature of the situation did anything to help Lucius's nerves. Still, he held himself together very admirably, sitting and waiting to be questioned like he did it every day of his life.

In fact, during Mr. Picton's questioning the detective sergeant came off something like impressive: he didn't leave out any details, didn't hesitate in his answers, and didn't even sweat, or, at least, not much more than anyone else on that warm, humid August morning. In a funny kind of way I was proud of him, being as I knew how much he hated the position he'd been forced into; it wasn't until the very end of his testimony that things started to get a little bumpy.

"Just a few more details, Detective Sergeant," Mr. Picton said. "You've told us approximately when the revolver was last fired, how many shots were expended, how just two bullets could have been responsible for the wounds inflicted on the three children, and how closely the bullet removed from the Hatches' wagon matches the barrel of Daniel Hatch's gun. But was there anything you came across during your inspection of the weapon that might lead you to hazard a guess as to *who* fired it last?"

"Yes, there was," Lucius answered quickly.

"And what was that?"

"We performed a dactyloscopy test. We compared the results to samples taken from household objects that belonged to the defendant. The match was perfect."

Once again, Mr. Darrow was out of his chair like a shot. "I object to this line of questioning, Your Honor," he said. "The state is attempting to enter evidence of a type that has *never* been accepted in an American court of law, and I'm sure they know it."

"Quite right," Judge Brown replied, turning what was becoming his usual critical glance to Mr. Picton. "Unless the assistant district attorney is in possession of some new scientific data that establish fingerprinting—which, for the benefit of the jury, is what he's talking about—as absolutely reliable, or unless he can provide me with a precedent for its being allowed in an American court, I cannot permit this testimony to continue."

"Your Honor need not allow it to continue," Mr. Picton said. "In fact, the state does not *wish* to continue. We acknowledge that fingerprinting is not yet accepted in American courts of law, despite the fact that it has been effectively used as evidence in courtrooms in Argentina—"

"Mr. Picton," the judge warned, leveling his gavel.

"—and despite the fact, as well, that the British government in India has ordered its use throughout that colony by police and prosecutors—"

"Mr. Picton, enough!" the judge yelled, banging the gavel.

"Your Honor," Mr. Picton said, putting his innocent look on again. "I beg the court's pardon, yet I feel I am misunderstood. I only *mention* these rather interesting and, to some ways of thinking, important facts. I do not say that the jury should give any weight to them, simply because Argentines, Indians, and Englishmen do. After all, this is America, and things take time to be accepted, here. I do *not* offer these tests as evidence—I offer them simply as a rather remarkable coincidence that may interest the jury." Sitting down very quickly, Mr. Picton added, "I have no further questions, Your Honor."

By now Judge Brown was rubbing hard at the leathery, wrinkled skin of his face with both hands. "Mr. Picton," he said, trying to keep his voice under control, "if I have ever heard such bald sophistry in a courtroom before, I cannot recollect it. You know perfectly well that anything offered by a witness in testimony must be considered evidence, or it is improper! I ought to hold you in contempt, sir—and if you try that kind of semantic trickery again, I *will* hold you in contempt! You are here to present acceptable evidence, not remark on interesting, unproven theories!" Turning to the jury box, the judge bellowed, "The jury will disregard everything that was just said, and it will be stricken from the record!" Then it was Lucius's turn: the judge spun on him and hollered, "And if you mention the subject of fingerprinting again, Detective Sergeant, I'll hold *you* in contempt, too!"

Lucius's forehead began to glow bright under the heat of those words. "Yes, sir," he said sheepishly.

Hissing in exasperation, Judge Brown turned to the defense table. "All right, Mr. Darrow, the witness is yours! And since I'm in a warning mood, let me tell *you,* sir—I don't want to see any hysterical theatrics of the variety that I witnessed yesterday! This trial is going to be run in an orthodox manner from here on out, and if either side crosses the line again I'm going to lock *everybody* up!" Mr. Darrow couldn't hide a smile, at that; and the judge pointed straight at his head with the gavel when he saw it. "Don't make the mistake of taking this lightly, Mr. Darrow, or you'll find yourself on a train back to Chicago, smarting like a whipped cur!"

Mr. Darrow wiped the smile from his face as he came out from behind his table. "Yes, Your Honor. I do apologize—you've been extremely patient."

"You're damned right I have!" the judge said, causing the galleries to ripple with laughter. At the sound the judge got to his feet and banged his gavel like a madman. "And that goes for the rest of you, too!" As quiet returned, the judge began to calm down; but only when the room was absolutely still did he sit, mumbling something about "all my forty years on the bench." Then he pointed at Mr. Darrow again with the gavel. "Well? Get a move on, Counselor, I don't want to *die* before this trial is over!"

Nodding, Mr. Darrow approached Lucius. "Detective Sergeant, in how many legal cases, would you say, has ballistics played an important role?"

"In the United States?" Lucius asked.

"Ah, yes, Detective Sergeant," Mr. Darrow answered, "for the sake of His Honor's nervous health, I think we'd better confine our discussion to the United States." There were a lot of people who *wanted* to laugh, just then, but nobody did.

Lucius shrugged. "There are some."

"Can you give me a number?"

"No. I'm afraid I can't."

"But all this business about your being able to determine when a gun was fired by the mold and rust on the thing—that's been used before?"

"Several times. It began with the Moughon case, in 1879. The defendant was exonerated when a gunsmith determined that, because of the mold and rust accumulations in his pistol, the weapon could not have been fired in at least a year and a half. The murder in question had taken place during that time period."

Mr. Darrow shook his head, wandering over to the jury box. "I don't know, Detective Sergeant—maybe it's just me, but—I've seen a lot of mold and rust, in my life. Seems pretty amazing that you can date its growth as accurately as if it were a living creature."

"Molds *are* living creatures," Lucius answered, taking the chance to needle Mr. Darrow in spite of his nervousness. "And rust is simply the oxidization of metal, which conforms to known timetables. Once you have the training, it's not terribly complex."

"So you say, Detective, so you say. And I guess we have to accept your word on it—for the moment. So—the gun was fired about three years ago, give or take a few months. And one of the bullets was found embedded in the wagon." Mr. Darrow's face wrinkled up again. "I don't mean to sound dense, Detective, but what *about* that? The matching of the bullet to the gun, I mean? How many cases have been solved using *those* techniques?"

"Well," Lucius answered, a bit more uneasily, "gunsmiths having been matching bullets to gun barrels for decades—"

"So it's an exact science, then?"

"That would depend on what you mean by exact."

"I mean *exact,* Detective," Mr. Darrow said, walking back over to Lucius. "Containing no margin for error."

Lucius shifted in his seat, and then pulled out a handkerchief to wipe his forehead. "There aren't many sciences that contain no margin for error."

"I see," Mr. Darrow said. "So it *isn't* exact. And what about that bullet? Any sign that it was actually involved in the murders?"

"There were traces of blood on it."

"Any idea what kind of blood?"

Lucius started to sweat even more visibly and wiped his head again. "There—aren't any tests, as yet, that can distinguish one type of blood from another."

"Oh." Doing his level best to look like he was honestly wrestling with the problem, Mr. Darrow moved back to the jury box. "So what you are, in sum, saying, is that we have a gun that was fired *about* three years ago— by *whom* we certainly cannot say—and that was found at the bottom of a well behind the Hatches' house. It may or may not have been the gun that fired a bullet that was found in the Hatches' wagon—a bullet that may or may not have been involved in the murders. Is that about it, Detective?"

"I wouldn't characterize it that way," Lucius said. "The odds are—"

"The *odds* are high enough to leave room for reasonable doubt, Detective. At least in *my* mind. But let's try a question that maybe you can answer a little more precisely: In how many trials have you offered expert ballistic testimony?"

Lucius was obviously taken completely off guard. "How many?"

"It's a simple question, Detective."

Glancing down and going at his forehead one more time with the handkerchief, Lucius quietly said, "This is the first."

"The first?" Mr. Darrow answered, glancing quickly to the witness box, then back at the jury. "You're jumping into some pretty deep water for your first time swimming, don't you think?"

Trying to put up a fight, Lucius answered, "I've been studying ballistics for many years—"

"Oh, no doubt, no doubt. It's just that nobody's thought to ask you for your opinion yet. I wonder why." Finally taking his eyes from the jurors, Mr. Darrow loped back over to his table. "That's all, sir."

Lucius started to get up, but Mr. Darrow raised a hand. "Oh—there *is* one more thing, Detective Sergeant. You stated during your opening remarks that you're a member of the New York City Police Department. Would you mind my asking—what's your current assignment?"

Looking very startled, Lucius leaned back in the witness chair and tried to stall: "My current assignment? I was asked by the assistant district attorney to analyze—"

"I mean for *your* department," Mr. Darrow said.

Lucius took a deep breath. "My current assignment is unconnected to this case, and it would be inappropriate—"

"Isn't it true, Detective," Mr. Darrow interrupted, his voice rolling in a righteous way, "that you were assigned several weeks ago to investigate Dr. Laszlo Kreizler—specifically, his role in the suicide of one of the children in his care at the Kreizler Institute in New York City?"

The crowd couldn't keep quiet at that, and as they started to chatter in surprise Mr. Picton bolted out of his chair. "Objection! Your Honor, the state objects most strenuously! What possible bearing can the detective sergeant's current assignment have on this case?!"

The judge gaveled the galleries back to silence, then grabbed one of his ears and turned to Mr. Darrow. "Counselor, I *had* hoped that you were leaving the job of insinuation up to the assistant district attorney. What do you mean, sir, by bringing up such an apparently unrelated matter?"

"Your Honor," Mr. Darrow answered, "I'm afraid I can't agree with the court's assessment of this information as unrelated. When the state's case rests so heavily on the work of one expert, and when that expert's integrity and competence are the subject of an investigation being conducted by *another* of the state's experts—well, Your Honor, the assistant district attorney is not the only man who can spot a remarkable coincidence."

The judge bashed his gavel down, his eyes getting hot. "Perhaps not, sir—but this court will not tolerate the introduction of coincidences by the defense any more than it will condone similar behavior by the state! If the matters you're touching on have some direct bearing on this case, then explain it right now, sir."

Mr. Darrow just held up his hands, taking his turn at playing innocent. "I apologize, Your Honor, if my remarks were inappropriate."

"Inappropriate *and* inadmissible," the judge fired back. "The jury will ignore the defense's remarks concerning the witness's current assignment for the New York City Police Department, and those remarks will be stricken from the record." The warning gavel was lifted once more, toward the defense table. "And don't try that kind of thing with me again, Mr. Darrow. I will tolerate no mention or exploration of any subject that does not concern this case and this case alone. Now proceed with your questions."

"I have no further questions, Your Honor," Mr. Darrow answered, sitting down.

"Mr. Picton?" the judge said. "Do you wish to redirect?"

"If redirection could wipe the jury's memory clean of aspersions, Your Honor," Mr. Picton said, "then I would redirect. As it cannot, I will not."

"Then the detective sergeant is excused," Judge Brown answered, "and the state may call its next witness."

"The state," Mr. Picton announced, "calls Mrs. Louisa Wright."

There was a small commotion at the back of the room, as Mrs. Wright made her way in through the mahogany doors.

CHAPTER 46

W hile the former housekeeper was walking down the aisle, the Doctor leaned over to ask Mr. Picton:

"What about Parker?"

Mr. Picton shrugged. "Two of Dunning's deputies were supposed to escort him up on the early train this morning. They should have arrived by now. I'll have to get to him this afternoon."

Wearing an old-style blue dress, Mrs. Wright walked steadily and proudly through the gate in the oak railing, turning her grey-haired head and sharp features to the defense table just once and registering no emotion of any kind when she saw Libby Hatch. To Bailiff Coffey's oath she near yelled a solid "I do!" and then stated her name like she expected somebody to challenge her on it. It was an attitude what she never lost through all of Mr. Picton's opening questions, during which time he established a very clear picture of what life in the Hatch house had been like. Libby had been a woman of very changeable temperament, Mrs. Wright said, and when she felt that her own desires were being frustrated, she was capable of flying into extreme rages. Mr. Picton made sure the jury understood that Louisa Wright had no great love for Daniel Hatch and felt no jealousy toward her former mistress: as she'd told Miss Howard when we first got to town, the only people that she felt any genuine sympathy for or attachment to in the house were the three kids, who'd grown up so rattled by their father's crankiness and their mother's changeable moods that they sometimes seemed to be in a constant state of nervousness.

"Now, then, Mrs. Wright," Mr. Picton finally asked, after he'd painted this none-too-pleasing picture of the Hatch home, "when would you say that the Reverend Clayton Parker became a regular visitor to the house?"

"Well," the old girl answered, mulling it over, "he generally dropped by at holidays, Christmas and such, and of course he took care of christening Clara—but he didn't start paying what you'd call regular social visits until later. Clara's first birthday, I think, was the first night he actually stayed to dinner."

"And how often did he visit after that?"

"Oh, at least once a week, and sometimes more often. Mr. Hatch was taking more of an interest in the church's business by then, you see. A lot of people'll do that, when they start thinking that they don't have much time left." Mrs. Wright hadn't meant the statement as a joke, and she was surprised when it got a laugh from the galleries. "They will!" she insisted, folding her hands tightly, like she was embarrassed. "I've seen it happen."

"Of course you have," Mr. Picton answered. "But was Mr. Hatch's interest in the church the main reason for Reverend Parker's increased presence at the house?"

"Objection, Your Honor," Mr. Darrow droned. "The question calls for a speculative answer."

"I shall rephrase it, then," Mr. Picton said, before the Judge could order him to. "Mrs. Wright, was it *Mr.* Hatch that the reverend spent the greater portion of time with during his visits?"

"No, sir," Mrs. Wright answered with a little scoff. "After all, how long does it take to write a check?"

That got more laughs out of the crowd, and the judge responded in his usual manner: with irritated raps of his gavel. Leaning over, he scolded Mrs. Wright gently: "The witness will please try to keep the element of sarcasm out of her responses."

"I *am,* sir!" she answered, looking a little offended. "That's all Mr. Hatch did when the reverend came—write checks, and maybe talk for a few minutes about theology. The rest of the time it was the missus that looked after their—*guest.*"

"And why was that?" Mr. Picton asked.

"I'm sure I couldn't say," Mrs. Wright replied. "I only know what I saw, six or seven times."

"And what did you see?"

Stiffening her back and narrowing her eyes, Mrs. Wright lifted a pointing finger in the direction of the defense table. "I saw *that* woman and the

Reverend Parker. Out in the birch grove, about a quarter of a mile from the house."

"And what were they doing?"

"They were not doing the sorts of thing that a reverend generally does with a married woman!" Mrs. Wright answered, as offended as she would've been if the incidents had occurred just yesterday.

The judge sighed wearily. "Mrs. Wright, the question is a direct one. Do *please* try to make your answers follow suit. I've got enough wordplay to contend with in this case."

Mrs. Wright looked up at the bench, a shocked look on her face. "Do you mean—I should just *say* what I mean?"

The judge tried to smile. "It would be most refreshing."

Mrs. Wright folded her hands in her lap. "Well, I don't know as—but if you order me to, Judge, well . . ." She took a deep breath and went on. "The first time, I went looking for the missus, being as Clara'd been taken sick. I saw her in the birch grove with the reverend. They had their arms around each other. They were—kissing."

More mumbles in the crowd netted more raps of the gavel from the judge.

"And the other times?" Mr. Picton asked.

"The other times—well—" Mrs. Wright shifted uneasily. "Some of them were the same. But others—well, it was the middle of summer, those times. Warm, like now. The ground's soft in that grove, with a fine moss bed. And that's all I'm going to say, judge or no judge, court or no court. I'm a decent woman!"

Mr. Picton nodded. "And we certainly wouldn't ask you to behave in an indecent manner. But let me put the question to you this way, Mrs. Wright: Would it be accurate to say that you observed the defendant and Reverend Parker in a state of partial or complete undress?"

Now starting to positively squirm, Mrs. Wright nodded. "Yes, sir. It would."

"And engaged in physical intimacy?"

Her discomfort seeming to turn to anger, Mrs. Wright barked, "Yes, sir—and her with a husband and the sweetest little girl anybody could ever wish for back at the house! Disgraceful, I call it!"

Nodding as he started to pace before the witness chair, Mr. Picton slowly asked, "I don't suppose you could give me precise dates for these events?"

"Not precise, sir, no."

"No. But let me ask you this—would you feel sure saying that they preceded the births of Matthew and Thomas Hatch by at least nine months?"

"Your Honor!" Mr. Darrow called out. "I'm afraid the state is indulging its taste for suggestion again."

"I'm not so sure I agree with you this time, Counselor," the judge answered. "The state, though they have been an infernal nuisance about it, have introduced evidence that speaks to opportunity and means, in this case. I'm going to allow them to start approaching the question of motive. But you do it *carefully,* Mr. Picton."

Looking like he could've kissed that white, fuzzy head what was bobbing behind the bench, Mr. Picton said, "Yes, Your Honor," and then turned back to his witness. "Well, Mrs. Wright? Would you say that the timing was about right, with respect to the birth of the two younger Hatch children?"

"It was awfully close," Mrs. Wright replied with a nod. "I remember remarking on it to myself at the time. And when the boys came out looking the way they did, well . . . I drew my own conclusions."

"And how was it that they looked?" Mr. Picton stole a glance up at the bench. "I ask you not to be presumptuous here, Mrs. Wright."

Wagging a finger toward the defense table again, Mrs. Wright said, "Those boys didn't get their coloring—their eyes, their skin, their hair— from Mr. or Mrs. Hatch. Anybody could see that. And there was something else, too—when you live in the house that you work in, you get to know its rhythms, so to speak. Mrs. Hatch slept in a separate bedroom from Mr. Hatch. When they were first married, they spent some nights together in his room, but after Clara came . . . well, Mr. Hatch never slept anywhere but in his own bed. And if the missus ever went into Mr. Hatch's room again, other than to take him food and medicine when he was dying, I certainly didn't witness it."

"I see. Then when *was* the last time you saw Mrs. Hatch go into her husband's room?"

"The night the children were shot," Mrs. Wright answered. "She was flying all through the house—I couldn't stop her, I was too busy trying to help the children. But she locked herself into Mr. Hatch's old room for a good five minutes."

"Locked herself?" Mr. Picton repeated. "How did you know that she locked the door?"

"She was in there when the sheriff and Dr. Lawrence came," Mrs. Wright answered with a shrug. "They tried to get to her, so Dr. Lawrence could give her something to calm her down. But the door was locked. After a few more minutes she came back out, still screaming and running all around. She said she'd found her husband's gun, and that she was afraid she was going to do herself some injury with it. She told me to get rid of the thing— so I wrapped it up in a paper bag and dropped it down the old well."

"And do you remember what kind of paper bag it was?"

Mrs. Wright nodded. "Mr. Hatch'd bought everything in bulk, to save money. We still had a whole crate of bags from Mr. West's factory."

Mr. Picton moved to his table and picked up the piece of paper bag what Lucius had cut away from the Colt revolver the evening he found the thing. "So the bag would have borne this imprint?" He handed her the snippet of brown paper.

Studying the thing, Mrs. Wright nodded. "Yes, that's right."

"You're sure?"

"Certainly I'm sure. You see, two years ago West's bag company moved this writing, here, from the bottom of the bags to up around the top. If you have enough of the things, you notice."

"And do you have enough of the things?"

"Yes, sir, I never throw them away. A widow living on an army pension can't be too careful about expenses."

"No, of course not. Well, thank you, Mrs. Wright. I have no more questions."

Mr. Picton sat down, still looking very pleased that none of Mrs. Wright's testimony had been excluded from the record. Mr. Darrow, on the other hand, seemed to be going through one of those on-the-spot strategy shifts of his: holding his hands in front of his face and knitting his brows tight over his eyes, he waited a minute or two before saying anything or moving.

"Mr. Darrow?" the judge asked. "Do you have questions for this witness?"

Finally showing some movement, but only in his eyes, Mr. Darrow mumbled, "Just one or two, Your Honor." Then, after another pause, he stood up. "Mrs. Wright, did you ever observe anything in the defendant's behavior that would've led you to believe that she might've been capable of murdering her own children?"

Mr. Picton, who'd only just settled into his chair, got right back up. "I must object to that, Your Honor. The witness is not qualified to speak to such matters. We have alienists who will tell us what the defendant might or might not have been capable of."

"Yes," the judge replied, "and no doubt they'll contradict each other and get us absolutely nowhere. The witness is a woman of uncommon good sense, it seems to me, Mr. Picton—and it was *you*, after all, who argued to have her impressions included in the record. I'll let her answer."

"Thank you, Your Honor," Mr. Darrow said. "Well, Mrs. Wright?"

Taking a moment to think it over, and stealing another look at Libby as she did, Mrs. Wright said, "I—hadn't counted on being asked that question."

"Oh?" Mr. Darrow said. "Well, I'm sorry to surprise you. But try to come up with an answer, all the same. *Did* you ever, during all the years that you were in her employ, suspect that Mrs. Hatch was capable of murdering her own children?"

Mrs. Wright looked to Mr. Picton, and the struggle what was going on in her mind was plain to see in her face.

"What the hell's Darrow doing?" Mr. Moore whispered. "I thought that was supposed to be one of *our* questions!"

"He's seen what the jury's inferring from her testimony," the Doctor answered. "He wants to rattle her by attempting to force her to make an outright accusation." He leaned forward anxiously. "But will she *be* rattled . . . ?"

Mr. Darrow folded his arms. "I'm still here, Mrs. Wright."

"It—" Louisa Wright wrung her hands for a few seconds. "It's not the kind of thing to bandy around—"

"Really?" Mr. Darrow replied. "It seems to me you've done an awful lot of 'bandying' already. I wouldn't think this would give you any pause. But let me make it easier for you. You claim that Mrs. Hatch was engaged in what sounds like it was a pretty torrid affair with the Reverend Parker. Don't you think it would've been easier for her to run off with him, once her husband was dead, if she didn't have three children to drag along?"

"That's a hard way to put it," Mrs. Wright answered, glancing at Libby again.

"If you can think of an easy way to put such accusations," Mr. Darrow said, "you just let me know. Well, Mrs. Wright?"

"You don't understand," the woman said, a little more defiantly.

"And what don't I understand?"

Mrs. Wright leaned forward, eyeing Mr. Darrow. "I have children, sir. My husband and I had two, before he was killed in the war. I can't imagine what would drive a woman to do something like that. It isn't natural. For a mother to end any life that she brought into the world—it just isn't natural."

"Your Honor, I'm forced to ask for your help here," Mr. Darrow said. "The question was, I think, pretty close to clear."

"Mrs. Wright," Judge Brown said, "you're only being asked for your opinion."

"But it's a terrible thing, Your Honor, to accuse someone of!" Mrs. Wright said.

Mr. Darrow, smelling her fear, moved in closer to the witness stand. "But the state *is* accusing her, Mrs. Wright, and you're a witness *for* the state. Come, now, you knew that Mrs. Hatch had been written out of her husband's will—that the only way she could inherit his money was if the children died. Didn't that make you at all suspicious?"

"All right, then!" the woman finally hollered. "It *does* make me suspicious—but it's still an awful thing to accuse someone of!"

"It *does* make you suspicious, Mrs. Wright?" Mr. Darrow asked quietly. "Or it *did*? Let me see if I follow you. You say that Mrs. Hatch had a violent temper sometimes. You say that she was romantically involved with the Reverend Parker. And you say that she wanted her husband's money. And all of this, you *now* say, is grounds for believing that she killed her children—although you didn't make any such accusations at the time."

"Of course I didn't!" Mrs. Wright protested. "I was only asked for my opinion a week or so ago!"

"Exactly, Mrs. Wright," Mr. Darrow answered, very satisfied. "Tell me—have you ever known any other women who raised a hand to their children?"

Mrs. Wright's face grew puzzled. "Yes, of course."

"Ever heard of any who were unfaithful to their husbands?"

Shifting nervously, Mrs. Wright tried to rein her voice in. "One or two, perhaps."

"How about any that married rich old men to get their hands on their money?"

"Perhaps."

"Do you think any of them would've been capable of murdering their own children?"

"What do you mean?"

"Just what I say, Mrs. Wright."

"I—I don't know."

"But you've got pretty definite suspicions about Mrs. Hatch. *Now*, I mean."

"I don't understand you."

"Oh, I think you do," Mr. Darrow replied, coming in close again. "Mrs. Wright, isn't it true that you only think Mrs. Hatch might have killed her children *now* because the assistant district attorney and his investigators *suggested* to you that she might have done it?"

"Your Honor!" Mr. Picton shouted, popping up. "If the counsel for the defense is implying that the witness is lying—"

"Your Honor, I am implying no such thing," Mr. Darrow answered. "I'm simply trying to trace the origins of Mrs. Wright's suspicions, and to show that they, like so many other things in this case, seem to lead back to the assistant district attorney—and to the people who are advising him in this matter."

"Mr. Darrow," Judge Brown said, "I thought we had seen the last of insinuation, here—"

"And so we have, Your Honor," Mr. Darrow answered obligingly. "I have no further questions for this witness."

There was a long pause, during which Mr. Picton watched Mr. Darrow sit back down with a combination of anger and temporary confusion in his face.

"Mr. Picton?" Judge Brown finally said. "Do you wish to redirect?"

Mr. Picton turned to the bench. "No, Your Honor."

"Then the witness is excused," the judge said, at which the shaken Mrs. Wright made her way down from the stand. Judge Brown looked to Mr. Picton again. "Do you have another witness for us, sir?"

Trying to get himself fully composed, Mr. Picton looked anxiously to the door and then to Sheriff Dunning, who only shrugged once. "Actually, Your Honor," Mr. Picton replied, "the state's next witness has apparently not arrived yet. He was due to be escorted to town by two of Sheriff Dunning's deputies, but I don't know—"

Just then a young boy slipped through the mahogany doors. He was wearing the uniform of the Western Union company, and in his hand he was clutching an envelope. After asking the guard at the door a question, he was directed toward Mr. Picton's table, and made his way down the aisle.

Seeing him, Mr. Picton said, "This may be word of the witness now, Your Honor—if I may have just a moment."

"A *moment*, Mr. Picton," the judge said, sitting back.

The delivery boy passed by our two rows of seats, then handed the envelope to Mr. Picton and asked him to sign for it. Doing so quickly, Mr. Picton tore the telegram open and read it quickly; then he read it again, as if its contents made no sense to him. Finally, on the third reading, his face lost all its color, and he sank into the chair behind him.

"Picton," the Doctor whispered, watching him, "what is it?"

Judge Brown leaned forward in his chair, looking both concerned and a little irritated. "Mr. Picton? Are you well, sir?"

"Your—Your Honor," Mr. Picton breathed, struggling to get back to his feet. "I—" Staring at the floor underneath him without really seeming to see it, Mr. Picton finally caught his breath, cleared his throat, and looked up. "I'm sorry, Your Honor. At this time the state was to have called the Reverend Clayton Parker. He was due to take the early train this morning in the company of two of Sheriff Dunning's deputies. Apparently there was an—accident—"

"An accident?" the judge echoed. "What kind of an accident?"

Pausing and looking at the telegram again, Mr. Picton said slowly, "Apparently Reverend Parker fell under the wheels of an approaching train at the Grand Central Terminal this morning. He was severely injured and taken to a nearby hospital. He died there forty-five minutes ago."

The news hit the room as hard as the train must've hit the reverend. The people in the galleries—some of who'd been members of Parker's congregation—broke into open commotion, and a few were moved to tears. As for our group, we were all too stunned to say or do anything at all. There was no confusion among us, of course: we all knew that there was no chance that the death had actually been an accident. Getting killed by a train at Grand Central was almost impossible, unless somebody was helping you: somebody experienced at such things, somebody strong, somebody crazy enough to pull such a job in the middle of a large crowd, and somebody who wasn't worried about the presence of two sheriff's deputies. Somebody wound up on burny, for instance; somebody like a Hudson Duster.

As for Libby Hatch, she erupted with a short, loud sound that I could've sworn was a laugh; but when I looked over, she had her face buried in her hands, and seemed to be crying.

Judge Brown went to work restoring order, though he did so more gently than usual. As the crowd started to quiet down, he looked around the room with a somber face.

"The court is indeed sorry to receive this news," he said. "Reverend Parker was well known and respected in this community, despite any allegations that have been made in this room. Under the circumstances, I would suggest that we call a recess until two o'clock—at which hour, Mr. Picton, you can call your next witness. Or, if you need more time—"

Still looking very shaken, Mr. Picton began to shake his head. "No, Your Honor. Thank you. The state will be ready at two o'clock. With its next witness . . ."

The judge banged away, and as soon as he'd left the courtroom the place came alive again. Mr. Picton collapsed back into his chair, and none of us made any move toward him, not really knowing what we could possibly say. Once again, things were not going the way he'd planned, and the future of our case looked like it was in doubt—especially in light of the way Mr. Darrow had handled Louisa Wright, a witness whose testimony wouldn't ever receive corroboration now. Knowing all this, Mr. Picton just sat there in his chair for what seemed a long time, staring at the telegram in his hand; finally, he lifted his face and looked over to the rest of us—and to one of us in particular.

"Well, Doctor," he said, very quietly. "I hope you can be ready by two, because I can't let the jury sleep on what they've heard today." He paused, raising an eyebrow. "You're all we've got left."

The Doctor nodded, realizing, it seemed, just what a tight spot he was now in. But his voice when he spoke was very controlled—calm, even. "That's all right, Mr. Picton," he said, touching the hair under his lower lip. "I may have learned a thing or two from our friend Darrow . . ."

CHAPTER 47

Coming back into the courtroom that afternoon, I took note of a change in the positioning of the guards in the place, one what didn't make much of an impression on me at the time. The big man who'd usually stood behind Iphegeneia Blaylock was now at the door, while Henry, our old friend with the narrow head and the slow brain, was standing inside the oak railing, near the defense table. Writing the switch off to each man wanting a change of pace, I didn't, like I say, think much of it; but now, looking back, I can see that it was the first indication of something much more sinister, something that would eventually result in an unexpected and terrible conclusion to the trial. It would've saved a lot of heartache if I could've seen what the shift really signaled, if any of our group could have; but the only one who might've logically been expected to read it correctly was the Doctor, and he was much too focused on his coming showdown with Mr. Darrow to pay attention to those kind of seemingly small details.

Taking the stand at just past two, the Doctor spent most of the next hour answering Mr. Picton's questions about the work he'd done with Clara Hatch, proceeding from there into a discussion of his assessment of Libby Hatch's mental condition. The jury, like the people in the galleries around them, were pretty obviously disposed to view the Doctor's statements with what you might call skepticism, when he first began to speak; but as was so often the case when he appeared in court, he slowly began to win at least some of them over with his clear and compassionate statements, especially when it came to the subject of Clara. Making it clear that while treating the girl he'd simply followed his standard procedure for dealing with such cases—and also making it clear just how many similar cases he *had* dealt with—the Doctor painted a picture of a very bright, very sensitive girl, one whose mind had been terribly jumbled but not broken by the events what'd occurred on the night of May 31st, 1894. His description of Clara had the effect of softening the jury up to the point where they became interested in the details of his medical diagnosis, instead of being put off by them; and as he talked about spending long days sitting and drawing with her, making it clear that he'd neither tried to force her to speak nor put words in her mouth once she did begin to communicate, those twelve men became more and more what you might call receptive, so that by the time Mr. Picton began to inquire about Libby Hatch, they were ready to hear whatever the Doctor had to say. There was no clever maneuvering involved in all this: the simple fact was that for all the Doctor's unusual appearance, his accent, and the strange nature of much of his work, when he talked about children his attitude was so honest and caring that even the most skeptical types couldn't question that he honestly cared about what was best for his young charges.

Mr. Picton's queries about Libby Hatch were all designed for one basic purpose: to show that the woman was calculating, not insane, and that she was very capable of using a variety of methods to get what she wanted. The Doctor told about the three different approaches she'd employed to try to gain his sympathy—playing the victim, the seductress, and finally the wrathful punisher—and he explained how none of them was what he called "pathological" by nature. They were, in fact, methods what were very commonly used by many different sorts of women when they were trying to get the upper hand in a given situation—especially a situation what involved men. Playing Devil's advocate for a moment, Mr. Picton asked if a woman's murdering her own kids could really be included as part of such efforts—if it could actually be looked at as her trying to gain greater control over her life and her world. Here the Doctor launched into a long recital of similar cases he'd seen and read about over the years, cases where women had indeed done away with their offspring when said kids stood in the way of what their mothers perceived as their own basic needs.

Part of this conversation was a long examination of a case we'd all come to know well: the life and killings of Lydia Sherman, "Queen Poisoner." The Doctor noted some very interesting similarities between that murderess and Libby Hatch: Lydia Sherman had been what the Doctor referred to as "temperamentally as well as constitutionally unsuited to either marriage or motherhood," but that hadn't stopped her from going hunting for husbands and bearing children over and over. Whenever things'd gotten intolerable—as they were always bound to do, given her personality—she just killed each family off, instead of accepting that the problem might lie inside herself. The same sort of "dynamic," the Doctor said, controlled Libby Hatch's behavior: for whatever reason (and he made sure to mention the fact that Libby never would discuss her childhood with him) the defendant just couldn't tolerate the gap between what she wanted and what she thought society expected of a woman. Headstrong and absorbed with her own needs and desires as she was, Libby couldn't let even children stand in the way of her plans; but she also felt a desperate need to have people perceive her as a good woman, a caring mother, a loving wife. Looked at from this angle, the strange story about the phantom Negro on the Charlton road really wasn't so odd: only a tale so fantastic could make her look like a hero to the people in her town, instead of a woman who'd murdered three kids what were in her way. But there was nothing, the Doctor emphasized, insane in any of this: members of the male sex very often went to the gallows for similar crimes, without anybody ever suggesting that they were crazy.

But weren't there differences, Mr. Picton asked, between women and men, so far as these things went? Only in the eyes of society, the Doctor answered. The world at large didn't want to accept the idea that what most people considered the only truly reliable blood relationship in the world—that between a mother and her children—was in fact anything but sacred. Not done giving voice to the questions he was sure were in the jury's minds, Mr. Picton proceeded to ask why Libby hadn't just abandoned the kids and disappeared to start a new existence somewhere else, the way other women often did. Was it just the money that she expected to get from her husband's estate when they died that'd driven her to bloodshed? These questions were designed to let the Doctor repeat the main theme of his testimony, to hammer it into the jury's thinking—and the Doctor took the opportunity to pound away. Stronger even than Libby's desire for wealth, he said, was the desire to be accepted by the world as a good mother. Every human being, he explained, wants to believe—and wants the rest of the world to believe—that he (or she) can perform life's most primitive functions. For women trained by American society, this was especially true—the message to young girls (and here the Doctor borrowed from Miss Howard, who had, after all, been responsible for his own realization of the fact) was that if you couldn't attend to the propagation of the species, nothing else you did would really make up for the failure. Libby Hatch had been especially "indoctrinated" with this belief, probably by her own family. She just could not tolerate being seen as the sort of person who wouldn't or couldn't care for her children adequately; in her mind, it was better that they die than that she be tarred with that particular brush. But, said Mr. Picton, such thinking might be interpreted by some people as insanity—and *wasn't* it insanity, really, of *some* kind? No, answered the Doctor, it was intolerance. Of a raging, vengeful variety, true; but intolerance had not yet—and, to his way of thinking, never would be—classified as a mental disorder.

Those of us in the first two rows had, of course, heard all this many times, in recent weeks; but the Doctor and Mr. Picton managed to pump enough new blood into the discussion so that even we became wrapped up in the talk. The effect that it had on the jury was even stronger, from the look of them—and that, I guess, is why Mr. Darrow went straight for the throat once Mr. Picton sat down.

"Dr. Kreizler," he said, moving toward the witness box with a hard look on his face, "isn't it true that you and your associates have recently been trying to prove that the defendant is responsible for the unexplained deaths of a number of children in New York City?"

Mr. Picton didn't even need to get up: before he could register an objection, Judge Brown slammed down his gavel, silencing the loud chatter that the question had sparked in both the galleries and the jury box. "*Mr. Darrow!*" he hollered. "I've had just about enough of this kind of irresponsible questioning, from *both* sides! I want to see you and Mr. Picton in my chambers—*now!*" As he got up, the judge turned to the jury box. "And *you* gentlemen will ignore that last question, which will be stricken from the record!" Turning again, the Judge looked down at the Doctor. "The witness may feel free to move about—but you'll still be under oath, Doctor, when we get back under way. Let's go, gentlemen!"

Moving so fast that he didn't look like much more than a black blur, Judge Brown disappeared through the back door of the courtroom, followed quickly by Mr. Darrow and Mr. Picton. As soon as they'd gone, the crowd came alive with animated conversation. The doctor, not wanting to look shocked, slowly rose and drifted over to where we were all sitting.

"So, Doctor," Lucius said. "I guess this is when the *real* trial begins."

"He's laying the groundwork for his experts," Marcus added, looking across the room to Mrs. Cady Stanton, Dr. White, and "Dr." Hamilton. "He knows he can't come at you with incompetence, so he'll go for the ulterior motive. But I didn't think he'd do it so fast."

"It was his only choice," the Doctor answered. "If he'd gradually led up to the accusation, the judge never would have allowed him to reach it. This way, he at least makes sure that the jury hears his charge. It's worth a lecture in chambers."

"Speaking of his witnesses, it looks like there's more bad doings over there," Cyrus said, pointing to the defense table. Libby Hatch had gotten up to introduce herself to Mrs. Cady Stanton, and as they shook hands I could make out the old girl saying, "Thank you, thank you," in answer to what were almost certainly some very flattering comments from the defendant—the same sort of comments she'd made to the Doctor on first meeting him.

"Maybe I should try to break that up," Miss Howard said, as she watched the pair continue to chat. "Now that the subject's been broached, so to speak, I'm sure Mrs. Cady Stanton will understand—"

"I wouldn't, Sara," the Doctor said. "Let's not give Darrow any more ammunition by attempting to fraternize with his witnesses." His black eyes wandered to the back door of the courtroom, and he smiled as he said, "I can only imagine what's going on in there . . ."

What was going on in there, we later learned from Mr. Picton, was a full accounting to the judge by the assistant district attorney of just what had brought all of us to Ballston Spa. It seemed that Mr. Darrow's private detectives (who, it turned out, were actually Mr. Vanderbilt's private detectives), with help from the Bureau of Detectives in New York and various employees of both the Lying-in and St. Luke's Hospitals, had put together a pretty good picture of our recent moves with regard to Libby Hatch. The only thing that Mr. Darrow didn't seem to know about was the Linares case, and Mr. Picton made sure he didn't let any information slip, on that score. Judge Brown received all this news in an air of exasperation, and though it didn't make him any better disposed toward Mr. Picton or the rest of us, it did make him all the more determined to keep any unrelated matters out of the record of the case currently being tried. He was very firm with Mr. Darrow about that: the defense could say whatever it wanted to about the Doctor's personal or professional motives and methods, but it could not bring up the subject of other allegations or investigations. Mr. Darrow argued that it would be tough to paint an accurate picture of the Doctor's true motivations without bringing up those other investigations, but the judge stuck to his guns, as Mr. Picton had predicted he would, and said that the Hatch case had to be tried on its own merits. He warned Mr. Darrow against trying to poison the jury's ears with any more surprise questions what would have to be stricken from the record (but could never, of course, truly be stricken from the jury's memories), and then the three men returned to the courtroom, where the defense's examination of the Doctor continued.

"Dr. Kreizler," Mr. Darrow said, once the galleries had gotten themselves resettled. "What exactly is your occupation, sir?"

"I am an alienist and a psychologist," the Doctor answered. "I work in most of the hospitals in New York in that capacity. In addition, I perform mental competency assessments for the city, when asked, and I appear as an expert witness at trials such as this one. Most of my time, however, is spent at an institute for children which I founded several years ago." Mr. Darrow, looking eager, was about to ask another question, when the Doctor showed just what he'd meant when he said he'd learned a few lessons from the counsel for the defense: "I should add, however, that I am not currently serving as the active director of the Institute, due to a court investigation into its affairs which was initiated following the suicide of a young boy we recently took in."

Looking disappointed at not getting a chance to force this last information out of the Doctor, Mr. Darrow asked, "You were, in fact, ordered not to return to your Institute for a period of sixty days, were you not?"

"Yes," the Doctor answered. "It's not an uncommon action for a court to take under such circumstances. It allows the investigation into what drove the boy to take his own life to be conducted more freely and effectively."

"And has the investigation turned up any answers to the question of why the boy took his own life?"

The Doctor lowered his eyes just a bit. "No. It has not."

"That must be particularly frustrating, for a man who's spent most of his life trying to help children."

"I don't know that it's frustrating," the Doctor answered. "Puzzling, certainly. And distressing."

"Well, I'm no alienist, Doctor," Mr. Darrow said, walking over to the jury. "But I'd say that puzzling and distressing, when put together, can add up to frustrating without much trouble. Wouldn't you agree?"

The Doctor shrugged. "They might."

"And a person who's frustrated on one front might be tempted to seek satisfaction on another—at least, that's how it's always seemed to me." Returning to his table, Mr. Darrow picked up a book. "Tell me—do you know of a Dr. Adolf Meyer?"

Nodding, the Doctor said, "Certainly. He's a colleague of mine. And a friend."

"Children seem to be an area of special interest for him, too, to judge by his writings." The Doctor nodded silently. "I take it you've read what he has to say about children with what he calls 'morbid imaginations'?" After another nod from the Doctor, Mr. Darrow said, "Maybe you could tell the jury just what that refers to."

"Morbid imagination," the Doctor answered, turning to the jury box, "is characteristic of children whose fantasies cannot be controlled, even by conscious exertion. Such children often suffer from nightmares and night terrors, and the condition can even lead, in its most extreme variant, to delusions."

Picking up a second book, Mr. Darrow walked toward the witness stand. "How about these two European doctors—Breuer and Freud? Do you know about them?"

"Yes."

"They seem to've made quite a study of hysteria and its effects. I confess I didn't really know what that word meant, until I started in on this volume. I always thought it referred to overexcited ladies."

Quiet laughter floated through the galleries at that, and the Doctor waited for it to calm down before he said, "Yes, the word originated with the Greeks, who thought that violent nervous disorders were peculiar to women and originated in the uterus."

Mr. Darrow smiled and shook his head, putting the books down. "Well—we've learned better, haven't we? Just about *anybody* can be hysterical nowadays. I'm afraid I may unintentionally have driven His Honor pretty close to it." The crowd laughed a little louder this time, but the judge didn't do anything except give Mr. Darrow an icy stare. "And I do apologize for it," the counselor said, holding up a hand. Then he looked at the Doctor again. "But I'm interested in what these gentlemen—Breuer and Freud—have to say about hysteria. They seem to think it originates in childhood, like the morbid imagination. Doctor, is there any chance that Clara Hatch suffers from either a morbid imagination or hysteria?"

I could see the Doctor working hard to keep from scoffing at the question. "No," he said. "Not in my opinion. As I told the state's attorney, Clara has experienced what I refer to as 'protracted hysterical disassociation.' It's quite distinct from the kind of hysteria Breuer and Freud discuss."

"You seem awfully sure, after spending—*how* many days with the girl?"

"Ten in all."

"Quick work," Mr. Darrow judged, playing at being impressed. "How about Paul McPherson—the boy who killed himself at your Institute?"

The Doctor kept his features very still at the mention of the unfortunate kid. "What about him, specifically?"

"Did he suffer from those pathologies?"

"I can't say. He was only with us a short time, before his death."

"Oh? How long?"

"A few weeks."

"A few weeks? Shouldn't that have been enough time for you to formulate an accurate diagnosis? After all, with Clara Hatch it only took you ten *days*."

The Doctor's eyes thinned up as he realized where Mr. Darrow was going. "I attend to dozens of children at my Institute. Clara, by contrast, had my undivided attention."

"I'm sure she did, Doctor. I'm sure she did. And you told her that the work you were doing together would help her, am I correct?" The Doctor nodded. "And did you tell her it would help her mother, too?"

"In a child like Clara," the Doctor explained, "the memory of a terrifying experience causes a division within the psyche. She divorced herself from the reality of it by refusing to communicate with the rest of the world—"

"That's very interesting, Doctor," Mr. Darrow said. "But if you'd answer the question?"

Pausing and then nodding reluctantly, the Doctor replied, "Yes. I told her that if she could bring herself to speak of what happened it would help her—and her mother."

"Helping her mother was very important to her, then?"

"It was. Clara loves her mother."

"Even though she seems to think that her mother tried to kill her? And *did* kill her brothers?" Without waiting for an answer, Mr. Darrow pressed on: "Tell me, Doctor—when you were working with Clara, who first mentioned the idea that her mother'd been the actual attacker on the Charlton road? Was it you or her?"

The Doctor reeled back a bit, looking very indignant. "She did, of course."

"But you already believed her mother was responsible, is that right?"

"I—" The Doctor was having trouble finding words: a rare sight. "I wasn't certain."

"You came all the way to Ballston Spa at the request of the assistant district attorney because you *weren't certain*? Let's try the question another way, Doctor: Did you *suspect* that Clara's mother was responsible for the attack?"

"Yes. I did."

"I see. And so you come to Ballston Spa, and you spend every waking hour with a girl who hasn't spoken to another soul in three years, and you use all the tricks and techniques of your profession—"

"I do not use tricks," the Doctor said, getting riled.

But Mr. Darrow didn't pause: "—to get this little girl to trust in you and believe that you're trying to help her, while all the time you suspect that her mother was in fact the person who shot her. And you honestly ask us to believe that none of your suspicions ever bled over into your handling of the child, at any time during those ten days?"

The Doctor set his jaw so hard that his next words could barely be made out: "I don't *ask* you to believe anything. I'm telling you what *happened*."

But again Mr. Darrow ignored the statement. "Doctor, you've described your own mental condition after losing Paul McPherson as 'puzzled' and 'distressed.' Would it be fair to say that you're still puzzled and distressed about it?"

"Yes."

"Puzzled, distressed—and potentially disgraced in the eyes of your colleagues, I'd think, if the investigation shows that Paul McPherson died because he didn't get the amount of care, the amount of time, he needed at your Institute. For, as you say, you couldn't give that boy your 'undivided attention.' And so he died. And then you come up here, full of guilt about the dead boy and suspicions about the defendant. And you find yourself faced with a young girl whom you *can* give your 'undivided attention' to—whom you can *save* from the fate that befell Paul McPherson. But only, *only* if there's an answer to the mystery that's kept the girl silent all these years. And so—you *create* an answer."

"I created nothing!" the Doctor protested, grabbing at his left arm without realizing it.

"Are you so sure, Doctor?" Mr. Darrow asked, his own voice rising. "Are you certain that you didn't *plant* the idea in Clara Hatch's mind, as only a clever alienist could, that it was her mother, not some lunatic who'd disappeared and could never be caught, who was responsible—all so that she can talk and enjoy a happy life again?!"

"Your Honor!" Mr. Picton called out. "This is blatant badgering of the witness!"

But Judge Brown only waved him off.

Seeing that, Mr. Darrow kept going: "There's just one problem, though, Doctor, one thing that gets in the way. For your scheme, your and the state's scheme, to work, my client has to go to the electrical chair! But then, what does that matter to you? You'll be vindicated—in your own mind and in the eyes of your colleagues, the McPherson case will be more than balanced out by the Hatch case! Your precious integrity will be restored, and the state can close the books on an unsolved murder! Well, forgive me, Doctor, but I'm not willing to make that trade. There are tragedies in this life that don't *have* answers!"

Suddenly, in a move what caused Miss Howard, Mr. Moore, Cyrus, and me to gasp, Mr. Darrow grabbed his own left arm, mirroring what the Doctor was doing; then he held it out, making it clear that he knew, he somehow *knew*, the secret of the Doctor's past.

"Yes—tragedies without answers, Doctor, as you well know! And trying to balance the books isn't going to change that! Tying the guilt for this case around my client's neck won't put movement back into Clara Hatch's paralyzed arm, and it won't bring Paul McPherson back to life. Things just aren't that neat, Doctor, not that *explicable*. A madman committed a crime and disappeared. A boy walked into a washroom and hanged himself. Horrifying, inexplicable events—but I won't let you and the state nail my client to the cross, just because you can't live without explanations! No, sir—I will not do it!" Turning to the jury, Mr. Darrow lifted a thick finger toward the heavens, then let it fall, as if he were suddenly completely exhausted. "And I hope—maybe I even *pray*—that *you* gentlemen won't do it, either." He took a deep breath and wandered back to his seat. "I have no further questions."

It seemed like a very long time since Mr. Darrow had started talking, and I don't think I ever felt more sympathy for the Doctor than I did when he was excused from the witness stand and had to make the long walk back over to where the rest of us were sitting. I knew how he felt, how deeply Mr. Darrow's words had cut into him; and so when he didn't pause at his seat, but just kept moving on toward the mahogany doors, I wasn't at all surprised. I didn't make any move to follow just yet, knowing he'd want to be alone for a few minutes; but as soon as the judge had ordered court recessed until ten o'clock the next morning I bolted for the exit, Cyrus and Mr. Moore following close behind me.

We found the Doctor across the street, standing under a tree and smoking a cigarette. He made no move at all when we approached, just kept staring at the court house with narrow, squinting eyes. Cyrus and I each stood to one side, while Mr. Moore faced him head-on.

"Well, Laszlo," he said, gently but with a smile. "I guess you've got more to learn from him than you thought."

The Doctor just blew out a smoky sigh, and smiled ever-so-slightly back at his childhood friend. "Yes, John. I suppose so . . ."

Then we heard Mr. Picton's voice calling and saw him appear on the courthouse steps with Miss Howard, the Isaacsons, and El Niño. When they caught sight of us, they rushed on over, Mr. Picton smoking his pipe and swinging one fist at empty air.

"Damn the man!" he said, once he was sure that the Doctor was okay. "Of all the blasted cheek! I *am* sorry, Doctor. He was wrong—terribly wrong."

The Doctor's eyes moved to Mr. Picton, while his head remained still. "Wrong?" he said quietly. "Yes, he was wrong—about Libby Hatch. And this case. But about me?"

Shrugging just once, the Doctor threw his cigarette into the gutter and began to walk down High Street alone.

———

CHAPTER 48

By midnight on that Thursday the odds against our convicting Libby Hatch had risen to a hundred to one at Canfield's Casino, and it wasn't hard to understand why: Mr. Darrow'd managed to plant doubts in the jury's minds about Lucius's ballistic testimony even before his own "expert," Albert Hamilton, had taken the stand, while Mrs. Louisa Wright's thoughts about a possible romantic motive for the killings had been reduced to unprovable by the sudden and shocking "accident" what had befallen the Reverend Clayton Parker that morning at Grand Central. Mr. Darrow's very effective questions about the Doctor's motivations and techniques had been the icing on this bleak cake, and it was plain to all of us that if things kept going the way they were, defeat was just around the corner.

It was no wonder, then, that the atmosphere at Mr. Picton's house that night moved past gloomy, until it almost seemed like there was a wake going on. Feeling what you might call resigned about the legal case as such, we began to focus our energies not on what remained to be done in court (which was just about nothing, so far as our side was concerned, except for Mr. Picton's official announcement that the state was resting its case) but on what steps we'd need to take to try to get Ana Linares out of the Dusters' place before Libby made her way back to New York. This meant getting word to Kat by way of the go-between Mr. Moore'd engaged: Kat's pal Betty, who was supposedly waiting for us to send a wire to Frankie's joint as soon as we knew it was time for

Kat to make her move. Just talking about this possibility played hell with my nerves again, and for a few minutes I actually toyed with the idea of heading down to New York and making sure everything was set and in place; but the sight of me hanging around would, I knew, only make Kat's situation even more dicey. So I stayed put, waiting with the others for what looked like it was going to be the dismal end of our business in Ballston Spa.

"And so the new century will bring a new kind of law," was how Mr. Picton summed things up, as we all sat out on the front porch of his house late that night. "Proceedings where victims and witnesses are put on trial instead of defendants, where a murderer is identified as 'a woman' instead of an individual . . . ah, Doctor, it's no step forward, that I can tell you, and I don't think I want to be party to it. If things go on like this, we'll find ourselves in some shadow world, where lawyers use the ignorance of the average citizen to manipulate justice the way priests did in the Middle Ages. No, if we lose this case—*when* we lose this case—it'll be my last, I suspect."

"I wish I could find some aspect of the affair that might offer you solace," the Doctor answered quietly. "But I'm afraid I see none. Darrow is the legal man of the future, that much is indeed clear."

"And I'm a relic," Mr. Picton agreed with a nod; then he laughed once. "A relic at forty-one! Hardly seems fair, does it? Ah, well—such are the fortunes of the new age."

You had to hand it to the man: unlike many other sporting bloods I've known, he was a genuinely graceful loser, and I don't think there was one of us who failed to appreciate his ability to receive the head what'd been handed to him (his own) in court and still come up philosophical—except, of course, for Miss Howard, who was always the last member of our company to accept failure or defeat of any kind.

"You two can just stop acting like the whole thing's over," she said, sitting on the steps of the porch with a small kerosene lamp and a large map of New York State. "Darrow hasn't even opened his case yet, for God's sake—we've still got time to come up with *something*."

"Oh? And what would *that* be?" Mr. Moore asked. "Face it, Sara—you can't fight the prejudices of an entire society, *and* a woman who's as lethally cunning as this one, *and* one of the most vicious gangs in New York, *and* a legal wizard like Darrow, all at one and the same time, and expect to survive." He turned to Mr. Picton, lowering his eyes. "No offense intended, Rupert."

But Mr. Picton only saluted his friend with his pipe. "None taken, John, I assure you. You're absolutely right—the man's turned what should have been a disaster into a triumph. My hat's off to him."

"Yes, well, before you fall all over each other lining up to pay homage to that legal snake," Miss Howard shot back, "do you mind if I suggest some further efforts to salvage our cause?" She looked back down at her map. "We're still missing the one big piece—somebody who knows something about Libby Hatch's family."

"Sara," Marcus said, pointing toward the court house, "that jury is not going to be very receptive to a psychological examination of Libby Hatch's childhood context, just at the moment."

"No," Miss Howard answered, "and that's not what I'm proposing. Don't forget, she went to the Muhlenbergs as a wet nurse. She had to've had a child, and that child has got to be somewhere, either above or below the ground."

"But you looked for days, Sara," Lucius said. "You covered practically every inch of Washington County—"

"And that may be just where I went wrong," Miss Howard replied. "Think about it Lucius—if you were Libby, and you'd landed yourself the kind of job she had at the Muhlenbergs, would you give them any way to check on the actual facts of your past?"

Before Lucius could answer, the Doctor asked, "What are you saying, Sara?"

"That she's too smart for that," Miss Howard answered. "If she left some secret behind in her hometown, or even if she only left her family behind, that family would probably have known things that Libby wouldn't have wanted to get out, especially not to people who might hire her as a wet nurse. You've said it yourself, Doctor, the woman's characteristic behaviors *must* extend back into her childhood. So Libby had to make sure that no one ever knew where she actually came from. On the other hand, she had to say she came from someplace that she could actually describe, someplace that she knew at least *something* about, to make her story hold water."

"That's true," Cyrus said, considering it. "She *would* have covered herself, at least that far."

"But she could've come from anywhere!" Mr. Moore protested.

"John, do try to listen for more than thirty seconds running," Miss Howard spat back. "She *couldn't* have come from anywhere. She was a woman who learned that the Muhlenbergs needed a wet nurse from an advertisement—that makes her local. She talked a lot about towns in

Washington County—so she must have spent some time there. But if she was trying to conceal her roots, she didn't actually *come* from Washington County—which means—"

Mr. Picton snapped his fingers. "Which means you may want to get back down to Troy, Sara. It's the seat of Rensselaer County, which is to the south of Washington County—on the *east* bank of the river. And Stillwater sits directly across the water from the line that separates the two counties."

Miss Howard slapped her map hard and set the kerosene lamp down. "Which is exactly what I realized five minutes ago," she said, with a big, satisfied smile.

"It's still a long shot," Marcus said, shaking his head wearily. "And you'll have to go tomorrow, which means missing—"

"Which means missing what?" Miss Howard cut in. "Darrow's 'experts'? Mrs. Cady Stanton? I know what they're going to say, Marcus, and so do you. It's obvious—maybe even gratuitous, at this point. But we *do* have to work fast. Cyrus, I could use you, if you'll come—Stevie, too."

"And El Niño to protect you!" the aborigine near shouted, getting caught up in Miss Howard's enthusiasm.

"Naturally," she answered, rubbing his bushy head. Then she looked to the Doctor and Mr. Picton. "Well?"

Mr. Picton paused and smoked, shrugging his shoulders. "Nothing to be lost, I suppose. I say go to it."

"And you, Doctor?"

The Doctor looked at her with just the faintest trace of hope in his features; more, at least, than'd been there all night. "I'd say that you're all going to need some rest. You'll want to catch the earliest possible train, if you intend to have the full day in Troy."

At that the four of us—Miss Howard, me, Cyrus, and El Niño—got up and headed for the screen door. We weren't exactly confident, I couldn't say that, but the prospect of actually doing something, instead of spending another day watching Mr. Darrow turn the Ballston court house into his private stomping grounds, was some kind of a relief, and I was glad to be included in the plan. The reasoning behind it did seem promising, too, even if the time we had to test it wasn't much; and as we went into the house and up the stairs to our respective rooms, I took the opportunity to pay my own sort of compliment to Miss Howard's brainwork:

"So," I said, as we got to the second floor. "I guess being a 'spinster detective lady' leaves you plenty of time for thinking, anyway."

I barely got into my room without catching a playful but well-aimed clip to the side of the head.

So began a new round of searching the Hudson Valley countryside, one what was both tighter in terms of schedule and less tedious in terms of method than all the riding around Miss Howard, El Niño, and I'd done before the start of the trial. We caught the first train to Troy the next morning, and managed to get to the Rensselaer County offices without too much trouble. Housed in a building what bore more than a passing resemblance to a bank, the offices looked out over a small park at the center of town, and from the windows in the records room the city didn't look half so ugly as it had from the train. In fact, it had a sort of charm about it, or at least that particular part of it did. I suppose that impression could've just been due to the unseasonably cool weather and my thankfulness at not having to sit in the Ballston court house; whatever the case, I found that the first two or three hours we spent going through birth and death records passed pretty quickly. There wasn't anybody else in the spacious room with us, except for a clerk whose biggest chore, besides fetching files for us, seemed to be staying awake. So we were able to talk and act pretty freely, a fact what quickly led El Niño (who couldn't read English) and me (who wasn't much use with official documents) to start clowning around among the chairs and tables, letting Cyrus and Miss Howard attend to the real work and only straightening up at those moments when we were told to roust the clerk and tell him to fetch another batch of files and bound records.

By one o'clock or so our horseplay had the aborigine and me pretty hungry, and we set out to find someplace to buy boxed lunches for everybody. Our behavior didn't improve any as we went about this job, and on our way back to the county offices with the food we were taken aside by a cop, who, I think, was more bewildered by the sight of El Niño than he was interested in what we were up to. The bull walked us back to the county building, just to make sure our story held water, and told Miss Howard not to let us "run wild" in the streets. I had to resist the temptation to tell him that if such as what we'd been doing was his idea of "running wild," he needed to spend some time in New York; after that he finally left, and we all went outside to the little park to eat.

Once we were back in the records room Cyrus quickly struck gold, in the shape of a small, beat-up book what listed births and deaths for a town with the peculiar name of Schaghticoke during the years 1850 to 1860. Searching for any entry containing the unusual name "Elspeth," Cyrus found one not under the name "Fraser," but "Franklin," which had been the father's handle. It was the *mother* who, it seemed, bore the name Libby Hatch had used when she moved to Stillwater.

"Do you mean they weren't married?" Miss Howard asked Cyrus, as we all gathered around to look over his shoulders at the faded pages of the record book. "Libby's illegitimate?"

Cyrus shrugged. "That might explain a few things about her behavior. And it ought to be easy enough to confirm. Stevie, wake our friend up"— Cyrus threw a thumb in the direction of the dozing clerk—"and tell him we'll need the marriage records for the same town, covering, say, the ten years previous to—what's the date of her birth? March eighteenth, 1858. Ten years previous to that."

"Got it," I said, running over to the clerk's counter and rousting him by banging my hands on the surface of the thing, where he'd nestled his lazy head on a few books. Grumbling and cursing as he got to his feet, the mug dragged himself off to fetch the requested item, which turned out to be another small, dusty record book. I ran it back over to Miss Howard, who sat beside Cyrus and quickly started examining it, looking for any mention of people named either Franklin or Fraser.

"Here it is," she said, after about ten minutes of searching. "Formalization of a common-law marriage—George Franklin and Clementine Fraser, April twenty-second, 1852."

"There's two other children listed here," Cyrus said, still going over his volume. "George Junior, born September of 1852, and Elijah, born two years later."

"Well," Miss Howard said, looking almost disappointed, "there goes the bastard theory. It looks as though she simply adopted her mother's maiden name as an alias when she left home."

"And how do we find out when that was?" I asked. "Supposing we can't locate the parents, I mean."

"We know that she was working for the Muhlenbergs in 1886," Miss Howard answered. "We could check the 1880 census—that'll narrow things down a bit."

"On it!" I said, heading back over to the clerk's counter. The man heard me coming this time, and jerked his head up before I had a chance to give him another start; and when he reappeared from some faraway corner behind the counter, he evened things up some by dropping an enormous book onto my hands. Yelping as I grabbed the thing and turned to carry it away, I mumbled, "Nothing like a government job for improving your sense of humor, hunh?" then went back to the others.

From the 1880 census we learned that Libby Hatch had in fact still been living with her family in that year, when she would've been twenty-one. We also learned that George Franklin's occupation had been "farmer" (no thundering shock), and that the two Franklin boys were also still living at home, where they worked as hands for their old man. The only other question what we figured could be answered in the records office was whether or not Libby'd ever been married while she was living in Rensselaer County: another check of wedding records, though, came up blank, leaving us wondering if she'd taken the vows in some other county in the years between 1880 and 1886, or if the kid we knew she must have given birth to had been born out of wedlock. We got no help with this last mystery from the birth records for those years, which didn't mention anybody named either Franklin or Fraser bringing any babies into the world; and so, with all those questions still hanging in the air, we returned our pile of books and files to the clerk and headed back to the train station.

We caught the four o'clock local back to Ballston Spa, and the trip turned out to be a pretty merry and exciting one, given the information we'd come up with. True, there was every chance it would lead nowhere: it was impossible to say what the fortunes of the Franklin family had been in the years since 1880 (I still thought the odds were even that Libby'd done the whole bunch in), but at least now we had a legitimate place to start a reasonable search. Anxious to let the Doctor and the others know all this, we raced up the hill from the Ballston train depot to the court house once we reached town, only to find that court had already adjourned. So it was on down to Mr. Picton's house at what became a dead run, to spread the word that hope for new information wasn't dead yet.

But we found that this news didn't encourage the rest of our troops much, given what'd gone on in court during the day. As expected, Mr. Darrow'd opened the defense's case with his three experts, who'd each done their level best to reinforce the jury's already strong inclination to find Libby Hatch not guilty. Albert Hamilton, the snake-oil salesman–turned–forensics expert, had managed to lay out enough confusing information about guns and bullets to make Lucius's testimony seem, if not mistaken, at least unprovable. To start with, he'd said, the slug what the state'd found in the Hatches' wagon *might* have come from Daniel Hatch's Colt, or it might not have: because there was no central registry for firearms (just as Lucius and Marcus had told us) and because the Colt Peacemaker had been such a popular model of revolver for so many years, the odds that the bullet had in fact come from some other gun were nothing close to the million to one what Lucius had estimated. As for the identifying marks on the missile itself, Hamilton took great pains to explain just how high production standards at Samuel Colt's factory were, and how the specifications of every piece turned out were consistent with all those of the same model. Even the nick inside the muzzle of Hatch's gun what produced the small mark on the bullets that we'd seen could've been the result of a factory defect, "Dr." Hamilton said, a defect shared by dozens and maybe hundreds of other Peacemakers. Mr. Picton, on cross-examination, had asked how a factory what had such high production standards could turn out hundreds of revolvers with the same muzzle flaw, a question what Hamilton hadn't been able to answer; but, incompetent as the man obviously was to anybody who knew anything about ballistics, he'd done a lot of damage with the laymen of the jury, and Mr. Darrow's claim that the state's ballistic evidence was untrustworthy had seemed proved.

As for the Doctor's associate, William Alanson White, it'd been his job to dispute the state's contention that a sane woman could plan and carry out the murders of her own children—and he had, it seemed, seen to his task pretty effectively. He was helped by the fact that during his career he hadn't dabbled much in the psychology of family relationships, certainly not in the controversial way what the Doctor and others of his breed (like Dr. Adolf Meyer) had; because White's business was pretty strictly criminals and their mental disorders, he was seen from the beginning as less peculiar than the Doctor, and therefore more trustworthy. On top of that, he hadn't done any direct personal work with Clara Hatch, a fact what under ordinary circumstances might've made him look something less than fully informed, but what in this troubling, topsy-turvy case made him seem more detached and reliable. On being asked by Mr. Darrow for his "educated opinion" about Clara's mental condition, Dr. White'd answered that he didn't really believe that the memories of a girl who'd been through such an ordeal—and who was still, after all, very young—could be relied on. Such was what the jury wanted to hear—it was a lot easier than accepting that what Clara'd said was true—and so they'd seemed to ignore Dr. White's own statements about not being an expert on kids and accepted the rest of what he had to say.

The main part of his testimony, though, had focused on Libby Hatch herself, and on the notion of whether she was capable of the crime what the state'd charged her with. Dr. White said that, after spending some three hours with the woman, he'd formed the same opinion as Dr. Kreizler: that Libby, though emotional and impulsive, was free from any mental disease and was, especially as far as the legal definition of the word went, sane. But the conclusion Dr. White drew from this was the opposite of what Dr. Kreizler's had been: Libby's sanity was a very strong indication—if not outright proof—that she couldn't have shot her kids. In his experience, he said, there were only three reasons women committed such crimes: insanity, poverty, or the children being illegitimate. Since none of these reasons was in extreme evidence in this case, the state's explanation of what'd happened was "not credible." "The very character of the crime," Dr. White had said, using words Mr. Picton'd found so outrageous he'd written them down, "is sufficient to warrant a diagnosis of mental disease." Libby Hatch *had* no mental disease; so, using logic what, again, was flawed to professional ears but very appealing to a jury, she couldn't have done it.

But what about all the other cases what Mr. Picton and Dr. Kreizler had brought up, Mr. Darrow'd then asked, cases involving women who'd unquestionably murdered their own children and been found sane by courts and juries? What about Lydia Sherman, for instance? Lydia Sherman, Dr. White'd replied, had unfortunately committed her crimes during a time when mental science was in a much more primitive state; on top of that, people had been so disgusted by the killings that "Queen Poisoner" had been accused of, and there'd been so much evidence and so many witnesses to speak against her, that the possibility of her getting a fair trial, much less being found mentally incompetent, had been about zero. The alienists of the time had been too unsophisticated to understand what'd been wrong with the woman, and the public had been desperate for revenge: this was Dr. White's simple explanation for why Lydia Sherman's fate had been sealed. Mr. Darrow'd then asked Dr. White if, in his opinion, this injustice was now being repeated, maybe even outdone, by the state of New York's attempt to convict and execute Libby Hatch? Yes, Dr. White had solemnly answered; in fact, since Libby Hatch was, in his opinion, innocent, the injustice was even greater.

Finally, there'd been Mrs. Cady Stanton to seal the deal for the defense. Mr. Darrow's questioning of her had been particularly clever: as a lifelong battler for woman's rights, he'd asked, didn't Mrs. Cady Stanton feel that members of her sex had to accept all of the burdens as well as the advantages of equality? Didn't she think that they shouldn't be allowed to "hide behind their skirts," to use their gender as an excuse or even an explanation for certain crimes? Of course, Mrs. Cady Stanton had said; and if the crime Libby Hatch had been accused of had been anything other than murdering her own children, the old suffragist wouldn't have bothered traveling to Ballston Spa to give testimony. But in this one thing, childbirth and parenting, she said, men and women were not and never could be equal. Repeating what she'd told us when she came to Number 808 Broadway, Mrs. Cady Stanton had lectured the jury and the galleries about the "divine creative power" of women that was made manifest in the connection between a mother and child. If that power was used for evil purposes, she said, it could not be the woman's doing—after all, no woman could possibly betray a force what, being divine, was greater than her own will. No, if a woman did commit violence against her own child, it was either because she was insane or because the society of men had forced her into it somehow; probably both.

This last point was tough for Mr. Picton to argue on cross-examination; for he, during his time with Dr. Kreizler, had come to understand how very much Libby Hatch's actions might indeed have been affected by the society of men. But both Mr. Picton and the Doctor held that, such effects aside, Libby was still legally responsible for her own actions, and Mr. Picton had asked Mrs. Cady Stanton if she didn't agree. No, she'd answered, throwing the Doctor a look what said that, though she wasn't allowed to speak of it, she did believe that he was involved in some kind of mysterious witch-hunt. No, she said, a woman so harried and hounded as to be capable of murdering her own children must certainly have been driven insane—certainly *legally* insane, meaning unaware of the nature of her acts or that they were wrong—by man's society. And since neither the prosecution's nor the defense's expert mental witnesses had found Libby to in fact be insane, she could not have committed the crimes.

It had taken only a day to get all this testimony in, and measured as a whole it represented, Mr. Picton said, further proof (not that we needed any) that Mr. Darrow was truly the master of arguing in the negative. Without ever putting his client on the stand (always a dangerous thing for the defense to do in a murder trial), he'd managed to tear apart the state's assertions with logic what was so turned around—ass-backwards, even—that it seemed to make some kind of sense. Confused at first, the jury'd slowly become convinced; and all Mr. Picton's desperate efforts to point out that it was plain verbal trickery to say that someone had to be innocent just because they were sane while the crime they were accused of was *insane* just made him look, as he'd said the night before, like the voice of an older age. Mr. Darrow's reverse and negative logic had the feel of a new century, of modern thinking, and so, indeed, it was; but as Mr. Picton had also said the night before, being new didn't make it any more honorable or respectable—just more effective with juries. Which in the end, I suppose, is the only thing what most lawyers have ever considered progress.

Mr. Darrow hadn't yet closed his case, and he could theoretically call Libby Hatch to the stand on Monday if he wanted to; but there really wasn't any reason for it. Her little performance when Clara'd been on the stand had been more effective than any testimony she might give about how much she cared for her children; and allowing Mr. Picton a shot at her during cross-examination (the state wasn't itself allowed to call the defendant) could only lead to trouble. No, from Mr. Darrow's point of view it was better to keep her where she was: the teary-eyed widow and loving mother at the defense table, whose life had been scarred by terrible losses and tragedies, and who, for all her heroic attempts to overcome a sea of troubles, was now being persecuted by a state government embarrassed by its failure to solve an old and savage crime and an alienist bent on restoring his reputation.

It wasn't hard, then, to see why the news we brought back from Troy offered so little in the way of consolation to our friends: the question of what in her past had made Libby Hatch the woman she was today, or on the night she'd shot her three children, appeared to be a ship what'd already sailed. As Marcus had said the night before, the jury was past caring about any psychological explanations of what *context* had produced a normal, sane girl who would one day be capable of murdering her own children; in fact, they were past believing that she had murdered her children in the first place, and if we tried to introduce such testimony we'd just be grasping at air. The only useful thing, it seemed, that might come out of the search was if Libby had committed some other violent act during the years before she'd gone to the Muhlenbergs and we could find some way to tie that act to the present proceedings.

That possibility seemed pretty remote, though, to everybody—everybody except, again, Miss Howard, who just refused to give up on whatever horse she was riding until it was good and dead. And so early Saturday morning she had the four of us who'd made the Troy trip up and aboard Mr. Picton's surrey. (The Doctor'd wanted to come along, but he felt a personal responsibility to head out to the Westons' farm that day and see how Clara was doing.) The town of Schaghticoke was located about half a dozen miles inland from the east bank of the Hudson, which meant another ferry crossing and another monotonous ride through farm country what wasn't much different from the territory we'd covered in Saratoga and Washington Counties. We arrived in the place to find that the locals were getting a few big fields ready for the Rensselaer County Fair, a fact what made the general atmosphere, along with the attitudes of the town's residents, more cheery than they likely were ordinarily: we didn't have to ask but a few people about the Franklin farm before we found one helpful old soul who gave us very exact instructions on how to get there.

The spread lay to the east of the town, alongside a shadowy back road what was painful to travel, and what made Miss Howard and me figure that we were on our way to yet another gloomy house haunted by the ghosts of past violence and tragedy. You can imagine our shock, then, when we came around one bend in the bumpy road to find ourselves faced with a couple of very well-tended corn fields on our left, and some cow pastures with newly strung wire fences on our right. Most surprising of all was the sight, between the corn fields, of a small but pleasant-looking little house, its clapboards bearing a fresh coat of white paint and its neatly clipped lawn bordered by pretty little flower patches.

We turned up the short drive to the house, seeing no sign of life at first, but then finally spying a man in overalls walking from the house to a large green barn what was hidden behind one of the corn fields. He looked to be about forty-five or so, and seemed a decent, friendly enough type: as he spread chicken feed from a bucket around to a group of hens what were clucking in the barnyard, he made some pleasant, maybe even affectionate little noises, smiling as he watched the birds scurry around to peck at the food. Watching him, I pulled the surrey to a stop in front of the house.

"We're in the wrong place" was all I could say.

Miss Howard just studied the scene for a few minutes, looking troubled; then she got down off the buckboard and moved up to a gate in the white picket fence what bordered the front lawn.

"Stay here," she said, passing through the little gate in the fence. El Niño didn't much like the idea of her going to talk to the unknown man in the barnyard by herself, but I told him to just relax, pointing out that she was almost certainly carrying some kind of firearm. All the same, he produced his little bow and one of his short arrows from inside his dinner jacket (he'd rigged the lining of the garment to accommodate his weapons) and kept a steady eye on what went on across the yard.

"Excuse me!" Miss Howard called as she reached the corner of the house. At the sound the man turned and, smiling pleasantly, trotted on over to where she was standing, which was just within earshot of the rest of us.

"Hello," he said, setting his bucket down and wiping his hands on his overalls. "Something I can do for you?" Looking past Miss Howard, he caught sight of the rest of us in the surrey; and though I don't think the sight of two black men made him feel exactly easy, he didn't seem to get overly nervous about it.

"I hope so," Miss Howard answered. "My name is Sara Howard. I'm an investigator working with the Saratoga County District Attorney's office. I'm looking for Mr. and Mrs. George Franklin."

The mention of the Saratoga D.A. also didn't seem to rattle the man as much as it should have, certainly not as much as it had the other people we'd visited in the area. The fellow's eyes grew puzzled, but he didn't lose his smile completely. "They're my folks," he said. "Or were. My father died five years ago."

"Oh," Miss Howard answered. "I am sorry. And your mother?"

"Over in Hoosick Falls, visiting my brother and his wife," the man answered. "They've got a store there. She won't be back 'til tomorrow afternoon, I'm afraid. What's this all about?"

Matching the man's pleasant tone, Miss Howard asked, "Would you be George Franklin, then? Or Elijah?"

The man cocked his head in surprise. "Looks like you know all about us, miss. I'm Eli—that's what I'm called. Is there something wrong?"

"I—" Miss Howard glanced back to the rest of us, looking like she wasn't quite sure how to proceed. "Mr. Franklin—if I may ask, have you had any communication from your sister recently?"

"Libby?" For the first time, a cloud seemed to pass over Eli Franklin's features, and he glanced at the ground uneasily. "No. No, we haven't any of us heard from Libby for—well, for quite a few years, now." When he looked up again, the fellow wasn't smiling anymore. "She in some kind of trouble?"

"I'd—really rather discuss the matter when your mother's here," Miss Howard answered.

"Look," Franklin said, "if there's something my mother needs to hear, I think you'd better let me be the one to tell her. What's Libby done?"

"You assume she's done something?" Miss Howard asked curiously. "Why not that something's been done to her?"

Franklin's eyes got wider with surprise as he considered this possibility. "*Has* something happened to her? Is she all right?"

"Mr. Franklin . . ." Miss Howard folded her arms, her green eyes focusing right in on the man's brown ones. "I'm afraid I have to tell you that your sister is right now on trial in Ballston Spa. On a very serious charge."

Franklin absorbed this news, what should have been pretty rattling, with much less alarm than I would've thought possible. "So," he said, after a few silent minutes. "So that's it." His voice wasn't outraged or even stunned, just sort of—well, sad was the only way to put it. "What happened? There's a man mixed up in it, I guess. Is he married, something like that?"

"Something like that," Miss Howard lied coolly, figuring, I knew, that she was likely to get more information out of the farmer if she went along with his assumptions instead of telling him the truth. "Why? Was she ever in that sort of trouble before?"

"Libby?" Franklin grunted. "When it came to men, Libby was *always* in trouble." Looking away and making a little hissing sound of disappointment, Franklin said, "So why are you here? Are we going to be called into court? I don't see why—"

"No," Miss Howard answered quickly. "Nothing like that. I just thought that perhaps you and your family could provide us with some information about your sister's past. She's rather reluctant to talk about it herself."

Franklin shook his head. "Nothing surprising in that, I'm afraid," he said. "Well . . . you probably *should* wait for my mother, if that's the kind of thing you want. She'll know more than I can remember. You could come back tomorrow—"

"Oh, we'll come back," Miss Howard answered quickly. "But if you could just tell me a few basic facts." She turned to walk across the lawn toward the door of the little house. "Have you always lived here?"

"Yes," Franklin answered; then he caught himself. "I'm sorry—can I get you anything? Something to drink, maybe, or—"

"Yes, that'd be very nice of you," Miss Howard said. "I'm afraid it's been a long, dusty drive."

"And your—your people, there?" Franklin said, indicating the surrey.

"Hmm?" Miss Howard noised. "Oh. No, I wouldn't worry about them. I won't be long, anyway. I'll save most of my questions for tomorrow, when your mother's here."

"Well, then—please, come inside," Franklin said.

Giving us a quick glance and a nod what said to stay put, Miss Howard vanished into the little house, her host scraping the mud and manure off his boots on an old mother's helper what was bolted to the stone steps outside the door.

"I don't get it," I said as they went in. "*This* was where Libby Hatch grew up?"

"Doesn't quite seem to match, does it?" Cyrus answered, as he got down off the surrey to stretch his legs. "But there's never any way of knowing . . ."

"Señorito Stevie," El Niño said to me, moving to put his bow away. "This man—he will not hurt the lady?"

"I don't think so," I answered, scratching my head.

"So," the aborigine said with a nod, lying down on the back seat of the surrey. "Then El Niño will sleep." Before closing his eyes, though, he picked his head up to look at me one more time. "Señorito Stevie—the path we are taking to baby Ana is a strange one, yes? Or is it only that El Niño does not understand?"

"No, you understand all right," I told him, lighting up a smoke. "One strange path, is the truth . . ."

CHAPTER 49

Miss Howard wound up spending just half an hour inside the Franklin place, but it was long enough to learn a few interesting little nuggets of information, ones she refused to tell the rest of us in the surrey until we'd gotten back to Mr. Picton's house that evening and had collected around the chalkboard along with the Doctor and everyone else.

It seemed that the house we'd seen was very old, and contained only a few rooms—and out of these, just two were for sleeping. The Franklin brothers had shared one of them, while Libby had spent all of her childhood and early adult years sleeping in a small bed in her parents' room. There'd been no dividing curtain or partition of any kind in this chamber, and so for most of her life Libby had lived with a total lack of privacy, a fact what the Doctor considered extremely important. Apparently both he and Dr. Meyer had done a lot of work concerning children who were almost never out of sight of their parents, and had discovered that such kids developed a whole batch of problems when it came time to deal with the outside world: they were generally short-tempered, viciously sensitive to any kind of criticism, and, as the Doctor put it, "pathologically afraid of embarrassment, almost to the point of what Dr. Krafft-Ebing has labeled 'paranoia.'" And yet, underneath all that, these same types, when grown, could be strangely doubtful about their ability to make their own way in the world: they generally grew up with a strong need to have people around them, but at the same time they resented and even hated those people.

"We are not speaking of something precisely similar to violent physical or verbal abuse, of course," the Doctor explained, as he began, for the first time, to fill in the section of the chalkboard what had been set aside for facts concerning Libby's childhood. "But such a lack of privacy can produce many of the same results—primarily, the failure of the psyche to develop into a truly unified, integrated, and independent entity." Again I thought back to Miss Howard's words about Libby's personality being broken, at an early age, into pieces what she could never reassemble. "It's difficult to conceive of," the Doctor went on. "The stifling horror of being forced to spend every waking and sleeping hour in the intimate, watchful company of some other human being, of rarely if ever knowing solitude. Think of the incredible frustration and anger, the sense of complete—complete—"

"*Suffocation*," Cyrus finished for the Doctor; and I knew he was thinking back to the various babies what Libby'd done in through that very method.

"Precisely, Cyrus," the Doctor said, writing the word on the board in big letters and underlining it. "Here, indeed, we have the first key that fits both the enigma of Libby's mind and the apparent puzzle of her behavior—suffocation. But what did it lead to, Sara, in her early adulthood? Did the brother give you any idea at all?"

"There *was* one subject he was willing to discuss," Miss Howard said. "Primarily, I think, because he didn't want his mother to have to hear about it. It seems that Libby had a lot to do with boys, and from a very early age. She was extremely precocious, romantically and sexually."

"Again, it's logical," the Doctor said, considering it. "Such behavior would of necessity be secret, and therefore private—yet it reflects her inability, her very frustrating inability, to achieve such privacy and independence on her own." As he scribbled these thoughts, the Doctor added, "I don't imagine, as a result, that she was particularly kind to the unsuspecting young men who became involved with her."

"No," Miss Howard answered. "Quite a heartbreaker, would be the most—*charitable* way to put it."

"Good," the Doctor judged, nodding. "Very good."

Mr. Moore, who'd been sitting in the corner with a big glass pitcher full of martinis what he'd mixed for himself, let out a big groan at that; and the sound seemed to be echoed by the wail of a train whistle off in the distance. Listening to it, Mr. Moore held up a finger.

"You hear that, Kreizler? That's the sound of this damned case getting away from us. It's fading into the night, and what are *you* doing? Still sitting around with your blasted chalkboard, acting like there's some way you're going to *think* your way out of losing. We're *finished*—who the hell cares *why* Libby Hatch is the way she is, at this point?"

"The eternal voice of encouragement," Mr. Picton said, glancing over to Mr. Moore. "Have six or seven more of those foul concoctions, John, and perhaps you'll nod off—then we can go on in peace."

"I know it seems late in the race, Moore," the Doctor said, lighting a cigarette as he studied the blackboard. "But we must do what we can, while we can. We *must*."

"Why?" Mr. Moore grumbled. "Nobody *wants* the damned woman to be guilty, they've made that much clear. Who the hell are we carrying on *for*, at this point?"

"There's still the problem of Ana Linares, John," Lucius said.

Mr. Moore let out another grunt. "A girl whose own father doesn't care if she lives or dies. She'll probably have as good a chance with Libby as she would with him, the Spanish bastard."

"I wasn't actually thinking of Ana Linares, just now," the Doctor said, his voice going very quiet.

"No," Miss Howard said, "it's Clara, isn't it? How was she? I didn't even think to ask."

The Doctor shrugged, looking uneasy. "Bewildered. And not very talkative, though I don't blame her for that. I promised her that this ordeal would help both her and her mother. It's done neither—and now her terror at the memory of what happened three years ago is being matched by her fear of what *will* happen if her mother goes free. She's not so young as to be blind to the danger she may be in if Libby is loose to take revenge on what she no doubt sees as a treacherous child who was the only witness to her bloody act." Setting his piece of chalk down, the Doctor picked up a glass of wine and tried to take a sip; but he stopped in mid-action, as if he had no interest in any kind of relief.

"You can't blame yourself, Doctor," Marcus said. "The case looked solid. There was no reason to believe it would go this way."

"Perhaps," the Doctor said, sitting down and putting his glass aside.

"And may I remind everyone again—" Miss Howard said. But she got only that far before Mr. Moore let out another big groan.

"Yes, yes, we know, Sara, it's not over yet! My God, don't you ever get tired of that saw?"

"If you mean don't I wish it would end so I'd have a good excuse to sink to the bottom of a glass and live there, John, then no," Miss Howard snapped. "It's true that we may not have gotten very much information today—but the mother must know more, and she returns tomorrow. So will we." She looked to the Doctor. "Will you come with us? I'm not sure I'll know all the right questions to ask."

From somewhere deep, the Doctor managed to stir the final traces of what passed for encouragement. "Of course," he said, putting his hands on his legs and then standing up. "But now, if you all don't mind, I'll think I'll retire before dinner. I'm not particularly hungry. We don't need to be at the Franklins' until the afternoon, you say, Sara?"

"That's right."

"Then there's no reason to rise early, at least." He looked around the room a little awkwardly. "Good night."

We all mumbled replies, and then grew silent as the Doctor slowly climbed the stairs.

Once she'd heard his bedroom door close, Miss Howard took a piece of chalk from the board and flung it at Mr. Moore's head, catching him very nicely between the eyes and making him yelp.

"You know, John," she said, "if the *Times* won't take you back, you could always open a new business kicking injured dogs or knocking the crutches out from under cripples."

"Someday," Mr. Moore moaned, rubbing the chalk mark on his head, "you're going to do me some serious physical injury, Sara—and I promise you, I'll sue! Look, I'm sorry if you all think I'm being a defeatist, but I just don't see what you're going to find out from Libby Hatch's *mother* that's going to change things."

"Maybe nothing!" Miss Howard shot back. "But you've seen what the Doctor's been through this week—and remember, *we* drew him into this case, to help him forget his troubles in New York. Now it looks like we've only made things worse. You might at least try to be encouraging."

Mr. Moore glanced over at the stairway, looking a little ashamed of himself. "Well—I suppose that's true . . ." He poured himself another drink and then turned to Miss Howard. "Do you want me to come along tomorrow?" He did his best to sound sincere. "I promise you, I will try to keep things hopeful."

Miss Howard sighed and shook her head. "I don't think you could be hopeful right now if your life depended on it. No, it'll be better if just Stevie and I go—the fewer people, the less awkward the silence will be." She looked up at the ceiling. "And I've a feeling there's going to be a *lot* of silence . . ."

It was a sound prediction. The Doctor didn't come down from his room 'til close to noon on Sunday, and he still didn't seem to have much of an appetite. He did his level best to take an interest in the job what lay ahead of us, but it was a pretty hopeless cause: he seemed to know just how unlikely it would be that we'd discover anything so crucial at the Franklins' farm that it would swing our fate in court. By the time we climbed aboard the surrey, he'd dropped any effort at conversation and grown very quiet and thoughtful again, and he stayed that way through all of the long drive over to Schaghticoke.

The Franklin house was just as peaceful as it'd been the day before; but this time, in addition to Eli Franklin working around the barnyard, there was an elderly woman—fleshy but not fat—weeding one of the flower patches by the house. Her white-haired head was shielded from the sun by a wide-brimmed straw hat, and her gingham dress was covered by a slightly soiled apron. Even from halfway up the drive we could hear her singing to herself, and a small dog was happily prancing around, letting out a little yap occasionally to get the woman's attention and receiving a pat on the head and a few kindly words in return.

As the Doctor took in the scene before him, his black eyes began to glow with a light what I hadn't seen in evidence for a couple of days. "So . . ." he said, as I drew the surrey to a stop beside the gate in the white picket fence; and when he got down to the ground, he smiled just a little.

"Not precisely what you expected?" Miss Howard asked, joining him.

"Tragedy and horror do not always come with the appropriate trappings, Sara," the Doctor answered softly. "If they did, mine would be a useless profession."

As I tied off our horse's reins, I saw that Eli Franklin had caught sight of us and was running out to the gate. He seemed to be moving with real purpose.

"Hello, Miss Howard," he said, his face full of worry.

"Mr. Franklin," she answered with a nod. "This is Dr. Kreizler, who's also working on the case. And I don't think you met our young associate Stevie Taggert yesterday—"

Eli Franklin just shook our hands quickly without saying anything, then turned to Miss Howard again. "My mother—when I told her—"

But by then the woman who was tending the flowers had turned and seen us. Her little dog was yapping louder and faster as he, too, registered the presence of strangers. "Oh!" the woman called, in a voice what was both very loud and sort of melodious. "Oh, are these Elspeth's friends, Eli, dear?"

She started toward us, and Eli Franklin spoke even faster and with more urgency: "I couldn't tell her that Libby was actually in trouble—it would set her nerves off, and her heart's not so strong anymore. Is there any way that you can find out what you need to know without—"

"We shall try, Mr. Franklin," the Doctor answered good-naturedly. "It may be that your mother can tell us all we need to know without our revealing our true purpose."

Eli Franklin's face filled with relief, and he just had time to say, "Thank you, Doctor, I do appreciate—" before his mother arrived at the gate.

The little dog was yapping louder than ever, and as Mrs. Franklin held her hat in place on her head she looked down to scold him gently: "Leopold, stop that, these are visitors!" The dog tried to calm down, but it was an effort. "I'm sorry," the woman said to us, her singsong voice growing a little addled. "He's *very* protective! Well! So you're all friends of my daughter's? And trying to find her, my son says?" Back behind her amber-colored eyes you could see that Mrs. Franklin—who must have been very handsome in her day—didn't quite believe the story, but that it was easier for her to accept it than to contemplate other, less pleasant possibilities. "I'm afraid we can't help you," she went on, before the Doctor or Miss Howard could answer. "As Eli told you yesterday, we haven't heard from Libby in several years. Not that I'm surprised! So careless, that girl! She never could take care of the simplest little—"

"Yes, Mother," Eli Franklin said, touching her elbow to quiet her down. "This is Miss Howard and Dr.—Kreizler, was it? And the boy is called—"

"Just Stevie'll do," I said, looking at the woman and getting a big smile in return.

"Oh, just Stevie, eh?" she said, reaching out to touch my cheek. "Well, that's good enough—you're a fine-looking boy!"

"They think maybe something we know about her past will help them locate Libby," Eli Franklin went on.

Miss Howard nodded. "You see, she hasn't contacted *us* in quite some time, either. Perhaps if we knew a little more of what her usual habits were—"

Mrs. Franklin nodded. "Hasn't contacted you? Well, that doesn't surprise me, either! I don't know why that girl never could take care of the smallest details. We've gotten one or two little notes, over the years, but never so much as a single visit! She just dances through life, doing as she pleases. Ah, well, some people are that way, I suppose." She pulled the picket gate open. "Please, please, come in and sit on the porch out back— we've screened it in, so you won't have to fight off these terrible flies. What with all the moisture this summer, I'm afraid the insects have been positively thriving!" We started to follow her around the side of the house, none of us getting a word in. "Now, I've made lemonade and iced tea—I thought it would be too warm for anything else. There's some ginger-bread, too, and we might find something even sweeter for you, Stevie, if you crave sweets as much as *my* boys did! But as for Libby, I don't know how much help I can be . . ." Moving onto the back porch of the house, we found that the big screen panels did in fact remove us from the an-noying black flies what had started to swarm in the afternoon sun. "It may be that *you* can tell *me* more, really. As I say, we haven't even *seen* her in—how long has it been, Eli?"

Eli Franklin looked at Miss Howard what you might call pointedly. "Ten years," he said.

"*Ten?*" his mother repeated. "That can't be right. No, you must be mis-taken Eli, I can't believe that even Libby, careless as she is, would go ten years without a visit! Has it *really* been that long? Well, sit down, sit down, everyone, and have something to drink!"

I took a seat in a big wicker chair, sighing a little to myself: getting in-formation out of this biddy was going to be a job, all right.

"Thank you, Mrs. Franklin," the Doctor said, taking a seat in another of the wicker chairs. "The afternoon is warm, and the drive was a long one."

"Yes," Mrs. Franklin answered, pouring out glasses of her cool refresh-ments and handing them around. "All the way from Ballston Spa! I must confess, I never would've guessed that Elspeth would be the center of so much attention." In the words, and also in their tone, there was some-thing what reminded me in a chilling way of the first time we'd ever heard Libby Hatch speak, outside her house on Bethune Street. "She was never the kind of girl that people took much interest in." Eli Franklin shot Miss Howard a quick look again, asking her with his eyes not to bring up the things he'd mentioned the day before. "Her brothers were more outgo-ing, of course, more social—they got that from me, I suppose. But El-speth was more like her father—a daydreamer, too busy in her own mind to ever be of much use, really."

"I understand your husband is no longer with us," Miss Howard said.

"No, bless his heart," the woman answered, reaching around from the table to slip sprigs of fresh-cut mint into all our glasses and then passing around a plate of gingerbread. "He's been gone almost five years, now. Poor George worked himself into the grave, keeping the farm going. He never was much good at it, really—if he hadn't had the boys to help him . . . but they're born workers, both of them. They get that from me, too, I expect. Practical heads. But George was a dreamer, like Elspeth. It was all we could do to raise three children and keep this place afloat."

"And Elspeth?" the Doctor asked carefully. "Surely she was *some* help to you."

Mrs. Franklin laughed: the light, well-oiled sound of a woman what was used to handling men. "Well, I don't know how many ways I can say it, Doctor, but the girl was never really any good to *anyone,* not when it came to the practical business of living. Oh, she was pretty enough. And clever, too, especially with her studies. But not useful in any way that would have really been important for a young lady." I saw Miss Howard near choke on her piece of gingerbread, but she managed to keep a pleasant expression on her face. "A positive fright in the kitchen," Mrs. Franklin went on. "And as for housework, well . . . I couldn't even put her to *dusting* without her breaking whatever we had that *could* be broken. A sweet thing, but what does sweetness matter when you're all grown up? It was no wonder she never had any suitors. Lived with us until she was near an old maid, and not one man ever came to ask for her hand. I didn't wonder. Men around here work hard—they need a woman who can tend house, not a clever dreamer. And prettiness fades, Doctor, prettiness fades . . ." The little dog, who'd followed us onto the porch and was panting in excitement beside Mrs. Franklin's chair, let out another yap. "Oh! Leopold, you want gingerbread, I'm so sorry! Here . . ." Handing the dog a piece of the cake—which I had to admit was as good as any I'd ever had—Mrs. Franklin began to stroke his head. "Yes, there, my sweet boy. You don't remember Libby, do you, Leopold? She left before you came to live with us . . ." The woman looked back up, lost in thought. "We had another dog, then—*Libby's* dog. What was his name, Eli?"

"Fitz," Eli Franklin answered, munching on his gingerbread and swilling his third glass of lemonade.

"Yes, that's right. Fitz. Oh, she loved that dog. Cried awfully when he died—I thought she might expire herself! Remember, Eli?"

Suddenly Eli Franklin stopped chewing: he looked around at all of us what you might call guardedly, then slowly got the gingerbread in his mouth down his gullet. "No," he answered, quickly and quietly.

"Well, of course you do!" Mrs. Franklin said. "Don't be silly—it was just before she left to work with that family in Stillwater—"

"The Muhlenbergs?" Miss Howard said hopefully.

"Oh, then you know the Muhlenbergs, Miss Howard?" Mrs. Franklin replied, happily surprised. "Fine people, Elspeth said—she wrote from there once. Very fine. And just before she left, she had that attack of bilious fever—"

"Mother—" Eli Franklin said, still looking a little alarmed.

"—and the morning after that Fitz died. I'm *sure* you remember, Eli— we buried him out by the barn. You built a little coffin, and Libby painted a headstone—"

"Mother!" Eli Franklin said, a little harshly now; then he smiled around at the rest of us, though it was a strain. "I'm sure these people don't want to hear about every little thing that happened to Libby while she was living here—they're interested in what's happening to her *now.*"

"Well . . ." Mrs. Franklin looked at her son in some shock; but along with the shock there was a trace of sudden, cold anger, of the variety what I'd sometimes seen come into Libby Hatch's face. "I certainly *apologize* if I'm embarrassing my own *son.* But I was telling them about the Muhlenbergs—"

"You were telling them—" Eli Franklin said; then, catching his mother's look, he dropped it. "All right. Go ahead, tell them—about the Muhlenbergs."

"They were very fine people," Mrs. Franklin went on, giving her son one last warning look as her tone became musical again. "That's what she said in her letter. And of course I was glad, because it seemed the perfect sort of work for her!"

Miss Howard's face near dropped, and I imagine mine did the same. For anybody to say that being a wet nurse was the "perfect sort of work" for Libby Hatch indicated that they didn't know her at all; and Mrs. Franklin, however addled she might've seemed at moments, did appear to be aware of her daughter's strengths and weaknesses. Before either of us could give voice to our confusion, though, the Doctor, suspecting that the story'd undergone a change somewhere along the line of communication, asked, "And what sort of work was that, Mrs. Franklin?"

"Why, don't you know?" she answered, surprised. "Surely if you know the Muhlenbergs, you know that Libby was their son's tutor—before she went to New York, that is. But perhaps you met them after she'd already left?"

"Yes," Miss Howard said, quickly and nervously. "Just recently, in fact. And we didn't meet your daughter until she'd arrived in the city—you see, that's where we're all from."

"Oh, is that so?" Mrs. Franklin answered. "Well, if you're from New York, then you certainly know more about my daughter than I do. You see, I've had only one letter from her since she moved there, and that was so long ago—it's been years since I've heard anything at all. But then, as I say, Elspeth was always that way—I doubt she even realizes she hasn't written! So very careless, that girl, always daydreaming about something . . ."

For a moment Mrs. Franklin's mind seemed to wander in that way we'd already witnessed; but when it did so this time around, I began to see that what I'd taken for addle-headedness was really just a way of avoiding subjects what she wouldn't or couldn't discuss, maybe because they were too painful, or maybe because they would've revealed things about *her* what she didn't want known, especially to strangers. Such being the case, I expected the Doctor to start pressing harder for information: he wasn't one to let people get away from the point. I was doubly surprised, then, when he just stood up, studied Mrs. Franklin's eyes as they stared into the distance, and finally said, "Yes. I suspect you are right, Mrs. Franklin. Thank you so much for the refreshment—we shall continue to look for your daughter in New York."

Snapping out of her seeming daze quickly and looking very relieved, Mrs. Franklin also stood up. "I *am* sorry I can't be of more help to you all, truly I am. And if you do run across Elspeth, you might just tell her that her family's curious to know what she's up to." With that she started to walk us toward the screen door.

"Doctor," Miss Howard said, looking concerned, "I'm not sure that we've—"

"Oh, I think Mrs. Franklin's told us all she can," the Doctor answered pleasantly. "And it will prove *extremely* helpful, I'm sure." As he said these last words, he gave Miss Howard a very meaningful look; and she, taking it on faith that what he said was true, just shrugged and moved to the screen door. As for me, I had no idea what they were talking about; but then, I hadn't really expected to. I hadn't even been sure I'd be let into the house, and once I was there, I figured I'd have to wait 'til the ride home for explanations.

As we passed back out onto the lawn from the porch, Mrs. Franklin held up a finger. "Do you know, Doctor—you might try the theaters. I always had an idea that Elspeth would end up on the stage—I can't imagine why, but I always did! Well, good-bye, now! It was so pleasant to talk with you all!"

Miss Howard and I tried not to look even more confused as we said good-bye to Mrs. Franklin, who called to her little dog and then vanished into the small house.

"I'll see you to your rig," Eli Franklin said, himself looking pretty relieved that we were departing. "And I thank you for not mentioning the matter of Libby's being in trouble to my mother. You see how she is, and—"

"Yes, Mr. Franklin." The Doctor's voice had suddenly lost the soft, polite tone he'd used with the man's mother. "We do indeed, as you say, 'see how your mother is.' Perhaps more than you know. And I'm afraid I shall require a service for concealing our true purpose from her."

The words and the way the Doctor said them struck new nervousness, maybe even fear, into Eli Franklin. "Service?" he mumbled. "What do you—"

"The barnyard, Mr. Franklin," the Doctor answered. "We should like to inspect the barnyard."

"The barnyard?" Franklin tried to muster up a laugh. "Why in the world would you want to see *that*, there's nothing—"

"Mr. Franklin." The Doctor's black eyes struck the man's features dead still. "If you please."

Franklin started to shake his head slowly, a movement what quickly became agitated. "No. I'm sorry, but I don't even know what you want, I'm not going to let you—"

"Very well." The Doctor turned back toward the porch. "You make it necessary for me to ask your mother . . ." He seized hold of the handle on the door, only to have Franklin grab his forearm with one of his powerful hands: not roughly, but with desperation, all the same.

"Wait!" Franklin said; then, as the Doctor spun a scowl on him again, he released his grip. "You—you just want to look around the barnyard?"

"Mr. Franklin, you know perfectly well what we want to see," the Doctor answered; and as he did, Miss Howard suddenly clutched at her forehead, apparently realizing whatever it was that the Doctor was driving at.

Swallowing hard, Franklin looked to her. "Libby's in a lot more trouble than you said she was, isn't she?"

"Yes," Miss Howard said, "I'm afraid so."

Seeming a little pained by that information, Franklin nodded once or twice. "All right. Come on, then."

Leading the way with long, slow steps, Franklin guided us off the back lawn of the house and across the dusty drive, then into the manure- and mud-covered barnyard. As he did, Miss Howard and I pulled up close to the Doctor.

"You suspect—" Miss Howard asked.

"I suspect nothing," the Doctor finished for her. "I'm certain. We need only an accurate description of the site, to demonstrate to the woman that we have actually been here and are in earnest."

"Description of what site?" said yours truly, now the only member of our group who didn't know what was going on; but Miss Howard and the Doctor both kept following Franklin silently, around to the far side of the barn.

There was a muddy water hole to one end of the structure, round back, and a large patch of prickly raspberry bushes at the other. Franklin walked over to one section of the raspberries and then, sighing as he looked to us again, grabbed an old branch that'd fallen off of a gnarled crab-apple tree what stood not far from the water hole. He used the branch to slash and pry at the thick, thorny stems of the bushes in front of him, and as he did a small object came into view on the ground:

It was a wooden headstone, maybe two feet high. The thing was cracked in a few spots, but not badly, and the lettering what'd been painted on it, though faded, was easy to read:

FITZ

1879–1887

LOVE ALWAYS, FROM MAMA

As I read the last line, I felt as though somebody'd run along my back with the hard end of a goose quill: they were the very same words what were carved on Thomas and Matthew Hatch's graves in Ballston Spa.

"Sure," I whispered to nobody, taking a couple of frightened steps back as I kept staring at the headstone. "Of course—she was a *wet nurse* . . ."

At the sound of the Doctor's voice I finally looked up. "What did the dog die of, Mr. Franklin?" he said.

Franklin just shook his head. "I don't know. She brought him to me—dead. Not a mark on him. I built her the coffin, and she took it off and sealed it up. Then I helped her bury it."

"And your sister's—'bilious fever'?" the Doctor asked.

"It lasted all night," Franklin answered, turning to stare at the headstone. His voice became what you might call detached as he added: "Came on her after we'd all gone to sleep . . . nearly killed her. But do you know? She never said a word, until morning. Never made a sound. . . . My mother and father, they slept right through it. Right through it."

The Doctor nodded. "You understand, Mr. Franklin, that a person who destroys evidence of a crime can be indicted as an accessory?"

Franklin nodded, his face still blank. "It's only a dog . . ."

The Doctor moved closer to the man. "I hope, for your sake, that your sister will see reason, and make it unnecessary for us to return with a court order authorizing an exhumation of this—*dog*. In the meantime, I advise you to make very sure that the grave is not tampered with."

Franklin didn't say anything to that, just kept nodding and staring at the headstone. Satisfied that the fellow'd gotten his point, the Doctor looked to Miss Howard and me, then turned and started back for the surrey.

"Doctor," Franklin mumbled as we went, causing us to stop and turn back to him. "She never—Libby, I mean—she never had much. You heard my mother—she was just a servant in this house. Not even that—a servant gets her own quarters." He looked down at the grave again. "She had men—boys, really—who chased her. She was foolish. But it was something of her own. She deserved to have that much, without it ruining her life. She deserved to have more than just a *dog* . . ."

The Doctor nodded once, and then we kept moving to our rig.

"Do you think," Miss Howard said quietly, "that Judge Brown will give us a court order?"

"It's my belief that such action won't be necessary," the Doctor answered. "Darrow and Maxon will be able to see reason, even if Libby can't."

As we climbed up onto the rig, Miss Howard looked back toward the barn. "And the brother—did he know? *Does* he know?"

"He suspects, certainly," the Doctor answered, as I started our horse moving. "But as to whether or not he's sure . . ."

"What about the mother?" I asked. "She ain't so harebrained as she makes out—she might know, too."

"It's possible, of course," the Doctor answered. "She, too, suspects much about her daughter, and wouldn't be altogether surprised by this. But I don't think she's aware of it. A woman like Libby Hatch would have found ways to conceal the pregnancy—and you heard what happened when she finally delivered the child. She *never made a sound*. In most cases I wouldn't believe it, but in this instance we are dealing with a person capable of incredible discipline when she finds herself trapped."

"But who was the father?" Miss Howard asked.

"All questions to be answered later," the Doctor replied. "Stevie—I saw an inn on our way through the town. They may have a telephone. We must call Mr. Picton, and tell him to meet us at his office as soon as we return. Then he must contact Darrow and Maxon and have them, along with their client, join us at, say—" Pulling out his watch and checking the time, the Doctor made a quick calculation. "Nine o'clock. Yes, that should leave us enough time to work out the details." Tucking the timepiece away again, the Doctor folded his arms anxiously. "And then we shall see."

CHAPTER 50

By seven-thirty that evening our entire team was packed into Mr. Picton's office one more time, to weigh the results of our trip to the Franklins' farm and determine what we should do about it all. Even El Niño was present: as usual, it wasn't that he understood most of what was going on or had anything to contribute, but he was always concerned that "the lady," "Mr. Mont-*rose*," Mr. Picton (his future "*jefe*"), or one of the rest of us might be set upon by some villainous characters. He'd come to believe that it was his personal mission and responsibility to prevent any such assault; and as those of us what actually had something to say about the case sat in a circle around Mr. Picton's desk, the aborigine stood by the door, weapons at the ready. At the time I considered this, like so much of his behavior, amusing and touching, nothing more; later, I'd come to wish that we'd all followed his cautious lead.

The main topic of conversation—a conversation what rapidly turned into a debate—was how we were going to present our discovery to the defense lawyers, and what the best deal to try to strike with them in light of it was. The general thought was that Mr. Picton would tell Libby Hatch that the state'd be willing to forget about the coffin what was buried behind her family's barn in return for her changing her plea to one of guilty—but guilty of what? Mr. Picton was very reluctant to abandon the first-degree murder charge, what would've sent Libby to the electrical chair; but he knew that giving someone a choice between death now and death later wasn't really much of a carrot. So, he tried to reconcile himself to the next best thing: second-degree murder and a sentence of life imprisonment without the possibility of parole. Some of our group—Marcus and Mr. Moore, mainly—didn't see why Libby'd go for that option, either, given her personality: a woman who seemed to enjoy her freedom in as many different ways as this one did wasn't likely to look on the prospect of spending the rest of her days behind bars with much enthusiasm.

But the Doctor disagreed. He figured that, though the woman might rebel at the idea of such a sentence on the surface, some deeper part of her soul would accept and maybe even welcome it. Mr. Moore and Marcus were skeptical about this thought, too, until the Doctor explained it further. Prison, he said, would actually satisfy the conflicting longings of Libby's spirit: the need to be isolated while at the same time having people around; the need to perform what she saw as some sort of useful task (for a woman as clever as Libby would no doubt be assigned to a position of some authority among the prisoners in, say, the women's block at Sing Sing) while at the same time feeling like she was defying accepted social customs and authority (she would, after all, be a jailbird). And then there was the question of her desire to control what went on around her: many criminals, the Doctor said, especially those of Libby's stripe, secretly craved some kind of regulation and discipline in their lives (she had, he reminded us all, been able to go through hours of labor without ever making a sound loud enough to wake her parents); and though physical control in this case would actually be administered by the prison, Libby, with her talent for self-delusion, would quickly convince herself that in fact she was the one who was dictating what went on. And in a way, the Doctor said, she'd be right, being as it would be her own criminal actions what would've landed her in jail. But one consideration weighed above all others in convincing the Doctor that Libby would take the deal what Mr. Picton planned to offer: over and over we'd seen her demonstrate that she prized her own life above all things, including the health and safety of her own offspring—the chance to escape execution would be enough, the Doctor said, to make Libby play along, even without the other influences.

Marcus was satisfied by this reasoning, but Mr. Moore still had his doubts; and Mr. Picton, though he knew they were taking the only sensible course, continued to feel a little cheated by not being able to secure a death sentence. But the Doctor insisted to all of them that the only thing what was truly important was for Libby Hatch to be put into a place where she'd never again have any contact with children—especially her own child. On top of that, knowing that her mother was going to be jailed for life instead of executed would only help Clara Hatch's recovery, since the girl wouldn't have to carry the enormous weight for the rest of her life of having played a part in sending her mother to the chair. Miss Howard stated that this was the best reason of all for making the deal; indeed, she said, considering what effect her mother's execution might've had on Clara, she wondered why Mr. Picton hadn't made life imprisonment for Libby his goal in the first place. This comment led to some pretty passionate statements from the assistant district attorney about the unknowable future, and how he couldn't trust that some governor might not get suckered—say, twenty or thirty years down the line—by one of Libby's effective performances into reversing the part of her sentence what specified that there was to be no parole. The Doctor and Miss Howard might have done a lot that day to *explain* her evil, he said, but they hadn't done anything to *remove* it: only death could provide that kind of solution.

That set the Doctor off again, on the subject of how was science ever supposed to learn anything from criminals like Libby if the state went around frying and hanging them all; and this discussion, along with all others related to it, went on and on as the sun set beyond the train depot down the hill from Mr. Picton's window. Finally, at a few minutes after nine, there was a knock at the door of Mr. Picton's outer office. El Niño pulled the thing open, and in wandered Mr. Darrow and Mr. Maxon, the first looking curious but confident as he took in the scene around him, the second seeming, as ever, very nervous. With formal little movements El Niño showed the pair into Mr. Picton's inner office, and we all stood up.

"Ah! Maxon, Darrow," Mr. Picton said. "Good of you to come so late on a Sunday evening."

"Quite a conference you've got going here," Mr. Darrow said, glancing around at us all and nodding a polite greeting. "Having trouble planning your summation, Mr. Picton?"

"Summation?" Mr. Picton said, playing at surprise. "Oh! Great jumping cats, do you know, with all that's happened today, I'm afraid I completely forgot about closing arguments! But then, I'm not entirely sure we're going to need them." He pulled out his pipe and clamped it between his teeth, looking very pleased with himself.

Mr. Maxon—who'd had a lot of run-ins with Mr. Picton in court, and was in a position to know when the man was up to something—started to look even more jittery than he had when he came in. "What is it, Picton?"

he asked, pushing his pince-nez down tighter on his skinny nose. "What have you got?"

"What *can* he have?" Mr. Darrow asked with a chuckle. "The state's closed its case in chief, Mr. Picton. I hope you didn't make the mistake of saving anything for last-minute theatricals. Judge Brown doesn't seem like the kind of man that'll go for them."

"I know it," Mr. Picton answered. "And your colleague Maxon, there, *knows* I know it. So whatever I've 'got,' it must be something fairly good to warrant my asking you here tonight—don't you think so, Maxon?" Mr. Maxon, unlike Mr. Darrow, seemed to take this statement straight to heart; and, pleased by that fact, Mr. Picton looked over to me. "Stevie? I wonder if you'd just run down and tell Henry to have Mrs. Hatch—I beg your pardon, Mrs. Hunter—brought up from her cell."

"Got it," I said, making for the door.

As I went out I heard Mr. Picton continuing, "Doctor, why don't you stay in here with the three of us? The rest of you might just have a seat in the outer office—we don't want to overwhelm the defendant, after all . . ."

After bolting down the hall, I dashed onto the marble stairs, taking them two at a time on my way down to the guard's station in the entryway. Running to it without looking up, I began to say, "Mr. Picton wants—"

Then I saw who I was talking to. It wasn't the guard Henry at all, but one of the other big men what'd watched the courtroom doors all through the trial.

"Where's Henry?" I asked.

The man looked at me with a sour expression. "What's it to you, kid?"

I shrugged. "Nothing. But what it is to Mr. *Picton* is he's got orders for him."

Looking even more irritated, the guard nodded toward a doorway behind him. "Henry's downstairs. Guarding the prisoner."

I heard the statement; I accepted it with a simple nod of my head, and never thought twice about it. But now, looking back across the gap of so many years, I find myself once again wishing desperately that something could have made me see what was going on.

"Well," I told the guard, "Mr. Picton wants he should bring the prisoner up to his office."

"What, *now*?" the guard asked.

"I don't figure as he meant next Thursday," I said, turning around and heading back to the staircase. "If I was you I'd get moving—they're all up there waiting."

"Hey!" the guard called after me, as I started up the stairs. "Just remember, I don't get paid to take orders from any kid!" Then he turned to go through the door behind him.

"You just *took* one, mug," I mumbled, smiling as I got back to the second floor. "So go chase yourself."

Back in Mr. Picton's outer office I found that Cyrus, the detective sergeants, Mr. Moore, Miss Howard, and El Niño were all crowded around the closed oak door to the inner chamber. Cyrus had the aborigine up on his shoulders, from which spot El Niño was looking through a partly open transom, spying on what was going on among the three lawyers and the Doctor and trying to whisper his intelligence back to the others; the only problem was that his English wasn't good enough to understand much more than half of what the men inside were saying.

"They are speaking of the girl, Clara, now," El Niño whispered as I came in.

"What about her?" Miss Howard asked.

"Something—something—" El Niño shook his head in frustration. "The Señor Doctor is saying things I do not understand—some things about sickness, and about the mother—she who is the killer . . ."

"Oh, this is useless," Mr. Moore said in frustration. Then he signaled to me. "Stevie, trade places with your friend. I want to know what the hell's happening in there."

I was about to follow the order when there came a knock at the outer door. Waiting for El Niño to get down off of Cyrus's shoulders, I opened the thing, and found myself facing the guard Henry and Libby Hatch. Better than a week in jail hadn't done anything to damage the way the woman carried herself—her black dress looked as crisp as it had on the night she got off the train—or to dull the devilish gleam in her golden eyes. I'd never been so close to those eyes, before, nor had them focused directly on me; and I found that their general effect was to cause me to back up, slowly and silently, until I near fell over the unused secretary's desk what sat in that outer office. This reaction caused Libby to smile at me in a way what I hope never to see in another person, a way what brought Mr. Moore's earthy language at the Café Lafayette back into my mind: you really couldn't tell, from the look in her face, just what this woman might have in store for you. Love, hate, life, death— all of them, it seemed like, were very possible, so long as they served her purposes.

And from the proud way that she moved through the others to get to the thick door to the inner office, it was pretty clear that Libby Hatch felt like her purposes were being very well served, just at that juncture. She glanced at each of the silent faces before her and kept smiling, then started to shake her head, as if to say that we'd all been terribly foolish to even think about taking her on. Henry kept one hand on her arm (she wasn't wearing any manacles, another fact what should've struck me as odd but didn't) as he knocked on the inner office door and Mr. Picton told him to enter. He opened the door and indicated to Libby that she should go on in. He did this by way of a single look, the kind of quick, meaningful glance what only people who know each other very well use to communicate.

"Come in, Mrs. Hunter," I heard Mr. Picton call. "Thank you, Henry. I'll send someone down when we're finished."

"You don't want me to wait?" the guard asked.

Mr. Picton just sighed. "Henry, am I speaking Greek? If I wanted you to wait, I'd ask you to wait. Go back downstairs, and I'll send someone when we're finished, thank you very much!"

Looking the way he always did when Mr. Picton gave him a hard time—like some kind of injured animal—the guard glanced at Libby again, and she nodded at him once. Only at that signal did Henry turn around to storm moodily out of the room. As for Libby, she went on in and took a seat before Mr. Picton's desk next to Mr. Darrow, while Mr. Maxon closed the door on the rest of us.

"All right, Stevie," Mr. Moore whispered. "Up you go!"

In a quick move I stepped into a cradle what Marcus made with his hands, then grabbed Cyrus's hands and let him pull me onto his shoulders. Once comfortably seated, with Cyrus holding on to my legs, I carefully moved my face up to the transom, which was open just far enough for me to see all the players in the room, along with a swatch of Mr. Picton's desk. Whispering down to the others at regular intervals, I witnessed and narrated the following scene:

"Why've I been called up here at this hour?" Libby asked softly and sadly. Her expression, what I could only see in profile, looked much more timid than it had in the outer office. "Is it Clara? Has something happened to my baby?"

"Now, now, Mrs. Hatch," Mr. Maxon said, putting a hand to her arm. "I beg your pardon—Mrs. Hunter. Please, calm yourself."

"Yes, do spare yourself the effort, Mrs. Hunter," Mr. Picton said, without any trace of sympathy in his voice. "You're not in court now, nor are there any members of the press lurking about. Your usual histrionics are not required."

"Instead of being insulting, Picton," Mr. Darrow said, crossing one leg over the other and then leaning back in his chair, "you might tell us what the hell it is you want."

"Yes," Mr. Picton answered, lighting his pipe with quick little moves of his arms and hands. "I don't see that there's any reason to beat around the bush." Letting out big blasts of smoke, he sat forward. "The *raspberry* bush, to be precise, Mrs. Hunter—the one behind your family's barn in Schaghticoke." He opened his eyes a bit wider. "Or weren't the bushes there when you were still living at home? No, I don't suppose they would have been—too difficult to get under them to do all that digging. Still, they grow like weeds, do raspberries—quite tall, now. They almost hide the thing. *Almost.*"

Libby's head had frozen, and her hands were clutching tightly at the arms of her chair. I could only see one of the golden eyes, but it had opened wide, wider than I'd ever seen before: wide enough to make me believe that for once she might have been truly surprised and at a loss.

"Picton," Mr. Darrow said, scratching at his head and looking very annoyed, "have you taken complete leave of your senses, or does all this babbling actually mean something?"

But Mr. Maxon's face revealed a very different kind of reaction; he may not've understood exactly what his opponent was talking about, but he obviously knew that the assistant district attorney didn't spend a lot of time ranting pointlessly about nothing at all.

"Picton," Mr. Maxon said quietly, "*do* you have new information you plan to introduce?"

Mr. Picton didn't answer either of the questions, just continued to stare at Libby, his grey eyes turning that strange silvery color they did when he was excited. After a few seconds, he started to nod. "Yes, Mrs. Hunter. We've found them—your mother, and your brother Elijah. And, more importantly, we've found *it,* and heard the whole story." This last statement contained a bit of a bluff, I knew—but all good lawyers know the value of a calculated bluff.

Libby continued to say nothing, causing both of her counsels to turn to her in some concern. "What's he talking about?" Mr. Darrow said, his deep voice sounding like he, too, was beginning to suspect that Mr. Picton might have hold of something real.

Libby just kept staring silently at Mr. Picton; but she seemed to sense that he wasn't the real cause of her predicament, and soon the golden eyes moved over to fix on the Doctor.

"Who—*what* in hell *are* you?" she near whispered, in a voice so icy-mean that it seemed to shock both Mr. Maxon and Mr. Darrow.

For his part, the Doctor just shrugged and stared back at the woman. "Only a man who knows what you are capable of, Mrs. Hunter. Nothing more."

Growing very uneasy, Mr. Darrow stood up and shoved his hands into his pockets. "All right, look—is somebody going to tell us what's going on here, or not?"

"It's fairly simple, Darrow," Mr. Picton answered, finally looking away from Libby. "Though horrifying, in its simplicity. Ten years ago—I'm afraid I can't give you an exact date, though we suspect it was in the spring—your client bore a child. An illegitimate child. She murdered it, and buried the body behind her family's barn in a coffin that also contained the body of her dog. Which, I'm sure, she also killed, to provide a cover for the burial. We've seen the grave site, and have corroborating statements from members of her family. We're prepared to discuss a deal."

Mr. Darrow's eyes went wide. "Well, of all the desperate, eleventh-hour tricks—"

He stopped as Libby silently raised a hand to him. "And if we don't take your deal?" she asked.

"Then," Mr. Picton replied, smoking again, "we exhume the child's body, making your mother—who is still, by the way, ignorant of our discovery—fully aware of the crime, and arrest you as soon as the current trial is over. We may also arrest your brother as an accessory—he did, after all, build the coffin and dig the grave—"

"He knew nothing about it!" Libby said without thinking.

Moving automatically, Mr. Darrow put a firm hand to his client's shoulder. "Say absolutely *nothing*, Mrs. Hunter." Satisfied that she would obey him, Mr. Darrow turned to Mr. Picton again. "Are you finished?"

"Yes, just about," Mr. Picton answered.

Sitting back down and rubbing his furrowed brow, Mr. Darrow studied Libby's face carefully for what seemed like a long time. There was obviously something there what he didn't like, something what told him that maybe Mr. Picton wasn't talking through his hat. "Hypothetically speaking," Mr. Darrow said slowly, without turning away from Libby. "What kind of a 'deal' are you talking about?"

"We will reduce the charge in the current case to second-degree murder if she will change her plea to guilty."

"*And,*" the Doctor added carefully, "contact her associates in New York tomorrow morning, and instruct them to release the child Ana Linares into our custody, when we return."

Mr. Picton nodded. "In return, she receives a life sentence without the possibility of parole."

Libby seemed like she was about to respond; but Mr. Darrow moved one of his big hands back to her shoulder. "Don't say *anything,*" he told her again, even more firmly this time; then he glanced over at Mr. Picton. "Do you suppose Mr. Maxon and I could discuss this privately with our client—maybe have some time to think about it?"

"You can discuss it in this office for the next fifteen minutes," Mr. Picton answered. "That's how long the deal's good for. The Doctor and I will leave you."

Rising, Mr. Picton nodded to the Doctor, who slowly followed him toward the door. Not wanting to get caught spying, I quickly slipped off Cyrus's shoulders and jumped to the floor with a bump. When the door opened, I'd just managed to get myself upright again; and as the Doctor came out, he gave me a curious look what said he suspected I'd been up to something. When Mr. Picton closed the door, though, all attention turned to other subjects.

"Well?" Mr. Moore said; though I'd already told him and the others where things stood, I guess he figured he ought to observe the formalities.

"Well," Mr. Picton echoed quietly in response, "I think we've got a very decent chance. She seems to be taking us quite seriously. I don't think she wants to have her mother made aware of what her only daughter's done with her life, or dragged into court to testify about an infanticide that took place right under her nose. The possibility of her brother's being prosecuted seemed to strike a nerve, too."

"There's no reading the woman, though," the Doctor added, considering it. "Something in her tone was—*wrong*. She was shocked, certainly, but—she doesn't have the manner of someone who feels the trap closing. Not yet."

"Maybe what you said is true, then, Doctor," Lucius answered. "Maybe some part of her unconscious mind *is* drawn to the idea of prison."

The Doctor shook his head quickly, struggling with something. "No, there was a different quality. I can't quite define it. And I don't think I'll be able to. Not, at any rate"—he pulled out his watch—"for another fourteen minutes . . ."

Those fourteen minutes passed in almost complete silence. The three people in Mr. Picton's office kept their voices very low, making it impossible for us to tell what they were talking about; and as for our group, I think we were all too nervous to speculate any further about what might happen. Both the Doctor and Mr. Picton checked their watches every minute or so, always breathing heavily when they found how little time had passed. Finally, though, the moment did come for them to head back into the office. Mr. Picton gave the Doctor a little nod of his head, and then he rapped on the door gently. Not waiting for a reply, he headed in, holding the door open for the Doctor and then closing it on the rest of us.

"Stevie!" Mr. Moore whispered; but I'd already gotten halfway up Cyrus's back, and was looking through the transom by the time Mr. Picton said:

"Well, Darrow? Do you have a decision?"

Looking at the floor and going through his pockets in a busy but meaningless sort of way, Mr. Darrow said, "I'm afraid you'll have to direct your questions to Mr. Maxon from now on, Picton."

Mr. Picton looked surprised. "Oh?"

"Yes," Mr. Darrow answered, still not wanting to look either Mr. Picton or the Doctor in the face. "Mrs. Hunter has seen fit to dispense with my advice. Such being the case, I intend to return to Chicago by the next available train."

Trading what you might call astonished looks, Mr. Picton and the Doctor both did their best not to show any obvious signs of relief or gloating. "Oh, surely not!" Mr. Picton said.

"You can spare me the professional courtesy, Picton," Mr. Darrow said. "But if you want to crow, feel free—you've managed to pull off one hell of a stunt."

Through all this, Libby Hatch just sat staring straight ahead, with a look on her face what said she'd pretty well had done with Mr. Darrow. As for Mr. Maxon, his usually nervous face showed, for the first time, a certain sort of relief.

"I've got to catch the trolley and get my things," Mr. Darrow went on as he headed for the door. His big shoulders looked more stooped to me than usual, though I could've been imagining it. "There's a midnight train, I think, to Buffalo—I can catch a connection there."

"Well!" Mr. Picton said, relighting his pipe. "I *am* sorry you won't be here—"

"Oh, I'm sure you are, Picton," Mr. Darrow said, smiling a bit; then, before I had a chance to do anything but rap on Cyrus's head, the lawyer grabbed hold of the knob on the door and pulled. Cyrus jumped to the left, so that at least the rest of the people in the office wouldn't be able to see us; but when Mr. Darrow came out and closed the door behind him, he looked up to see me still perched on Cyrus's shoulders. I half expected him to give out with some kind of outraged lecture concerning the ethics of our behavior; so I was very surprised when he just shook his head, causing one of those locks of hair of his to fall forward, and then chuckled in a very friendly fashion.

"I have *never* seen anything to beat *this*," he said, saluting our group with two fingers and then exiting through the outer office door.

As soon as he was gone, Cyrus stepped back over to his right, positioning me by the transom again. I carefully peered into the office once more, to find that the Doctor, Mr. Picton, and Mr. Maxon were all staring at the still-silent Libby Hatch.

"Mrs. Hunter has decided that she will accept your terms," Mr. Maxon said, looking calmer by the second. "Mr. Darrow advised against it, but I—"

"You don't need to explain, Maxon," Mr. Picton said good-naturedly. "Darrow's a big-city lawyer who wants to make a national name for himself. Not much publicity in accepting a plea bargain, is there? Not when you had every reason to expect a dramatic victory. But I'm sure Mrs. Hunter knows that you have her best interests, rather than your own reputation, at heart."

"Thank you, Picton," Mr. Maxon said with a nod. "That's very decent of you. Yes, all things considered, I do think acceptance of your terms is the wisest choice. Do you need anything else from us right now, or shall we leave the rest for court tomorrow?"

Shaking his head, Mr. Picton said, "No, I have nothing more—unless Mrs. Hunter wants to make some kind of a statement?"

Still sitting very still, Libby slowly began to shake her head; then, thinking of something, she held up a finger. "There's just one point," she said quietly. "My brother Eli. I don't want you going after him. He didn't know anything about it."

"Surely he suspected something?" Mr. Picton asked.

"Do you prosecute people for being suspicious these days?" Libby countered. "No—I want your guarantee, on that."

Mr. Picton nodded. "Don't worry, Mrs. Hunter. By accepting this deal, you abort any investigation into the business at your family's house. If that isn't too unfortunate a choice of words . . ." Looking to the door, Mr. Picton then called, "Stevie!"

"Lemme down!" I whispered to Cyrus, who grabbed my arms and lowered me to the floor, more gracefully this time. I opened the office door and stuck my head in to see Mr. Maxon helping Libby to her feet.

"Stevie, would you ask Henry to come back up and escort Mrs. Hunter back to her cell?" Mr. Picton asked.

I just nodded and bolted off again—though this time, I got only as far as the second-floor hallway:

There, pacing nervously, was Henry, smoking on a cigarette what he held in one hand and biting the fingernails of his other paw between drags.

"Say!" I called to him. "Mr. Picton says Mrs. Hunter's supposed to go back to her cell."

Throwing his cigarette onto the floor and stamping it out with one of his heavy boots, Henry rushed past me into the office. I didn't even have time to get back in myself before he'd reappeared with his charge, who looked for all the world as though the roof of her world had just caved in. I had no reason to think that she didn't really feel that way; and as I watched her wander toward the stairs, my own spirits began to pick up considerably, though in a quiet sort of way. The speedy departure of Mr. Maxon only increased this mood; and when I finally got back into Mr. Picton's office, I found that everybody else was feeling about the same: happy, yes, but sort of stunned at how quickly the whole thing had turned around.

Mr. Moore was the first one to actually say anything: "Well, what's the procedure, here, Rupert? Is it time to celebrate, or . . ." His words trailed off as he looked to his friend.

Mr. Picton just smiled, shrugged, and tried not to look too excited. "Guardedly, John—guardedly. Judge Brown still has to approve the deal, and he's not very fond of surprises."

"Still," Miss Howard said, also not sure just how happy she ought to let herself get, "he can't quash it, can he? Not when the defendant herself has agreed."

"I, Sara," Mr. Picton answered, starting to organize some papers on his desk, "am a particularly superstitious person. Which I'm sure hasn't escaped you. I would not care to make any predictions about what will happen tomorrow morning."

"What about you, Doctor?" Lucius asked.

The Doctor had wandered over to Mr. Picton's window, and was looking down at the Presbyterian church. "Hmm?" he noised.

"Any prediction to make?" Lucius said. "Or is there still something that doesn't feel right about it to you?"

"Not about *it*, Lucius," the Doctor answered. "About *her*. The deal itself is quite sound, and I'm convinced that Judge Brown, though possessed of a singularly rigid mind, will approve it."

Mr. Picton made a little hissing noise; and though he was smiling, he seemed more than a bit uneasy. "I do wish you wouldn't say things like that, Doctor . . ."

"Oh, come on, Rupert!" Mr. Moore said, allowing his spirits to rise a bit. "Leave all that mumbo jumbo to the darker regions of the world! You're the master of your own fate in this case, I don't know how you could have demonstrated that any more clearly. You and Kreizler—yes, and you, too, Sara. You've pulled off a coup, and I say we ought to get back to your house and crack open some of that very excellent champagne I saw hidden away in one corner of your cellar."

"Hear, hear," Marcus agreed. "Come on, all of you. We've been on the ropes for so long that we've forgotten what it feels like to land a solid blow. Solid blow, hell—we've knocked the stuffing out of them!"

Watching the Doctor carefully, Cyrus said, "It *does* seem like the tide's turned."

I was starting to get swept up in the growing mood of victory, myself; but then a practical thought struck me. "What about Kat?" I said. "Shouldn't we try to get word to her?"

"Not yet, Stevie," the Doctor answered quickly. "Not until Judge Brown has made the arrangement official. Miss Devlin will only put herself in danger, if she makes any unusual moves before we have returned to New York to assist her."

I nodded to that; and as I proceeded to think the rest of the matter over, I really couldn't see any reason why we shouldn't go home and celebrate. "So why are we standing around here?" I asked. "And how come it doesn't feel like we can just cut loose?"

Miss Howard turned to me. "Remember those men in Stillwater, Stevie?" she said. "You wouldn't have thought they'd have had anything to fear, either—it's been *years* since the Muhlenbergs' house burned down. But the feeling never went away . . ."

"Oh, fiddle-faddle, as my grandmother used to say," was Mr. Moore's answer to that. "We've got the woman caged, and her fate is sealed. Come on, all of you, let's get back home and start patting ourselves on the back!"

"Yes," Mr. Picton finally agreed with a nod. "I do think we owe ourselves at least one evening free of anxiety. Why don't you all go along and get started? I just want to review a few things and get my proposal to

Judge Brown ready—and I'll thank you not to dispose of all the champagne before I join you, John."

So the rest of us departed, passing out into the warm night and starting the walk home at a good clip. Our spirits continued to pick up as we moved down High Street, and though I can't say that we were exactly ecstatic when we reached Mr. Picton's house, we were feeling sound enough to break into general cheers when we discovered that our host had called ahead and had Mrs. Hastings bring a few bottles of the champagne up from the cellar and put them on ice. Dinner was laid out and waiting, and the amiable old housekeeper's handiwork had never looked so inviting: there was roast capon, cold curried lamb with raisins, a variety of delicious potatoes (included salty fried ones for me), and a positive bounty of young vegetables what had come in just that day from local farms. Add to that fresh strawberry shortcake and homemade ices, and you had a feast what we simply couldn't wait for our host before diving into. Laughter and high spirits filled the dining room in ever-greater amounts as we ate and drank; and though I was only downing root beer, my behavior, before long, was just as loose as that of the wine-swilling adults. Caught up in this mood, I don't think any of us were really conscious of how much time was slipping by: we might've stayed at that table all night, so powerful was the general feeling of relief at knowing that we were finally on the verge of what looked to be a happy conclusion to the case of Libby Hatch.

Then, just before midnight, we began to hear a bell tolling in the distance.

Marcus was the first to take note of it: in the middle of laughing at a story what Mr. Moore was relating about being chased around Abingdon Square by a bunch of Hudson Dusters during his recent trip to New York, the detective sergeant suddenly cocked his head and looked toward the front of the house. He didn't stop smiling, but his laughter died down pretty quickly.

"What the hell," he mumbled. "Do you hear that?"

"Hear what?" Mr. Moore answered, going for more champagne. "You're delusional, Marcus—"

"No, listen," the detective sergeant replied, taking his napkin from his lap and standing up. "It's a bell . . ."

Out of the corner of my eye I saw the Doctor's head jerk up: in an instant he, too, had registered the noise, and the rest of us soon did likewise.

"What in the world?" Lucius said.

El Niño moved quickly to the screen door out front. "It comes from one of the churches!" he called back to us.

"*Services?*" Cyrus said. "A midnight mass in *August?*"

Feeling suddenly uneasy, I looked to the Doctor, who was holding out a hand in an effort to get the rest of us to be quiet. As we followed his instruction, another sound began to rise over the pulsing chirp of the crickets and grasshoppers outside:

It was a man's voice, calling desperately for help.

"Picton," the Doctor whispered.

"That's not Rupert's voice," Mr. Moore answered quickly.

"I know," the Doctor said. "And that is precisely what frightens me." With that he raced for the front door, while the rest of us followed close behind.

CHAPTER 51

Moving with a sense of purpose what wiped out all the growing joy we'd felt during dinner (and also seemed to sober the adults up at a quick pace), we ran back up High Street toward the court house. About halfway there it became pretty clear that the bell we were hearing was the one in the steeple of the Presbyterian church: not a good sign. As we ran along the sidewalk, lights came on and lamps were lit in various houses along the way, though only a few daring souls came outside in their nightclothes to try to find out what was going on. The whole thing remained very mysterious until we'd almost gotten to the court house, when I suddenly realized that I recognized the voice what was screaming for help.

"It's the other guard!" I called to the Doctor. "The one what was on the front door when we left!"

"Are you certain?" the Doctor called back to me.

"I talked to him before they brought Libby up from her cell!" I answered, listening to the voice again. "Yeah, that's him, all right!"

Peering into the near darkness ahead of us—there were only two or three streetlamps between Mr. Picton's place and the court house—I tried to make out any signs of activity; then I noted that the bell had stopped ringing. When we got near the court house lawn, I caught sight of a figure on the front steps of the building, one whose arms were frantically waving to us.

"There he is!" I called out, when I could see for sure that it was in fact the guard what I'd had words with earlier.

The Doctor's face opened wide with horror when he saw that I was right, but he never let up his pace; and soon we were face to face with the panic-stricken man.

"For God's sake!" the guard said, pointing. "Get downstairs! Try to help them, Doctor! I've got to go for Sheriff Dunning!"

"But what's—" the Doctor started to ask; the guard, though, was already shooting away.

"Help them, Doctor, *please!*" he cried as he left.

Marcus watched him go, wondering, "Why the hell didn't he use the telephone?"

"He's terrified past reason," the Doctor answered quickly, catching his breath. "And I can only think of one reason why—come!"

Leading the way again, the Doctor entered the courthouse, shooting over to the doorway behind the guard station. It opened onto a set of stone stairs what the Doctor had no trouble negotiating, given the many times he'd been down them during his interviews with Libby Hatch. As his feet danced quickly along, leading us into the bowels of the building, he kept muttering to himself, over and over again, "Stupidity—stupidity!"

Bursting into a central room in the basement what was the receiving area for the various jail cells beyond, the Doctor suddenly stopped—as did the rest of us, when we followed him to take in the scene in that dimly lit stone chamber:

Propped up against one wall was the guard Henry. His eyes were open wide, and his jaw was hanging away from his head at an awkward sort of angle. His throat had been cut from ear to ear, and there were a few other stab wounds in his chest. He wasn't bleeding, though—at least, not anymore. Every drop of blood in his body, it seemed, had oozed out to drench his clothes and create a huge, dark pool on the floor under and around his body.

Across from him, also propped up against a wall, was Mr. Picton. He, too, had a few ugly wounds in his chest, and a nasty cut on one side of his neck; but unlike Henry's, his open eyes held a faint glimmer of life, while his mouth seemed to be taking air in, even if it was only in fitful little gasps.

The pool of blood what surrounded him, though, was near as big as the one what the dead guard lay in.

While the rest of us were studying this scene in shock, the Doctor got straight over to Mr. Picton and made a quick examination of his wounds. "Cyrus!" he called. "I'll need my medical bag from the house!" Without a word, Cyrus vanished back into and up the staircase. "Detective Sergeant!" the doctor went on, looking to Lucius. "You, too, Sara—help me! John, Marcus, we'll need bandages—shred your shirts, both of you!"

As everybody else moved to do what they were told, El Niño and I wandered slowly over to stand behind them. It was an awful sight, so awful as to be past immediate comprehending, at least for me. El Niño, on the other hand—who'd seen a lot of brutal bloodshed in his life—seemed to grasp it all right away: he fell helplessly to his knees, hung his head for a moment, then raised it to stare at the ceiling with wide, despairing eyes. All of a sudden he let out a long, terrible wail, one what cut through the night like a wolf's howl and made me realize, for the first time, the true meaning of what I was looking at.

"*Jefe!*" the aborigine wailed, beginning to weep. "Señor Picton, no! *No!*"

The sound of El Niño's grief caused Mr. Picton to turn his head ever so slightly, a movement what appeared to cause him great pain. As he glanced up to see the Doctor, Lucius, and Miss Howard working on his wounds, he tried to get enough spit into his mouth to speak.

"My God . . ." he gasped, "that's a hell of a noise, for such a little man to make . . ."

"You've got to keep quiet, Rupert," Mr. Moore said, as he and Marcus frantically tore their shirts into bandage strips. The sight of his old friend lying there so badly wounded seemed to move our journalist friend to the point of tears; but he ground the reaction away with his teeth and just kept ripping. "You're going to be all right, but for once in your life, *please* keep quiet!"

Mr. Picton choked out a small chuckle, at that, then winced once hard. "I'm sorry, John," he breathed. "I'm sorry I always talked too much. . . . I know it embarrassed you sometimes . . ."

"Don't be an idiot," Mr. Moore said, having a harder time, now, keeping the tears back.

"And the Doctor . . ." Mr. Picton went on, glancing at the man who was feverishly trying to bind his wounds and stop his bleeding. "You always wanted to . . . to know, Doctor . . . why I was that way . . . my *context* . . ." A sudden cough brought a splatter of blood up and onto the Doctor's chest, but he kept working on his patient. "I was going to tell you . . ." Mr. Picton went on. "I meant to tell you . . ."

"Mr. Picton, you must listen to John," the Doctor answered. "It's imperative that you remain quiet."

"Heard *that* before . . ." Mr. Picton breathed. Then he took in one or two desperate gulps of air, his chest going into some kind of a spasm; it seemed to subside, though, and as it did, he let his eyes drift over to the guard Henry's body. "I've . . . been lying here . . . watching him . . ." Another small laugh got out. "The idiot . . . how many stories . . . true *and* fictitious, Doctor . . . would you imagine involve jailers being . . . seduced by their captives . . . ?"

"Please, Rupert," Miss Howard said, herself seeming close to tears. She reached up to put two bloody fingers to his lips, then smiled weakly. "Do try to lie still. I know it's difficult for you—"

Mr. Picton pulled his head away from her fingers, then smiled back at her. "Sara . . . I would prefer . . . as little interference . . . with my death scene . . . as possible . . ." Looking at Henry again and taking another difficult, wheezing breath, Mr. Picton went on, "I . . . would calculate that there are hundreds . . . of such stories. . . . It's a measure . . . of the man's illiteracy, you see. . . . That's what's so interesting . . ." He began to cough up blood again, and this time the action caused him much more agony: he grabbed at the lapel of the Doctor's jacket, eyes bulging wide, and pulled hard. "It wasn't . . . her . . ." he gasped, blood now pouring from his mouth and drenching his ginger beard. "She told *him* . . . to kill me. . . . But the pinheaded fool . . . couldn't even manage *that* properly . . ." Sitting back as his face went terribly pale, Mr. Picton added, "Then *she* killed *him* . . . over an hour ago. . . . She's got the jump on you, Doctor. . . . You've got to go . . . *go* . . ."

"Rupert, in the name of heaven, *shut up!*" Mr. Moore said, the tears now out of his eyes and streaming down his cheeks.

Mr. Picton smiled over at him once more, then tried to look around to the rest of us. "You've all . . . I want to thank you . . ." Taking hold of the Doctor's lapel again, he whispered, "When they bury me, Doctor . . . look at the graves . . . my family . . . a clue . . ."

Then his head fell to one side, and all the silvery spark of recognition slipped out of his eyes.

The Doctor put his fingers to Mr. Picton's throat, then pulled out his watch and, opening it, held the shiny cover under the man's bloody nostrils. "He's still breathing," the Doctor announced, going back to work. "But just."

The sound of footsteps came echoing down the stone stairs, and then Cyrus reappeared, carrying the Doctor's black medical bag. Mrs. Hastings followed along behind him in a few seconds, and when she saw the bloody scene on the floor her hands flew up to cover her mouth.

"Oh, Your Honor!" she cried quietly, rushing over to stand by the Doctor. "Oh, Your Honor, no!"

"Mrs. Hastings," the Doctor said, trying hard to keep everybody on track. "Mrs. Hastings!" he repeated, grabbing the woman's arm and getting her attention. "Do you know if Dr. Lawrence has any sort of surgical equipment in his office? Mr. Picton cannot be moved as far as Saratoga, but we can't give him the help he needs here."

Trying to stifle her own weeping, Mrs. Hastings nodded. "Yes—I think so—that is, we took my husband there when he—oh, Your Honor, I can't bear it!"

"Listen to me!" the Doctor said. "Take the detective sergeant with you." With a nod of his head he indicated Marcus, who had put his jacket back on over his undershirt. "Telephone Dr. Lawrence, and tell him to prepare. Then get over to Mr. Wooley, at the stables. Have him ready his gentlest wagon, and fit it out with whatever padding he can. Mrs. Hastings!" The Doctor grasped the grief-stricken woman's arm harder. "Can you do this?"

"I—" She began to nod, and tried to pull herself together. "Yes, Doctor. If the detective sergeant will help me."

"Come on, Mrs. Hastings," Marcus said, guiding her to the door. "If we move quickly enough, everything will be fine."

As the pair left the room, the Doctor went back to work bandaging Mr. Picton's wounds. "Yes—*if* they move quickly enough . . ." he said quietly, in a voice what didn't contain much hope.

Hearing those words, I considered for the first time the possibility that Mr. Picton might die; and along with the terrible sadness of that thought came the full realization of who had attacked him, and what that attack meant: Libby Hatch was loose, and on her way, almost certainly, back to New York.

"What about the woman, Doctor?" Lucius asked, as he continued to help with the bandaging. "Mr. Picton's right—she's got a good jump on us."

"That can't be helped," the Doctor answered quickly. "We owe this man too much—whatever can be done must be done. We need to talk to Sheriff Dunning, as well. I want it to be absolutely clear what happened here, so that when we go after her this time we can do it openly."

Hearing all this talk, and struck cold by the sight of all the blood in the room, I could think of only one thing: What would happen to Kat when Libby got back to New York? It was past midnight—a tough, maybe impossible, hour to get a message through to Betty in time for her to get over to the Dusters' and warn Kat who was coming. What would happen?

I wondered with mounting fear, my hands going cold and my feet shifting nervously. If the woman could do this to poor Mr. Picton, not to mention the big, dead man lying against the wall across the room, what would happen when she—

I felt a tug at the back of my shirt. Turning, I saw El Niño, who seemed to have put his bout of grief aside, at least as much as he could: instead of tears, there was now a glaring fire in his dark eyes, and his face, for the first time since I'd known him, seemed to show what kind of violence he was capable of once his blood was up. At that moment I wasn't looking at an amiable little aborigine; I was looking at a man who'd been violently torn away from his people at an early age, sold into bondage, and then escaped to become a wandering mercenary.

"Señorito Stevie," he whispered, urging me into the stairway while the others continued to fix their attention on Mr. Picton. I followed him in, keeping my own eyes on the Doctor's fast-moving hands.

"Señorito Stevie," El Niño repeated, once we were out of earshot of the others. "I must go."

"Go?" I said, glancing at him quickly to see his face setting even harder. "Go where?"

"The *jefe* will die," El Niño said, in a matter-of-fact way what still betrayed much of his grief. "I have seen such wounds before. And I have read it in the Señor Doctor's eyes. He will try to save Señor Picton—but he will fail. And his failure will take hours. My future here will die with the *jefe*. I must go." Suddenly his gleaming *kris* appeared from under the dinner jacket. "Before the trail of the woman becomes lost. I owe this to Señor Picton. He was to give me a life—I shall avenge his."

"Why are you telling me this?" I asked, turning fully to him.

"They will not let me go," he said, nodding at the others. "They will try to stop me—and they will try to stop you, too."

"*Me?*" I said.

"You cannot wait for the *jefe* to die," the aborigine said. "Not if you are to save your friend, and baby Ana. It is for *us* to do this thing, Señorito Stevie, and we must do it *now*. You know the places we must go. And I have the skills"—he glanced down at the knife in his hand—"to do what must be done. But they will not permit it, if they know."

I turned again to look at the Doctor, knowing just what El Niño meant. If I'd even suggested that I be allowed to go ahead on my own and see to Kat's safety, the doctor would never have agreed. He'd let me stay involved in the case from the beginning because I'd promised not to put myself in danger unnecessarily—and there was every chance that he'd view me bolting off to New York on my own to try to protect Kat as too high of a risk. He'd probably be right, too.

"But," I whispered, "how would we—where—"

"It is no great difficulty," El Niño said. "You and I, we are people who know the ways of such things."

I gave the matter a few seconds' consideration. "They'd be expecting us to try to get on a train," I thought out loud. "So they'd try to stop us at the station. We could steal a horse from the stables, ride to Troy, and catch an express from there—"

The aborigine put a firm hand to my shoulder. "Yes. You see, Señorito Stevie, it is for you and I to do this thing. It is we who know the way of it."

Taking two or three heavy breaths to try to calm the pounding in my chest brought on by the possible death of Mr. Picton and the definite danger that Kat had suddenly been placed in, I nodded. "Okay," I said. "There's just one thing . . ."

Going to the staircase doorway, I made a little hissing sound in Mr. Moore's direction. I had to do it two or three times before I got his attention, and then finally he turned.

"Mr. Moore!" I whispered; then I urged him over with a wave of my hands.

Moving slowly and keeping his eyes locked on Mr. Picton, he joined us in the staircase. "What is it, Stevie?"

"Mr. Moore," I said, shuffling in my anxiousness, "I've—we've—we're going. *Now.*"

That got his attention, and he turned his tear-stained face to me fully. "What do you mean?"

"She's got a long lead," I answered. "The rest of you have to take care of Mr. Picton and clear things with the sheriff. By the time all that happens . . ."

Mr. Moore pondered that for a second, then grabbed another quick look at Mr. Picton. "But what can you—" Turning back to us and looking down, he suddenly caught sight of El Nino's *kris.* When he did, his face filled with darkness—but not disapproval. "How will you go?"

"We'll manage," I answered. "But we'll need a little bit of a start."

Looking to his blood-soaked friend again, Mr. Moore reached into his pocket and pulled out his billfold. "You'll need money, too," he said, matter-of-factly.

"You'll *help* us?" I said, a slight tremble of relief coursing through me.

Mr. Moore nodded once. "Kreizler'll have my guts for garters," he whispered. "But it's the only way." He forked over a wad of bills, everything he had, then put one hand on my shoulder and the other on El Niño's. "Don't tell me how you'll get there—I can't reveal what I don't know. And watch yourselves. We'll follow as soon as we can. As soon as—"

"I know," I said. "And tell the Doctor—" I glanced into the room once more to look at the man who'd done so much for me in my life, and who I was now defying. "Tell the Doctor I'm sorry . . ."

"I know," Mr. Moore answered. "Don't worry—and don't waste any more time. Just go, and do what you have to." He gave me a hard, meaningful stare. "*Go*, Stevepipe . . ."

Then he turned and went back to the others, while El Niño and I quietly but quickly took to the stone steps, moving with the practiced skill of two people who'd spent many years mastering the art of stealth.

CHAPTER 52

W hen El Niño and I reached Mr. Wooley's stables, we found the liveryman up and sending Mrs. Hastings and Marcus off in the specially padded rig (he'd put a feather mattress in the bed) what the
Doctor'd ordered. We waited for the man to go back into his house, figuring he would never have agreed to hire one of his animals out to a pair
like us; then we shot over to the barn, where I made short work of a big
but simple padlock with the set of picks in my pocket. Once inside, I
looked around for the little Morgan what I knew to be such a strong, reliable animal; finding him, I told El Niño to get a bridle and saddle ready,
while I scrounged around in an old desk by the door for a pencil and a
scrap of paper. I wrote out a note explaining where Mr. Wooley could locate his animal—at the Troy train station—and then folded the note up
with more than enough cash to cover the "loan."

By the time I was finished, El Niño had the horse ready to ride; and as
it turned out that he'd done some time with a band of horse-riding raiders
in French Indochina, I helped him shorten the stirrups and then let him
take the front of the saddle and the reins, while I got behind and grabbed
onto his shoulders. Moving at a quiet walk out past Mr. Wooley's house,
we picked up a little speed as we trotted toward the southeast edge of
town; and once on the Malta road, the aborigine turned the Morgan
loose, so that we began to fly along at a pace what was both jarring and
reassuring.

It was better than twenty miles to Troy, but that little Morgan—
though loaded down with two riders—made short work of it, as I'd ex-

pected and hoped he would. Less encouraging was the news we received
at the station: we'd missed the last passenger train to New York for the
night, and we wouldn't be able to secure seats on another until six A.M.
But there was a West Shore Railroad freight train due through in another
twenty minutes; and so, leaving our trusted mount behind, the aborigine
and I made our way to the edge of the station yard, where we waited to
hop aboard one of the boxcars of the train as it slowed to pass through
the city. This arrangement, though less comfortable and picturesque than
a ride in a passenger car (the West Shore traveled on inland tracks as far
south as Poughkeepsie), turned out to be far better suited to our purposes, being as the freighter only made a few stops on its journey south;
and though its final destination was Weehawken, New Jersey, across the
Hudson from Manhattan, there was a ferry line based in that town, one
whose boats ran all night across the water to Franklin Street, which was
only some twenty-five blocks south of the Dusters' headquarters on
Hudson Street.

None of which made the trip any easier on our spirits. For the first part
of the train journey El Niño just sat in the open doorway of our box car,
staring at the black countryside what was passing around us. Sometimes
he looked like the hate he now felt for Libby Hatch had turned him to
stone; other times his face softened and he wept quietly into his hands or
knocked his head against the wooden doorway. Nothing I found to say
consoled him, though I'll admit my efforts weren't the most determined;
besides still being nearly heartbroken myself over what'd happened to Mr.
Picton, I was far too worried about Kat to make any claim that things
would all turn out all right in the end. And so when the west bank of the
Hudson came back into view below Poughkeepsie, I just sat beside the
aborigine and took to staring out at the river, trying but failing not to calculate how much blood Mr. Picton must've lost in the long minutes he'd
lay there alone on the basement floor of the courthouse or how fast Libby
Hatch might've gotten out of Ballston Spa.

That Libby'd arrive in New York considerably ahead of us was a given;
the only question was what she would do when she got there. Was her
main concern now getting rid of all traces of Ana Linares, securing what
money she could from Goo Goo Knox, and then heading out of the state,
probably to the West, where wanted criminals could and often did disappear into new lives under assumed names? Such would've been the most
logical set of moves, but nobody'd ever accused Libby Hatch of being logical. Clever and devious, yes, to a point what sometimes made her look
brilliant; but at bottom her actions—her whole life—were deathly non-

sensical, and I knew that if I was going to predict her next steps I'd have to think like the Doctor, instead of drawing on my lifelong experience with criminals whose goals were more practical.

As we crossed into New Jersey and dawn started to turn the sky a strange, glowing blue I put my mind to this task and came up with only one consideration what I figured was cause for hope: with all that she'd been through upstate, with all that'd been discovered and revealed about her life of murder and destruction, Libby's desire and even need to keep Ana alive—to nurture her as a way of proving that she could, finally, care properly for a child—would be increased. She'd try to escape the city, there was no question about that; but I figured she'd make the attempt *with* the baby, and so long as she didn't try to do Ana any harm, there wouldn't be any cause for Kat to try to step in and maybe get herself killed. This reasoning was, I told myself, sound; and I clung to it as tightly as our train hugged the inner side of the Palisades on its way into Wee-hawken.

El Niño and I jumped off the train as soon as it came within sight of the Weehawken yard, then ran full out for the ferry station, still not exchanging a word. More and more the aborigine was becoming all business: having rested his hopes for a new life on Mr. Picton, he was determined to have his revenge, an act what, it seemed, was very important in the part of the world where he came from. All the way across the Hudson on the ferry he took to sharpening his arrows and knife and readying his short bow, along with mixing ingredients from a few small pouches into a small wooden vial what held a sticky, gluelike substance. This, I figured, was the poison what he used to coat the tips of his missiles, and I could only guess that he was tampering with the mixture to make it more deadly than it'd been on any of the occasions when I'd seen him use it. So dark and determined did his face become as he went about this process that I began to feel that I needed to get a few things straight with him.

"El Niño," I said, "nobody knows better than me how you feel. But our first worry is making sure that we get Ana and Kat out alive, right?" The aborigine just nodded slowly as he dipped the points of his arrows into the wooden vial. "And you know what the rest of them—the Doctor and Miss Howard and the others—would say about what comes after, don't you? They'd say that if we get the chance, we should take Libby Hatch alive and hold her for trial."

"She has *had* her trial," El Niño mumbled back. "Because of the trial she almost went free. I know that the others believe this, Señorito Stevie . . ." Tucking his last arrow carefully inside his jacket, he looked me dead in the eye. "But do you?"

I just shook my head. "I'm telling you what *they'd* say. Once we're sure Kat and the baby are okay, what you do is your business, so far as I'm concerned."

He nodded, looking toward the Franklin Street ferry station as it began to loom up large before us. "Yes. You and I understand these things . . ."

There wasn't any other way to handle it. If I'd tried to stop El Niño from doing what he believed he had to, I'd've only ended up at odds with him; besides, I wasn't at all sure that his way wasn't best. Libby Hatch was like a snake, one what seemed able to squirm or kill her way out of any predicament she found herself in; and I couldn't imagine anybody better suited to deal with such a strange, deadly serpent than the little man from across the seas what was sitting next to me.

New York City is never uglier than at daybreak, and it never smells worse than during the month of August: both of these facts were more than demonstrated that morning as we sloshed and bumped our way into the Franklin Street ferry terminal. Sure, in the distance we could see all the sights what gave suckers from out of town such a jolt—the Western Union Building, the towers of Printing House Square, the steeple of Trinity Church—but none of it made up for the stench of rotting garbage and filthy water what infested the waterfront, or for the sight of those miserable, dirty blocks what lay beyond the ferry station. Of course, the mood what my companion and I were in when we arrived didn't help our impression of the city any; after a night as horrifying—and sleepless—as ours'd been, there wasn't much of a way *any* town could've looked good. The only thing I could be grateful for was that the mission we were on left little or no time for letting the miserable feeling of being back among the dirt and dangers of the metropolis get to us: as soon as we were ashore, we began to run the mile or so to our destination, never once thinking about taking a hansom.

The first order of business, pretty obviously, was to try to get some kind of an idea of what was going on inside the Dusters' place. At that early hour of the morning the joint would likely be pretty dead (though you never could be sure, given that the Dusters were all burny fiends, and such people, when they *do* sleep, tend to do so at odd hours), so I thought our smartest move was to get ourselves hidden someplace where we could keep an eye on the comings and goings around the building. This would be easiest to do from a rooftop across Hudson

Street: there wouldn't be many street corners or such where we could lurk in broad daylight without getting spotted by some member of the gang. Working our way up through the warehouses, trade stores, and boardinghouses of Hudson Street, then past little St. Luke's Chapel (the same route, I noted, what Cyrus, the detective sergeants and I'd driven the first night of the case) we eventually reached the heart of Duster country, making sure to cut over west of Hudson Street itself as we approached the gang's headquarters. Coming back around on Horatio Street, El Niño and I picked a likely building on the west side of Hudson that would give us a good view of what was happening in and around the gang's filthy but fashionable dive; then we got into the building's backyard by way of an old loading alley. I picked the lock of the back door, and in a few minutes we'd made it up onto the rooftop, where we quickly moved over to crouch down behind the little wall what rose up at the front of the thing.

It wasn't yet eight o'clock, and the only signs of life at the Dusters' were a few slummers leaving the place. These well-dressed types were obviously wound up on burny and hadn't yet gotten their fill of rolling around in the muck of the gang's violent, earthy life: but the big Duster who was pushing them out made it pretty clear that the "hosts" themselves'd had enough of entertaining such people and wanted some rest. This was good news for us, as it provided some time to figure how we were going to get a message inside to Kat and find out if Libby Hatch was in fact in the place. Obviously, *I* couldn't go in and start asking questions; and if El Niño tried there was always the chance that Libby would catch sight of him provided she was there. The quickest way to attend to the problem seemed to be for me to head down to Frankie's joint and find Kat's pal Betty: she could enter the Dusters' without much trouble and get the lay of things. El Niño, in the meantime, would stay on the rooftop, and if Libby Hatch appeared and tried to make good her escape, he'd set himself to following, making a move against her only if he could be sure of getting Ana Linares away safely.

So it was back down onto the street for me, where I hailed the first hansom what came into sight. The driver of the rig was just starting his day after retrieving his horse from a stable a couple of blocks away, and I knew that I wouldn't be able to get him to drive to Frankie's place on Worth Street for any amount of money. It wasn't a neighborhood what cabbies operated in, unless they were looking to get robbed and probably killed; so I directed the mug to the nearest destination I could think of what I figured he'd be willing to take on: old Boss Tweed's court house just north of City Hall. The court house wasn't but a few blocks from Frankie's (though those few might as well have been fifty, considering the change in scenery what took over as you traveled them), but I'd managed to time my trip just so's it collided with the morning rush: I gave the cabbie every tip I knew about taking side streets and staying off the main routes, but it still took a frustrating amount of time to get downtown.

Morning was never a happy time to find yourself entering a joint like Frankie's, and that day was no exception. It being summer, there were kids lying "asleep"—or, to put it plain, hammered unconscious by the foul brew what Frankie served up at his bar—all over the street outside; and them what were awake were busy throwing up into the gutter and moaning like they were ready to die. Stepping over bodies and every kind of human waste as I made my way down into the dive, I was at least relieved to hear that all was quiet in the dog-and-rat pit; in fact, there wasn't a soul awake inside the joint except the bartender, a tough-looking Italian kid of about fifteen with a very nasty scar along the side of his face, one what seemed to glow angrily even in the darkness of that black, dirty hole.

I asked him if Frankie was around, only to be told that "the boss" was asleep in one of the back rooms—with, as my luck would have it, Betty. I told the barkeep I needed to have a few words with Betty, to which the kid just shook his head, saying that Frankie'd left word he didn't want anybody disturbing either of them. Knowing I couldn't let this stand in my way, I started to carefully let my eyes drift around the room, studying the kids and trying to figure out if one of them was carrying a sap of some kind. There was one boy toward the back of the room—he couldn't've been more than ten—who had a telltale leather handle hanging out of his pants pocket; and being as he was lying with his head on a table in a pool of his own vomit, I didn't figure as he'd give me much of a hard time about borrowing his weapon. So I just made straight for the little doorway what led to the "bedrooms" in the back, with the bartender moving fast behind me and starting to curse. But I got to the sleeping kid's sap before the bartender got to me, and in about three seconds my pursuer had a nice lump on his head to go with the scar on his face, and was lying on the floor.

A quick check of the back rooms revealed that Frankie and Betty were out cold in one of the last little pens, and I got the girl up and dragged her out to the bar, where I managed to find some water to splash on her face. She produced a three-inch knife pretty quick, at that, having no idea what in the hell was going on; and it was only quick wits and quicker reflexes what prevented me from getting the blade in my gut. Once she saw it was me she put the knife away, though her mood didn't improve much; but when I told her what the situation was regarding Kat she tried hard to get herself pulled together, and then agreed to come with me and be part of our plan—after, of course, I offered her a few bucks. Friendship was friendship, for a girl like that, but money was also money, and if there was a chance to combine the two, well, there wasn't anybody what would've criticized her for it.

Walking as quick as Betty could manage, we got back over to the Tweed court house, hailed another hansom, and headed back up to Hudson Street: "Hudson Street Hospital," was what I told the driver, again to make him feel more secure about the ride. The hospital was close to the Dusters' joint, and by the time we reached the little medical facility Betty had managed to get herself more alert by blowing some burny what she had in her ratty little bag. I didn't even try to lecture her or stop her—my lookout was Kat, just then—but it wasn't ever what you'd call a heartening thing to see a girl so young beating her body up with that vicious white powder, especially in the morning. Still, it helped her face the idea of going into the Dusters' with a little more courage, so that by the time I left her and raced back up onto the rooftop where El Niño was still positioned, I had good reason to think that the plan would be successful.

This outlook was reinforced when the aborigine reported that he had, in fact, laid eyes on Libby Hatch: she'd appeared very briefly just after I left, to flag down a passing milk wagon. She hadn't looked any too pleased about being up and attending to what were pretty obviously baby Ana's needs at that early hour, but the fact that she'd headed back inside seemed to indicate that, at least for the moment, she wasn't contemplating any drastic move. Not that there was any real reason for her to yet: she knew that it would take time for the Doctor and the others to catch up with her, and that even when they did they'd have to relate what'd happened to the cops and then convince somebody at headquarters on Mulberry Street to raid the Dusters' headquarters: not the kind of thing any cop or squad of cops in their right minds were likely to undertake without one hell of a lot of persuading. But just knowing where the woman and the baby were was cause for some satisfaction.

Less encouraging was the fact that Betty came back out of the Dusters' in just fifteen minutes, looking confused, disappointed—and not a little concerned. I whistled to her from our high perch, then directed her to meet me around the corner, at the mouth of the trucking alley. There she told me a story what was peculiar, to say the least: Libby Hatch had arrived at the Dusters' at just past three that morning, and had immediately locked herself away in Goo Goo Knox's chamber with Ana Linares. Kat, true to her word to Mr. Moore, had right away gone upstairs, and talked her way into Knox's room by asking Goo Goo if she could be any help with the baby. But Libby'd remembered only too well that Kat was a friend of mine, and she'd flown into a rage, saying that Kat was a spy whose real purpose was to steal Ana away and bring the law after her. Now, Goo Goo would ordinarily have solved this problem by having Kat taken over to the river, killed, and thrown in; but at that point Ding Dong—as much, I figured, out of a desire to save face in the gang as out of any true concern for Kat—had stepped in, saying that nobody was going to do away with one of his girls without his say-so. Knox and Ding Dong had then gotten into a hell of a scrape, one what'd apparently been very entertaining to all those slummers we'd seen. At first Kat'd joined in the fight, trying to defend Ding Dong; but after about half an hour Libby herself, with that unpredictability what we'd all come to know so well (and what usually didn't indicate anything good), had put a stop to the battle by saying that she'd be satisfied if Kat would just get out of the joint. This Kat'd done, removing herself exactly as far as the nearest corner. I figured this meant that Kat'd intended to keep right on watching things from outside the place, so's she'd be able to tell whichever of our party came back to the city first (she'd have been able to figure out that we wouldn't be far behind Libby) where our adversary'd got to, if she'd left the building, and whether or not she still had the baby with her.

But then, for some reason what nobody inside the dive could figure, Kat'd suddenly disappeared, not long before El Niño and I'd arrived on the scene. Betty'd tried to find out if anybody had any idea where she might've gone; she even went so far as to have a conversation with Ding Dong, who, while nursing his bruises and cuts, said he didn't much know nor care where "the little hellcat" was. Kat's sudden disappearance was the most disturbing part of the story, being as, though she was at least safely out of Libby Hatch's direct reach, there was every chance Knox'd found out that she was lurking around and had dispatched somebody to take care of her. On top of that, if Kat'd been safe, there were only a few joints where she probably would've gone, and Frankie's was at the top of that very short list. Obviously, she hadn't turned up there. On the other hand, it *was* August, and though the hot, heavy sky had been threatening a thunderstorm all morning, it hadn't broken yet—Kat could've been hiding out in any of the city's parks or the dozens of other outdoor havens what were available to kids on the run during the warm months. So, since things were quiet inside the Dusters' for the time being, I decided to assume that Kat was okay and lying low somewhere: I'd make a quick round of some of the more obvious hiding spots downtown, and then check with those acquaintances of mine—including Hickie the Hun—who might've already seen her, or could reasonably be expected to catch sight of her during the day.

I gave Betty the telephone number of the Doctor's house before letting her go back to Frankie's, and made her promise to call and keep calling if Kat should turn up. Then I went back up onto the rooftop to tell El Niño what my plan was. I knew he'd want to stay right where he was and keep watching the Dusters', just in case Libby did make a move, so I also gave him the Doctor's telephone number, though I warned him that I wasn't likely to show up at the house for at least another hour or two. But in the event that Libby did get out and get moving, I told him to stay close to her and to keep trying to report. Then, figuring that the aborigine was broke, I handed over half of the cash what Mr. Moore'd given me, and finally started out on my search.

The first and most nerve-racking part of this job was a quick trip over to the Hudson waterfront to see if anybody'd noticed a struggle going on that morning or if any bodies'd been spotted in the water. I talked to a few gangs of longshoremen as I worked my way down as far as the Cunard pier, but none of them'd heard of any trouble. I even ran into my old pal Nosy, who was, as usual, poking around in the midst of all the early morning debarking and unloading what was going on, and he likewise said he hadn't seen Kat nor heard about any violence on the waterfront. This news, like the information I'd gotten from Betty, had the effect of both reassuring me and making me even more nervous about where Kat could've gone or what she might be doing. More than anything else, one question stuck in my head: Why had Libby Hatch been willing to let Kat walk away, instead of insisting that she share the fate what'd befallen the poor, dumb guard Henry, and maybe Mr. Picton, too? Of all Libby's many complicated characteristics, mercy didn't seem one what made an appearance all that often, especially not where her own safety and schemes were concerned. Why had she let Kat go?

Working my way downtown and through my old neighborhood, stopping in at half a dozen other kid dives what weren't much different from Frankie's, I continued to find no trace of Kat. Hickie was over at the Fulton Fish Market, cramming a morning swim in before the coming storm unloaded on the city, and he told me that he'd been working a string of houses on the West Side with a collection of our old pals the night before. They hadn't made their way home 'til early in the morning, and they'd stopped off for a few pails of beer at a dive on Bleecker Street on their way. But he, too, hadn't seen or heard anything of Kat, a fact what seemed to be cause for hope: if something *had* happened to her, word would've gotten around our circuit pretty fast. But where in the hell *was* the girl?

Another swing past Frankie's (where the Italian kid I'd laid out was, thankfully, nowhere to be seen) finally gave me the beginnings of an answer: when Betty'd gotten back from giving me a hand at the Dusters, she'd found Kat waiting for her. Kat had, it seemed, been feeling very poorly, which was why she'd left off watching the Dusters' place: a severe pain in her stomach and gut had struck her, a mysterious ailment what neither she nor Betty could identify or ease. On hearing that I was back in town, Kat'd decided to head on up to the Doctor's house and wait for me, since, as she'd told Betty, I could lay hands on some medicine what was especially useful for the kind of trouble she was in (meaning the Doctor's supply of paregoric). Betty'd wanted to go with Kat, who was starting to vomit pretty violently by the time she left; but Frankie was still angry at her for leaving that morning, and so Kat'd had to set out on her own, and was probably at Seventeenth Street now.

I ran back over toward City Hall Park to hire a cab, picturing in my mind Kat all huddled up where she'd hidden once before, in among the hedges what ran along the border of the Doctor's front yard. She'd looked pretty awful then, and what with Betty's strange report I didn't expect her to appear much better when I found her this time: her sudden exit from the Dusters' probably indicated another lack of burny, from which she was now feeling the effects. We'd have to repeat the treatment what'd helped her the last time around, though it would cost me another lecture from the Doctor; but at least I'd be able to help her once I got her into the house.

I found her just where I'd figured to, balled up like a newborn kitten in among the greenery to the side of the front yard, wearing the dress she always did in summer: an old, light job that showed off the curves what were still forming in her young body. She was asleep, clutching her bag tight to her stomach and breathing in quick little gasps. There were a couple of pools of vomit—really not much more than bile, given that she'd been retching for so long—lying on the ground behind her curled back, and her face was the color of old ashes. Big charcoal-colored circles had formed under her eyes, and as I took her hand I noted that her fingernails were starting to turn a strange and disturbing sort of color, like they'd been stepped on.

Even *I* could see that she was much sicker than she'd been last time.

As I wiped a few sweat-drenched strands of blond hair out of Kat's face, I noted that her skin was strangely cool to the touch; and when I tried to get her to wake up, it took a good minute of gently slapping her palms and calling her name to do the job. As soon as she started to come around she grabbed at her gut especially hard, then retched again, bringing up nothing at all this time. Her head swaying as I helped her to sit up, she seemed to have trouble focusing her blue eyes.

"Stevie . . ." she breathed, falling against my chest. "Oh, God, I've got a awful pain in my gut . . ."

"I know," I said, trying to pull her up so's I could get her inside. "Betty told me. How long you been without the burny, Kat?"

She shook her head as much as she could, which wasn't but a little. "It ain't that. I've got a whole tin of the stuff, and I been blowing it all morning. This is something else . . ." As she stood up, the pain in her midsection seemed to ease a little bit, and she looked up to really see my face for the first time. "Well," she whispered, with a small smile, "I ain't generally at my best when we see each other, am I?"

I smiled back at her as best I could, and brushed some more hair out of her face. "You'll be fine. Just got to get you inside and fixed up."

She tightened her grip on my shirt, looking very worried and maybe a little ashamed. "I tried, Stevie—I told your friend Mr. Moore I'd look out for the kid, and I really did try, but the pain got so bad—"

"It's okay, Kat," I said, holding on to her tighter. "You done good—we got somebody else watching the place now. Somebody Libby won't be able to get away from."

"Yeah, but will *he* be able to get away from *her*, Stevie?" Kat said hoarsely.

"Won't need to," I answered. "This mug's different, Kat—he can match her play for play."

Nodding and then stumbling a little as I pulled her toward the front door, Kat tried to swallow: an action what appeared to give her a lot of difficulty. "He *must* be good, then," she said, coughing some. "'Cause I'll tell you, Stevie—that woman is the end of the damned world . . ."

Taking out my key, I opened the front door and guided Kat into the warm, stale air of the house. Just as soon as we'd reached the bottom of the staircase, she doubled over again, vomiting up some yellow bile and then screaming once in agony. But the shrieking itself seemed to call for more strength than she had, and as she fell out of my arms to sit on one of the stairs she just began to weep quietly.

"Stevie," she managed to say, as I sat next to her and held her tight, "I know you ain't supposed to, and I don't want you to get in no trouble—"

I'd forgotten all about the paregoric. "Right," I said, leaning her against the stairway wall and then standing up to head for the Doctor's consulting room. "You wait here, I'll get the stuff."

As I tried to move down the hall, I felt her clinging to one of my hands, like if she let go I might never come back. Turning around, I saw tears still streaming down her terribly pale face. She was staring at me in a way what sort of seemed like she'd never really seen me before. "I ain't never deserved your being so good to me," she whispered; and something in the words made me rush back to her for a second and hold her as tight as I thought she could stand.

"You pipe down with that," I said, trying hard to keep my own eyes dry. Maybe it was the long night catching up with me; maybe it was the awful thing what had happened to Mr. Picton; and maybe it was fearful joy at hearing her actually admit to some kind of a deep and pure connection between us at a moment when she was in such desperate pain; whatever the explanation, the thought of losing her just then was the worst thing I could imagine. "You're gonna be fine," I went on, drying her face with my sleeve and looking deep into those blue eyes. "We got through this once, didn't we? And we will again. But this time," I added with a smile, "after we do, *I'm* putting you on the damned train *myself*—and you are getting *out* of this town."

She nodded once, then looked down. "Maybe—maybe you'll come with me, even, hunh?" she said.

Having no idea at all what I was saying, I just whispered, "Yeah. Maybe."

Looking a little ashamed, Kat mumbled, "I never meant to go back to him, Stevie. But I didn't hear nothing from my aunt, and I didn't know what to—"

"Forget that," I said. "All we gotta worry about right now's getting you better."

And then I bolted off into the Doctor's consulting room to fetch the big bottle of paregoric, what I proceeded to liberally dose Kat with. She didn't complain at all about the taste, knowing the good effect it'd had on her cramping the last time around; but her problem with swallowing only seemed to be getting worse, and it wasn't easy for her to get the stuff down. Once she had, though, it appeared to take hold of her pretty quick, easing her pain up enough so that she could stand back up, put one arm around my neck, and start moving up the stairs. But the effect turned out to be temporary: we'd only gotten to the third floor of the house before she doubled over and screamed again, this time in a way what made me afraid to move her much farther. We were just outside the door to the Doctor's bedroom, and I decided the best thing would be to take her in and get her laid down on his big four-poster bed.

"No!" Kat gasped, as I half carried her along. "No, Stevie, I can't! It's *his* bed, he'll skin you!"

"Kat," I answered, laying her out on top of the thin, deep blue spread what covered the bed, "how many times you gotta be wrong about the man before you get it? He *ain't* that way." As her head sank into the Doctor's big mountain of soft goose-down pillows, I glanced around the room for something to cover her with, eventually catching sight of a comforter covered in green-and-silver Chinese satin what was folded up on a divan by the window. "Here," I said, spreading the thing over her. "You got to keep warm and let the medicine go to work."

Even with all her pain, Kat managed to pull the comforter up so's she could rub the satin against her cheek. "He's got nice things," she mumbled. "Genuine satin—hot as the air gets, it still stays so cool. . . . How come that is, Stevie?"

I crouched down on my knees next to the bed and touched her forehead, smiling. "I don't know. Them Chinamen got tricks." She winced once more, and I held up the paregoric bottle. "You wanna see if you can get some more down?"

"Yeah," she said; but, try as she might, she just couldn't swallow more than a little of the stuff, and finally she gave up trying. Writhing around with her hands on her stomach, she cried out again, then started to gnash her teeth in a frightful way.

It was beginning to occur to me that this might not be something what was going to pass with a dose of paregoric; and so, telling Kat to try to hold on, I ran into the Doctor's study and opened his book of addresses and telephone numbers, eventually finding the listing for Dr. Osborne, a good-hearted colleague of the Doctor's what I knew lived nearby, and who'd often done us good turns when somebody in the house was hurt or sick. Racing down to the telephone outside the kitchen, I got hold of an operator and had her connect me; but the maid at Dr. Osborne's said that he'd gone off to do his rounds at St. Luke's Hospital and wasn't expected back for a couple of hours. I told the woman to have him telephone as soon as he returned, and then I went back up to the bedroom again. Breathing a big sigh of a relief when I saw that Kat's painful spasms seemed to have passed, at least for the moment, I went to kneel by the bed again, and took her cold left hand in both of mine.

She turned her head over and smiled at me. "I heard you down there. Trying to get me a doctor . . ."

"He'll come in a little bit," I answered with a nod. Then I joked quietly, "Figure you can make it that long?"

Kat nodded. "I'll make it a lot longer than that, Stevie Taggert," she whispered, still smiling. "You watch." Glancing around the room, Kat took in a deep, sudden breath. "I ain't never had a doctor tend to me. And I sure ain't never had no satin comforter. Feels nice . . ." Then she lost the smile, and for a minute I got scared that the pain was coming back; but it was only curiosity that filled her face. "Stevie—one thing I never asked you . . ."

"Yeah, Kat?"

"How come? I mean, you looking out for me all this time?"

I gripped her hand tighter. "That don't sound like the girl with the big plans what *I* know," I said. "How can I expect you to hire me as a servant if I ain't nice to you now?"

She picked up her right hand and weakly slapped at my arm. "I'm serious," she said. "Why, Stevie?"

"Ask Dr. Kreizler when he gets here. He's full of explanations."

"I'm askin' *you*. *Why?*"

I just shook my head and shrugged a little bit, then turned my face down to look at her hand. "'Cause. I care about you, that's why."

"Maybe," she breathed, "maybe you even love me some, hunh?"

I shrugged again. "Yeah. Maybe I even do."

I looked up when she put a finger gently to my face. "Well," she said, her mouth playing at a frown but then smiling gently, "it ain't gonna *kill* you to *say* it, you know . . ." Then she turned toward the window, her blue eyes catching the grey light of the cloud-filled sky. "So Stevie Taggert loves me, maybe," she whispered, in what you might call amazement. "What do you know about *that* . . . ?"

The windows shook a little as the storm's first clap of thunder finally boomed over the city. Kat didn't seem to hear it, though; with those last words she'd drifted off to sleep, a sign, I figured, that the paregoric had finally taken real hold. Keeping my two hands on her one, tight enough to feel the blood pulsing through her wrist, I lay my head down on the satin comforter and waited for Dr. Osborne to call . . .

But what woke me wasn't the telephone. It was the gentle but firm touch of Dr. Kreizler, prying my fingers off of Kat's dead hand.

CHAPTER 53

If my mind hadn't been clouded by all the things I felt for and about Kat, I might've been able to see what was really wrong in time to help her: that's the thought that's haunted me ever since, anyway. I'd been right in supposing that Libby's letting Kat go from the Dusters' had been just a little too easy, a little too merciful. When the Doctor and the others arrived at the house at about noon, Kat was already dead, and even before they woke me Lucius, tipped off by Kat's awful appearance, had taken a sample of the little pool of vomit what she'd spat up at the foot of the stairs on the first floor and performed one of his chemical tests. The result had been definite: the burny what Kat had been blowing ever since leaving the Dusters' early that morning had been laced with arsenic. There wasn't any question who'd done the lacing, of course, nor much mystery as to when or how: while Goo Goo Knox and Ding Dong'd been knocking the stuffing out of each other and Kat'd been trying to bust it up, Libby'd got hold of Kat's bag and slipped the poison into her burny tin, counting on Kat not being able to spot the very slight difference in color between the two powders.

Still dazed by a lack of sleep and the shocks of the last twenty-four hours, I just sat on the edge of the Doctor's bed as I listened to all this, staring at Kat's strangely peaceful face and waiting for a couple of men from the city morgue to come and take her body away. The others—excepting Marcus, who'd gone straight from Grand Central to Police Headquarters on Mulberry Street to explain to his bosses that a fugitive was loose in the city—quietly moved around the house, talking among themselves about what should be done next and knowing that it would be best not to say anything to me until I came out of the horrible fog I was in.

This didn't even start to happen until I heard the sound of the van from the morgue arriving outside. When the two attendants who were driving it entered the house, I began to realize for the first time that they were going to take Kat away, and that the face what, dead or no, still lay in front of me would soon be gone from my sight forever. There wasn't any way to stop it, I knew that; but in my continued state of confusion I found that what I needed most was some way to say the good-bye what Libby Hatch had robbed me of. Glancing feverishly around the room, my eyes settled on Kat's worn old bag. I snatched the thing up, praying that it contained the few items in the world what she actually cared about—her dead father's wallet, her dead mother's picture, and her train ticket to California—and thanking God when I found that it did. I told the Doctor that we couldn't let the city plant Kat in any potter's field without those things, but he told me not to worry, that he'd arrange for her to have a decent burial out in Calvary Cemetery in Queens.

The sound of the word "burial" cut through the last of the strange haze I'd been drifting through ever since waking up, and a pronounced lump began to grow in my throat. Running out to the morgue van in the rain what'd finally started to fall, I stopped the two attendants as they were loading Kat's body in, then pulled back the sheet what covered her. Touching her cold face one last time, I leaned down to whisper into her dead ear:

"Not *maybe,* Kat—I *did.* I *do* . . ."

Then I slowly pulled the sheet back up, and stepped back to let the two attendants go about their business. As I watched the van pull away from the house, cold, clear reality swept over me in a terrible wave, one so powerful that when I turned to see Miss Howard standing inside the front door, giving me a look what said she knew just how much Kat'd meant to me and how I was feeling, I couldn't help but run over, bury my face in her dress, and let myself have at least a couple of minutes of tears.

"She did try, Stevie," Miss Howard whispered, putting her arms around my shoulders. "In the end she tried very hard."

"Couldn't beat the odds, though," I managed to mumble through my grief.

"There were no odds to beat," Miss Howard answered. "The game was rigged against her. From the very start . . ."

I nodded, sniffling away as much sorrow as I could. "I know," I said.

The Doctor, having seen the van out of sight, walked through the front yard to join us. "Life did not offer her many chances," he said quietly, standing by us and looking out the open door. "But it was not life, finally, that took her last chance away. Left to her own devices, she might have escaped all that she'd known here, Stevie." He put a hand to my head. "That knowledge must be foremost in your thoughts, in the days to come."

Nodding again, I wiped at my face and tried to get myself pulled together; then a thought entered my head, one what'd been shoved aside by all the turmoil of Kat's death. "What about Mr. Picton?" I asked. "Is he—?"

"Dead," the Doctor answered, plainly but gently. "He died where we found him—the loss of blood was simply too great."

I suddenly felt like the ground underneath me was just melting away. "Oh, God . . ." I moaned; then I slid down the wall to the floor, grabbing at my forehead with one hand and quietly crying again. "*Why?* What the hell is all this *for* . . . ?"

The Doctor crouched down in front of me. "Stevie," he said, his own eyes red around their black cores, "you grew up in a world where people robbed for money, killed for advantage or out of rage, assaulted to satisfy lust—a world where crime seemed to make some terrible sort of sense. And this woman's actions seem very different to you. But they aren't. It is all a result of *perception*. A man rapes because he sees no other way to satisfy an urgent, terrible need. Libby kills because she sees no other way to reach goals that are as vital to her as the very air she breathes, and were planted in her mind when she was too young to know what was taking place. She, like the rapist, is wrong, horrifically wrong, and it is our job—yours, mine, Sara's, *all* of ours—to understand the perceptions that lead to such misbegotten actions, so that we may have some hope of keeping others from being enslaved by them." Reaching out to touch my knee, the Doctor looked into my eyes with an expression what showed all the pain he'd felt when his beloved Mary Palmer had died just steps from where I was sitting. "You have lost someone you cared for deeply to those wretched perceptions, and to that enslavement. Can you now go on? We haven't much time, and if you wish to stay out of what's left to be done—"

He was cut off by a pair of sounds: a clap of thunder from the sky above, then the ringing of the telephone beyond the kitchen. I couldn't and can't say exactly why, but for some reason the pairing of those noises reminded me that El Niño was still out and at work, and that I still hadn't heard anything from him. With that realization I stopped crying for the moment, and struggled to get to my feet.

"I'd better answer that," I said, starting back toward the kitchen. "It might be El Niño—I left him to watch over the Dusters' place."

"Stevie." I stopped and turned to see the Doctor still studying me, sympathetically, but with real purpose. "If you cannot go on, no one will blame you. But if you choose to go on, then remember what our work is."

I just nodded, then headed into and past the kitchen, picking up the receiver of the 'phone and pulling the mouthpiece down. "Yeah?" I said.

"Señorito Stevie." It was El Niño, all right, his voice still very businesslike and determined. "Do you have news of your friend?"

I sighed once, trying to hold back more tears. "The woman got to her," I said. "She's dead. Mr. Picton, too."

El Niño muttered something softly in a language what I couldn't place: neither English nor Spanish, I figured it for the native tongue of his people. "So," he went on, after a moment's pause. "The need for justice has grown. I am sorry for that, Señorito Stevie."

"Where are you?" I asked.

"In the stables across from the house of the woman. She has returned there with baby Ana. I paid the man here for to use his telephone."

"And the Dusters?"

"They are everywhere on the street."

"Don't make any play, then," I told him. "If you can see some of them, that means there's even more what you *can't* see. Stay out of sight."

"Yes. But if the chance comes—she dies, yes?"

Looking back into the kitchen, I saw that the Doctor and Miss Howard had come into it. They were watching me as I talked, probably knowing full well who was on the other end of the line.

"I don't know about that," I said, looking to the Doctor.

"But Señorito Stevie—your friend has *died*—"

"I know," I answered. "But it might be more complicated than we thought. We need to know—to know why she's doing this."

The aborigine gave that a moment's thought and a sigh before answering, "I tell you, Señorito Stevie—in jungles I have seen in my journies, there are villagers who live near the lairs and hunting grounds of tigers. Some of these tigers kill men—some do not. No one knows why. But all know that the tigers who *do* kill must die—for once they drink the blood of man, they never lose the taste for it." I couldn't figure how to answer him: half of me knew that what he was saying, terrible as it was, made very real sense. "Señorito Stevie? You are there?"

"I'm here."

"Will you hunt the tiger with me, or will you try to 'understand' it?"

I looked to the Doctor again, knowing, even in my sorrow, what I had to do. "I can't," I said, turning away so that the Doctor and Miss Howard wouldn't hear me. "I can't do it with you. But you go on. And don't call here again—they'll try to stop you."

There was another pause; then El Niño said, "Yes. It is best, this. It is not for us to decide what is the way—only the gods and fate can determine who will reach her first. I understand you, my friend."

"Yeah," I whispered. "I understand you, too."

"I hope I shall see you again. If I do not—remember that I still wear the clothes you gave me. And when I do, I see your face, and feel your friendship. I am proud of this."

The words put me near to tears again. "I've got to go," I said, replacing the receiver on its little hook before El Niño had a chance to say anything more.

"The aborigine?" the Doctor asked.

I nodded, moving into the kitchen. "He's down on Bethune Street. She's back there with Ana. But the neighborhood's crawling with Dusters."

"I see." The Doctor started pacing around the kitchen table. "Has she returned to the house simply to collect her things? Or to rid herself of the burden of Ana Linares in the safety of her secret hideaway?" After pondering this for a few seconds, the Doctor rapped a fist on the table. "In either case, we have run out of time—the crisis will play out *tonight*. If Marcus is successful, we can use the full power of the Police Department to enter the house. If not—"

"But even if he is," Miss Howard added, "can we be sure she won't harm the child before we get there? Or while we're trying to get in?"

"We can be sure of nothing," the Doctor answered. "But we must try to attend to what we can. With that in mind, Sara, I suggest that you call Señora Linares. Advise her that we must now take action, and that its results may not please her husband. She may wish to seek safety in some place other than her own home." Nodding in agreement, Miss Howard moved to the 'phone just as Cyrus entered the kitchen and put a strong, comforting hand to my shoulder. "Ah, Cyrus," the Doctor went on. "Some of your excellent coffee is called for, I think—we won't be catching up on our sleep anytime soon, and clear heads will be needed."

"Yes, sir," Cyrus answered. Then he looked down at me. "Might be enough time for *you* to get a little rest, Stevie. You could use it."

I just shook my head. "I don't want to sleep," I said, remembering what'd happened the last time I'd drifted off. "Make that coffee strong, though."

"Always do," Cyrus said. "Oh, and Doctor—the detective sergeant asked me to tell you that he's gone down to headquarters to give his brother a hand. Says he's worried about how long it's taking."

"As am I," the Doctor answered, checking his watch. "It would seem, on the surface, to be a fairly straightforward matter. Like so many things about this case . . ."

Not really feeling ready yet to talk about the particulars of what we were going to do next, I wandered on upstairs, where I found Mr. Moore in the parlor. He'd turned one of the Doctor's easy chairs around to face a window what he'd opened, so's he could get a good view of the storm what was continuing to batter the city. Collapsing onto the nearby settee, I joined him in quietly studying the wind-tossed trees in Stuyvesant Park.

"Hell of a storm," I mumbled, looking over to see that Mr. Moore's face was full of the same kind of sadness and confusion that was eating away at my own soul.

"Hell of a *summer*," he answered. "But the weather's always crazy in this goddamned town . . ." He managed to turn to me for just a few quick seconds. "I really am sorry, Stevie."

"Yeah," I answered. "Me, too. I mean, about Mr. Picton . . ."

Mr. Moore nodded and let out a big gush of air, shaking his head. "So now we're supposed to catch this woman," he mumbled. "Catch her and study her. It's not exactly what I'm in the mood for."

"No," I agreed.

He held a finger up like he was lecturing the angry heavens. "Rupert," he said, "never believed you could learn anything from killers after you'd caught them. He said it was like trying to study the hunting habits of wild animals by watching feeding time at a menagerie. He'd have been the first to say that we should kill this bitch if we get the chance."

"It might happen," I said with a shrug. "El Niño's still out there somewhere. And he won't stop to ask her why she does the things she does. All he'll want is a clear shot when she's not holding the baby."

"Well, I hope he gets one," Mr. Moore answered flatly. "Or, for that matter, that *I* do."

I looked at him again. "You really think you could kill her?"

"Could you?" he answered, going for a cigarette.

I shrugged. "I been thinking about that. Might as well be me as some electrician at Sing Sing, if she's gonna die. But . . . I don't know. Won't bring anybody back."

Mr. Moore hissed out smoke as he lit his stick. "You know," he said, his face still looking sad, but irritated, too, "I've always hated that expression."

For a few more minutes we sat quietly, starting every now and then when a big clap of thunder boomed or a bolt of lightning shot down into what seemed like the heart of the city. Then the other three joined us, Cyrus carrying a coffee service and setting it down on the rolling cocktail cart. The Doctor could read Mr. Moore's and my moods well enough not to start talking about any plans right away, so we all just drank the coffee and watched the storm for another half hour or so—until a hansom pulled up at the curb outside and produced the two detective sergeants. They'd pretty obviously been bickering inside the cab, and they kept right on going when they got into the house: things, it seemed, had not gone well downtown.

"It's cowardice," Marcus explained, after taking a careful moment to tell me how sorry he was about Kat. "Absolute cowardice! Oh, they'll get the warrant authorized, all right, but if apprehending the woman means going up against the Dusters, they're not interested."

"I've been trying to remind my brother," Lucius said, pouring himself a cup of coffee, "of what happened the last time the Police Department attempted a large-scale confrontation with the Hudson Dusters. An embarrassing number of officers ended up in the hospital. Kids on the West Side still taunt patrolmen by singing little ditties about it."

"And let's not forget who can generally be found hanging around the Dusters' place," Miss Howard added. "A lot of well-connected people in this town like to go down there to take cocaine and romanticize about the lives of gangsters. The fools."

"That doesn't excuse cowardice," Marcus insisted, himself going for some of Cyrus's brew. "Damn it, we're talking about *one woman* who is a *mass murderer,* for God's sake. And the department doesn't want to get involved because they're afraid they'll *lose face*?"

"The department doesn't want to get involved," the Doctor said, "because no one that they view as being of any importance has yet been killed. You know as well as I do that such has always been the rule in this city, Marcus—we had a brief respite under Roosevelt, but none of the reforms really took hold."

"Then what's our answer?" Lucius asked, looking around the room.

I knew what *I* was thinking, and I knew that Mr. Moore and Marcus probably felt the same way: if nobody else was going to take care of the job, it was up to us to go down there, bust into that hell house on Bethune

Street, and do what had to be done. But none of the three of us was going to give voice to this opinion while the Doctor was in the room, knowing, as we did, that he placed such a high value on our taking Libby Hatch alive.

Which was why his next line of thought came as kind of a surprise: "The navy," he said quietly, his black eyes lighting up.

"The *what*?" Mr. Moore responded, looking dumbfounded.

"The *navy*," the Doctor repeated, turning to Marcus. "Detective Sergeant—we know that the Hudson Dusters relish conflict with the New York City Police Department. How would they feel, do you suppose, about an encounter with the United States Navy?"

"Kreizler," Mr. Moore said, "you have obviously gone around some bend—"

Ignoring Mr. Moore, Marcus began to nod. "Offhand, I'd say they'd back off—navy men are, as you know, pretty renowned brawlers. And they carry the authority of the federal government, not just the city—political connections and local rivalries wouldn't get into the thing."

The Doctor began to bounce the knuckles of his right hand against his mouth. "Yes," he said quietly. Then another thought seemed to flash in his head. "The White Star Line's pier is, I believe, just a few blocks around the corner from Libby Hatch's house on Bethune Street, isn't that right?"

"Yes, it is," Miss Howard said, looking puzzled. "At Tenth Street. Why, Doctor?"

Seeing a copy of the morning edition of the *Times* tucked into Marcus's jacket pocket, the Doctor stood up and snatched it away. Quickly ruffling its pages, he searched for what seemed like some small but important piece of information. "No White Star ships currently in port," he eventually said with a nod. "Then he could have a vessel land there, and we could approach the house from the rear—taking the gang by relative surprise."

"*Who* could?" Mr. Moore near shouted. "Laszlo, what in hell—" All of a sudden, his jaw dropped as he got it. "Oh, no. Oh, no, Kreizler, that is insane, you can't—not *Roosevelt*!"

"Yes," the Doctor answered, looking up from the paper with a smile. "Roosevelt."

Mr. Moore scrambled to his feet. "Get *Theodore* involved in this case? Once he finds out what's going on, he'll start his damned war against Spain right here in this city!"

"Precisely why," the Doctor replied, "he must not be told all the details. Ana Linares's name and lineage need not concern him. The fact that we are attempting to solve a string of murders and a kidnapping and can get no satisfaction from the New York police will be more than enough to rouse Theodore's interest."

"But," said Miss Howard, who, like Mr. Moore and the Doctor, had known Mr. Roosevelt for most of her life, "what can even Theodore possibly do? He's assistant secretary of the navy, yes, but—"

"And just now he's treating the entire fleet as if it were his own," the Doctor replied, holding up an envelope. "A letter from him came during our absence. It seems that Secretary Long is on vacation for the month of August, and Theodore has been making bold moves. He's becoming known as 'the warm-weather secretary' around Washington, a fact of which he is inordinately—and typically—proud. I'm certain there are one or two serviceable vessels and crews out at the Brooklyn Navy Yard—perhaps even closer. More than enough men to meet our purposes. An order from Roosevelt is all the thing would require."

Mr. Moore was gently slapping his own face, trying to come to grips with the notion. "Let me get this straight: You're proposing that Roosevelt order the United States *Navy* to *invade* Greenwich Village and engage the Hudson Dusters?"

The Doctor's mouth curled up gently again. "Essentially, yes."

Marcus stepped in quickly. "It may sound outlandish, John," he said, looking encouraged by the idea. "But it won't play that way in reports. If any violence should occur, it'll just read like a typical brawl between sailors and gangsters. And while it goes on, we'll be able to do what we need to."

Tucking his letter from Mr. Roosevelt into his jacket, the Doctor dashed for the stairs. "I'm going to telephone him in Washington straightway," he said, heading down toward the kitchen. "There's no time to be lost—the woman must even now be planning her flight from the city!"

Suddenly there was a new feeling of life in the house, one brought on, I knew, by the bare possibility of even indirect involvement in the case on the part of Mr. Roosevelt. He had that effect on people, did the former police commissioner: of all the Doctor's close friends there wasn't one with a purer love of life, of action—and most especially of a good fight, whether boxing or politics or war. But he was a kind man, too, was Mr. Roosevelt, as kind as anyone what ever came to the Doctor's house in all the years I lived there; and I found that even I, in my saddened state, took a lot of heart from the thought that he might give us a hand in bringing Libby Hatch to justice. Oh, the idea was a crazy one, Mr. Moore was right about that much; but practically every undertaking Mr. Roosevelt got involved with seemed crazy, at the start—yet most of them ended up being not only important but happy achievements. So as we waited for the Doctor to return from the pantry, we began to talk over the details of the plan with an interest what bordered on enthusiasm—enthusiasm what was very surprising, considering all we'd been through.

When the Doctor came back upstairs, he was, if not out-and-out excited, at least very satisfied. "He'll do it. He wants us to wait here—he'll have someone from the navy yard inform us of what vessel will be available and when. But he promises action *tonight*."

Mr. Moore let out another moan of disbelief, but even he was smiling a bit by that point. "May God help us . . ."

So began more long hours of waiting. During the first couple of these our quiet anticipation grew, fed by more of Cyrus's coffee, into a strange sort of hopeful fidgeting; but as the afternoon wore on this feeling started to ebb, mostly because the telephone and the doorbell remained notably silent. Mr. Roosevelt was not a man to waste time; and the fact that we weren't getting word from any of his people, in Brooklyn or anywhere else, seemed what you might call mystifying. The rain didn't let up, and eventually its steady rhythm helped exhaustion take hold of each of us: eager we might've been, but that didn't change the fact that nobody'd really slept for more than an hour or so since Saturday night. One by one members of our group began to drift off to bedrooms for catnaps, and each, including me, woke from these fitful spells of slumber to the disappointing news that there'd still been no message from either Washington or Brooklyn.

Finally, as five o'clock drew near, the Doctor went back downstairs to call Mr. Roosevelt again; and when he returned this time his mood was very different from what it'd been earlier. He hadn't gotten through to his friend, but he *had* come away from a conversation with Mr. Roosevelt's secretary with the distinct impression that the man was in his office and avoiding the Doctor's call specifically. No one could make any sense out of this at all: Mr. Roosevelt was not a man to avoid a straight, nose-to-nose jawing with anybody, especially someone he cared about and respected. If he'd found he couldn't deliver on his earlier pledge to the Doctor, he would certainly have gotten on the telephone to say so. What, then, could be the explanation? Had he discovered the Spanish connection to the case of Libby Hatch somehow, and decided to pursue a separate course on his own?

Such questions were not exactly the kind what would've revived our weakened enthusiasm; and by seven o'clock the whole bunch of us were strewn around the Doctor's parlor, dozing. The rain had finally lightened up, and I was lying in front of one of the open French windows on the carpeted floor, letting the cool air that the storm had brought into the city play over my face and lull me into the first really decent rest I'd had all day. Still, it was a light sleep, one easily interrupted by noises from outside; and the noise what I heard coming from that direction at about seven-thirty was one what was at once so familiar yet so out of place that I honestly couldn't tell if I was asleep or awake:

It was the forceful, high-pitched sound of Mr. Roosevelt's voice.

"Wait here!" it was saying; then I heard the sound of a carriage door closing. "I shall want you to take us to the yard as soon as we've had a chance to speak with the others!"

"Yes, sir!" came a crisp, efficient answer, one what caused me to roll over and look outside.

And there he was, all right, the assistant secretary of the navy, done up in his best black linen and walking side by side with an older man who wore a navy officer's uniform.

"Holy Christ," I mumbled, rubbing my eyes to make sure I wasn't see-ing things. "Holy Christ!" I repeated, loud enough for the others to start coming out of their slumbers. Unable to stop myself from breaking into a smile, I scrambled to my feet and began shaking whatever shoulders I could grab fastest. "He's here! Doctor—Miss Howard—it's Mr. Roo-sevelt! He's *here*! Holy *Christ*!"

At this news the others got to their feet, looking just as confused and unsure of their senses as I'd felt—that is, until they heard the sound of the front door opening.

"Doctor?" came the bark from downstairs. "Moore! Where in thunder are you all?" Heavy footsteps pounded on the stairs as the shouting con-tinued. "And where is the brilliant Sara Howard, that former secretary of mine?"

A few more heavy steps, and then those unmistakable features began to appear in the shadows at the top of the stairs: in a sort of reversed version of Mr. Lewis Carroll's Cheshire Cat, Mr. Roosevelt generally became vis-ible grin first, his big teeth standing out in even the deepest blackness. Next to be seen were the small, squinting eyes behind the little steel-rimmed spectacles, and finally the square head, the broad mustache, and the huge barrel chest, the last of which had been built up, after enduring a childhood of terrible asthma, to become one of the most powerful in the world.

"Well!" he cried out, as he moved down the hall followed by the much calmer—and very wise-looking—navy officer. "I like *this*! Crime and out-rage running rampant, and you all lollygagging about as if there were no action to be gotten!" He put his hands to his hips as he came into the parlor, still grinning from ear to ear; then he shot his right paw out to the Doctor. "Kreizler! Delighted to see you, Doctor, *dee-lighted!*"

"Hello, Roosevelt," the Doctor answered with a smile. "I suppose I should've known you wouldn't miss this chance."

"Hell," Mr. Moore said, "we *all* should've known."

Making his way around the room, Mr. Roosevelt pressed the flesh hard with everybody, and accepted a warm hug from Miss Howard. He was especially glad, it seemed to me, to find that the Isaacson brothers were there, and still on the police force—for it was himself who'd brought them in, as part of his effort to loosen the grip what the Irish clan of Tammany hirelings had on Mulberry Street. When he finally got around to saying hello to me, I'd gotten so excited by his presence and the new hope it seemed to bring that I was shifting from foot to foot nervously. Still, there must have been much of the morning's sadness left in my face, for Mr. Roosevelt's smile shrank a little as he leaned down to shake my hand and look into my eyes.

"Well, young Stevie," he said, with real sympathy. "You've had a hard time of all this, I understand. But don't doubt this, my boy—" He put one of his tough hands on my shoulder. "We have come here to see that *justice* is done!"

CHAPTER 54

A s the Isaacsons began to sort through all their housebreaking equipment and weapons, figuring out what we'd need for our final assault
on Number 39 Bethune Street, the rest of us rushed to get into suitable
clothes for the mission: you didn't often stand still, and you never wasted
time, when Mr. Roosevelt was around. Once we were reassembled in the
parlor, the former police commissioner took a moment to introduce us to
his companion.

"Lieutenant William W. Kimball of the United States Navy," Mr. Roosevelt said proudly, almost as if the officer was one of his own kids, instead
of a man what obviously had a few years on him. Quite a few years, in
fact: when it came my turn to shake hands with the officer I wondered
why, at his age (almost fifty, it turned out), he was still stuck with such a
low rank. It wasn't until later that somebody explained to me that his situation wasn't unusual: being as the navy hadn't seen any real action since
the Civil War, advancement had gotten to be a very slow process. "Lieutenant Kimball lectures at the Naval War College," Mr. Roosevelt continued, "and has no equal when it comes to the business of war plans."

"Why, Roosevelt," Mr. Moore mocked, "are you planning a *war*?"

Mr. Roosevelt held up a finger. "Now, now, Moore, you won't snare me
with any of your reporter's questions. The navy is *always* developing con-
tingency plans, in the event of conflict with *any* power."

"I shouldn't have thought that we required any strategic planning for
what we are to undertake tonight," the Doctor said, studying Lieutenant
Kimball curiously. "Though you are of course welcome, Lieutenant."

"Thank you, Doctor," the lieutenant answered gamely; but even though he seemed to have some of the swagger (along with the usual large mustache) of a sailor, you could tell from his voice that he also had far more brains than your garden-variety naval man. "It's not my war planning, though, that prompted Mr. Roosevelt to ask me along. I have some other areas of expertise that he thought might be useful."

"Indeed!" Mr. Roosevelt agreed, pounding on the lieutenant's back. "Kimball, here, is a man ahead of his time. I hear nothing but battleships, battleships, battleships, from most of our officers, but Kimball has put his mind to developing the weapons that will determine the course of naval warfare in the *next* century, rather than the *last*. Torpedoes! Submarines! I tell you, that French novelist Verne has nothing on the lieutenant, here."

That comment snagged my interest, for the Doctor'd often given me books by Mr. Jules Verne to read, and the Frenchman's tales of life under the sea, trips to the moon, and powerful new weapons had kept me up late more than one night, wondering just what sort of a world we were actually heading for. "Is that true, Lieutenant?" I asked, as respectfully as I knew how. "Will we really fight underwater, like Captain Nemo?"

The lieutenant smiled and reached out to tousle my hair some. "Oh, yes, Master Taggert—but without Nemo's electrical guns, I'm afraid. At least for the moment. The *torpedo* will be the submarine's principal armament, and together with torpedo boats they will become the deadliest enemies of *all* ships."

"Torpedo boats?" I echoed. "What are those?"

"*Those*," Mr. Roosevelt answered, "are the reason that Lieutenant Kimball is here, Stevie. Small, lightly armored craft, capable of remarkable speeds. I cruised in one from Oyster Bay to Newport a few weeks ago, and I don't mind telling you all—it was bully! Like riding a high-mettled horse—agile, quick, capable of striking without warning and then disappearing." He turned to the Doctor. "Just the sort of thing, it seemed to me, that your business tonight requires, Kreizler."

The Doctor considered that idea. "Yes—yes, the ability to arrive suddenly and depart at high speed will be a great asset. And where are these craft at the moment?"

"We have several out at the navy yard," Lieutenant Kimball answered. "They require relatively small crews, but more men can be taken on, if we feel we need them."

"The more the better, if we're going up against the Dusters," Mr. Moore said. "I don't suppose there's any chance these 'torpedoes' can reach a few blocks inland, Lieutenant?"

"I'm afraid not, Mr. Moore," Lieutenant Kimball answered with a smile. "Once ashore, we'll have to rely on ourselves."

"Yes," Mr. Moore said, not very enthusiastically. "I was afraid of that."

"Take heart, John!" Mr. Roosevelt said, thumping his old friend on the back the way he had Lieutenant Kimball. Mr. Moore, though, didn't look too pleased by the action. "Why, we can put three score sailors against those—"

"Teddy," Mr. Moore interrupted, using the childhood name what Mr. Roosevelt was known to dislike. "It's going to be a hell of an evening, and if you start slapping me now I won't be able to stand up by the time it's all over."

"Ha! You don't fool me with that talk. I know the true measure of your abilities, Moore—I saw them amply displayed on our last adventure together!" Walking over to Miss Howard, Mr. Roosevelt took her hands in his warmly. "And you, Sara—that dress may be plain, but I'll wager it has room enough for a certain pearl-handled Colt of yours!"

"Along with a considerable supply of cartridges," Miss Howard replied with a nod. "So don't anyone think of jeopardizing themselves by keeping a special eye out for me."

"As if we don't know *that*," Lucius said, shaking his head.

"Ah, and my Maccabees!" Mr. Roosevelt said, moving over to the Isaacsons. "Kimball, you will never meet two men who combine bravery and brains more than the detective sergeants, here. I was called a lot of things for bringing Jews onto the police force, but I stand by the decision. Why, if we had six or seven men like these in Naval Intelligence, I daresay—ah." Realizing that he was about to say too much about his business in Washington, Mr. Roosevelt smiled and raised a hand. "But I'm straying from the affairs of the moment. Cyrus!" he went on, approaching my big friend. "What about you—will you rely on those fists alone, or will you take along something a little more substantial?"

"Fists'll suit me fine, sir," Cyrus answered with a smile. "I owe a couple of those Dusters a few good licks."

"And you'll get them in, I don't doubt it for an instant. You know, we must go a few rounds in the ring, someday, you and I!" Curling up his arms, Mr. Roosevelt took a few light jabs in Cyrus's direction. "It would be fine sport, don't you think?"

"I'm at your disposal, sir," Cyrus replied, bowing a little and still smiling.

"First rate," Mr. Roosevelt answered. "That's bully. Well, now, we're expected at the yard! The crews have been alerted and are standing by.

Everyone prepared? Good! I have a carriage waiting, Doctor, one that can accommodate most of us, and perhaps the rest can travel in one of yours."

"I fear cabs will be necessary," the Doctor answered, "as we've had no time to retrieve our horses from the boarding stables."

"Well, then, who's to ride with the lieutenant and myself?" Mr. Roosevelt asked. "What about you, Stevie? Like to hear more stories about the wondrous weapons Lieutenant Kimball dreams of loosing on the world?"

I looked quickly and eagerly to the Doctor, who nodded, knowing, I think, how much I did want to go with the navy man, and why. The discussion of weapons and destruction, far from thrilling me in any boyish way, was speaking to a dark, determined desire, one what'd been planted by Kat's death and had been growing all day: the hope that we might finally be able to strike at Libby Hatch in a way what even *she* wouldn't be prepared for.

"Yes, sir," I told Mr. Roosevelt. "I'd like that."

"Good! Kimball, I appoint young Taggert your aide for this operation. Don't underestimate him—several officers of this city's police force made that mistake, and some of them still can't walk correctly." As Mr. Roosevelt turned to the Doctor, his expression grew more serious. "I hope *you'll* ride with us, too, Doctor," he said; then he looked to Miss Howard. "And you, Sara, as well—for I confess I'd like to know more about this devilish woman we're chasing."

With the thick grey layers of storm clouds what'd hung over the city that day now breaking up into separate black clusters that stood out boldly against a moonlit sky, we all filed out of the house and moved to the corner of Second Avenue, followed by Mr. Roosevelt's big landau, what had its two canopies pulled up against the weather. Once we'd secured two hansoms for Mr. Moore, the detective sergeants, and Cyrus, the rest of us got into the landau behind Mr. Roosevelt and Lieutenant Kimball, and before long conversation was filling the roomy shell under the canopies. The Doctor, Miss Howard, and Mr. Roosevelt spoke about Libby Hatch and the case in quiet tones what showed consideration for my feelings, consideration I appreciated greatly. As for the amiable Lieutenant Kimball, he seemed so determined to keep me entertained that I wondered if maybe Mr. Roosevelt—who obviously knew at least the basic facts of what I'd been through that day—hadn't given him instructions to try to give my spirits a lift. If so, the lieutenant followed his orders admirably. From a description of all the wondrous things what he expected to take place on the seas in the next ten or twenty years, he moved on to tales of foreign lands he'd served in, and of the strange people he'd met there: stories that, while they couldn't and didn't really cheer me up as such, at least diverted my attention from the bleak thoughts what were still standing ready to flood back into my soul.

We took the Brooklyn Bridge across the lower portion of the East River, then made a hard left and traveled along the waterfront until we reached Wallabout Bay and the entrance to the great maze of dry docks, piers, cranes, railroad tracks, ordnance docks, foundries, and construction sheds what was the Brooklyn Navy Yard. The place was pretty much a New York institution, dating back to the beginning of the century and as familiar to natives of the city as any part of the harbor; but for some reason it looked very different to me that night. Maybe it was just my mood, I thought to myself, or maybe it was visiting the place in the company of the man who, for all practical purposes, was the most important naval official in the country at that moment. But very soon I realized that neither of these was the real explanation:

It was the lights—there were lights on everywhere and, underneath the lights, scores of men hard at work. All this at near ten o'clock on a Monday night. And as I noticed the men, I noticed what it was that they were working *on:* armored warships—some of them half built, some near ready to sail, all of them big and impressive—were crammed into every slip and corner of the joint.

"An awful lot of building going on out here, Mr. Roosevelt," I said, watching fire tenders and riveters holler to each other and toss red-hot plugs of steel through the black night.

"Yes," Mr. Roosevelt answered, looking around like a kid on Christmas morning. "We launched the *Maine* from here two years ago, and there have been several others since. Many more to come, as well!"

Out of the corner of my eye I caught the Doctor giving Miss Howard a look: a quiet reminder of how important it was that Mr. Roosevelt *not* find out just whose baby it was we were trying to rescue or why we'd been forced to go about it the way we had. The daughter of a high Spanish official, missing; that same official beating his wife and not seeming to care if he never saw his child again; the lies about the case what'd been issued by the Spanish consulate; suddenly all these things seemed very connectable to the humming activity in the navy yard, in a way what could have spelled bigger trouble than even *we'd* experienced lately.

The torpedo boats what Mr. Roosevelt and Lieutenant Kimball had spoken of were tucked away along one concrete wharf at the far end of the yard—and quite a collection they were, too. Not all that much bigger than the steam yachts and launches what generally shot around the harbor, the boats had much more powerful engines what required two and even three smokestacks; at the same time, they were much sleeker in design than the private and commercial vessels, having a graceful bullet shape what made it seem impossible that they were actually plated with steel. Not that there *was* much plating on them—as Mr. Roosevelt'd said, the boats sacrificed safety for speed, and they could go better than thirty miles an hour when required. Each boat appeared to be manned by just twenty-five or thirty men, and at various spots on their decks they carried the deadly weapons what gave them their names: torpedoes, fourteen-foot steel cylinders filled with compressed air and tipped with powerful explosive devices. The air, when it was released, shot the missiles on their way out of the boats' torpedo tubes and through the water for upwards of hundreds of yards: plenty of time for the fast little boats what delivered them to get clear of the resulting explosions. All in all, a very ingenious bit of inventing, one what stood in very great contrast to the enormous battleships with their huge artillery turrets what were being built in other parts of the yard. It would certainly be interesting to see, I thought to myself, if the battleships of other countries would one day be laid low by the same kind of fast, hard-hitting little craft as we were on our way to board that night.

Along with the crews of the torpedo boats, there were another twenty or so sailors lined up on the wharf, men who looked like they'd been specially selected for the job ahead of us. I'd seen a lot of brawling seamen in my day and in my neighborhood, and watched more than one dive and concert saloon get dismantled when a group of them were taken by some fast-talking "dancer" or quick-handed faro dealer; but no bunch I'd ever come across could've matched those boys what were waiting for us at the yard that night. Muscle-bound, scarred, and obviously itching for a genuine, top-drawer brawl, the men appeared to be having a tough time controlling their high spirits enough to stand to attention when Lieutenant Kimball and Mr. Roosevelt got out of the landau. Lieutenant Kimball had some words with the three torpedo boat commanders, who then mustered their crews on the wharf next to the bruisers what were already there. Stepping in front of this collected force—which, I had to admit, looked to be a fair match even for the Dusters—Lieutenant Kimball ordered them to stand at ease, then began to walk up and down the wharf as he explained the evening's business.

"Gentlemen!" he called out, his strong voice giving no hint of either his near fifty years or his usual assignment as a strategy planner. "Most of you, I'm sure, know that it is absolutely impossible to sail salt water in Uncle Sam's service for thirty, ten, or even five years without becoming imbued with the feeling that the United States of America is the finest and most glorious thing that has ever happened, and that it must lead—in *everything!*" Here the men broke into cheers, cheers what Mr. Roosevelt heartily joined. The rest of us held back, feeling that it wasn't really our place to take part—though I felt an urge to. "But," the lieutenant went on, "I suspect you also know that the United States cannot lead in everything so long as enemies stand in its way. Enemies *without*—who will, with any luck, soon feel the power of the great ships being built around us—and enemies *within,* who must feel our power on this very night!" That got the boys going again, and Lieutenant Kimball had to work hard to get them to quiet back down. "I ask you now to give your attention to the honorable assistant secretary of the navy, Mr. Theodore Roosevelt!"

Stepping to the fore, Mr. Roosevelt narrowed his eyes and took the measure of the company before him. "Men," he said, in that crisp, choppy way of his, "some of you may find the job ahead of us a strange one. Why, you might reasonably ask yourselves, should we be assigned the task of enforcing the laws of this great nation on our own soil?" Balling up one fist, Mr. Roosevelt began to smack it into his other palm as he continued to bellow over the sounds of the construction what was going on all around the yard: "The answer, men, is a simple one—because those persons to whom the safety of the public and the enforcement of justice in *this* part of our nation have been entrusted are failing to perform their duty! And who is it that the United States invariably calls on when its citizens are in danger—anywhere in the world—and no one else can or will assume the responsibility of protecting them?!"

With a unity of voice what was both very shocking (given the men) and very thrilling (given the situation), the sailors all roared out, "*The United States Navy, sir!*" The sound nearly knocked those of us behind Mr. Roosevelt over, but he only grinned and shook his fist in the air.

"Indeed!" he called out. "I expect you to fight fairly, men, but I expect you to fight *hard!* Thank you all!" Then Mr. Roosevelt stepped aside to let Lieutenant Kimball speak again.

"Officers will carry sidearms, petty officers and seamen will carry night-sticks! Force will be applied when force is encountered! This is a military police action, gentlemen—I know you will conduct yourselves accordingly. Now—fall out to board your boats!"

With another mighty roar, this one of pure excitement and lust for action, the men broke ranks and started for the torpedo boats, jumping into them as the engineers let off loud, hissing blasts of steam from the power plants of each vessel. Lieutenant Kimball directed our party to the lead boat, where we took up positions just behind the steering house. Orders to cast off were barked out over the rising grind of the steam pistons, and then—very suddenly, it seemed—the boat's propellers began to churn up the waters of the bay and we shot out toward the river, at a speed I'd certainly never experienced on the water and what made me stumble back a bit. As the air forced against our faces and bodies by the quickening pace of the boat became ever more powerful, Mr. Roosevelt put one of his strong arms around my shoulders and held me steady. Smiling up at him, I turned to watch the other two boats fall in behind us.

I don't know that I've ever truly been able to describe the feeling what came over me at that moment, though I've tried many times. I was heartened past words by the sight of the two boats behind us, and by the rumble of the powerful engines in our own vessel: all the emotions of the night and the day what'd just passed—not to mention those of the tough and often frightening weeks what'd come before—suddenly jumped out of my mouth in a loud holler, one what Mr. Roosevelt joined me in. Turning forward again, I caught sight of the same Brooklyn Bridge what we'd crossed just half an hour earlier, and which we were currently moving toward at a speed what was beginning to seem impossible. Viewing the bridge from below was so peculiar as to seem like a dream, especially given how fast we passed under it; yet we were about to go faster still. As we motored past Hickie the Hun's best-loved swimming spot, the Fulton Fish Market, and on toward the base of Manhattan and Battery Park, the commander of our boat gave the signal to turn the engine fully loose, so that by the time Lady Liberty came into view it seemed that we could've reached her island in just a matter of seconds.

Glancing over at the rest of our group, I could see that they, too, were impressed by the speed and maneuverability of the wondrous little craft we were riding in: the Doctor, Mr. Moore and the Isaacsons were all taking turns peppering Lieutenant Kimball with questions what were often hard to hear over the ever-greater din of the boat's powerful engines. As for me, I had no questions, only more emotions, ones as irresistible as the floating weapon we were traveling aboard. When we turned north to enter the waters of the Hudson and I saw all those spots on the waterfront where I'd so often come to brood about Kat, I turned those feelings loose, letting tears of sadness, rage, and determination mix with those what were being drawn out of my eyes by the powerful rush of air what was slamming ever harder against our faces.

"We've got you now, Libby Hatch," I began to whisper to myself through clenched teeth. "We've got you, we've *got* you!"

CHAPTER 55

Just as the Doctor'd figured, the gigantic, two-story housing of the White Star Line pier provided us with the kind of cover an ordinary, open wharf couldn't have. As the torpedo boats closed in on Tenth Street, the commander of our vessel ordered our little fleet to slow up some, and then we cruised quietly in toward the waterfront, slipping alongside the long, green shed of the pier and tying up on pilings near some ladders what led up from the water to a doorway into the structure. Leaving behind about half of the crews to watch over the boats—but taking all the additional sailors what'd been assigned to the job—we scrambled quickly up the rungs of those perilous approaches and then into the bottom floor of the pier: the baggage claim area, an enormous, open space what was usually a madhouse of crazed activity. Empty as it was that night, it had a very ghostly feel to it, and for the first time my feeling that we were on an unstoppable mission began to mix with a healthy dose of anxiousness. The few guards and White Star officials what were in the place had, it seemed, been alerted to our coming, as they cooperated with Mr. Roosevelt (whose face was all the identification he needed in New York City, just as it would soon be all over the United States and the world) by guiding us out to the front door without any questions at all.

As we walked, the Doctor pulled alongside me. "I have not," he said quietly, "brought up the subject of your sudden departure from Ballston Spa, Stevie, given the events of the day. Nor shall I do so now. I ask only this: please stay close to someone larger or better armed than yourself at all times. It's not that I doubt your ability to defend yourself, but this woman—"

"You don't have to tell *me*," I said, trying to reassure both him and myself as we moved out of the pier and into the darkness of the waterfront. "I got no ideas about going up against her alone. Though I might like to."

The Doctor reached around to give me a quick embrace. "I know. But she is a creature of infinite resource. In fact, even with *this* force, I hope that we are adequately prepared."

There were some gangs of longshoremen roaming the waterfront, but they knew better than to tangle with or mouth off to fifty or sixty armed sailors who looked as full of purpose as our men did. We decided to stick to West Street, what ran alongside the river, for the five blocks between the pier and Bethune Street, figuring that the Dusters wouldn't be expecting anybody to enter their territory from that direction and we'd be able to at least get close to Libby Hatch's place without being detected. We hadn't gone two blocks, though, before dark, mysterious shapes began to move around on the inland side of the wide street. They appeared in pairs at first, but those pairs quickly grew to become packs, the way mangy, tight-ribbed dogs'll do when they spot a possible source of food. It didn't seem like they had any idea of why we'd come, because before long the usual idiot taunts and challenges began to echo out across to us: it was just gang members pissing on their territory to let other animals know it was taken, I knew that—but I also knew that, given our mission, it could quickly turn into something much worse.

By the time we'd reached Eleventh Street, the shadows across from us had grown to about fifteen in number, and they were feeling bold enough to start throwing rocks and bottles over our way. Mr. Roosevelt and Lieutenant Kimball weren't standing for any such behavior, and they made as much clear pretty quick: as soon as the first missile landed, Mr. Roosevelt barked out, "Kimball!"

The lieutenant responded by turning to one of his officers. "Lieutenant Commander Simmons! Take ten men, sir, and deal with those persons!"

Now, I didn't want to pipe up and tell those navy boys their business; but it seemed to me that this might've been a wrong move, being as the Dusters were not likely to be expecting such a response, and the forcefulness of it could very well tip them off to the fact that they weren't just watching a party of sailors on shore leave making their way uptown for a night of gambling and whoring. Still, there was no small satisfaction in watching one of the torpedo boat commanders and his detachment move at double time across the cobblestones of West Street, sidearm and night-sticks at the ready, and plow into the burny-crazed, confused Dusters with such determination that what followed couldn't really have been classified as a fight. One or two of the gang members took nice shots across the head, and a couple more got good swift pokes in the gut; but the rest, alarmed by the sight of the lieutenant commander's pistol, just ran. Un-fortunately, I knew only too well that they were running back to Hudson Street, to fetch reinforcements and weapons and let Goo Goo Knox and Ding Dong know what was going on.

"Here we go," I whispered to myself nervously, as we crossed West Street at Bethune and the detachment what'd sent the first group of Dusters running rejoined us. All of a sudden the block and a half to Libby Hatch's house was looking very long to me, now that contact had been made, and when I saw Miss Howard and Lucius pull out their revolvers, I decided to move in behind them. Cyrus, meanwhile, slipped his right hand into his jacket pocket and got his brass knuckles on: something ugly, we both knew, was most definitely coming.

We saw a few more shadowy figures bolt out of doorways and alleys on the north side of Bethune Street, and also out of the construction site of the new Bell Telephone Laboratories on our side. The sailors with us seemed to take all this scurrying as a sign that the Dusters had already gotten the message and weren't going to be any trouble; unfortunately, we civilians knew better. Like most gangs, the Dusters didn't favor any fight where they didn't enjoy an advantage in both numbers and weapons, and it was pretty obvious that they were just regrouping, probably for some kind of a stand at Washington Street. This collecting of forces would, I was sure, only take place after a considerable amount of burny blowing, which meant that when we faced the gang they'd be wound up to the point where they figured they'd be a match for the en-tire U.S. Navy, let alone the few men what were now entering their ter-ritory.

For several long minutes, though, Bethune Street in front of us re-mained quiet and empty, a fact what struck me as odd; and my nervous-ness began to let up a bit, as I allowed myself the thought that maybe I was just being what you might call an alarmist.

But, of course, I wasn't.

Just before we reached the intersection of Washington Street, they began to fan out in a thick line in front of us: more Dusters—maybe sixty or seventy in all—than I'd ever seen gathered in any one spot in my life. Ding Dong'd brought out most of the kid auxiliaries, and these young hell-raisers were all making the same kinds of moves what we'd seen them get up to when we'd first come to Libby Hatch's place: slapping big slabs of wood into their palms, polishing up brass knuckles, and looking like it was all they could do to keep from rushing straight at us. To top it all off, every member of the gang's eyes were lit up like the windows at Mc-Creery's department store on a Thursday night, showing that I hadn't been wrong in supposing they'd gotten themselves good and wound up before they moved out to meet us.

Leading this very dangerous-looking mob were Goo Goo Knox and Ding Dong, who had, it seemed, patched up their squabble of earlier in the day—or, more likely, they'd just put off one good scrape in favor of a better one. As usual, Ding Dong was grinning like an idiot, in that way what, to my everlasting confusion, Kat'd found so charming. Knox, on the other hand, though the look on his face and the axe handle in his hand said that he was ready to go at it, was wearing an expression what also made it clear that he had a much better idea of who he was up against. This was understandable: for, as leader of the Hudson Dusters, he'd crossed paths with Mr. Roosevelt during our friend's term as police commissioner many times, and he knew that if the burly swell with the spectacles showed up looking like he was ready for trouble, you could count on the fact that such wasn't a bluff.

Knox was a scary-looking little package, wild-eyed and strong-armed, to be sure, but with skin so pale as to make him seem like a ghost. This was due partly to his heritage, but mostly to the fact that he almost never saw daylight: before becoming one of the founders of the Dusters, he'd been a member of the Gophers, another frightening, unpredictable group of violent Irishmen who ruled in Hell's Kitchen and got their name from the fact that they spent their days in the cellars of that neighborhood, drinking, carousing, and doing whatever else passed for "living" in their book. Only at night did they come outside, to raid the train yards on the West Side, lock horns with other gangs, or engage in their other favorite outdoor sport: beating cops unconscious and stealing their uniforms to give to their girlfriends as trophies. It was partly because so many Dusters were former Gophers that the newer gang was feared by the Police Department: along with the practice of raiding the train yards on the West Side, the Dusters'd maintained the Gophers' taste for going after men in uniform. I didn't know whether that taste included the uniform of the

U.S. Navy; but from the look on Knox's face that night, I figured we could be pretty sure that it did.

"Mr. Roosy-velt," Goo Goo called, as our party drew up close to the gang. "I heard you was in Washington, playin' wit' boats. What brings you ta Duster territory?"

"When last I checked, Knox," Mr. Roosevelt answered, "the West Side of New York City was still part of the United States. These are men of the United States Navy, and they are here to assist the detective sergeants"— he pointed a thick finger at the Isaacsons—"in the performance of their duty."

"And what duty might that be?" Knox asked, though it was easy to see that he knew the answer.

"What it might be is none of your business," Mr. Roosevelt answered. "You and your—*followers* had better step aside."

"I don't think you get it," Knox answered, looking to his boys with a smile, then sniffling and running his tongue around his upper gums. This was a sure sign that he'd been blowing a lot of burny: the drug, taken that way, had the effect of making the upper part of people's mouths go numb, so that they seemed to have to check and see that their parts were all there every few seconds. "Like I said," he went on, "this is *Duster* territory— other gangs don't come in here, city cops don't come in here, don't *nobody* come in here, if they don't wanna take a beating."

"Really?" Mr. Roosevelt said.

"Yeah," Knox answered, with a confident nod. "Really."

"Well," Mr. Roosevelt declared, glaring at Knox, "I'm afraid there's one exception to that rule which you may have overlooked."

"Oh? And what might *that* be, you piece of—"

As he said these last words, Knox made a sudden sweeping move and tried to swing the axe handle on Mr. Roosevelt: a bad mistake. With a speed what was always surprising, given his size and thickness, Mr. Roosevelt snatched the stick of wood out of Knox's hands, making all of the Dusters' eyes go wide. Then, in another quick motion, Mr. Roosevelt gave Goo Goo a wicked smack across the side of the head with the weapon. "*That* might be the United States *federal government*!" Mr. Roosevelt bellowed, as Knox fell to his knees, moaning like the injured animal he was.

The other Dusters took a couple of steps forward, like they might charge; but they were still too confused to take definite action. I could tell, though, that said situation wasn't going to last very long: I pulled on the Doctor's sleeve, nodding my head in the direction of the river and trying to tell him I knew a full-scale battle was about to break out and that while it was raging we'd do best to get back down to West Street and come at Libby Hatch's house from another direction. He got the message, and as the sailors closed ranks and got ready to receive the coming attack, all of our group started to walk slowly backward—all, that is, excepting Cyrus, who'd locked eyes with Ding Dong and wasn't going anywhere.

Second by second the air got more and more charged; then Knox, his forehead bleeding, gathered his wits, looked up at his boys, and shouted, "Well? What the hell're you waiting for?"

At that the storm finally broke. In a solid, screaming wall the Dusters rushed forward, and the sailors did likewise. Both sides mixed it up so fast that the use of pistols by either group became pretty near an impossibility from the start. It'd be a contest of fists and sticks, that much was obvious, and it'd likely take up the whole block we were standing on: we had to get away fast.

"Run!" I told Mr. Moore, who nodded and, together with the detective sergeants, started to dash west. Miss Howard and the Doctor, though, hung back, waiting for Cyrus.

"Cyrus!" the Doctor commanded, as Miss Howard covered our big friend with her Colt. "Come with us, *now*!"

But Cyrus was way beyond taking any orders: as soon as the brawl'd erupted he'd reached out to grab Ding Dong by the shirt, then literally lifted him off the ground and thrown him about six feet behind the line of our sailors, where he wouldn't be able to get any help from his pals. Hitting the ground hard, Ding Dong'd dropped the stick he was carrying, and Cyrus quickly kicked it away. Then he pulled Ding Dong to his feet and said:

"No sticks, no knives, no guns—and I'm no fourteen-year-old girl, either. Now let's see how you do."

With that he started to pummel the Duster, who had to work hard to cover himself and get in a few shots of his own.

Sighing once, the Doctor turned to Miss Howard. "We'll have to leave him, Sara—there is the matter of accounts to be settled. He'll be all right, but *we* must go!"

Nodding reluctantly, Miss Howard turned her body west but kept her eyes on Cyrus—and it was a good thing she did, being as just as we started to move away two Dusters managed to break out of the brawl further up the street and ran over to try to give Ding Dong a hand. They were both carrying metal bars wrapped in burlap, and Cyrus had his back to them: once again, it looked like he might get blindsided by the gang.

Miss Howard, though, smoothly spun back around toward the fight, then raised her Colt and, holding it steady with both hands, let off two rounds, their explosions echoing off the buildings and the cobblestones thunderously. When the smoke of the shots cleared, the two Dusters with the metal bars were lying on the ground, each one clutching at a shattered kneecap. Miss Howard smiled and, seeing that Cyrus was now pretty well having his way with Ding Dong, turned to follow the rest of us.

Catching me staring at her in amazement, she said only, "I told you, Stevie—there is nothing like a bullet in the leg to make men mind their manners." Then she pushed me along toward West Street.

The howls of rage and pain from the brawl were now filling the whole neighborhood; and as the six of us ran around the corner to Bank Street, it began to sound like Hell itself had opened up on Bethune Street. Even the longshoremen on the waterfront were keeping clear of the action, and the residents of the neighborhood stayed locked up very tight in their homes: we could hear bolts being thrown on doors as we passed by on our way to Greenwich Street. But the overall effect of the battle turned out to be a helpful one, for as we turned north again and approached Bethune Street, we didn't catch sight of a single Duster: they'd all gone to join in the "fun." This left us an open road to Libby Hatch's place from the east, and in just a few more seconds we'd reached it.

"I doubt," the Doctor said breathlessly, "whether knocking will prove useful. Detective Sergeants?"

Marcus quickly produced his crowbar, and wedged it into the jamb of the door just to the right of the knob. He and Lucius both laid hold of the thing and got ready to put their full weight and strength into heaving away at it. "When we pull," Marcus said, sweating as much as his brother by that point, "the rest of you try to push on the door itself. Sara, I think you'd better keep your Colt at the ready." As Miss Howard stood back to obey this request, the Doctor, Mr. Moore, and I gathered around to fit into whatever spots we could reach on the door. "Ready?" Marcus asked, and we all grunted replies in the affirmative. "All right, then, one—two—"

As he called out "three!" he pulled hard on the crowbar with Lucius, and the rest of us shoved. The frame of the old door began to crack and splinter almost right away, and a few more good blows and yanks destroyed the right side of the structure completely. With a kick Marcus burst the door open, and then we all stepped to either side very fast, so that Miss Howard could train her gun immediately on—

Nothing. There was no sign of life in the little entryway to the house, and the steps against the right-hand wall led up into darkness what showed a similar lack of human activity. Miss Howard led the way in, still keeping her Colt trained on the darkness, and then the rest of us followed, frightened, yes, but also starting to feel tremendous disappointment.

"She can't," the Doctor whispered. "She *can't* have slipped away *again* . . ."

Inching our way into the dark house, we began to spread out, Lucius producing his revolver and taking a couple of steps up the stairway. He would've gone farther, followed by Mr. Moore and Marcus—but then we heard the sudden sound of a door slamming in the sitting room. There was only one such structure in that area, I knew that from my last visit:

"The basement door," I whispered, and then the three men on the stairs came back down. Again on Marcus's count, we all burst into the sitting area, led by Miss Howard and Lucius.

But the room was too dark to reveal much of anything, at first, except the general outlines of the furniture nearest to us and the entrance to the kitchen hallway at the back. Which was why the voice, when we heard it come out of the shadows, was all the more frightening:

"It doesn't matter, now," said Libby Hatch, very quietly. "You've found your way into the house—but you'll never find what you came for."

Lucius opened his mouth, seeming like he wanted to announce to the woman that she was under arrest, but the Doctor touched his arm, and spoke in a calm voice: "Listen to me, Elspeth Franklin—you need not face death—"

But Libby Hatch only spat and cursed, "Damn you all!"

Then we saw the sudden movement of a shadow in the hallway, going toward the kitchen. It was nothing more than the briefest blur, and it was followed, much to our increasing confusion and frustration, by the sound of feet climbing upwards.

"Stairs," the Doctor said. "There are *back stairs*!"

"I sure as hell never saw 'em," I said.

"She may have had a concealed passageway built," Marcus offered, "when she had Bates reconstruct the basement."

"One which will no doubt prove as difficult to enter as the chamber below," the Doctor agreed with an agitated nod. "Quickly, then—Marcus, you, Lucius, and Moore get downstairs! See what you can do to break into the chamber! Sara, you and Stevie come with me!"

With the sounds of the brawl still echoing out on the street, we all exploded off in our assigned directions, the men heading down the basement steps and Miss Howard and I following the Doctor up the staircase, past the second floor and on to the third. There we found a steel ladder what led to a hatchway in the ceiling. Miss Howard led the way up it and, opening the thing, tried to quickly jump out onto the roof.

We might have known better than to go chasing an enemy as clever as Libby in such an obvious way. Being the last one up, it was hard for me to see exactly what happened next, but the Doctor later related it to me. Once she'd stuck her head out of the hatchway Miss Howard got pistol-whipped hard, a blow what forced her to let go of her Colt (which fell back down to the floor at the base of the ladder) and rendered her unconscious right away. With surprising strength—increased, to be sure, by the desperateness of her situation—our enemy hauled Miss Howard's body up and out of the hatchway, laid it out on the tar-covered roof, and then trained a pistol of her own on the Doctor.

"You, of all people, should know that I'll use this, Dr. Kreizler," I heard Libby Hatch say. "Now get up here—and move very slowly."

As the Doctor climbed on up, I saw that I had a moment where I'd be out of view; so I scrambled down and fetched Miss Howard's gun, shoving it into my pants and covering it with my shirt so's to make it look as if I was still unarmed. Then I hurried back up the ladder, hoping to make Libby think that I hadn't had time to make the play.

It worked. Once the Doctor was up on the roof I saw Libby's golden eyes—wide and crazed by this point—move into the hatchway and fix on me. "You, too, boy," she said, obviously not knowing I was now armed. "Get up here!"

I followed the order, making sure to keep my movements slow and easy enough so as not to shake the Colt loose. When I'd got clear of the hatchway, Libby slammed it closed and, pointing the gun first at the Doctor and then at me, used her free hand to drag Miss Howard's body over on top of the hatch cover, a move what would make it tough for anybody to open the thing from below. Standing up straight, Libby kept moving her gun back and forth from me to the Doctor, trying to decide what to do and looking more unbalanced and wild than I'd ever seen her.

"Which one, which one," she mumbled. Then she grabbed the Doctor's arm and stuck the pistol to his head. "Put your hands in the air. You do the same, boy, and then stay very still, if you want to keep the Doctor's great brain in one piece."

Looking over to see that Miss Howard, though out cold, was still breathing regularly, I raised my hands halfway up: any higher, and I would've revealed the Colt tucked into my pants. Believing that both the Doctor and I were going to do what she told us, Libby seemed to relax a little: she used one hand to straighten first her hair and then her dress, which I noted was the same red-with-black-lace job what we'd first seen her in. At that point her look of craziness gave way to something what might've almost passed for regret.

"*Why?*" she asked, looking at the Doctor.

"I should have thought that would be obvious," he answered, keeping his hands up.

Before Libby could answer, a particularly loud round of hollering and screaming came rising up from the street, and she turned toward it. "Do you hear that?" she said. "That's *your* fault—*all* of yours! None of this had to happen!"

"If we'd left you free to continue murdering children, you mean?" the Doctor asked.

"Murdering them?" Libby answered, now looking positively injured. "All I did, all I ever tried to do, was *help* them!"

The Doctor gave her a sideways glance. "I believe you mean that in some way, Elspeth Franklin," he said quietly.

She nodded once, her golden eyes filling with tears; then she stamped a foot suddenly and angrily. "If you believe that, then why have you been *hounding* me like this?"

"Listen to me, Elspeth," the Doctor went on. "If you surrender yourself, there may be a way to help you—"

Libby's voice grew cold and mean: "Of course—in the *electrical chair*, you lying bastard!"

"No," the Doctor insisted, still quietly. "I can help you. I can try to make the authorities understand why you've done these things—"

"*But I've done nothing!*" Libby hollered, full of new desperation. "Can't you *see* that?" She paused, studying the Doctor's face. "No. No, of course you can't. You're a *man*. What *man* could understand what my life has been like—why I've had to make the choices I have? Do you think I *wanted* any of this? It wasn't my fault that it happened!"

I figured the only way I was going to be able to make a move for the Colt was to try to get the woman even more upset and off balance than she already was: so, though I knew the Doctor wouldn't have approved, I began to taunt her. "Yeah? What about the kid you buried with the dog? Whose fault was *that?*"

"You be quiet!" she seethed, turning to me. "You're not even a man—just a *boy*! All *you* understand are your own damned needs, your own damned *wants*! A woman probably worked herself raw raising you, and how did you ever repay her, except by spitting in her face? By disobeying, by whining, by—" Tightening her grip on her pistol, Libby glared at me hotter than ever with those gold eyes. "You want to know about the boy in the grave, do you? I didn't ask for him, and I didn't want him. I had a beau—a respectable boy, from a family that had a place in our world—the kind of boy I could have brought home to my mother, to show that I could—that I could—" Her voice starting to wander, Libby glanced down at the tarred roof for an instant. "He would've done anything for me. And I *did* do anything for him—but then his family found out, and they wouldn't . . ." Quickly, she looked back up. "And I was left with his lying, dirty *seed* in me! It wasn't wrong, to prevent the disgrace! What could it have been but a bastard—something else, something *more,* that I'd done *wrong*? So I did what was *right*—but I couldn't even *tell* anyone!"

Seeing that my plan was having the desired effect, I kept pressing: "And when you shot Matthew and Thomas and Clara? I suppose you didn't want to do that, either—your finger slipped on the trigger, or they *asked* you to shoot them—"

The Doctor was by now staring at me, perplexed and alarmed. "Stevie, what are you—"

I ignored him. "What *about* that?" I went on harshly. "How did you do the right thing *there*?"

Her breath now coming in quick heaves, Libby shouted, "It was *better* for them! Do you think I *wanted* to shoot them? It was better for them, to be finished with this world—"

"Yeah!" I shouted back at her. "Better so's you could take their money and go off with your boyfriend the preacher!"

"Be quiet! Goddamn you children, can't any of you ever just be quiet?" Swallowing hard, Libby tried without much success to get a firmer grip on herself. "You know what this leads to! I've warned you, and now I have to show you!"

Looking at me all of a sudden the way she must, I figured, have looked at all the children she'd killed just before the act, she raised her pistol into the air and brought it down on the Doctor's head, causing him to tumble to the ground, still conscious but bleeding from a cut above his temple. Brutal as the deed was, it gave me all the time I needed: when Libby yanked the Doctor back up by his collar, she turned again to find me holding Miss Howard's Colt with both hands and training its barrel on her.

"Okay," I said, my own heart racing. "Now, you want to start killing people, you go ahead. But I promise—you'll be the *second* one to go."

———

CHAPTER 56

She was looking at me with the same expression what'd been on her face when Mr. Picton had revealed that we knew about the grave behind her family's barn: surprise and shock. Again I got the feeling that she hadn't been in such positions many times in her life; and that fact, I knew, might lead her to do some unpredictable things. But I had my own little dose of unpredictability up my sleeve, one what I was getting set to administer.

Her eyes dancing in fear and anger, Libby's mouth first tightened up, then cracked open long enough for her to say, "I'll kill him! I swear I will!"

I nodded to her. "I know," I said. "Question is, do you wanna go, too?"

"What choice do I have?" the woman shouted back. "Damn you, you're just like the others—you don't leave me any *choice*!"

"I'll give you a choice," I said. "You let the Doctor walk over here, then you run. We won't follow."

The Doctor, still reeling a little from the blow to the head he'd taken, looked as confused as Libby Hatch. "Stevie, what are you saying?"

Once again I paid him no mind. "Well?" I said, keeping my eyes on Libby.

She did a little dance in her head with the idea, looking tempted. Then I got some unexpected help when Mr. Roosevelt's voice boomed up from down in the street:

"They're retreating! Lieutenant Kimball! Detail some of your men—I want Knox taken into custody!"

I let myself have a little smile just then. "You hear that?" I said, nodding toward the front edge of the roof. "Your pal Goo Goo's beating it out of here. So what's it gonna be? You gonna play smart and go with him?"

"How do I know you won't follow me?" Libby asked.

The next part of my performance had to be the best: I took a deep breath, kept my eyes on hers, then said, "You can take this gun. It's the only one we got."

The Doctor wasn't so dazed as not to understand that. "No!" he said. "Stevie, do not—"

But Libby cut him off: "You slide it over here first."

I shook my head. "You let go. Let him take two steps clear. Then I will."

"Stevie," the Doctor insisted, "you can't trust—"

He stopped as Libby jammed the barrel of her pistol hard against his head. "Oh, yes, that's right, isn't it, Doctor? You can't trust Libby—you can't trust the *woman*. She'll break her word. She'll shoot you in the back. After all, she killed her own children, didn't she? And all those others, too. How can you possibly trust someone who could do all that? Well, let me tell you, Dr. Kreizler . . ." Moving the barrel of the gun a couple of inches away from the Doctor's skull, Libby swayed a bit, like things were really starting to get to her. "Let me tell you," she said again, her voice getting softer and what you might call detached. "I did *everything* for those children. My own, I went through the agony of bearing. The others, I went through the long, sleepless, *endless* hours of caring for. Feeding, cleaning, changing . . . and for what? For *what*, Doctor? They never stopped crying. They never stopped getting sick. They never stopped needing." With her free hand Libby clutched at her hair, as her face and voice filled with truly desperate anger and sorrow. "Needing—always *needing*. It never stopped. I did everything I could, *everything,* but it never stopped! It should have been enough. It was *all I could do*—it should have been enough! But it never was . . . it never was. And so—can't you see? They were better off after I—" Suddenly she glanced down at the roof and mumbled, "They didn't need *anything,* then . . ." Shaking herself hard, Libby looked back up, the gold light of the clever killer suddenly back in her eyes. "All right, boy. He takes two steps, then you slide the gun over."

I nodded. "That's the deal."

The Doctor tried one more time to stop me: "Stevie, do not do this—"

"Go on, Doctor," Libby almost chuckled in her most frightening voice. "Take your two steps . . ."

As the Doctor started to move, Libby kept her gun trained squarely on his head. When he'd gotten what I figured was far enough from her, I leaned down and placed Miss Howard's revolver on the tar.

"Stevie—" the Doctor tried again; but I just looked up at him, hoping that he could read the message in my eyes. It took him a second or two, but he did eventually get it. Then he closed his mouth and nodded.

"All right," Libby said. "Slide it over."

I did as I was told. The Colt came to a stop just at Libby's feet, and she quickly leaned over to pick it up. Then she stood again, without either turning to run or lowering her own weapon.

"Actually, Doctor," she said, with one of her most cunning, seductive little smiles, "you were quite right." Her revolver clicked loudly as she pulled back the hammer. "I've no intention of allowing any of you—"

She never finished the sentence. A small hissing sound cut through the night air, and I jumped over to grab the Doctor's legs and pull him down to the roof. A shot went off, but it struck only an iron furnace chimney on the house next door with a loud clang. Then both the Doctor and I looked up.

Libby's smile was gone now, but her eyes were still open and she was still clutching her smoking gun. The better part of a small, crude arrow was sticking out of the side of her neck, and I knew that, though she was still on her feet, there was a good chance that she was already dead: the strychnine could've killed her before the muscles of her legs had a chance to give way. After another second or two she did collapse, first to her knees and then, after another pause, over onto her side.

The Doctor and I ran over to her immediately, myself taking care to quickly pry the pistol from her hand. For his part, the Doctor lifted her head and examined her eyes, then felt her neck for a pulse. He must've sensed something, being as he said, "Elspeth? Elspeth Franklin?"

As the last air left her lungs, Libby managed to form the words *always needing.* Then she was gone, and the Doctor reached out to close the golden eyes for the last time.

I don't know how long the pair of us crouched there looking at her, but I do know that what finally brought us around was the sound of knocking on the underside of the hatchway cover.

"Sara?" It was Mr. Moore's voice, shouting up from below the closed entryway. "Stevie, Kreizler—what the hell happened, are you all right?"

Both the hatchway cover and Miss Howard's body jumped a bit as Mr. Moore tried to get up onto the roof; and with the bumping movement

Miss Howard began to come around, first groaning and then, as her eyes opened, rolling over and falling onto the roof with a small grunt.

"Sara," the Doctor said urgently. He lay Libby Hatch out on the roof quickly, then ran over to where Miss Howard lay just as Mr. Moore leapt up and out of the hatchway.

"Good Christ," he said, taking in the scene. "What the hell happened here?"

Ignoring the question, the Doctor pulled a handkerchief out of his pocket and lifted Miss Howard's shoulders up onto his knee. Then he began to wipe at and examine the spot on her head where she'd been hit, soon satisfying himself that it wasn't a serious wound. Gently rubbing and patting her cheeks with his hand, he finally got her to focus on him.

"Doctor," she breathed. Looking around, she tried dizzily to make a move. "What happened—where—"

The Doctor held her still. "Be calm, Sara," he said with a smile, brushing her hair out of her face as Mr. Moore and I gathered round. "It's over. At least, *this* part of it is." Then he turned her so that, without moving her head much, she could see Libby Hatch's body.

"She's—dead?" Miss Howard said; and in spite of the fact that she was still a little groggy, I could hear a faint touch of sadness in her voice.

"Yes," the Doctor answered gently, sensing, I think, how she felt.

Miss Howard watched the body for a few more seconds; then, in a quick sort of spasm, she made a noise what seemed like a combination of a gasp and a lone, deep sob. She turned her head back toward us, and I could see a tear on her cheek. "I'm sorry," she whispered, wiping the tear away as fast as she was able. "I know I shouldn't—"

The Doctor quieted her with a little shushing sound, and rubbed her cheek softly again. "Don't apologize. Someone *should* shed a tear at this moment." He paused, then looked over at Libby Hatch. "But I confess that I cannot. I cannot . . ."

Miss Howard suddenly looked puzzled. "But—" she said, trying to sit up, "who—"

"That's what *I'd* like to know," Mr. Moore said, glancing at the Doctor and me.

"Take a look at her neck," I told him.

Making his way carefully across the roof, as if Libby might still jump up and have at him, Mr. Moore carefully examined the body, then nodded. "Oh . . . so it was the aborigine, after all." He retrieved Miss Howard's Colt, then glanced at the rooftops around us. "Where is he?" he asked.

"Don't know," I said with a shrug. "Pretty far, by now, and still moving. I hope."

"Well, we'd better have that arrow," Mr. Moore answered, cautiously reaching down to remove the thing from Libby's neck. "I wouldn't want to try to explain it to Roosevelt," he added, tossing the missile over the edge of the roof into the back yard. "And I'm sure the wound will be mysterious enough to confound whatever fool coroner the police engage." Walking back across the roof quickly, he gave me a questioning but approving look. "Did the two of you plan this, Stevie?"

"I wouldn't exactly say we *planned* it," I answered.

The Doctor looked up at me, uncertainty and pride showing together in a slight smile. "Your gambling instincts seem to be intractable, Stevie."

"It wasn't a gamble," I said. "Not if you knew him like I did."

Miss Howard, her head clearing, reached up to touch the side of the Doctor's slightly bloodied face. "You're hurt," she said.

"That, too, is thanks to our young friend," the Doctor replied, nodding my way. "But it's not serious—all part of Stevie's plan, it seems."

"Hey, wait a minute," I protested quickly. "I didn't know she'd actually *smack* you—"

The Doctor already had a hand up. "It was well worth it—an appropriate punishment for ever doubting your judgment in such matters." Then his black eyes gave me a more serious look. "I mean it, Stevie. It was a brilliant bit of work."

As if to punctuate the remark, Mr. Moore gave my head a rub and Miss Howard smiled at me—all of which, of course, was just the sort of attention what's always made my skin crawl. Fortunately, I quickly thought of a way to change the topic:

"What about Ana?" I asked, looking up at Mr. Moore.

His face suddenly went straight. "Oh, God," he said, with what sounded like dread. "Yes, Ana." He looked to the Doctor and Miss Howard. "Can you two make it downstairs?"

Miss Howard began to struggle to her feet. "I think so," she said, finally standing. "Why, John? What is it?"

Mr. Moore, still looking what you might call inscrutable, just shook his head. "I could tell you," he said. "But you'd never believe it."

———

CHAPTER 57

By the time we got back down to the first floor of the building the action out on the street seemed to've calmed down quite a bit, and from the cheering sounds being made by our sailors, it seemed like they truly had come away from the encounter winners. As we passed by the front door, Marcus came in through it, confirming that the Dusters had fled the scene, a result what he, too, seemed to find very heartening. It was up to me to be the spoilsport, by informing everybody that if in fact the Dusters had disappeared for the moment, they'd likely be back: soon, in greater numbers (they'd probably call in more auxiliaries), and better armed, which meant guns.

"What makes you think that, Stevie?" Mr. Moore said, poking his head outside the door and looking around. "Those navy boys gave them one hell of a black eye—I wouldn't think they'd be any too anxious to come back for more."

"They have to," I answered. "We took them on right in the middle of their own territory. They let this stand, and they'll *lose* that territory, to every gang what borders them. It's a sign of weakness, and they can't afford it."

"Stevie's logic, once again, is sound," the Doctor said. "Let's not forget that he knows this world far better than the rest of us. Marcus, I suggest you find Roosevelt. Tell him to forget about arresting Knox or anyone else, and simply detach a group of men to retrieve Libby Hatch's body from the roof. Then we shall return to the boats."

Nodding in agreement, Marcus turned to Mr. Moore. "Are you taking them down, John?" Mr. Moore just nodded back, and then Marcus turned to me. "It was the garden that gave me the tip, Stevie. Remember the way it seemed so untended? And how unused you said those tools downstairs looked?"

Puzzled, I furrowed my eyebrows at him. "Yeah?"

"Well," the detective sergeant said, heading back out into the street, "there was a reason."

Further bewildered by that last comment, the Doctor, Miss Howard, and I followed Mr. Moore to the basement door, then down into the dusty cave below.

The one electrical bulb was lit, showing things pretty well the way I'd left them the night I'd been there: in other words, there was no sign of any secret doorway having been forced open, a fact what surprised not only me, but the Doctor and Miss Howard, too.

"Moore," the Doctor said, "I thought you intimated—"

Mr. Moore held up a hand. "We closed it again to give you the full effect," he said, going past the rack of preserves to the collection of old, rusty garden tools. "We did everything we could to try to move this thing manually," he said, indicating the rack. "And *you* might actually have moved it, Stevie, if you'd picked something other than that old hoe to try to wedge behind it."

"What do you mean?" I said, not getting the hint.

Mr. Moore pointed at the two tallest of the tools—a shovel and an iron rake—what stood side by side. "Open," he said, indicating the shovel, "and close," at which point he touched the rake.

"Moore, we've no time for games," the Doctor said. "What the devil are you talking about?"

By way of an answer Mr. Moore just held up a finger, then grabbed hold of the shovel's handle. The tool didn't come away from its resting spot at his touch; instead, it pivoted at a point on the floor, to which it was, it seemed, anchored. As Mr. Moore lowered the thing on that pivot, lo and behold, the rack of preserves began to move, as if by itself: it swung away from the brick dividing wall by the furnace and revealed a three-foot-square hole leading down through the stone floor and into the ground below the building.

"Oh, my God," Miss Howard whispered, stepping forward toward the hole. The Doctor and I followed, shocked past speech.

"Just big enough for an average adult to negotiate," Mr. Moore said, picking up one of the Isaacsons' portable torches what lay nearby. "As is the entire passageway."

"Passageway?" the Doctor echoed.

"Come on," Mr. Moore said, taking a few steps down onto an iron ladder what was fixed to the side of a deep shaftway what led downwards from the hole. "I'll show you."

With that he disappeared below ground, while the rest of us looked nervously to each other.

"How come I got no big desire to go down there?" I said quietly.

"You've been through an awful lot, Stevie," Miss Howard answered, putting a hand to my arm. "And what's down there may not be too pleasant."

"It would be completely understandable if you wished to wait here," the Doctor agreed.

I shook my head. "It ain't that. I want to see it, but . . ." Trying to shake off my severe jitters, I stepped down onto the ladder. "Aw, hell," I said, "how much worse can this thing get?"

Moving carefully, I followed Mr. Moore's torch, which appeared to come to a stop about fifteen feet down. "Wait for one second before you come all the way down, Stevie," he called to me, "so I can get into the side passage. Each of you will have to do the same."

"The side passage?" I repeated.

"You'll see when you get here."

And I did. At the base of the shaftway, the walls of which were rough concrete, was an opening into a narrow tunnel what ran sideways. The thing was just high enough for a person to crouch in, so's you could kind of scurry along without actually crawling. Mr. Moore guided me into this space when I got down, then did the same for Miss Howard and the Doctor when they arrived. After that, he turned his torch in what I calculated to be the direction of the backyard, revealing that the passageway—what was also concrete—went on for another forty feet. There was a dank smell to it, but it wasn't nearly as stifling as it should've been.

"Is that a draft?" Miss Howard asked, licking her finger and holding it up.

"It becomes almost a breeze," Mr. Moore answered, his face lit up like a jack-o'-lantern by the light of the torch, "once you get to the other end."

"But what produces it?" the Doctor asked.

"All part of the surprise, Laszlo," Mr. Moore answered, starting down the tunnel toward a small glow of light that filled its far end. He cupped his free hand in front of his mouth. "Lucius! You still there?"

"Yes, John," came Lucius's whispering reply. "But keep your voice down, dammit!"

We kept scuffling along, crooked over like coal miners, and as we went, a thought occurred to me: "I don't hear any baby crying," I said grimly.

"No," Mr. Moore answered, in that same inscrutable tone of voice he'd used on the roof. "You don't."

In another few seconds we'd reached the end of the passageway and arrived at a small wooden doorway. It was cracked open just a bit, and the crack was producing the light we'd seen from the other end. It appeared that this entranceway led into yet another chamber; and as we collected ourselves to go on in, my nerves fluttered worse than ever. Pictures of torture chambers in castle dungeons began to flash through my head: racks, iron maidens, red-hot irons, exposure to filth and rats—who knew what Libby Hatch had used to try to get the unruly kids she kidnapped to behave? I began to wonder if maybe I shouldn't have taken the chance to just wait up top—but once again, I swallowed all such hesitations.

"All right," Mr. Moore said. "Everyone set?" Nobody said they were, but nobody said they weren't, either, and Mr. Moore took that as a sign to proceed. "Then follow me."

He swung the little door open, and we entered the room.

The first thing you noticed about the space was light: bright light, produced not by bare electrical bulbs but by very pleasant little lamps what sat on a pair of wooden night tables and a small chest of drawers what was painted a gentle pink. The walls had been covered with patterned paper what showed little pictures of smiling baby animals against a white ground. The paper reflected the light of the lamps and made the glare, especially as you came out of the dark passageway, all the harsher. As Mr. Moore had said, the draft we'd felt became a kind of breeze once we'd entered the room, one what was actually very refreshing: it was produced, he told us, by electrical fans inside smaller ventilation shafts what led up to the backyard and drew air down from there. On the wall opposite the chest of drawers was a handsome crib with a white lace canopy over its top. In a third wall a window frame had been installed, complete with glass, and behind this some talented person had painted a quiet country scene, one what resembled the rolling hills and open pasturelands of Saratoga County. There was a handmade carpet on the floor, and a fine oak rocking chair in one corner; and all over the place there were mountains of toys, everything from an expensive musical box to stuffed animals to building blocks.

In fact, if you'd been above ground, it would've been a first-class nursery.

"Holy Christ," I mumbled, too shocked to offer anything else by way of an opinion. My dumbfoundedness was only increased when I looked into the corner and at the rocking chair:

In it was sitting Detective Sergeant Lucius, gently rocking back and forth as he held a content Ana Linares in his arms.

Faced with three stunned faces, the detective sergeant blushed a bit. "I had to change her diaper to get her to stop crying," he said with some embarrassment. "But it was all right—I've had a lot of practice with my sister's children."

"Apparently," the Doctor said, approaching the pair and bending down to put a finger to Ana's face. "You've done very well, Detective Sergeant. My compliments."

Miss Howard and I gathered around. "She's all right, then?" Miss Howard asked.

"Well, she's undernourished, certainly," Lucius answered. "And slightly colicky. But that was to be expected, I suppose." His eyes suddenly lit up with interest. "What about Mrs. Hatch?"

"The aborigine got her," Mr. Moore announced. "The navy boys are fetching her body now. And according to our resident gangland expert, here"—he pointed my way—"we've *all* got to get moving, before the Dusters come back looking for even bigger trouble."

"Yes," Lucius replied nervously, as he carefully stood up with the baby. "I think that would be a wise idea. Sara, would you like to—"

Miss Howard, though, made no move to take the child; instead she just smiled a little deviously. "You're doing extremely well, Lucius. And I've had a rather nasty bump on the head, I'm afraid—I might lose my balance on the way out."

"Do you *mind* taking her, Detective Sergeant?" the Doctor asked, roaming around the room and trying, it seemed to me, to burn the startling image of it into his mind before we had to leave.

"No, no," Lucius answered, still rocking the baby. Then he turned a warning look on the rest of us. "I just don't want to hear about it for years to come, that's all." Taking a few steps forward, he stood by the Doctor and gazed around the room with him. "A little difficult to accept, isn't it?"

The Doctor only shrugged. "Is it? I wonder . . ."

"What do you mean, Laszlo?" Mr. Moore said, picking up a little stuffed dog and rubbing it against his nose. "Given who we've been dealing with, I would've expected something a lot more—*austere*. And that's putting it euphemistically."

"That was only one side of her, John," Miss Howard said, running a finger over the grinning baby animals of the room's wallpaper.

"Indeed, Sara," the Doctor agreed quietly.

"Well," I offered, finally getting over my own amazement, "one thing's for sure, anyway."

"Stevie?" the Doctor asked, looking my way.

I shrugged. "She finally got some privacy. Had to dig halfway to China to get it, but . . ."

The Doctor nodded. "True." He glanced at Ana Linares. "And yet, even here, sealed off from the world, she could not—could not . . ." The Doctor's words trailed off as he stared into the baby's enormous round eyes, which were almost as dark as his own. "You," he said, forgetting his last thought and putting a hand to Ana's chin, making her smile that big, game grin what we'd come to know so well from the photograph her mother'd given us. "You have been a very difficult young lady to find, Señorita Linares. But thank God you're safe. Thank God . . ."

"Well," Mr. Moore said, "she won't *stay* safe if we all don't get out of here. So get a good last look, Kreizler—something tells me we won't be coming back into Duster territory for quite a while."

With that we all started back into the passageway, leaving the Doctor behind for a few seconds to give him just a little more time to mentally memorize the strange hideaway what had been Libby Hatch's obsession, and what was now, being as she was dead, the only remaining blueprint he had to the workings of her tangled mind.

Back upstairs, we found that Mr. Roosevelt and Lieutenant Kimball had come into the house, along with Marcus. The rest of the navy boys were gathered around the steps outside, and a couple of them were carrying a folding stretcher what they must've fetched from one of the torpedo boats. Strapped to the stretcher was Libby Hatch's body, draped in a bedsheet. The general mood of the bunch seemed to have changed from celebration to concern: apparently a couple of sailors had seen a few Dusters making moves what indicated that the gang was in fact preparing a new attack. So we got out onto the sidewalk quickly, the sailors forming a circle around Lucius, who still had the baby, and the men what were carrying the stretcher. Then, at double time, we began to trot back toward the river.

As we went, I fell in beside Cyrus. His clothes were a little rearranged, but otherwise he looked hale, hearty—and very satisfied. "Ain't many people what come away from locking horns with Ding Dong looking as healthy as you do, Cyrus," I said, smiling up to him.

He shrugged, though he couldn't help but grin a bit, himself. "That's because there aren't many people who get him in a fair fight," he answered.

"So I'm guessing you came out on top?"

Glancing up ahead to the construction site of the Bell Laboratories, what was now on our left, Cyrus answered, "I'll let you be the judge of that."

He nodded in the direction of a big pile of bricks: propped up against them was Ding Dong, his face a patchwork of bruises and his arms and legs sticking out at what you might call angles.

"Jesus," I breathed, whistling low. "Is he alive?"

"Oh, he's alive, all right," Cyrus answered. "Though in the morning he may wish he wasn't." I nodded grimly at that, feeling some deep sense of justice; and as we trotted on toward the river, Cyrus looked down at me meaningfully. "You know I always thought she was trouble, Stevie," he said. "I won't deny that now. But she did right by you, by us, and by the baby, in the end—so I guess I was wrong."

I gave him a look what I hoped was as full of thanks as I felt. "You weren't wrong," I said. "Trouble she was. But she was other things, too."

Cyrus nodded. "That's so . . ."

The general mood of our little army improved considerably once we got back across West Street and started to move, at the same double-time pace, south on the waterfront. As the huge black outline of the White Star Line pier began to grow bigger, you could start to feel the cloud of the anxiousness lifting from over us; but it was up to Mr. Roosevelt to give the official signal that it was okay to breathe easier.

"Well, then, Doctor!" he boomed as we trotted past Perry Street. "It would seem that we've enjoyed a victory!"

"I shall reserve final judgment until we are safely cast off," the Doctor answered cautiously, still watching the streets around us. "But the preliminary results are encouraging."

Mr. Roosevelt roared with laughter. "By God, Kreizler, if I ever met a man more apt to see the dark side of a situation, I'm not aware of it! True, we didn't take that infernal scoundrel Knox into custody—but we delivered a message that those swine won't soon forget, and at the cost of only a few bruises to our own men! Enjoy the moment, Doctor—savor it!"

"Our casualties were no greater than bruises?" the Doctor asked, still not ready to give in to celebrating.

"Well, all right, two men's arms were broken," Mr. Roosevelt conceded. "And another suffered a fractured jaw. But I assure you, the culprits were paid back with interest. So I'll have none of your melancholy, my friend, none at all! You must learn to *enjoy* your triumphs!"

The Doctor did smile at that, though I think it was as much out of amusement at his old friend's incorrigible attitude as any real joy over what had just taken place at Number 39 Bethune Street. Oh, he was happy we'd rescued little Ana, I didn't doubt that; but the final secrets of why all the horrors we'd experienced had been necessary in the first place were now lying forever hidden on the stretcher what the two sailors next to Detective Sergeant Lucius were carrying. Legally prevented, for the time being, from using the operating theater at his Institute, the Doctor had no place to perform a postmortem on Libby Hatch's brain, to see if it'd been abnormal in some way; and even if he hadn't been so restricted, the detective sergeants couldn't exactly deliver a body with a dissected head to their superiors. Coming on top of Libby's death, these considerations would, I knew, always prevent the Doctor from seeing our experience as "a triumph," just as Kat's death would always make the memory of the adventure especially bittersweet for me.

We got to the torpedo boats without any trouble, and got Libby Hatch's body stowed aboard the closest of them. The Isaacsons planned to accompany said boat to a police pier down by the Battery, where they'd be able to close the case what their department had been so unwilling to open in the first place. Miss Howard, in the meantime, would take Ana Linares in the lead boat with the rest of us, first back to the Brooklyn Navy Yard and from there on to the Doctor's house. Once safely home, Miss Howard would telephone the señora, who, since that afternoon, had been waiting for a message at the French consulate, where she'd gone to hide from her husband.

Her head now completely clear, Miss Howard got into the lead torpedo boat without any trouble, and waited for Lucius to bring Ana down the ladder to her; but, not unpredictably, Mr. Roosevelt stepped in to do the honors.

"You get back to your boat, Detective Sergeant," he said, taking the baby. "I've had quite a lot of experience with such little bundles as this one, and you may rest assured that I shall get her safely aboard!" Cradling Ana in one arm, Mr. Roosevelt then made his way nimbly down the long ladder from the pier to our boat. He moved with much greater ease, considering his cargo, than any of us could have done; and I remembered, watching him, that he had five young kids of his own, who he must have toted around in similar if not identical situations many times.

Once he'd gotten aboard and was handing the baby over to Miss Howard, Mr. Roosevelt took a moment to actually look at Ana's appealing little features. "Why," he said, in a soft way what wasn't at all like his usual manner, "what an extraordinary face. Look at her eyes, Doctor!"

"Yes," the Doctor said, as he jumped down from the ladder into the boat. "I've seen them, Roosevelt. A beautiful child."

Letting one of his big fingers play around little Ana's face, Mr. Roosevelt offhandedly asked, "Whose is she?"

Mr. Moore, Miss Howard, the Doctor, Cyrus, and I all froze; but fortunately Mr. Roosevelt was too proccupied to notice.

"Whose?" the Doctor repeated smoothly, as our boat's engines rumbled to life and our crew began to cast off. "Does it matter, Roosevelt?"

"Matter?" Mr. Roosevelt answered with a shrug. "I don't know that it *matters,* but after what we've been through, I should like to meet the parents." He grinned wide as Ana reached out to grasp hold of his finger. "And tell them how lucky they are to have engaged you all."

"Her parents," Miss Howard said, coolly and quickly, "are consular officials. *French* consular officials. Unfortunately, they plan to return home as soon as they're reunited with the child. Understandably."

"Ah. Yes." Mr. Roosevelt nodded, looking serious for a moment. "That *is* understandable, I suppose—quite understandable. But I hope you'll emphasize to them, Sara, that this sort of incident is hardly typical of our nation."

"Of course," Miss Howard answered.

Grinning again as he went back to studying Ana, Mr. Roosevelt said, "French, you say? What a pity they weren't Spanish. She has something of a Spanish look about her, this little one. It might have been useful to show those blackguards how a *free* people handles a problem like this!"

"Mmm, yes," Mr. Moore said casually. "It might have been."

"Still," Mr. Roosevelt went on, as our boat cruised out into the center of the Hudson, "as you say, Doctor, it hardly matters who her family is. She is a child, and she is safe now." At that Ana reached out again to clutch Mr. Roosevelt's playful finger, causing his smile to widen. "Do you know," he said quietly, "I think a baby's hand is the most beautiful thing in the world."

CHAPTER 58

O nce we were all back at Seventeenth Street, Lucius discovered that the Doctor had a nursing bottle in his consulting room (he used it, what you might call ironically enough, to lecture women who were having trouble weaning their kids) and began to mix a concoction in it what he thought might help Ana Linares get over the touch of colic what was continuing, every few minutes, to take away her usual happy smile and playful laughter. Milk, honey, and the little paregoric what was left over from my attempts to dose Kat all went into the brew, and as the detective sergeant fed it to the baby she did seem to regain her full color and spriteliness of spirit. It was a breath of fresh air, to have a contented, even happy, symbol of new life among a group of people who'd experienced nothing but violence and killing for days and nights on end. In fact, so potent was the effect of Ana's presence that we all took turns holding and feeding her, letting the little girl's unspoiled joy at being alive and our knowledge that we'd rescued her from a close brush with death perform the kind of healing magic what only children can bring.

Along toward one A.M. Mr. Roosevelt and Lieutenant Kimball took their leave and headed back for Washington, to resume the business of planning the war with Spain what they believed and hoped was on its way. I don't know to this day if anyone ever told the former police commissioner just how much our business that night might've been connected, if things had broken only a hair differently, to the outbreak of that war; something tells me that he and the Doctor must have had words about it before Mr. Roosevelt's death earlier this year. But the most important fact,

then as now, was that Mr. Roosevelt had come to our aid without knowing anything more than that his friends and an innocent child were in
trouble. It only made me like and respect the man all the more; and as I
think of him now, pulling away from the house in his landau on his way
to Grand Central, flashing us that wonderful grin what would one day
keep political cartoonists in such clover, I wondered why it was that so few
men had his kind of strength: that particular ability to be gentle and loving with a baby on the one hand, and to crack the heads of mugs like the
Hudson Dusters on the other. It's a question what still dogs me.

At about one-thirty the detective sergeants returned from the First
Precinct house down on New Street, where the body of Libby Hatch'd
been taken after its arrival at the police pier. From the First the corpse
would be shipped on up to the morgue, a fact what made my spirit burn:
I didn't much like the idea of the murderess being in so much as the same
building as Kat, even if they were both dead. Still, there was nothing to do
about it, as an autopsy had to be performed on Libby. (The conclusions of
said procedure, we later found out, were "inconclusive," just as Mr.
Moore'd suspected they would be.) As for El Niño, I half expected that he
might telephone the house that night, just to make sure everything'd
turned out okay; but then I realized that, so far as he was concerned,
everything already had. His *jefe* had been avenged, and baby Ana would
be returned to her mother; all that was left for him in New York was trouble with the law, and when I took the time to consider it I realized that I'd
much rather he move fast to get safely out of town—and maybe out of the
country—than slow down to risk contact with us.

For her part, Miss Howard had, according to plan, 'phoned uptown to
the French consulate straightway when we returned to the Doctor's
house, to inform Señora Linares that all was well and that, as soon as she
had police protection, she'd bring Ana to her. We all knew that the detective sergeants were needed for this job, and that they'd best be armed
when they carried it out: there was no way of saying what new servants
Señor Linares had hired when El Niño'd come over to our side, or if they,
like the aborigine, had been keeping watch over the Doctor's house. But
as it turned out, such caution wasn't necessary: Miss Howard, Marcus,
and Lucius got the baby back to her mother without any sign of trouble.
When they returned, they told us that the señora was in the process of deciding whether to go back to her family in Spain or to head west, to those
parts of the United States where new beginnings were the common coin,
and where, I'd once hoped, Kat might've been able to get a fresh start on
life. But the great and inexpressible joy the señora'd experienced when

she'd been reunited with Ana, Miss Howard and the Isaacsons said, was enough to make such decisions seem of small importance for the moment, and had given our three teammates the powerful feeling that everything we'd been through had been well worth it.

Such may have been true, too—for them. For Mr. Moore and me, though, there would always be questions, questions about whether we'd been right in getting people we cared deeply about involved in a case what ended up costing them their lives. Such questions seldom come with easy answers, and they never go away: as I sit here writing these words, I can't say as I'm any closer to quieting those doubts than I was at three A.M. that morning, when everyone finally went their separate ways and I sat for an hour in my windowsill, tearfully smoking cigarettes and seeing Kat's eyes all over the starry sky.

There were, of course, the funerals to attend to, and after a simple ceremony for Kat at Calvary Cemetery on Wednesday afternoon—one what I was grateful to every member of our group for attending—we all boarded a train early Thursday morning to head back up to Ballston Spa and watch Mr. Picton get planted in the ground of the same cemetery on Ballston Avenue what we had, only weeks earlier, violated. It was sadness, affection, and respect, of course, what drew us so far to say our last good-byes to the agitated little man with the ever-blasting pipe who'd refused to let the case of the murders on the Charlton road die, and who, in death, had given us the legal leverage we'd needed to openly pursue Libby Hatch in New York. But curiosity pulled us north, too: curiosity about what Mr. Picton's final words about "a clue" in the cemetery had meant.

Standing by his open grave as his casket was lowered in, each of us sneaked a peek at the headstones of the other members of his family; and we were all slightly shocked to find that every person in that plot—not only Mr. Picton's parents, but a younger sister and brother, as well—had died on exactly the same day. This led the Doctor to put some gentle questions to Mrs. Hastings after the ceremony, which she answered by saying that indeed, Mr. Picton's family had all been killed one night as they slept, by a gas leak in the big house at the end of High Street. Mr. Picton had been away at law school when it'd happened, and he'd never spoken of the matter in later years; and while Mrs. Hastings wouldn't comment on the odd coincidence of gas leaking in so many rooms of the Picton house at one and the same time, she did say that it was after the tragedy that Mr. Picton'd decided to pursue a career in prosecution. This was enough for the Doctor, who knew—as did, I think, Mrs. Hastings—that the "coincidence" of the several gas leaks was so incredible as to be dismissable.

Someone had deliberately done away with the family, and the fact that all the doors of the house had been bolted when it'd happened indicated that it'd been one of the Pictons themselves.

Beyond that, though, neither the Doctor nor anyone else could do more than speculate. Had Mr. Picton's mother, in a fit of some kind of despondency, done away with her husband, her offspring, and herself by means of gas—not an uncommon practice, according to the Doctor, among lethally melancholic women? Had Mr. Picton suspected the truth about the matter, and had that suspicion not only made him endlessly anxious for the rest of his days, but driven him for so many years to convict Libby Hatch? We would never know. But just the possibility, combined with the sad occasion of the funeral itself, was enough to keep us all very quiet during the train ride back to New York.

Things calmed down eerily around Seventeenth Street in the days what immediately followed—the case was over, but there was no possibility of returning to a normal routine, being as, even if our spirits had been strong enough to bounce back so quickly, we were still waiting to find out the results of the court investigation into affairs at the Doctor's Institute. On Friday morning the Isaacsons—who'd put off giving their testimony ever since we'd gotten back to town—finally went before the closed court and told their tale. That same afternoon the Reverend Bancroft was called to give his opinion about how the Institute was set up, whether the staff were up to snuff, and if, in general, the place was a sound proposition. The court waited until Monday to hand down its decision, and I'm not exaggerating when I say that those two days were among the longest of my life. The weather turned foully humid, coating every person in the city in the kind of thin sheet of heavy sweat what seems impossible to get off and always sends tempers flaring. Monday was no better: the thermometer'd already climbed into the high eighties by ten, and when Cyrus, the Doctor, and I boarded the calash to head down to the Tweed court house at two I wasn't sure that either Frederick—whose weeks of boarding had made him a touch lazy—or any of the rest of us was going to make it.

But make it we did, in every sense of the word. Not only did Judge Samuel Welles surprise us by declaring that the affairs of the Institute were in order and the case of Paulie McPherson was "an obvious aberration," but he went on to shock the entire courtroom by giving those city fathers what had brought on the investigation a tongue-lashing. Dr. Kreizler's methods might be unorthodox, Judge Welles said, and some people might not be comfortable with them; in fact, he wasn't so sure that he was comfortable with all of them himself. But you couldn't argue with results, and the plain fact was that in all his years of operation the Doctor had lost exactly one kid, one who, as the detective sergeants' investigation had plainly revealed, had been at least thinking about suicide before coming to the Institute, and who'd brought the instrument of the "crime" with him when he was enrolled. Reminding the Doctor's critics that New York's courts had better things to do than pursue unwarranted investigations, Judge Welles declared the whole matter dismissed.

We'd known that Welles was an unpredictable character; but no public official had ever made that kind of statement in support of the Doctor's work, and the event was enough to make you think that maybe there was some kind of justice in the world, after all. Mr. Moore'd taken the hopeful chance of engaging a private room at Mr. Delmonico's restaurant for after the hearing (such rooms being the only places in the joint where Cyrus and I were allowed to eat), and during the meal that followed the adults stuffed themselves on more kinds of strangely named French food than I could possibly rattle off all these years later. As for me, I made do with a steak and fried potatoes, and Mr. Delmonico even rounded me up a bottle of root beer (though I think he had to send one of his boys out to fetch it from a local grocer). But even if I can't remember just what it was that everybody ate, I *can* remember that it was an evening of a type what was rare for us: there'd been no killings or kidnappings, and no great mystery was the main topic of conversation. In fact, crime didn't come up much at all—it was just a time to be happy in each other's company, and remember that terrible events were not the only things that bonded us together.

Being as the rest of the day had gone so well, we probably should've known that some unpleasant or at least disturbing surprise would be waiting for us at its end. The Doctor invited everyone back to his house after the meal at Delmonico's, and when we arrived we discovered a very handsome brougham sitting at the curb in front of the front yard. But the two men sitting up on the driving seat didn't exactly match the rig: wearing rough sailor's jackets what indicated a familiarity with the seamier parts of the waterfront, they had the kind of deep brown features, thin, drooping mustaches, and large, dark eyes what immediately suggested they were from India, or that general part of the world. I was riding in a cab with Detective Sergeant Lucius, whose face—always jolly and rosy after a big meal and lots of red wine at Mr. Delmonico's—suddenly went straight, even a little pale, when he saw the carriage and the men.

"What the—" he whispered. "Oh, no."

"Oh, no?" I answered, looking at the brougham and then back at the detective sergeant. "What's 'oh, no' about it? Who are they?"

Taking a deep breath, Lucius said, "They look like lascars."

"Lascars?" I repeated, now a little disturbed myself: even *I* knew about the tough breed of sailors and pirates whose home waters were the Indian Ocean and the South China Sea. "What the hell are they doing *here*?"

"Care to guess?" the detective sergeant said. "Lascars are a very common sight—on the Manila waterfront."

"Oh," I noised, glancing again at the two mugs on the brougham. Then I just sank down into my seat. "Aw, shit . . ."

By the time Lucius's and my cab stopped, the others had already gotten out of a second hansom and the Doctor's calash, and were gathered around the door of the brougham. There was no sign of life from inside the thing yet, and the first such that we got was a question:

"Dr. Kreizler?" said a deep voice, one what bore a strong Spanish accent.

The Doctor stepped forward. "I am Dr. Laszlo Kreizler. May I be of assistance?"

The door of the brougham finally opened, and out stepped a very dark, handsome man of medium height and build, his hair carefully fixed with pomade. His clothes looked to be about the best that money could buy, and had that formal cut what seems to always mark the diplomat. In his hand he carried a walking stick what had a heavy ball of silver for a handle.

"I am Señor Narciso Linares. I believe you know of me."

The Doctor just nodded with a small smile, having already guessed, like the rest of us, who the caller was. "Señor."

Señor Linares flicked his stick toward the house. "Is there a place where we may speak? The matter is most urgent."

"Please," the Doctor said, indicating the front door. The señor moved toward it and the Doctor followed, after which the rest of us moved to do the same: but then the two lascars jumped down off the brougham and stood in our way at the gate to the front yard, folding their arms and seeming ready for an argument.

The Doctor turned around, an expression of shock coming into his face. "Señor," he said, very sternly. "What is the meaning of this behavior? These people are residents of and guests in this house."

Considering the matter for a moment, the señor just nodded and said, "So." Then he mouthed some words in Spanish to the lascars, who glumly moved back toward the carriage. After that we all went inside, Cyrus keeping a very careful eye on the two boys at the curb as we did.

The Doctor led Señor Linares up into the parlor and offered him a drink. When the visitor requested a glass of brandy, Mr. Moore fetched it, while the rest of us took seats. Cyrus stood by one window and opened it, still watching the lascars.

"Dr. Kreizler," Señor Linares said in some surprise, when he saw that we all intended on staying in the parlor. "My business with you is of a *private* nature—it is certainly not for the ears of servants."

"There are no servants here," the Doctor replied. "These are my colleagues."

The señor glanced at Cyrus. "The black, as well?"

Trying hard not to get openly irritated, the Doctor just said, "If you have something you wish to discuss, señor, you must do so in front of our collected company. Otherwise, I must bid you good evening."

Shrugging, Señor Linares drained his brandy and put the glass aside. "I shall come to the point, then. I have reason to believe, Doctor, that you know the whereabouts of my wife and child."

"Indeed?"

"Yes. If this is so, I most strongly recommend that you reveal those whereabouts to me, unless you wish to provoke a diplomatic incident."

The Doctor paused and took out his cigarette case. "I had always understood that diplomats were tactful men," he said. "Perhaps I was misinformed."

"The time for tact is long past," Señor Linares answered testily. "I know that, some time ago, my wife sought the assistance of this woman—" He waved his stick in Miss Howard's general direction. "Since then, my life has been a succession of difficulties. I warn you, sir, I am most sincere in my threat of an official protest."

As he lit one of his smokes, the Doctor studied the señor for a few more seconds, then sat back. "Actually, you are not."

Señor Linares looked like he'd been slapped. "You call me a liar?" he demanded, getting to his feet.

"Please, sir," the Doctor replied, waving his cigarette and not at all concerned. "Spare me your Latin pride—or what is the term that men such as yourself use? Your *machismo*? It is wasted here, I assure you."

"Dr. Kreizler," the señor answered, "I am not a man to endure such words—"

"Señor Linares," the Doctor said, "please do sit down. I submit that if you had any intention of actually involving either your consulate or your government in this matter, you would have done so long ago. And you would certainly not have arrived at my house in the company of such creatures as those two men"—he threw a hand lightly in the direction of the window—"whose presence was undoubtedly intended to extract through physical intimidation the information you seek. Fortunately for myself— less fortunately for you—I did not return home alone. Shall we dispense, then, with talk of diplomatic incidents?"

The señor gave himself a couple of seconds, then sat back down and even managed a small, what you might call begrudging smile. "Yes. I heard that you were a clever man."

The Doctor's face suddenly went hard. "And I have heard that you, sir, are a man who does not shrink from beating women, as well as anyone else who might be smaller and weaker than yourself. And that you have been perfectly willing, anxious even, to conceal the abduction of your own child. So perhaps you can tell me, señor—why is it that you come here now, as if you were the governor of some far-off Spanish colony, in an attempt to bully me into giving you information that I do not possess?"

The señor looked up quickly. "Then you do not know what has become of my wife and daughter?"

"If I knew, sir, I should hardly be likely to tell you. But you have my word that I do not." Which was true: Señora Linares had left New York over the weekend but hadn't made her final destination known to Miss Howard before going. She planned to write when she was resettled and all was well.

Taking the Doctor's statement, it seemed to me, more lightly than a man in his position might've been expected to, Señor Linares rested himself against his stick and said, "I see. So. It seems that I have wasted my time coming here." Then he glanced up at Mr. Moore, almost like he was annoyed that he hadn't been given another brandy yet.

Pouring it for him, Mr. Moore couldn't help but get into the action: "Was it just because she was a girl? They don't count for much in your part of the world, do they—female offspring?"

The señor shook his head. "You Americans—such provincial moralists. Do you imagine I would conduct myself as I have without compelling reasons?"

"What reasons," Miss Howard asked, quietly but what you might call disdainfully, "could possibly be 'compelling' enough to make you abandon Ana?"

Glancing around the room at each of our faces, Señor Linares downed his second brandy, then began to nod his head slowly. "I suppose my motives must seem horrifying, to your rather naïve way of thinking."

"We're not sure what your motives *are,*" Marcus offered.

"We've been trying to determine that since the beginning," Lucius added. "Without success."

Still nodding as Mr. Moore poured him yet another shot of brandy, Señor Linares said, "I can understand the difficulty. You, like the rest of your countrymen, believe what is in your newspapers. The Spanish Empire is a decadent collection of arrogant militarists, who would like nothing better than to prove their virility against whatever nation offends them. Well . . ." He took a smaller sip of brandy. "You are right, in part— but only in part." Indicating the Doctor's silver cigarette box, the señor said, "May I?" to which the Doctor, now very interested in what the man was saying, nodded. The señor lit up one of the number inside the box, drew on it, and let the smoke out with a look of satisfaction. "Very fine," he said. "Russian?"

The Doctor nodded again. "Georgian. Blended with Virginia."

The señor took another drag. "Yes. Very fine indeed. . . . Tell me, Doctor. Have you ever heard of a cousin of mine—General Arsenio Linares?" The Doctor shook his head. "He commands at Santiago de Cuba. Or of Admiral Pascual Cervera y Topete, commander of our naval squadron at Cádiz?" Again the Doctor came up blank. "I did not think so. But you know—you *all* know—of the 'butcher' General Weyler, and of the belligerent clique of monarchists and military officers that surround the queen regent. . . . They are the men who are quoted in your newspapers. Your Mr. Hearst and Mr. Pulitzer—they will not sell their product by printing voices of reason."

"Reason?" the Doctor asked, looking puzzled.

The señor gave him a tough, straight look. "You don't really suppose, Doctor, that we are *all* so blind as to be unable to recognize the reality which surrounds us? Yes, there are many Spaniards in Cuba, and in Spain, and even in my boyhood home of the Philippines, who believe that your country has meddled in our affairs and insulted our leaders past the point of toleration. And they are right. But they wish to resolve the matter through war—they wish it almost as much as do many Americans. There are those in our country, however, who know what the inevitable result of such a war would be. The men I have mentioned, for example, know. And *I* know."

"Would you mind telling *us*?" Mr. Moore said.

Señor Linares looked over at him and chuckled. "This country . . . it is like a youth who has suddenly grown into manhood, and does not yet realize the extent of his own strength. If Spain goes to war with your country, señor, the result will be disastrous for our empire. We will lose what little we still possess in this hemisphere, and probably a great deal more. But such arguments are lost on those who wish to defend our pride with arms. They pay no attention to the warnings of experienced officers like my cousin, or Admiral Cervera, who know how great our weakness is. Nor do they listen to mere consular secretaries, who have seen your great ships under construction in Brooklyn, in Newport, and in Virginia." Staring into his glass, Señor Linares seemed to grow bitterly downcast. "They do not listen."

The Doctor's eyes had gone wide. "Are you saying," he asked quietly, "that you deliberately tried to suppress knowledge of your daughter's abduction in order to keep political extremists in your country from obtaining further rationalizations for declaring war on the United States?"

Looking not at all ashamed of it, the señor answered, "What would *you* have done, Doctor? The Spanish Empire is sick—dying of its own arrogance, which seeks any excuse to be unleashed. I know this. Yet at the same time, I was raised to be a *part* of that empire. My family has served it for three hundred years. I must do all that I can to hold off the final destruction."

"Including letting your own daughter quite possibly die?" Miss Howard said.

Señor Linares didn't look at her as he answered. "Spain needs sons—not daughters. The cost had to be weighed against the return, as you Americans say."

"So now," Marcus went on for him, "you're just trying to make sure that they won't resurface somewhere. You want to be certain the matter is really ended."

The señor shrugged. "I should like an annulment from my wife, if she will not return to me. I shall marry again. As I say, Spain needs sons."

Suddenly standing up, his eyes burning, the Doctor said, "I have told you that we know nothing of the whereabouts of your family, Señor Linares. That is the truth. And now I must ask that you leave my house."

The señor didn't look like the fairly rude order came as much of a surprise: he got up, leaning on his stick, then nodded and walked into the hall.

"Señor," Miss Howard called after him. The man stopped at the top of the staircase and turned. "If a man can place a greater priority on his country than his own child—and if his country not only tolerates but encourages such a choice—then hasn't that country *already* been destroyed?"

"In the months to come," Señor Linares answered quietly, "I suspect that we shall learn the answer to that question."

Stepping quickly, almost lightly, the señor made his way out of the house and back to his carriage, leaving the rest of us to sit quietly and think over this, the last missing piece in the case of Libby Hatch.

CHAPTER 59

O f course, war between the United States and the Empire of Spain did come, just months after we sat in the Doctor's parlor with Señor Linares; and in spite of what a lot of people seem to've taken to believing since, what the señor had called Spanish "arrogance" was just as responsible for the bloodbath as were all the rantings and ravings of those Americans what favored the idea. Señor Linares's predictions about the outcome of the thing proved just as accurate as his ideas about its causes: the Spanish Empire was pretty well destroyed, and the United States found itself in possession of a whole string of new foreign possessions—including the Philippine Islands. I don't guess that much of anybody, even in Washington, had a really sound idea of what they were getting themselves into by taking over such places: as Mr. Finley P. Dunne, the newspaper wag, wrote at the time, most Americans couldn't have told you whether the Philippines "were islands or canned goods" before the war. As for me, I had only one thought—a question, really—when I heard that we were the new rulers of the place: Had El Niño returned to his homeland before we invaded, and had he then become part of the native army what quickly began to fight against our country for independence? I never found out; but it would've been like him.

The detective sergeants returned to their regular duties at the Police Department after they'd finished their investigation of the Doctor's Institute, but their position there remained as troubled as it'd always been. Over the years there've been commissions what've investigated corruption in the department—in fact, it sometimes seems like there's *always* a commission investigating said corruption—and Marcus and Lucius have given testimony before all of them, in an attempt to get at least the Bureau of Detectives cleaned up. But the only real result of their efforts has been to isolate them even more from their "peers," and I'm sure that, if it wasn't for the brilliance what they've demonstrated on so many cases, they would've gotten the axe a long time ago. But they keep on going, squabbling, experimenting, and generally trying to use forensic science to push police work forward; and many's the thief, killer, rapist, and mad bomber what wishes that the Irish brass'd been able to get rid of the "Jew boys" a long time ago.

Miss Howard kept her operation at Number 808 Broadway going after the Hatch case; in fact, she and it are *still* going, though she eventually expanded its services so that both men and women could gain the benefit of her skills. Over time she's gotten to be kind of a legend in the detection world, a fact what makes her very proud, though she'd never admit as much. And, despite all her talk about men's defects, she's actually taken the time to get herself mixed up with one or two of them along the way, though it's not for me to reveal the details of those experiences. What I *can* say is that she remains the most singular woman I've ever come across, always displaying a combination of deep friendship and independence what many members of her sex are as incapable of achieving today as Libby Hatch was twenty-two years ago. I guess that this situation exists, as Miss Howard has always maintained, because of all the guff that women are fed as young girls—and maybe the solution is for more females to carry guns, I don't know: Miss Howard's certainly put quite a few more bullets into men's legs over the years, and it's only helped her stay her own person.

Cyrus's and my friendship, well, that's always been one of the rocks of my life. He got married, not too long after the business of Libby Hatch was completed, and his wife, Merle Spotswood, came to live with us, ending our long search to find a decent cook. She was and remains one of the best ever born, besides being as personally decent and strong as her husband. I was still living in the Doctor's house when their three kids came into the world, and though they turned the top floor of the place into a noisy nursery (the young ones moved into the room what had once belonged to Mary Palmer), I didn't mind. It did sometimes drive the Doctor a little crazy; but the kids always made sure to walk softly when they passed by his study door, and having children around the house did a lot of good for everyone's spirits. Seventeenth Street was a happy place during those years, one what I was not a little sorry to leave when it came time for me to move out into the back room of my store and start life on my own.

As for the Doctor, once his name'd been cleared he dived back into affairs at his Institute like a man what'd been deprived of life's necessities. That's not to say that there weren't questions raised during that spring and summer of 1897 what stayed with him—there certainly were. Some of them—What had driven Paulie McPherson to hang himself? What'd actually happened to Mr. Picton's family? How many children had Libby Hatch killed that we didn't even know about?—were unanswerable, and faded with the years; but others were more personal, and didn't go anywhere. In fact, they seem to occupy the Doctor still, at times, as he sits in his parlor of a late night and ponders the complications of life. You couldn't say that those questions were put into his head by the clever Clarence Darrow, exactly, for the Doctor had always vexed himself with nagging doubts; but Mr. Darrow's skilled statement of those doubts during Libby Hatch's trial gave voice to what might otherwise have stayed unspoken ideas. Most of all, the question of *why* the Doctor had—and has—always worked so hard to find explanations for the terrible events he's encountered in his professional life seems to have been tough for him to come to grips with. Mr. Darrow's suggestion that maybe he was at heart using his work as a way of quieting the doubts what he had about himself obviously struck a deep chord; and as the Doctor watched his onetime opponent go on to great fame in courtrooms all across America, I think the idea only haunted him all the more. But it never stopped him from working, from pressing ahead, and it's that ability—to work through the self-doubts what any worthwhile human being feels—that is, so far as I can tell, the only thing what separates a meaningful life from a useless one.

And then there's Mr. Moore. I have the luxury of writing these final words because, for the first time since opening this shop, I have an assistant: sportsman that he is, Mr. Moore has conceded the bet after reading the rest of my manuscript, though he was careful to tell me that whatever spirit the narrative may have has been "regrettably marred by an appalling lack of style." Says him. Anyway, he's out there now, apron and all, selling smokes to swells and, I think, enjoying the opportunity what it offers him to badger such people in the way what only a shopkeeper can: nothing's ever pleased my old friend more than being given a chance to spit in the face of the upper crust from which he hails.

His return to the *Times* after the Hatch case wasn't easy for him: he would've liked to've chronicled our recent exploits in the pages of the paper, but he knew that his editors wouldn't touch the thing with a very long stick. So he decided to console himself by taking over coverage of the legal proceedings what followed "the mystery of the headless body." It was Mr. Moore's hope that he'd be able to inject some of the lessons we'd learned from pursuing Libby Hatch into that second story of intimate murder, though he really should've known better. The victim of the crime, the dismembered Mr. Guldensuppe, was soon forgotten by just about everybody, while his former lover, Mrs. Nack, and her most recent conquest and partner in crime, Martin Thorn, found themselves the subject of a full-blown public melodrama. Mrs. Nack quickly became, so far as the press, the public, and the district attorney's office were concerned, a damsel in distress: she passed herself off as having been misled and corrupted by Thorn, when in fact she'd helped plan the killing and assisted in the job of dismembering the corpse. To top it all off, by giving the state everything it needed to send the unfortunate sap Thorn to the electrical chair at Sing Sing, Mrs. Nack managed to get the district attorney to ask the judge in the case to impose the lightest possible sentence on her, which he did: she got fifteen years at Auburn, which, with good behavior, could and did end up being only nine.

When the day came for Thorn to go to the chair, Mr. Moore went up to Sing Sing, determined to get some kind of statement from the doomed prisoner to the effect that society was still willing to let women get away with brutal outrages just because it was too disturbing to believe that they were capable of them. He buttonholed Thorn as the condemned man was being led into the death chamber, and asked him what he thought about Mrs. Nack's light sentence.

"Oh, I don't know," Thorn answered, beaten down and resigned. "I don't care much about it one way or the other."

So ended Mr. Moore's little crusade to bring to light some few of the truths we'd learned from Libby Hatch. The "savage" Thorn and the "deluded but redeemed" Mrs. Nack (as the D.A. labeled them) turned out to be, in fact, very ordinary people, while the "monsters" what everyone in town had originally thought were responsible for the crime—the grave robbers, mad anatomists, bloodthirsty ghouls, and the like—were just shadows, dreamed up to glorify policemen, sell newspapers, and scare unruly kids. True to the Doctor's beliefs, the real monsters continued, then as now, to wander the streets unnoticed, going about their strange and desperate work with a fever what looks to the average citizen like nothing more than the ordinary effort required to get through an ordinary day.

As for me, I've done better than might've been expected, I suppose, given where I started out. Most of my old pals and associates ended up either in jail or dead on the streets, and while it's hard to feel sorry that the likes of Ding Dong and Goo Goo Knox went that way, it seems sad that someone as good-hearted as Hickie the Hun should've spent most of his adult life walking the yard at Sing Sing. My own life's pretty much been this shop; and while tobacco's done all right by me in terms of money, it's also left me—in an example of what the Doctor calls "horribly tragic irony"—with this wretched hack, a condition what will, very probably, keep eating away at my lungs until there's nothing left to cough up. I get the feeling, sometimes, that the Doctor feels guilty about never getting me to give up the smokes; but I was a nicotine fiend long before I ever met the man, and, caring and patient as he always was, there were just some things about my early life what even his kindness and wisdom couldn't undo. I don't hold him responsible, of course, or love him any the less for it, and it makes me sad to think that my physical predicament only gives him one more reason to vex himself; but again, I guess it's that very vexing, and the ability to keep working through it toward a better sort of life for our mostly miserable species, what makes him such a very unusual man.

There've been women in my life every now and again, but none who've filled me with the kind of dreams what I once shared with Kat in the Doctor's kitchen. All of that died with her, I guess; and if it seems strange that such should've happened so early in my life, I can only say that it sometimes occurs to me that those of us what grew up on the streets did *everything* too early—too early, and too fast. Once a week I take the subway out to Calvary Cemetery and put flowers on Kat's grave, and there's times— more and more often, these days—when I find myself sitting and chatting with her, much the way we did on that morning when she downed the better part of a bottle of paregoric. Wherever she is, I suppose she knows that I'll likely be joining her sometime fairly soon; and while I don't like to think about leaving my friends, and especially the Doctor, behind, there's a kind of a peculiar thrill in thinking that in the end I'll find her again, all grown up and free of her cravings for burny and the high life. We might even, at long last, be able to make some kind of a peaceful, pleasant life together—the kind of life what she never knew during her short time in this world. A lot of people, I guess, might consider that a silly sort of dream; but if you came from the world what Kat and I did, it wouldn't seem that way at all.

ACKNOWLEDGMENTS

While researching the prequel to this book, *The Alienist,* it became apparent to me that, contrary to popular belief, women are just as prone to violent crime as are men. But their victims are most often children—frequently their own children—and this disturbing fact seems to discourage the kind of sensationalist reporting that usually characterizes cases involving violent men, especially male serial killers. I discussed this matter with Dr. David Abrahamsen, who had given me much assistance during the preparation of *The Alienist,* and he confirmed that women generally abuse or murder people with whom they have strong personal connections (unlike men, who often select strangers as the victims of their violent tendencies, since they are easier to objectify). Once again, I thank Dr. Abrahamsen for his assistance and encouragement, without which this project would have gone astray early on.

Anyone familiar with the phenomenon of female violence will see in the case of Libby Hatch elements of crimes from not only the last century but our own time, as well. This similarity is quite intentional, and could not have been achieved without the important work of analysts who have chronicled the stories of some of the more noteworthy contemporary female killers. Of these writers I must mention Joyce Eggington for her powerful study of Marybeth Tinning, Ann Rule for her incisive work on the Diane Downs case, Andrea Peyser for her reporting on and analysis of the Susan Smith murders, and my friend John Coston for his examination of Ellen Boehm. All are to be commended for their refusal to sociologically rationalize the acts of their subjects, and for their insistence (to paraphrase Rupert Picton) on treating them as violent individuals first and women second.

Libraries, as always, make the difference between fantasy and reconstruction possible. I must thank the staffs of the New York Public Library, the New York Society Library, and the New-York Historical Society for their tireless help. I must also thank the staff of the Brookside Museum in Ballston Spa, New York, along with the staffs of the Ballston Spa Public Library, the Saratoga Springs Public Library, and the Saratoga County Historical Society.

Perrin Wright provided not only research assistance but companionship on some mental and physical journeys which, disturbing as they were for me, were in some ways more so for her. I thank her for being so insightful, open-minded, and supportive.

Dr. Laszlo Kreizler was born during a dinner I had long ago with John Therese, who has continued to offer his friendship and advice. Both are as highly valued now as they were then.

My path through the maze of the late nineteenth–century legal system in New York State was lit by the ever-insightful Julie Glynn, attorney-at-law. In addition, she and her husband, Andy Mattson, a keen analyst of American studies, were always willing to discuss ideas and listen to tirades, all of which kept the pressure from becoming explosive. Needless to say, whatever liberties I have taken with legal procedure for drama's sake are my own doing.

Once again, Tim Haldeman provided invaluable reactions and suggestions, as well as the friendship necessary to keep a long and difficult project going. I am in his debt.

For their supreme patience and constant encouragement, I thank my agent, Suzanne Gluck, and my editor, Ann Godoff. They endured what must sometimes have seemed the endless ramblings of a soul in torment, and I hope they know that I couldn't have gotten through it all without them. Marsinay Smith and Enrica Gadler also smoothed the path, and I deeply appreciate their efforts.

Heather Schroeder has worked tirelessly to oversee the fates of these stories abroad, and has always exhibited understanding and patience.

For helping me stay on course, as well as extending the hand of true friendship in Mother England, I offer my sincerest thanks to Hilary Hale.

I must also acknowledge the efforts of those physicians who took pains to keep me going through several very difficult years: Ernestina Saxton, Tirso del Junco, Jr., Frank Petito, and Bruce Yaffe exhibited the kind of committed and responsive behavior that all doctors should embody but with which most, tragically, cannot be bothered. I thank them all. I offer special gratitude to Vicki Hufnagel, a pioneering surgeon who offered me hope when many others could or would not. For her efforts to illuminate several dark corners of medicine Dr. Hufnagel has consistently been rewarded with the hostility of the medical establishment, which continues to protect its blind and backward members as assiduously as it did a hundred years ago.

While this book was in its infancy, it nearly suffered the fate of many of Libby Hatch's victims due to my wide-eyed wandering into a creative quagmire on another coast. For helping me first try to realize a difficult vision and then get back to the business of writing books I would like to thank, in order of appearance, Rene Garcia (and Risa Bramon Garcia), Betty Moos, Mike Finnell, Joe Dante, Kathy Lingg, Cynthia Schulte, Helen Mossler, Garry

Hart, Bob Eisele, Dan Dugan, Thom Polizzi, Jamie Freitag, Sandy Veneziano, Jason La Padura, Natalie Hart, Deborah Everton, Marshall Harvey, Michael Thau, Kathy Zatarga, Bill Millar, Hal Harrison and the rest of the crew at Paramount, along with—for they cannot be forgotten—John Corbett, John Pyper-Ferguson, Rod Taylor, J. Madison Wright, Darryl Theirse, Carolyn McCormick (and Byron Jennings and Cooper), Marjorie Monaghan, Joel Swetow and the rest of the cast of the Chronicles. That this book will be released before that project is evidence not of any shortcomings on their parts, but of why New York need never fear a certain desert village in Southern California as a rival for artistic innovation and cultural power.

Special gratitude goes to Lynn Freer and Jim Turner, along with my buddy and morning nemesis, Otto; John and Kathy von Hartz; my brother Simon and his wife, Cristina, along with my most reliable advisers Lydia, Sam, Ben, and Gabriella; my brother Ethan and his wife, Sarah; Marta von Hartz and Jay Shapiro; William von Hartz; Debbie Deuble; Ezequiel Vinao; Oren Jacoby; Meghann Haldeman; Ellen Blain; and the ever-reliable Tom Pivinski. I would also like to thank Marvin Cochran, and have faith that wherever he is, he'll hear me.

The completion of this book, along with the sanity of its author, were consistently aided by the remarkable sense and sensibility of Elisabeth Harnois.

PHOTO: © PATTY CLAYTON

CALEB CARR is a novelist and military historian, and the award-winning author of the *New York Times* and worldwide bestsellers *The Alienist* and *The Angel of Darkness,* as well as numerous other works of fiction and nonfiction, most recently *Surrender, New York.* His nonfiction works include the critically acclaimed T*he Lessons of Terror: A History of Warfare Against Civilians* and *The Devil Soldier: The Story of Frederick Townsend Ward.* A native of New York City, he has spent much of his life in upstate New York, where he now lives.

ABOUT THE TYPE

This book was set in Galliard, a typeface designed by Matthew Carter for the Mergenthaler Linotype Company in 1978. Galliard is based on the sixteenth-century typefaces of Robert Granjon, which give it classic lines yet interject a contemporary look.

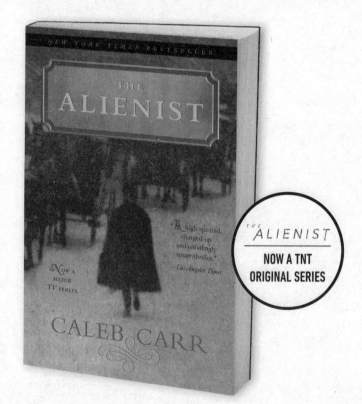